The Liar

The Hippopotamus

BY THE SAME AUTHOR

Autobiography
Moab is My Washpot

Novels
Making History

Miscellaneous
Paperweight
Hysteria (ed)

With Hugh Laurie
A Bit of Fry and Laurie
A Bit More Fry and Laur
Three Bits of Fry and Laurie

The Liar
The Hippopotamus

STEPHEN FRY

Quality Paperbacks Direct
London

This omnibus edition published 2000
By BCA
By arrangement with Arrow Books Limited
The Random House Group Limited

CN 8482

The Liar

The author and publishers are grateful to the following for permission to use copyright material:
Shakespeare and Tragedy © John Bayley quoted by kind permission of Routledge Ltd
'Maria' (Richard Rodgers/Oscar Hammerstein II) © 1959 Williamson Music International, USA
Reproduced by permission of EMI Music Publishing Ltd, London WC2 0EA
'Puppy Love' composed by Paul Anka
and reproduced by kind permission of M.A.M. Music Publishing Ltd
'I Don't Know How to Love Him' by Tim Rice
Reproduced by kind permission of MCA Music Ltd

The Hippopotamus

The lines quoted on page 419, 422 and 423 are from
'A Fathers Advice' by Mark Beaufoy

The lines of verse from 'The Hippopotamus' by T.S. Eliot are
taken from *The Complete Poems and Plays of T.S. Eliot*,
reproduced here by kind permission of Faber and Faber Limited
and the Estate of T.S. Eliot

Printed and bound in Germany by
GGP Media, Pössneck

CONTENTS

The Liar

To ....
(*insert full name here*)

Not one word of the following is true

A Fame *T*-shirt stopped outside the house where Mozart was born. He looked up at the building and his eyes shone. He stood quite still, gazing upwards and glowing with adoration as a party of Bleached Denims and Fluorescent Bermuda Shorts pushed past him and went in. Then he shook his head, dug into his hip pocket and moved forwards. A thin high voice behind him caused him to stop mid-stride.

'Have you ever contemplated, Adrian, the phenomenon of springs?'

'Coils, you mean?'

'Not coils, Adrian, no. Coils not. Think springs of water. Think wells and spas and sources. Well-springs in the widest and loveliest sense. Jerusalem, for instance, is a spring of religiosity. One small town in the desert, but the source of the world's three most powerful faiths. It is the capital of Judaism, the scene of Christ's crucifixion and the place from which Mohammed ascended into heaven. Religion seems to bubble from its sands.'

The Fame *T*-shirt smiled to himself and walked into the building.

A Tweed Jacket and a Blue Button-down Shirt of Oxford Cotton stopped in front of the steps. Now it was their turn to stare reverently upwards as the tide of human traffic streamed past them along the Getreidegasse.

1

'Take Salzburg. By no means the chief city of Austria, but a Jerusalem to any music lover. Haydn, Schubert and . . . oh dear me yes, here we are . . . and Mozart.'

'There's a theory that special lines criss-cross the earth and that where they coincide strange things happen,' said the Oxford Cotton Button-down Shirt. 'Ley-lines, I think they call them.'

'You'll think I'm grinding my axe,' said the Jacket, 'but I should say that it is the German language that is responsible.'

'Shall we go up?'

'By all means.' The pair moved into the interior shadows of the house.

'You see,' continued the Tweed, 'all the qualities of ironic abstraction that the language could not articulate found expression in their music.'

'I had never thought of Haydn as ironic.'

'It is of course quite possible that my theory is hopelessly wrong. Pay the nice Fräulein, Adrian.'

In a second-storey chamber where little Wolfgang had romped, whose walls he had covered with precocious arithmetic and whose rafters he had made tremble with infant minuets, the Fame T-shirt examined the display cases.

The ivory and tortoise-shell combs that once had smoothed the ruffled ringlets of the young genius appeared not to interest the T-shirt at all, nor the letters and laundry-lists, nor the child-size violins and violas. His attention was entirely taken up by the models of stage designs which were set into the wall in glass boxes all round the room.

One box in particular seemed to fascinate him. He stared at it with intensity and suspicion as if half expecting the little papier mâché figures inside to burst through the glass and punch him on the nose. He appeared to be oblivious of

2

*the group of Bleached Denims and Acid-coloured Shorts that
pressed around him, laughing and joking in a language he
didn't understand.*

*The model that so particularly engrossed him was of a
banqueting hall in which stood a dining table heaped high
with food. Two little men had been placed by the table, one
crouched in terror, the other standing with hand on hip, in
an attitude of cavalier contempt. Both figures looked upstage
at the model of a white statue which pointed down at them
with the accusing finger of an Italian traffic policeman or
wartime recruiting poster.*

*The Tweed Jacket and the Blue Button-down had just
entered the room.*

*'You start at that end, Adrian, and we'll meet in the
middle.'*

*The Jacket watched the Oxford Cotton move to the other
end of the room and then approached the cabinet, whose glass
was still being misted by the intense scrutiny of the* Fame *T-
shirt.*

*'Don Giovanni,' said the Tweed coming up behind him,
'a cenar teco m'invitasti, e son venuto. Don Giovanni,
you invited me to dinner, and here I am.'*

*The T-shirt still stared into the glass. 'Non si pasce di
cibo mortale, Chi si pasce di cibo celeste,' he whispered.
'He who dines on heavenly food has no need of mortal
sustenance.'*

'I believe you have something for me,' said the Tweed.

'Goldener Hirsch, name of Emburey. Small package.'

*'Emburey? Middlesex and England? I had no idea you
were interested in cricket.'*

*'I get it out from a newspaper. It looked a very English
name.'*

'And so it is. Goodbye.'

3

The Tweed moved on and joined the Blue Shirt, who had fallen into conversation with a Frenchwoman.

'I was telling this lady,' said the Shirt, 'that I thought the design for The Magic Flute over there was by David Hockney.'

'Certainly so,' said the Tweed. 'Hockney seems to me to paint in two styles. Wild and natural or cold and clinical. I seem to remember remarking that there are two kinds of Hockney. Field Hockney and Ice Hockney.'

'Please?'

'It's a joke,' explained the Blue Shirt.

'Ah.'

The Tweed was examining an exhibit.

'This figure here must be the Queen of the Night, surely.'

'She is a character altogether of the most extraordinary, I believe,' said the Frenchwoman. 'Her music – my God, how but that it is divine. I am myself singer and to play the Queen is the dearest dream of my bosom.'

'It's certainly one hell of a part,' said the Oxford Cotton. 'Pretty difficult I'd have thought. What's that incredibly high note she has to reach? It's a top C, isn't it?'

The Frenchwoman's answer to this question startled not just the Blue Button-down Shirt and his companion, but the whole room. For she stared at the Blue Shirt, her eyes round with fright, opened her mouth wide and let go a piercing soprano note of a purity and passion that she was never to repeat in the whole of her subsequent, and distinguished, operatic career.

'Good lord,' said the Tweed, 'is it really that high? As I remember it – '

'Donald!' said the Button-down Shirt. 'Look!'

The Tweed Jacket turned and saw the cause of the scream and the cause of other, less technically proficient, screams that were starting up everywhere.

4

In the middle of the room stood a man in a Fame *T-shirt, twitching and leaping like a puppet.*

It was not the crudity of such a dance in such a place that had set everyone off, it was the sight and sound of the blood that creamed and frothed from his throat. The man seemed, as he hopped and stamped about, to be trying to stem the flow by squeezing at his neck with both hands, but the very pressure of the blood as it pumped outwards made such a task impossible.

Time stands still at such moments.

Those who retold the scene afterwards to friends, to psychiatrists, to priests, to the press, all spoke of the noise. To some it was a rattling gargle, to others a bubbling croak: the old man in the tweed jacket and his young companion agreed that they could never bear again the sound of a cappuccino machine without being forced to think of that awful death wheeze.

All remembered the staggering quantity of the blood, the force of it pushing through the man's fingers. All remembered the chorus of bass voices upraised in panic as helping hands braved the red shower and leapt forward to ease the jerking figure to the floor. All recalled how nothing could staunch the ferocious jetting of the fountain that gushed from the man's neck and quenched the words 'I'm Going to Live For Ever' on his T-shirt with a dark stain. All remarked on how long it seemed to take him to die.

But only one of them remembered seeing an enormously fat man with a small head and lank hair leave the room, letting a knife leap from his hand like a live fish as he went.

Only one man saw that, and he kept it to himself. He grabbed his companion's hand and led him from the room.

'Come, Adrian. I think we should be otherwhere.'

One

I

Adrian checked the orchid at his buttonhole, inspected the spats at his feet, gave the lavender gloves a twitch, smoothed down his waistcoat, tucked the ebony Malacca-cane under his arm, swallowed twice and pushed wide the changing-room door.

'Ah, my dears,' he cried. 'Congratulations! Congratulations to you all! A triumph, an absolute triumph!'

'Well, what the fuck's he wearing now?' they snorted from the steamy end of the room.

'You're an arse and an idiot, Healey.'

Burkiss threw a flannel onto the shiny top hat. Adrian reached up and took it between forefinger and thumb.

'If there is the slightest possibility, Burkiss, that this flannel has absorbed any of the juices that leak from within you, that it has mopped up a single droplet of your revolting pubescent greases, that it has tickled and frotted even one of the hideously mired corners of your disgusting body then I shall have a spasm. I'm sorry but I shall.'

In spite of himself, Cartwright smiled. He moved

further along the bench and turned his back, but he smiled.

'Now, girls,' continued Healey, 'you're very high-spirited and that's as it should be but I won't have you getting out of hand. I just looked in to applaud a simply marvellous show and to tell you that you are certainly the loveliest chorus in town and that I intend to stand you all dinner at the Embassy one by one over the course of what I know will be a long and successful run.'

'I mean, what kind of coat is that?'

'It is called an astrakhan and I am sure you agree that it is absolutely the ratherest thing. You will observe it fits my sumptuous frame as snugly as if it were made for me . . . just as you do, you delicious Hopkinson.'

'Oh shut up.'

'Your whole body goes quite pink when you are flattered, like a small pig, it is utterly, utterly fetching.'

Adrian saw Cartwright turn away and face his locker, a locker to which Adrian had the key. The boy seemed now to be concentrating on pulling on his socks. Adrian took half a second to take a mental snapshot of the scrummy toes and heavenly ankle being sheathed by those lucky, lucky socks, a snapshot he could develop and pore over later with all the others that he had pasted into the private album of his memory.

Cartwright wondered why Healey sometimes stared at him like that. He could sense it when he did, even when he couldn't see, he could feel those cool eyes surveying him with pity and contempt for a

7

younger boy who didn't have so sharp a tongue, so acid a wit as almighty Healey. But there were others dumber than he was, why should Healey single him out for special treatment?

Setting a spatted foot on the bench that ran down the middle of the changing-room with elegant disdain, Adrian began to flip through a pile of Y-fronts and rugger shorts with his cane.

'I was particularly taken,' he said, 'with that number in the first act when you and the girls from Marlborough stood in a line and jumped up at that funny leather ball. It was too utterly utter for words. Lord how I laughed when you let the Marlborough chorus run off with it . . . dear me, this belongs to someone who doesn't appear to know how to wipe his bottom. Is there a name-tape? Madison, you really should pay more attention to your personal hygiene, you know. Two sheets of lavatory paper is all it takes. One to wipe and one to polish. Oh, how you skipped after that Marlborough pack, you blissful creatures! But they wouldn't give you the ball, would they? They kept banging it on the ground and kicking it over your lovely goalpost.'

'It was the referee,' said Gooderson. 'He had it in for us.'

'Well whatever, Gooderson darling, the fact is that after this wonderful matinée performance there is no doubt that you are all going to become simply the toast of the town. Certain unscrupulous men may call upon you here in your dressing- room. They will lavish you with flowers, with compliments, with phials of Hungary water and methuselahs of the costliest champagne. You must be wary of such men, my hearts, they are not to be trusted.'

'What, what will they do to us?'

'They will take the tender flower of your innocence, Jarvis, and they will bruise it.'

'Will it hurt?'

'Not if it is prepared beforehand. If you come to my study this evening I will ready you for the process with a soothing unguent of my own invention. Wear something green, you should always wear green, Jarvis.'

'Ooh, can I come too?' said Rundell, who was by way of being the Tart of the House.

'And me!' squeaked Harman.

'All are welcome.'

The voice of Robert Bennett-Jones bellowed from the showers. 'Just shut up and get bloody dressed.'

'You're invited too, R.B.-J., didn't I make that clear?'

Bennett-Jones, hairy and squat, came out of the shower and stumped up to Adrian.

Cartwright dropped his rugger shirt into the laundry bin and left the changing-room, trailing his dufflebag along the ground. As the doors flapped behind him he heard Bennett-Jones's harsh baritone.

'You are disgusting, Healey, you know that?'

He should stay to hear Healey's magnificent putdown, but what was the point? They said that when Healey arrived he had got the highest ever marks in a scholarship entrance. Once, in his first term, Cartwright had been bold enough to ask him why he was so clever, what exercises he did to keep his brain fit. Healey had laughed.

9

'It's memory, Cartwright, old dear. Memory, the mother of the Muses . . . at least that's what thing-ummy said.'

'Who?'

'You know, what's his name, Greek poet chap. Wrote the Theogony . . . what *was* he called? Begins with an "H".'

'Homer?'

'No, dear. Not Homer, the other one. No, it's gone. Anyway. Memory, that's the key.'

Cartwright went into the House library and took down the first volume of the Chambers Encyclopaedia. He had still only got as far as Bismarck.

In the changing-room, Bennett-Jones snarled into Adrian's face.

'Just plain fucking disgusting.'

The others, some of whom had been peacocking about the room, stroking their towels round their napes like boas, staggered to guilty halts.

'You're a fucking queer and you're turning the whole House into fucking queers.'

'Queer am I?' said Adrian. 'They called Oscar Wilde a queer, they called Michelangelo a queer, they called Tchaikovsky a –'

'And they were queers,' said Sargent, another prefect.

'Well, yes, there is that,' conceded Adrian, 'my argument rather falls down there I grant you, but what I say is this, my door is always open to you, R.B.-J., and to you as well, Sargent, naturally, and if either of you has any problems in coming to terms with your sexuality you mustn't hesitate to visit me and talk about it.'

'Oh for God's sake – '

'We can thrash it out together. Personally I think it's your habit of dressing up in shorts and prancing about on a field and this bizarre obsession with putting your arms round the other members of the scrum and forcing your head between the bottoms of the back row that is at the root of this insane fixation. The lady doth protest too much, methinks.'

'Let's fucking throw him out,' said Sargent, advancing.

'Now I warn you,' said Adrian, 'if either of you touches me . . .'

'Yes?' sneered Bennett-Jones. 'What'll you do?'

'I shall sustain a massive erection, that's what, and I shan't be answerable for the consequences. Some kind of ejaculation is almost bound to ensue and if either of you were to become pregnant I should never forgive myself.'

This was just enough to bring the others down onto his side and have the prefects laughed into retreat.

'Well, my lovelies, I shall have to leave you now. I am promised to the Princes Despina this evening. A little baccarat after supper is my guess. She means to win back the Kurzenauer Emeralds. Jarvis, you have a stiffy, this is most unpleasant, someone throw some cold water over him. Goonight, Lou. Goonight, May. Goonight. Ta ta. Good night, ladies, good night, sweet ladies, good night, good night.'

English boarding schools have much to recommend them. If boys are going to be adolescent, and science has failed to come up with a way of stopping them, then much better to herd them together and let them

11

get on with it in private. Six hundred suits of skin oozing with pustules, six hundred scalps weeping oil, twelve hundred armpits shooting out hair, twelve hundred inner thighs exploding with fungus and six hundred minds filling themselves with suicidal drivel: the world is best protected from this.

For the good of society, therefore, Adrian Healey, like many Healeys before him, had been sent to a prep school at the age of seven, had proceeded to his public school at twelve and now, fifteen years old, he stood trembling with pubertal confusion on the brink of life. There was little to admire. The ravages of puberty had attacked his mind more than his skin, which was some kind of a blessing. From time to time a large, yellow-crowned spot would pop from his forehead, or a blackhead worm its way from the sweaty shelter of the side of his nose, but generally the complexion was good enough not to betray the hormonal crisis and mental havoc that boiled within and the eyes were wide and sensual enough for him to be thought attractive. Too smart at exam passing to be kept out of the Sixth Form, too disrespectful and dishonourable to be a prefect, he had read and absorbed more than he could understand, so he lived by pastiche and pretence.

His constipation, furred tongue and foul-smelling feet were no more than conventional school attributes, passed down from generation to generation, like slang and sadism. Adrian might have been unorthodox, but he was not so blind to the proper decencies as to cultivate smooth-flowing bowels or healthy feet. His good nature prevented him from discovering the pleasures of bullying and his cowardice allowed him to ignore it in others.

The great advantage of English public school life lies of course in the quality of tutelage it provides. Adrian had received a decent and broad English education in the area of his loins. Not all the credit for this could go to his schoolmasters, although a few of them had not been afraid to give practical guidance and instruction of a kind which would gladden the heart of those who believe that the modern teacher is slipshod in his approach to the Whole Boy. Mostly he had been given space to make his own way and learn his own lessons of the flesh. He had quickly happened upon the truth which many lonely contemporaries would never discover, the truth that everybody, simply everybody, was panting for it and could, with patience, be *shown* that they were panting for it. So Adrian grabbed what was to hand and had the time of his life genitally – focusing exclusively on his own gender of course, for this was 1973 and girls had not yet been invented.

His love life, however, was less happy. Earlier that afternoon he had worshipped at his altar in a private welter of misery that his public swagger never hinted at.

It had been upstairs, in the Long Dorm. The room was empty, the floorboards squeaking more faintly than usual beneath his tread. Cartwright's cubicle had its curtain drawn. The distant moan of whistles and cheers on the Upper Games Field and the nearer bang of a downstairs door slamming shut had unsettled him. They were over-familiar, with a bogus, echoing quality, a staginess that put him on his guard. The whole school knew he was here. They knew he liked to creep about the House alone. They were watching, he was convinced of it The background shouts of rugger and hockey weren't real, they were part of a taped soundtrack played to deceive him. He was walking into a trap. It had always been a trap. No one had ever believed in him. They signed him off games and let him think that he had the House to himself. But they knew, they had always known. Tom, Bullock, Heydon-Bayley, even Cartwright. Especially Cartwright. They watched and they waited. They all knew and they all bided their time until the moment they had chosen for his exposure and disgrace.

Let them watch, let them know. Here was Cartwright's bed and under the pillow, here, yes, here the pyjamas. Soft brushed cotton, like Cartwright's soft brushed hair and a smell, a smell that was Cartwright to the last molecule. There was even a single gold hair shining on the collar, and there, just down there, a new aroma, an aroma, an essence that rippled outwards from the centre of the whole Cartwrightness of Cartwright.

For Adrian other people did not exist except as extras, as bit-players in the film of his life. No one but he had noted the splendour and agony of existence, no one else was truly or fully alive. He alone gasped at dew trapped in cobwebs, at spring buds squeaking into life. Afternoon light bouncing like a yo-yo in a stream of spittle dropping from a cow's lips, the slum-wallpaper peel of bark on birches, the mash of wet leaves pulped into pavements, they grew and burst only in him. Only he knew what it was to love.

Haaaaaaah . . . if they really were watching then now was the time to pull back the curtain and jeer, now was the time to howl contempt.

But nothing. No yells, no sneers, no sound at all to burst the swollen calm of the afternoon.

Adrian trembled as he stood and did himself up. It was an illusion. Of course it was an illusion. No one watched, no one judged, no one pointed or whispered. Who were they, after all? Low-browed, scarlet-naped rugger-buggers with no more grace and vision than a jockstrap.

Sighing, he had moved to his own cubicle and laid out the astrakhan coat and top hat.

If you can't join them, he thought, beat them.

He had fallen in love with Hugo Alexander Timothy Cartwright the moment he laid eyes on him, when, as one of a string of five new arrivals, the boy had trickled into evening hall the first night of Adrian's second year.

Heydon-Bayley nudged him.

'What do you reckon, Healey? Lush, or what?'

For once Adrian had remained silent. Something was terribly wrong.

It had taken him two painful terms to identify the symptoms. He looked them up in all the major textbooks. There was no doubt about it. All the authorities concurred: Shakespeare, Tennyson, Ovid, Keats, Georgette Heyer, Milton, they were of one opinion. It was love. The Big One.

Cartwright of the sapphire eyes and golden hair, Cartwright of the Limbs and Lips: he was Petrarch's Laura, Milton's Lycidas, Catullus's Lesbia, Tennyson's Hallam, Shakespeare's fair boy and dark lady, the moon's Endymion. Cartwright was Garbo's salary, the National Gallery, he was cellophane: he was the tender trap, the blank unholy surprise of it all and the bright golden haze on the meadow: he was honey-honey, sugar-sugar, chirpy chirpy cheep-cheep and his baby-love: the voice of the turtle could be heard in the land, there were angels dining at the Ritz and a nightingale sang in Berkeley Square.

Adrian had managed to coax Cartwright into an amusing half-hour in the House lavs two terms previously, but he had never doubted he could get the trousers down: that wasn't it. He wanted something more from him than the few spasms of pleasure that the limited activities of rubbing and licking and heaving and pushing could offer.

He wasn't sure what the thing was that he yearned for, but one thing he did know. It was less acceptable to love, to ache for eternal companionship, than it was to bounce and slurp and gasp behind the fives courts. Love was Adrian's guilty secret, sex his public pride.

He closed the changing-room door and fanned himself with the lavender gloves. It had been a close thing. Too close. The greater the lengths he went to to be liked, the more enemies he gathered on the way. If he fell, Bennett-Jones and others would be there to kick him. One thing was for certain, the Queer Pose was running dry and a new one was going to have to be dreamt up or there would be Trouble.

A gang of fags was mobbing about by the notice-boards. They fell silent as he approached. He patted one of them on the head.

'Pretty children,' he sighed, digging into his waist-coat pocket and pulling out a handful of change. 'Tonight you shall eat.'

Scattering the coins at their feet, he moved on.

Mad, he said to himself as he approached his study door. I think I must be mad.

Tom was there, in a yoga position, biting his toe-nails and listening to *Aqualung*. Adrian sank into a chair and removed his hat.

'Tom,' he said, 'you are looking at a crushed violet, a spent egg, a squeezed tube.'

'I'm looking at a git,' said Tom. 'What's with the coat?'

'You're right,' said Adrian, 'I *am* stupid today. And every day. Stupid, stupid, stupid. Horrid, horrid, horrid. Morbid, morbid, morbid. Torrid, torpid, turbid. Everying in my life ends in id. Get it?'

'Get what?'

'Id. It's Freud. You know.'

'Oh. Right. Yeah. Id.'

'Idealistic idiot, idiosyncratic idler. Everything *begins* in id as well.'

'Everything begins with "I", you mean. Which is ego,' said Tom, placing an ankle behind his ear, 'not id.'

'Well of course it's very easy to be clever. If you could just help me out of this coat, I'm beginning to sweat.'

'Sorry,' said Tom. 'I'm stuck.'

'Are you serious?'

'No.'

Adrian fought his way out of his costume and into

17

his uniform while Tom reverted to a half-lotus and recounted his day.

'Went into town and bought a couple of LPs this afternoon.'

'Don't tell me,' said Adrian, 'let me guess . . . *Parsifal* and *Lark Ascending*?'

'*Atom Heart Mother* and *Salty Dog*.'

'Close.'

Tom lit a cigarette.

'You know what pisses me off about this place?'

'The cuisine? The distressingly plain uniforms?'

'I bumped into Rosengard in the High Street and he asked me why I wasn't watching the match. I mean what?'

'You should've asked him why *he* wasn't.'

'I said I was just on my way.'

'Rebel.'

'I like to keep my nose clean.'

'Well, "I'm just on my way" isn't a very stylish handkerchief, is it? You could have said that the match was too exciting and that your nervous system simply couldn't bear any more suspense.'

'Well I didn't. I came back here, had a wank and finished that book.'

'*The Naked Lunch*?'

'Yeah.'

'What did you reckon?'

'Crap.'

'You're just saying that because you didn't understand it,' said Adrian.

'I'm just saying that because I did understand it,' said Tom. 'Any road up, we'd better start making some toast. I invited Bullock and Sampson over.'

'Oh, *what*?'

'We owe them a study tea.'

'You know I hate intellectuals.'

'You mean you hate people who are cleverer than you are.'

'Yes. I suppose that's why I like you so much, Tom.'

Tom gave him a pained, constipated stare.

'I'll boil the kettle,' he said.

Cartwright looked up from the Chambers Encyclopaedia and mouthed, 'Otto Von Bismarck born in . . . in 1815, the year of Waterloo and the Congress of Vienna. Founder of modern Germany . . .'

In his line of sight were hundreds of books, the only one of which he could remember reading was *To Kill a Mockingbird* in the company of the rest of his fifth form at prep school. Such a great many books and yet this was still only the House library. The School library had thousands and thousands more and university libraries . . . Time was so short and his memory so feeble. What was it Healey had said? Memory is the mother of the Muses.

Cartwright levered Malthus to Nantucket from off the shelf and looked up Muses. There were nine of them and they were the daughters of Zeus and Mnemosyne. If Healey was right then Mnemosyne must mean memory.

Of course! The English word 'mnemonic', something that reminds you of something. Mnemonic must be derived from Mnemosyne. Or the other way around. Cartwright made a note in his rough-book.

According to the encyclopaedia, most of what was

known of the Muses came down from the writings of Hesiod, particularly this Theogony. That must have been the poet Healey was referring to, Hesiod. But how did Healey *know* all that? He never seemed to be reading, at least no more than anyone else. Cartwright would never catch up with him. It just wasn't bloody fair.

He wrote down the names of the Muses and returned with a sigh to Bismarck. One day he would get right to the end, to zythum. Not that he needed to. He had peeped ahead and seen that it was a kind of ancient Egyptian beer, much recommended by Diodorus Siculus – whoever he was.

Everyone had been rather surprised the day Adrian announced that he was going to share a study with Tom.

'Thompson?' Heydon-Bayley had shrieked. 'But he's a complete dildo, surely?'

'I like him,' said Adrian, 'he's unusual.'

'Graceless, you mean. Wooden.'

Certainly there was nothing obviously appetising about Tom's appearance or manner, and he remained one of the few boys of his year with whom Adrian had never made the beast with two backs, or rather with whom he had never made the beast with one back and an interestingly shaped middle, but over the last year, more people had come to see that there was something arresting about Tom. He wasn't clever, but he worked hard and had set himself to read a great deal, in order, Adrian assumed, to acquire some of Adrian's dash and sparkle. Tom always went his own way with his own ideas. He managed to get away with the longest hair in the House and the most public nicotine habit in the school, somehow without ever drawing attention to himself. It was as if he grew his hair long and smoked cigarettes because he liked to, not because he liked being seen to. This was dangerously subversive.

Freda, the German undermatron, once discovered him sunbathing nude in the spinney.

'Thompson,' she had cried in outrage, 'you cannot be lying about naked!'

'Sorry, Matron, you're right,' Tom murmured, and he had reached out a hand and put on a pair of mirrored sunglasses. 'Don't know what I was thinking of.'

Adrian felt that it was he who had brought Tom into notice and popularity, that Tom was his own special creation. The silent spotty gink of the first year had been transformed into someone admired and imitated and Adrian wasn't sure how much he liked it.

He liked Tom all right. He was the only person he had ever spoken to about his love for Cartwright and Tom had the decency not to be interested or sympathetic enough to quench the pure holy flame of Adrian's passion with sympathy or advice. Sampson and Bullock he could do without, however. Especially Sampson, who was too much of a grammar-school- type swot ever to be quite the thing. Not an ideal tea-companion at all.

Tea was a very special institution, revolving as it did around the ceremony and worship of Toast. In a place where alcohol, tobacco and drugs were forbidden, it was essential that something should take their

21

place as a powerful and public totem of virility and cool. Toast, for reasons lost in time, was the substance chosen. Its name was dropped on every possible occasion, usually pronounced, in awful public school accents, 'taste'.

'I was just having some toast, when Burton and Hopwood came round . . .'

'Harman's not a bad fag actually. He makes really majorly good toast . . .'

'Yeah, you should come round to my study, maybe, we'll get some toast going . . .'

'God, I can hardly move. I've just completely overdone it on the toast . . .'

Adrian had been looking forward to toasting up with Tom in private and talking about Cartwright.

'Oh, Christ,' he said, clearing a space on his desk for the teapot. 'Oh, Christly Christ.'

'Problem?'

'I shall know no peace other than being kissed by him,' moaned Adrian.

'That a fact?'

'It is a fact, and I'll tell you what else is a fact. It's a fact that he is wearing his blue Shetland turtle-neck today. Even as we speak his body is moving inside it. Warm and quick. It's more than flesh and blood can stand.'

'Have a cold shower, then,' said Tom.

Adrian banged down the teapot and grabbed Tom by the shoulder.

'Cold shower?' he shouted. 'Jessica Christ, man, I'm talking about love! You know what it does to me? It shrinks my stomach, doesn't it, Tom? It pickles my guts, yeah. But what does it do to my mind? It tosses

22

the sandbags overboard so the balloon can soar. Suddenly I'm above the ordinary. I'm competent, supremely competent. I'm walking a tightrope over Niagara Falls. I'm one of the great ones. I'm Michelangelo, moulding the beard of Moses. I'm Van Gogh, painting pure sunlight. I'm Horowitz, playing the Emperor Concerto. I'm John Barrymore before the movies got him by the throat. I'm Jesse James and his two brothers – all three of them. I'm W. Shakespeare. And out there it's not the school any longer – it's the Nile, Tom, the Nile – and down it floats the barge of Cleopatra.'

'Not bad,' said Tom, 'not bad at all. Your own?'

'Ray Milland in *The Lost Weekend*. But he could have been talking about Cartwright.'

'But he was talking about alcohol,' said Tom, 'which should tell you a lot.'

'Meaning?'

'Meaning shut up and get buttering.'

'I shall put the *Liebestod* on the stereo, that's what I shall do, you horrid beastly man,' said Adrian, 'and still my beating heart with concord of sweet sounds. But quick, man! – I hear a hansom drawing up outside! And here, Watson, unless I am very much mistaken, is our client now upon the stair. Come in!'

Sampson appeared at the doorway, blinking through his spectacles, followed by Bullock who tossed a jar at Tom.

'Hi. I brought some lemon curd.'

'Lemon curd!' said Adrian. 'And what was I saying only this minute, Tom?' "If only we had some lemon curd for our guests." You're a mind-reader, Bollocks.'

'Some toast over there,' said Tom.

23

'Thanks, Thompson,' said Sampson, helping himself. 'Gooderson tells me you were not unadjacent to mobbing up R.B.-J. and Sargent in the changing-rooms, Healey.'

'Dame Rumour outstrides me yet again.'

Not unadjacent? Jesus . . .

Bullock slapped Tom on the back.

'Hey, Tommo!' he said. 'I see you've got *Atom Heart Mother* at last. What do you reckon? Far outsville or far insville?'

While Tom and Bullock talked about Pink Floyd, Sampson told Adrian why he thought Mahler was in actual fact wilder, in the sense of more controlled, than any rock group.

'That's an interesting point,' said Adrian, 'in the sense of not being interesting at all.'

When the tea and toast were finished, Bullock stood up and cleared his throat.

'I think I should announce my plan now, Sam.'

'Definitely,' said Sampson.

'What ho!' said Adrian, getting up to shut the door. 'Treasons, stratagems and spoils.'

'It's like this,' said Bullock. 'My brother, I don't know if you know, is at Radley, on account of my parents thinking it a bad idea to have us both at the same school.'

'On account of your being twins?' said Adrian.

'Right, on account of my mother OD-ing on fertility drugs. Any old way, he wrote to me last week telling me about an incredible bitch of a row blazing there on account of someone having been and gone and produced an unofficial magazine called *Raddled*, full of obscene libellous *Oz*-like filth. And what I

24

thought, what Sammy and I thought, was – why not?'

'Why not what?' said Tom.

'Why not do the same thing here?'

'You mean an underground magazine?'

'Yup.'

Tom opened and shut his mouth. Sampson smirked.

'Jesus suffering fuck,' said Adrian. 'It's not half a thought.'

'Face it, it's a wow.'

'These guys,' said Tom, 'the ones who put out this magazine at Radley. What happened to them?'

Sampson polished his spectacles with the end of his tie.

'Ah, now this is why we must proceed with great circumspection. They were both, hum, "put out" themselves. "Booted out" I believe is the technical phrase.'

'That means it's got to be a secret,' said Bullock. 'We write it in the holidays. You send me the material, typed onto stencils. I get it duplicated on my dad's office Gestetner, bring it back at the beginning of next term, we find a way of distributing it secretly round all the Houses.'

'All a bit Colditz, isn't it?' said Tom.

'No, no!' said Adrian. 'Don't you listen to Thompson, he's an old cynicky-boots. I'm in, Bollocks. I'm in for definite. What sort of material do you want?'

'Oh you know,' said Bullock, 'seditious, anti-public school. That kind of thing. Something to shake them up a bit.'

'I'm planning a sort of *fabliau* comparing this place

25

with a fascist state,' said Sampson, 'sort of *Animal Farm* meets *Arturo Ui* . . .'

'Stop it, Sammy, I'm wet at the very thought,' said Adrian.

He looked across at Tom.

'What do you reckon?'

'Yeah, why not? Sounds a laugh.'

'And remember,' said Bullock, 'not a word to *anyone*.'

'Our lips are sealed,' said Adrian. *Lips. Sealed.* Dangerous words. Not five minutes could pass without him thinking of Cartwright.

Bullock took a tobacco tin out of his pocket and looked around the room.

'Now,' he said, 'if someone would close the curtains and light a joss-stick, I have here for your delight some twenty-four-carat black Nepalese cannabis resin which should be smoked immediately on account of it being seriously good shit.'

II

Adrian threw himself along the corridor towards Biffen's formroom. Dr Meddlar, one of the school chaplains, stopped him.

'Late, Healey.'

'Really, sir? So am I.'

Meddlar took him by the shoulders. 'You're riding for a fall, Healey, you know that? There are hedges and ditches ahead and you are on course for an almighty cropper.'

'Sir.'

'And I shall be cheering and laughing as you tumble,' said Meddlar, his spectacles flashing.

'That's just the warm-hearted Christian in you, sir.'

'Listen to me!' spat Meddlar. 'You think you're very clever, don't you? Well let me tell you that this school has no room for creatures like you.'

'Why are you saying this to me, sir?'

'Because if you don't learn to live with others, if you don't conform, your life is going to be one long miserable hell.'

'Will that give you satisfaction, sir? Will that please you?'

Meddlar stared at him and gave a hollow little laugh. 'What gives you the right to talk to me like that, boy? What on earth do you think gives you the right?'

Adrian was furious to find that there were tears springing to his eyes. 'God gives me the right, sir, because God loves me. And God won't let me be judged by a f-f-fascist – hypocrite – bastard like you!' He squirmed away from Meddlar's grasp and ran on down the corridor. 'Bastard,' he tried to shout, but the words choked in his throat. 'Fucking bloody bastard.'

Meddlar laughed after him. 'You're evil, Healey, quite evil.'

Adrian ran on and out into the quad. Everyone was in morning school. The colonnade was empty, the Old School Room, the library, the headmaster's house, the Founder's lawn, all deserted. This again was Adrian's home, an empty world. He imagined the whole school with noses pressed up against their form-room windows staring out at him as he ran through the West Quad. Prefects with walkie-talkies striding down the corridor.

'This is Blue Seven. Subject proceeding along past the Cavendish library towards the Music School. Over.'

'Blue Seven this is Meddlar. Interview went according to plan, subject now unstable and in tears. Red Three will continue surveillance in the Music School. Over and out.'

Either they've got a life and I'm imaginary, thought Adrian, or I've got a life and they're imaginary.

He'd read all the books, he knew he was really the same as anyone else. But who else had snakes wrestling in their stomachs like this? Who was running beside him with the same desperation? Who else would remember this moment and every moment like it to the last day of their lives? No one. They were all at their desks thinking of rugger and lunch. He was different and alone.

The ground floor of the Music School was filled with little practice-rooms. As Adrian stumbled along the passageway he could hear lessons in progress. A cello pushed a protesting Saint-Saëns swan along the water. A trumpet further along farted out 'Thine be the glory'. And there, third from the end, Adrian saw through the glass panel, was Cartwright, making quite a decent fist of a Beethoven minuet.

Fate was always doing this. There were six hundred boys in the school and although Adrian went out of his way to intercept Cartwright and to engineer apparently accidental meetings – he had learnt his time table off by heart – he was sure that he bumped into him by genuine chance more often than was natural.

Cartwright appeared to be alone in the practice-room. Adrian pushed open the door and went in.

'Hi,' he said, 'don't stop, it's good.'

'Oh, it's terrible really,' said Cartwright, 'I can't get the left hand working smoothly.'

'That's not what I've heard,' said Adrian and immediately wanted to bite off his tongue.

Here he was, alone in a room with Cartwright, whose hair was even now leaping with light from the sunshine that poured in through the window, Cart-wright whom he loved with his whole life and being and all he could find to say was 'That's not what I've heard.' Jesus, what was the *matter* with him? He might just as well have put on an Eric Morecambe voice, shouted 'There's no answer to that' and slapped Cartwright's cheeks.

'Um, official lesson?' he said.

'Well, I've got my Grade Three exam in half an hour, so this is a practice. It lets me off double maths at least.'

'Lucky you.'

Lucky you? Oh, pure Oscar Wilde.

'Well, I'd better let you get on with it then, hadn't I?'

Great, Adrian, brilliant. Magisterial. 'I'd better let you get on with it then, hadn't I?' Change one syllable and the whole delicate epigram collapses.

'Right,' said Cartwright and turned back to his music.

'Cheerio, then. G'luck!'

'Bye.'

29

Adrian closed the door.

Oh God, Oh Godly God.

He wound a fraught trail back to the form-rooms. Thank God it was only Biffen.

'You're extraordinarily late, Healey.'

'Well, sir,' said Adrian, sitting at his desk, 'the way I look at it, better extraordinarily late than extraordinarily never.'

'Perhaps you'd like to tell me what kept you?'

'Not really, sir.'

Something of a gasp ran round the form-room. This was going it a bit strong, even for Healey.

'I beg your pardon?'

'Well, not in front of the whole form, sir. It's rather personal.'

'Oh I see. I see,' said Biffen. 'Well, in that case, you had better tell me afterwards.'

'Sir.'

Nothing like getting a schoolmaster's curiosity glands juicing.

Adrian looked out of the window.

'Oh to be in Cartwright, now that March is here.'

Any minute now, some lucky examiner was going to be watching a lovely little frown furrow Cartwright's brow as he skipped through his minuet. Watching the woollen sleeve of his winter jacket ride up his arms.

'Whenas in wool my Cartwright goes, Then, then methinks how sweetly flows, That liquefaction of his clothes.'

He became aware of Biffen's voice knocking at the door of his dreams.

'Can you give us an example, Healey?'

30

'Er, example, sir?'

'Yes, of a subjunctive following a superlative.'

'A superlative, you say, sir?'

'Yes.'

'A subjunctive following a superlative?'

'Yes, yes.'

'Um . . . how about "*le garçon le plus beau que je connaisse*"?'

'Er . . . the finest boy that I know? Yes that meets the case.'

'Finest, sir? I meant the most beautiful.'

Damn, he was supposed to be phasing out the queer pose. Well, at least it got a laugh.

'Thank you, Healey, that will do. Be quiet, the rest of you, he really doesn't need any encouragement.'

Oh but I do, thought Adrian, I need all the encouragement going.

The lesson moved on, Biffen leaving him alone to daydream.

At the end of the forty minutes he reacted to the bell as fast as he could, streaking to the doorway from the back of the form-room and trying to lose himself in the crowd, but Biffen called him back.

'Aren't you forgetting something, Healey?'

'Sir?'

'You owe me an explanation for your unpunctuality, I think.'

Adrian approached the dais.

'Oh yes, sir. The thing is, sir, I was going to be late anyway – only a bit, but I bumped into Dr Meddlar.'

'He kept you for twenty minutes?'

'Yes, sir – or rather no, sir. He was very rude to me. He upset me, sir.'

31

'Rude to you? The Chaplain was rude to you?'

'I'm sure that's not how he would put it, sir.' Adrian had a shot at his pure but troubled expression. It was particularly effective when looking up at someone, as he was now. It was loosely based on Dominic Guard's Leo in the film of *The Go-Between*. A sort of baffled honesty.

'He . . . he made me cry, sir, and I was too embarrassed to come in blubbing, so I went and hid in the music-room until I felt better.'

This was all terribly unfair on poor old Biffen, whom Adrian rather adored for his snowy hair and perpetual air of benign astonishment. And 'blubbing' . . . Blubbing went out with 'decent' and 'ripping'. Mind you, not a bad new language to start up. 1920s schoolboy slang could be due for a revival.

'Oh dear. But I'm sure the Chaplain must have had good reason to be . . . that is, Dr Meddlar wouldn't speak sharply to you without cause.'

'Well I admit I was cheeky to him, sir. But you know what he's like.'

'He is, I am sure, a scrupulously fair man.'

'Yes, sir. I – I wouldn't want you to think that I've been lying to you, sir. I'm sure Dr Meddlar will tell you his side of the story if you ask him.'

'I won't do that. I know whether a boy is telling me the truth or not.'

'Thank you, sir.'

Did he hell. They never bloody did.

'I don't want to lecture you, Healey, and I don't want to keep you from your morning break, but you must face the fact that many members of staff are beginning to lose their patience. Perhaps you feel they don't understand you?'

'I think the problem is that they do understand me, sir.'

'Yes. You see that is exactly the kind of remark that is guaranteed to put certain masters' backs up, isn't it? Sophistication is not an admired quality. Not only at school. Nobody likes it anywhere. In England at any rate.'

'Sir.'

'You're the cleverest boy in my French set. You know that perfectly well. But you've never worked. That makes you the stupidest boy in the school.'

Parable of the talents next, what was the betting?

'What are your university thoughts?'

'Oh, well sir . . . you know. After "A" levels I think I'll've had it with education, really. And it will probably have had it with me.'

'I see. Tell me, what do you do on Friday afternoons, Healey? I take it you're not in the Cadet Force.'

'Threw me out, sir. It was an outrage.'

'Yes, I'm sure it was. So it's Pioneering, is it?'

'Yes, sir. There's a little old lady I visit.'

'Well,' said Biffen filling his briefcase with exercise books, 'there's a little old lady and a little old man in the Morley Road you might also find time to visit one day. My wife and I always give tea on Fridays, you'd be most welcome.'

'Thank you, sir.'

'You don't have to let us know in advance. We shall expect you when we see you. Off you go then.'

'Thank you, Mr Biffen, thank you very much.'

Adrian instinctively offered his hand which Biffen took with tremendous firmness, looking him straight in the eye.

'I'm not Mr Chips, you know. I'm perfectly well aware that you feel sorry for me. It's bad enough from the staff, but I won't take pity from you. I won't.'

'No sir,' said Adrian, 'I wasn't . . .'

'Good.'

III

Tom and Adrian and Pigs Trotter, an occasional hanger-on, were walking into town. From time to time tracksuited boys ran past them, with all the deadly purpose and humourless concentration of those who enjoyed Games. Juniors twittered along, running sticks against palings and whispering. Adrian thought it worth while trying out his new slang.

'I say, you fellows, here's a rum go! Old Biffo was jolly odd this morning. He gave me a lot of pi-jaw about slacking and then invited me to tea. No rotting! He did really.'

'I expect he fancies you,' said Tom.

'That's beastly talk, Thompson. Jolly well take it back or expect a good scragging.'

They walked on for a bit, Adrian practising new phrases and Pigs Trotter lumbering behind laughing so indiscriminately that Adrian soon tired of the game.

'Anyway,' he said. 'Tell me about your parents, Tom.'

'What do you want to know?'

'Well, you never talk about them.'

34

'Nothing to say about my folks,' Thompson said. 'Dad works for British Steel, Mum is next in line for Mayor. Two sisters, both mad, and a brother who's coming here next term.'

'What about you, Healey?' said Pigs Trotter. 'What do your parents do?'

'Parent,' said Adrian. 'The mother is no more.'

Trotter was upset.

'Oh God,' he said, 'I'm sorry. I didn't realise . . .'

'No, that's fine. Car crash. When I was twelve.'

'That's . . . that's awful.'

'If we go to Gladys Winkworth, I'll tell you the whole story.'

The church in the town was perched on a hill and in the cemetery – which people of shattering wit like Sampson never tired of calling 'the dead centre of town' – there was an old wooden bench on which was a plaque which said 'Gladys Winkworth'. Nothing else. The assumption was that it had been erected by a doting widower as a lasting memorial to his dead wife. Tom thought she was actually buried under it. Adrian believed it was simply the bench's proper name and he stuck to that belief.

From Gladys, the Upper, Middle and Lower Games Fields, the science block, the sports hall, the theatre, the Old School Room, libraries, chapel, Hall and Art School were all visible. You felt like a general observing a battle.

The day was cold and the breath steamed from their mouths and nostrils as they climbed through the graveyard.

'Alas, regardless of their fate the little victims play,'

35

said Adrian. 'The quick and the young play peep-bo behind the marking stones of the cold and the dead.'

Tom and Adrian sat down and waited for Pigs Trotter to catch up.

'It's not a nice story, the story of my mother,' said Adrian as Trotter finally crashed down beside them, 'but I'll tell it if you promise to keep it to yourselves. Only Pa Tickford knows. My father told him when I arrived here.'

Trotter nodded breathlessly. 'I won't tell a soul, Healey. Honest.'

Adrian looked at Tom who nodded gravely.

'Very well then,' said Adrian. 'One evening about three years ago . . . almost exactly three years ago in fact, I was sitting at home watching television. It was *A Man Called Ironside*, I remember. My father is a Professor of Biochemistry at Bristol University and he often works late. My mother had been in the kitchen since three in the afternoon drinking vodka from a teacup. At ten o'clock she smashed the cup onto the floor and cried out so I could hear her in the sitting room.'

Trotter shifted uncomfortably.

'Look,' he said. 'You don't have to tell us this, you know.'

'No, no, I want to. She had been, as I say, drinking all afternoon and she suddenly howled, "Ten o'clock! It's ten o'fucking clock! Why doesn't he come? Why in God's name doesn't he come?" Something along those lines.

'I went into the kitchen and looked at her face all swollen, her tear-stained and mascara-blotched cheeks and her trembling lip and I remember thinking, "She's

36

like Shelley Winters but without the talent." Don't know why a thought like that should come to me, but it did. I turned back to the telly – couldn't bear to look at her like that – and said, "He's working, Mother. You know he's working."

'"Working?" She shrieked her stinking breath right into my face. "Working! Oh that's very good. Screwing that *cunt* of a lab assistant is what he's doing. The little bitch. I've seen her . . . with her stupid white coat and her stupid white teeth. Little *bitch whore*!"'

Tom and Trotter both stared at Adrian in disbelief as he screeched out the words, but his eyes were closed and he didn't seem to be aware of them.

'She really could scream, my mother. I thought her voice would fracture with the violence of it, but in fact it was my own which cracked. "You should go to bed, Mother," I said.

'"Bed! He's the one who's in fucking bed," she giggled, and she pulled at the bottle and the last of the vodka just dribbled down her mouth and mixed with the tears that ran down the folds of her fat face. She burped and tried to jam the bottle into the waste-hole of the waste-disposal thing, the thingummy.'

'Garburator,' said Pigs Trotter. 'I think they're called Garburators.'

'Garburator, that's it. She tried to jam the bottle down the Garburator.

'"I'm *going* to *catch* them at their little *game*," she chanted – she put on a kind of sing-song voice whenever she was pissed, it was one of the signs that she was really gone – "*That's* what *I'm* going to *do*. Where are the keys?"

'"Mother, you can't drive!" I said. "Just wait, he'll be back soon. You see."

'"Where are the keys? Where are the fucking car keys?"

'Well, I knew exactly where they were. In the hall, on the table, and I ran for them and stuffed them into my mouth. God knows why. That really got her going.

'"Come here you little bastard, give me those keys!"

'I said, "Mother, you can't drive like this, just leave it, will you?"

'And then . . . then she picked up a vase from off the table and flung it at me. Broke on the side of my head and sent me flying against the foot of the stairs where I tripped and fell. See that scar, just there?'

Adrian parted his hair and showed Trotter and Tom a small white scar.

'Five stitches. Anyway, there was blood all running down my face and she was shaking me and slapping my face, left and right, left and right.

'"Will you give me those fucking keys?" she kept screaming, shaking me on every syllable. I sprawled there, I was crying I don't mind telling you, really wailing. "Please, Mother, you can't go out, you can't. Please!"'

Adrian stopped and looked around.

'Dare we risk a cigarette, do you think?'

Tom lit three at once.

'Go on!' said Pigs Trotter. 'What happened then?'

'Well,' said Adrian inhaling deeply, 'what Mother hadn't seen was that the moment the vase hit me, the car keys had shot out of me like a clay-pigeon from a trap. She thought I still had them in my mouth so she started to try and wrench it open, you know, like a vet trying to give a pill to a dog.

'"So the little bugger's swallowed them has he?" she said.

'I shouted back, "Yes, I've swallowed them! I've swallowed them and you can't get them back! So . . . so just forget it." But like a pratt of a heroine in a Hammer horror film I couldn't help looking round for them myself, so of course she followed my eyes, crawled across the hallway and swooped on them. Then she was off. I kept shouting at her to come back. I heard the scrunch on the gravel as she drove away and then – again like some git in a film – I fainted.'

'Christ,' said Pigs Trotter.

'She killed a family of four as well as herself,' said Adrian. 'My father, who had never had an unfaithful thought in his life, has still not really recovered. She was a bitch, my mother. A real bitch.'

'Yes,' said Tom. 'Thing is, Ade, you may have forgotten, but I met your mother last term. Tall woman with a wide smile.'

'Fuck,' said Adrian. 'So you did. Oh well, it was a good try anyway.' He stood and flicked his cigarette behind a gravestone.

Trotter stared at him.

'You mean,' he said. 'You mean that you made that up?'

'"Fraid so,' said Adrian.

'All of it?'

'Well my father's a professor, that bit's true.'

'You fucking shitbag,' said Trotter, tears filling his

eyes. 'You fucking shitbag!' He stumbled away, choking with tears. Adrian watched him go with surprise.

'What's the matter with Pigs? He must have known it was a lie as soon as I began.'

'Oh nothing,' said Tom, turning his large brown eyes on Adrian. 'His mother and two brothers were killed in a car crash three years ago, that's all.'

'Oh no! No! You're kidding!'

'Yes I am, actually.'

An MCC Tie sat down next to a Powder Blue Safari suit at a window table in the Café Bazaar. White Shirts with Black Waistcoats hurried to and fro, the change jingling in their leather pouches.

'Herr Ober,' *called the MCC Tie.*

'Mein Herr?'

'Zwei Kaffee mit Schlag, bitte. Und Sachertorte. Zweimal.'

The waiter executed a trim Austrian bow and departed.

The Powder Blue Safari Suit mopped his brow.

'No exchange was made,' *he said.*

'Well now,' *said the MCC Tie.* 'Odysseus will certainly have got hold of the documents and will be preparing to take them out of Salzburg. He must be followed and relieved of them.'

'If the Trojans are prepared to kill Patrochlus in broad daylight . . .'

'They won't dare harm Odysseus.'

'He has a companion, you know. A young Englishman.'

The MCC Tie smiled.

'I'm fully aware of it. How shall we style him?'

'Telemachus?'

'Quite right. Telemachus. Remind me to tell you all about Telemachus.'

41

'You know him?'

'Intimately. I think we will find that it won't be necessary to inflict harm upon either Odysseus or Telemachus. Just so long as we can lay our hands on Mendax.'

'They are leaving tomorrow.'

'Are they now? What kind of chariot are they riding?'

'Odysseus has a red Wolseley.'

'Typical. Quite typical.'

The MCC Tie looked across at the Safari Suit with an expression of affectionate contempt.

'I don't suppose, Hermes, that you possess such a thing as a short-wave wireless?'

'A report to make?'

'Don't be foolish. BBC World Service. The West Indies are playing England at Old Trafford today.'

'Playing? Playing what?'

'Cricket, you arse of a man. Cricket.'

Two

I

'The periphrastic "do" was a superfluous tense-carrier,' said Adrian. 'Semantically empty yet widely used. The major theories of the origin of the periphrastic "do" are three: One) It was derived from the influence of the corresponding use of "faire" in French. Two) It developed out of the Old English causative "do". Three) It derived from semantic development of the full factitive verb "do". An examination of these three theories should tell us much about alternative approaches to diachronic syntax and generative grammar.'

He looked across to the sofa. Trefusis was lying on his back, an overflowing ashtray on his chest, lightweight earphones around his neck and a square of mauve silk over his face, through which he managed to smoke. If it weren't for the rise and fall of the ashtray and the clouds of smoke weaving through the silk, Adrian might have thought him dead. He hoped not, this was a good essay he was reading out and he had taken a lot of trouble over it.

Friends had warned against the Philology option.

'You'll get Craddock, who's useless,' they said.

43

'Trefusis only teaches research students and a few select undergraduates. Do the American paper like everyone else.'

But Trefusis had consented to see him.

'The Early Middle English periphrastic "do" could occur after modals and "have" + past participle. It was essentially a second position non-modal operator mutually exclusive with "be" + past participle and incompatible with a passive format. As late as eighteen-eighteen some grammarians wrote that it was a standard alternate to the simple form, but others denounced its use in any but empathic, interrogative and negative sentences. By the mid-eighteenth century it was obsolete.'

Adrian looked up from his sheaf of papers. A brown stain was forming in Trefusis's handkerchief, as the silk filtered the smoke.

'Um . . . that's it . . .'

Silence from the sofa. Far away all the bells of Cambridge began to chime the hour.

'Professor Trefusis?'

He couldn't have slept through an essay of that quality, surely? Adrian cleared his throat and tried again, more loudly.

'Professor Trefusis?'

From under the handkerchief came a sigh.

'So.'

Adrian wiped the palms of his hands on his knees.

'Was it all right?' he asked.

'Well constructed, well researched, well supported, well argued . . .'

'Oh. Thank you.'

'Original, concise, thoughtful, perceptive, incisive,

illuminating, cogent, lucid, compelling, charmingly read . . .'

'Er – good.'

'I should imagine,' said Trefusis, 'that it must have taken you almost an hour to copy out.'

'Sorry?'

'Come, come, Mr Healey. You've already insulted your own intelligence.'

'Oh.'

'Val Kirstlin, *Neue Philologische Abteilung*, July 1973, "The Origin and Nature of the Periphrastic Verb 'Do' in Middle and Early Modern English". Am I right?'

Adrian shifted uncomfortably. It was hard enough to know what Trefusis was thinking when his face was unveiled; with a handkerchief over him he was as unreadable as a doctor's prescription.

'Look, I'm terribly sorry,' he said. 'The thing is . . .'

'Please don't apologise. Had you bothered to do any work of your own I should have been obliged to sit through it just the same, and I can assure you that I had much rather listen to a good essay than a mediocre one.'

Adrian couldn't think of an adequate reply to this.

'You have a fine brain. A really excellent brain, Mr Healey.'

'Thank you.'

'A fine brain, but a dreadful mind. I have a fine brain *and* a fine mind. Likewise Russell. Leavis, a good mind, practically no brain at all. Shall we continue like this, I wonder?'

'Like what?'

'This fortnightly exhibition of stolen goods. It all

45

seems rather pointless. I don't find the pose of careless youth charming and engaging any more than you find the pose of careworn age fascinating and eccentric, I should imagine. Perhaps I should let you play the year away. I have no doubt that you will do very well in your final tests. Honesty, diligence and industry are wholly superfluous qualities in one such as you, as you have clearly grasped.'

'Well, it's just that I've been so . . .'

Trefusis pulled the handkerchief from his face and looked at Adrian.

'But of course you have! Frantically busy. Fran-tic-ally.'

Trefusis helped himself to another cigarette from a packet that lay on top of a tower of books next to the sofa and tapped it against his thumb-nail.

'My first meeting with you only confirmed what I first suspected. You are a fraud, a charlatan and a shyster. My favourite kind of person, in fact.'

'What makes you so sure?'

'I am a student of language, Mr Healey. You write with fluency and conviction, you talk with authority and control. A complex idea here, an abstract proposition there, you juggle with them, play with them, seduce them. There is no movement from doubt to comprehension, no breaking down, no questioning, no excitement. You try to persuade others, never yourself. You recognise patterns, but you rearrange them where you should analyse them. In short, you do not think. You have never thought. You have never said to me anything that you believe to be true, only things which sound true and perhaps even ought to be true: things that, for the moment, are in

46

character with whatever persona you have adopted for the afternoon. You cheat, you short-cut, you lie. It's too wonderful.'

'With respect, Professor . . .'

'Pigswill! You don't respect me. You fear me, are irritated by me, envy me . . . you everything me, but you do not respect me. And why should you? I am hardly respectable.'

'What I mean is, am I so different from anyone else? Doesn't everyone think the way I think? Doesn't everyone just rearrange patterns? Ideas can't be created or destroyed, surely.'

'Yes!' Trefusis clapped his hands with delight. 'Yes, yes, yes! But who else *knows* that they are doing that and nothing else? *You* know, you have always known. That is why you are a liar. Others try their best, when they speak they mean it. You never mean it. You extend this duplicity to your morals. You use and misuse people and ideas because you do not believe they exist. Just patterns for you to play with. You're a hound of hell and you know it.'

'So,' said Adrian, 'what's to become of me then?'

'Ah, well. I could ask you not to bother me any more. Let you get on with your boring little life while I get on with mine. Or I could write a note to your tutor. He would send you down from the university. Either course would deprive me of the income, however nugatory, that I receive for supervising you. What to do? What to do? Pour yourself a glass of Madeira, there's Sercial or Bual on the side. Hum! It's all so difficult.'

Adrian stood and picked his way across the room.

Trefusis's quarters could be described in one word.

Books.

Books and books and books. And then, just when an observer might be lured into thinking that that must be it, more books.

Barely a square inch of wood or wall or floor was visible. Walking was only allowed by pathways cut between the piles of books. Treading these pathways with books waist-high either side was like negotiating a maze. Trefusis called the room his 'librarinth'. Areas where seating was possible were like lagoons in a coral strand of books.

Adrian supposed that any man who could speak twenty-three languages and read forty was likely to collect a few improving volumes along the way. Trefusis himself was highly dismissive of them.

'Waste of trees,' he had once said. 'Stupid, ugly, clumsy, heavy things. The sooner technology comes up with a reliable alternative the better.'

Early in the term he had flung a book at Adrian's head in irritation at some crass comment. Adrian had caught it and been shocked to see that it was a first edition of *Les Fleurs du Mal*.

'Books are not holy relics,' Trefusis had said. 'Words may be my religion, but when it comes to worship, I am very low church. The temples and the graven images are of no interest to me. The superstitious mammetry of a bourgeois obsession for books is severely annoying. Think how many children are put off reading by prissy little people ticking them off whenever they turn a page carelessly. The world is so fond of saying that books should be "treated with respect". But when are we told that *words* should be treated with respect? From our earliest years we are taught to revere only the outward and visible. Ghastly literary types maundering on about books as "objects". Yes, that does happen to be a first edition. A present from Noël Annan, as a matter of fact. But I assure you that a foul yellow *livre de poche* would have been just as useful to me. Not that I fail to appreciate Noël's generosity. A book is a piece of technology. If people wish to amass them and pay high prices for this one or that, well and good. But they can't pretend that it is any higher or more intelligent a calling than collecting snuff-boxes or bubble-gum cards. I may read a book, I may use it as an ashtray, a paperweight, a doorstop or even as a missile to throw at silly young men who make fatuous remarks. So. Think again.' And Adrian had thought again.

Now he found his way back to the small clearing where Trefusis lay on his sofa blowing smoke-rings at the ceiling.

'Your very good health,' said Adrian sipping his Madeira.

Trefusis beamed at him.

'Don't be pert,' he said, 'it isn't at all becoming.'

'No, Professor.'

There followed a silence in which Adrian eagerly joined.

He had stood in many studies in his day, tracing arabesques on the carpet with his foot, while angry men had described his shortcomings and settled his future. Trefusis was not angry. Indeed he was rather cheerful. It was perfectly apparent that he couldn't care less whether Adrian lived or died.

'As your Senior Tutor, I am your moral guardian,'

he said at last. 'A moral guardian yearns for an immoral ward and the Lord has provided. I shall strike a bargain with you, that's what I shall do. I am going to leave you in uninterrupted peace for the rest of the year on one condition. I want you to set to work on producing something that will surprise me. You tell me that ideas cannot be created. Perhaps, but they can be discovered. I have a peculiar horror of the cliché – there! the phrase "I have a peculiar horror" is just such a revolting expression as most maddens me – and I think you owe it to yourself, to descend to an even more nauseating phrase, to devote your energies to forging something new in the dark smithy of your fine brain. I haven't produced anything original myself in years, most of my colleagues have lived from the nappy onwards without any thought at all making the short journey across their minds, leave alone a fresh one. But if you can furnish me with a piece of work that contains even the seed of novelty, the ghost of a shred of a scintilla of a germ of a suspicion of an iota of a shadow of a particle of something interesting and provoking, something that will amuse and astonish, then I think you will have repaid me for being forced to listen to you regurgitating the ideas of others and you will have done a proper service to yourself into the bargain. Do we have a deal?'

'I don't quite understand.'

'Perfectly simple! Any subject, any period. It can be a three-volume disquisition or a single phrase on a scrap of paper. I look forward to hearing from you before the end of term. That is all.'

Trefusis fitted the earphones over his ears and groped under the sofa for a cassette.

'Right,' said Adrian. 'Er . . .'

But Trefusis had put the handkerchief back over his face and settled back to the sound of Elvis Costello.

Adrian set down his empty glass and poked out his tongue at the reclining figure. Trefusis's hand came up and jabbed an American single-fingered salute.

Oh well, thought Adrian as he walked across Hawthorn Tree Court on his way to the porter's lodge. An original idea. That can't be too hard. The library must be full of them.

At the lodge he cleared his pigeon-hole. The largest object there was a jiffy-bag stuck with a hand-made label saying 'Toast by Post'. He opened it and a miniature serving of marmalade, two slices of soggy toast and a note fell out. He smiled: more flattering attentions from Hunt the Thimble, a relic from his days at Chartham Park a year ago. He had thought then that life at Cambridge was going to be so simple.

The note was written in an Old English Gothic which must have taken Hunt the Thimble hours to master.

'He took the bread and when he had given thanks, he toasted it and gave it to Mr Healey saying, Take, eat, this is my body which is given for you: eat this in remembrance of me. Likewise after supper he took the sachet of Marmalade and when he had given thanks, he gave it to them saying, scoff ye all of this; for this is my Marmalade of the New Testament, which is spread for you: do this as oft as ye shall taste it, in remembrance of me. *Amen*.'

Adrian smiled again. How old would Hunt the Thimble be now? Twelve or thirteen probably.

There was a letter from Uncle David.

'Hope you're enjoying life. How's the college doing in the Cuppers this year? Had a chance to inspect the Blues XI? Enclosed a little something. I know how mess bills can mount up . . .'

Mess bills? The man must be getting senile. Still, three hundred quid was surprising and useful.

'. . . I shall be in Cambridge next weekend, staying at the Garden House. I want you to visit me on Saturday night at eight. I have a proposition to put to you. Much love, Uncle David.'

The pigeon-hole was also stuffed with circulars and hand-bills.

'A tea-party will be held on Scholar's Lawn, St John's College, to protest at American support for the regime in El Salvador.'

'The Mummers present Artaud's *The Cenci* in a new translation by Bridget Arden. Incest! Violence! A play for our times in the Trinity Lecture Theatre.'

'Sir Ian Gilmour will talk to the Cambridge Tory Reform Group about his book *Inside Right*. Christ's College. Admission Free.'

'Dr Anderson will give a lecture to the Herrick Society entitled *The Punk Ethic As Radical Outside*. Non-members £1.50.'

After a judicious binning of these and other leaflets, Adrian was left with Uncle David's cheque, the toast, a bill from Heffer's bookshop and a Barclaycard statement, both of which he opened as he walked back to his rooms.

He was astounded to discover that he owed Heffers

£112 and Barclaycard £206. With the exception of one or two novels, all the books itemised on the Heffer's bill were on art history. A Thames and Hudson edition of Masaccio alone had cost £40.

Adrian frowned. The titles were very familiar, but he knew that he hadn't bought them.

He quickened his pace across the Sonnet Bridge and into the President's Court, only to charge straight into a shrivelled old don in a gown. With a cry of 'Whoops!' the man, whom he recognised as the mathematician Adrian Williams, fell sprawling on the ground, sending books and papers flying over the grass.

'Dr Williams!' Adrian helped him up. 'I am sorry . . .'

'Oh hello, Adrian,' said Williams, taking his hand and springing up to his feet. 'I'm afraid neither of us was looking where we were going. We Adrians are notoriously abstracted, are we not?'

They skipped about the lawn collecting Williams's papers.

'Do you know,' said Williams, 'I tried one of those packet soups yesterday. "Knorr" it was called, K–N–O–R–R, a very strange name indeed, but Lord, it was delicious. Chicken Noodle. Have you ever tried it?'

'Er, I don't think so,' said Adrian picking up the last of the books and handing it to Williams.

'Oh you should, you really should! Miraculous. You have a paper packet no larger than . . . well let me see . . . what is it no larger than?'

'A paperback?' said Adrian shuffling from foot to

foot. Once cornered by Williams, it was very hard to get away.

'Not really a paperback, it's squarer than that. I should say no larger than a single-play record. Of course in area that probably *is* the same size as a paperback, but a different shape, you see.'

'Great,' said Adrian. 'Well I must be . . .'

'And inside is the most unprepossessing heap of powder you can imagine. The dried constituents of the soup. Little lumps of chicken and small hard noodles. Very unusual.'

'I must try it,' said Adrian. 'Anyway . . .'

'You empty the packet into a pan, add two pints of water and heat it up.'

'Right, well, I think I'll go to the Rat Man now and buy some,' said Adrian, walking backwards.

'No, the Rat Man doesn't sell it!' Williams said. 'I had a word with him about it this morning and he said he might get it in next week. Give it a trial period, see if there's a demand. Sainsbury's in Sidney Street has a very large supply, however.'

Adrian had nearly reached the corner of the court.

'Sainsbury's?' he called, looking at his watch. 'Right. I should just be in time.'

'I had the happy notion of adding an egg,' Williams shouted back. 'It poaches in the soup. Not unlike an Italian *stracciatella*. Singularly toothsome. Oh, you'll discover that Sainsbury's display a vegetable soup on the same shelf, also made by Knorr. It's quite hard to tell the two packets apart, but be sure to get the Chicken Noodle . . .'

Adrian rounded the corner and streaked for his rooms. He could hear Williams's voice cheerily exhorting him not to let it boil, as this was certain to impair the flavour.

Perhaps that's what Trefusis meant about not lying. Williams wasn't raving about his bloody soup in order to be respected or admired, he genuinely meant to impart a sincerely felt enthusiasm. Adrian knew he could never be guilty of any such unfiltered openness but he was damned if he was going to be judged because of it.

Gary was listening to Abba's *Greatest Hits* and leafing through a book on Miró when Adrian came in.

'Hello, darlin',' he said. 'I've just boiled the kettle.'

Adrian went up to the stereo, took off the record and frisbee'd it out of the open window. Gary watched it skim across the Court.

'What's up with you, then?'

Adrian took the Heffers and Barclaycard bills from his pocket and spread them out on Gary's book.

'You are aware that theft, obtaining goods and monies by false pretences and forgery are all serious offences?' he said.

'I'll pay you back.'

Adrian went to his desk and opened a drawer. His Heffers card and Visa card were missing.

'I mean, you might at least have told me.'

'I wouldn't have thought of being so vulgar.'

'Well I don't want to be vulgar either, but you now owe me a grand total of . . .' Adrian leafed through his notebook, 'six hundred and eighteen pounds and sixty-three pence.'

'I said I'd pay you back, didn't I?'

'I'm busy wondering how.'

'You can afford to wait. You should be glad to do a member of the working classes a favour.'

'And you should have too much pride to allow me . . . oh for God's sake!'

The sound of Abba singing 'Dancing Queen' had started up in a room the other side of the court. Adrian slammed the window shut.

'That'll teach you to throw things out of the window,' said Gary.

'It'll teach me *not* to throw things out of the window.'

'Suppose I pay you back in portraits?'

Adrian looked round the room. The walls were covered with dozens of different portraits of himself. Oils, water-colours, gouaches, grisailles, pen and ink, chalk, silverpoint, charcoal, pastels, airbrushed acrylics, crayons and even Bic biro drawings, ranging in style from neo-plasticist to photorealist.

He had been given no choice in the matter of sharing rooms. Gary and he were drawn out of the tombola together, so together they were. The bondage trousers, henna'ed hair and virtual canteen of cutlery that hung from his ears told the world that Gary was a punk, the only one in St Matthew's and as such as fascinating and horrifying an addition to the college as the modern Stafford Court on the other side of the river. Gary was reading Modern and Medieval Languages, but intended to change to History of Art in his second year: meanwhile he expressed his devotion to Adrian – real or pretended, Adrian never knew which – by treating him as an idiot older brother from another world. He had never met a public school boy before coming to Cambridge and hadn't really believed that they existed. He had been more shocked by Adrian than Adrian had been by him.

'And you really used to have fagging and that?'

'Yes. It's on the way out now I believe, but when I was there you had to fag.'

'I can't bleeding believe it! Did you wear a boater?'

'When appropriate.'

'And striped trousers?'

'In the Sixth Form.'

'Fuck me!' Gary had wriggled with delight.

'I'm hardly the only one, you know. There are dozens here from my school alone, hundreds from Eton and Harrow and Winchester.'

'Yeah,' said Gary, 'but it's less than seven per cent of the population, isn't it? People like me never usually meet people like you except in a Crown Court, when you're wearing a wig.'

'This is nineteen-seventy-nine, Gary, people like you are forming the Thatcher cabinet.'

Adrian had told him about life at school, about the magazine, about Pigs Trotter's death. He had even told him about Cartwright.

Gary had immediately done a drawing of Adrian as he imagined him in a blazer and cricket whites, dawdling in front of a Gothic doorway, while capped and gowned beaks flitted in the background like crows. Adrian had bought it on the spot for ten pounds. Since then he had subsidised Gary's cannabis and vodka by buying at least three works of art a week. But he didn't now think he could take even one more view of himself, in any medium, from any angle, and he said so.

'Well then,' said Gary, 'you're going to have to wait for me to pay you back till the end of the year.'

'Yes, I suppose I am,' said Adrian. 'Oh coitus!'

'Oh come on, you can afford it.'

'No, it's not that. It's work.'

'Work? I thought this was supposed to be a university.'

'Yes, well, it's rapidly turning into a technical college,' said Adrian, falling into an armchair.

'Didn't Trefusis go for your essay then?'

'No, he loved it, that's the problem,' said Adrian. 'It was too good. He was very impressed. So now he wants me to do something major. Something startling and original.'

'Original? In philology?'

'No, any subject. I should be flattered really, I suppose.'

Honestly, what was the point? He could tell the truth to Gary, surely? He was lying as a matter of course. Was it pride? Fear? He closed his eyes. Trefusis was right. Right but ludicrously wrong.

Why wasn't he happy? Jenny loved him. Gary loved him. His mother sent him money. Uncle David sent him money. It was the May Term of his first year, the weather was fine and he had no examinations. Everything unpleasant was behind him. Cambridge was his. He had now made up his mind to stay here after Finals and become a don. All you had to do was memorise enough good essays and repeat them in three-hour bursts. Trefusis wasn't an examiner, thank God.

He hung Jeremy, his blazer, on Anthony, the peg.

'Let's have some toast,' he said. 'Hunt the Thimble has provided.'

II

'We come now gentlemen,' said President Clinton-Lacey, 'to the matter of JRFs and Bye-Fellowships. I wonder if – '

Garth Menzies, a Professor of Civil Law, coughed through a cloud of dense smoke which poured into his face from the pipe of Munroe, the Bursar.

'Excuse me, Mr President,' he said, 'I understood we had agreed to a no-smoking rule at Fellows' meetings?'

'Well, that is certainly true, yes. Admiral Munroe, I wonder if you would mind . . .?'

Munroe banged his pipe down on the table and gave Menzies a look charged with deepest venom. Menzies smiled and transferred a sweet from one side of his mouth to the other.

'Thank you,' said Clinton-Lacey. 'Now. JRFs and Bye-Fellowships. As this body is well aware, there has been – '

Munroe sniffed the air loudly.

'Excuse me, Mr President,' he said. 'Am I alone in detecting a nauseating smell of spearmint in this room?'

'Er . . .?'

'It really is most disagreeable. I wonder where it could be coming from?'

Menzies angrily took the mint from his mouth and dropped it into the ashtray in front of him. Munroe smiled beatifically.

'Thank you,' said Clinton-Lacey. 'Fellows, we have a problem in retaining our present levels of postgraduates. There is a large number of Junior Research Fellows and Bye-Fellows that benefits from our grants and disbursements as you know. You will be far from unaware of the nature of the economic weather system that blows towards us from Westminster.'

Admiral Munroe ostentatiously pushed the ashtray into the centre of the table, as if the smell of mint still offended him.

Alex Corder, a theologian down the end of the table, barked a rather harsh laugh.

'Barbarians,' he said. 'They're all barbarians.'

'The government,' said Clinton-Lacey, 'the justice of whose doctrines we are not assembled here to discourse upon, has certainly struck an attitude towards the universities which must give us cause for alarm.'

'The Prime Minister is a scientist,' said Corder.

Garth Menzies raised his eyebrows. 'I'm sure no one would accuse the Prime Minister of academic partiality.'

'Why ever not?' said Munroe.

'Well, whatever her possible bias,' said Clinton-Lacey, 'there is a feeling in government that the Arts side, oversubscribed by candidates for entrance as it already is, must be, er, honed, and extra encouragement given to the disciplines which can more productively . . . ah! Professor Trefusis!'

Trefusis stood in the doorway, a cigarette dangling from his lips, peering vaguely as if unsure whether this was the right room or the right meeting. The sight of Menzies' disapproving glare seemed to reassure him; he entered and slid down into the empty seat next to Admiral Munroe.

'Well, Donald, I am sorry that you seem to have been delayed again,' said Clinton-Lacey.

Trefusis was silent.

'Nothing serious I hope?'

Trefusis smiled affably around the room.

'Nothing serious I hope?' repeated the President.

Trefusis became aware that he was being addressed, opened his jacket, switched off the Walk-man that was attached to his belt and slipped off his earphones.

'I'm sorry, Master, did you speak?'

'Well yes . . . we were discussing the fall-off in resources for the Arts.'

'The Arts?'

'That's right. Now . . .'

Menzies coughed and pushed the ashtray towards Trefusis.

'Thank you, Garth,' said Trefusis, flicking the ash from his cigarette and taking another puff. 'Most thoughtful.'

The President persevered.

'We will not have enough money to create any more Junior Research Fellows in the Arts for at least two years.'

'Oh, how sad,' said Trefusis.

'You are not concerned for your department?'

'*My* department? My department is English, Master.'

'Well precisely.'

'What has English to do with "the Arts", whatever they may be? I deal in an exact science, philology.

61

My colleagues deal with an exact science, the analysis of literature.'

'Oh poppycock,' said Menzies.

'No, if anything it's hard shit,' said Trefusis.

'Really, Donald!' said the President. 'I am sure there is no need . . .'

'Professor Trefusis,' said Menzies, 'this is a minuted meeting of adults, if you feel you can't preserve the decencies of debate then perhaps you should leave.'

'My dear old Garth,' said Trefusis, 'I can only say that you started it. The English language is an arsenal of weapons; if you are going to brandish them without checking to see whether or not they are loaded you must expect to have them explode in your face from time to time. "Poppycock" means "soft shit" – from the Dutch, I need scarcely remind you, *pappe kak*.'

Menzies purpled and fell silent.

'Well, be that all as it may, Donald,' said the President, 'the subject was resourcing. Whatever our views on the rights and wrongs of government policy, the fiscal reality is such that . . .'

'The reality,' said Trefusis, offering cigarettes around the table, 'as we all know, is that more and more young people are begging to be admitted to *this* college in *this* university to read English. Our English department receives a higher number of applicants for each available place than any other department in any other university in the country. If the rules of the market place, which I understand to be sacred to the gabies, guffoons and flubberhaddocks in office, are to apply, then surely we should be entitled to *more* fellowships, not fewer.'

'The feeling, Donald,' said the President, 'is that

English graduates cannot offer an expertise of benefit to the country. The fruits of research in botany or genetics or even my own subject, economics, are recognised as having a palpable value to the world . . .'

'Hear, hear,' said Menzies.

'Poppycock,' said Munroe, accepting a box of matches from Trefusis.

'But you and your colleagues,' said the President, ignoring both interruptions, 'are seen more and more as an intolerable burden on the tax-payer. There is nothing for you to discover of interest, nothing you can offer your undergraduates that fits them usefully into industry or profitable enterprise. You know that those are not *my* views. Around this table we have rehearsed many times the arguments and counter-arguments and I do not propose to do so again. I can only tell you that the monies will not be available this year.'

'Mr President,' said a don at the end of the table, 'I would like you to register my view that this is an absolute disgrace. This Philistinism will do nothing but impoverish our country. I hope you will minute my utter disgust.'

'Well,' said Trefusis, 'that should make Sir Keith Joseph and his friends shake in their boots, shouldn't it? No, no. The time has come for action. With the Fellows' approval I can train a hand-picked company of crack undergraduates and be in Whitehall before June.'

'This pose of embittered and embattled artist,' said Menzies, 'is unseemly and out of date. Society can no longer afford its jesters and is weary of being hit over the head with empty pigs' bladders. The world is bored of the piffling excesses of the Arts, of its arrogance and irrelevance to the real world. Your fat could do with trimming.'

'You're right of course,' said Trefusis, 'I see that now. We need lawyers. Wave upon wave of them.'

'Well of course it's very easy to mock . . .'

'It's certainly easy to mock some things,' agreed Trefusis. 'Oddly enough though I've never found it easy to mock anything of value. Only things that are tawdry and fatuous – perhaps it's just me.'

III

'So you see my little honeypot baby-squeeze,' said Adrian, 'I have to come up with some bloody piece of research or I may be out on my rather divinely shaped ear.'

'Well it's about time you did some work,' said Jenny, biting his nipple.

'That's a horrid thing to say. Now go a bit lower down and get those lips working, it's my turn to come and I have to be off to the University Library.'

Jenny sat up.

'That reminds me,' she said. 'Mary and I have written a letter to all the Senior Tutors in Cambridge.'

'Good God,' said Adrian, pulling her head down again, 'this is no time to babble of schoolgirl crushes.'

'No listen,' she said popping up. 'It's the pornography.'

'What?'

'You know I've been going to Tim Anderson's lectures on Derrida and Sexual Difference?'

'Look, if your mouth's busy you could at least use your hands. There's some baby oil under the bed.'

'Well, he showed us some pornography last week. Boxfuls of it. From the University Library. It's a copyright library, you see, so they get a copy of everything published. Everything.'

'What, you mean . . . everything?'

'Everything. Centuries of pornography up to the present day. The cellars are packed with tons of the most degrading and disgusting . . . I'm talking about amputees, children, appliances, things you could never even imagine.'

'You don't know what I could imagine.'

'I went to have a look at some of it. All I needed was Helen Greenman's signature. Told her it was to do with Tim Anderson's lectures. Well I mean, this stuff shouldn't be at Cambridge. It has no possible academic justification. It's degrading to women and should be burnt.'

'And degrading to animals and children and appliances, I shouldn't wonder.'

'Adrian, it's not funny. I think the UL dignifies this shit by storing it. So Mary and I are trying to get it banned.'

'What sort of things did you see exactly?'

'Well you have to view it in a private room . . .'

'Describe it to me . . . and use your left hand. That's it. A bit faster. Yes! Oh yes *indeed*. Now, what did you see?'

'Well there was one where this woman took a pork-pie . . .'

'That's the posish, Gary,' said Adrian when he had walked back from Newnham to St Matthew's. 'It's all there, a whole *index expurgatorius* waiting to be drooled over. And *this* is what the librarian needs to be shown.'

He handed him a small piece of paper on which was written:

'I authorise access to Jennifer de Woolf, an undergraduate of this college, to the following titles of Special Research Material . . .'

Underneath were listed titles of books and magazines and at the bottom was the signature, 'Helen Greenman, Senior Tutor, Newnham College'.

Gary's mouth fell open.

'*Elsa and the Bull, Young Nuns, Concentration Camp Action* . . . you're joking . . . *My Hot Little Daughter, Hung, Young and Handsome, Tampon Tina, Fist Fuck Faggots, Clingfilm Fantasies. Clingfilm*? Bleeding Christ.'

Adrian was rifling in the drawer of his desk.

'Too good to be missed I think you'll agree. Where are we . . . ah, yes.' He took a piece of writing-paper from his drawer. 'Now then, Gary, my old chum, my old mate, my old mucker. Do you want to knock off say . . . fifty quid from your debt? Of course you do. I want you to examine this letter, paying particular attention to the signature at the bottom.'

Gary took it.

'Dear Mr Healey, Dr Pittaway tells me that you are in need of instruction for the Philology option in

the English Tripos. I have not forgotten your expertise as an umpire when we met at Chartham Park last
summer and remember you as an alert young person
bright with capability and promise. I would therefore
be most happy to offer you what help I may. My
rooms are in Hawthorn Tree Court, A3. I shall expect
you at ten o'clock on Wednesday the 4th unless I hear
otherwise. Please be sure to bring your mind with
you. Donald Trefusis.'

'What about it?' said Gary.

'You can forge my signature, which is delicate and
elegant. This scrawl can't be beyond you?'

'You dirty fucker.'

'Well quite.'

V

Adrian walked through Clare College towards the
University Library. The impertinence of the building, as it launched upwards like a rocket, had always
annoyed him. Compared to the feminine domed grace
of Oxford's Bodleian or London's British Museum, it
was hardly a thing of beauty. It strained up like a
swollen phallus, trying to penetrate the clouds. The
same principle as a Gothic spire, Adrian supposed.
But the union of the library and the heavens would be
a very secular Word-made-Flesh indeed.

He went inside and made his way up to the
catalogue room. He flipped through the card indices,
scribbling down hopeful titles. Everywhere grey-
faced research graduates and desperate third year
students with books under their arms and private
worlds of scholarship in their eyes hurried back and

forth. He spotted Germaine Greer clutching a pile of very old books and Stephen Hawking, the Lucasian Professor of Mathematics, steering his motor-driven chair into the next room.

Do I really have a place here? Adrian wondered. All this work? This sweat? No short cuts, no cheating, no copying out, no grafting? Of course I do. A physicist doesn't work any harder than I do. He just copies out God's ideas. *And* he usually gets them wrong.

Gary watched Trefusis leave his rooms, briefcase in hand, trailing a cloud of smoke. He waited until five minutes after he had crossed the Sonnet Bridge before climbing the stairs to the first floor.

The latch of the outer oak door surrendered easily to Adrian's Barclaycard, as Adrian had said it would. Gary turned on the lights and surveyed the Manhattan of books before him.

It's got to be in here somewhere, he said to himself. I suppose I'll just have to wait for it to reveal itself.

Adrian went to the desk in the reading-room and waited to be noticed. It was very tempting to slap the counter and shout 'Shop!' He managed a polite cough instead.

'Sir?'

Librarians always seemed to treat Adrian with as much apathy and contempt as was possible without being openly rude. He would sometimes ask any one of the UL staff for a book written in, say, a rare dialect of Winnebago Indian, just for the hell of it, and they would hand it over with wrinkled noses and an air of superior scorn, as if they'd read it years ago and had long got over the stage where such obvious and juvenile nonsense could possibly be of the remotest interest to *them*. Had they somehow seen through him or was their contempt for undergraduates universal? The specimen who had come forward now seemed more than usually spotty and aloof. Adrian favoured him with an amiable smile.

'I'd like,' he said in ringing tones, '*A Fulsome Pair of Funbags* and *Flesby Dimpled Botts* please, and *Davina's Fun with Donkeys* if it's not already out . . . oh and *Wheelchair Fellatio* I think . . .'

The librarian pushed his spectacles up his nose.

'What?'

'And *Brownies and Cubs on Camp*, *Fido Laps it Up*, *Drink My Piss, Bitch* and *A Crocodile of Choirboys*. I believe that's all. Oh, *The Diary of a Maryanne*, too. That's a Victorian one. Here's an authorisation slip for you.'

Adrian flourished a piece of paper.

The librarian swallowed as he read it.

Tut-tut, thought Adrian. Showing Concern And Confusion. Infraction of Rule One of the Librarian's Guild. He'll be drummed out if he's not careful.

'Whose signature is this please?'

'Oh, Donald Trefusis,' said Adrian. 'He's my Senior Tutor.'

'One moment.'

The librarian moved away and showed the paper to an older man in the background.

It was like trying to get a large cheque cashed, the same whispered conferences and sly glances. Adrian turned and took a leisurely look around the room.

Dozens of faces immediately buried themselves back in their work. Other dozens stared at him. He smiled benignly.

'Excuse me, Mr . . . Mr Healey, is it?'

The older librarian had approached the counter.

'Yes?'

'May I ask for what purpose you wish to look at these . . . er . . . publications?'

'Research. I'm doing a dissertation on "Manifestations of Erotic Deviancy In . . ."'

'Quite so. This *appears* to be Professor Trefusis's signature. However I think I should ring him up if you don't mind. Just to make sure.'

Adrian waved a casual hand.

'Oh, I'm sure he wouldn't want to be bothered about this, would he?'

'These authorisations are not usual for undergraduates, Mr Healey.'

'Adrian.'

'I would be much happier.'

Adrian swallowed.

'Well of course, if you think it's necessary. I can give you his number in college if you like. It's – '

The librarian scented triumph.

'No, no, sir. We can find it ourselves, I'm sure.'

Gary managed to track down the telephone under an ottoman. He answered it on the fifth ring.

'Yes?' he panted. 'Trefusis here, I was just taking a crap, what is it? . . . Who? . . . Speak up man . . . Healey? . . . "Manifestations of Erotic Desire . . ."? Yes, Is there some problem? . . . Of course it's my signature . . . I see. A little trust would not go amiss,

70

you know. You're running a library, not a weapons depository, this bureaucracy is . . . No doubt, but that's what the guards at Buchenwald said . . . Very well, very well. You catch me in a bad mood this morning, take no notice . . . All right. Goodbye then.'

'That appears to be fine, Mr Healey. You appreciate that we had to make sure?'

'Of course, of course.'

The librarian gulped.

'These will take some time to . . . er . . . locate, sir. If you'd like to come back in half an hour? We'll provide a private reading-room for you.'

'Thank you,' said Adrian. 'Most kind.'

He bounced springily along the corridor on his way down to the tea-room.

I can fool all of the people all of the time, he thought.

A man walked past him.

'Morning, Mr Healey.'

'Morning, Professor Trefusis,' said Adrian.

Trefusis! Adrian skidded to a halt. He was heading for the reading-room! Not even Trefusis could answer his telephone at St Matthew's and be in the UL at the same time.

He tried to shout after him but could manage only a hoarse whisper.

'Professor! . . . Professor!'

Trefusis had reached the door. He turned in surprise.

'Yes?'

Adrian ran up to him.

'Before you go in, sir, I wondered if I could have a word?'

'Very well. What is it?'

'Can I buy you a bun in the tea-room?'

'What?'

'Well, I wondered . . . are you going in for a book or to do some work?'

'To do some work as it happens.'

'Oh, I shouldn't if I were you.'

Trefusis smiled.

'You've tried it and find it a disagreeable pursuit? I'm afraid in my case it has to be done. Someone, after all, has to write articles for future undergraduates to copy out.'

He put his hand to the finger-plate of the door.

Adrian only just managed to stop himself from tugging at his sleeve.

'Full. Not a reading table to be had. That's why I wanted to speak to you. Wondered if you could show me a good place to work.'

'Well, I find the ninth-floor reading-room is generally free from distraction. You might try there. However I am bound to say that I would feel a little bothered working in the same room as you. I'll go and see if there are any private rooms free on this floor, I think.'

He pushed against the door. Adrian practically screamed.

'No that's all right, sir! You go to the ninth floor. I've just remembered, I've got to go anyway. Got a . . . meeting.'

Trefusis came away from the door, amused.

'Very well. I am greatly looking forward to your

masterwork, you know. People think our subject is airy-fairy, namby-pamby, arty, not to put too fine a point on it, farty. But as you are no doubt discovering, it is grind and toil from Beowulf to Bloomsbury. Grind, grind, grind. Toil, toil, toil. I like the Kickers. Good morning.'

Adrian looked down at his shoes. They were indeed smart.

'Thank you, Professor. And your brogues are a riot.'

With breathless relief he watched Trefusis disappear round the corner towards the lifts.

Adrian got back to St Matthew's to find that Gary had pushed all the furniture back to the walls and cleared the floor, which was covered with a vast sheet onto which he was drawing in charcoals.

'How'd it go?'

'Fabulous. Like a breeze. Did you put a handkerchief in your mouth?'

'Nah! If there's one thing Trefusis sounds like, it's a man with no handkerchief in his mouth. I just went up two octaves and sounded pissed off.'

Adrian scrutinised Gary's activities.

'So. Second question. What are you doing to my room?'

'Our room.'

'Our room, that I furnish and pay for?'

'This is a cartoon.'

'A cartoon.'

'In the original sense.'

'So the original sense of cartoon is "total fucking mess" is it?'

'The original sense of cartoon is a sheet of material onto which you draw the outlines of your fresco.'

Adrian picked his way through the debris and poured himself a glass of wine from a half-empty bottle on the mantelpiece. A half-empty bottle of the college's best white burgundy, he noted.

'Fresco?'

'Yeah. When I've designed it, I simply hang the sheet over the wall, prick the outline onto the wet plaster and get to work as quickly as possible before . . .'

'What wet plaster would that be?'

Gary pointed to a blank space of wall.

'I thought there. We just rip off the old plasterwork, bit of bonding on the laths, and Bob's your uncle.'

'Bob is not my uncle. I have never had an uncle called Bob. I never intend to have an uncle called Bob. If being Bob's nephew involves destroying a five-hundred-year-old . . .'

'Six hundred years actually. It's going to be a representation of Britain in the late seventies. Thatcher, Foot, CND marches, unemployment. Everything. I paint it, then we cover it with wood panelling. That's the expensive bit. The panelling will have to be hinged, see? In a hundred years' time this room will be priceless.'

'It's already priceless. Couldn't we leave it as it is? Henry James had tea here. Isherwood made love to a choral scholar in that very bedroom. A friend of Thomas Hardy's committed suicide here. Marlowe and Kydd danced a galliard on these exact floorboards.'

74

'And Adrian Healey commissioned Gary Collins's first fresco here. History is an on-going process.'

'And what's our bedder going to say?'

'It'll brighten her day. Better than picking up the manky Y-fronts of the economists opposite.'

'Fuck you, Gary. Why do you always make me sound so prissy and middle-class?'

'Bollocks.'

Adrian looked round the room and tried to fight down his bourgeois panic.

'So, hinged panelling, you say?'

'Shouldn't cost too much if that's what you're worrying about. I picked up this builder who's working on the site of Robinson College. He reckons he can get me some good stuff for under five hundred and he'll do all the rendering and plastering for free if I let him fuck me.'

'Not exactly in the great tradition is it? I mean, I don't think that Pope Julius and Michelangelo came to a similar kind of arrangement about the Sistine Chapel. Not unless I'm very much mistaken.'

'Don't bet on it. Anyway, someone's got to fuck me, haven't they?' Gary pointed out. 'Since you won't I've got to look elsewhere. Makes good sense.'

'Suddenly the whole logic becomes clear. But what about work? I'm supposed to be working this term, don't forget.'

Gary got to his feet and stretched.

'Bugger that, that's what I say. How was the porn?'

'Incredible. You've never in all your life seen anything like it.'

'Naughty pictures?'

'I'm not sure I'm ever going to be able to look a

75

labrador in the face again. But, ruined as my faith in humankind may be, I have to say that we of the twentieth century are a pretty normal bunch compared to the Victorians.'

'Victorian porn?'

'Certainly.'

'What did they *do*? I've often wondered. Did they have dicks and fannies and the rest of it?'

'Well of course they did, you silly child. And the zestier volumes indicate that they had a great deal more. There's a – '

Adrian broke off. He had suddenly given himself an idea. He looked at Gary's cartoon.

Why not? It was wild, it was dishonest, it was disgraceful, but it could be done. It would mean work. A hell of a lot of work, but work of the right kind. Why not?'

'Gary,' he said. 'I suddenly find myself at life's crossroads. I can feel it. One road points to madness and pleasure, the other to sanity and success. Which way do I turn?'

'You tell me, matey.'

'Let me put it this way. Do you want to pay off all your debt in one, plus the five hundred for wooden panelling? I've got a job for you.'

'Okay.'

'That's my boy.'

Trefusis approached the counter of the reading-room. The young librarian looked at him in surprise.

'Professor Trefusis!'

'Good morning! How wags the world with you today?'

'I'm very fit thank you, sir.'

'I wonder if you can help me?'

'That's what I'm here for, Professor.'

Trefusis leant forward and lowered his voice conspiratorially, not an easy task for him. Among his many gifts he had never been able to count speaking in hushed tones.

'Oblige the whim of a man old and mad before his time,' he said, quietly enough for only the first twelve rows of desks behind him to catch every word, 'and tell me if there is any reason why I shouldn't have come in here an hour ago?'

'Pardon?'

'Why should I not have come into this room an hour ago? Was something afoot?'

The librarian stared. A man who services academics is used to all forms of mental derangement and behavioural aberration. Trefusis had always struck him as blithely and refreshingly free from nervous disorder. But, as the saying had it, old professors never die, they merely lose their faculties.

'Well apart from the fact that an hour ago you couldn't have been here . . .' he said.

'I couldn't?'

'Well not while you were at St Matthew's talking to Mr Leyland on the telephone.'

'I was talking to Mr Leyland on the telephone?' said Trefusis. 'Of course I was! Dear me, my memory . . . Leyland rang me up, didn't he? On the telephone, as I recall. That's right, it was the telephone, I remember distinctly, because I spoke to him through it. He rang me up, on the telephone, to talk to me about . . . about . . . what was it now?'

'To check your authorisation for that undergraduate to read those . . . those Reserved Publications.'

'Mr Healey that would have been?'

'Yes. It was all right, wasn't it? I mean, you did confirm . . .'

'Oh yes. Quite all right, quite all right. I was merely . . . humour me once more and let me have a copy of the titles Mr Healey wanted to see, would you, dear boy?'

VI

'Bust me, Sir!' said Mr Polterneck. 'Bust me if I haven't just the little warmint for your most partic'lar requirements just now a-curling up in innocent slumber in the back room. You can bounce me from here to Cheapside if that ain't the truest truth that ever a man gave utterance of. Mrs Polterneck knows it to be so, my Uncle Polterneck knows it to be so and any man as is acquainted with me could never be conwinced to the contrary of it, not if you boiled him and baked him and twisted him on the rack for another opinion.'

'I am assured of your good faith in this matter?' asked Peter.

'Lord, Mr Flowerbuck. I'm in the way of weeping that you might have doubt of it! My good faith in this matter is the one sure fact you may most particular be assured of! My good faith is a flag, Mr Flowerbuck. It is a tower, Sir, a Monument. My good faith is not made of air, Mr Flowerbuck, it is an object such as you might touch and look upwards on with wonder and may you whip me until I bleed if that ain't so.'

'Then I suppose we might do business?'

'Now then, Sir,' said Mr Polterneck, producing a most preposterous handkerchief of bright vermilion silk with which he mopped his brow. 'He's a most especial warmint, is Joe Cotton. Most particular especial. To a gentleman like yourself as I can tell is most discerning in the nature of young warmints, he is a nonparelly. I could sonnet you sonnets, Mr Flowerbuck, about the gold of his tresses and the fair smoothness of his young skin. I could ballad you ballads, Sir, on the theme of the fair round softness of his rump and the garden of paradise that awaits a man within. I've a stable of young colts, Sir, as I can say the like would not be found in any district of the City, nor without the City too, and Master Cotton, Sir, is my Prize. If that ain't recommendation enough you can hang me by the neck right now, Sir, from old Uncle Polterneck's lintel, and have done with me for a lying rascal.'

It was all Peter could do to restrain himself from taking Polterneck fully at his word. The fear of what foul gases might ooze from the creature's lungs as he did so and what contamination he would suffer in the handling of him kept his vengeful fury at bay quite as much as the reflection that he must proceed as levelly as he might with the business in hand.

'I suppose you can tell me nothing of his provenance?' he asked indifferently.

'As to his provenance, Sir, I'm in the way of thinking, and Mrs Polterneck is the same, and Uncle Polterneck is hardly of a different persuasion, that he was sent down from Heaven, Sir. Sent down from Heaven itself to put bread in the mouths of my kinfolk and give pleasure and boon to gentlemen such as yourself, Sir. That is my opinion of his provenance and the man ain't been given birth to who could shake me out of it. You never seen such beauty in a lad, Sir. And how he's all compliance and skill in the Art he has been called to! A wonder to see him set to work, Sir. They say a young sister was sent down with him.'

'A girl? His twin, perhaps?'

'Well, now that you are in the line of remarking on the matter, I did hear mention as how the girl *was* his twin, Sir! A golden beauty of like complexion, for those that admires the same in the gentle sex. Where she might be, I have no knowledge, nor interest neither. Young cock-chicks is my game, Sir, the hen-birds is too devilish tickerly a proposition for a peaceable gentleman like myself. Bust me if they don't start a-breeding and a-parting with chicks of their own afore they've paid their way and how,' wheezed Mr Polterneck, 'is a man of business to procure the blessing of prosperity for his hearth when his stock is all a-laid up and a-breeding?'

'So you have no knowledge of this sister's whereabouts?'

'As to Whereabouts, whereabouts is different to provenance, Sir. Whereabouts is Mystery, and ask Mrs Polterneck and Uncle Polterneck if I don't deal in nothing but certainty. The whereabouts of Miss Judith is in doubt, the whereabouts of Master Joe is in the back room. If you are needful of a pretty little lady . . .'

'No, no. Your Joe will do.'

'Indeed, Sir, as I hope he *will* do.'

'As for price?'

'Ah now, Mr Flowerbuck,' said Polterneck, wagging a greasy finger. 'Seeing as we're agreed on the warmint's celestial provenance, I can't have my proper say in the affair of Fees. If he was my own I'd say a crown, and Mrs Polterneck and Uncle Polterneck would cry that I was a-cheating myself cruel and I would shake my head sorrowful and raise the fee another crown to please 'em! I should happily settle at that price, though Mrs P. and Uncle P. would complain I was cheating myself still. I was born generous and I can't help it and won't give apology to no man for it. But for all I can cheat myself, Mr Flowerbuck, I can't be cheating Heaven! It wouldn't be right, Sir. I could rob myself with a will an it pleased my gentlemen, for my customers is all to me, but I can't go robbing the Angels, Mr Flowerbuck, I can't. It ain't in me to do so. A full sovereign for the evening, back again by six next morning.'

Peter forbore once more to put a period to the rottenest life in the rottenest den in the rottenest borough in the rottenest city in all the rotten world. He pressed a coin into Polterneck's hand.

'Bring the boy to me!' he whispered.

Polterneck clapped his hands.

'Flinter!'

In the shadows at the back of the room a figure rose from out the straw. It was the figure of a boy, no older in appearance than fourteen years, although in a city where children of six have the eyes and gait of old men, indeed the same life of experience to look back upon, and where youths of twenty are so kept back in growth by filth and hunger that they retain the aspect of frail infants, it was impossible for Peter to determine the true age of this specimen. But that was never his concern, for his eyes were ever fixed upon the face. Or upon the part where the face ought by rights to have been. For it was not a face he fixed his gaze upon. A face, my Lords and Ladies and fine gentlemen, has eyes, does it not? A face must boast ears, a mouth, some arrangement of all the features that sniff and see and hear and taste before it can lay claim to that title. That they sniff the stench of villainy, see the deepest shame, hear the most degraded blasphemies and taste aught but the bitterest sorrows – that is never the face's affair! The face presents these organs each set in their place to look at what they will and listen where they please. What countenance deserves the name therefore – my lords who look upon gold plate, my ladies who breathe fine perfumes, my friends who taste plump mutton and hear the sweet harmony of a loving voice – what face can be called a face which has not a nose set upon it? What term might we invent to describe a face whose nose is all ate up? A face with a hole in its middle where a nose should have stood – be it a nose pinched and long, swollen and bulbous, or Roman and aloof, be it any kind of nose plain or pretty – a face, I say, with a black nullity where nostrils and bridge should be presenting themselves for admiration or disgust, that is no face but the face of Shame, no countenance but the countenance of Want. It is the visage of Sin and Lust, the aspect of Need and Despair but not – I beg the favour of your believing me – not, an hundred times never, the face of a human child.

'Flinter! Fetch down young Joe for the gentleman.

And Flinter! don't you never dream of touching no part of him neither, or bust me if you don't find your head a suddenly lacking of two ears also!'

Polterneck turned to Peter with an indulgent smile, for all the world as if to say 'Bless my buttons if I don't lavish more care on my young lads than they deserve!' He must then have caught sight of the expression of revulsion and horror on Peter's face, for he hastened to whisper an explanation.

'The pox, Mr Flowerbuck! The pox is a sore trial in my line of working. He was a good worker was Master Flinter and nor I don't have the heart to dismiss him now the pox has taken away his smeller.'

'I should imagine,' said Peter, 'that . . .'

'Slow down, for God's sake,' said Gary. 'My fucking wrist is about to drop off.'

Adrian stopped pacing the room.

'Sorry,' he said. 'I was getting carried away. What do you reckon so far?'

'Not sure about "bulbous".'

'You're right. I'll check it tomorrow.'

'It's two o'clock in the morning and I'm about to run out of ink. I'm going to crash.'

'Finish the chapter?'

'In the morning.'

*In a service-station car-park off the Stuttgart – Karlsruhe
Autobahn, a Tweed Jacket and a dark Blue Marks &
Spencer's Leisure Shirt were licking their wounds.*

'I just can't believe it,' *the Leisure Shirt was saying.* 'I
mean out of nowhere and for what?'

'Perhaps they fancy themselves as latter day highway
robbers,' *offered the Tweed.*

'Well that greasy one in a safari suit wasn't exactly my
idea of a Dick Turpin.'

'No,' *said the Tweed. He looked at the Leisure Shirt, who
had turned away and started kicking a tree stump.*

'Why did I have to go and suggest what is obviously the
most secluded bloody service-station on the whole sodding
Autobahn?'

'I blame myself, Adrian, I should have parked nearer the
main building, I do hope you are all right?'

'Well they didn't take my passport or wallet, at least. In
fact as far as I can see they didn't take anything.'

'Not quite true.'

*The Tweed gestured forlornly towards the back seat of the
Wolseley.*

'My briefcase, I regret to say.'

'Oh. Anything in it?'

'Some papers.'

'Phew. Lucky escape then, I suppose. Shall we call the police?'

Three

Three

I

At the front of the tractor, fed from its power-take-off, was a picker. A conveyor belt ran along the side and disgorged the potatoes onto a rolling rack. Adrian and Lucy's job was to 'dress' them, to pull out the rotten, green or squashed potatoes as they trundled on their way to Tony, who stood at the end of the line, bagging the survivors. Every twenty or thirty minutes they would stop and unload a dozen full sacks into a pile in the middle of the field.

It was revolting work. The rotten and the good looked alike, so Lucy and Adrian had to pick up and examine each potato that jigged and bounced along in front of them. The bad ones burst under the slightest pressure, exploding in a squelch of stinking mucus. When it rained, mud sprayed up from the wheels and spattered their faces and clothes; when it was dry, clouds of dust choked them and matted their hair. The endless clanking, grinding, whining roar could have been the soundtrack for one of those Hieronymous Bosch visions of Hell, Adrian thought, where the moaning damned stand with their hands over their ears while demons frolic gleefully around them, probing their intimate parts with forks.

But in hell the inmates would at least try to strike up conversations with each other, hard as it might be to make themselves heard above the rumble of the treadmills and the roar of the furnaces. Lucy and Tony, brother and sister, never said a word to Adrian beyond a "Ning' when he turned up, freezing, at dawn and a "Nernight, then' at dusk when, stiff as a statue, he mounted his bicycle to pound wearily home to bath and bed.

Lucy just stared at the potatoes. Tony just stared at his bagging apparatus. Sometimes Adrian caught them staring at each other, in a manner which reminded him of the joke definition of a Cotswold virgin: an ugly girl under twelve who can run faster than her brother.

Lucy was no beauty, but if the looks she exchanged with Tony were anything to go by, Adrian guessed that she was no sprinter either.

The fact that he was expected to work at all in the Easter holidays had come as a blow. He was quite used to being told to find a job for the summer: waiting on tables at the Cider With Rosie restaurant, folding bolts of baize at the wool factory, treadling the cardboard-box machine at the ICI plant in Dursley, picking currants at Uley, feeding the birds at the Wildfowl Trust in Slimbridge.

'But Easter!' he had moaned into his cereal, the first morning of the holidays. 'No, Mother, no!'

'You're fifteen, darling! Most boys of your age like the idea of some kind of light work. Father thinks it's a good idea.'

'I know he does, but I've already *got* work to do. My school project.' Adrian was thinking of the article he had promised Bullock he would write for the school underground magazine.

'He doesn't want you wasting your time loafing around indoors.'

'That's pretty rich coming from him. He spends the whole bloody year cooped up in his sodding laboratory.'

'That's not fair, Ade. You know it isn't.'

'I've never had to get a job in the Easter hols before.'

His mother poured herself a fourth cup of tea.

'Won't you try it for me, darling? See how it goes?'

'Well it just means I'll have to write my essay over the Easter weekend, doesn't it? Or am I expected to pick bloody potatoes all through the most important sacred festival in the whole bloody Christian bloody calendar as well?'

'Of course not, darling. I'm sure you'll enjoy working for Mr Sutcliffe, he's a very nice man. And Father will be so pleased.'

She brushed his cheek with the back of her hand. But Adrian wasn't going to take it gracefully. He stood up and washed his bowl under the tap.

'Don't bother, darling. Betsy will do that.'

'It's a bloody swizz. I mean, it's cricket next term. I've got to get some practice in.'

'Well I'm sure you'll get nice and fit at the farm, dear.'

'That's not the same as practising is it?'

'Don't whine, Ade. It's a very ugly sound. And I must say I'm not sure I know where this sudden enthusiasm for sports comes from, dear. Mr Mountford said in your report that you failed to attend a single rugby game or a single PE lesson last term.'

'Cricket's different,' said Adrian. 'I mean, you send me off to school for most of the year and then as soon as I come back you can't wait to get rid of me. I just hope you won't both be surprised if I lock you in an old people's home when you're old and smelly.'

'Darling! Don't be horrid.'

'And I'll only come and visit you to give you work to do. Shirts to iron and socks to darn.'

'Ade, that's an awful thing to say!'

'And only then will you know what it's like to be unloved by your own flesh and blood!' said Adrian, drying his hands. 'And don't giggle woman, because it isn't funny!'

'No darling, of course it isn't,' his mother said with her hand over her mouth.

'Oh I give up,' he had said and put a tea-towel on her head. 'I bloody give up.'

Human spirit, or lack of it, is such that, foul as the work was, Adrian found himself so lulled by the routine that sometimes the hours would pass like minutes. He tried hard to concentrate on composing in his head his contribution for the magazine. But he was always being distracted by other thoughts. He found himself playing a drama in which he cast himself as God and the potatoes as humans. This one he hurled into outer darkness, that one he sent to be garnered home.

'Well done, thou good and faithful spud, you may go to your reward.'

'Sinner! Corrupted one. I pluck thee out, I pluck thee out. Look, with a spot I damn thee.'

He wasn't sure if it was better to be a rotten potato or a healthy one, whether he would rather be safely bunched up in a warm bag with the goody-goodies or be thrown over the side and ploughed back into the soil. One thing was certain, either of those fates was preferable to being God.

The green potatoes were especially interesting. Donald Sutcliffe, the farmer, had explained them to him one lunchtime.

'Spuds have to grow underground, see. If they poke up through the soil and catch the rays of the sun you'll get photosynthesis and that gives you chlorophyll which'll turn them green. A green potato is a relative of Woody Nightshade. Not as poisonous, but he won't do you any good.'

This immediately made Adrian think that he was a green potato and Cartwright was the sun.

I have been kissed by the light and transformed, he thought. I am dangerous and God has rejected me.

He was always doing that these days. Everything he saw became a symbol of his own existence, from a rabbit caught in headlights to raindrops racing down a window-pane. Perhaps it was a sign that he was going to become a poet or a philosopher: the kind of person who, when he stood on the sea-shore, didn't see waves breaking on a beach, but saw the surge of human will or the rhythms of copulation, who didn't hear the sound of the tide but heard the eroding roar of time and the last moaning sigh of humanity fizzing into nothingness. But perhaps it was a sign, he also thought, that he was turning into a pretentious wanker.

On the last working day before Easter, Maundy Thursday, the four of them had been loading bags onto the trailer in thickening twilight when Adrian caught sight of a gathering of huge birds, as black as priests, pecking at rotten potatoes at the further end of the field.

'Look at the size of those crows!' he had cried.

'Boy,' said Mr Sutcliffe, tugging at a sack, 'when you see a load of crows together, them's rooks. And when you see a rook on its own, that's a fucking crow.'

'Oh,' said Adrian. 'Right. But supposing a rook gets lost or wanders off by itself. What would you call that?'

Mr Sutcliffe roared with laughter.

'Well I don't know about you, lad, but I'd call it a crook!'

II

'A SCHOOL FOR SCANDAL'
or
'The Education of an English Gentleman'
by
Woody Nightshade

The Daisy Chain Club is exclusive. Exclusive because you can only join if you sleep in a junior dormitory, one without cubicles. It isn't hard to become a member. Membership is enforced. If one person refuses, the club cannot meet.

The rules are simply learnt. After lights out you stretch out your right hand until it finds your neighbour's <u>membrum virile</u>. The same is being done to you by the boy on your left. At a given signal from the President of the club (always the Prefect whose duty it is to have to sleep in a junior dormitory), it's all hands to the pumps and last one home's on the bathroom-cleaning roster for a week.

It's a calm, civilised and amiable club, The Daisy Chain. There are ones like it in every house in the school and in every public school in the land. An acquaintance from Ampleforth tells me of the Hot Cupboard Society, another from Rugby of the Milk-Shake Club, whose name speaks for itself. A Wykhamist friend told me of a pursuit at Winchester called the Biscuit Game. The players stand around in a circle tossing off onto a Wholemeal Digestive. The last one to spit his stuff on the biscuit eats it. A new kind of cream filling well in advance of anything McVitie's have got round to thinking of. Packed with potassium and vitamins, too.

From time to time news of these little entertainments leaks out. A careless word from Bletchley-Titherton to his older sister, a letter home from a young Savonarola and the whistle is blown. There follow tears, recriminations and hasty expulsions.

This is strange. Let's face it boys, most of our fathers went, if not to this school, at least to others like it. Most of the staff too. Milk-Shake Clubs and their like are as old as the chapel steps.

But this is England, where the only crime is to be Found Out.

'My dear old fellow, we all know what goes on but it really doesn't do to shout about it. Upsets the apple-cart, muddies the water, what?'

I can't help thinking of the House of Commons. Six hundred or so men, most of them public school. They pronounce daily on the moral evils of the world, but just think my dears, just think of the things they have done and continue to do to their bodies and the bodies of others.

We are being groomed for power. In twenty years' time we will see fellow members of The Daisy Chain Club on television talking about oil prices, giving the Church's viewpoint on the IRA, presenting Blue Peter, closing down factories, handing down severe sentences from the bench.

Or will we?

The world is changing. We grow our hair long, we take drugs. How many people reading this have not smoked cannabis on school premises? We are not very interested in power, we are very interested in putting the world right.

Now that is really intolerable. No my-dear-old-fellowing for that kind of crime.

The Daisy Chain Club may provoke tears,

recriminations, hasty expulsions and even hastier cover-ups and laughings-off. But long hair, pot and real rebellion, they provoke anger, hatred and madness. When young people shag each other off in the dorms they are engaging in a charming old custom, a time-honoured ritual: the only reason that there are expulsions is that the tradition is hard to explain to tearful mothers and snide newspapers. But when boys say that they would rather be drummers than barristers, gardeners than businessmen, poets than soldiers, that they don't think much of examinations and authority and marriage, that when they are of age they intend to remake the world to fit them, not remake themselves to fit the world, then there is Trouble.

Someone once said that Capitalism is the exploitation of man by man and Communism is the exact reverse. I expect most of us agree with that. I don't know any schoolboy Communists, but I do know hundreds of schoolboy revolutionaries.

In the 60s the ideal was to overthrow by force. I don't know if you've seen the film 'If ...' I doubt it, every year the cinema club tries to show it and every year Headman forbids it. The film ends with a band of schoolboys turning into guerillas and assassinating parents and staff. People said that although it was set in a school it was supposed to be a metaphor for real life. Well I don't know about you, but for me school is real life. And probably will be for years. I have no interest in shooting any of the masters dead of course (well, no more than two or three, tops), but I have a lot of interest in challenging their authority. Not wresting it from them, necessarily, but <u>challenging</u> it. Asking where it comes from, how it is earned. If we are told that it is earnt on the basis of age and strength alone, then we know what kind of world we are living in and I hope we will know what to do about it. We are always being asked to show respect. Well, we can show respect with the best of them, what we find it hard to do is to <u>feel</u> respect.

Our generation, the 70s Generation, is calling for a social revolution, not a pol—

'Adrian!'

'Oh, bollocks!'

'We're ready to go now, darling.'

'Go? Go where?' shouted Adrian.

'To church, of course.'

'But you said I didn't have to!'

'What?'

Adrian came out of his room and looked down into the hall. His mother and father were standing by the door swathed in their dominical best.

'I'm in the middle of my school project. You said I didn't have to go to church.'

His father snorted.

'Don't be ridiculous! Of course you do.'

'But I was working . . .'

'You'll put on a tie and come down *now*!'

'You're a fucking maniac,' said Tom.

'*You're* a fucking maniac,' said Adrian.

'We're all fucking maniacs,' said Bullock.

They were in Bullock and Sampson's study leafing through copies of *Bollocks!*

The trunk they sat on felt to them like a powder keg. It contained seven hundred copies ready for distribution.

'Come on kids,' Bullock had said when Adrian had suggested the title at the end of the previous term, '*BUM* is much better. Bullock's Underground Magazine. Bollocks is my nickname for God's sake. Everyone will know I had something to do with it.'

'That's the whole idea, my little love-noodle,' Adrian had replied. 'No one is going to believe that Brainy Bollocks himself would be so stupid as to name a subversive underground magazine after himself.'

So *Bollocks!* it was. There was no artwork because only Sampson and Tom had much skill at drawing and their styles were too readily identifiable.

The magazine they now looked through was a simple fifteen pages of gestetnered typescript on green paper. No handwriting, no illustrations or distinguishing characteristics of any kind. It could have been done by any person or persons in any House in the school. Bullock had had no trouble typing and reproducing the stencils in total secrecy at home.

After many crossings-out and changes of direction, Adrian's piece had been sent off to Bullock's address in Highgate the Tuesday after Easter: reading it back now he found it rather tame and half-hearted next to the libretto of a rock opera on school life that Bullock had contributed and Tom's frankly hairy analysis of the heroin counter-culture in *The Naked Lunch*. Sampson's allegory of red and grey squirrels was simply incomprehensible.

'Now,' said Tom, 'we face the problemette of distribution.'

'More of a problemola than a problemette,' said Bullock.

'A problerama, even,' said Sampson.

'I'd go so far as to call it a problemellaroni,' said Bullock.

'It's a real cunt,' said Tom, 'no question.'

'I don't know though,' said Adrian, 'we've all been on cube calls, haven't we? We should know how to break into the Houses.'

'I've never been on one actually,' said Sampson.

'Well, I've been on plenty,' said Adrian. 'In fact, I believe I hold the House record.'

Discipline is a sensitive subject in public schools; the flogging of offenders, the toasting of small boys in front of fires, the forcing of uncomfortable objects up their bottoms, the hanging of them upside down by their ankles, all these cruel and unusual forms of punishment had died out at Adrian's school by the time he arrived. Headman sometimes flicked a cane, masters gave lines, detentions or remissions of privilege and prefects gave cube calls, but imaginative violence and cunning torture were things of the past. It had been three years since a boy had been emptied upside down in a lavatory or had his dick slammed in a desk. With this kind of leniency and liberalism in sentencing in our premier educational establishments, many thought that it was no wonder the country was going to the dogs.

When the cube call, whose violence was bureaucratic rather than physical, had been invented, no one could say. A single cube call was a small slip of paper given by a prefect to an offender. It contained the name of another prefect, always from another House. A double cube call contained two names of two different prefects, again from two different Houses. Adrian was the only boy in living memory who had been given a sextuple cube call.

The recipient of the call had to get up early, change into games clothes, run to the House of the first prefect on the list, enter the prefect's cubicle, wake him up and get him to sign next to his name. Then on to the next prefect on the list, who was usually in a House right at the other end of the town. When all the signatures had been collected, it was back to his own House and into uniform in time for breakfast at ten to eight. So that offenders couldn't cheat by going round in the most convenient geographical order, or by getting up before seven o'clock, the official start time, the prefects on the list had to put down the exact time at which they were woken up next to their signatures.

Adrian detested cube calls, though a psychologist might have tried to persuade him otherwise, considering how far out of his way to collect them he seemed to go. He thought it an illogical form of punishment, as irritating for the prefects who were shaken from their slumbers as for the offenders.

The system was open to massive abuse. Prefects

could settle scores with colleagues they disliked by sending them cube callers every day for a week. Tit-for-tat cube call wars between prefects could go on like this for whole terms. In Adrian's House, Sargent had once had a feud with a prefect in Dashwood House called Purdy. On every day of one horrendous week Adrian had collected single cube calls from Sargent for absurd minor offences: whistling in his study during prep; having his hands in his pockets while watching a match; failing to cap a retired schoolmaster who had been walking down the High Street and whom Adrian had never even had pointed out to him before as a cappable entity. On each of Sargent's cube calls that particular week Purdy's had been the name listed. On the fifth day Adrian had sidled apologetically into Purdy's cube to find it empty.

'The bird had flown, my old love,' he had tried to explain to Sargent when returning his unsigned chit. 'But I did abstract Purdy's sponge-bag from his bedside, just to prove that I was in his cube.'

That afternoon Sargent and Purdy had fought each other on the Upper. After that Adrian was left alone.

Of course prefects could do each other favours as well.

'Oh Hancock, there's a not-half scrummy scrum-half in your Colts Fifteen, what's his name?'

'What, Yelland you mean?'

'That's the one. Rather fabulous. You . . . er . . . couldn't find your way clear to sending him over one morning, could you? As a little cubie?'

'Oh all right. If you'll send me Finlay.'

'Done.'

Adrian as a new boy had been startled to find, on his first ever cube call, that the prefect whose signature he needed slept naked with only one sheet to cover him and was extremely hard to wake up.

'Excuse me, Hollis, Hollis!' he had squeaked desperately in his ear.

But Hollis had just groaned in his sleep, rolled an arm over him and pulled him into his bed.

The only really enjoyable part of the cube call for Adrian was the burglary. Officially all the Houses were locked until seven, which was supposed to make it pointless to set off early on a cube call and take the thing at a leisurely pace. But there were larder, kitchen and changing-room windows that could be prised open and latches that could yield to a flexible sheet of mica. Once inside all you had to do was creep up to the dorm, tiptoe into the target prefect's cube, adjust his alarm clock and wake him. That way you could start the call at half past five or six and save yourself all the flap and hurry of trying to complete it in forty minutes.

'Yup,' Adrian told Bullock. 'Don't you worry your pretty little head about it. I reckon I know a way into every House.'

Two days later the whole school awoke to *Bollocks!*

From three in the morning until half past six, Tom, Adrian, Bullock and Sampson, working from maps and instructions drawn up by Adrian, had invaded the Houses and left copies in studies, common rooms, libraries and in piles at the foot of staircases. They had seen no one and been seen by no one. They had come down to breakfast in their House as apparently amazed and excited by the appearance of the magazine as everyone else.

In school, before morning chapel, they joined the knots of people under the noticeboards in the colonnade, twittering about its contents and trying to guess who the authors were.

He had been wrong to worry that the sophistication of the others' contributions would outshine his. His brand of salacious populism was far more interesting to the school than the recondite pedantry of Bullock and Sampson, and much less aggressive than Tom's style of Open Field Beat. The most feverish speculation of the day centred around the identity of Woody Nightshade. Everywhere Adrian went he heard snatches of his article being quoted.

'Hey there, Marchant. Fancy a quick round of the Biscuit Game?'

'They can chop off your hair, my children, but they can't chop off your spirit. We are winning and they know it.'

'A school isn't an ante-room for real life, it is real life.'

'Passive resistance!'

'Let's set our own syllabus. Fail their exams, pass our own.'

The school had never known anything like this. At the eleven o'clock break on the morning of its appearance there was no other topic of conversation in the Butteries.

'Go on, admit it, Healey,' Heydon-Bayley said to Adrian, his mouth full of cream-slice, 'it was you wasn't it? That's what everyone's saying.'

'That's odd, someone told me it was you,' said Adrian.

He found it achingly frustrating not to be able to crow about his part in it. Bullock, Sampson and Tom revelled in the anonymity, but Adrian longed for applause and recognition. Even jeering and hissing would have been something. He wondered if Cartwright had read his article. What would he think of it? What would he think of the *author* of it?

He watched very closely to see how people reacted when accused of being a contributor. He was always trying to improve his mastery of the delicate art of lying and the spectacle of people telling the truth under pressure repaid close study.

He noticed that people said things like:

'Yeah, it was me actually.'

'Piss off, Aitcheson! Everyone knows it was you.'

'Oh God! How did you find out? Do you think Headman knows?'

Adrian memorised all the replies and reproduced them as faithfully as he could.

And then the authorities had struck back.

Adrian's Housemaster, Tickford, rose to his feet after lunch that same day, as did the other eleven Housemasters in the other eleven Houses.

'All copies of this magazine will be collected from studies by the prefects before Games this afternoon and destroyed. Anyone found in possession of a copy after three o'clock will be severely punished.'

Adrian had never seen Tickford look so furious. He wondered if he could possibly have guessed that *Bollocks!* had originated in his House.

He and Tom had handed their two copies in cheerfully.

'There you go, Hauptmann Bennett-Jones,' said Adrian, 'we have also an edition of *The Trial*, by the notorious Jew, Kafka. Berlin would appreciate it, I am thinking, if this too was added to the bonfire. Also the works of that decadent lesbian Bolshevik, Jane Austen.'

'You'd better watch it, Healey. You're on the list. If you had anything to do with this piece of shit then you are in trouble.'

'Thank you, Sargent. You needn't take up any more of our valuable time. I'm sure you have many calls of a similar nature to make in the neighbourhood.'

But for all the sensational impact of the magazine, Adrian felt somehow a sense of anti-climax. His article would never make a shred of difference to anything. He hadn't exactly expected open warfare in the form-rooms, but it was depressing to realise that if he and Bullock and the others were exposed tomorrow they would be expelled, talked about for a while and then completely forgotten. Boys were cowardly and conventional. That's why the system worked, he supposed.

He sensed too that if he came across the article in later life, as a twenty-year-old, he would shudder with embarrassment at the pretension of it. But why should his future self sneer at what he was now? It was terrible to know that time would lead him to betray everything he now believed in.

What I am now is *right*, he told himself. I will never

see things as clearly again, I will never understand everything as fully as I do at this minute.

The world would never change if people got sucked into it.

He tried to explain his feelings to Tom, but Tom was not in communicative mood.

'Seems to me there's only one way to change the world,' said Tom.

'And what's that?' asked Adrian.

'Change yourself.'

'Oh, that's bollocks!'

'And *Bollocks!* tells the truth.'

He went to the library and read up his symptoms in more detail. Cyril Connolly, Robin Maugham, T.C. Worsley, Robert Graves, Simon Raven: they had all had their Cartwrights. And the novels! Dozens of them. *Lord Dismiss Us*, *The Loom of Youth*, *The Fourth of June*, *Sandel*, *Les Amitiés Particulières*, *The Hill* . . .

He was one of a long line of mimsy and embittered middle-class sensitives who disguised their feeble and decadent lust as something spiritual and Socratic.

And why not? If it meant he had to end his days on some Mediterranean island writing lyric prose for Faber and Faber and literary criticism for the *New Statesman*, running through successions of houseboys and 'secretaries', getting sloshed on Fernet Branca and having to pay off the Chief of Police every six months, then so be it. Better than driving to the office in the rain.

In a temper, he took out a large Bible, opened it at random and wrote 'Irony' down the margin in red biro. In the fly-leaf he scribbled anagrams of his name. Air and an arid nadir, a drain, a radian.

He decided to go and see Gladys. *She* would understand.

On his way he was ambushed from behind a gravestone by Rundell.

'Ha, ha! It's Woody Nightshade!'

'You took the words right out of my mouth, Tarty. Only you would know about something as disgusting as the Biscuit Game.'

'Takes one to know one.'

Adriam mimed taking out a notebook.

'"Takes one to know one," I must write that down. It might come in useful if I ever enter a competition to come up with the Most Witless Remark in the English Language.'

'Well I beg yours.'

'You can't have it.'

Rundell beckoned with a curled finger. 'New wheeze,' he said. 'Come here.'

Adrian approached cautiously.

'What foul thing is this?'

'No, I'm serious. Come here.'

He pointed to his trouser pocket. 'Put your hand in there.'

'Well frankly . . . even from you, Tarty, that's a bit . . .'

Rundell stamped his foot.

'This is serious! I've had a brilliant idea. Feel in there.'

Adrian hesitated.

'Go *on*!'

Adrian dipped his hand in the pocket.

Rundell giggled.

'You see! I've cut the pockets out. And no undies. Isn't that brilliant?'

'You tarty great tart . . .'

'Keep going now you've started, for God's sake.'

Adrian reached Gladys and sat down with a thump. Down below, Rundell blew an extravagant kiss and skipped off to replenish his strength before trying the game on someone else.

Why can't I be satisfied with Tarty? Adrain asked himself, wiping his fingers on a handkerchief. He's sexy. He's fun. I can do things with him I wouldn't dream of doing with Cartwright. Oh hell, here comes someone else.

'Friend or foe?'

Pigs Trotter lumbered into view.

'Friend!' he panted.

'La! You are quite done up, my lord. Come and sit this one out with me.'

Trotter sat down while Adrian fanned himself with a dock-leaf.

'I always think the cotillion too fatiguing for the summer months. Persons of consequence should avoid it. When I have danced a cotillion, I know for a fact that I look plain beyond example. The minuet is, I believe, the only dance for gentlemen of rank and tone. You agree with me there, my lord, I make no doubt? I think it was Horry Walpole who remarked, "In this life one should try everything once except incest and country dancing." It is an excellent rule, as I remarked to my mother in bed last night. Perhaps you will do me the honour of accompanying me to the card room later? A game of Deep Bassett is promised and I mean to take my lord Darrow for five hundred guineas.'

'Healey,' said Trotter. 'I'm not saying you did and I'm not saying you didn't, I don't really care. But Woody Nightshade . . .'

'Woody Nightshade,' said Adrian. '*Solanum dulcamara*, the common wayside bitter-sweet:

> They seek him here, they seek him there,
> Those masters seek him everywhere.
> Isn't he nimble, isn't he neat,
> That demmed elusive bitter-sweet.

'A poor thing, but mine own.'

'You've read his article, I suppose?' said Pigs Trotter.

'I may have glanced through it a few times in an idle hour,' said Adrian. 'Why do you ask?'

'Well . . .'

There was a catch in Trotter's throat. Adrian looked at him in alarm. Tears were starting up in his piggy eyes.

Oh hell. Other people's tears were more than Adrian could cope with. Did you put an arm round them? Did you pretend not to notice? He tried the friendly, cajoling approach.

'Hey, hey, hey! What's the matter?'

'I'm sorry, Healey. I'm really sorry b-but . . .'

'You can tell me. What is it?'

Trotter shook his head miserably and sniffed.

'Here look,' said Adrian, 'there's a handkerchief. Oh . . . no, second thoughts this one's not so clean. But I have got a cigarette. Blow your nose on that.'

'No thanks, Healey.'

'I'll have it then.'

He eyed Trotter nervously. It was cheating to let your emotions out like this. And what was a lump like Pigs doing with emotions anyway? He had found a handkerchief of his own and was blowing his nose with a horrible mucous squelch. Adrian lit his cigarette and tried to sound casual.

'So what's troubling you, Trot? Is it something in the article?'

'It's nothing. It's just that bit where he starts talking about . . .'

Trotter drew a copy of *Bollocks!* from his pocket. It was already folded open on the second page of Adrian's article.

Adrian looked at him in surprise.

'I wouldn't get caught with this if I were you.'

'It's all right, I'm going to throw it away. I've copied it all out by hand anyway.'

Trotter dabbed a finger down on a paragraph.

'There,' he said, 'read that bit.'

'"And they call it puppy-love,"' Adrian read, '"well I'll guess they'll never know how the young heart really feels." The words of Donny Osmond, philosopher and wit, strike home as ever. How can they punish us and grind us down when we are capable of feelings strong enough to burst the world open? Either they know what we go through when we are in love, in which case their callousness in not warning us and helping us through it is inexcusable, or they have never felt what we feel and we have every right to call them dead. Love shrinks your stomach. It pickles your guts. But what does it do to your mind? It tosses the sandbags overboard so the balloon can soar. Suddenly, you're above the ordinary . . .'

Adrian looked across at Pigs Trotter who was rocking forwards and tightly gripping his handkerchief as if it were the safety-bar of a roller-coaster.

'It's a misquotation from *The Lost Weekend* that bit, I think,' said Adrian. 'Ray Milland talking about alcohol. So. You . . . er . . . you're in love then?'

Trotter nodded.

'Um . . . anyone . . . anyone I'd know? You don't have to say if you don't want to.' Adrian was maddened by the huskiness in his throat.

Trotter nodded again.

'It . . . must be pretty tough.'

'I don't mind telling you who it is,' said Trotter.

I'll kill him if it's Cartwright, Adrian thought to himself. I'll kill the fat bastard.

'Who is it then?' he asked, as lightly as he could.

Trotter stared at him.

'You of course,' he said and burst into tears.

They walked slowly back towards the House. Adrian wanted desperately to run away and leave Pigs Trotter to welter in the salt bath of his fatuous misery, but he couldn't.

He didn't know how to react. He didn't know the form. He supposed that he owed Trotter something. The object of love should feel honoured or flattered, responsible in some way. Instead he felt insulted, degraded and revolted. More than that, he felt put upon.

Trotter?

Pigs can fly. This one could, anyway.

It isn't the same, he kept saying to himself. It isn't

the same as me and Cartwright. It can't be. Jesus, if I were to declare my love to Cartwright and he felt a tenth as pissed off as I do now . . .

'It's all right, you know,' said Pigs Trotter, 'I know you don't feel the same way about me.'

Feel the same way about me? Christ.

'Well,' said Adrian, 'the thing is, you know, I mean it's a phase, isn't it?'

How could he say that? How could he *say* that?

'It doesn't make it any better though,' said Trotter.

'Right,' said Adrian.

'Don't worry. I won't bother you. I won't tag onto you and Tom any more. I'm sure it'll be all right.'

Well there you are. If he could be so sure that it would be 'all right' then how could it be love? Adrian knew that it would never be 'all right' with him and Cartwright.

Trotter's wasn't the Real Thing, it was just Pepsi.

They were nearing the House. Pigs Trotter dried his eyes on the sleeve of his blazer.

'I'm very sorry,' said Adrian, 'I wish . . .'

'That's okay, Healey,' said Trotter. 'But I ought to tell you that I have read *The Scarlet Pimpernel*, you know.'

'What do you mean?'

'Well, in the book, everyone wanted to know who the Scarlet Pimpernel was and so Percy Blakeney made up that rhyme: the one you just did a version of: "They seek him here, they seek him there, Those Frenchies seek him everywhere . . ."'

'Yes?' What on earth was he on about?

'The thing is,' said Trotter, 'that it was Percy Blakeney himself who was the Scarlet Pimpernel all the time, wasn't it? The one who made up the rhyme. That's all.'

IV

Adrian managed to get into Chapel early next morning, so that he could sit behind Cartwright and ponder the beauty of the back of his head, the set of his shoulders and the perfection of his buttocks as they tightened when he leant forward to pray.

It was a strange thing about beauty, the way that it transformed everything in and around a person. Cartwright's blazer was outstandingly the most beautiful blazer in Chapel, but it came from Gorringe's like everyone else's. The backs of his ears, peeping through the soft golden tangle of his hair, were skin and capillary and fleshy tissue like any ears, but nobody else's ears set fire to Adrian's blood and flooded his stomach with hot lead.

The hymn was 'Jerusalem the Golden'. Adrian as usual fitted his own words.

'O Cartwright you are golden, With milk and honey blest. Beneath thy contemplation Sink heart and voice opprest. I know well, O I know well, What lovely joys are there, What radiancy of glory, What light beyond compare.'

Tom, next to him, heard and gave a nudge. Adrian obediently returned to the text, but lapsed again into his own version for the final verse.

'O sweet and blessed Cartwright, Shall I ever see thy face? O sweet and blessed Cartwright, Shall I ever win thy grace? Exult O golden Cartwright! The

Lord shall play my part: Mine only, mine for ever, Thou shalt be, and thou art.'

Six hundred hymn-books were shelved and six hundred bodies rustled down onto their seats. At the east end, Headman's heels rang out on the stone floor as he stepped forward for Notices, hitching up the shoulder of his gown.

'Boys have been seen using a short cut from the Upper to Alperton Road. You are cordially reminded that this path goes through Brandiston Field, which is private property and out of bounds. The sermon on Sunday will be given by Rex Anderson, Suffragan Bishop of Kampala. The Bateman Medal for Greek Prose has been won by W.E.St. J. Hooper, Rosengard's House. That is all.'

He turned as if to go, then checked himself and turned back.

'Oh, there is one more thing. It has come to my notice that a more than usually juvenile magazine of some description has been circulating about the school. Until the authors of this nonsense have come forward there will be no exeats, no club activities and all boys will be confined to their Houses in free time. Nothing else.'

'It's a fucking outrage,' said Adrian as they streamed out of the Chapel into the sunshine. 'And so pathetic, so completely pathetic. "A juvenile magazine of some description!" As if he hasn't read it a hundred times and trembled with fury as he read it!'

'He just wants to make it sound as if it isn't such a big deal,' said Tom.

'Does he really think we're going to fall for that? He's scared, he's bloody scared.'

Heydon-Bayley came up.

'Gated for the rest of term! The bastard!'

'It's just a feeble attempt to try and get the school to turn against the magazine and do his detective work for him,' said Bullock. 'It won't work. Whoever's responsible is too clever.'

Adrian was once more at a loose end that afternoon. It was a Corps day so there was no cricket and he didn't dare climb up to Gladys Winkworth in case he bumped into Trotter again. Officially he should be visiting his old lady and doing odd jobs for her, but she had died of hypothermia the previous term and he hadn't been supplied with a replacement yet. He had just decided to go down to the School Gramophone Library and practise conducting to records, a favourite legal pastime, when he remembered he had a standing invitation to tea from Biffen the French master.

Biffen lived in rather a grand house in its own grounds on the edge of town.

'Hello, sir,' said Adrian. 'It's a Friday, so I thought . . .'

'Healey! How splendid. Come in, come in.'

'I've brought some lemon curd, sir.'

There were about six boys already in the sitting room, talking to Biffen's wife, Lady Helen. Biffen had married her at Cambridge and then taken her back to his old school when he joined as a junior master. They had been here ever since, objects of great pity to the school: an Earl's daughter tied to a no-hope, slow-lane pedagogue.

'I know you!' boomed Lady Helen from the sofa.

'You are Healey from Tickford's House. You were Mosca in the School Play.'

'Healey is in my Lower Sixth French set,' said Biffen.

'And he mobs·you appallingly, Humphrey dear. I know.'

'Er, I've brought some lemon curd,' said Adrian.

'How kind. Now, who do you know here?'

Adrian looked round the room.

'Um . . .'

'You'll certainly know Hugo. He's in your House. Go and sit next to him, and get him to stop spoiling my dog.'

Adrian hadn't noticed Cartwright sitting at a window seat, apart from the main group, tossing bits of cake at a spaniel.

'Hi,' he said, sitting down next to him.

'Hi,' said Cartwright.

'Did you pass your exam then?'

'Sorry?'

'Your Grade Three piano. You remember. Last term.'

'Oh, that. Yes thanks.'

'Great.'

More immortal dialogue from the Noël Coward of the seventies.

'So,' said Adrian, 'do you come here . . . er . . . is this something you've been to many times?'

'Most Fridays,' said Cartwright. 'I've never seen you here before.'

'No, well . . . I've not been invited before.'

'Right.'

'So . . . er . . . what happens exactly?'

'Well, you know, it's just a tea-party, really.'

And so it had proved. Biffen had instigated a book game in which everyone had to own up to books they'd never read. Biffen and Lady Helen called out titles of classic novels and plays and if you hadn't read them you had to put your hand up. *Pride and Prejudice*, *David Copperfield*, *Animal Farm*, *Madame Bovary*, *1984*, *Lucky Jim*, *Sons and Lovers*, *Othello*, *Oliver Twist*, *Decline and Fall*, *Howards End*, *Hamlet*, *Anna Karenina*, *Tess of the D'Urbervilles*, the list of unread books that they managed to compile had made them all giggle. They had agreed that by the end of term the list would have to be much more obscure. The only two books that had been read by everyone present were *Lord of the Flies* and *Catch 22* which, Biffen remarked, said much about English teaching at prep schools. It was all a transparent, and to Adrian rather wet, device to get everyone to read more, but it worked.

Adrian, despite the gentility of it all, had rather enjoyed himself and was fired with an enthusiasm for outreading everyone on the Russians, who always sounded the most impressive and impenetrable.

'I mean,' he said to Cartwright as they walked back to Tickford's, 'this place can really get you down. It's not a bad idea to have a sanctuary like that to go to, is it?'

'He's going to be my tutor next year when I'm in the Sixth Form,' said Cartwright. 'I want to go to Cambridge and he's the best at getting you through Oxbridge Entrance apparently.'

'Really? *I* want to go to Cambridge too!' said Adrian. 'Which college?'

'Trinity, I think.'

'God, me too! My father was there!'

Adrian's father in fact had been to Oxford.

'But Biffo thinks I should apply to St Matthew's. He has a friend there he was in the war with, a Professor Trefusis, supposed to be very good. Anyway, we'd better get a move on. Don't forget we're gated. It's nearly five already.'

'Oh shit,' said Adrian, as they broke into a run.

'Did you read the magazine, then?' he asked as they jogged up the hill to Tickford's.

'Yes,' said Cartwright.

And that was that.

'It was practically a conversation, Tom!'

'Great,' said Tom. 'Thing is . . .'

'It's all settled. He'll join me at Cambridge in my second year. After we've graduated we'll fly to Los Angeles or Amsterdam to get married – you can there, you know. Then we'll set up house in the country. I'll write poetry, Hugo will play the piano and look beautiful. We'll have two cats called Spasm and Clitoris. And a spaniel. Hugo likes spaniels. A spaniel called Biffen.'

Tom was unimpressed.

'Sargent was in here ten minutes ago,' he said.

'Oh pissly piss. What was he after?'

'Tickford wants to see you in his study straight away.'

'What for?'

'Dunno.'

'It can't be . . . does he want to see you as well? Or Sammy or Bollocks?'

Tom shook his head.

116

'He's got nothing on me,' said Adrian. 'He can't have.'

'Stout denial,' said Tom. 'It works every time.'

'Exactly. Brazen it out.'

'But I tell you,' warned Tom, 'there's definitely something up. Sargent looked scared.'

'Rubbish,' said Adrian, 'he hasn't the imagination.'

'Shit-scared,' said Tom.

The Housemaster's study was through the Hall. Adrian was surprised to see all the Prefects standing about in a cluster near the door that connected the boys' side of the House to Mr and Mrs Tickford's living quarters. They stared at him as he went through. They didn't jeer or look hostile. They looked . . . they looked shit-scared.

Adrian knocked on Tickford's door.

'Come in!'

Adrian swallowed nervously and entered.

Tickford was sitting behind his desk, fiddling with a letter-opener.

Like a psychopath toying with a dagger, thought Adrian.

The window was at Tickford's back, darkening his face too much for Adrian to be able to read his expression.

'Adrian, thank you for coming to see me,' he said. 'Sit down, please sit down.'

'Thank you, sir.'

'Oh dear . . . oh dear.'

'Sir?'

'I don't suppose you have any idea why I have sent for you?'

Adrian shook his head, a picture of round-eyed innocence.

'No, I should imagine not. No. I hope word has not got out.'

Tickford took off his glasses and breathed anxiously on the lenses.

'I have to ask you now, Adrian . . . oh dear . . . it's all very . . .'

He replaced the glasses and stood up. Adrian could see his face clearly now, but still he couldn't read it.

'Yes, sir?'

'I'm going to have to ask you about your relationship with Paul Trotter.'

So *that* was it!

The moron had gone and blabbed to someone. The Chaplain probably. And vicious Dr Meddlar would have been only too keen to repeat it to Tickford.

'I don't know what you mean, sir.'

'It's a very simple question, Adrian. It really is. I'm asking you about your relationship with Paul Trotter.'

'Well, I haven't really . . . really got one, sir. I mean, we're sort of friends. He hangs around with me and Thompson sometimes. But I don't know him very well.'

'And that's it?'

'Well yes, sir.'

'It is terribly important that you tell me the truth. Terribly important.'

A boy can always tell when a master is lying, Adrian thought to himself. And Tickford isn't lying. It *is* very important.

'Well, there is one thing, sir.'

'Yes?'

'I really don't know that I should repeat this to you, sir. I mean Trotter did tell me something in confidence . . .'

Tickford leant forward and took Adrian's hand by the wrist.

'I promise you this, Adrian. Whatever Trotter may have said to you, you *must* now tell me. Do you understand? You must!'

'It's a bit embarrassing, sir . . . couldn't you ask him yourself?'

'No, no. I want to hear from you.'

Adrian swallowed.

'Well sir, I bumped into Trotter yesterday afternoon and he suddenly . . . he suddenly started crying and so I asked him what the matter was and he said he was very unhappy because he was . . . well he had a sort of . . .'

God this was hard.

'. . . he was . . . well he said he was in love with someone . . . he, you know, had a pash on them.'

'I see. Yes, of course. Yes I see. He thought he was in love with someone. Another boy, I suppose?'

'That's what he said, sir.'

'Trotter was found in a barn in Brandiston Field this afternoon,' he said, pushing a piece of paper across the desk. 'This note was in his pocket.'

Adrian stared.

'Sir?'

Tickford nodded sadly.

'The stupid boy,' he said. 'The stupid boy hanged himself.'

Adrian looked at the note.

'I'm very sorry but I couldn't bear it any more,' it read. 'Healey knows why.'

'His mother and father are on their way down from Harrogate,' said Tickford. 'What am I going to say?'

Adrian looked at him in panic.

'Why, sir? Why would he kill himself?'

'Tell me the name of the boy he was . . . he had this thing for, Adrian.'

'Well, sir . . .'

'I must know.'

'It was Cartwright, sir. Hugo Cartwright.'

Two Savile Row suits, a Tommy Nutter and a Bennett, Tovey and Steele, faced each other over a table at Wiltons.

'Good to see the Native back again,' said the Bennett, Tovey and Steele. 'I was beginning to think it extinct.'

'Now you say that,' said the Tommy Nutter suit, 'but I've got rather a soft spot for the Pacific chaps myself. They're sort of wetter somehow, don't you think? Fleshlier if there is such a word.'

The Bennet, Tovey and Steele did not agree. He considered it typical of the Tommy Nutter to have a loud taste in oysters.

'This Montrachet's a bit warm, isn't it?'

The Bennett, Tovey and Steele sighed. He had been brought up from his nanny's knee to believe that white Burgundies should not be overchilled. They knew him at Wiltons and took great care to present his wines just so. The Tommy Nutter would resent a lecture, however. Men of his stamp were absurdly sensitive.

'Still,' said the other. 'Who's complaining? Now then. Let's talk Mendax. GDS has had no joy, I'm sorry to say, with the Odysseus material. No joy at all.'

'No decrypt whatsoever?'

'Oh, they opened it up all right. It was an old twist-cypher. Pre-war. Absolute antique.'

'That figures,' grunted the Bennett, Tovey and Steele. 'And what was inside?'

'Names, addresses and telephone numbers. Load of harmless Osties. Lifted straight from the bloody Salzburg directory, would you believe?'

'The old bastard.'

'So the thing is,' the Tommy Nutter twisted the stem of his wine-glass coyly, 'did this Odysseus of yours bring the material out or did he leave it behind?'

'He's had nothing in the mail. We know that.'

'Your friend on the inside still paying his way?'

'Oh yes.'

'Good, because he's a greedy son of a bitch.'

The Bennett, Tovey and Steele suit ignored this. It wasn't as if the Tommy Nutter suit was paying for Telemachus. He thought he was, of course, and would probably never notice that it came directly out of the Bennett, Tovey and Steele's pocket, never to be reclaimed from the fund. It was a purely private business, but Cabinet liaison had to believe there was honey in it for them. It would not do for them to find out that the Service was being used entirely for the Bennett, Tovey and Steele's private ends.

'I think the Mendax material is still over there,' he said, 'without the walls of Ilium.'

'In Salzburg, you mean?' asked the Tommy Nutter, whose grip on codenames was weak at the best of times.

'That's right. In Salzburg.'

'This is all very much your own pigeon, you know. You are the only one who believes in Mendax. I am reminded of the operation you ran in seventy-six, also against Odysseus. What did that game come to?'

The Bennett, Tovey and Steele shot the Tommy Nutter a suspicious glare.

'What do you mean game?' he said. 'Why do you say game?'

'Keep your hair on, old man. I just meant that you seem to have a bit of a maggot in your head on the subject of Trefusis. Some of us are wondering why. That's all.'

'You'll find out yet. Listen. The point is this. I never said I did believe in Mendax. But if it doesn't exist why should the Trojans and Odysseus want us to believe that it does? That's worth pursuing surely?'

'Humph,' said the Tommy Nutter. 'It has at least been a cheap operation so far, that I will grant you. But we haven't a shred of proof that Szabó – what's he called again?'

'Helen.'

'We haven't a shred of evidence to suggest that Helen is anything other than a loyal servant of his state. The Trojans have just given him a medal for God's sake.'

'All the more reason to suspect Odysseus.'

'Why "Helen" by the way? Odd codename for a man.'

The Bennett, Tovey and Steele suit was not going to give the Tommy Nutter a free lesson in Homeric mythology. Where did the man go to school? The tie was no indication. Beaconsfield Conservatives or something equally foul, probably. Hadley Wood Golf Club. Carshalton Rotarians. Yuk.

'It seemed to make sense at the time,' he said.

'Oh ah,' the Tommy Nutter pressed a crumb into the table cloth. 'So tell me about these grandchildren.'

'Stefan is a chess-player. He's coming over here to play in a couple of months. They'll keep him on a long leash I shouldn't wonder.'

'And you want me to allocate resourcing?'

'I'd quite like some money made available, if that's what you mean. Grade Two surveillance should do it.'

'I have to interface, as they say, with the Treasury

tomorrow. Cabinet next week. Oh, look, you're not going to smoke are you?'

Christ! *thought the Bennett, Tovey and Steele. Roll on the next Labour government.*

Four

I

Tim Anderson considered the question with great care.

'I don't believe that the comparison with *Oliver Twist*, seductive and engaging as I would be the last to deny it being, is as valid as a first glance might allow.'

'But surely, Dr Anderson, the similarities *are* very clear. What we have here is a secret workhouse birth, we have a gang of boys set to work by the character Polterneck, we have the character of Peter Flowerbuck, who traces his own family connection with the Cotton twins, not unlike Mr Brownlow's quest in *Oliver Twist*, we have Flinter, who like Nancy is an agent of revenge. The parallels are surely most striking?'

Gary poured some more Meursault for Jenny and Adrian, never at any time taking his eyes off the screen.

'I am not going to consider failing to grant you the presence of narrative echoes,' Tim Anderson replied, 'but I would certainly find myself presented with personal difficulties if asked to deny that this is the mature Dickens of *Little Dorrit* and *Bleak House*. I'm sensing a fuller picture of a connected world here than we are allowed in *Twist*. I'm sensing a deeper anger, I find myself responding to a more complete symphonic vision. The chapter which describes the flood, the scene depicting the bursting of the Thames's banks and the sweeping away of the Den is a more proleptic and organic event than the reader has been confronted with in earlier novels. I would be laying myself open to a charge of being mistaken if I attempted to resist the argument that the character of Flinter is a development of both Nancy and the Artful Dodger which we can't be afraid to recognise takes us into a more terrified Dickens, a more, if you like, Kafkaesque Dickens.'

The interviewer nodded.

'I understand that the University has already sold the film and television rights of *Peter Flowerbuck*?'

'That is not substantially incorrect.'

'Are you worried that to do this before the manuscript has been officially authenticated might lay you open to future embarrassment, should it prove to be a fake?'

'As you know, we have taken on a number of new research fellows at St Matthew's who are working extensively on the text to determine its authenticity-level. They will be running linguistic particles and image-clusters through a computer program which is as reliable as any chemical test.'

'Authorial fingerprinting?'

'Authorial is the term often used, fingerprinting, that is far from wrong.'

'And how confident are you that this is genuine Dickens?'

'Let me turn that question round and say that I am not confident that it isn't Dickens.'

'Let me turn that answer round and say "bullshit",' said Adrian.

'Hush!' said Jenny.

'Well, I mean. Symphonic visions.'

'I don't think it insignificant,' Anderson continued, 'that at a time when English departments at my university and hundreds of others are being threatened with cuts, a discovery of pure scholarship like this should attract such attention and validate so completely what has quite properly been perceived as the beleaguered discipline of English studies.'

'It's a very lucrative discovery, certainly. How in fact was it made?'

'I was alerted to the existence of the text by a student of mine from Newnham College. She had been participating in my seminars on Derrida and Sexual Difference and had been pursuing a number of independent lines of enquiry into the Victorian Deviant Ethic. She found the papers in the St Matthew's College Library hidden amongst old copies of *Cornhill* magazine.'

'Did she realise what she had stumbled across?'

'She was not unaware of its potential lack of insignificance.'

'I understand that a philologist from your own department, and indeed college, Donald Trefusis, has expressed doubts as to the genuineness of the find?'

'I believe that I think it of immense value to express doubts. It is because of the Professor's repeated queries that we have been granted the necessary funding to research the manuscript.'

'Dr Anderson, many people like myself, who have read *Peter Flowerbuck* have been struck by the candour and detail with which sexual activity and the nature of Victorian child-prostitution is described. Do you think Dickens ever intended to publish?'

'We are currently trawling all biographical source materials for some clue as to the answer to that highly legitimate question. Perhaps I can turn it round, however, and ask, "Would he not have destroyed the manuscript if he never wanted it read?" Yeah?'

'I see.'

'I cannot deny myself the right to believe that he left it to be found. We therefore owe it to him to publish now.'

'It is not of course a completed work. What you have is only a fragment.'

'There is truth in that remark.'

'Do you think there is a chance of discovering the rest of the manuscript?'

'If it exists we are not doubtful of locating the residue.'

'Dr Anderson, thank you very much indeed. The three currently extant chapters of *Peter Flowerbuck*, edited and annotated by Tim Anderson, will be available from the Cambridge University Press in October, priced fourteen pounds ninety-five. The BBC serialisation, currently in production, with an ending by Malcolm Bradbury, is due to reach our screens sometime in the spring of nineteen-eighty-one.'

Jenny got up and switched off the television.

'Well,' said Gary, 'that's set the apple-cart amongst the pigeons and no mistake. What do we do now?'

'Now,' said Adrian, 'we wait.'

II

Adrian put down the cane and loosened the cravat. Gary sat down on the step and mopped his brow with a most preposterous handkerchief of bright vermilion silk. Jenny addressed them from the fire-escape.

'I have very few notes to give,' she said. 'There's an old theatrical saying, "Bad dress, good performance"; I'm sorry to have to tell you that this was an excellent dress. The mechanics of the show are all there. The greatest imponderable is the time it will take for the audience to follow Adrian into this yard. That's something we'll discover tonight. It's all there: just pace and enjoy it. We're all just waiting for the final director now – the audience. If you don't mind standing here in the sun I'll come amongst you now with individual notes.'

Jenny had approached Tim Anderson for permission to mount a production of *Peter Flowerbuck* and his gratitude to her for the discovery of the manuscript had made it impossible for him to refuse.

'Jenny, can I ask at this stage how you imagine presenting on stage what is, ultimately, not a play?'

'Didn't you once say yourself, Dr Anderson, that all the theatrical energy in Victorian Britain went not into drama but into the novel?'

'That is something I did say, yes.'

'The RSC is apparently planning a dramatisation of *Nicholas Nickleby*, surely *Peter Flowerbuck* is even more suited to the theatre? If we use the ADC we can take the audience outside with Peter as he goes to the Den. The yard at the side of the theatre is pretty much a Victorian slum already.'

'I'm insanely excited.'

'Good.'

'Jenny, may I ask you, do you need any help with the preparation or finalisation of a playtext?'

'Oh, I'm not writing it. Adrian Healey is.'

'Healey? I wasn't aware he'd been authorised to read the manuscript.'

'Oh, he's read it all right.'

She climbed down the fire-escape now and approached Adrian and Gary with a sheaf of notes.

'The Polterneck scenes are basically fine,' she told Gary. 'But for God's sake learn that scene twelve speech properly.'

'What happens in scene twelve?'

'It's where you buy Joe. Which reminds me, where's Hugo?'

'Here I am.'

'I want to rehearse the Russell Square scene with you and Adrian. It's still not right. Let's see . . . I've got some more notes for the others. If you go and run through it on stage now I'll send Bridget over and be with you in ten minutes.'

Hugo and Adrian walked into the theatre together.

'Nervous?' said Adrian.

'A bit. My mother's coming. I don't know what she'll think.'

'Your mother?'

'She's an actress.'

'Why did I never know that?'

'Why should you have done?'

'No reason, I suppose.'

It would have been a difficult scene even if Hugo hadn't been playing Joe. Adrian ran through it in his mind, like a Radio 3 announcer giving the synopsis of an opera.

Flowerbuck, he intoned to himself, has taken the boy Joe Cotton back to his house in Russell Square, convinced that he is his sister's son. Joe on arrival immediately tries to take off his clothes, unable to imagine that he would be expected to do anything else in a gentleman's house. Peter and Mrs Twimp, his housekeeper, calm him down and give him a bath. Mrs Twimp, played by Bridget Arden, injects into the scene her own brand of malapropistic comedy as they try to question Joe on the details of his early childhood. His memory is very uncertain. He recalls a garden, a large house and a fair-haired sister but very little else. At this stage, and indeed *on* this stage, Adrian Healey, playing Flowerbuck, finds his memory to be uncertain too and often starts to forget his lines.

After the bath Joe is taken to the dining room to eat. Or rather the dining room comes to them. It is that kind of production. Joe recognises in horror a portrait of Sir Christian Flowerbuck, Peter's uncle.

'That gentleman hurt me!' he cries.

It transpires that Sir Christian, Peter's benefactor and godfather, whose baronetcy and money Peter is in line to inherit, had been the first man to violate Joe.

The scene ends at night with Joe creeping from his room and slipping into Peter's bed. He knows no other form of companionship or love.

Peter awakes next morning, horrified to realise that he has lain with the boy who he is now more sure than ever is his nephew.

Adrian had had nothing to do with the casting of Hugo, at least as far as anyone knew. Jenny had bounced into his rooms one afternoon, full of excitement.

'I've just seen a perfect Joe Cotton! We don't need to get a real boy after all.'

'Who is this child?'

'He's not a child, he's a Trinity first year, but on stage he'll look fourteen or fifteen easily. And, Adrian, he's exactly as you . . . hum . . . as Dickens describes Joe. Same hair, same blue eyes, everything. Even the same walk, though I don't know if from the same cause. He came to see me this morning, it was rather embarrassing, he thought I was expecting him. Bridget must have arranged it without telling me. His name's Hugo Cartwright.'

'Really?' said Adrian. 'Hugo Cartwright, eh?'

'Do you know him?'

'If it's the one I'm thinking of, we were in the same House at school.'

Gary opened his mouth to speak, but he met Adrian's eye and subsided.

'I dimly remember him,' said Adrian.

'Don't you think he's ideal casting for Joe?'

'Well in many ways I suppose he is, yes. Fairly ideal.'

If Hugo was unnerved by correspondences between a hundred-and-twenty-year-old Victorian manuscript and an incident from his own and Adrian's life he made no mention of the fact. But there was no doubt that his acting in the scene was awkward and formal.

'This is your home now, Joe. Mrs Twimp is to be your mother.'

'Yes, sir.'

'How should you like Mrs Twimp as a mother?'

'Does she want to join us, sir?'

'Join us, Joe? Join us in what?'

'In the bed, sir.'

'Bless me, Mr Flowerbuck, the lad is so manured to a life of shame, that's the fact of it, that he can't conceive no other!'

'There is no necessity for you to sleep with anyone but yourself and your Saviour, Joe. In peace and innocence.'

'No, Sir, no indeed! Mr Polterneck and Mrs Polterneck and Uncle Polterneck must have their boy-money. I am their gold sovereign, Sir.'

'Keep your clothes on, Joe, I beg of you!'

'Lord love the poor child, Mr Flowerbuck. Look at the condition of him! He should be washed and given fresh arraignments.'

'You're right, Mrs Twimp. Bring a bath and a robe.'

'I shall return percipiently.'

Jenny called across from the stalls.

'What do you think your feelings towards Joe are here?'

Adrian shaded his eyes across the lights.

'Well revulsion, I'd've thought. Horror, pity, indignation . . . you know. All that.'

'Good, yes. But what about desire?'

'Um . . .'

'You see, I think it's implicit that Peter is sexually attracted to Joe from the first.'

'Well I really don't . . .'

'I feel Dickens makes it very clear.'

'But he's his nephew! I don't think *Dickens* had any such thought in *Dickens's* head, do you?'

'I don't think we can be so sure.'

'Oh can't we?'

'Look at Joe now. He's standing in front of you, half naked. I think we should sense a sense of . . . we should sense a sense of . . . of . . . some kind of latent, repressed desire.'

'Right-ho. One sense of latent, repressed desire coming up. Do you want a side-order of self-disgust too, or hold on that?'

'Adrian, we go up in three hours, please don't start fucking about.'

'Okay. Fine.'

'Now, Hugo, what about you?'

'Well . . .'

'What's your attitude to Adrian, do you think?'

'Well he's just another man, isn't he?'

'I don't know how to love him,' sang Adrian. 'What to do, how to move him. He's a man, he's just a man and I've had so many men before, in very many ways. He's just one more.'

'I think Adrian's right there,' said Jenny. 'Despite being a quarter-tone flat. Imagine all the peculiar things you've had to do for your customers. Being bathed and clothed probably doesn't seem that new or different. You've been trained to please: your complaisance is the complaisance of a whore, your smile is the smile of a whore. I think you can afford a

134

touch more assuredness. At the moment you're rather stiff.'

'He's only flesh and blood,' said Adrian. 'Look at who he's standing next to.'

'Adrian, please!'

'Sorry, Miss.'

Mrs Twimp entered with the breakfast tray.

—Sir, the lad can't be found . . . ooh!'

She started in surprise at the sight of Joe's head nestling on the sleeping Flowerbuck's bare chest.

—Sir! Sir!

—Oh . . . good morning, Mrs Twimp . . .

—Bless me! I never saw such licence! Mr Flowerbuck, Sir, I cannot credit the account of my eyes. That you should stand exposed as an amuser of children, nought but a correcter of youth, a pedestal! A vile producer, a libertarian! That I should gaze upon such naked immortality, such disillusion.

—Calm yourself, Mrs Twimp. The child crept in at night when I was asleep. I had not the first idea that he was with me until just now.

—Sir! I beg your pardon . . . but the sight of him. I could only jump to one confusion.

—Leave us, Mrs Twimp.

—Shall you try to arouse him, sir? I think he should be aroused directly.

Adrian could feel Hugo's body tense at the laugh from the audience that greeted this line.

—I will wake him and send him down to you, Mrs Twimp.

—I shall draw some water for his absolutions.

She exited to a warm round of applause.

Adrian sat up and stared in front of him.

—Oh Lord! What have I done? What in God's name have I done?

—Good morning, sir.

—Ah Joe, Joe! Why did you come to me last night?

—You are my saviour, sir. Mrs Twimp bade me remember it most carefully. And you told me I should sleep only with my saviour.

—Child, I meant . . .

—Did I do wrong, sir? Did I not please you?

—I dreamt . . . I know not what I dreamt. Say I was asleep, Joe. Say I slept all night.

—You were very gentle to me, sir.

—No! No! No!

In the blackout and in the thunder of applause that marked the end of the act, they lay there while the bed was trundled into the wings where Jenny stood jumping up and down with excitement.

'Wonderful!' she said. 'Listen to that! The Grauniad is out there and the *Financial Times*.'

'The *Financial Times*?' said Adrian. 'Is Tim Anderson thinking of starting a Flowerbuck limited company?'

'Their drama critic.'

'I didn't know they had one. Who the hell reads drama criticism in the *Financial Times*?'

'Everyone will if it's a good notice, because I'll have it blown up and put outside the theatre.'

'How long's the interval?' asked Hugo.

No one at the party was going to deny that it had been the finest production in the history of Cambridge drama, that Hugo and Gary in particular were bound for West End glory in weeks, that Adrian had done a fine job in translating Dickens to the stage and that he must write a new play for Jenny to direct the moment she joined the National, which appointment must be only days away.

'My dear Healey!' a hand was placed on Adrian's shoulder. He turned to see the smiling face of Donald Trefusis.

'Hello, Professor. Did you enjoy it?'

'Triumphant, Adrian. Absolutely triumphant. A most creditable piece of adaptation.'

'Will it do as my piece of original work?'

Trefusis looked puzzled.

'You know, the task you set me earlier this term?'

'Adapting someone's novel? Will that do as your piece of original work? You must have misunderstood me.'

Adrian was slightly drunk and, although he had planned this moment a hundred times in his head, it was always in Trefusis's rooms and without 'Hit Me With Your Rhythm Stick' playing in the background.

'Well, Professor, no. That's not what I mean,' he cleared his throat. 'I mean will *Peter Flowerbuck* the novel count as my original piece of work?'

'Oh certainly, certainly. By all means. I thought for a moment that you were . . .'

Bridget Arden, the voluptuous actress who had played Mrs Twimp with such éclat, came up and kissed Adrian on the mouth.

'Julian's rolling a joint in the downstairs dressing-room, Adey. Come and join us.'

'Ha! Very good! Rolling a joint! That's a great one!

'Love it . . . er, she's just . . . you know,' explained Adrian, as they watched her falling downstairs.

'Of course she is, my dear fellow! No, I was saying. I thought for a moment you expected that I would take just the *adapting* of your novel as a satisfactory task. I accept the *writing* of it, gladly. A splendid conception. It exceeded my most optimistic expectations.'

'You mean you know?'

'Aside from the three hundred and forty-seven anachronisms that Dr Anderson and his team will uncover in time, I had the good fortune to be in your rooms one afternoon. How I could have mistaken D staircase for A, I have no idea. I am not usually so inattentive. But before I realised my error, I had stumbled across the manuscript.'

'You stumbled across a bundle of papers wrapped in a blanket hidden on top of a bookcase?'

'I am quite a stumbler when the mood is on me. I stumbled for Cambridge as an undergraduate.'

'I bet you did.'

'Absurdly remiss of me, I know. Not solely an affliction of the elderly however. I believe your friend Gary Collins once accidentally stumbled into my rooms in just the same way. In his case, I understand he even stumbled across a telephone before he noticed where he was. These confusions are not so rare as one might imagine.'

'Oh God. But if you've known all along, why haven't you . . .'

'Blown the whistle? I have my reasons and your manuscript serves them perfectly. The English department at St Matthew's has never had so many research fellows or been flooded with so many grants. The Dickens Society of Chicago alone . . . but that is of no interest to you. I am sincerely delighted. This is the second time you have failed to disappoint me. It's so hard to find a good crook these days. You're a treasure, Adrian, a real treasure. One thing I am unclear on, though. Why did you hit upon the happy idea of having the manuscript discovered in St Matthew's and not in the University Library?'

'Well, I wanted it to be college property. I assumed then that you would be the one to publicise it.'

'And *I* would be the one with egg on my face when the truth came out? I suspected as much. You are too splendid. I know we shall become friends.'

'No I didn't exactly mean . . .'

'You have done your college a great service. I will leave now, to allow space for carnival, riot, drugs and carnal frenzy to develop. Silenus and his leering wrinkles are not required when youth is sporting. Oh look, there is that man from Narborough, the one you routed on the cricket field the first time ever we met. Excellent performance, my dear Cartwright! I am not ashamed to say that I wept openly.'

Hugo nodded vaguely and came up to Adrian, flushed and swaying, a bottle in one hand, a cigarette in the other.

'Look where he comes,' said Adrian, 'the Allegory of Dissipation and Ruin.'

Hugo burped happily and gestured at Trefusis who was saying his farewells to Jenny.

'I know that old fart from somewhere,' he said.

'You are talking about the old fart that I love. That old fart is a genius. That old fart won a thousand pounds by backing Chartham Park against Narborough Hall. You must remember the cricket match.'

'Oh yes, that's right. You cheated.'

'Cheated?'

'Donald Trefusis. Philip Slattery's uncle. Friend of old Biffo Biffen's from school. I don't forget anything, me. Mnemosyne was, let us not forget it, the mother of the Muses.'

Adrian looked at him in surprise. 'Well, quite.'

'At least according to Hesiod. So what is the old fart that you love doing here?'

'He's the ADC treasurer.'

Jenny came up with Gary.

'For God's sake stop drinking, Hugo. You'll look forty tomorrow instead of fourteen if you carry on at this rate.'

'A man who has just exposed himself to four hundred people, including his mother, has every right to drink.'

'God yes, I forgot the famous Helen Lewis was in,' said Adrian. 'How did she like it?'

'She was highly complimentary about everyone except me.'

'She didn't like you?' Jenny asked.

'She just didn't mention me, that's all.'

Jenny consoled him with the thought that it was probably professional jealousy. Adrian beckoned to Gary, who was pogo-ing with a lighting technician.

'Trefusis knows all,' he said. 'The bugger burglarised our rooms. But it's all all right.'

'What does Trefusis know?' said Hugo, who had overheard.

'Nothing, nothing.'

'He's the old fart that Adrian loves,' Hugo confided to Jenny and the rest of the room. 'I used to be the old fart that he loves. Now it's Trefusisisisis.'

'That's right, Hugo, time for bye-byes.'

'Really?' said Jenny. 'I thought *I* was the old fart he loved.'

'Adrian loves everybody, didn't you know? He even loves Lucy.'

'And who the hell is Lucy?'

'Oh my goodness, is that the time? Jenny, if we're going to hit Newnham tonight we should . . .'

'Lucy is his dog. He loves Lucy.'

'That's right. I love Lucy. Starring Lucille Ball and Desi Arnaz. Now I really think . . .'

'Do you know what he did once? In Harrogate. He pretended to . . .'

'Oh shit, he's about to throw,' said Gary.

Adrian caught the brunt of the vomit, which, in an unusual fit of humility, he rather thought he deserved.

III

'So let me see if I understood you, Dr Anderson.' Menzies removed his spectacles and pinched the bridge of his nose like a rep actor in a court-room drama. 'Not one word, not one syllable of this document is in fact the work of Charles Dickens?'

'It certainly looks as if the paper and writing materials are modern. The handwriting however . . .'

'Oh for goodness' sake, if the ink is twentieth-century how can the manuscript be in Dickens's own hand? Or are we now to authorise research grants that will establish the use of the retractable biro in Victorian Britain? Perhaps you even believe that Dickens is still alive?'

'I think I should remind the governing body,' said Clinton-Lacey, 'that the film is due to be premièred next week. Some kind of statement is going to have to be made.'

'The college will be a laughing-stock.'

'Yes indeed,' said Trefusis. 'Sketches on *Not The Nine o'Clock News*, a cartoon by Marc. Calamitous.'

'Well it's your department, Donald,' said Menzies. 'Rather than sit back and enjoy this cataclysm, why don't you come up with a solution?'

Trefusis stubbed out his cigarette.

'Well now, that is precisely what I have taken the liberty of doing,' he said. 'With your permission I shall read a statement that the press might be offered without too much embarrassment.'

Everyone around the table murmured assent. Trefusis took a piece of paper from his satchel.

'"Using a linguistic analysis program pioneered by the English faculty in collaboration with the Department of Computing Science,"' he read, '"Dr Tim Anderson, Fellow of St Matthew's College and Lecturer in English at the University, has refined and perfected techniques which have allowed him to determine precisely which parts of the play *The Two Noble Kinsmen* were written by Shakespeare and which by Fletcher."'

'Er . . . I have?' asked Tim Anderson.

'Yes, Tim, you have.'

'What on earth has Shakespeare got to do with it?' cried Menzies. 'We are talking about . . .'

'"Comparing textual samples of known Shakespeare

against the writings of the Earl of Oxford, Francis Bacon and Christopher Marlowe, he is also in a position to prove that all the plays of the Shakespearean canon are the work of one hand, William Shakespeare's, and that Oxford, Bacon and Marlowe are responsible for none of it. There are, however, some intriguing passages in three of the plays which would appear not to be by Shakespeare. Dr Anderson and his team are working on them now and should soon have positive results. An interesting by-product of this important work is the discovery that the novel *Peter Flowerbuck* is not by Charles Dickens, but is almost certainly the work of a twentieth-century writer. There is evidence, however, that the story is based on an original Dickens plot. Dr Anderson's team is following up this suggestion with great energy." I think that should meet the case.'

'Ingenious, Donald,' said Clinton-Lacey. 'Quite ingenious.'

'You're too kind.'

'I don't see what's so ingenious about it. Why bring Shakespeare in?'

'He's diverting attention, Garth,' Clinton-Lacey explained. 'Bring out the name Shakespeare and it's even bigger copy than Dickens.'

'But all this guff about Dr Anderson working on bits of Shakespeare and the plot lines being original Dickens? What's that about?'

'Well you see,' said Trefusis. 'It shows that we are currently researching all this important material, that there may be *something* in *Peter Flowerbuck* after all.'

'But there isn't!'

'We know that, but the newspapers don't. In a

couple of months' time the whole thing will be forgotten. If they do make enquiries about our progress we can say that Dr Anderson is still working on the problem. I'm sure Tim will be able to bemuse the press.'

'He will be the one to make the announcement then?'

'Certainly,' said Trefusis. '*I* have nothing to do with the affair.'

'I'm unsure as to what the tension between the ethical boundaries and the margins of pragmatism might announce themselves to be in a situation which . . .' Anderson began.

'You see? Tim will do splendidly. His is the only major European language I still find myself utterly unable to comprehend. The press will be bored. It isn't quite enough of a hoax story to excite them and is too rigorous and scientific to have any human interest.'

'But all this means that we will have to keep funding the extra staff,' Menzies complained. 'For appearances' sake.'

'Yes,' said Trefusis dreamily, 'there is that drawback of course.'

'That's outrageous.'

'Oh I don't know. As long as they're kept busy lecturing, teaching undergraduates and authenticating documents that will be sent to us from all over the world – now that we are acknowledged as the leading university for authorial fingerprinting – I'm sure we'll find a use for them. They may even pay their way.'

'You're lying,' said Gary. 'You've got to be lying.'

'I wish I were,' said Adrian. 'No, that's not true, I wouldn't have missed it for worlds.'

'You're telling me that you sold your arse down the Dilly?'

'Why not? Someone's got to. Anyway it wasn't my arse exactly.'

Gary paced up and down the room while Adrian watched him. He didn't know why he had told him. He supposed because he had been stung once too often by the accusation that he had no idea what the real world was like.

It had started when Adrian had mentioned that he was seriously considering marrying Jenny.

'Do you love her?'

'Look Gary. I'm twenty-two years old. I got here by the skin of my teeth, because I awoke from the bad dream of adolescence in the nick of time. Every morning for the next, God knows, fifty years, I'm going to have to get out of bed and participate in the day. I simply do not trust myself to be able to do that on my own. I'll need someone to get up for.'

'But do you love her?'

'I am magnificently prepared for the long littleness of life. There is diddley-squat for me to look forward to. Zilch, zero, zip-all, sweet lipperty-pipperty nothing. The only thought that will give me the energy to carry on is that someone has a life which would be diminished by my departure from it.'

'Yes, but do you love her?'

'You're beginning to sound like Olivier in *The Marathon Man*, "Is it safe? Is it safe?" "Sure it's safe. It's real safe." "Is it safe?" "No, it's not safe. It's incredibly unsafe." "Is it safe?" How the hell do I know?'

'You don't love her.'

'Oh piss off, Gary. I don't love anyone, anything, or anybody. Well, "anyone" and "anybody" are the same, but I can't think of a third "any". Which reminds me . . . that bloody Martini advert, it's bugged me for years. "Any time, any place, anywhere." What the fuck difference is there between any place and anywhere? Some advertising copywriter was paid thousands for that piece of rubbish.'

'This is a change of subject on a cosmic scale. You don't love her, do you?'

'I just said. I don't love anyone, anything or anybody, any time, any place, anywhere. Who does?'

'Jenny does.'

'Women are different, you know that.'

'I do as well.'

'Men are different too.'

'Gay men, you mean.'

'I cannot believe I am having this conversation. You think I'm like Emma, don't you? "Adrian Healey, handsome, clever and rich, with a comfortable home and happy disposition, seemed to unite some of the best blessings of existence; and had lived nearly twenty-three years in the world with very little to disturb or vex him."'

'*Distress* or vex, I think you'll find. It's as good a description as any.'

'Really? Well, I may have missed some of Jane

Austen's subtler hints, but I don't think Emma Wood-house spent part of her seventeenth year as a harlot in Piccadilly. I haven't read it for a couple of years of course, and some of the obliquer references could have passed over my head. Miss Austen also seems to fight very shy of describing Emma's time in chokey on remand for possession of cocaine. Again I'm perfectly prepared to concede that she *did* and that I have simply failed to pick up the clues.'

'What the fuck are you going on about?'

And Adrian had told him something of his life between school and Cambridge.

Gary was still indignant. 'You plan to marry Jenny without telling her any of this?'

'Don't be so bourgeois, my dear. It doesn't suit you at all.'

Adrian was growing disillusioned with Gary. He had started on his History of Art, or History O Fart, as Adrian liked to call it, at the beginning of the year and ever since he had begun to evolve into something else. Bondage trousers had given way to second-hand tweed jackets with Hermès silk flourishing from the breast pockets. The hair returned to its natural dark, slicked back with KY jelly; knives and forks dangled no more from the lobes. The Damned and The Clash were less likely to blast across the court from the rooms now than Couperin and Bruckner.

'It only needs a moustache for you to look like Roy Strong,' Adrian had told him once, but Gary hadn't been moved. He wasn't going to be the world's little piece of pet rough any more and that was that. And now he was lecturing Adrian on the ethics of personal relations.

'Anyway, why should I tell her? What difference would it make?'

'Why should you marry her? What difference would it make?'

'Oh let's not go round in circles. I've tried to tell you. I've done all my living. There's nothing to look forward to. Do I go into advertising? Do I teach? Do I apply to the BBC? Do I write plays and become the voice of the Bland Young Man generation? Do I consider journalism? Do I go to an acting school? Do I have a shot at industry? The only justification for my existence is that I am loved. Whether or not I like it, I am responsible for Jenny and that is something to get up in the morning for.'

'So it's a life of sacrifice. You're afraid that if you don't marry her, she'll top herself? I hate to wound your vanity but people don't behave like that.'

'Oh don't they? Don't people kill themselves?'

Jenny entered without knocking.

'Hiya, bum-holes, I cleared your pigeon-holes on the way in. Exciting jiffy-bag for you, big boy. Could it be the clitoral exciter we ordered?'

'Morning toast more like,' said Gary, taking the package and passing it over.

Adrian opened it while Gary explained to Jenny the history of Toast By Post.

'You taught a boy two years ago and he *still* has this crush on you?'

'His faithful little heart overflows with love.'

'Nonsense,' said Adrian. 'It was never more than an elaborate joke. If anything the parcels mock me.'

'Do you think he wanks into them before he seals them up?'

'Gary!' Jenny was shocked.

'As in "I'm coming in a jiffy", you mean? No, I do not, though I grant you the toast is a bit soggy. What else have we? A little pot of apricot jam, a pat of butter, a note which says, "And Conradin made himself another piece of toast . . ."'

'That boy is weird.'

'Who's Conradin?' Jenny asked.

'Reach down my index, Watson, and look under "C". Dear me, what villainy is grouped under this letter alone! There's Callaghan, the politician to whose door we traced what you in your memoirs gave the somewhat fanciful title the "Winter of Discontent", Watson. Here's Callow, the second most dangerous actor in London, any one of whose grimaces may be fatal, Lewis Collins, Charlie Chester, Leslie Crowther of dread memory, Marti Caine, what a catalogue of infamy is here . . . but no Conradin. Peter Conrad, who invented opera, William Conrad, whose Cannon was a Quinn Martin Production, but no Conradin.'

'I think it's from a Saki short story,' said Gary. 'Sredni Vashtar, the polecat.'

'Oh yes, you're quite right. Or was he a ferret?'

'And what's the relevance to you?' asked Jenny.

'Well, there we have to peer into the dark, dripping mind of Hunt the Thimble. The chances are that it is simply a literary reference to toast, and he is fast running out of those. But there could be a Meaning.'

'Conradin was a boy who had a horrible, repressive aunt,' said Gary. 'So he prayed to Sredni Vashtar, his polecat . . .'

'Or ferret.'

149

'He prayed to his polecat or ferret and his prayers were answered. Sredni Vashtar killed the aunt.'

'And meanwhile Conradin calmly made himself another piece of toast.'

'I see,' said Jenny. 'The polecat is a kind of phallic symbol, do we think?'

'Honestly, dear,' said Gary, 'you're so obsessed, you'd think a *penis* was phallic.'

'Well Sredni Vashtar is a monster from the Id, at the very least,' said Adrian. 'The dark, hot-breathed stink of the animal that Conradin would one day release from its dark hiding-place to wreak its revenge on the chintz and teacups of his aunt's drawing-room life.'

'Do you think this boy is trying to tell you something?'

'Perhaps his thimble is a thimble no more, but a long, furry savage beast that wriggles and spits and mauls aunts. I'll write and ask him.'

He looked through the rest of his post. A cheque from his mother was always welcome, a cheque from Uncle David for five hundred pounds even more so. He slipped it quickly into his jacket pocket. Reminders that Billy Graham was in Cambridge and would preach in Great St Mary's were always monumentally unwelcome, as were invitations to hear *Acis and Galatea* played on original instruments.

'But not sung,' he suggested, looking through the rest of his mail, 'on original voices. I suppose in two hundred years' time they'll be giving Beatles concerts on ancient Marshall . . . oh and a letter from old Biffo, bless him.'

Biffen was the only master from school with whom

Adrian stayed in touch. The man was so fluffy and white and decent and had taken so much pleasure in the news of Adrian's scholarship to St Matthew's which had somehow filtered through to the school the year before, that it would have been a positive cruelty not to write to him from time to time to let him know how it was all going.

He glanced through the letter. Biffen was full of the news of the Dickens manuscript.

'Donald writes me that there may be some doubt about it. I do hope not.'

'I'd forgotten Biffo knew Trefusis,' said Adrian, laying the letter aside. 'Hello! What have we here?'

There was a crumpled handwritten note for him. 'Please come to tea at C5, Great Court, Trinity. Alone. Hugo.'

'How is Hugo?' asked Jenny. 'I haven't seen much of him since *Flowerbuck*.'

'I remember him being rather naff in Bridget's production of *Sexual Perversity In Chicago*,' said Gary. 'He kept forgetting his lines and tripping over. He hasn't been in anything since.'

Adrian put the note down and yawned.

'He's probably been swotting for his Part One's. He was always that kind of creep. Hand me Justin and Miroslav.'

Adrian noticed that the permanent puddle in the passageway between King's and St Catharine's had iced over. Spring was having to make a fight of it. He wrapped Miroslav, his cashmere scarf, closer round him as he stepped out into the icy gale that blasted along King's Parade. They used to say that Cambridge was the first stopping place for the wind that swept down from the Urals: in the thirties that was as true of the politics as the weather.

Adrian wondered whether he mightn't become political himself. Always one to walk the other way from trends, he sensed that left-wingery was about to become very unfashionable. Long hair was out, flared jeans were out, soon there would be no more cakes and ale, canapés and Sancerre at best, Ryvita and mineral water at worst. Trefusis complained that the modern undergraduate was a cruel disappointment to him.

'They're all getting firsts and married these days, if you'll forgive the syllepsis,' he had said once. 'Decency, discipline and dullness. There's no lightness of touch any more, no irresponsibility. Do you remember that damning description of Leonard Bast in *Howards End*? "He had given up the glory of the animal for a tail-coat and a set of ideas." Change tail-coat to pin-stripe and you have modern Cambridge. There's no lack of respect today, that's what I miss.'

As Adrian hurried past the Senate House he noticed two old men standing outside Bowes and Bowes. He put an extra spring in his step, a thing he often did when walking near the elderly. He imagined old people would look at his athletic bounce with a misty longing for their own youth. Not that he was trying to show off or rub salt into the wounds of the infirm, he really believed he was offering a service, an opportunity for nostalgia, like whistling the theme tune from *Happidrome* or spinning a Diabolo.

He skipped past them with carefree ease, missed

his footing and fell to the ground with a thump. One of the old men helped him up.

'You all right, lad?'

'Yes fine . . . I must have slipped on the ice.'

Using Justin, his umbrella, as a walking-stick, he hobbled down Trinity Street, ruthlessly mocking himself.

'Adrian, you're an arse. In a world of arses, you are the arsiest by a mile. Stop being an arse at once, or I'll never talk to you again. So there.'

'Is there a problem, sir?'

'Oh sorry, no . . . I was just . . . humming to myself.'

He hadn't realised he'd been talking out loud. The Trinity porter stared at him suspiciously, so as Adrian limped into Great Court, he broke into more definite and deliberate song to prove his point.

'How do you solve a problem like Maria?' he fluted. 'How do you catch a cloud and pin it down? How do you find a word that means Maria? A flibbertigibbet, a will o'the wisp, a clown.'

Hugo's rooms were in the corner tower. The same tower where Lord Byron had kept his bear, arousing the wrath of the college authorities, who had told him sniffily that the keeping of domestic animals in rooms was strictly forbidden. Byron had assured them that it was far from a domestic animal. It was an untamed bear, as wild and savage as could be, and they had been reluctantly obliged to let him keep it.

'How do you solve a problem like Maria? How do you hold a moonbeam in your hand?'

Hugo opened the door.

'I brought a jar of anchovy paste, half a dozen

potato farls and a packet of my own special blend of Formosan Oolong and Orange Pekoe,' said Adrian, 'but I was set upon by a gang of footpads outside Caius and they stole it all.'

'That's all right,' said Hugo. 'I've got some wine.'

Which was about all he seemed to have. He poured out two mugfuls.

'Very nice,' said Adrian, sipping appreciatively. 'I wonder how they got the cat to sit on the bottle.'

'It's cheap, that's the main thing.'

Adrian looked round the room. From the quantity of empty bottles about the place he supposed that cheapness must indeed have been the deciding factor in Hugo's wine-buying policy. The place was very meanly appointed; apart from the usual college tables and chairs, the only things of interest that met Adrian's inquisitive scrutiny were a photograph of Hugo's actress mother on the table, a *Peter Flowerbuck* poster on the wall which showed Adrian in a tall hat leading Hugo away from a snarling Gary, a handful of Penguin classics, a guitar, some LPs and a record-player.

'So anyway Hugo, my old penny bun. How is everything?'

'Everything,' said Hugo, 'is terrible.'

It didn't look it. Drink never shows in the faces of the young. Hugo's eye was bright, his complexion fine and his figure trim.

'Work is it?'

'No, no. I've just been thinking a lot lately.'

'Well, that's what we're here for, I suppose.'

Hugo filled up his mug with more wine.

'I just want to see if I've got you straight. You

seduce me in my first year at school and then ignore me completely until you make up a lie about Pigs Trotter having been in love with me . . . Julian Rundell told me the truth about that, by the way. Then you seduce me again by pretending to be asleep. Years later, after having cheated my prep school out of a cricket victory, you tell me that you weren't really asleep that night, which I *didn't* in fact know, even though I said I did. Then what happens? Oh yes, you write a fake Dickens novel describing a character who looks like me and just happens to make love to someone who looks like you while that person just happens to be asleep. I think that's everything. You see, all I want to know is . . . what have I done?'

'Hugo, I know it seems . . .'

'It worries me, you see. I must have done something terrible to you without knowing it and I'd like it all to stop now, please.'

'Oh God,' said Adrian.

It was so hard to connect this man with Cartwright. If Hugo had taught at another prep school and gone to another university, the memory of him wouldn't be muddied by a sight like this alien Hugo who trembled and wept into his wine. It *was* another person of course, molecularly every part of the old Cartwright must have been replaced dozens of times since he had been the most beautiful person who ever walked the earth. And the old Adrian who had loved him was not the same as the Adrian who beheld him now. It was like the philosopher's axe. After a few years the philosopher replaces the head, later he replaces the shaft. Then the head wears out and he replaces it again, next the shaft again. Can he go on calling it the same axe? Why should this new Adrian be responsible for the sins of the old?

'It's so easy to explain, Hugo. Easy and very hard. Just one word covers it all.'

'What word? *No* word could explain it. Not a whole Bible of words.'

'It's a common enough word, but it might mean something different to you than it does to me. Language is a bastard. So let's invent a new word. "Libb" will do. I libbed you. That's all there is to it. I was in libb with you. My libb for you informed my every waking and sleeping hour for . . . for God knows how many years. Nothing has ever been as powerful as that libb. It was the guiding force of my life, it haunted me then and haunts me still.'

'You were in *love* with me?'

'Well now, that's your word. Libb has a great deal in common with love, I admit. But love is supposed to be creative, not destructive, and as you have found out, my libb turned out to be very harmful indeed.'

Hugo gripped the rim of his mug and stared into his wine.

'Why can't you . . .'

'Yes?'

'I mean . . . everything you do . . . that bloody magazine, the being asleep, the cricket match, that Dickens novel . . . everything you do is . . . is . . . I don't know what it is.'

'Duplicitous? Covert? Underhand? Sly? Devious? Evasive?'

'All of those things. Why have you never come out and said anything or done anything in the open?'

'I'm fucked if I know, Hugo. I'm seriously fucked

if I know. Perhaps because I'm a coward. Perhaps because I don't exist except in borrowed clothes. I used to think everyone but me was a fraud. It's simple logic to realise that, except to a madman, the opposite must have been the truth.'

'Hell's bells, Adrian. Have you any idea how much I admired you? Any idea at all? Your talent? You used to come into the changing-room sometimes dressed as Oscar Wilde or Noël Coward or whoever and stride up and down like a prince. You used to make me feel so *small*. All the things you can do. My mother thinks I'm a bore. I used to wish I could be you. I fantasised being you. I would lie awake at night imagining what it would be like to have your tall body and your smile, your wit and words. And of course I loved you. I didn't libb you or lobb you or lubb you or labb you, I loved you.'

'Oh lord,' sighed Adrian. 'If I find a way of expressing adequately now what I am thinking and feeling you will take it to be a piece of verbal dexterity and the latest in a long line of verbal malversations. You see! I can't even say "deceit". I have to say "verbal malversations". Everyone's honest but me. So perhaps I should just whine and moan wordlessly.'

Adrian opened the window and howled into Great Court like a demented muezzin, taking the perform-ance so far as to produce real tears. When he turned to face back into the room Hugo was laughing.

'What they call keening, I believe,' said Adrian.

'Well, there's always the cliché,' Hugo said, extend-ing his hand. 'We can be just good friends now.'

'Here's looking at you, kid.'

'Here's looking at you, kid.'

'We'll always have Paris.'

'We'll always have Paris.'

Adrian raised his mug of wine. 'Here's death to the past.'

'Death to the past.'

A Tweed, a Shapeless Green Needlecord Jacket and an Eau de Nil Chanel Suit sat in conference in the Savile Club Sand Pit.

'I'm very much afraid that someone in St Matthew's is not to be trusted.'

'Garth, you think?' asked the Shapeless Green Needlecord.

'Garth is much as he was in your day, Humphrey. Maddening, sour, truculent and asper. Not a natural player, I feel. Not a concealer. It is also very unlikely that he would have been introduced at this late stage.'

'Have you heard from Bela?' the Chanel Suit wanted to know.

'Not a whisper. He knows that the Budapest network have him under the tightest possible surveillance. Pearce is playing for very high stakes this time.'

'Don't I know it!' said the Eau de Nil Suit. 'My bag burst in the middle of Waitrose's yesterday.'

The others giggled like schoolchildren.

'Oh dear me,' said the Tweed. 'However did you explain it?'

'I didn't. I just fled, leaving my shopping behind. I don't know if I can ever show my face in there again.'

They drank tea in companionable silence.

'Who then?' asked the Needlecord suddenly. 'If not Garth?'

The Tweed made a suggestion.

'Donald, no!' protested the Eau de Nil Suit.

The Tweed shrugged apologetically.

'What a howling shit.'

'Well, perhaps his insertion into play may turn out to be rather a useful development.'

'I don't see how.'

'He's plasticine.'

'Outdated you mean?'

'Not Pleistocene, Humphrey. Plasticine. We had all considered him as a possible player for the future, had we not? We know what a shifty little soul he is. Much better to have him as an enemy than as a friend. This is all turning out to be much more fun and much more complex than I had anticipated. The plot thickens like finest Devon cream.'

'If Pearce is going to play dirty like this, Donald, shouldn't we do the same?'

'Humphrey's right, you know,' said the Chanel Suit. 'Why don't I ask Nancy and Simon if they can't lend a hand?'

'Tug of loyalties?' the Tweed wondered. 'I mean Simon works for Pearce, after all.'

'I like to hope,' said the Eau de Nil Chanel Suit, 'that Simon's real loyalties go deeper than that.'

'Very well then. Recruit them and familiarise them with the ground rules. Stefan is due in England soon. He will have news from and of Bela. You know, this is all highly satisfactory.'

'It's not going to get out of control is it?' asked the Needlecord. 'I'm not sure I like the introduction of killing. Pearce cannot bear to be beaten, you know.'

'No more can I,' said the Tweed. 'And I won't be.'

Five

'You were his best friend,' Mrs Trotter said. 'He talked about you a great deal, how clever and amusing you were. He was very fond of you.'

'Well, Mrs Trotter,' said Adrian, 'I was very fond of him. We all were.'

'I do hope you and . . . and the other boy . . . Cartwright . . . can come to the funeral.'

She looked just like Pigs when she cried.

That evening the whole House was already in a slightly hysterical state by the time Tickford broke the news officially at House Compline.

'Some of you, I don't know . . . may know,' he said, '. . . may have heard, I don't know, that there has been a tragedy here. Paul Trotter took his own life this afternoon. We have no idea why. We don't know. We just don't know. We can't know.'

Fifty pairs of eyes swivelled towards Adrian, wondering. Why had be been sent for first? Why had he been shut up with Tickford and Pigs's parents for so long?

Cartwright had not yet been spoken to. He knew nothing and his eyes turned towards Adrian too, large and full of awe.

'I'm afraid he must have been very unhappy,'

continued Tickford, apparently to the ceiling. 'Very unhappy, I don't know why. But we shall say a prayer for him and commend his soul to God. Almighty Father . . .'

Adrian felt a thigh being pressed against his as he knelt to pray. It was Rundell.

'What?'

'I saw him,' whispered Rundell. 'Yesterday afternoon in the cemetery, he went up and sat next to you!'

'So what?'

'Refresh him with your Mercy, cleanse him with your Love . . .'

'And then you came down together and he was crying.'

'That has nothing to do with it.'

'In the name of your Son who died that all might have eternal life . . .'

'Oh, yeah?'

'Amen.'

Tom asked no questions and Adrian couldn't bring himself to tell him anything.

Biffo had sent a note the next morning. 'What terribly upsetting news, terribly upsetting. Helen and I were so distressed. I taught Trotter last year; such a delightful boy. I do hope you feel free to come and talk to me about it. If you would like to, of course. Helen and I would be delighted if you could make more of our Friday afternoon visits this term. With every sympathy at this dreadful time. Humphrey Biffen.'

Tom and Adrian were playing cribbage during the afternoon when there was a knock at the door.

'Avanti!'

It was Cartwright, looking frightened.

'Can I have a word with you, Healey?'

Tom saw the expression on Cartwright's face and reached for a book and a pair of sunglasses.

'I'd better grow.'

'Thanks, Thompson.' Cartwright stood looking at the floor and waited for Tom to close the door behind him.

'Sit down do,' said Adrian.

'I've just been to see Tickford,' said Cartwright, either not hearing or not heeding the invitation.

'Oh, ah?'

'He said Trotter had some sort of . . . a kind of crush on me. And that you told him that.'

'Well, that's what Trotter told me.'

'But I didn't even know him!'

Adrian shrugged.

'I'm sorry, Cartwright, but you know what this place is like.'

Cartwright sat down in Tom's chair and stared out of the window.

'Oh hell's bells. It'll be all over the school.'

'Of course it won't be,' said Adrian. 'Tickford won't tell anyone. I certainly won't tell anyone. I mean, I haven't even told Thompson and I tell him everything.'

'But Tick says I've got to go to the funeral. What will people think of that?'

'Well . . .' said Adrian, thinking fast. 'I'm going to

163

the funeral too. I'll put it around that your parents are friends of Trotter's parents.'

'I suppose that'll do,' said Cartwright, 'but why did you have to tell Tick in the first place?'

'It was suicide! He left a note. It said "Healey will explain" or something like that. What else could I do but tell the truth?'

Cartwright looked up at him.

'Did Pigs, did Trotter say . . . did he tell you how long he'd had this, this *thing* for me?'

'Since you came to the school apparently.'

Cartwright dropped his head and stared at the floor. When he looked up again there were tears in his eyes. He looked angry. Angry and to Adrian more beautiful than ever.

'Why did he tell *you*?' he cried. 'Why couldn't he have told me? And what did he have to go and kill himself for?'

Adrian felt taken aback by the anger in Cartwright's voice.

'Well, I suppose he was scared in case . . . in case you rejected him or something. I don't know how these things work.'

'More scared of me rejecting him than he was of killing himself?'

Adrian nodded.

'So now I'm going to have to wake up every morning for the rest of my life knowing that I'm responsible for someone's suicide.'

The tears splashed down his face. Adrian leant forward and held his shoulder.

'You must never think of it like that, Hugo. You mustn't!' he said.

He had never called him Hugo before and he hadn't touched him since their brief how-do-you-do in the House lavs, which was before Adrian had known he was in love.

'I'm as responsible as you are, really,' Adrian said. 'More responsible, if anything.'

Cartwright stared in surprise.

'How do you mean?'

'Well,' said Adrian, 'I could have advised Trotter to tell you, couldn't I? I could have told him not to bottle it up.'

'But you weren't to know what was going to happen.'

'And nor were you, Hugo. Now come on, dry your eyes, or people will really know something is wrong. We'll go to the funeral and then in a couple of weeks we'll have forgotten all about it.'

'Thanks, Healey. I'm sorry to be so . . .'

'Adrian. And there's nothing to be sorry about.'

Between that day and the day they travelled up to Harrogate they hadn't exchanged a word. Adrian had seen him mobbing around with his friends as if nothing had happened. The House did its best to forget the whole embarrassment. Trotter was thought of with the kind of contempt and revulsion young Englishmen of the right type reserve for the sick, the mad, the poor and the old.

The funeral was set for ten in the morning, so Tickford had decided that they should travel up the evening before and spend the night in a hotel. For the whole duration of the journey Cartwright stared out of the window.

He's beginning to resent Trotter's posthumous power over him, Adrian thought.

The Tickfords didn't speak much either. This was a duty they did not relish. Adrian, never a tidy traveller, twice had to ask Ma Tickford, who was driving, to stop the car so that he could be sick.

He couldn't imagine why he had dropped Cartwright in it the way he had. A kind of revenge he supposed. But revenge for what? And on whom? A revenge on the ghost of Trotter or on the living, breathing Cartwright?

He wasn't Woody Nightshade, he was Deadly Nightshade. Everybody who had anything to do with him was lethally poisoned.

But they don't exist, he kept repeating to himself as they rattled up the A1. Other people don't exist. Trotter isn't really dead because he was never really alive. It's all just a clever way of testing me. There's no one in these cars and lorries driving south. There can't be that many individual souls. Not souls like mine. There isn't room. There can't be.

But suppose Trotter's ghost watched him? Trotter would know everything by now. Would he forgive him?

From now on, I conform.

He should have guessed that Tickford would give him and Cartwright a twin room at the hotel. The bill was being settled by the school, after all.

Their room was at the end of a creaking corridor. Adrian opened the door and bowed Cartwright in.

Manly, unconcerned and businesslike, he told himself. Two healthy English school chums sharing digs.

166

Holmes and Watson, Bunny and Raffles. Nothing else.

'So, Cartwright old boy – which bed do you fancy?'

'I don't mind really. This one'll do fine.'

'Okay. Bags the bathroom first, then.'

Like all the English hotels Adrian had ever stayed in, this one was appallingly overheated. He undressed and slipped naked into bed while Cartwright brushed his teeth in the bathroom.

Now then, Healey, he warned himself. You're to behave. Understand?

He switched out the light above his bed just as Cartwright came out, magnificently clad in sky-blue pyjamas of brushed cotton, swinging a sponge-bag from his wrist.

'Night then, Cartwright.'

'Night.'

Adrian closed his eyes. He heard Cartwright shuffle off his slippers and get into bed.

Don't let him turn his light off. Make him pick up a book. Please, God, please.

He strained his ears and caught the sound of a page turning.

Thank you, God. You're a treasure.

During the next five minutes Adrian allowed his breathing naturally to deepen into a slow rhythm until any observer would swear that he was fast asleep.

He then began to give the impression of a more troubled rest. He turned and gave a small moan. The eiderdown fell to the floor. He rolled over far to one side, causing the top sheet to come away. A minute later he turned the other way violently, kicking with his foot so that the sheet joined the eiderdown.

He was now naked on the bed, breathing heavily and writhing. Cartwright's light was still on but the pages had stopped turning.

'Adrian?'

It had been a light whisper, but Cartwright had definitely spoken.

'Adrian . . .' Adrian mumbled in return, half snoring the word as he turned to face Cartwright, mouth open, eyes closed.

'Adrian, are you all right?'

'No one left in the valley,' said Adrian, flinging out a hand.

He heard Cartwright's bed creak.

Here we go, he thought to himself, here we bloody well go!

Cartwright's feet padded across the room.

He's next to me, I can sense it!

'I'll eat them later . . . later,' he moaned.

He heard the rustle of a sheet and felt the eiderdown being pulled on top of him.

He can't just be going to tuck me up! He can't be. I've got a stiffy like a milk-bottle. Is he flesh and blood or what? Oh well, here goes. Nothing ventured, nothing gained.

He arched his body and thrashed his legs up and down.

'Lucy?' he called, quite loudly this time.

Where he got the name Lucy from, he had no idea.

'Lucy?'

He swept out an arm and found Cartwright's shoulder.

'Lucy, is that you?'

The eiderdown was slowly pulled away from him

again. Suddenly he felt a warm hand between his thighs.

'Yes,' he said, 'yes.'

Then soft hair brushing against his chest and a tongue licking his stomach.

Hugo, he sighed to himself. Hugo! and out loud, 'Oh Lucy – *Lucy!*'

He was awoken by the sound of a lavatory flushing. The eiderdown was on top of him and the sun was shining through a gap in the curtains.

'Oh God. What have I done?'

Cartwright came out of the bathroom.

'Morning,' he said brightly.

'Hi,' mumbled Adrian, 'what the hell time is it?'

'Seven thirty. Sleep all right?'

'Jesus, like a log. And you?'

'Not too badly. You talked a lot.'

'Oh sorry,' said Adrian, 'I do that sometimes. I hope it didn't keep you awake.'

'You kept saying Lucy. Who's Lucy?'

'Really?' Adrian frowned. 'Well, I used to have a dog called Lucy . . .'

'Oh, right,' said Cartwright. 'I wondered.'

'Works every time,' Adrian said to himself, turning over and going back to sleep.

It was a small funeral. A small funeral for a small life. Trotter's parents were pleased to see Adrian again and were polite to Cartwright, but they couldn't entirely disguise their distaste for him. His beauty, pale in a dark suit, was an affront to the memory of their pudgy and ordinary son.

After the ceremony they drove to the Trotters'

farmhouse five miles outside Harrogate. One of Pigs Trotter's sisters gave Adrian a photograph of himself. It showed him lying on his stomach watching a cricket match. Adrian tried hard but couldn't remember Pigs Trotter taking it. No one commented on the fact that Trotter kept no photographs of Cartwright.

Mr Trotter asked Adrian if he would come and stay in the summer holidays.

'You ever sheared sheep before?'

'No, sir.'

'You'll enjoy it.'

Tickford took the wheel for the homeward journey. Adrian was allowed in the front next to him. They didn't want to risk him being sick again.

'A sorry business,' said Tickford.

'Yes, sir.'

Tickford gestured over his shoulder towards Cartwright, who was leaning against Ma Tickford and snoring gently.

'I hope you haven't told anyone,' he said.

'No, sir.'

'You must get on with the term now, Adrian. It has not started well. That disgusting magazine and now this . . . all in the first week. There's a bad spirit abroad, I wonder if I can look to you to help combat it?'

'Well, sir . . .'

'This may be just the jolt you need to start taking yourself seriously at last. Boys like you have a profound influence. Whether it is used for good or evil can make the difference between a happy and an unhappy school.'

'Yes, sir.'

Tickford patted Adrian's knee.

'I have a feeling that I can rely on you,' he said.

'You can, sir,' said Adrian. 'I promise.'

It was four o'clock when they got back. Adrian returned to his study to find it empty. Tom was obviously having tea somewhere else.

He couldn't be bothered to track him down, so he made toast on his own and started on some overdue Latin prep. If he was going to turn over a new leaf then there was no time like the present. Then he would write back to Biffo. Attend all his Friday afernoons. Read more. Think more.

He had hardly begun before there came a knock at the door.

'Come in!'

It was Bennett-Jones.

'Really, R.B.-J. Flattered as I am by your fawning attentions I must ask you to find another playmate. I am a busy man. Virgil calls to me from across the centuries.'

'Yeah?' said Bennett-Jones with a nasty leer. 'Well it just so happens that Mr Tickford calls to you from across his study, an'all.'

'Dear me! Five minutes' separation and already he pines for me. Perhaps he wants my advice on demoting some of the prefecture. Well, I am always happy to look in on dear Jeremy. Lead the way, young man, lead the way.'

Tickford was standing behind his desk, his face deathly white.

'This book,' he said, holding up a paperback, 'does it belong to you?'

Oh Christ . . . oh Jesus Christ . . .

It was Adrian's copy of *The Naked Lunch*.

'I . . . I don't know, sir.'

'It was found in your study. It has your name written in it. No other boy in the school has a copy in their study. On the instructions of the headmaster the prefects checked this morning. Now, answer me again. Is this your book?'

'Yes, sir.'

'Just tell me one thing, Healey. Did you write the magazine alone or were there others?'

'I –'

'Answer me!' shouted Tickford, slamming the book down onto the desk.

'Alone, sir.'

There was a pause. Tickford stared at Adrian, breathing heavily from his nostrils like a cornered bull.

Oh cuntly cunt. He's going to hit me. He's out of control.

'Go to your study,' said Tickford at last. 'Stay there until your parents come for you. No one is to see you or talk to you.'

'Sir, I –'

'Now get out of my sight, you poisonous little shit.'

A Peaked Cap, waving a sheet of typescript, hurried into the Customs office where a Dark Grey Suit was watching television.

'Comrade Captain,' he said. 'I have the inventory of the delegation's luggage.'

'You can cut out the Comrade crap for a start,' said the Dark Grey Suit, taking the proffered sheet.

'Szabó's articles are itemised at the top, sir.'

'I can read.'

The Dark Grey Suit scanned the list.

'And you searched the rest of the team just as thoroughly?'

'Just as thoroughly Com— Captain Molgar, sir.'

'The chess books have been checked?'

'They have all been checked and replaced with identical copies in case of . . .' the Peaked Cap gestured hopefully. He had no idea what the original chess books might have contained. 'In case of . . . microdots?' he whispered.

The Dark Grey Suit snorted contemptuously.

'This radio in Ribli's luggage?'

'A perfectly ordinary radio, Captain. Comrade Ribli has taken it abroad many times. He is not under suspicion also?'

The Dark Grey Suit ignored the question.

'Csom's suitcase seems to be very heavy.'

'It is an old case. Leather.'

173

'Have it X-rayed.'

'Yes, sir.'

'Yes, Captain.'

'Yes, Captain.'

'That's better.'

The Peaked Cap coughed.

'Captain, sir, why do you let this Szabó out of the country if he is . . .?'

'If he is what?'

'I-I don't quite know, sir.'

'Szabó is one of the most talented young grandmasters in the world. The next Portisch. All this checking is simply a routine test of your efficiency, nothing more. You understand?'

'Yes, Captain.'

'Yes, Comrade Captain.'

'Yes, Comrade Captain.'

The Dark Grey Suit hummed to himself. He did not know what they were looking for either. But the British had been paying him a great deal for many years and now that they suddenly wanted him to work for his money he supposed he had no business complaining. This was not dangerous work, after all. He was doing no more than his usual duty and if the authorities discovered his unusual interest in Szabó they would be more likely to reward him for his zeal than shoot him for his treachery.

He had hoiked out Szabó's file that morning to see if there was anything there to justify this sudden British directive. There was nothing there: Stefan Szabó, a perfectly blameless citizen, grandson of a Hungarian hero and a great chess hope.

The solution came to the Dark Grey Suit in a blinding flash. Stefan Szabó was planning, sometime during the tournament in Hastings, to defect. The British needed to check that he was an honest defector, that he was not bringing any equipment out with him that would suggest a darker purpose.

But why should a successful chess-player need to defect? They made plenty of money, which they were allowed to keep, they were granted unlimited travel abroad, foreign bank accounts. Hungary was not Russia or Czechoslovakia, for God's sake. The Dark Grey Suit, who had betrayed his country for years, felt a stab of resentment and anger against this young traitor.

'Little shit,' he thought to himself. 'What's wrong with Hungary that he needs to run away to England?'

Six

Just as Adrian was getting thoroughly bored, the President started to wind up the meeting.

'Now,' he said, 'it's getting rather late. If there is no further business, I would like to – '

Garth Menzies rose to his feet and smiled the smile of the just.

'There is one thing, Master.'

'Can't it wait?'

'No, sir. I don't believe it can.'

'Oh, very well then.'

Adrian cursed inwardly. They all knew the subject Menzies was going to raise and Menzies knew that they knew. They had been given the chance to raise it themselves but they hadn't. So be it. Very well. Other men might shrink from their duty, but not Garth Menzies.

He barked his throat clear.

'I am amazed, Mr President, absolutely amazed that this meeting can contemplate adjournment without first discussing the Trefusis Affair.'

A dozen heads looked sharply down at their agenda papers. A dozen pairs of buttocks clenched tightly together.

He had said it. The man had said it. Such a want of delicacy. Such wounding impropriety.

At the far end of the table a mathematician specialising in fluid dynamics and the seduction of first year Newnham girls blew his nose in a hurt manner.

Those parts of Adrian that weren't already looking sharply down or clenching tightly together contrived to quiver with disfavour.

How incredibly like Garth to bring up the one subject that everyone else in the room had been so elegantly avoiding. How childish the rhetoric with which he claimed to be amazed at that avoidance.

'I find myself wondering,' said Menzies, 'how we feel about having a criminal amongst us?'

'Now, really Garth – '

'Oh yes, Master, a criminal.'

Menzies, tall and thin, face as white, shiny and bold Roman as the cover page of the quarterly journal of civil law it was his pride to edit, had placed his left thumb along the lapel of his coat and now he stooped forwards from the waist, waving in his right hand, in what he hoped was a brandish, a copy of the *Cambridge Evening News*.

Adrian found himself chilled by the sight of a grown man trying so transparently to strike the forensic pose of a glamorous barrister. No matter how he aged, and there was not now one dark hair on his head, Menzies could never look any grander than a smart-arsed sixth-former. A smart-arsed *grammar-school* sixth-former, Adrian thought. He cut a dreadful sort of Enoch Powell figure. A kind of adolescent Malvolio, all elbows and shiny temples. Adrian found

Menzies as tiresome as his archetypes; unspeakable to behold, dangerous to discount.

Menzies resented his widespread popularity because he felt it sprang from illogical and irrelevant factors like his breath, his voice, his sniffs, his gait, his clothes, his whole atmosphere. For that reason he devoted himself with all the dismal diligence of the dull to giving the world more legitimate grounds for dislike. That, at least, was Adrian's interpretation. Donald always claimed to like the man.

If Donald had been present to witness him now, newspaper in hand and destruction in mind, Adrian was sure he would have altered his opinion.

President Clinton-Lacey, at the head of the table, looked down at his agenda and shaded his eyes. From under his hand he waggled a covert eyebrow at Adrian like a schoolboy sharing a joke under a desk-lid. But there was an urgency and seriousness in the look which told Adrian that he was being given some kind of signal.

Adrian wasn't sure if he could interpret it. He stared ahead of him, perplexed. Did the President want him, as a friend of Donald's, to speak up? Was he warning Adrian not to let his feelings get the better of him? What? He returned the look with a questioning lift of his own eyebrows.

In reply the President gave a 'yackety-yack' gesture with his hand.

Clinton-Lacey's Boltonian sense of humour was notorious but surely he meant something more than 'Oh, that Menzies, he does go on, doesn't he?'

Adrian decided it must be a demand for him to do some filibustering. He swallowed nervously. He was only an undergraduate after all and these were not the sixties. The days of genuine student representation on the boards of governors of the colleges were long gone. It was understood that he was a constitutional hiccough that it would have been embarrassing to cure. He was there to listen, not to comment.

However.

'Don't you think, Dr Menzies,' he began, not daring to look up, 'that the word "criminal" is a bit strong?'

Menzies rounded on him.

'Forgive me, Mr Healey, you are the English student. I am just a lawyer. What on earth would I know about the word criminal? In my profession, out of ignorance no doubt, we use the word to describe someone who has broken the law. I am sure you could entertain us with an essay on the word's origin that would prove conclusively that a criminal is some kind of medieval crossbow. For my purposes however, in law, the man is a criminal.'

'Now, gentlemen . . .'

'Dr Menzies' clumsy sarcasm aside,' said Adrian, 'I have to say that I know full well what criminal means and it is a perfectly ordinary English word, not a legal term, and I resent it being used of Donald. It makes him sound like a professional. One crime doesn't make a criminal. It would be like calling Dr Menzies a lawyer just because thirty years ago he practised briefly at the Bar.'

'I have every right in the world, Mr President,' shrilled Menzies, 'to call myself a lawyer. I believe my reputation in the legal field has done nothing but reflect credit on this institution – '

'Perhaps it wouldn't be unfitting if I said something

here,' said Tim Anderson. His book on Jean-Luc Godard had recently been exceptionally well reviewed by his wife in *Granta* magazine and he was in a less solemn mood than usual.

'I think it would be immensely unfitting,' snapped Menzies.

'Well that's a not uninteresting point, certainly,' said Anderson, 'but I was thinking more that I don't know many people who couldn't express doubt about the strategies that the authorities adopt in situations not a million miles dissimilar to this one and I just don't think that's something we shouldn't be unafraid to shirk addressing or confronting. That's all.'

'I have just been told by a student that I have no right to call myself a lawyer, Master,' said Menzies. 'I await an apology.'

'Dr Menzies is an academic,' said Adrian. 'He is a teacher. I'd have thought that that was quite enough of a profession for one man. I maintain that he is not a lawyer. Law just happens to be the subject he teaches.'

'I am not absolutely sure that I see the relevance of this,' said the President and something in the tone of his voice made Adrian look at him again. He was rolling an eye in the direction of the corner of the room.

The cameras!

Since the beginning of this, Adrian's third and final year, St Matthew's had put up with a television crew on the premises. Their technique, that of becoming part of the furniture, was working so well that they had become appallingly easy to ignore. They had lived up to the name of fly-on-the-wall and only the odd irritating buzz reminded the college of their existence.

It was clear that the President did not want Adrian to forget them. He could not possibly allow anything of the Trefusis Affair to be seen on national television. Adrian's duty lay clear ahead of him. He had to find a way of doing or saying something that would make the film of the meeting, or this part of it, unsuitable for family viewing.

He took a deep breath.

'I'm sorry, Master,' he said, snapping a pencil, 'but the point is that I won't sit here and hear my friend insulted, not if the accuser is the Director of Public Prosecutions, the Procurator Pissing Fiscal and the Witchfinder Fucking General all rolled into one.'

A splutter of incredulity from a middle-aged Orientalist met this unusual outburst.

'Donald has been called a criminal,' Adrian went on, warming to his theme. 'If I run down the street to catch a bus, does that make me an athlete? If you yodel in the bath, Master, does that make you a singer? Dr Menzies has a tongue like a supermarket pricing-gun.'

'Twisting my words won't help.'

'Untwisting them might.'

'Well untwist these words, then,' said Menzies, forcing his copy of the newspaper under Adrian's nose.

'What the yellow rubbery fuck do you think you're up to now?' said Adrian, pushing the newspaper away. 'If I want to blow my nose, I'll use a frigging snot-rag.'

'Healey, have you run mad?' hissed Corder, a theologian, sitting next to Adrian.

'Stick it up your heretical arse.'

'Well!'

'Explain it to you later,' said Adrian in an undertone.

'Oh, it's a game!'

'Sh!'

'Splendid!' whispered Corder, and then sang out, 'Oh, do come on, Garth, get a sodding move on.'

'Well,' said Menzies. 'I have no idea what childish motive you have for hurling abuse at me, Mr Healey. Perhaps you think it is funny. At the risk of being told that I have no sense of humour I am quite prepared to suggest that even an undergraduate audience would remain unmoved by the spectacle of a student insulting one more than twice his age. As for Dr Corder, I can only assume that the man is drunk.'

'Piss off, you fat tit,' said Corder primly.

'Mr President, are they to be allowed to continue in this fashion?'

'Dr Corder, Mr Healey, let Dr Menzies have his say, please,' said the President.

'Right you fucking are, Mr President,' said Adrian, standing up and immediately sitting down again. He had noticed that the microphone boom was only a few inches higher than his head. If he kept standing up he had a notion it would appear in shot and spoil the footage.

'You have the floor, farty,' said Corder.

'I think I'd better say for my own part,' said Tim Anderson, 'that notwithstanding – '

'Thank you,' said Menzies.

Adrian burped loudly and felt with his feet for the TV cabling which ran under the table.

'Now, for those of you have not seen it,' Menzies continued, fishing his spectacles out of his jacket pocket, 'there is an article in this evening's local paper which is of exceptional interest to this college. I shall read it to you.

'"Professor Donald Trefusis,"' he intoned, in that awful declamatory chant reserved by politicians for public readings of I Corinthians 13, '"holder of the Regius Chair in Philology and Senior Tutor of St Matthew's College, appeared at Cambridge magistrate's court this morning charged with gross indecency . . ."'

Menzies broke off. While he had been speaking a large electric lamp in the corner of the room had begun to totter on its base. It creaked on its stand, unable to make up its mind whether to crash to the ground or return to an upright position. By the time a technician had noticed and started to run across to save it, it had decided on the floor. It was the noise of the ten kilowatt bulb exploding that had interrupted Menzies' flow.

'Oh dear,' said Adrian, standing up, distraught. 'I think my feet may inadvertently have become tangled up in your cables for a moment. I'm so sorry . . .'

The BBC director smiled at him through clenched teeth.

'If Mr Healey can manage to sit still for just three minutes,' Menzies continued, 'I shall resume . . .'

'You had got as far as gross indecency,' said Adrian.

'Thank you. ". . . charged with gross indecency. The Professor had been arrested in the Parker's Piece men's toilet at three o'clock the previous night. A youth, described as in his late teens, escaped after a struggle with police. The Professor (66) pleaded guilty. The President of St Matthew's College was unavailable for comment this morning. Donald Trefusis, who is well-known for his articles and broadcasts, told the *Evening News* that life was very extraordinary."'

'Yes, well thank you, Garth,' said the President, 'I think we're all pretty much aware of the details of this morning's court-room drama. I suppose you think something should be done about it?'

'Done?' said Menzies. 'Of course something should be done!'

Adrian stood up.

'Hoover, Wrigleys, Magicote, Benson and Hedges, Sellotape, Persil, Shake and Vac, Nestlés Milky Bar,' he said and sat down again. He had a vague idea that brand names couldn't be mentioned on the BBC.

'Thank you, Adrian,' said the President, 'that will do.'

'Yes sir, Mr President, sir!' said Adrian.

Tim Anderson spoke.

'I don't think I'd be wrong in detecting – '

'If an undergraduate were compromised in this fashion,' said Menzies, 'we would have no hesitation in sending him down. Professor Trefusis is a member of the college just like any student. I submit that under the college ordinance of 1273 and subsequent statutes of 1791 and 1902 we are duty bound to take disciplinary action against any Fellow who brings the good name of the college into disrepute. I move that this meeting of the Fellows immediately invite Professor Trefusis to relinquish the post of Senior Tutor and furthermore I move that they insist he withdraw from any active teaching post in this college for one year. At the very least.'

'Nice subjunctives,' murmured Adrian.

'Now steady on, Garth,' said the President. 'I'm sure we're all as shocked as you are by Donald's . . . Donald's . . . well, his behaviour. But remember where we are. This is Cambridge. We have a tradition of buggery here.'

'Bottomy is everywhere, you know,' the ninety-year-old treble of Emeritus Professor Adrian Williams sang out. 'Wittgenstein was a bottomist, they tell me. I read the other day that Morgan Forster, you remember Morgan? Next door, at King's. Wrote *A Passage to India* and *Howards End*. Wore slippers into Hall once. I read that *he* was a bottomite too. Extraordinary! I think everyone is now. Simply everyone.'

A red-faced statistician thumped the table angrily.

'Not I, sir, not I!' he thundered.

'I don't think we should be unafraid not to discuss the gay dialectic as an energy and the homophobic constraints that endorse its marginalisation as a functionally reactive discourse,' said Tim Anderson.

The cameraman in the corner tilted his camera from one end of the table to the other, quite unable to decide on whom to concentrate his lens.

'If I can speak,' said Adrian.

He had just unwrapped a packet of cigarettes and now scrunched up the cellophane so loudly that the microphone boom, which had just reached him, swung away like a startled giraffe and struck Menzies on the head.

A production assistant with a clipboard giggled and was rewarded with a look of foul contempt from the President.

Menzies was not to be put off.

'The fact is this, Master. There are laws. Homosexual acts are only permitted amongst consenting adults in private.'

'Are you allowed in law, Dr Menzies,' asked Adrian, 'to defecate in public?'

'Certainly not!'

'How would I be charged if I did?'

'Gross indecency, beyond question, the case of the Earl of Oxford – '

'Exactly. But would I be arrested for taking a crap in a public lavatory?'

'Don't be ridiculous.'

'So a public lavatory is, in law, a private place?'

'You're twisting words again, Healey.'

'But again, the words are already twisted. Either a municipal bog is a private place or it isn't. If it is a private place in which to shit, how is it not a private place in which to fellate?'

'Oh, it was fellatio, was it?' the President seemed surprised.

'Well, whatever.'

'Who was doing it to whom, I wonder?'

Menzies' hold on his temper was weakening.

'Either the law is the law or it is not! If it is your intention to campaign for a change in that law, Healey, very good luck to you. The fact remains that Professor Trefusis has brought into disrepute the good name of this college.'

'You never liked him did you?' Adrian couldn't

help saying. 'Well, here's your chance. He's down. Kick him good and hard.'

'Mr President,' said Menzies, 'I have proposed a motion to the Fellows. That Donald Trefusis be stripped of his Senior Tutorship and suspended from the college for a full year. I demand it to be put to the question.'

'Mr President,' said Adrian, 'surely Dr Menzies can't have forgotten that a motion cannot be voted on unless saving that it howmay shall as thus *nem con*, *ne plus ultra* before these presents, as witness the hand thereunto, be seconded?'

'Er . . . quite right,' said the President. 'I think. Do we have a seconder?'

Silence.

'I ask again. Do we have a seconder for Dr Menzies' proposal that Donald Trefusis be relieved of his college duties for the period of one year?'

Silence.

Menzies' chalk-white cheeks were lit with the pin-prick of crimson which, for him, passed for a manly blush.

'Madness, absolute madness! The college will live to regret it.'

'Thank you, Dr Menzies,' said the President.

He turned to the film crew.

'That is the end of the meeting. I'll ask you to go now, as we have one or two private college matters to discuss which cannot possibly be of relevance to your film.'

The crew silently gathered their equipment. The director glared at Adrian as he left the room. The female assistant with the clipboard winked.

'I'm in there,' Adrian thought to himself.

'Now then,' said the President, when the last of the crew had gone. 'I'm sorry to keep you all, but I received a letter from Professor Trefusis this morning and I think you had better hear it.'

He took a letter from his inside pocket.

'"Henry,"' he read. '"By the time you read this I am very much afraid that my improvidence will already have been made known to you. I feel I must first offer the profoundest of apologies for the embarrassment I have caused to you and the college.

'"I will not burden you with reasons, excuses, denials or explanations. I have no doubt in my mind however that it would be a sensible thing for me to ask you if I might take advantage of my right to a sabbatical year. I had intended to ask this of you in any case, as my book on the Great Fricative Shift impels me to visit Europe for research materials. May I therefore take this opportunity to beg your permission to leave Cambridge immediately a sentence, which I am assured will at worst take the form of nothing more inconvenient than a small fine and at best a reprimand from the bench, has been passed upon me?

'"Perhaps you will be so kind as to let me know of your decision in this matter as soon as possible, Henry, for there are many arrangements to be made. Meanwhile, in all contrition I remain, Your good friend Donald."'

'Well,' said Menzies at last, 'how ironic. It seems that Professor Trefusis can be credited, in some regards at least, with more decency than the rest of the fellowship.'

'Up your crack, you fat runt,' said Corder.

'The game's over now, Alex,' said Adrian. 'The film crew has gone.'

'I know,' said Corder, stuffing his briefcase with detritus from the meeting. 'That was for real.'

In a small bedroom a Striped Nightgown had been talking to a Donkey Jacket.

The tape of the conversation was being listened to by a Dark Grey Suit. He felt sorry for the Donkey Jacket having to cope with the ruined husk of a once fine mind.

The old fool was babbling of bacon and cheese.

'It's all right, Grandfather, you should rest now.'

'Steffi's cheese is in the ice-box, you see,' whimpered the Striped Nightgown.

'That's right,' soothed the Donkey Jacket. 'Of course it is.'

'Your cheese is in the pantry.'

'In the pantry, that's right.'

'I saw God yesterday, he's very kind. I think he likes me.'

'I really think you should sleep, you know.'

The Donkey Jacket sounded very distressed. The Dark Grey Suit heard the sound of the old man crying.

'Told him that I hadn't had a shit in two weeks, Martin. "You won't need to in Heaven," he said. Wasn't that kind?'

'Very kind. Very kind indeed.'

'Take two kinds of cheese. Always two kinds. One for the mouse and one for the ice-box.'

'That's right.'

'Bit of pörkelt wouldn't hurt. With some egg-dumplings and red cabbage. No sugar though.'

'Off to sleep now.'

The Dark Grey Suit heard the Donkey Jacket rise from the bed. Heard him kiss the forehead of the Striped Nightgown. Heard the Donkey Jacket's footsteps make for the door. Heard . . . a strained whisper? The Dark Grey Suit turned up the volume of his tape-recorder to maximum.

'Martin! Martin!' A hoarse, urgent command from the old man.

The Donkey Jacket's footsteps stopped near the door.

'Sew it into the lining of your jacket!'

So the old bastard was sane after all. The Dark Grey Suit reached for a pad and composed a cypher for London.

Seven

Crossing the river by way of the Sonnet Bridge on a direct course from the President's Lodge to Donald Trefusis's room in Hawthorn Tree Court, Adrian slapped each stone ball that marched along that noble structure's span in frustration. He had hated that meeting, hated the relish with which Garth Menzies had read out the article in the *Cambridge Evening News*, hated the bubbling looks of salacious amusement on the faces of the BBC crew. All of them laughing at Trefusis.

Hell and hot shit, he said to himself, Donald of all people.

The Tea Room Trade they called it in America; in English, Cottaging. Putting yourself up for quick sex in a public loo.

'Bad news, Adrian,' the President had said that morning. 'Donald has gone and popped up in the guise of a lavatory cowboy. He tells me he's due in court at ten thirty. The *Evening News* is sure to cover it. And tomorrow the nationals. What the hell are we going to do?'

Adrian remembered the times he had sprawled on Donald's chesterfield of a summer evening, hot from a game of cricket. Or the weeks they had shared hotel rooms in Venice and Florence and Salzburg during last year's long vacation. The man had never so much as touched Adrian's shoulder. But then why on earth should he have? There were plenty of lanky, languid undergraduates in the University more appetising than Adrian. Anyway, maybe Donald's tastes were more Orton than Auden. Perhaps it was only anonymous rough trade that lit his fire. Live and let live, of course: but better he should paw Adrian than kneel before some greasy truck driver to whom the name Levi Strauss meant nothing but jeans and, by blowing him, blow a reputation, a career and a way of life.

It was Adrian's last summer, but whenever he crossed the bridge, no matter how occupied he might be, he could never prevent himself from looking across at the Backs, the green train of lawn and willow that swept along the river behind the colleges. With a late afternoon mist descending on the Cam, the absurd beauty of the place depressed him deeply. Depressed him because he caught himself failing to react properly to it. There had been a time when that blend of natural and human perfection would have caused him to writhe with pleasure. But now human affairs and the responsibilities of friendship had claimed that part of him that was capable of feeling and there was nothing left over for nature or the abstract.

Donald Trefusis, a urinal Uranian, a bog bugger. Who'd've thought it?

Adrian, no stranger to sexual adventurism, had never been struck by the charms of the public lavatory as an erotic salon. There had been an occasion, not long after his expulsion from school, when he had found himself forced to answer the griping of his bowels in a Gents in the bus-station at Gloucester.

Sitting there, gently encouraging his colon, he had suddenly become aware of a note being fed through an uncomfortably large hole in the wall that divided him from the neighbouring cubicle. He had taken and read it more in an innocent spirit of good citizenship than anything else. Perhaps some unfortunate disabled person had got into trouble.

'I like young cock,' the note said.

Shocked, Adrian looked at the hole. Where the note had been there was now a human eye. Because he couldn't think of anything else to do under the circumstances, or because he was born foolish, Adrian smiled. A winning smile, accompanied by a friendly, faintly patronising wink: the kind of beaming encouragement you might give a toddler who has presented you with an incompetent drawing.

There immediately followed a shuffle of feet next door and a clink of belt buckle hitting concrete. After a brief pause, a bulky and rather excited penis pushed itself through the hole and twitched urgently.

Without pausing for hygiene and comfort, Adrian had yanked up his trousers and fled in panic. For the next half-hour he wandered Gloucester looking for a place in which he might wipe himself, not daring to risk another public convenience. To this day Adrian failed to see any allure in the lavatory. Apart from anything else the smell. And the risk . . . but risk was the whole point, he supposed.

But nonetheless, the Trefusis that he knew – the man with startled white hair and Irish thorn-proof jackets, patched at the elbows, Trefusis the Elvis

Costello fan and Wolseley driver, Trefusis the sports
fan and polyglot – it wasn't easy to imagine that
Trefusis frenziedly gobbling at a trucker. It was like
trying to picture Malcolm Muggeridge masturbating
or Margaret and Denis Thatcher locked in coital
ecstasy. But hard to imagine or not, these things had
all presumably happened.

Adrian hopped across the lawn of Hawthorn Tree
Court, a precaution learnt from schooldays.

'Healey, can't you read?' they used to shout after
him.

'Oh yes, sir. I'm very good at reading, sir.'

'Then can't you see that it clearly says, Don't Walk
On The Grass?'

'I'm not walking, sir. I'm hopping.'

'Don't be clever, boy.'

'All right, sir. How stupid would you like me to
be, sir? Very stupid or only quite stupid?'

He threw himself up the stairs and thumped on
Trefusis's oak. College rooms had two doors and if
the oak, the outer door, was closed, it was generally
held to be bad form to clamour for entrance. Adrian
reckoned that circumstances warranted the solecism.

From within he heard a muffled curse.

'Donald, it's me. Adrian. Won't you let me in?'

After a sigh and a creak of floorboards the door
opened.

'Really, couldn't you see that my oak was sported?'

'I'm sorry, but I thought – '

'I know. I know what you thought. Come in, come
in. I was recording.'

'Oh, sorry.'

Donald's irregular broadcasts on the radio, his

'wireless essays' as he called them, had recently given him a modest amount of fame that had kindled the resentment felt by men like Garth Menzies. Adrian found it hard to believe that, after the events of last night and this morning, Trefusis could contemplate continuing with them. He was even now rewinding the tape on his Uher recorder.

'Sit down,' he said. 'There's a rather comical Bâtard-Montrachet on the side. You might pour out two glasses.'

Now he poured out two glasses of wine and threaded his way through the librarinth towards the small study-within-a-study which contained Donald, his desk, his computer and his tape-recorder. The study was in the centre of the room and made up an inner sanctum no more than six foot square and eight foot high entirely constructed of books, mostly books in Romanian, it appeared. There was even a door. This had been made as part of the set for a student production of *Travesties*, which Trefusis had enjoyed. The director, Bridget Arden, a pupil of his, gave him the door as a present. It had required large stage weights to keep it upright at first, but with books stacked all round its frame it was soon as firmly wedged in place as could be.

One advantage of this strange inner room, Trefusis claimed, was that it made an excellent soundproof chamber for his broadcasts. Adrian's view was that it satisfied a vague agoraphobia, or at least claustraphilia, that he would never admit to.

Trefusis was speaking into the microphone as Adrian tiptoed through with the glasses.

'. . . and since this embarrassment in all its noble

and monumental proportions will be known to you by now through the kind offices of the press, I shall, for the moment, spare you a description of its more gaudy details, although I look forward to sharing them with you in a frank, straightforward and manly way before the year is quite out. For the time being I will, if I may, take a break from these wireless essays and see something of the world. When I have found out what the world is like, be sure that I will let you know, those of you who are interested, of course, the others will simply have to guess. Meanwhile if you have been, then continue to and don't even think of stopping.'

He sighed and put the microphone down.

'Well, it's all very sad,' he said.

'Where shall I put the wine?' said Adrian, looking around for a free space.

'I should try your throat, dear boy,' said Trefusis, taking his glass and drinking it down. 'Now. I suppose you have come to tell me about the meeting?'

'It was outrageous,' said Adrian. 'Menzies was after your blood.'

'The dear man. How silly of him, it wasn't there, it was in here all the time, running through my body. He should have come and asked for it. Was he terribly cross?'

'He wasn't too pleased by my tactics, anyway.'

Trefusis looked at him in alarm.

'You didn't say anything reckless?'

Adrian explained how the meeting had gone. Trefusis shook his head.

'You are a very silly boy. Clinton-Lacey read out my letter, I suppose?'

'Yes, it rather took the wind out of Menzies' sails. But it wasn't necessary, Donald, no one else wanted you to step down. Why did you write it?'

'The heart has its reasons.'

'You've got to watch Menzies. I bet he'll fight your reappointment next year.'

'Nonsense, Garth and I simply overflow with love for each other.'

'He's your enemy, Donald!'

'He most certainly is not,' said Trefusis. 'Not unless I say so. He may dearly want to be my enemy, he may beg on bended knee for open hostility of the most violent kind, but it takes two to tangle. I choose my own enemies.'

'If you say so . . .'

'I do say so.'

Adrian sipped at the wine.

'Buttery, isn't it? The vanilla comes as a late surprise.'

'Yes, yes it's excellent . . . um . . .'

'You have a question?'

This was rather difficult.

'Donald?'

'Yes?'

'About last night . . .'

Trefusis gazed at Adrian sadly.

'Oh dear, you are not going to ask me an embarrassing question, are you?'

'Well, no,' said Adrian, 'not if it does embarrass you.'

'I meant *you*,' said Trefusis. 'You are not going to embarrass yourself, are you?'

Adrian gestured helplessly.

'It just seems so . . . so . . .'

'So squalid?'

'No!' said Adrian. 'I didn't mean that, I meant it seemed so . . .'

'So *unlike* me?'

'Well . . .'

Trefusis patted him on the shoulder.

'Let's go to the Shoulder,' he said. 'I'm sure Bob will find a nice quiet table for us.'

The Shoulder of Lamb was very crowded. Choral Scholars from St John's, limp with Pimms from an early May Week garden party, were singing an *a capella* version of 'Message in A Bottle' in one corner, a pair of millionaire computer designers poked each other heatedly on the chest in another. Adrian remembered how two years ago one of them had bummed cigarettes off him in the Eagle. Now his company was worth sixty million pounds.

The landlord stepped crisply forward and winked.

'Professor Trefusis, sir, and young Mr Healey!' he said, rolling his head back on his neck like a sunstruck sergeant-major. 'Bit busy this evening, sir.'

'So I see, Bob,' said Donald. 'Is there somewhere . . .?'

'I'll take you upstairs, sir.'

Bob led them through the front bar. One or two people stopped talking when they caught sight of Trefusis. Adrian was amazed at the blithe calm with which he greeted them.

'Evening, Michael! I did so enjoy your Serjeant Musgrave. Quite to the purpose. Such boots, too.'

'Simon! I see that your results were posted. A Third! You must be thrilled.'

Bob took them up the stairs.

'We was all most proud to read of your exploits in the paper, sir.'

'Why, thank you, Bob.'

'Reminds me of my old Adjutant when we was on household duties at the Palace. Fuckingham Palace we used to call it then, of course.'

'I'm sure.'

'Dear oh dear, St James's Park was a sink in those days, sir. Wasn't a bush that didn't have at least one guardsman and customer in it. Course, you'll remember Colonel Bramall, won't you, sir?'

'Thank you Bob, this room will do splendidly. Perhaps Nigel could be induced to bring up a couple of the Gruaud Larose?'

'Certainly, sir. How about a nice veal and ham pie? Spot of chutney?'

'Ludicrously ideal.'

'He'll be with you in a breath, sir.'

When they had disposed of the veal and ham pie, but not the chutney, which Trefusis warned would have a most ruinous effect on the palate, he poured out two glasses of wine.

Adrian gulped at his greedily, determining that drunkenness was the only state in which to cope with his discomfort. If the Wizard of Oz was going to reveal himself as a sad and bewildered old man, Adrian didn't want to be sober when it happened.

To be fair, Donald looked about as sad and bewildered as the Laughing Cavalier as he sipped his claret and dipped his head in appreciation.

'A purist might recommend another year of ageing

for the tannin to smooth out its rougher edges,' he said. 'I think it already supernacular, however.'

'It's fine,' said Adrian, pouring himself another glass.

Trefusis watched him contentedly.

'A good wine is like a woman,' he said. 'Except of course it doesn't have breasts. Or arms and a head. And it can't speak or bear children. In fact, come to think of it, a good wine isn't remotely like a woman at all. A good wine is like a good wine.'

'I'm rather like a good wine too,' said Adrian.

'You improve with age?'

'No,' said Adrian, 'whenever I'm taken out I get drunk.'

'Except that in your case you get laid down after drinking, not before.'

Adrian blushed.

'Oh dear,' said Trefusis, 'that was not a sexual allusion. Merely frivolous paronomasy on the theme of alcoholically induced unconsciousness. I was particularly pleased with "in your case". Are you to be discomfited by the potential for erotic interpretation of every remark I might make?'

'I'm sorry,' said Adrian. 'I've a feeling I'm a bad vintage.'

'That's nonsense, but very graceful. We were talking of drink, I've always believed it right for young people to drink. Not be alcoholic of course, that is a passive state of being, not a positive action. But it is good to drink to excess. That sounds like a toast. To excess.'

'To excess,' said Adrian, bumpering. 'Nothing exceeds like it.'

'Your strenuous tongue is bursting Joy's grape against your palate fine, and that's just as it should be.'

'Keats,' burped Adrian. 'Ode to Melancholy.'

'Keats indeed,' said Trefusis, refilling their glasses. 'Ode *on* Melancholy in fact, but we are beyond pedantry here, I hope.'

'Bollocks,' said Adrian, who hated being corrected, even kindly.

'Now,' said Trefusis, 'we should talk.'

'For the moment,' he said, 'I have nothing to say on the subject of last night. One day, when the world is pinker, I will a tale unfold, whose lightest word would harrow up thy soul, freeze thy young blood, make thy two eyes, like stars, start from their spheres, thy knotted and combined locks to part, and each particular hair to stand on end, like quills upon the fretful porpentine, and generally make you go all of a dither. But for the moment, shtum, you can keep all thoughts on the topic to yourself: zip your lip. However I do have a proposition to put to you which I would like you to consider very seriously. You have no fixed plans for next year, I think?'

'That's right.'

Adrian had made up his mind to wait until after his Finals before deciding what to do with himself. If he got a First he still planned to stay at Cambridge, otherwise he supposed he would look for a teaching job somewhere.

'How would it be, I wonder, if you were to spend the summer travelling with me?'

Adrian goggled. 'Well, I . . .'

'As you know, I shall be doing a little research for

my book. But I have something else to do. There is a problem that needs sorting out, a noisesome problem but not unchallenging. I believe you will be able to offer me material assistance with it. In return I will naturally take care of all expenses, hotels, flights and so forth. It will, I think, be a tour not wholly devoid of interest and amusement. At journey's end we will both deposit ourselves back in England, you to become Prime Minister or whatever lowly ambition you have set your sights on, me to pick up the threads of a ruined and disappointed career. How does that strike you as a plan?'

It struck Adrian as Roscoe Tanner struck a tennis-ball, but how it struck him as a plan he couldn't say. His mind reeled with questions. Had Trefusis run mad? What would his parents say? Should he tell them? Did Donald expect him to share his bed? Is that what it was all about?

'Well?'

'It's . . . it's unbelievable.'

'You don't like it?'

'Like it? Of course I like it, but – '

'Excellent!' Trefusis poured out two more glasses of wine. 'Then you're game?'

If I refused to sleep with him, thought Adrian, would he just kick me out and abandon me in the middle of Europe without a penny? Surely not.

'God yes!' he said. 'I'm game.'

'Wonderful!' said Trefusis. 'Then let us drink to our Grand Tour.'

'Right,' said Adrian draining his glass, 'our Grand Tour.'

Trefusis smiled.

'I'm so very pleased,' he said.

'Me too,' said Adrian, 'but . . .'

'Yes?'

'This problem you mentioned. That I may be able to help you with. What exactly . . .?'

'Ah,' said Donald. 'I'm afraid I am not yet fully at liberty, as they say, to disclose the details.'

'Oh.'

'But I don't suppose there's any harm in my asking you to cast your mind back to last summer. You remember the Salzburg Festival?'

'Vividly.'

'I am sure you haven't forgotten that terrible business in the Getreidegasse?'

'The man in the Mozart museum?'

'That same.'

'I'm hardly likely to forget it. All that blood.'

Bob appeared at the door.

'Sorry to disturb, gents. Thought you might appreciate some of this superior Armagnac brandy.'

'How solicitous!' said Trefusis.

'May I enquire, sir, whether everything went well?'

'Everything went splendidly, Bob. Splendidly.'

'Oh goody-good,' said Bob, taking three small brandy glasses from his jacket pocket. 'I'll join you then, if I may.'

'Please do, Bob, please do. Desperate times call for desperate measures, so pour us each one desperate measure.'

Bob complied.

'We were just talking about Salzburg.'

'Ooh, nasty business that, sir. Poor old Moltaj.

Throat slit from ear to ear, they tell me. But then you both saw it in the flesh, didn't you, sirs?'

Adrian stared at him.

'I know you'll do right by old Moltaj, Mr Healey,' said Bob, clapping him on the shoulder. 'Course you will, sir.'

*A St Matthew's Tie with Liberty silk handkerchief flamboy-
antly thrust into the breast pocket was bent double in
Corridor Four of the third floor of Reddaway House next to
the door marked '3.4.CabCom'. He seemed to be taking an
unconscionable time in doing up the laces of his black Oxford
shoes. It was almost impossible for him not to hear voices
coming from behind the door.*

*'I was just thinking, sir, that what with the Bikini alert
over Iran and everything . . .'*

*'Bugger the bloody Persians, Reeve – I have a Limit Zero
Cabinet Appro on this.'*

'Copeland is very keen that we should co-operate.'

*'Listen to me. The Hairy Mullah is there to stay. You
know it, I know it. Neither Copeland nor anyone at Langley
nor over here has got a choirboy's chance in Winchester of
doing anything about it. Checkmate, d'you see? I don't
suppose you know what checkmate means?'*

'Well . . .'

*'Of course you don't, you went to Oxford. Checkmate
comes from the Arabic "shah mat" – the King is dead. Well
the Shah is mat, all right, he's as mat as a bloody doornail,
and I don't propose to waste time feeding the ambitions of his
whining progeny – they can live it up in Monaco and Gstaad
for the rest of their lives as far as I'm concerned. Clear the*

board, put the chessmen back in their box, we've got bigger capon to baste.'

'Right, sir.'

'Right. So. Report?'

'Well, sir. I'm sorry to have to make report that the ObSquad lost Castor for a day.'

'What?'

'Er . . . if you take a look at this, sir. It's a Cambridge police report.'

The St Matthew's Tie heard the wobble of a cardboard wallet being opened.

'Castor and Odysseus, eh?'

'We rather think so, sir.'

'So are you telling me that Odysseus has got the whole box of tricks now?'

'No, sir . . . if you remember our signal from Locksmith in Budapest, Castor may have given one part of Mendax to Odysseus but the other half will be with Pollux, sewn into the lining of his jacket.'

'And Pollux is still in Troy?'

'Not exactly sir. Vienna Station received another signal from Locksmith this morning, fully prioritised.'

'Fully whatted?'

'Er . . . prioritised, sir.'

'Christ.'

'It seems that Pollux left Troy last night.'

'Headed for the Greek camp?'

'Best guess, sir.'

There was a long pause.

The St Matthew's Tie straightened himself to allow a little blood to flow down from his head.

'If you're right, Reeve, Odysseus will make his way Greekwards in the next few days too.'

'With Telemachus, do you think?'

Another long pause was followed by the sound of a folder being dropped on a desk.

The St Matthew's Tie stooped to do up another shoe-lace.

'Well, nothing to keep me in England now that Botham seems to have lost us the blasted Ashes. I'll fly over the moment anything develops.'

'Cricket not going too well then, sir?'

'The man's a bloody disgrace. He couldn't captain a paraplegic netball team.'

'Will you be around for initialling appropriation orders later in the afternoon, sir?'

'Well, young Reeve, after a brief luncherising and half an hour's memorandorising Cabinet, I'll be at Lord's.'

'Right, sir.'

'So if you want me to signatorise anything, send Simon Hesketh-Harvey round, he's a member. Now I must go and lavatorise. And while I'm away for God's sake try and learn to speak English.'

The St Matthew's Tie hurried along the corridor to his office. He heard the door of 3.4.CabCom opening. A voice hailed him.

'Ho there, young Hesketh-H!'

The St Matthew's Tie turned. A Bennett, Tovey and Steele Suit was standing in the corridor.

'Morning, sir.'

'Snap.'

They looked at each other's neck-ties with a smile.

'You may have to change that for the good old orange and yellow this pip emma,' said the Bennett, Tovey and Steele.

'Sir?'

'If you're a good boy, Reeve will send you over to me at Lord's this afternoon to watch the final death throes.'

'*Good-o,*' said the St Matthew's Tie. '*I shall enjoy that, sir.*'

'*Right. Oh, by the way –* '

'*Sir?*'

'*Prioritise. Ever come across that one?*'

'*Ugh!*' said the St Matthew's Tie. '*Langley?*'

'*No, that arse Reeve, of course. Last week it was "having a meet-up with", God knows what new linguistic macédoine he's going to serve up next.*'

'*One shudders to think, sir.*'

'*All right then, Simon, off you pop.*'

Eight

I

'I have taken much care in packing,' said Trefusis as he pushed shut the boot of the Wolseley. 'A tin of barley-sugar for you, Castrol GTX for the car, figgy oatcakes for me.'

'Figgy oatcakes?'

'Oatcakes are very healthy. Hotels, restaurants, cafés, they all take their toll. Salzburg is not kind to the figure. At my age travel broadens the behind. A steatopygous Trefusis is an unhappy Trefusis. The buns and tortes of Austria are whoreson binders of your whoreson stool. But a figgy oatcake laughs at constipation and favours rectal carcinoma with a haughty stare. In the grammar of health, while cream may hasten the full stop, porridge will ease the colon.'

'Oh, ah,' said Adrian. 'And curry creates the dash, I suppose.'

'Oh, I like that. Very good. "Curry creates the dash." Yes, indeed. Most . . . most . . . er, what is the word?'

'Amusing?'

'No . . . it'll come to me.'

The interior of the car smelt of Merton Park

thrillers, Bakelite headsets and the Clothes Ration. It only needed the profile of Edgar Wallace or the voice of Edgar Lustgarten to sweep Adrian and Trefusis, with bells ringing, into a raincoat and Horlicks Britain of glistening pavements, trilbied police inspectors and poplin shirts. So familiar was the odour, so complete the vision it evoked as they swung with a whine of gears out of the college gates and onto the Trumpington Road, that Adrian could almost believe in reincarnation. He had never smelt that precise smell before, yet it was as known to him as the smell of his own socks.

Trefusis would not be drawn on the purpose of their mission to Salzburg.

'You knew that man who was killed then?'

'Knew him? No.'

'But Bob said . . .'

'I do hope the Bendix doesn't give out. The Wolseley 15/50 is a marvellous saloon, but the Bendix is most terribly susceptible to trouble.'

'Well if you didn't know him, how come you know his name?'

'I suppose one could call such an affliction bendicitis.'

'When I first arrived in Cambridge there was a rumour that you recruited for MI5. Either that or for the KGB.'

'My dear fellow, there is not a don over the age of sixty who is not said to be the fourth, fifth, sixth or seventh man in some improbable circle of spies, double agents and ruthless traitors. You should pay no attention.'

'You worked at Bletchley during the war though, didn't you? On the Enigma code.'

'So did Beryl Ayliffe the college librarian. Are we to believe that she is an MI5 . . . what's the word . . . operative?'

Adrian pictured the chain-smoking chatelaine of the St Matthew's library.

'Well no, of course not,' he conceded. 'But . . .'

'Ha, ha. More fool you, because she *is*!'

'What?'

'Or is she?' mused Trefusis. 'So damned difficult to tell in this damned deadly game we play. Anyway, what does it matter? Isn't it all the bloody same? Left, right? Right, wrong? The old distinctions don't matter a damned damn any more, damn it.'

'All right, all right,' said Adrian, stung by the mockery. 'I grant you it all sounds a bit stupid. But we did see a man killed last year. You can't get away from that.'

'Assuredly.'

'And that's why we're going back to Salzburg?'

'I don't think we'll eat until we get to France. There's a surprisingly good restaurant at the railway station at Arras. See if you can find it on your map, there's a dear.'

II

Adrian had never eaten *foie gras* before.

'I thought it was just pâté,' he said.

'Oh no, the pâté is quite inferior. These are the livers themselves. Flash fried. I think you'll be pleased.'

Adrian was.

'It just literally melts in the mouth!' he exclaimed. 'Unbelievable!'

'You'll find the Corton Charlemagne an excellent accompaniment. Perfectly served at last. I have an ex-student who is likely to become the next editor of the *Spectator*. On his succession I shall offer for publication a little article on the iniquity of the British habit of over-chilling white Burgundies. If one's young friends are going to disgrace themselves by writing for such low periodicals the least they can do is assuage their guilt by providing a platform for advanced ideas. I make it a point to teach all my pupils to believe in properly served wine.'

Adrian listened with half an ear to the Professor's flow of conversation. A young man and woman had entered the restaurant a moment earlier and now floundered in the middle of the room, waiting for someone to show them to a table. Adrian's eyes narrowed suddenly. He leant across to Trefusis.

'Don't look now, but that couple behind you who've just come in . . .' He lowered his voice to a whisper. '*They were on the boat with us!* I swear it's the same two. They were behind us in the car queue. In a green BMW.'

Trefusis tore a bread roll in half and looked speculatively into a large mirror over Adrian's shoulder.

'Really? Bless my soul, it's a small world and no mistake.'

'You don't think . . . you don't think they might be . . . *following* us?'

Trefusis raised his eyebrows. 'It's possible of course. It's always possible.'

Adrian grabbed Trefusis's arm across the table. 'I could go and have a pee and put their car out of action. What do you say?'

'You think micturating over their car would put it out of action?'

'No, I mean *pretend* to have a pee but actually wrench out the rotor arm or take the distributor cap or whatever it is you do.'

Trefusis gazed at him with only the trace of a smile on his face. 'Do you know how they make *foie gras*?'

'Donald, I'm serious. I'm sure they're following us.'

With a sigh, Trefusis put down the fragment of *brioche* he had been buttering.

'I'm serious too. It's time, young Healey, that you knew what this trip was all about.'

'Really?'

'Really. Now, I'll ask you again. Do you know how to make *foie gras*?'

Adrian stared at Trefusis. 'Er . . . no. No I don't.'

'Very well then, I'll tell you. You rear a goose from a puppy or calf or whatver a goose is when young.'

'Chick? Gosling?'

'Quite possibly. You take a young Strasbourg goose-cub, chick or gosling and you feed it rich grain in a mashy pulp.'

'Fatten it up, you mean?'

'That's right, but the mashy pulp is placed, you see, in a bag.'

'A bag?'

'That's right. A bag or sack. The bag or sack has some species of nozzle or protuberance at the narrow end, which is forced down the goose's gullet or throat. The bag or sack is then squeezed or compressed and the meal or fodder thus introduced or thrust into the creature or animal's crop or stomach.'

'Why not just let it feed normally?'

'Because this procedure is undertaken many times a day for the whole of the poor animal's life. It is force fed on a massive scale. Force fed until it is so gorged and gross that it can no longer move. Its liver becomes pulpy and distended. Ideal, in fact, for flash frying and presenting with a glass of spacious Montrachet or fat, buttery Corton Charlemagne.'

'That's horrific!' said Adrian. 'Why didn't you tell me that before?'

'I wanted you to taste it. It is one of the highest pleasures known to man. Wasn't it Sydney Smith who had a friend whose idea of heaven was eating it to the sound of trumpets? Like most of our highest pleasures, however, it is rooted in suffering; founded in an unnatural, almost perverted, process.'

Adrian's mind raced forward, trying to think of the relevance of this to their situation. He ran a storyline through his head. A European cartel of *foie gras* manufacturers, determined to prevent the Common Market from outlawing their product. Prepared to kill in order to protect what they saw as their God-given right to torture geese for the tables of the rich. Surely not? That sort of thing simply did not happen. And even if it did, it was scarcely the sort of affair in which Trefusis would interest himself.

'So what exactly . . .?'

'This forcing of a goose is an image I want you to hold in your head while I tell you of something else . . . ah . . . *le poisson est arrivé*.'

Trefusis beamed as two large dishes, each covered

with an immense silver *cloche*, were set before them. The waiter looked from Adrian to Trefusis with an expectant smile and – now sure of their attention – he swept each *cloche* clear with a flourish, releasing clouds of delicately fishy steam.

'*Voilà! Bon appetit, messieurs!*'

'Enlightening that what we call John Dory the French call Saint Pierre, the Italians San Pietro and the Spanish San Pedro.'

'Who was John Dory, do you think?'

'Oh, I imagine the Dory is from *doré*, gilded or golden. Of course we do sometimes call it St Peter's fish, I believe. *Merci bien.*'

'*M'sieur!*' The waiter bowed smartly and strutted away.

'Howsomever that may be,' said Trefusis. 'Some time ago I was contacted – I believe that's the right word? – by an old friend of mine, Tom Daly. Tom used to be the garden steward at St Matthew's and a fine gardener he was too, as green-fingered as . . . as . . .'

'As a Martian with septicaemia?'

'If that pleases you. It fell out that in nineteen-sixty-two Tom pleached, plashed and entwined himself with one Eileen Bishop. In due course he pollinated her and there sprung up a fine young son. In a simple but affecting ceremony in Little St Mary's later that year I agreed to renounce the world, the flesh and the devil in order to cleanse my soul in readiness for the task of standing sponsor to their freshly budded sprig, whom they had decided to baptise Christopher Donald Henry.'

'This gardener married and had a son and you are his godfather?'

'I believe that's what I said,' said Trefusis. 'Then in nineteen-seventy-six, to the distress of us all, Tom left the college to take up the post of chief borough gardener in West Norfolk. When next you admire the gay rampage of tulips at a roundabout in King's Lynn or the giddy riot of wayside lobelia in central Hunstanton, you'll know whom to thank. Be that as it may. Beyond the usual silver porringer at birth and the bi-annual five-pound note, my contribution to Christopher's moral welfare has been scant. I have to confess that Christopher, my godson, is a child of whom I stand rather in awe.'

Adrian tried to picture the Professor standing rather in awe of anything.

'The boy is remarkably gifted you see,' said Trefusis, gently laying a sliver of fish-bone on the side of his plate. 'His mathematical ability as an infant was simply astounding. From an early age he exhibited almost supernatural powers. He could multiply and divide long numbers in seconds, calculate square and cube roots in his head, do all the circus tricks. But he had a fine mind as well as an arithmetically prodigious brain and it was assumed that he would make his way to Trinity and contribute something to the field of pure mathematics before he was thirty or whatever age it is that marks the Anno Domini of mathematicians.'

'I believe they're pretty much over the hill by twenty-six these days,' said Adrian. 'How old is he now?'

'Eighteen or so. He is lucky, you might think, to

have a father proud of his gifts and who, moreover, would have been happy for him to employ them academically, in the service of scholarship, for the sake of the pure art of pure mathematics. Many fathers of comparably modest incomes would have looked on a clever son as a route to riches. My son the financier, my son the barrister, my son the accountant. Tom stood quite ready and without rancour to explain the child away as my son the loopy mathematician with the scurfy hair and bottle-end spectacles.'

'And . . .?'

'Three years ago Christopher was awarded a scholarship to a public school in Suffolk: the money came from an organisation Tom Daly had never heard of. It now seems that this organisation is proposing to put Christopher through Cambridge. He will read not Pure Maths there, but Engineering. What is worrying Tom is that the organisation is only interested in Christopher because of his potential as a brain. After university they want him to go into industry.'

'What is the organisation?'

'I'll come to that. Tom believes that Christopher shouldn't be committed so early. He is frightened that this organisation is, in effect, buying his son. So he came to me and asked if I knew anything of them. I was able to confirm that I did. I have known of them for some time.'

'Who are they?'

'Let's settle up. I will tell you the rest on the road. What would be an adequate lagniappe, do you think?'

Adrian looked out of the rear window.

'They *are* following us!'

'How frustrating for them. All that power under

their bonnet and they are forced to hold their pace down to our niggardly fifty-five miles per hour.'

As Trefusis spoke, the BMW moved out to the left and swept past them. Adrian caught a glimpse of the driver's face, alert and tense behind the wheel.

'The same man all right. British number plates. Right hand drive. GB sticker on the back. Why's he passed us, though?'

'Perhaps a relay,' said Trefusis, 'someone else will take up the pursuit. It is scarcely a problem to identify a car of this age and distinction.'

Adrian looked at him sharply. 'You admit that we're being followed then?'

'It was always a possibility.'

Adrian popped a lump of barley-sugar into his mouth. 'You were telling me about this organisation. That paid for your godson to go through school.'

'I have become increasingly aware in recent years,' said Trefusis, 'of what can only be called a conspiracy on a massive scale. I have watched the most talented, the most able and most promising students that come through St Matthew's and other colleges in Cambridge and other universities in England . . . I have watched them being bought up.'

'Bought up?'

'Purchased. Procured. Acquired. Gotten. Let us say an undergraduate arrives with phenomenal ability in, for example, English. A natural candidate for a doctorate, a teaching post, a life of scholarship or, failing those, a creative existence as poet, novelist or dramatist. He arrives full of just such ambitions and sparkling ideals but then . . . they get to him.'

'They?'

'Two years after graduation this first class mind is being paid eighty thousand pounds a year to devise advertising slogans for a proprietary brand of peanut butter or is writing snobbish articles in glossy magazines about exiled European monarchs and their children or some such catastrophic drivel. I see it year after year. Perhaps a chemist will arrive in the college. Great hopes are held out for his future. Nobel Prizes and who knows what else besides? He himself is full of the highest aspirations. Yet even before his final exams he has been locked and contracted into a job for life concocting synthetic pine-fresh biological soap powder fragrances for a detergent company. Adrian, someone is getting at our best minds! Someone is preventing them from achieving their full potential. This organisation I told you of is denying them a chance to grow and flourish. A university education should be broad and general. But these students are being *trained*, not *educated*. They are being stuffed like Strasbourg geese. Pappy mush is forced into them, just so one part of their brains can be fattened. Their whole minds are being ignored for the sake of that part of them which is marketable. Thus they have persuaded my godson Christopher to read Engineering instead of Mathematics.'

'How long has this been going on?'

'I cannot tell how long. Years, I suspect. I first began to take real notice fifteen or twenty years ago. But it is getting worse. More and more brilliant students are being diverted from work that could be of real benefit to mankind and their country. They are being battery farmed. Young Christopher Daly is just one of thousands.'

'My God!' said Adrian. 'You know who's behind this? We've got to stop them!'

'It's a conspiracy of industrialists, of certain highly placed economists and of members of governments of all political colours,' said Trefusis.

'But how can we prevent it? And what has it got to do with Salzburg?'

Trefusis looked across at Adrian, his eyes filled with grave concern. Suddenly he burst out laughing. Shaking his head from side to side, he snorted and struck the steering wheel. 'Oh Adrian, I *am* cruel! I'm wicked, naughty, dreadful and digraceful. Please forgive me.'

'What's so funny?'

'You silly, *silly* boy. What I have just described is the way the world works! It's not a conspiracy. It is called Modern Western Civilisation.'

'W-what do you mean?'

'Of *course* the best brains are lured into industry, advertising, journalism and the rest of it. Of *course* universities are adapting to the demands of commerce. It's regrettable and there's little we can do about it. But I think only a Marxist would call it an international conspiracy.'

'But you said an organisation . . . you told me that a specific organisation had offered that boy Christopher a scholarship.' .

'The state, Adrian. A state scholarship. And the state will hope in return that he goes into something productive once he has obtained his degree. He will be incented by money, recruitment drives and the general thrust and tenor of the times. That is all.'

Adrian fumed in silence for a while.

'And this has nothing to do with what we're going to Salzburg for?'

'Nothing at all.'

'You are impossible, you know that?'

'Improbable perhaps, but not impossible. Besides, whilst what I described may not be a conscious intrigue, it is happening nonetheless and is vexatious in the extreme.'

'So you're still not going to tell me what we are in actual fact doing here?'

'All in actual good time,' said Trefusis. 'Now the Cardinal is getting thirsty; if memory has not fully quit her throne I believe there should be an amenable garage and *routier* in about eighty kilometres or so. In the meantime, we can tell each other the story of our lives.'

'All right,' said Adrian. 'You first. Tell me about Bletchley.'

'Little *to* tell. It was set up as a wartime decrypting station and filled up with mainly Cambridge personnel.'

'Why Cambridge?'

'The closest university town. At first they recruited philologists and linguists like myself.'

'This was when?'

'Nineteen-forty. Round about the time of the Battle of Britain.'

'And you were how old?'

'Tush and bibble! Is this then to be an interrogation? I was twenty-two.'

'Right. Just wondered.'

'Young and fizzing at the brim with ideals and theories about language. Now, who else was there with me? Dozens of girls who filed and clerked away with great brilliance and flair. The chess master Harry Golombek was on the team of course, and H.F.O. Alexander, also a magnificently dashing player. It was all rather cosy and fun at first, wrestling with enemy cyphers that had been intercepted all over Europe and Africa. It soon became clear, however, that the Enigma encryption device that German Naval Intelligence was using would need mathematicians to crack it. Acquaintanceship with the decryption techniques of the last war, the ability to do the *Times* crossword while shaving and a mastery of Russian verbs of motion were not enough any more. So they brought in Alan Turing, of whom you may have heard.'

Adrian had not.

'No? What a pity. Brilliant man. Quite brilliant, but very sad. Killed himself later. Many credit him with the invention of the digital computer. I can't quite remember how it came about. There was some pure mathematical problem which had faced the world of numbers for fifty years, I think, and he had solved it as a young man by positing the existence of a number-crunching machine. It was never his intention to build such a thing, it was merely hypothesised as a model to help solve an abstract difficulty. But unlike many mathematicians he relished the physical application of numbers. His hut in Bletchley was soon filled with rows and rows of valves. You remember valves? Tubes they call them in America. Little vacuum bulbs that glowed orange.'

'I remember,' said Adrian. 'It used to take televisions ages to warm up.'

'That's right. Well Alan had thousands of them all

linked together in some impossibly complicated fashion. Got them from the Post Office.'

'The Post Office?'

'Yes, the GPO had been experimenting in electronics before the war and they seemed to be the only people who really knew about it. The clever thing about the Enigma machine was that, although it was purely mechanical, it changed daily and the number of permutations was so grotesquely huge that the old techniques of decryption wouldn't work. Alan cracked it quite brilliantly. But that was only the first stage of course. He still needed to know the code before he could read the cypher.'

'What's the difference between a cypher and a code then?'

'Well, that is readily explained,' said Trefusis. 'Imagine a system in which a number refers to a letter of the alphabet. A equals one, B equals two, C equals three and so on, thus "Adrian" would be "One – four – eighteen – nine – one – fourteen", you understand?'

'Right . . .'

'That is a very basic form of cypher and a message written in it could be cracked by anyone of the meanest intelligence in seconds. But suppose that between us we two had personally prearranged that a word . . . "Biscuits", for example, was going to mean "nineteen-hundred hours", and that another word, for instance "Desmond", should signify "The Café Florian in St Mark's Square, Venice".'

'Got you . . .'

'I would then only have to signal to you: "Please send me some biscuits today, love Desmond," and you would know that I wanted to meet you at seven o'clock that evening at Florian's. That is a code and would be impossible to crack unless someone overheard us arranging it, or one of us was foolish enough to commit it to paper.'

'I see,' said Adrian. 'Then why not only use codes if they're uncrackable?'

'Unfortunately in wartime one needs to signal an enormous amount of unpredictable and detailed information. The receiver couldn't be expected to memorise thousands of different code words, and to write them down would be insecure. So it became practice to mix the two systems. A complicated cypher would be used which could only be cracked if one knew a key word, a code, which would change daily. That is how Enigma operated. So even when Enigma had been solved we needed Intelligence to help provide us with clues so that we could crack the daily code. That is where I came in, and of course, your old friend Humphrey Biffen.'

'Humphrey Biffen?'

'I believe he taught you French once.'

'Good Lord! Did Biffo work at Bletchley too?'

'Oh indeed. And Helen Sorrel-Cameron whom he later married. Guessing the daily key words was very much our speciality.'

'But however did you manage?'

'Well now, the Germans were so very confident that Enigma was uncrackable that they became remarkably sloppy about the assignation of the daily key. Intelligence furnished us with the names of operators and cypher clerks in German Naval Intelligence and Humphrey and I would make guesses. We used to keep immensely detailed files on each clerk:

225

their likes, their loves, their families, mistresses, lovers, pets, tastes in music and food . . . oh, everything. Each day we would try out different ideas, the name of that particular operator's dog, their favourite kind of pastry, their maiden surname, that sort of thing. We usually got there in the end.'

'But the Germans must have discovered that you had cracked it, surely?'

'Well that's the peculiarity of this kind of work. Our job was simply to furnish Military Intelligence with everything we decrypted. They would then, as a rule, fail to act upon it.'

'Why?'

'Because they could on no account let the enemy know that they were reading their most secret transmissions. It is generally believed, for instance, that Churchill had prior warning of the impending Luftwaffe raid on Coventry but neglected to tell the army and air force for fear of extra defences in the area revealing to the Germans that it had been known about in advance. This is not strictly true, but it demonstrates the principle. Some believe, of course, that Admiral Kanaris, the head of German Naval Intelligence, was perfectly well aware that we were reading Enigma all along, but that he was so pro-British and distressed at the behaviour of the Führer that he simply let it happen.'

'Fascinating,' said Adrian. 'God I wish I could have been around at a time like that.'

'Oh, I don't know,' said Trefusis. 'I think you might have been bored.'

Trefusis peered at the landscape and the road-signs. 'Still another fifty or so kilometres before our service station. Now it's your turn. What has happened in your young life? Plenty, I make no doubt.'

'Oh not so much,' said Adrian. 'I was arrested for the possession of cocaine once.'

'Really?'

'Yes. I had been living with an actor after a few months of being a rent-boy.'

'A rent-boy?' said Trefusis. 'How enterprising! And possession of cocaine? Were you imprisoned?'

'Well first I should tell you how I was expelled from school. That should take us twenty kilometres. Then I'll tell you what happened after that.'

Nine

I

He had stared at the first paper for the whole three hours, unable to write a thing. One of the girls came up to him afterwards.

'I saw you, Adrian Healey! Couldn't you answer any of the questions, then?'

Two years in this stupid college that called its pupils 'students' and its lessons 'lectures'. How had he stood it? He should never have given way.

'I think it's the right thing, darling. It'll give you so much more independence than a school. Father agrees. You can get the bus in to Gloucester and be home with me every night. And then after you've got the "A" levels, you can sit the Cambridge entrance. Everyone says it's an awfully good college. The Fawcetts' boy – David is it? – he went there after he was . . . after he left Harrow, so I'm sure it's all right.'

'What you mean is, it's the only place for miles around that'll take boys that've been expelled.'

'Darling, that's not . . .'

'Anyway, I don't want "A" levels and I don't want to go to Cambridge.'

'Ade, of course you do! Just think how you'd regret it if you missed the opportunity.'

He had missed the opportunity, and the lectures. Instead there had been the ABC cinema and the Star Café, where he played pin-ball and three-card brag.

Discuss Lawrence's use of external landscape in relation to the internal drama of Sons and Lovers.

Only connect . . . How are the Schlegels and Wilcoxes connected in Howards End?

Compare and contrast the different uses of landscape and nature in the poetry of Seamus Heaney and Ted Hughes.

Suddenly his plausible wit was of no use to him. Suddenly the world was dull and sticky and unkind. His future was behind him and he had nothing to look forward to but the past.

Goodbye Gloucester, goodbye Stroud. He was at least following a literary example. When Laurie Lee had walked out on his midsummer's morning he had had a guitar and the blessings of his family to accompany him. Adrian had a paperback copy of Anouilh's *Antigone*, which he had intended to read at lunchtime as some kind of feeble preparation for the afternoon's French literature paper, and fifteen pounds from his mother's handbag.

In the end he got a lift from a lorry driver who was going all the way to Stanmore.

'I can drop you somewhere on the North Circular, if you like.'

'Thanks.'

North Circular . . . North Circular. It was some kind of road, wasn't it?

'Er . . . is the North Circular anywhere near Highgate?'

'You can catch a bus from Golder's Green pretty quick.'

Bollocks lived in Highgate. He might be able to cadge a couple of nights there while he sorted himself out.

'I'm Jack, by the way,' said the driver.

'Er . . . Bullock, Hugo Bullock.'

'Bullock? That's a funny one.'

'I once met a girl called Jane Heffer. We should've got married.'

'Yeah? What went wrong?'

'No, I mean her being called Heffer. It's the female of bullock.'

'Oh right, right.'

They drove on in silence. Adrian offered Jack a cigarette.

'No thanks, mate. Trying to give 'em up. Don't do you any good in this game.'

'No, I suppose not.'

'So, what, you running away then, are you?'

'Running away?'

'Yeah. How old are you?'

'Eighteen.'

'Get away!'

'Well, I will be.'

Bullock's mother stood in the doorway and eyed him suspiciously. He supposed his hair was rather long.

'I'm a friend of William's. From school.'

'He's in Australia. It's his year off before going to Oxford.'

'Oh yes, of course. I just . . . wondered, you know. Not to worry. Happened to be passing.'

'I'll tell him you called if he rings. Are you staying in London?'

'Yes, in Piccadilly.'

'Piccadilly?'

What was wrong with that?

'Well, you know, more just *off*.'

The pin-ball machines in Piccadilly had more sensitive tilt mechanisms than those he was used to in Gloucester, and he wasn't getting many replays. At this rate he wouldn't be able to afford to carry on for more than an hour.

A man in a blue suit came down behind him and put down a fifty-pence piece.

'It's yours,' said Adrian, smacking the flipper buttons in frustration as his last silver ball rolled out of play. 'That was my last. I just can't seem to get the hang of the bloody thing.'

'No, no, no,' said the man in the blue suit, 'the fifty is for you. Have another go.'

Adrian turned in surprise.

'Well, that's awfully kind . . . are you sure?'

'Yes indeed.'

The fifty was soon used up.

'Come and have a drink,' said the man. 'I know a bar just round the corner.'

They left the chimes and buzzes and intense, haunted concentration of the amusement arcade and walked up Old Compton Street and into a small pub in a side street. The barman didn't question Adrian's age, which was an unusual relief.

'Haven't seen you before. Always good to meet a new face. Yes, indeed.'

'I'd've thought everyone was a stranger in London,'

said Adrian. 'I mean, it's mostly tourists round here, isn't it?'

'Oh, I don't know,' said the man. 'You'd be surprised. It's a village really.'

'Do you often play pin-ball?'

'Me? No. Got an office up the Charing Cross Road. I just like to look in most evenings on my way home. Yes, indeed.'

'Right.'

'I thought you were a girl at first with your hair and . . . everything.'

Adrian blushed. He didn't like to be reminded how long beard growth was in coming.

'No offence. I like it . . . it suits you.'

'Thanks.'

'Yes indeed. Yes indeedy-do.'

Adrian made a note, somewhere in the back of his mind, to get a haircut the next day.

'You sound a bit public school to me. Am I right?'

Adrian nodded.

'Harrow,' he said. He thought it a safe bet.

'Harrow, you say? Harrow! Dear me, I think you're going to be a bit of a hit. Yes indeed. You got anywhere to stay?'

'Well . . .'

'You can put up with me, if you like. It's just a small flat in Brewer Street, but it's local.'

'It's terribly kind of you . . . I'm looking for a job, you see.'

That's how simple it had been. One day a lazy student, the next a busy prostitute.

'Thing is, Hugo,' said Don, 'soon as I clapped eyes on you I thought, "That's not rent, that's the real

232

thing." I've been around the Dilly for fifteen years and I can spot 'em, indeedy-dumplings, I can. Now I'm sorry to say that I won't fancy you next week. Unplucked chicken is my speciality and I'll be bored stiff with you Thursday. Bored limp, more like. Hur, hur! But you cut your hair a bit – not too much – keep your Harrovian accent fit and you'll be clearing two ton a week. Yes indeed.'

'Two ton?'

'Two hundred, sunshine.'

'But what do I have to do?'

And Don told him. There were two principal amusement arcades, there was the Meat Rack, which was an iron pedestrian grille outside Playland, the more active of the arcades, and there was the Piccadilly Underground itself.

'But you want to watch that. Crawling with the law.'

Don wasn't a pimp. He worked at a perfectly respectable music publishing house in Denmark Street. Adrian paid him thirty pounds a week which covered his own accommodation and the use of the flat for tricks during the day. At night it was up to the tricks to provide the venue.

'Just don't start chewing gum, shooting horse or looking streetwise, that's all.'

At first the days passed slowly, each transaction nerve-racking and remarkable, but soon the quiet pulse of routine quickened the days. The young can become accustomed to the greatest drudgeries, like potato-harvesting or schoolwork, with surprising speed. Prostitution had at least the advantage of variety.

Adrian got on pretty well with the other rent-boys. Most of them were tougher and beefier than he was, skinheads with tattoos, braces and mean looks. They didn't regard him as direct competition and sometimes they even recommended him.

'Do you know of anyone less . . . chunky?' a punter might ask.

'You want to try Hugo, he'll be doing the *Times* crossword down the Bar Italia this time of the morning. Flared jumbo cords and a blazer. Can't miss him.'

Adrian was intrigued by the fact that the most prosperous, pin-striped clients went for the rough trade, while the wilder, less respectable tricks wanted more lightly muscled boys like him. Opposite poles attracted. The Jacobs wanted hairy men and the Esaus wanted smooth. It meant that he more than most had to learn to spot the sadists and nutters who were on the lookout for a sex-slave. One of the last things Adrian wanted was to be chained up, flogged and urinated over.

He liked to think that his rates were competitive but not insulting. A blow-job was ten quid to give, fifteen to receive. After a week he made up his mind to forbid anything up the anus. Some could take it and some couldn't: Adrian decided that he belonged to the latter category. A couple of boys tried to convince him, as he hobbled down Coventry Street after a particularly heavy night complaining that his back passage felt like a windsock, that he would soon get used to it, but he resolved – financially disadvantageous as it might be – that his rear section was to be firmly labelled a no-poking compartment. This was a proviso he had to make clear to clients at the opening of negotiations: between the thighs was fine – the intercrural method was, after all, endorsed by no less an authoritative source than the Ancient Greeks themselves – but he was buggered if he was going to be buggered. As long as he could get it up he didn't mind sodomising a client, but his own bronze eye was closed to all comers.

When business was slack he and some of the others would mix with the journalists and professional Soho drinkers in the French House in Dean Street. Gaston, the implausibly named landlord, had no objection to their presence so long as they didn't tout for custom there. The Golden Lion next door was for that. The regulars however – embittered painters and poets for whom the seventies were an unwelcome vacuum to be filled with vodka and argument – could be savagely impolite.

'We don't need your kind of filth in here,' a radio producer, whose watery seed Adrian had spat out only the previous night, shouted one afternoon. 'Get the fuck out!'

'How ill-bred!' Adrian had exclaimed as Gaston ejected the radio producer instead.

Like Adrian, most of the boys were self-employed; one or two had ponces, but in general pimping was a feature of the more highly structured sister profession of female prostitution. The boys were free to come and go as they pleased, no one was going to tell them where they could set up their stall, no one was going to take a cut of their hard-earned cash. The cash did come in at a pleasing rate but Adrian found he had little to spend it on. Drink didn't really appeal to him much and he was too afraid of drugs to be tempted to take so much as a single pill or a single puff of anything illegal. Every day he would walk to the post office behind St Martin's-in-the-Field and deposit his earnings into an account he had opened under the name of Hugo Bullock. It was all building up rather nicely.

Chickens worried him, though. These were the children of eleven, twelve and thirteen. Some were even younger. Adrian was no Mother Teresa and far too much of a coward to beg them to go home. They were tougher than he was and would have told him to get lost anyway. Besides, they had left their homes because life there was worse, in their eyes at least, than life on the streets. If there was one thing those children knew, it was where and when they were unhappy: there was no cloud of morality obscuring the clarity of their states of mind. They weren't popular with the majority of rent-boys, however, because they attracted television documentaries, clean-up campaigns and police attention, all of which interfered with and militated against the free flow of trade. Their customers, known not unnaturally as chickenhawks, were more nervous and cautious than Adrian's brand of client, so the chickens would have to do much more of the running than he could ever have dared to do. They would spot when they were being eyed up and step boldly forward.

'Lend us ten p for the machine, mister.'

'Oh, yes. Right. There you are.'

'Second thoughts, Dad, let's go away from here.'

It was unsettling to think of them being the same age as Cartwright. Cartwright would be sixteen going on seventeen now of course, but the Cartwright he would always know was thirteen going on fourteen.

The chickens leant up against the Meat Rack pushing their tightly denimed bums against the rails when, if only the stork had dropped them down a different chimney, they could have been clothed in white flannels, driving the ball past extra cover for four runs or wrestling with ablative absolutes in panelled class-rooms. If there was an accurate means of measuring happiness, with electrodes or chemicals, Adrian wondered if the schoolboy would prove to be happier than the rent-boy. Would he feel less exploited, less shat upon? Adrian himself felt freer than he ever had, but he had never been sure that he was representative.

After three weeks he decided to take advantage of his flexible hours and spend five days at Lord's watching Thompson and Lillee tear the heart out of the English batting in the second Test. He arrived at the Grace Gate early and walked round to the back to see if he could get a glimpse of the players warming up in the nets.

As he made his way past the Stewards' Offices and the members' stands he thought he caught a glimpse of a familiar figure striding towards him. He turned and started to walk in the opposite direction.

'Adrian! My God, Adrian!'

He quickened his step, but found himself blocked by the incoming tide of spectators.

'Adrian!'

'Oh, hello, Uncle David.' Adrian smiled weakly up into the thunderous face of his mother's brother.

'Where the hell have you been this last month?'

'Oh, you know . . .'

'Have you been in touch with your mother and father yet?'

'Well . . . I have been meaning to write.'

Uncle David grabbed him by the arm.

'You come along with me, young man. *Sick* with worry your mother's been. *Sick*. How you could have *dared* . . .'

Adrian had the lowering experience of being publicly dragged into the MCC offices like an errant schoolboy, which he supposed was by and large what he was.

'Morning, David, caught a yobbo have you?' someone called as he was pulled up the steps.

'I certainly have!'

They bumped into a tall blond man in a blazer coming the other way who smiled at them.

'Morning, Sir David,' he said.

'Morning, Tony, best of luck.'

'Thanks,' said the tall man and walked on. Adrian stopped dead as it suddenly dawned on him who it had been.

'That was Tony Greig!'

'Well who did you expect to see here, you idiot? Ilie Nastase? This way.'

They had reached a small office whose walls were covered with prints of heroes from the Golden Age of cricket. Uncle David closed the door and pushed Adrian into a chair.

'Now then. Tell me where you are living.'

'Muswell Hill.'

'Address?'

'Fourteen Endicott Gardens.'

'Whose house is that?'

'It's a bed and breakfast place.'

'Do you have a job?'

Adrian nodded.

'Where?'

'I'm working in the West End.' The 'in' was redundant, but Uncle David was unlikely to be impressed by the truth.

'Doing what?'

'It's a theatrical agency in Denmark Street. I make the coffee, that kind of thing.'

'Right. There's a pen, there's paper. I want you to write down the address in Muswell Hill and the address in Denmark Street. Then you are to write a letter to your parents. Have you any idea what you've put them through? They went to the police, for God's sake! What the hell was it all about, Adrian?'

Here he was in another study, in another chair, facing another angry man and being asked another set of impossible questions. 'Why do you do this sort of thing?' 'Why can't you concentrate?' 'Why can't you behave like everyone else?' 'What's the matter with you?'

Adrian knew that if he answered 'I don't know' in a sulky voice, Uncle David would, like dozens before him, snort and bang the table and shout back, 'What do you *mean*, you don't know? You must know. Answer me!'

Adrian stared at the carpet.

'Well?' asked Uncle David.

'I don't know,' Adrian said sulkily.

'What do you *mean*, you don't know? You must know. Answer me!'

'I was unhappy.'

'Unhappy? Well why couldn't you have *told* someone? Can you imagine how your mother felt when you didn't come home? When no one knew where you were? That's *unhappy* for you. Can you imagine it? No, of course you can't.'

Beyond a pewter mug at his Christening, a Bible at his Confirmation, a copy of Wisden every birthday and regular bluff shoulder-clapping and by-Christ-you've-grown-ing, Uncle David hadn't taken his sponsorial duties to Adrian with any spectacular seriousness, and it was unsettling to see him now glaring and breathing heavily down his nostrils as if he had been personally affronted by his godson's flight. Adrian didn't think he'd earned the right to look that angry.

'I just felt I had to get away.'

'I dare say. But to be so underhand, so . . . sly. To sneak away without saying a word. That was the act of a coward and a rotter. You'll write that letter.'

Uncle David left the room, locking the door behind him. Adrian sighed and turned to the desk. He noticed a silver letter-opener on the desk in the shape of a cricket bat. He held it to the light and saw the engraved signature of Donald Bradman running obliquely across the splice. Adrian slipped it into the inside pocket of his blazer and settled down to write.

Under a Portrait of Prince Ranjitsinhji,
A funny little office near the Long Room,
Lord's Cricket Ground,
June 1975

Dear Mother and Father,

I'm so sorry I ran away without saying goodbye. Uncle David tells me that you have been worrying about me, not too much I hope.

I'm living in a Bed and Breakfast place in 14 Endicott Gardens, Highgate, and I have a job in a theatrical agency called Leon Bright's, 59 Denmark Street, WC2. I'm a sort of messenger and office-boy, but it's a good job and I hope to rent a flat soon.

I am well and happy and truly sorry if I have upset you. I will write soon and at length to explain why I felt I had to leave. Please try and forgive

Your doting son

Adrian

PS I met the new England Captain, Tony Greig, today.

Twenty minutes later, Uncle David returned and read it through.

'I suppose that will do. Leave it with me and I'll see that it's posted.'

He looked Adrian up and down.

'If you looked halfway decent I'd invite you to watch from the Members' Stand.'

'That's all right.'

'Come tomorrow wearing a tie and I'll see what I can do.'

'That's awfully kind. I'd love to.'

'They give you days off to watch cricket, do they? From this place in Denmark Street? Just like that?'

'Like the Foreign Office, you mean?'

'Fair point, you cheeky little rat. And get your hair cut. You look like a tart.'

'Heavens! Do I?'

Adrian did not return to Lord's the next day, nor any of the other days. Instead he had gone back to work and found time to hang around the Tottenham Court Road catching Tony Greig's ninety-six and Lillee's maddening seventy-three on the banks of televisions in the electrical appliance shop windows.

The risk of meeting people he knew was acute. He remembered how Dr Watson in the first Sherlock Holmes story had described Piccadilly Circus as a great cesspool into which every idler and lounger of the Empire was irresistibly drained. It seemed now that as the Empire had dwindled in size, so the strength of the Circus's pull had grown. Britain was a draining bath and Piccadilly, its plug-hole, now seemed almost audibly to gurgle as it sucked in the last few gallons of waste.

It was part of Adrian's job, in the centre of the whirlpool, to scrutinise every face that eddied past. Innocent passers-by tended not to meet the glances of strangers, so he usually found himself able to turn away in time if there was someone he knew in the area.

One rainy afternoon, however, about a fortnight after the meeting with his Uncle David, while sheltering in a favourite pitch under the columns of Swan and Edgar, touting for business, he caught sight of Dr Meddlar, without his dog collar but unmistakable nevertheless, coming up the steps from the Underground.

Term must be over, Adrian thought as he concealed himself behind a pillar.

He watched Meddlar look left and right before crossing over to Boots the Chemists under the neon signs. Greg and Mark, a couple of skinheads that Adrian knew, were going about their unlawful business there, and he was amazed to see Meddlar stop and talk to one of them. He was trying to look casual, but to Adrian's knowing eye it was perfectly clear that formal discussions were taking place.

Hopping through the traffic, Adrian approached from behind.

'Why, Dr Meddlar!' he cried, slapping him bonhomously on the back.

Meddlar spun round.

'Healey!'

'My dear old Chaplain, how simply splendid to see you!' Adrian shook him warmly by the hand. 'But let me give you a piece of advice – *verb sap* as we used to say at the dear old school – if they're asking more than a tenner for you to suck their cocks, you're being ripped off.'

Meddlar went white and stepped backwards off the kerb.

'You're leaving?' Adrian was disappointed. 'Oh, if you must. But any time you're in need of rough sex let me know and I'll fix you up with something. But as the man said in *Casablanca*, "Beware, there are vultures everywhere. Everywhere, vultures."'

Meddlar disappeared into a mess of spray and car horns.

'Remember the Green Cross Code,' Adrian called

after him. 'Because I won't be there when you cross the road.'

The skinheads were not pleased.

'You bastard, Hugo! We were about to score.'

'I'll pay you in full, my dears,' said Adrian. 'It was worth it. Meanwhile let me stand you both a Fanta in the Wimpy. There's no action going on in this bloody rain.'

They sat by the window, automatically scanning the crowds that blurred past.

'Why did he call you "Healey"?' asked Greg. 'I thought your name was Bullock?'

'Healey was my nickname,' said Adrian. 'I used to do impressions of Denis Healey the politician, you see. It sort of stuck.'

'Oh.'

'What a silly billy,' Adrian added, by way of proof.

'That's just like him!'

'Well, it's just like Mike Yarwood anyway.'

'And that guy really was a vicar?'

'School Chaplain, on my life.'

'Bloody hell. He was asking Terry and me if we'd tie him up. And him a bleeding Collar.'

'"I struck the board and cried No More!"' said Adrian, folding his hands in prayer.

'You what?'

'George Herbert. A poem called "The Collar". It must have passed you by somehow. "Have I no garlands gay? All blasted? All wasted? Not so my heart: but there is fruit, and thou hast hands."'

'Oh. Right. Yeah.'

'You were the garlands gay, the fruit. And his hands were about to lay themselves on you, I suspect.

244

He must have forgotten how it ends. "At every word, Methought I heard one calling, *Child!* And I replied, *My Lord.*"'

'You don't half rabbit, do you?'

'It's a splendid poem, you'd love it. I can sprint down to Hatchards and buy a copy if you'd like.'

'Fuck off.'

'Yes, well, there is that side to it too, of course,' Adrian conceded. 'Now, if you'll forgive me, I've got to nip next door to Boots and get myself some more lotion for the old crabs.'

About two months later he was picked up by an actor.

'I know you,' Adrian said, as they sat back in the taxi.

The actor took off his sunglasses.

'Christ!' Adrian giggled. 'You're – '

'Just call me Guy,' said the actor. 'It's my real name.'

A famous trick! Adrian thought to himself. I've turned a famous trick!

He stayed the night, something he had been warned against. Guy had woken him up with smoked salmon and scrambled eggs and a kiss.

'I couldn't believe you were trade, honey,' he said. 'I saw you walk from Playland to the Dilly and I couldn't fucking *believe* it.'

'Oh well,' said Adrian modestly, 'I haven't been at it long.'

'And Hugo, too! My favourite name. It's always been my favourite name.'

'One does one's best.'

'Will you stay with me, Hugo baby?'

The invitation couldn't have come at a better time for Adrian. Three days before he had caught sight of himself in the mirror of the Regent Palace Hotel cloakroom and been shocked to see the face of a whore looking back at him.

He didn't know how or why he had changed, but he had. Only the tiniest amount of bumfluff grew on his chin and when he shaved it off he was still as smooth as a ten-year-old. His hair was shorter, but not coiffured or poncey. His jeans were tight, but no tighter than any student's. Yet the face had screamed 'Rent'.

He smiled engagingly at the mirror. A cheap invitation leered back.

He raised his eyebrows and tried a lost, innocent look.

Fifteen quid for a blow-job. Nothing up the arse, his reflection replied.

A couple of weeks out of the Dilly would give him a chance to bring back some of the peaches and cream.

Guy lived in a small house in Chelsea and was about to start shooting a film at Shepperton Studios. He had been cruising Piccadilly for a last treat before throwing himself into five weeks of rising at six and working till eight.

'But now I've got a friend to come home to. It's wonderful, honey, wonderful!'

Adrian thought that to have someone to answer the telephone, do the shopping and keep the place tidy for him was indeed wonderful.

'I had an Irish cleaner once, but the bitch threatened to go to the press, so I don't trust anyone to come in now. I trust you, though, cutie-pie.'

The public school accent. If only they knew.

'I may be right, I may be wrong,' he sang to himself in the shower, 'But I'm perfectly willing to swear, That when you turned and smiled at me, A prostitute wept in Soho Square.'

So Adrian stayed and learnt how to cook and shop and be charming at dinner parties. Guy's friends were mostly producers and writers and actors, only a few of them gay. Adrian was the only one who called him Guy, which added a special and publicly endearing touch to the friendship. Guy was thirty-five and had been married at the age of nineteen. The child from this marriage lived with the ex-wife, an actress who had taken Guy's announcement of homosexuality very badly, instantly remarrying and denying Guy any access to his son.

'He must be about your age now, couple of years younger perhaps. I bet he's a screaming madam. It would serve the bitch right.'

One evening Guy's agent, Michael Morahan, and his wife Angela came to dinner. They arrived before Guy had returned from Shepperton so Adrian did his best to entertain them in the kitchen where he was chopping peppers.

'We've heard a lot about you,' said Angela, dropping her ocelot stole onto the kitchen table.

'Golden opinions, I trust?'

'Oh yes, you've done Tony nothing but good.'

Michael Morahan opened a bottle of wine.

'That's a seventy-four,' said Adrian. 'It'll need to be decanted or at least breathe for an hour. There's a Sancerre in the fridge if you'd rather.'

'Thank you, this will be fine,' was the blunt reply. 'I understand from Tony that you're an O.H.?'

Adrian had already noticed the Old Harrovian tie around Morahan's neck and had his answer prepared.

'Well, to tell you the truth,' he said, 'that's a rumour that I sort of allowed to get around. Security,' he said, tapping the side of his nose. 'I may as well tell you that Hugo Bullock isn't my real name either.'

Morahan stared unpleasantly.

'So. A mystery man from nowhere. Does Tony know that?'

'Oh dear, do you think he should?'

'I'm sure not,' said Angela. 'Anyone can tell you're trustworthy.'

They went through to the sitting room, Adrian wiping his hands on a blue-and-white-striped butcher's apron he liked to wear when cooking.

'I have to look after him, you see,' said Morahan. 'Under age and anonymous is worrying.'

'I'll be eighteen in a couple of weeks.'

'You'll still be under age by three years. A man's career can be ruined. It nearly happened last year.'

'It wouldn't exactly do *my* career any good either, would it? So we're in a position of mutual trust, I'd've thought.'

'What do you have to lose exactly?'

'The bubble, reputation.'

'Really?'

'Yes, really.'

Angela intervened.

'It's just that we have to be sure . . . I'm sure you understand, Hugo darling . . . we have to be sure that you're not going to . . . to *hurt* Tony.'

'But why on earth should I?'

'Oh come on, man!' Morahan snorted. 'You know what we're saying.'

'You're saying that Guy, who is thirty-five years old, rich, famous and experienced in the ways of the world, is a poor trusting innocent to be protected and I, half his age, am a corrupting devil who might hurt him? Blackmail him, I suppose is what you mean.'

'I'm sure Michael never meant that . . .'

'I shall go to the kitchen and crush a garlic.'

Angela followed him in.

'It's his job, Hugo. You must understand.'

It might have been the garlic and the onions that he was chopping, it might have been anger, it might have been nothing more than performance – because it seemed dramatically the right thing to do under the circumstances – but for whatever reason, tears were in Adrian's eyes. He wiped them away. 'I'm sorry, Angela.'

'Darling, don't be ridiculous. Everything's going to be fine. Michael just wanted to . . . find me a cigarette would you? . . . he just wanted to be sure.'

They heard Guy coming up the stairs.

'Yoo-hoo, honey-bear! Daddy's home.'

Adrian winced at the language. Angela squeezed his arm.

'You love him, don't you, darling?' she whispered.

Adrian nodded. He might as well have this awful woman on his side.

'Everything's going to be fine,' she said, kissing him on the cheek.

Adrian displayed just the right kind of affection towards Guy over dinner. Not whorish, but adoring;

not clinging or possessive, but happy and trusting. Michael and Angela went away full of praise for his cooking, his wit and his discretion.

Guy was very touched. He nuzzled up to Adrian on the sofa.

'You're my very special puppy and I don't deserve you. You're magical and wonderful and you're never to leave.'

'Never?'

'Never.'

'What about when I'm fat and hairy?'

'Don't be a silly baby. Come bye-byes with Guy-Guy.'

On the evening before his last day of filming, Guy asked Adrian to take an envelope to a house in Battersea and bring back the reply. Zak, the man to whom he was to deliver the envelope, would be expecting him, but he was a famous Dutch pop-star, shy of publicity, so Adrian shouldn't be surprised if he behaved oddly.

Adrian couldn't think of any Dutch pop-stars who needed to be shy of publicity in South London, but Guy's manner and lack of soupy terms of endearment suggested that this was a serious business, so he said nothing and next morning went happily on his way.

Zak was friendly enough.

'Boyfriend of Tony? Hi, good to meet you. You got something for me?'

Adrian handed him the envelope.

'Guy . . . I mean Tony . . . said there'd be a reply.'

'A reply? Sure, I've got a reply. You wait here one moment.'

The envelope containing the reply was sealed and

Adrian walked back over Chelsea Bridge, debating with himself whether or not to steam it open and read it when he got back to the house. He decided against it. Guy trusted him and it would be exhilarating to be so honest for a change. Instead he pulled out his copy of *Antigone* and read as he walked. It was something of a pose, he liked the idea of being seen reading a book in French, but he also wanted to keep fluent. It always caused a sensation in the Dilly when he was able to give directions to French tourists or, indeed, to do business with them.

He reached the King's Road and turned left. There was some kind of a scuffle going on outside the King's Tavern. A group of glue-sniffers was fighting with spray cans. One of them sprayed red paint over Adrian as he tried to hurry past.

'Oh, look what you've done!' he cried.

'Oh, look what you've done!' they shouted back, mimicking his accent. 'Fuck off, arsehole.'

They were not in a mood to be spoken to, so Adrian moved smartly away. But they decided to abandon their game and give chase.

Oh shit, Adrian thought to himself, as he ran into Bywater Street. Why did I say anything at all? You idiot, Adrian! You're going to get twenty types of crap beaten out of you now. He could hear them catching up with him. But then . . . joy of joys! He heard the wee-waa, wee-waa of a police car drawing up.

Two of the kids scattered, with an officer sprinting after them. But the other three were pushed against a wall and searched.

'Thank God,' panted Adrian.

'Against that wall,' said a sergeant.

'Sorry?'

'Against that wall.'

'But I'm the one they were chasing!'

'You heard me.'

Adrian spread his legs against the wall and assumed the position.

'What's this?'

'What's what?' said Adrian. All he could see was a brick wall.

'This,' said the policeman, turning him round and holding up an envelope.

'Oh, it's a message. Belongs to a friend of mine. It's private.'

'A message?'

'That's right.'

The policeman ripped the envelope open and pulled out a polythene sachet of white powder.

'Funny kind of message.'

'What is it?' asked Adrian.

The policeman opened the sachet and dipped a finger into the powder.

'Well, flower,' he said as he sucked the finger, 'I'd say it was two years. Two years easy.'

A table, two chairs, a door that squeaked, cigarette smoke, no window, yellowing gloss paint, the distant murmur of the King's Road, the unblinking brown eyes of Detective Sergeant Canter of the Drug Squad.

'Look, you say it's not yours. You were delivering it for a friend. You've never used the stuff yourself. You didn't even know what it was. Frankly, Hugo, I believe you. But if you don't tell us the name of this friend, then I'm sorry to say that you'll be drowning in a bucket of hot shit without a life-belt.'

'But I *can't*, I really can't. It would ruin him.'

'It's not going to do you a lot of good, either, is it?'

Adrian clutched his head in his hands. Canter was friendly, amused, indifferent and tenacious.

'I've got to think up a charge, you see. What can I choose? There's possession. Let me see . . . how much was it? Seven grammes of Charlie . . . bit dodgy, that. Rather a lot for personal use. But first offence, you're young. Reckon we could get away with six months DC.'

'DC?'

'Detention Centre, Hugo. Not nice, but quick. Short sharp shock. Then there's possession with intent to supply. You're looking at two years straight away, now. Then we have to think about trafficking. They throw away the key for that one.'

'But . . .'

'The thing is, Hugo, I've got a problem here you have to help me with. You've already told me that you don't take it yourself, so I can't really charge you with possession, can I? If you don't powder your own nose, you must have been intending to flog it to someone else. Stands to reason.'

'But he wasn't paying me! It was just an errand, I didn't know what it was.'

'Mm.' Sergeant Canter looked down at his notes. 'Rather a lot of cash in your post-office account, isn't there? Where's all that from, then?'

'That's mine! I've . . . I've saved it. I've never had anything to do with drugs. I promise!'

'But I look down at my notes and I don't see any

names. All I see is "Hugo Bullock nicked in possession of a quarter ounce of best Bolivian Marching Powder." No one else for my charge-sheet. Just Hugo Bullock. I need the name of the man you collected it from and I need the name of your friend, don't I?'

Adrian shook his head.

The detective sergeant patted him on the shoulder.

'Lover is he?'

Adrian blushed.

'He's just . . . a friend.'

'Yeah. That's right. Yeah. How old are you, Hugo?'

'Eighteen next week.'

'There you go. I think I better have his name, don't you? He corrupts a nice well-brought-up young kid and he sends him to pick up his cocaine for him. The court will weep big tears for you, my son. Probation and sympathy.'

Adrian stared down at the table.

'The other man,' he said. 'The man I got it off. I'll give you his name.'

'Well, that's a start.'

'But he mustn't know that I told you.'

He had a sudden vision of a Godfather-like revenge being wreaked against him. Adrian, the man who grassed, beaten to a pulp in a prison, a brown-paper parcel of two dead fishes sent to his parents.

'I mean he won't ever know, will he? I won't have to give evidence against him or anything?'

'Calm down, Hugo, old lad. If he's a dealer we put him under surveillance and we catch him in the act. Your name never comes into it.'

Sergeant Canter leant forward, gently raised Adrian's chin with a finger, and looked into his eyes.

'That's a promise, Hugo. Believe me.'

Adrian nodded.

'But you'd better start talking quick. Your boy-friend is going to be wondering where you are by now. We don't want him to call his dealer friend up on the blower, do we?'

'No.'

'No. He'll be out of it quick as shit off a shovel and then Hugo Bullock will still be the only name on my list.'

'He . . . my friend won't miss me until the evening.'

'I see, what's his job?'

'Look, I said. I'm only going to tell you about the other man.'

'My pencil is poised, Hugo.'

After Adrian had signed his statement they brought him a cup of tea. A detective inspector came in to read through it. He glanced at Adrian.

'Looks like you're in a bit of luck, Bullock. Zak is not exactly a stranger to us. About five nine, you say?'

'Well I said I thought he was about the same size as Sergeant Canter.'

'Stud in the left ear?'

'I'm pretty sure it was the left.'

'Yeah. We lost the bastard a couple of months ago. If he's where you say he is you've done us a bit of a favour.'

'Oh well. Anything to help.'

The detective inspector laughed.

'Get him charged and sorted out with a brief, John. Possession.'

'What's a brief?' asked Adrian when the inspector had gone.

'Solicitor.'

'Oh. I thought . . . you know, legal aid. Don't you provide one?'

'A boy like you . . . your parents are going to want to appoint one.'

'My parents?'

'Yeah. What's their address?'

'I'd . . . I'd much rather keep my parents out of it. They don't know where I am you see and I've put them through enough really.'

'They file you as a missing person?'

'Yes . . . I mean, I think they did go to the police. I bumped into my godfather and he said they had.'

'I think they'd be happier knowing where you are then, don't you?'

But Adrian remained firm and was led to the desk to be charged as Hugo Bullock.

'Empty your pockets on the desk, please.'

His possessions were examined and itemised in a ledger.

'You have to sign so that when you get them back you know we haven't robbed you,' said Canter.

'Oh lordy lord, I trust you,' said Adrian, who was beginning to enjoy himself. 'If a chap can't consign his chattels to an honest constable without suspicion then what has the world come to?'

'Yeah, right. We'll need your signature anyway. Oh, and there's one other thing, Adrian.'

'Yes?'

'Ah,' said Canter. 'So it's Adrian Healey, is it? Not Hugo Bullock.'

Damn, shit, bollocks and buggery-fuck.

D.S. Canter was holding up Anouilh's *Antigone*. Adrian's name was written on the fly-leaf.

'Clever lad like you, falling for a trick like that,' he tutted. 'No Bullock on the missing persons list, you see. But I bet there'll be a Healey, won't there?'

II

A bell rang in the corridor, doors slammed and voices rose in anger.

'Watch yourself, Ashcroft, one more sound out of you and you're on report.'

'But what did I do?'

Adrian shut his eyes and tried to concentrate on the letter he was writing.

'Right! I warned you. Loss of privileges for a week.'

He took a piece of paper and spread it flat on the table. A cold wind blew outside and the sky had darkened to gunmetal grey. Snow was on the way.

'Please Mr Annendale, may I get a book from the library?'

'If you hurry.'

Adrian picked up a pen and began.

13th February 1978

Dear Guy,

I have been meaning to pluck up the nerve to write to you for some time. I was finally pricked into action by seeing you in *The Likeness* the other night. You were brilliant as always. I loved you in both parts – though the Good Shelford reminded me more of the Guy I Know (up in the gallery) . . .

I wonder if you found out what happened to me? I have a feeling that you imagined me skipping off with your money. But perhaps you heard the truth. The fact is that after I had been to see your friend Zak I was arrested by the police in possession of your end-of-shoot cocaine – you were just finishing *The Red Roof* if you remember. You'll be pleased to know, by the way, that Zak wasn't ripping you off – the haul was described in court as seven grammes of highest quality Andean flake.

It may be that you've been suffering from a guilty conscience about my innocent involvement in the whole affair, but if you have, I can now cheerfully relieve you of that burden. I was treated well and never put under pressure to reveal any names.

The old parents rallied round with character witnesses – godfathers, bishops, generals, even my old Housemaster at school would you believe? – and with squads of armed and dangerous solicitors. What chance did the magistrates stand? It was only by calling on all their reserves of pride and self-control that they managed to summon up the nerve even to put me on probation. I think one of them was so overcome by my quiet dignity and round-eyed innocence that he came within an ace of recommending some kind of civilian award for me.

Since then I have been to a crammer's in Stroud, passed exams and find myself filling in time teaching at a prep school in Norfolk before going off to St Matthew's College, Cambridge – not quite poacher turned game-keeper . . . slave turned slave-master? Something like it. Boy turned man, I suppose.

My name, as you probably know, is as far from Hugo Bullock as a name can be without actually falling over, but I won't bother you with it. This is just to wish you well and thank you for a month or two of unsurpassable fun and frolic.

I hope you are now treating your nostrils as well as you treated

Your very own

Hugo Bullock

There was a knock on the door.
  'Please, sir, can I ask a question?'
  'Newton, I distinctly heard with my own two ears – these, the ones I put on this morning because they go so well with my eyes – that Mr Annendale gave you permission to go to the library and get a book. I did not hear him give you permission to come to my room.'
  'It's just a quick question . . .'

'Oh, very well.'

'Is it true, sir, that you and Matron are having an affair?'

'Out, out! Get out! Out before I slash your throat with a knife and hang you dripping with blood from the flag-pole. Out, before I pull your guts from your body and stuff them down your mouth. Out, before I become mildly irritated. Go, hence, begone. Stand not upon the order of your going, but go at once. Run! run quickly from here, run to the other side of Europe, flee for your life nor give not one backward glance. I never hope to see you again in this world or the next. Never speak to me, never approach me, never advertise your presence to me by the smallest sound, or by the living God that made me I will do such things . . . I know not what they are but they will be the terrors of the earth. Flee hence, be not here, but somewhere in a vast Elsewhere to which I have no access. Boys who rub me up the wrong way, Newton, come to a sticky end. Be removed, piss off, *heraus*, get utterly outly out.'

'Thought so.'

'Grr!'

Adrian flung a book at the hastily closing door, signed the letter and lit a pipe. The snow had started to fall.

He had no more duties for the day so he decided to do a bit more work on *The Aunt That Exploded*, a play for the end of term that he had been cajoled into writing.

If Harvey-Potter was going to play Aunt Bewinda, something would have to be done about preserving his soprano. A definite fissure had appeared in his larynx at breakfast and a tenor Bewinda would be worse than useless. He should talk to Clare about deliberately shrinking the boy's underpants in the laundry. Anything to keep nature at bay for two months.

He still had to work on Maxted, the only master who had so far refused to participate.

'You can kick my arse from here to Norwich, Adrian, I'm not going to dress up in shorts for any man living.'

The principal idea of the play was that boys played grown-ups, parents, aunts, doctors and schoolmasters, and the staff played boys and, in the case of Matron, a little girl.

'Come on Oliver, even the Brigadier has agreed. It'll be wonderful.'

'If you can tell me in one word what's wrong with *The Mikado*?'

'No, can't do that. "It's crap" is two words and "It's complete crap" is three.'

'Of course *The Mikado* is crap, but it's good healthy stodgy crap. Your blasted play is either going to be horrible pebbly crap or a great gush of liquid crap.'

'I'll do all your duties this term. How about that?'

'No you bloody won't.'

That hadn't been such a clever offer. Maxted *enjoyed* being on duty.

'Well I think you're a heel and a stinker and I hope that one day you'll be found out.'

'Found out? What do you mean?'

'Ho hee!' said Adrian, who knew that everyone lived in fear of being found out.

But Maxted was not to be moved, which was a

nuisance because, set off in shorts and school-cap, his paunch and purple complexion would have been terrifically striking. Perhaps Adrian himself would have to play Bewinda's nephew. Not ideal casting: he was still closer in age to the boys than to any of the staff.

But it was a snug problem, the perfect sort of problem for a man in a tweed jacket, sitting in a fire-lit room with a good briar pipe between his teeth, a glass of Glennfiddich at his elbow and a blizzard whipping up outside, to ponder over. A clean problem for a clean man with a clean mind in the clean countryside.

He rubbed his fingers against the grain of his stubble and thought.

All gone. All anger quelled, all desire drained, all thirst slaked, all madness past.

There would be cricket next term, coaching and umpiring, teaching the young idea how to deal with the ball that goes on with the arm, reading them Browning and Heaney on the lawn when the sun shone and it was too hot to teach indoors. The rest of the summer would be spent discovering Milton and Proust and Tolstoy ready for Cambridge in October where, like Cranmer – but with a bicycle instead of a horse – his mind and thighs would find exercise. A handful of civilised friends, not too close.

'What do you make of that bloke in your college, Healey?'

'He's hard to get to know. I *like* him, but he's private, he's unfathomable.'

'Detached somehow . . . almost serene.'

Then a degree and back here or to another school –

his own perhaps. Stay on at Cambridge even . . . if he got a First.

All gone.

He didn't believe himself for a moment, of course.

He looked at his reflection in the window. 'It's no good trying to fool me, Healey,' he said, 'an Adrian always knows when an Adrian is lying.'

But an Adrian also knew that an Adrian's lies were real: they were lived and felt and acted out as thoroughly as another man's truths – if other men had truths – and he believed it possible that this last lie might see him through to the grave.

He watched the snow building up against the window and his mind caught the tube to Piccadilly and climbed the steps from the Underground.

There stood Eros, the boy with the bow poised to shoot, and there stood Adrian, the schoolmaster in tweeds and cavalry twills, looking up at him and slowly shaking his head.

'Of course you know why Eros was put in the Circus in the first place, don't you?' he remembered saying to a sixteen-year-old who was sharing his pitch outside the London Pavilion one July evening.

'Named after the Eros Strip Club, was it?'

'Oh that's close, but I'm afraid I can't give it you, I'll have to pass the question over. It was part of a tribute to the Earl of Shaftesbury: a grateful nation honours the man who abolished child labour. Alfred Gilbert, the sculptor, positioned Eros with his bow and arrow aiming up Shaftesbury Avenue.'

'Yeah? Well, fuck all that, there's a trick over there been eyeing you up for the past five minutes.'

'Had him. Overuses the teeth. He can find someone

else to circumcise. The point is, it's a kind of visual pun, Eros burying his shaft up Shaftesbury Avenue. You see?'

'Then why's he pointing down Lower Regent Street?'

'He was taken down and cleaned during the war and the fools who put him back up didn't know buggery ding-dong shit.'

'He could do with cleaning again.'

'I don't know. I think Eros should be dirty. In Greek legend, as I'm sure you are aware, he fell in love with the minor deity Psyche. It was the Greek way of saying that, in spite of what it may believe, Love pursues the Soul, not the body; the Erotic desires the Psychic. If Love was clean and wholesome he wouldn't lust after Psyche.'

'He's still looking this way.'

'His bottom is, at any rate.'

'No, the trick. He's started cruising me now.'

'I will clear away for you. Too many cocks spoil the brothel. Have him with my blessing. Just don't come crawling to me with your glans half hanging off, that's all.'

'I'll give him a minute to make up his mind.'

'Do that. I'm bound to wonder, meanwhile, was there any life more futile and perfectly representative than that of Lord Shaftesbury? His own adored son killed in a schoolboy fight at Eton while his national monument daily supervises child labour of a nature and intensity he would never have guessed at.'

'I'm definitely on here. See you later.'

Adrian dropped a log on the fire and stared into the flames. He was as secure as anyone: a real teacher with a real name, real references and real qualifications. No forgeries or tricks had brought him here, only merit. No one on earth could bang into the room and drag him to judgement. He really was a schoolmaster in a real school, really stirring a real fire in a safe and snug common room that was as real as the winter weather that really raged in the real world outside. He had as much right to pour a finger of ten-year-old malt and puff a soothing pipeful of the ready-rubbed as anyone in England. The grown-up didn't live who had the power to snatch away the bottle, confiscate the pipe or reduce him to stammered excuses.

Yet the sparks that spat up the flue spelt Wrigleys and Coke and Toshiba in Piccadilly neon; the escape of steam from the logs hissed a meeting of prefects plotting punishment.

He knew he could never jingle change in his pocket or park his car like a confident adult, he was the Adrian he had always been, casting a guilty look over a furtive shoulder, living in eternal dread of a grown-up striding forward to clip his ear.

But there again, when he sipped at the whisky his eyes failed to water and his throat forgot to burn. The body shamelessly welcomed what once it would have rejected. At breakfast he demanded not Ricicles and chocolate spread, but coffee and unbuttered toast. And if the coffee was sugared he leapt from it like a colt from an electric fence. He ate the crust and left the filling, guzzled the olives and spurned the cherries. Yet inside he remained the same Adrian who fought down the urge to stand and shout 'Bollocks' during church services, smelt his own farts and wasted hours skimming through *National Geographic* on the off-chance of seeing a few naked bodies.

He turned back to his work with a sigh. God could worry about what he was and what he wasn't. There was the tea-party scene to be written.

He hadn't been working for more than ten minutes when there came another knock at the door.

'If that is anyone under the age of thirteen they have my permission to go and drown themselves.'

The door opened and a cheery face peered round.

'Wotcher, cock, thought I'd come and cadge a drink.'

'My dear Matron, you can't have run out of Gees linctus again.'

She came and looked over his shoulder.

'How's it going?'

'The agony of composition. Got to keep everyone satisfied. I'm preparing a huge part for you.'

She massaged his neck.

'I can take it.'

'Oh you proud, snorting beauty, how I love you.'

It was a private joke that the boys had somehow got wind of. She was a thoroughbred filly and he was her trainer. Adrian had started it when he found out that her father bred race-horses for a living. She looked the part too, with a great mane of chestnut hair and dark eyes that she rolled in mock passion when Adrian patted her hindquarters.

She had come to Chartham as an assistant matron at the age of sixteen and had been there ever since. There were rumours amongst the staff that she was a lesbian, but Adrian put that down to wishful thinking on their part. She was now such an attractive twenty-five-year-old that they had to find some excuse for not desiring her and her liking for jeans and jackets over skirts and blouses made sapphic preferences an obvious escape route for them.

She had latched onto Adrian as soon as he had arrived.

'She always pretends to pant after new masters,' Maxted had said. 'It's just showing off to the boys to disguise her dykery. Tell her to bog off.'

But Adrian enjoyed her company: she was brisk and clean. Her breasts were high and handsome, her thighs strong and supple and she was teaching him to drive. Despite the heat of their language they had never come close to anything physical, but the thought beat its wings in the air whenever they were together.

He watched her wandering around his room, picking things up, examining them and putting them down again in the wrong place.

'She's restless, she needs a good gallop over the downs,' he said.

She went to the window.

'It's really settling, isn't it?'

'What is?'

'The snow.'

'I find it unsettling as a matter of fact. I'm on duty tomorrow and I shall have to find something for the boys to do. The rugger pitch will be four foot under if it carries on at this rate.'

'The school was cut off from the outside world for a whole week in seventy-four.'

'And it's been cut off ever since.'

She sat on the bed.

267

'I'm leaving at the end of the year.'

'Really? Why?'

'I'll have been here nearly ten years. It's enough. I'll go home.'

Every member of staff spoke regularly about leaving at the end of the year. It was their way of showing that they weren't stuck, that they had a choice. It meant nothing, they always came back.

'But who will spoon out the little darlings' malt? Who will paint their warts and kiss the place and make it well? Chartham needs you.'

'I mean it, Ade. Clare is fretting in her loose-box.'

'It's time some stallion was found to cover you, certainly,' Adrian agreed. 'The colts here have been very disappointing and the staff are all geldings.'

'Except you.'

'Ah, but I've still a few seasons of racing left in me before I get put out. After I've won the Cambridge Hurdles my stud fees will be that much higher.'

'You're not a queer are you, Adrian?'

He was startled by the question.

'Well,' he said, 'I know what I like.'

'And do you like me?'

'Do I like you? I'm flesh and blood aren't I? How could anyone not be thrilled by your tightly fleshed points, your twitching hocks, your quivering neck, your shining hindquarters, your heaving, shimmering flanks?'

'Then for God's sake, fuck me. I'm going mad.'

For all his talk, Adrian had never experienced a human being of another gender before and writhing around with Clare, he was astonished by the strength of her desire. He hadn't expected that women actually felt the kind of urge and appetite that drove men. Everyone knew, surely, that females went for personality, strength and security and were resigned to the need to be penetrated only if that was the price for keeping the man they loved? That they should arch their backs, spread wide the lips of their sex in hunger and urge him in was something for which he was not prepared. Adrian's room was at the top of the school and they had locked the door, but he couldn't help feeling that everyone would be able to hear her squeals and roars of pleasure.

'Bang me, you bastard, bang me hard! Harder! Deeper and harder, you lump of shit. God that's good.'

It explained all those jokes about bedsprings. The sex he had taken part in up until now didn't build up these colossal pounding rhythms. He found himself driving faster and faster and joining in her shouts.

'I . . . think . . . that . . . I'm . . . about . . . to . . . wheeeeeee! . . . whooooo! . . . haaaaaaa . . .'

He collapsed on her as she thrashed herself calm. Panting and sweating, they wound down together into a kind of breathless quiet.

She gripped his shoulders.

'You beautiful fucking son of a bitch. My God I needed that. Woof!'

'As a matter of fact,' gasped Adrian, 'I think I did too.'

Clare taught him a great deal that term.

'Sex is meaningless,' she said, 'if it's silent and mechanical. You have to think about it and plan it, like a dinner party or a cricket match. I tell you when to put in, how it's feeling, you tell me what you like, when you're coming, how you want me to move. Just remember that you have never thought a thought or imagined an act that is so dirty and depraved that I won't have thought of it thousands of times myself. That's true of everyone. When we stop talking and joking we'll know it's over.'

Two nights after the last day of term the head-master and his wife had gone out to a dinner party, so Clare and Adrian found they had the whole school to themselves. It was cold, but they had run naked around the classrooms where she had thrown herself over a desk to be spanked, into the kitchens where they had hurled jam and lard at each other, into the staff common room where he had pumped her up with the football pump, into the boys' showers where she had urinated over his face and finally into the gymnasium where they had rolled and rolled over the mats, shrieking and slithering and jerking in frenzy.

He lay looking up at the climbing ropes that hung from the ceiling. During the act all his senses had been suspended, but now it was over he felt the bruise on his shoulder where he had barged into a door, smelt the sour lard and urine and jam that was all over him and heard the hot-water pipes rattling under the floor and the bubbles of wind building up in Clare's bowels.

'Bath,' he said. 'Bath then bed. God I'm going to need these holidays.'

'Stay with me here for a while.'

It was their one point of disagreement. Adrian had never been able to luxuriate in the afterglow.

'Time for my tub.'

'Why do you always want to have a bath the

moment after you've made love to me? Why can't w
wriggle in our dirt for a while?' she said.

He fought down his customary post-coital irritation
and contempt.

'Don't go looking for something psychological that
isn't there. I have a bath after any kind of strenuous
exercise. It doesn't mean I feel dirty,' though he did,
'it doesn't mean I'm trying to wash you out of my
life,' though he was, 'it doesn't mean guilt, shame,
repentance or anything like that,' though it did. 'It
just means I want a bath.'

'Queer!' she shouted after him.

'Lesbian!' he yelled back.

When he came back next term, she was gone. Her
replacement was a forty-year-old with one breast who
most certainly *was* lesbian, which allowed the rest of
the staff the free luxury of finding her irresistibly
desirable. They spent their days saying she was a
grand old girl and their evenings attempting to coax
her down to the pub.

'Your girlfriend has gone, sir,' said Newton. 'Whatever are you going to do?'

'I shall devote the rest of my life to beating you into
a purée,' said Adrian. 'It will help me forget.'

III

The morning of the match, Hunt had put a message
under Adrian's toast as usual. This time it was a large
heart-shaped piece of paper covered in kisses. This
was going too far.

In theory, the boy on clearing duty should be the
one to make masters' toast, but Hunt had long since

decided that no one but he was going to make Adrian's. He fought everyone for the right. Whenever Adrian came down there would be two pieces on his side plate, and under them would be a message, usually nothing more dreadful than 'Your toast, sir . . .' or 'Each slice hand-grilled the traditional way by heritage craftsmen'. But love-hearts were too much.

Adrian looked round the hall to where Hunt was sitting. The boy pinkened and gave a small wave.

'What's Hunt the Thimble given you today, sir?' asked Rudder, the prefect next to Adrian. Hunt was known as the Thimble for the obvious reason and because he was said to be rather under-endowed.

'Oh nothing, nothing . . . the usual drivel.'

'I bet it isn't, sir. We told him that it was Valentine's Day today.'

'But Valentine's Day, Rudder dearest, falls on February the fourteenth and lies there until the fifteenth of that month. Unless I have become so bored by your anserine conversation and fallen asleep for four months, this is currently the month of June we are enjoying. What else, after all, could explain your cricket whites?'

'I know, sir. But we told him Valentine's Day was *today*. That's the joke.'

'Ah! Well, if the Queen can have two birthdays, why cannot Hunt the Thimble be granted the right to celebrate two Valentine's Days?'

'He told me,' said Rudder, 'that if he didn't get one back from you, he was going to hang himself.'

'He said *what*?' said Adrian, going white.

'Sir?'

Adrian grabbed Rudder's arm.

'*What* did he say?'

'Sir, you're hurting! It was just a joke.'

'You find the idea of suicide amusing, do you?'

'Well no, sir, but it was just . . .'

There was a silence. The boys at his table looked down at their cereal bowls. It wasn't like Adrian to be angry or violent.

'I'm sorry my angels,' he said, with an attempt at a laugh. 'No sleep last night. Working on the play. Either that or I'm turning mad. It was a full moon you know, and there's a history of lycanthropy in my family. Uncle Everard turns into a wolf every time he hears the *Crossroads* theme tune.'

Rudder giggled. The uncomfortable moment passed.

'Well, looks like a fine day today. I vote we load a crate of Coke onto the minibus before we go. You know what Narborough match teas are like.'

A mighty cheer now. The other tables looked across enviously. Healey's lot was always having fun.

The atmosphere in the minibus was tense. Adrian sat with them and tried to appear sunny and confident. It was no good his telling them to remember that it was only a game when he was as nervous as a kitten himself.

'We'll take a look at the pitch,' he told Hooper, the captain, 'and we'll decide then. But unless it's decidedly moist, put them in the field if you win the toss. "Knock 'em up, bowl 'em out" . . . it never fails.'

He was pleased with what he had done to the cricket eleven. He had never been much of a player himself but he knew and loved the game well enough to be able to make a difference to a schoolboy team. Everyone had agreed, watching his first eleven play a warm-up match against a scratch Rest of the School side, that he had done a tremendous job in two weeks.

But now they faced their first real opposition and he was worried that against another school they would fall to pieces. Last year, Hooper told him, Chartham Park was the laughing- stock of the whole area.

The bus whined up the Narborough driveway.

'Who's been here before?'

'I have, sir, for a rugger match,' said Rudder.

'Why are other schools always so forbidding? They seem infinitely bigger and more serious and their boys all look at least forty years old.'

'It's not a bad place, sir. Quite friendly.'

'Friendly? The maws of the heffalump are open wide, but don't believe that it betokens friendliness. Trust no one, speak to no one. As soon as you've heard this communication, eat it.'

There was a boy in a Narborough blazer waiting to show the team where to go. Adrian watched them stream off to the back of the house.

'See you there, my honeys. Don't accept any hand-rolled cigarettes from them.'

An old master bustled out to welcome Adrian.

'You're Chartham Park, yes?'

'That's right. Adrian Healey.'

'Staveley. I'm not Cricket. Our man's giving the team a pep talk. It's morning break at the moment. Come through to the staff room and savage a Chelsea bun with us.'

The staff room was baronial and crowded with

what seemed to Adrian like a greater number of masters than Chartham had boys.

'Ah, Chartham's new blood!' boomed the headmaster. 'Come to give us a spanking, have you?'

'Oh well, I don't know about that, sir,' Adrian shook his hand. 'They tell me that you're hot stuff. Double figures would satisfy us.'

'That false modesty doesn't do, you know. I can smell your confidence. You're St Matthew's bound, I understand?'

'That's right, sir.'

'Well then, you'll be pleased to meet my Uncle Donald who's staying here until Cambridge term begins. He'll be your Senior Tutor at St Matthew's of course. Where is he? Uncle Donald, meet Adrian Healey, Chartham Park's new secret weapon, he's joining you at Michaelmas. Adrian Healey, Professor Trefusis.'

A short man with white hair and a startled expression turned and surveyed Adrian.

'Healey? Yes indeed, Healey. How do you do?'

'How do you do, Professor?'

'Healey, that's right. Quite right. Your entrance paper was very encouraging. Pregnant with promise, gravid with wit.'

'Thank you.'

'And you're a cricketer?'

'Well, not really. I've been trying to coach a bit, though.'

'Well best of luck, my dear. My nephew Philip has a youth like yourself on the staff – he'll be going to Trinity – who is said to have done much with the

Narborough side. Quite the young thaumaturge, they tell me.'

'Oh dear. I think that means we can expect to be marmalised. I was hoping Narborough would have sunk into over-confidence.'

'Here he comes now, you'll be umpiring together. Let me introduce you.'

Adrian turned to see a young man in a cricket-sweater making his way towards them.

It had to happen one day. It was bound to have done. Adrian always imagined that it would be in the street or on a train. But here? Today? In this place?

'I already know Hugo Cartwright,'· he said. 'We were at school together.'

'Hello, Adrian,' said Hugo. 'Ready to be pounded into the dust?'

They put on their white coats and walked down to the ground.

'What sort of a wicket have you got for us?' Adrian asked.

'Not bad, slight leg-to-off slope from the pavilion end.'

'Got any bowlers who can use it?'

'We've a little leg-spinner I have hopes for.'

Adrian winced: he hadn't properly inoculated his team against leg-spin. It could run through a prep-school batting line-up like cholera through a slum.

'Does he have a googlie?'

'Ha-ha!' said Hugo.

'Bastard.'

He looked different but the same. Adrian's eyes could see the real Cartwright not too far beneath the surface. Behind the strengthened features he saw the smoother lines of the boy, within the firmer stride he read the former grace. His memory could scrub off four years of tarnish and restore the shining original. But no one else would have been able to.

If Clare had been with him and he had said, 'What do you think of that man there?' she would probably have wrinkled her nose and replied, 'Okay, I suppose. But I always think blond men look sinister.'

Everyone has their time, Adrian thought. You can meet people of thirty and know that when their hair is grey and their face lined, they will look wonderfully at their best. That Professor, for one, Donald Trefusis. He must have looked ridiculous as a teenager, but now he has come into his own. Others, whose proper age was twenty-five, grew old grotesquely, their baldness and thickening waistlines an affront to what they once were. There were men like that on the staff at Chartham, fifty or sixty years old, but whose true characters were only discernible in hints of some former passion and vigour that would come out when they were excited. The headmaster, on the other hand, was a pompous forty-one, waiting to ripen into a delicious sixty-five. What Adrian's own proper age was, he had no idea. Sometimes he felt he had left himself behind at school, at other times he thought he would be at his best in tubby and contented middle age. But Hugo . . . Hugo he knew would always be growing away from his fourteen-year-old perfection: the clues to his former beauty would become harder to find as each year passed, the golden hair would seem pale and weak at thirty, the liquid blue of the eyes would harden and set at thirty-five.

Summer's lease hath all too short a date, Hugo old boy, thought Adrian, but your eternal summer shall not fade. In my imagination you are immortal. The man walking beside me is merely The Picture of Hugo Cartwright, ageing and coarsening: I have the real Hugo in my head and he will live as long as I do.

'I think we'll bat first, sir,' the Narborough captain announced after winning the toss.

'That's it, Malthouse,' said Hugo. 'Knock 'em up and bowl 'em out.'

'Trust me to lose the toss,' said Hooper. 'Sorry, sir.'

'Don't be a dafty-trousers,' said Adrian. 'It's a good wicket to bat second on, it'll dry out all through the afternoon.'

He threw the ball to Rudder, Chartham's opening bowler, before taking his position at the stumps.

'Remember, Simon,' he said, 'straight and on a length, that's all you have to do.'

'Yes, sir,' said Rudder, swallowing.

The ground was in a kind of valley, with the looming Gothic of Narborough Hall on one rise and the church and village of Narborough on another. The pavilion was whitewashed and thatched, the weather perfect with only the faintest of breezes luffing the fielders' shirtsleeves. The grim seriousness of the children preparing to play, the detached amusement of Hugo at square leg, the church clock chiming mid-day, the round circles of fine gang-mown cuttings in the outfield, the sun winking off the roller by the sight-screen, the distant clatter of spiked shoes on the pavilion concrete, the open blue of the wide Norfolk sky, the six pebbles in the hand of Adrian's outstretched arm, this whole monstrous illusion froze, while to Adrian the world seemed to hold its breath as if uncertain that such a picture could last. This fantasy of England that old men took with them to their death-beds, this England without factories and sewers or council houses, this England of leather and wood and flannel, this England circumscribed by a white boundary and laws that said that each team shall field eleven men and each man shall bat, this England of shooting-sticks, weather-vanes and rectory teas, it was like Cartwright's beauty, he thought, a momentary vision glimpsed for a second in an adolescent dream, then dispersed like steam into the real atmosphere of traffic-jams, serial murderers, prime ministers and Soho rent. But its spectral haze was sharper and clearer than the glare of the everyday and, against all evidence, was taken to be the only reality, its vapour trapped and distilled in the mind, its image, scents and textures bottled and laid down against the long, lonely melancholy of adulthood.

Adrian brought down his arm.

'Play!'

Rudder bowled a ball of full length and the batsman swept his bat elegantly forward in defence. But the ball had already gone through him and Rice the wicket-keeper was leaping in glee. The batsman looked round in disbelief to see his off-stump lying on the ground. He returned to the pavilion shaking his head, as if Rudder had been guilty of some appalling social blunder. There was a liquid spatter of applause from the boundary. The school were in lessons and wouldn't be watching until after lunch.

Adrian tossed a pebble into his right hand and smiled across at Hugo.

'I got him, sir!' said Rudder, polishing the ball against his leg. 'I bloody got him. Golden bloody duck.'

'You beat him for pace, old love,' said Adrian, drawing him aside. 'The next batsman will be scared, bowl him two very quick ones just outside the line of off-stump and then a slower ball on middle, but disguise it.'

'All right, sir.'

Adrian wondered if it was a breach of etiquette for an umpire to coach during play. But then he saw Hugo, who had been replacing the bails at the other end, whispering urgently to the incoming number three. Very well then, they would fight it out between them, like First World War generals.

Rudder did as he was told for the first two balls, letting them fly at the new batsman, who played and missed at the first and left the second alone. He came thundering up for the third ball, grunting and stamping like a buffalo. The batsman quaked.

'Subtle disguise I don't think,' Adrian said to himself.

The ball was let go of early and seemed to float in at half the speed. The batsman had nearly completed his defensive stroke by the time it got to him, with the result that the ball was knocked from his bat gently back to Rudder who threw it up in the air with a yell of triumph.

'Caught and bowled! And hast thou slain the number three? Come to my arms, my beamish boy. Two for none, oh frabjous day, calloo callay!'

Hugo was furious at lunch. His side had been bowled out for fourteen runs. He couldn't believe it.

'I'll kill them!' he said. 'I'll castrate them and hang their scrotums from the score-board.'

'Don't worry,' said Adrian. 'We'll probably be all out for ten.'

'I'm going to replace the whole team with boys from the scholarship Sixth. At least they'll have some brains. What good is ball sense without common sense? I mean, trying to square cut a straight half-volley! It makes me want to throw up.'

Adrian was sure that he himself wouldn't sulk quite as gracelessly if it had been his side that had been dismissed for fourteen. But then Cartwright had always been ambitious. He remembered the time they had walked back from Biffen's tea-party and Cartwright had talked about going to Cambridge. That had been the same day that Trotter had hanged himself.

Adrian smothered a sudden desire to rap his spoon on the table, call for quiet and announce, 'This man opposite me here, my fellow umpire, I thought you might like to know that he sucked me off one night in a hotel when he thought I was asleep.'

'Funny old game,' he remarked instead.

'Look,' said Hugo. 'If you do cream us straight after lunch, how would you feel about making it a two-innings match?'

'Well . . .'

'It'll go down as your victory of course, but we do need the practice.'

'All right,' said Adrian. 'I'll check with my team first.'

Hooper was doubtful.

'We've never played two innings before, sir. What happens when we pass their first score?'

'We make as many runs as possible before we're all out.'

'Sir, suppose they can't get us all out?'

'That's when you have to declare, dear. Make sure you judge it so that there's time to put them in again, bowl them out and then pass their total before stumps. We don't want a draw.'

'When are stumps?'

'Narborough's Mr Cartwright and I agreed on seven o'clock. I'll have to ring the school and check with the headmaster. You'll be late for bed of course, but it'll all be the most super-duper fun.'

The whole school turned out to watch after lunch. As Adrian had feared, Narborough's leg-spinner, Ellis, completely baffled his boys. Once they had got used to the ball bouncing and spinning one way, he would send down top-spin and undetectable googlies that made the ball fly off to the waiting close field. Chartham was all out for thirty-nine after an hour and a half of tortured embarrassment. Hugo looked very smug as Narborough prepared for their second innings.

'We're only twenty-five ahead,' said Adrian.

'That's all right, isn't it, sir?' said Rudder. 'If we get them out for fourteen again we'll have won by an innings and eleven runs.'

'If.'

The Narborough openers stalked to the wicket looking determined and confident. They were playing in front of their home crowd now and had experienced the satisfaction of seeing the Chartham team writhe.

Rudder's first ball was a wide. Adrian signalled it, with raised eyebrows.

'Sorry, sir,' said Rudder with a grin.

His next ball was driven to the mid-off boundary, the next was hooked for six. The fourth, a no-ball, was late-cut for two which became six after four overthrows had been added. The next two were both glanced for four. Rudder turned to Adrian to collect his sweater.

'Two more balls yet, Simon.'

'Sir?'

'There was a wide and a no-ball in there. Two more balls.'

'Oh. Yes, sir. I forgot.'

The next two were each smacked for four over Rudder's head.

'What's going wrong, sir?'

'What's going wrong is you're not bowling properly. Line and length, darling, line and length.'

For the next two hours the opening pair batted freely and fiercely, putting on a hundred and seventy-four, until one of the batsmen, the same man Rudder had clean bowled first ball of the morning, retired to let some of his friends enjoy the slaughter.

Hugo's merriment was unbearable over tea, for all the whiteness of his teeth and the sparkle in his eyes.

'Well that's a bit more like it,' he said. 'I was beginning to get worried this morning.'

'Dear old friend of my youth,' said Adrian, 'I'm afraid you've discovered our principal weakness.'

'What, you can't bowl you mean?'

'No, no. Sympathy. My boys were simply devastated by your glumness at lunch, so we decided to cheer you up by letting you have some batting practice. I take it you're declaring over tea?'

'You bet. Have you out of here, tail between your legs, by half past five.'

'Is that a promise?' said a voice behind them. It was Professor Trefusis.

'Certainly, sir,' said Hugo.

'What do you think, Mr Healey?'

'Well let me see . . . two hundred and thirty-nine to make before seven. I think we can do it all right, if we don't panic.'

'Ellis isn't tired, you know,' said Hugo. 'He can bowl for hours at a stretch.'

'My boys were beginning to read him by the end,' said Adrian. 'We can do it.'

'I have just placed a bet with my nephew Philip,' said Trefusis. 'Two hundred pounds on Chartham to win at odds of five to one against.'

'What?' said Adrian. 'I mean . . . what?'

'I liked your entrance papers, most amusing. I don't see how you can fail.'

'Well,' said Hugo, as Trefusis ambled away, 'what a bloody idiot.'

'Oh, I don't know,' said Adrian, popping a sandwich into his mouth, 'smart investment if you ask me. Now, if you'll forgive me, I have to go and brief my platoon.'

'Want a side bet?' Hugo called out after him.

'Right,' said Adrian to his team. 'There's a man out there who is so sure, based on the evidence of what he's seen, that you can do it, that he has bet two hundred pounds that you will blow these bastards out of the water.'

They were padding up in the pavilion, forlorn but brave, like Christians preparing for an away match against Lions.

'But what do we do about Ellis, sir!' said Hooper. 'He's impossible.'

'That's a trough of piss. You step up to him and you cart him all over the park, is what you do. Just don't get pushed against your stumps. Aim for the close-in fielders, if you miss the ball you might manage to belt them with your bat on the follow-through.'

'Isn't that a bit unsporting, sir?'

'Arseholes. Whistle, hum, look unconcerned, look bored. When he's ready to bowl, you step forward and say you're not ready. Disturb his rhythm, demonstrate contempt. Don't forget, I'm out there, and he'll want to bowl from my end because of the slope.'

'You won't *cheat* will you, sir?'

'Cheat? Good heavens. This is an amateur cricket match amongst leading prep schools, I'm an Englishman and a schoolmaster supposedly setting an example to his young charges. We are playing the most artistic and beautiful game man ever devised. Of course I'll cunting well cheat. Now, give me my robe and put on my crown. I have immortal longings in me.'

Out in the middle, little Ellis took the ball and flipped it from hand to hand with the disturbing competence of a born spinner of the ball.

Adrian patted his head.

'Good luck, little chap,' he said. 'Don't get upset if they punish you a bit. It's only a game, eh?'

Ellis looked puzzled. 'Yes, sir.'

A sporting round of applause from the Narborough boys welcomed Chartham's opening pair to the wicket.

'Here they come now. They're both rather savage hitters of the ball, I'm afraid. But if you don't lose your head you should be able to cut it down to ten or so an over. A word of advice, though. Try and do something about disguising that googlie of yours a bit better . . . sticks out like a sore thumb.'

Ellis tweaked the ball out of the side of his hand uncertainly.

'Thank you, sir.'

'All right, here we go. Don't be nervous.'

Frowde and Colville, the openers, had certainly taken the game-plan literally. They surveyed the field with lofty disdain and smiled faint patronising smiles at the short leg and silly point crowded around them, nicely blending admiration for their physical courage and doubt for their mental capacity. They were welcome to stand there and be cut in two, but they had been warned.

'Play!' said Adrian.

Ellis stepped forward. Frowde at the other end threw up a hand and bent to do up his shoe-laces.

'Sorry!' he called. 'Won't be a sec.'

Ellis turned back to his mark and waited.

'All right, Frowde?' said Adrian.

'Fine thank you, sir. Just don't want to get tangled up when I start running.'

'Quite so,' Adrian dropped his arm. 'Play!!' he boomed.

Ellis bowled a full toss which Frowde hooked straight over the boundary. The short leg fielder glared at Ellis: the ball had nearly decapitated him.

Adrian signalled a four to the scorer.

'It was a six,' said Hugo at square leg.

'Sorry?'

'It was a six!'

'Are you sure?'

'Of course I'm sure! It went clean over.'

'Well if you're sure,' said Adrian, signalling a six. 'I didn't want to give ourselves two extra runs. That was a six, scorer!' he yelled, just as Ellis next to him was catching the return from deep mid-wicket. The blast in his ear made him drop the ball. Adrian picked it up for him.

'Try and get them to bounce on the ground first,' he said helpfully. 'That way it's harder for the batsman to hit quite so far.'

Ellis's second was a long hop square-cut for four.

'You see?' said Adrian. 'That's two fewer already.'

The next was on a good length and driven straight to close extra cover.

'There might be a couple here,' shouted Frowde to his partner.

'Genius,' thought Adrian, as they ran one run after the extra cover fielder fumbled the ball in his amazement at the possibility that anyone was going to run at all.

Ellis was made of stout stuff. His next ball was an excellent leg-break that nearly had Colville stumped.

Adrian stepped forward and patted the pitch.

'You must watch your feet after you've bowled,' he said to him. 'You're not allowed to run on in the area between the two wickets. It kicks up rough stuff and helps the bowler at the other end.'

Little Ellis was aghast at the possibility that Adrian might think he had been trying to cheat.

'I'm very sorry, sir,' he said. 'I didn't mean . . .'

'I'm sure you didn't, my dear fellow. That was just a warning, that's all. I'm sure it won't happen again.'

Ellis knocked the next ball from so wide of the stumps that it glanced straight across Colville for four byes.

He was taken off after three more catastrophic overs and retired to long on, blinking back tears and fending off the jeers of his home supporters on the boundary.

Cricket, thought Adrian. It's so character-building.

After the collapse of Ellis the outcome was never really in doubt. The fast man at the other end was competent but soon exhausted. Weirder and wilder alternatives were tried, boys who dropped slow balls from a great height, boys with violent actions like windmills that produced gentle long hops, boys who bowled balls that bounced twice before reaching the middle of the pitch, but to no avail. The openers put on a stand of a hundred and twelve and the fourth-wicket partnership of Rice and Hooper scored the final runs as Narborough church clock struck six.

Adrian watched it all with raised eyebrows and an impartial smile. Hugo boiled and seethed and glared, glancing miserably from time to time at the stony figure of his headmaster who sat perched on a shooting-stick next to Professor Trefusis.

'An instructive match,' said Adrian as he and Hugo

pulled up the stumps. 'I thought we were in real trouble at one stage.'

'I can't understand what the hell went wrong with Ellis,' said Hugo. 'I really thought he was the most gifted cricketer in the school. An England prospect even.'

'He's young yet. Temperament is the problem there, I fancy. I tried to calm him down and encourage him to get on with his natural game, but he was a bit overawed. Don't give up on him, he's learnt a lot today.'

'He'll learn a bloody sight more after I'm through with him.'

The Narborough team, hot and limp with exertion and defeat, saw them off in the driveway. Hugo stood with them, sipping at a can of beer.

'Three cheers for Chartham Park,' called Malthouse, their captain, raising his arm with an attempt at casual gallantry. 'Hip-ip.'

'Ray!' murmured Narborough.

'Hip-ip!'

'Ray!'

'Hip-ip.'

'Ray.'

'Three cheers for Narborough Hall,' shouted a flushed and triumphant Hooper, punching the air. 'Hip-Hip!'

'Hooray!' bellowed Chartham.

'Hip-Hip-Hip!'

'Hooray!'

'Hip-Hip-Hip-Hip!'

'HOORAY!'

'Goodbye then, Hugo. See you for the return match.'

'We'll pulverise you.'

'Of course you will.'

A madness suddenly possessed Adrian. With a pounding heart he leant forward and whispered in Hugo's ear.

'I was awake, you know.'

'What?'

'That night in Harrogate. I was awake all the time.'

Hugo looked annoyed.

'I know you bloody were. Do you think I'm an idiot?'

Adrian stared open-mouthed and then burst out laughing.

'You total . . . you complete . . . you . . .'

Trefusis stepped forward.

'Well, young man, you've earned me a thousand pounds. Here's two hundred, my original stake.'

'Oh really,' said Adrian. 'I couldn't.'

'Of course you could,' he pushed a bundle of notes at him. 'Tremendous display.'

'Yes, they're not a bad bunch, are they?' Adrian looked on affectionately as his team climbed into the minibus.

'No, no, no. You!'

'Professor?'

'I knew that the man who wrote those artfully disguised second-hand essays, who disgorged such specious and ill-thought-out nonsense with such persuasive and brilliant flair wouldn't let me down. You've clearly a genius for deceit and chicanery. I look forward to seeing you next term.'

Ten

'Well!' said Trefusis when Adrian had finished. 'Did I really say that? "A genius for deceit and chicanery"? Did I really? And we had only just been introduced. How rude.'

'I didn't take it so.'

'Well of course not.'

Trefusis groped about with his right hand in the driver's side glove compartment until he found a figgy oatcake, which he inspected carefully, blowing off a piece of fluff before popping it into his mouth. 'My goodness, Adrian,' he mumbled through the crumbs, 'that was all so much more than I had bargained for. Tell me . . .'

'Yes?'

'The girl who was the Matron at Chartham . . .'

'Clare? What about her?'

'Did you really . . .? I mean the lard and the football pump and the jam and the urine and so . . . and so on . . . you really *did* . . .?'

'Oh yes,' said Adrian. 'Isn't that usual?'

'Well now, *usual*. Usual isn't the word I'd've . . .' Trefusis wound down the window distractedly.

'Well anyway,' said Adrian, 'there it all is.'

'Young people sometimes give me the impression that I have never lived at all.'

'Surely you must have had experiences of a similar nature?'

'Oddly, no. Of a similar nature? No. It is profoundly strange I know, but I have not.'

'Well apart from . . .'

'Apart from what, dear boy?'

'Apart from, you know . . . that night in the lavs in Cambridge.'

'I *beg* your pardon? Oh . . . oh yes, of course. Apart from that, obviously.' Trefusis nodded contentedly. 'Now, unless I am more hugely mistaken than God, our service-station should be just around the corner. Ah! here we are. Petrol and lemon tea, I think. The car could do with a fill up and we could do with a fillip, hee-ho.'

Adrian, as the car swung off the road, marvelled, like many an English traveller before him, at the trimness and appealing order of continental service-stations. Euro-colours might be a little too bright and primary, but better this luminous cleanliness than the drab squalor of British motorway stops. How could they afford to have all the litter swept up and the paintwork so freshly maintained? Everything neat, from the little hanging-baskets of geraniums to the merry pantiled roofs that offered shaded parking to hot and weary travellers . . . a metallic gleam suddenly caught Adrian's eye. He gaped in astonishment.

Down the end of the same row into which Trefusis was inexpertly manoeuvring the Wolseley was parked a green BMW with British licence plates and a Hoverspeed 'GB' sticker.

'Donald, look! It's them.'

'I should hope so too. I was most specific as to time.'

'You were what?'

'And don't forget, dearest lad, that the verb "to be" takes a nominative complement.'

'What?'

'You said "it's them". What you meant of course was, "it's they".' Trefusis pulled up the handbrake and opened the door. 'But that's unbearable pedantry. Who, in their right mind, says "it's they"? No one. Well? Are you going to sit in the car or are you going to come along with me and hear me practise my Luxembourgeois?'

They took their trays of tea and buns to a table near the window. The couple from the BMW was sitting in a non-smoking section at the other end of the dining area.

'It won't do to talk to them,' said Trefusis. 'But it's good to know they are there.'

'Who *are* they?'

'Their names are Nancy and Simon Hesketh-Harvey and they have been kindly provided by an old friend of mine.'

'They're on our side then?'

Trefusis didn't answer. He bobbed his teabag up and down in its glass and thought for a moment.

'After the war,' he said at length, 'Humphrey Biffen, Helen Sorrel-Cameron, a mathematician called Bela Szabó and I had an idea.'

'At last,' said Adrian. 'The truth.'

'You shall judge. We had all of us worked together

on Enigma and become increasingly interested, in our own ways, in the possibilities of language and machines. Bela knew very well that the path to what is now called computing had been opened up in Britain and America and that digital machines would one day be capable of linguistic programming. Turing's work at Bletchley had shown that the old Höllerin-based punched-card systems would soon be a thing of the past. Algorithmic, low-level mathematical languages would be followed by higher level modular intelligent languages giving rise, ultimately, to heuristic machines.'

'Heuristic?'

'Capable of learning by mistakes, of operating, like human beings, through trial and error. My interest in all this was not mathematical, nor especially social. I was not frightened of machines becoming cleverer than human beings, nor of their in some way "taking over". I was however *very* interested in the development of new languages.'

'On account of your having learnt all the existing ones and being in danger of growing bored?'

'You exaggerate charmingly. Bela returned to Hungary after the war, Humphrey married Lady Helen, as you know, and became a schoolmaster. I stayed on at Cambridge. But we continued to work, where possible, on our idea for a perfect high level language that could be spoken by both machines and human beings. The dream, you see, was to invent an international language, like Esperanto, that would also serve as a *lingua franca* between man and machine.'

'But surely the ideal solution would be to teach a machine to speak English?'

'Well I'm very much afraid that this is what will happen. We had no way of predicting the arrival of the microprocessor, or perhaps I should say, we lacked the imagination to predict its arrival. The cost of computing has been reduced by a factor of a million in ten years. It is simply astonishing. This means that you can now buy for one pound processing ability that would have cost you a million pounds in nineteen-seventy-one.'

'But isn't that good?'

'Marvellous, simply marvellous. But of no use to me. There are now dozens of languages at work in computing. Cobol, Forth, C, Lisp, Superlisp, Fortran, BASIC, Pascal, Logo, simply scores of the wretched things. We have a new Babel. This will sort itself out as soon as computing power comes still further down in price. Before the end of the century we shall have computers that recognise existing human languages.'

'So what's the problem?'

'Oh, there's no problem. None at all. We spent thirty years mining what turned out to be a barren seam, that's all. Nothing wrong with that. That's academe-biz, as they say. I tell you this to give you the background of my relationship with Szabó. We stayed in touch, do you see? He in Budapest, I in Cambridge.'

Adrian said that he saw.

'Two years ago Szabó made a curious discovery. He had shifted the focus of his attentions over the years from pure mathematics to electronics, acoustic engineering and any number of invigorating related fields. Hungary is very good about that sort of thing.

That coloured cube that everyone is playing with at the moment is Hungarian, of course. I suspect that it is the advantage of speaking a language understood by so few that has turned the Magyars into such experts in numbers and shapes and dimensions. There is even a Hungarian mathematician at the moment who is close to achieving what was once thought to be the impossible. He is on the brink of squaring the circle. Or is it circling the square? Whichever.'

'A Hungarian is the only man who can follow you into a revolving door and come out first,' quoted Adrian.

'Exactly. Szabó is just one such hornery cuss. He had been working, during the seventies, on cures for the common stutter, experimenting with ways of playing back the speech of a stutterer into their ears as they spoke. Apparently if a subject hears his own voice back a split second after he has spoken and while he is moving on to the next thing he wants to say, his stutter will be eliminated.'

'How baroque.'

'Baroque? If you say so.'

'But not very practical to go about the place in headphones, I should have thought.'

'Quite so. Far from a feasible cure for the affliction. Experience in this area, however, did lead Bela towards what turned out to be immensely fruitful researches into the speech centres of the brain. The subject that most interested him was that of lying or, as it were, *saying the thing which is not*. He wanted to find out what happened in the brain when people said things which were not true; to see, for example, whether there is any difference between telling a lie, making a mistake in memory and inventing a fiction, all of which involve, in one way or another, saying the thing which is not. Thus a man might say: "I have to work late tonight, darling," or "The German for a chive is *ein Zwiebel*," or "Once upon a time there was a fabulous trouser-eating dragon called Geoffrey." These might all be taken to be examples of a lie. The speaker is in fact *not* going to be working late that night, he is instead going to the flat of his mistress there to conjoin with her in carnal riot. That is an Alpha-type lie. In the second case the man's *brain* knows full well that *Zwiebel* is in fact the German for "onion" and that the word he is groping for is *Schnittlauch*, but his mind is unable for the moment to gain access to that information. His statement that *ein Zwiebel* is the German for "a chive" is therefore a Beta-type lie. And lastly, there never was a fabulous trouser-eating dragon called Geoffrey, once upon any time and what is more the speaker knows it: a Gamma-type pseudology. The Alpha-type, the first kind of lie, the moral lie, if you like, the lie that disturbs the conscience of the speaker, might well be detectable using a polygram machine, the other two most certainly will not be.'

'Your friends are leaving,' said Adrian.

The BMW couple had stood up and were making for the exit.

'Excellent!' said Trefusis. 'That means we really *are* being followed.'

'How do you mean?'

'If Nancy and Simon leave the rendezvous first it is a sign that we are not alone. If they let *us* leave first, it means that we go unobserved.'

'Moscow Rules, George. Moscow Rules all the way.'

'I beg your pardon?'

'Nothing. So who is following us?'

'I dare say we shall find out. Drink your tea precipitately. We must not lag too far behind.'

Out in the car park the BMW had gone. Trefusis opened the driver's side door of the Wolseley, while Adrian looked around for signs of other cars preparing to start up in pursuit.

'Can't see any likely looking candidates,' he said.

Trefusis stooped and picked something from the ground. He came up holding a thick oblong of folded paper which he handed to Adrian across the top of the Wolseley.

'This was wedged in the hinges of the door. What does it say?'

Adrian unfolded the oblong and spread it over the roof.

'I think it must be in code, or cypher, rather. Or whichever one was which. Either way it's gibberish to me. You take a look.'

Adrian revolved the sheet of paper to face Trefusis.

'Young Nancy takes after her mother,' he said. 'It's in Volapük.'

'In what?'

'Volapük. A very silly international language devised at least a hundred years ago by a charming man called Johann Schleyer. "Vol" means world in his language and "pük" means speak. If he had known that in English it meant vomit, he might have chosen more carefully.'

'And what does the note say?'

'It seems that we are being followed by two cars, one a French-registered blue Lemon BX, whatever that might be, the other a white Swiss Audi Four.'

'They must mean a Citroën BX and an Audi Quattro, I should think.'

'That would seem to make sense. Well, this is refreshing to know, is it not?'

'What, that we're being followed?'

'Yes.'

'But we stick out like a sore thumb in this bloody jalopy.'

'I hope so. The element of surprise is absolutely crucial.'

'What element of surprise?'

'Exactly!' beamed Trefusis as he edged onto the autoroute and pointed the Wolseley towards Germany. 'That is what is so surprising.'

The staccato rush of cars travelling in the opposite direction reminded Adrian of interminable childhood journeys to the coast. He would gaze at his father's cocked wrists on the steering wheel or count all the four-legged animals in the fields as they passed, one for a sheep or cow, two for a horse, yawning repeatedly in a giddy cloud of car-sickness. He had had a trick of covering his ears with his hands and removing them rhythmically in time to the whoosh of each car as it passed the window.

He tried it again now.

'Are we there yet, Daddy?'

'Why do people always say that on car journeys?' asked Trefusis.

'It reminds them of when they were young.'

'Humph.'

'Anyway,' said Adrian. 'We were talking about lies.'

'So we were. Light me a cigarette, there's a good fellow.'

Adrian lit two from Trefusis's cigarette case and passed one over.

Trefusis took in a deep lungful of Gold Leaf.

'We can be fairly certain,' he said, 'that animals do not lie. It has been both their salvation and their downfall. Lies, fictions and untrue suppositions can create new human truths which build technology, art, language, everything that is distinctly of Man. The word "stone" for instance is not a stone, it is an oral pattern of vocal, dental and labial sounds or a scriptive arrangement of ink on a white surface, but man pretends that it is actually the thing it refers to. Every time he wishes to tell another man about a stone he can use the word instead of the thing itself. The word bodies forth the object in the mind of the listener and both speaker and listener are able to imagine a stone without seeing one. All the qualities of stone can be metaphorically and metonymically expressed. "I was stoned, stony broke, stone blind, stone cold sober, stonily silent," oh, whatever occurs. More than that, a man can look at a stone and call it a weapon, a paperweight, a doorstep, a jewel, an idol. He can give it function, he can possess it.'

'Surely when a bird uses a twig for nesting material it is doing the same thing?'

'Birds collect for nests much as we expand our lungs a dozen or so times a minute in order to suck in air or, in our case, tobacco smoke. It is, or so I am reliably informed by those who know, an entirely instinctive mechanism. Animals do not have the lying capability of man.'

'Keats's negative capability?'

'To some extent, yes. Within our brains connections are made and stored all the time. This word signifies this thing, this fact actually occurred, this experience was in truth undergone; the whatness and whichness of everything is established. Thus I ask you, "What did you drink just now?" and you reply "lemon tea" because lemon tea and your recent drinking are connected. If you deliberately wish to lie you *think* "lemon tea" – you can't help that because the link is there – but you search for some other drinking material and say, for example, "apple juice". A link is now made between your recent drinking activities, lemon tea and apple juice. The strongest link, however, is between the drinking activity and lemon tea because it is the true one. The link between what you drank and apple juice exists, because you created it. But it only exists through the link with the lemon tea. Are you following me?'

'Like a panther,' lied Adrian.

'The details of a lie are harder to recall than the truth, because they are less strongly linked in the mind. The act of remembering is literally just that: the act of reassembling the members of something. If the members are illusory it is naturally more difficult to enact this mental reconstruction.'

'So your friend Szabó discovered what happens in the brains of people when they lie and has invented some kind of lie-detector, is that it?'

'No, no. He did much more than that. He discovered a lie-*deflector*!'

Adrian watched the smoke from his cigarette being sucked through the quarter-light of the car. He had an awful feeling, deep down inside him, that he was somehow more than a passenger on this journey, more than an observer.

'A lie-deflector?' he said.

'Let us suppose that all true things are connected in the brain by pathways called A-type pathways and all untrue things are connected by B-type pathways.'

'Okay.'

'Imagine a machine which inhibits the brain from making any B-type connections. When under the influence of such a machine, the subject is simply unable to lie.'

'And this is what your friend Szabó has come up with?'

'Such is his claim.'

Adrian thought for a moment.

'There are some lies,' he said, 'which you tell . . . which people tell . . . so often that they believe them themselves. What about those?'

'However much you may consciously believe what you are saying, your brain knows the truth, and has made connections accordingly. You may imagine, for instance, that on holiday in Sardinia you witnessed a gang of twelve bandits robbing a bank with machine guns and hand grenades, you may repeat this story to the dismay of all your acquaintances at every dinner party to which those friends have made the rash mistake of inviting you, such that you believe it surely and wholly. Nonetheless, buried under the dead neural weight of all these convictions, your brain knows perfectly well that in fact there were only two

302

bandits with nothing more than a water-pistol and a spud-gun between them. Your brain was there too, you see, and it has registered the truth.'

'I do see. I do.'

'Szabó claims the machine is in fact as much a memory- retrieval device as a lie-inhibitor. It can just as easily make the subject disinter the German for "chive" as disgorge the details of his true whereabouts on the night in question.'

'Wow.'

'W, as you rightly remark, ow. Or, as they say in Poland, "Vov".'

'And where do *you* fit into all this?'

'Nowhere in the development of the machine. Bela and I have corresponded over the decades, and a little over a year ago he began to include in his letters to me references to his development of Mendax, as he has fancifully dubbed this fruit of his intellectual loins. Last July Istvan Moltaj, a violinist friend of his, left Hungary to take part in the Salzburg Festival. Bela entrusted him with a sheaf of papers relating to Mendax. The idea was that Moltaj should give the papers to me. We had an appointment to meet at Mozart's Geburtshaus in the Getreidegasse. It is apparent that someone had either been following Moltaj or had intercepted Bela's letter to me arranging the rendezvous. He was there most unpleasantly killed, not ten yards away from us, as we both have cause to remember.'

'And he never got to give you the papers?'

'Moltaj had taken the sensible precaution of leaving a package for my collection at the reception desk of the Goldener Hirsch Hotel. The package contained a sheaf of musical manuscript paper. A duet for piano and violin. The music was cacophonous in the extreme but the notes corresponded to letters which spelt out a text in classical Volapük.'

'So you got it?'

'You may remember that on our return to England last year we were robbed?'

'They took your briefcase!'

'They did indeed.'

'But, Donald, if I may say so . . .'

'Yes?'

'Why didn't you post the papers or something? If they were willing to cut a man's throat in broad daylight . . . I mean just to go round with them in a briefcase in your car! Not exactly tradecraft, old man.'

'Tradecraft?'

'You know. Not how Sarratt would train Circus men to operate in the field.'

'Adrian, I'm rather afraid that you are gibbering.'

'Le Carré. Operational procedures. A good field man would have taken the papers and shoved them in a DLB or DLD.'

'A what?'

'A Dead Letter Box or Dead Letter Drop.'

'Oh.'

'Moscow Rules, George, old boy. Moscow Rules all the way.'

'Yes, no doubt a Dead Letter Drop would have answered perfectly. I should have thought of that. Instead I made a false copy of the manuscript and left the real one in Salzburg.'

'You did?'

'It seemed sensible,' said Trefusis.

'So the papers in the briefcase that was stolen . . .?'

'Were drivel. It must have taken them a long time to discover, read it which way they might, that the manuscript they took from us contained nothing more illuminating than pages three-two-three to three-six-seven of the Salzburg telephone directory.'

'And what exactly did you do with the real manuscript?'

'There was a very nice chambermaid at the hotel. She said she would look after it for me. Was that bad tradecraft too?'

'Well,' said Adrian. 'If she's still got it, it was good tradecraft, if she hasn't, it wasn't.'

Trefusis inclined his head gratefully. 'Don't look behind you,' he said, 'but there has been a white Citroën two cars behind us for the last twelve kilometres. As to whether it's a BX or not, I really couldn't say.'

Adrian looked behind him.

'You still haven't told me,' he said, 'who was responsible for cutting this violinist's throat . . . what was his name again?'

'Moltaj.'

'Right. Do you know who killed him?'

'So many people would love to get their hands on a machine that can inhibit pseudology, mendacity and falsehood. The police, Intelligence services, all sorts and conditions of interested agencies and institutions. Bela, like any good scientist, is worried that he may have opened the door to something rather frantic, something rather ghastly.'

'What have I done? What have I done? Have we

305

any business taking away people's right to lie? That sort of thing.'

'Questions of free will certainly do seem to arise. It is perfectly possible to live a life from cradle to grave that is entirely dishonest. One might never reveal one's true identity, the yearnings and cravings of one's innermost self, even to the most intimate circle of family and friends; never really speak the truth to anyone. Priests and psychotherapists may believe that the confessional-box or the analysis session reveals truths, but you know and I know and every human being knows that we lie all the time to all the world. Lying is as much a part of us as wearing clothes. Indeed, Man's first act in Eden was to give names to everything on earth, our first act of possession and falsehood was to take away a stone's right to be a stone by imprisoning it with the name "stone". There are in reality, as Fenellosa said, no nouns in the Universe. Man's next great act was to cover himself up. We have been doing so ever since. We feel that our true identities shame us. Lying is a deep part of us. To take it away is to make us something less than, not more than, human. So at least Bela fears.'

'Yes,' said Adrian. 'You still haven't told me who killed Moltaj.'

'The Hungarians have a wonderful word,' said Trefusis. 'It is *puszipajtás* and means roughly "someone you know well enough to kiss in the street". They are a demonstrative and affectionate people, the Hungarians, and enthusiastic social kissers. "Do you know young Adrian?" you might ask and they might reply, "I *know* him, but we're not exactly *puszipajtás*."'

'I have no doubt whatever in my mind,' said Adrian, 'that all this is leading somewhere.'

'A few weeks ago Bela's grandson arrived in England. He is a chess-player of some renown, having achieved grandmaster status at last year's Olympiad in Buenos Aires. No doubt you followed his excellent match against Bent Larsen?'

'No,' said Adrian. 'I missed his match against Bent Larsen and somehow his matches against Queer Karpov and Faggoty Smyslov and Poofy Petrosian also managed to pass me by.'

'Tish and hiccups. Bent is a perfectly common Danish Christian name and it would do you no harm, Master Healey, to acquire a little more patience.'

'I'm sorry, Donald, but you do talk *around* a subject so.'

'Would you have said that?' Trefusis sounded surprised.

'I would.'

'I will then straight to the heart of the matter hie me. Stefan, the grandson of Bela, came to England a fortnight ago to play in the tournament at Hastings. I received a message to meet him in a park at Cambridge. Parker's Piece to be exact. It was ten o'clock of a fine June night. That is not extraneous colour, I mention the evening to give you the idea that it was *light*, you understand?'

Adrian nodded.

'I walked to the rendezvous point. I saw Stefan by an elm tree clutching a briefcase and looking anxious. My specifying that the tree was an elm,' said Trefusis, 'is of no consequence and was added, like this explanation of it, simply to vex you. The mention of the lad's anxiety, however, has a bearing. The existence of the briefcase is likewise germane.'

'Right.'

'As I approached, he pointed to a small shed or hut-like building behind him and disappeared into it. I followed him.'

'Ah! Don't tell me . . . the small shed or hut-like building was in fact a gentlemen's lavatory?'

'Meeting for the first time one of his grandfather's oldest friends, a man of whom he had heard much, Stefan naturally embraced me, bestowing a friendly kiss on each cheek. We were *puszipajtás*, do you see? Stefan then knelt to open his briefcase. It was at this point that two policemen emerged from a cubicle, making unpleasant insinuations and an arrest.'

'Is that a zeugma or a syllepsis?'

'It was an impertinence and an inconvenience.'

'It was in a convenience certainly . . . But you can hardly blame them. I mean, two men kissing in a lavatory and then one of them getting down on his knees . . . what was he thinking of?'

'The job in hand,' said Trefusis coldly.

'Oo-er!'

'Adrian, it is a long walk back to England. I suggest you keep your putrid sense of humour in check.'

'I'm sorry.' Adrian clamped his mouth shut.

'It is possible, I grant you,' Trefusis continued, 'that a person stumbling upon such a *tableau* might be tempted to place constructions of a deleterious nature upon it, but only if their minds were already composed of stuff so gross and rank in nature as to be themselves guilty of as much impropriety as the most shameless erotic miscreant in the land. Stefan, at any rate, found himself wholly perplexed by events. I managed to communicate to him in Hungarian, however, as we awaited the police van. I . . . er . . . created a scene and he was able to grab his briefcase and "make good his escape" as the newspapers have it.'

'What sort of a scene?'

'A scene-y sort of a scene. Just a general, you know, scene.'

'What sort of a scene?'

'Does it matter what sort of a scene?'

'Come on, Donald. What sort of a scene?'

'Oh very well. If you must know, I let out a screech of animal lust and attempted to remove the trousers of the officer detaining me.'

'You did *what*?'

'Well I have no doubt you could have dreamt up a dozen more appropriate schemes, Adrian, but it was all that occurred to me under the duress of the moment. I scrabbled at the unfortunate man's trouserings and while his companion leapt forward to rescue him from this parlous circumstance, Stefan found himself temporarily deoppilated. He returned to the Shoulder of Lamb where he left the item he had come up expressly to deliver and which I have with me now. Bob then arranged for his safe return to Hastings'

'Yes, I was meaning to ask you. How come Bob is involved in all this?'

'Bob is a friend.'

'Bletchley?'

'Bob has been involved in all kinds of things in his time. He had his tongue ripped out by the Japanese.'

'*What?*'

'Yes, but he doesn't talk about it.'

'Oh ha frigging ha. You *still* haven't told me who the enemy is.'

Trefusis reached for a figgy oatcake.

'Enemy?'

'Yes, enemy. The people who robbed us in Germany and stole your briefcase. The people who killed Moltaj and who are,' Adrian craned his neck round, 'still hot on our arses.'

'Well now, it would seem we have two "enemies", Adrian. Moltaj was killed by a servant of the Magyar Republic of Hungary, I think there is no doubt of that. Bela's employers have no intention of letting his invention leave their country.'

'And now they are following us?'

'No, we are being followed by enemy number two. It was they who robbed us in Germany last year.'

'And who are they?'

'Well,' said Trefusis, 'I was rather hoping *you* might know that, Adrian.'

Eleven

I

In the corridor, Rudi nearly collided with an enormously fat man with a small head and lank hair. Rudi managed, with a supreme effort of balance and coordination, learnt on the ski-slopes of Innsbruck, to avoid the calamity of dropping the drinks tray he was carrying and proceeded, trembling, on his way, cursing under his breath the rudeness and clumsiness of the guests as he went. Probably a music journalist in Salzburg for the Festival; such gracelessness was to be expected from the press.

Rudi tapped gently on the door to the sitting room of the Franz-Josef Suite and listened for a reply. This was his first week at the Österreichischer Hof and he was not certain if it was done simply to knock and enter as he would have done at the Hotel der Post in Fuschl-am-See where he had learnt his trade. The Österreichischer Hof was altogether smarter than the Hotel der Post and things were done here on the international scale, with taste, style, courtliness, discretion and just a *Schluck* of Austrian *Gemütlichkeit*.

There was no reply from within. Yet someone had ordered a bottle of Absolut lemon vodka and three glasses, someone had commanded room-service. Surely it was reasonable to suppose that someone was in the room? He knocked again and waited.

Still nothing. Most puzzling.

Rudi balanced the tray on his shoulder, leant forward towards the door, and coughed purposefully.

From inside he heard a voice. An English voice.

'*Entschuldigen Sie* . . .' Rudi called through the keyhole.

He could sense that his husky tones were not penetrating the thick wood of the door. Rudi was a little nervous. In the kitchens yesterday he had caused a beautiful puff-ball of Salzburger Nockerl, the hotel's speciality, to deflate by dropping a fork into it by mistake, and two days ago – Rudi blushed at the memory – two days ago in the dining room he had spilt some kirsch down the shirt-front of Signor Muti, the famous conductor. Fortunately the *maestro* had been wearing one of his famous black polo-neck shirts and the stain had not shown up so much, but the memory was painful to Rudi.

English people. Were they deaf?

'Excusing me!'

Rudi knocked again, his head leaning against the door. He heard the voice still.

'. . . incontinently and savagely beautiful, not unlike a small chaffinch, but much larger and with less of a salty after-tang . . .'

This Rudi could not understand. The word 'beautiful' was familiar certainly. English girls who came to stay with their families at the Hotel der Post liked to say that it was 'a very beautiful morning this morning, Rudi', that the mountain and the lake and the Schloss were 'simply beautiful' and sometimes, when he had been lucky, that his hair and eyes and his legs and his *Schwanz* were so 'beautiful'. Beautiful he knew, but what was this 'chaffinch'? Of course! a green vegetable, like *Kohl* or *Kraut*, that was chaffinch. A strange conversation this man was having.

'. . . a certain degree of *Schadenfreude* under the circumstances is inevitable perhaps . . .'

'*Schadenfreude!*' He could speak German.

Rudi knocked until his knuckles were raw.

'*Entschuldigen Sie bitte, mein Herr. Hier ist der Kellner mit Ihren Getränken!*'

'. . . a message delivered by motor-bicycle. A curious new phenomenon these despatch riders . . .'

Rudi could wait no longer. He swallowed twice, turned the handle and entered.

A beautiful suite, the Franz-Josef. Herr Brendel the pianist had stayed there last week and the Bösendorfer Grand that had been installed for him had not yet been collected. They should keep the piano here always, Rudi thought. With the flowers and the cigarette boxes and long flowing curtains, it conspired to give the room the look of a film set from the nineteen-thirties. With great care he set down his drinks tray on top of the piano and listened again to the English voice.

'. . . this rider, standing in the threshold holding out a clipboard to be signed, reminded me at first of a copy of Izaac Walton's *Compleat Angler* that I have in my possession. Bound in leather, lavishly tooled and a lasting joy . . .'

'Your drinks are arrived, my sir.'

313

'. . . of the package that he delivered I can say only this . . .'

The voice was coming through from the bedroom. Rudi approached nervously.

'. . . it shocked me right down to my foundation garments. From stem to stern I quivered . . .'

Rudi straightened his bow-tie and tapped loosely on the half-open bedroom door with the back of his hand.

'Sir, your drinks that you have ordered . . .'

Rudi broke off.

The door he had knocked on so lightly had swung open to reveal a man sitting on the end of the bed, soaked from head to foot in blood. He faced a writing table on which stood a small radio.

'. . . I suppose there are degrees of startlement, much as there are degrees of anything. If there is an official scale comparable to, for example, the Beaufort, Moh or Richter Scales and if that scale be measured from one to ten, I would say that on this Trefusian Scale of Abject Bestartlement I scored at least a creditable 9.7, certainly from the European judges. The East Germans would probably have been less generous, but even they could not have failed to give me 9.5 for artistic impression . . .'

Rudi hugged the door-handle and half swung from the door, staring at the dead man with innocent surprise and wonder, like a child watching donkeys copulate.

A knock on the sitting-room door brought him to his senses.

A high English voice called through the sitting room.

'Martin! Are you there? Martin!'

Rudi jumped. This was witchcraft.

Two men had entered the sitting room, one silver-haired, the other closer to Rudi's age. They were smiling.

'Ah, lemon vodka on the piano. Very much Martin's poison.'

Rudi gasped.

'*Sie sind . . . sie sind!*' said Rudi, pointing at the older man.

'*Was bin ich?*' the man asked in surprise.

So he was German, this man. But the voice. The voice was . . .

Rudi pointed to the bedroom.

'*Da drinnen sitzt ein Mann!*'

'Is there something wrong with him, Donald?'

'*Er ist tot!*'

'Oh dear,' said Trefusis, hurrying forwards. 'Please not. Please not!'

Adrian followed him into the bedroom.

'. . . I will let you know, those of you who are interested, of course, the others will simply have to guess. Meanwhile if you have been, then continue to and don't even think of stopping.'

'Well, as the Professor has just told us, that was the last of the current series of *Wireless Essays from the Desk of Donald Trefusis*. Half an hour of World News in a moment, followed by *Meridian*. BBC World Service. This is Lond – '

Adrian switched off the radio and brought his gaze to bear upon the young man on the bed.

His throat had been cut in a wide crescent from one ear to the other. It was as if a second mouth had been

315

cut beneath the chin. Even the lining of the poor man's jacket had been ripped open. As with Moltaj the previous year, the flap of skin had a gruesomely false, plastic, made-up appearance. Adrian supposed that just as genuine gunfire was said not to sound realistic, so genuine death had a falser air than the gore of the movies.

Rudi gestured towards the radio: *'Das waren Sie, nicht wahr?'*

Trefusis nodded vaguely. *'Jawohl, das war ich.'*

'Sind Sie Österreicher oder Deutscher?'

'Engländer.'

'Echt?'

'Echt,' said Trefusis. *'Hast du die Polizei schon telefoniert?'*

'Nein . . . ich bin nur zwei Minuten da . . .'

'Also.'

Trefusis crossed over to the writing table and picked up the radio.

'Und hast du jemanden gesehen?'

'Nein . . . nie – Moment! Ja, ein dicker Mann . . . sehr dick . . .'

'Mit kleinem Kopf and schlichten Haaren?'

'Ganz genau!'

'This young gentleman and I will await the police, Adrian.'

Adrian nodded. He felt sick, deeply sick. Sicker than when he had witnessed the death of Moltaj in Mozart's house, sicker than he had ever felt in his life. It was his fault. It was all his fault. From liar to murderer, like in the Æsop fable.

Trefusis had sat at the table and was scribbling on a sheet of hotel writing-paper. Adrian steeled himself to turn and look at the dead man again. The torn throat and the blood soaking into the sheets were disgusting enough, but somehow the savage shredding of the viscose lining of the jacket seemed a world more obscene. It revealed a wanton animal fury that struck fear into Adrian's soul.

'Adrian, I want you to deliver this note to the British Consulate,' said Trefusis. 'It is to be placed into the hands of the addressee himself. None other.'

Adrian looked at the name written on the envelope.

'Are you sure, Donald?'

'Quite sure, thank you. The Consulate is situated in number four Alter Markt. This has all gone quite far enough.'

II

Adrian made his way across the Makart Steg bridge that connected the Österreichischer Hof with the old town. The Salzach flowed beneath him, traffic flowed past him on the Staatsbrücke, crowds of holiday-makers flowed around him and dark, dreadful thoughts flowed within him.

Some of the shops on the Franz-Josef Kai had begun to place posters in their windows of the con-ductors and soloists due to appear in the Festival. An umbrella and luggage shop by the taxi-rank where Adrian waited was tricolated in the yellow and black livery of the Deutsche Gramophon Gesellschaft. A huge photograph of von Karajan glowered out at him, distrust apparent in the deep frown and clenched brows, contempt all too clear in the upward thrust of the chin and the sour wrinkle about the mouth. Two-horse fiacres flicked past him, bearing tourists and Festival-goers along the Müllner Hauptstraße. A bruised sky bore down. Adrian saw an image of the whole scene through a camera that was zooming outwards and outwards with himself in the centre diminishing and diminishing until he was a frozen part of a postcard pinned to a cork noticeboard in a warm suburban kitchen in England, eternally trapped, blessedly unable to move forwards or backwards in time or space.

At last, after twenty minutes, just as he was preparing to go in the shop and ask about buses, a Mercedes taxi drew up into the empty rank beside him.

'*Britisches Konsulat, bitte. Alter Markt vier.*'

'*Aber man kann es in zwei Minuten spazieren.*'

'*Scheiße.* Never mind. *Das macht nichts.* Take me there anyway. *Es sieht nach Regen aus.*'

Indeed, as Adrian spoke, the first drops began to fall, and by the time the cab drew up outside the Alter Markt, which would indeed have taken only a few minutes to reach on foot, the rain was pouring heavily. The taxi had not been able to go right to the door of the Consulate, so Adrian had to thread his way through the market itself, where people were gathering for shelter under a stall that sold artificial flowers. Number four itself was a small doorway next to the Oberbank a few doors down from Holzermayer's, which sold the *Mozartkugeln*, small chocolate marzipans wrapped in silver-foil portraits of Salzburg's most famous son. Adrian had bought a box for his mother there the previous summer.

'Sir David who?'

The woman at the desk was not helpful.

'Pearce. I know he's here, could you just tell him that . . . hang on.' Adrian took a Festival brochure from a pile on the desk and wrote in a white space on the back. 'Just show him that. I'm sure he'll see me.'

'Well I'm sorry, Mr . . . Telemackles, does it say?'

'Telemachus.'

'No one called Sir David anything at the Consulate. Never has been.'

'He's here. He must be here.'

'You're in trouble, I suppose? Want to borrow money?'

'No, no, no. Look, could you call the Consul and tell him that Telemachus insists on seing Sir David Pearce. Just tell him that.'

'I'll try his secretary,' she said, with a sniff.

Adrian tapped the desk with his fingers.

'Hello, Mitzi? It's Dinah at the front desk. Have a young gentleman here who says he wants to see a Sir David Pearce. I told him we . . . oh . . . I'll ask him.'

The receptionist favoured Adrian with a combative scowl.

'What was that name again, please?'

'Oh, Healey. Adrian Healey.'

'That's not what you said.'

'Never mind, just say Adrian Healey.'

'Mitzi? He says Adrian Healey . . . yes, I'll hold.'

She turned to Adrian again. 'Could you not do that?'

Adrian smiled. His fingers stopped tapping against the desk.

'Yes, dear? All right. You'll send someone down will you?'

319

'Everything all right?' Adrian asked.

'You're to wait. Chair over there.'

The words had hardly left her lips before Adrian heard a door closing upstairs and footsteps descending the stairs. A greasy-haired man in a powder-blue safari suit bounded towards him with hand outstretched.

'Adrian Healey?'

'We've met before, I think,' Adrian said. 'On the Stuttgart to Karlsruhe Autobahn.'

'Dickon Lister. Simply delighted. Come on up, why don't you?'

Adrian followed Lister up the central staircase and into a vast reception room. Sitting on a sofa, hunched over a small radio set, an earpiece plugged into his left ear, was a man in a Savile Row suit and St Matthew's College tie. Dickon Lister winked at Adrian and left the room.

'Hello, Uncle David.'

'It's unbelievable, Adrian, simply unbelievable!'

'I really don't see how . . .'

Uncle David waved him to silence.

'That's it! That must be it. Lillee has gone, that *must* be it.'

'What . . .'

'Haven't you heard? *Headingley*, man! Botham and Dilley put on one hundred and seventeen for the eighth wicket yesterday. Simply unbelievable. And now . . .' He clapped his thighs ecstatically. 'You won't believe this, Adrian, but Australia needed only one hundred and thirty to win today and they went from fifty-six for one to seventy-five for eight. Willis

320

has run through them like a tornado. What? No . . .
Chilly, you *cunt!*'

'What is it?'

'Chris Old has just dropped Bright. Wake up man!'
he boomed at the radio. 'It was five hundred to one
against an England victory in the betting tent today,
can you credit it? And if it wasn't for you and your
bloody Trefusis I'd be up there now watching the
most exciting Test Match in history. But oh no . . .'

He relapsed into silence again, wincing and grim-
acing at the radio.

Adrian settled himself on the edge of the sofa and
stared into the empty fireplace. He could hear a faint
hiss from Uncle David's earpiece. A clock ticked
slowly on the mantelpiece. Adrian felt the same
molten surge of guilt in his stomach he had felt so
often in the past. He could not for anything imagine
the outcome of the next twenty-four hours, but he
knew that it would be dreadful. Simply dreadful.

Finally Uncle David let out a great roar.

'That's it, that's it! Willis has taken eight for forty-
three! England have won! Ha, ha! Come on, my boy,
cheer up! Let's get Dickon to bring us in some
champagne, what do you say?'

'I think you should read this first.'

'What is it?' Uncle David took the envelope. 'A
demand for more money, Ade?'

Adrian watched Uncle David's face, as he read the
letter through, change from benign indifference to
irritation, anxiety and anger.

'Damn him! Damn him to Spitzburg in a cork-
bottomed raft. Where is he now?'

'Österreichischer Hof.'

'With Pollux?'

'No,' said Adrian. 'The thing is Pollux was dead when we got there. His throat had been . . . you know . . . like Moltaj.'

'Shitty damn. Police?'

'Not yet. There was a waiter though, so I suppose . . .'

'Doublefuck, hell and arse-tits. *Lister!* Where the hell is that man when you need him? *Lister!!*'

'Sir?'

'Get on to Dunwoody at Vienna. Tell him to fix the Salzburg Polizei soon, sooner, soonest. Pollux has been bollocksed in the Österreichischer Hof. Suite?' He clicked his fingers at Adrian. 'Come on boy! Suite? Room number!'

'Franz-Josef it was called, I think,' said Adrian. And don't call me sweet, he added to himself.

'You *think*? Was it or wasn't it?' Uncle David shook him by the shoulders.

'Yes!' shouted Adrian. 'The Franz-Josef.'

'Got that Lister? Full diplo tarpaulin over the whole farting mess. And a car for me and laughing boy here to be at the Goldener Hirsch by six o'clock this pip emma. You'd better come along as well.'

'Armed?'

'No,' said Adrian.

Uncle David's right hand slammed lazily into the side of Adrian's face.

'Don't give orders to my men, Ade, there's a dear.'

'Right,' said Adrian, sitting down on the edge of the sofa. 'I'm sorry.' Uncle David's signet-ring had caught the flesh above his left eyebrow and he blinked as a drop of blood oozed into his eye. The blinking

only caused the blood to sting his eyes more, so tears
sprang up to wash it away.

Uncle David nodded to Lister.

'Armed,' he said, 'and ever so slightly dangerous.'

Twelve

At one end of the Schubert Banqueting Room at the Goldener Hirsch Hotel a small platform had been arranged on which stood a chair and a table. On the table were set a gavel, a medicine bottle of purple liquid, a metal waste-paper bin, a box of matches, two small radio sets and a pair of headphones. The chair was set to one side, facing out into the rest of the room. Behind the stage a grey curtain obscured the back wall, trimly pleated like a schoolgirl's skirt. The impression given might have been that of a village hall in Kent preparing to host a Women's Institute lecture. Only the tondo portrait of Franz Schubert who gazed down at the room over round spectacles with an affable, academic and Pickwickian air and the collection of antlers distributed on the walls betrayed the Austrian bloodlines of the setting.

A cluster of people stood against the tall window at one side and twittered quietly to each other like shy early arrivals at a suburban orgy. Humphrey Biffen, white-haired and awkwardly tall, stooped like an attentive stork to hear his son-in-law Simon Hesketh-Harvey relate the details of the extraordinary cricket match that had taken place earlier that day in Yorkshire. Lady Helen Biffen was clucking sympathetically at a pale young man with red-rimmed eyes. Amidst them bustled Trefusis with a bottle of Eiswein.

At precisely the moment a gilt and porcelain clock on a plaster corbel by the window chimed six o'clock with dainty Austrian insistence, Sir David Pearce strode in, followed by a smiling Dickon Lister and an ovine Adrian.

Pearce looked about him, failing quite to conceal his satisfaction at the silence his arrival had caused to descend on the room. His manufactured angry glance flashed across at Biffen and his son-in-law, then back to Trefusis who was hurrying forward with three glasses and a bottle.

'Donald, you old barrel of piss!' barked Sir David. 'What are you doing with my man Hesketh-Harvey?'

'Ah, David. Prompt almost to the second! So grateful, so grateful.'

Trefusis proffered Lister a glass, blinking up at him.

'Have we . . .?'

'Lister, Professor. How do you do?'

'If you take hold of these two glasses, Adrian, then I can pour.'

Trefusis looked enquiringly at the swelling over Adrian's eye. Adrian inclined his head minimally towards Pearce and twisted his own ring-finger to indicate the cause of the cut. Trefusis bobbed with comprehension and began gingerly to pour the wine.

'I think you'll like this, Mr Lister . . . oh dear, "Mr Lister"! How inelegant of me. That's worse than "Lord Claude" isn't it? Or "Professor Lesser", come to that. This is called Eiswein, by the way. Are you familiar with it?'

'Ice vine?'

'Eiswein, yes.' Adrian watched with amusement the light of lecture come into Trefusis's eyes as he backed Lister into a corner and began to preach. 'They allow, you know, the full effects of the *pourriture noble*, or *Edelfäule* as they call it here, to take effect on the grape, such that the fruit simply glistens with rot and sugar. They then take the most audacious risk. They leave the grape on the vine and await the first frost. Sometimes, of course, the frost comes too late and the fruit has withered; sometimes too early – before it is yet fully purulent with botrytis. But when, as in this vintage, the conditions concatenate ideally, the result is – I'm sure you'll agree – vivid and appealing. One's sweet tooth returns with age, you know.'

Lister sipped his wine with every evidence of appreciation. Trefusis poured a glass for Sir David and one for Adrian. The overpowering bouquet of thick, honeyed grape almost made Adrian, his head still buzzing from the blow he had received from Uncle David, his mind still dizzy with apprehension, swoon. As he blinked and steadied himself, his focusing eyes met the sad, solemn gaze of Humphrey Biffen who smiled sweetly from the corner and looked away.

'Hum ho,' said Trefusis. 'I am supposing that we had better proceed. Adrian, I wonder if you wouldn't mind accompanying me to the dais?'

Adrian drained his wine-glass, handed it with what he hoped was a flourish to Dickon Lister and followed

Trefusis to the platform. He could not rid himself of the suspicion that this whole charade had been rigged to expose him. But exposure as what, to whom or to what end, he could not for the life of him figure out.

'If you would sit here,' said Trefusis indicating the single chair. 'I think we might be ready to bully off.'

Facing his audience like a conjuror's stooge, with Trefusis behind him at his prop-table, Adrian looked down at his shoes to avoid the stare of expectant faces that were turned towards him. Enticing sounds floated up through the window from the central courtyard bar below; the prattle of drinkers; tinkles of ice and glasses and laughter; a horn concerto by that same Mozart who was born three and half centuries after this hotel had been built and almost exactly two centuries before Adrian had gulped his first lungful of air. The funeral march of Siegfried would have suited his mood better than this foolishly exuberant gallop.

Behind him Trefusis cleared his throat. 'If I might have everyone's attention . . .?'

An unnecessary request, thought Adrian. Every eye in the room was already fixed firmly on the stage.

'Do sit down, everyone, I beg. There are chairs for all. So! That is much better.' Lister had ignored Trefusis's invitation to be seated and stood in the doorway with his legs apart. Whether he imagined he was deterring entrance or egress, Adrian could not decide.

'Perhaps I can prevail upon you to lock the door, Mr Lister . . . ah, I see that you have already done so. Excellent! Now then, I think we all know Adrian Healey. He is Sir David Pearce's nephew, on the distaff. Sir David, of course, is a well-known servant of the government, by which I mean he is not well-known at all, for his department is a clandestine one. His assistant Dickon Lister you see guarding the doorway like Cerberus. They, on behalf of their government, are most interested in a system devised by my friend Bela Szabó. Sir David as an old tutee of mine from university has long known of my association with Szabó, whose distinguished grandson, Grandmaster Stefan Szabó, is with us today.'

Adrian looked at the young man with eyes fresh from weeping who sat between Biffen and Lady Helen. Nothing in the shape of his head or the set of his expression indicated anything of the abstract or logical genius that marked out the chess champion. A rather ordinary, innocent looking fellow. But sad: very, very sad.

'I had hoped that Bela's other grandson, Martin, would be with us too. As I think you all know he was killed today.'

Five sets of eyes bored into Adrian, who coloured and looked down again.

'Also with us are Humphrey Biffen and his wife Lady Helen, old friends and colleagues of Bela and myself. Their son-in-law, Simon Hesketh-Harvey, is here too. As it falls out Simon works in the same department as Sir David.'

'Or at least did until six o'clock this evening,' growled Sir David. 'I'll have your arse for a plate-rack, Hesketh-Harvey.'

'But then of course Simon and Mr Lister are not the only people to have been in your employ, are they, Sir David? I believe I am right in saying that young Master Healey here has been drawing a stipend from you for the last two years at least.'

Adrian closed his eyes and tried to concentrate on Mozart.

'But let us get things in order. Two years ago, Szabó, when still an obedient Hungarian scientist, had been to Salzburg for a conference. There he had hidden papers relating to his Mendax machine. And not a moment too soon. Six months following his return to Budapest, the Hungarian authorities had found out about his work and were demanding to be shown the fruits of it. Your department, David, had heard of Mendax too and became determined that Britain must certainly do its best to gain possession of so intriguing a device – if only as a means of impressing your American *confrères*. The world had just learnt about poor dear Anthony Blunt, we must remember, and I am sure there must have been an overwhelming desire within your Service to win gorgeous trophies to lay before the feet of your betters. You supposed that were Szabó to try to dispose of Mendax then I, as his oldest friend outside Hungary, would in some manner be involved.'

'And so you were, old love.'

'It is true that Szabó sent me a letter last year. He wrote of his wish for me to collect the documents he had hidden in Salzburg. I was requested to be at Mozart's Geburtshaus at two p.m. on the seventh of July where a contact would be awaiting me by a diorama of the supper scene from *Don Giovanni*. I have no doubt you intercepted this letter to me, Sir David. Quite right too, I don't complain of that.'

'Too bloody bad if you did, Professor.'

'Neatly put. So, what happened next? Well, Adrian, the eyes and ears of Sir David Pearce, accompanied me to the rendezvous. My contact at the Geburtshaus was to be a friend of Szabó's named Istvan Moltaj, a violinist officially present in Salzburg for the Festival. So far so splendid.'

'So far so obvious.'

'Well, now to something rather less obvious perhaps.'

Adrian wondered why this meeting seemed to be developing into a public dialogue between Donald and Uncle David.

'I wonder if you have ever heard, Sir David, of Walton's Third Law?'

'No matter how much you shake it, the last drop always runs down your leg?'

'Not quite. It was a wartime SIS convention. If a meeting is set up and a time for it given in the twelve-hour clock − using an a.m. or p.m. suffix − then the meeting is understood to be called for a time thirty-three minutes earlier than that designated. What Adrian would call tradecraft, I believe. Accordingly Moltaj met me not at two p.m. on the appointed day, but at one twenty-seven p.m. At this meeting he told me where to find the Mendax papers. They were to be collected by me from the reception desk here at the Goldener Hirsch. Moments after imparting this information, Moltaj's throat was cut by someone, I must assume, who was blessedly unfamiliar with Walton's Third Law. A few days later, your man Lister, acting, I have no doubt, on information received from Adrian, made a rather vulgar attempt to relieve me of the papers in an Autobahn lay-by in West Germany.'

Sir David leant back in his chair and looked round at Lister, still standing in the doorway. 'Were you vulgar, Lister? I'm sorry to hear that. See me afterwards.'

'Vulgar and unsuccessful. I had left the papers here. I knew perfectly well that Adrian was not to be trusted. That is why I ensured that he was always by my side. Was it not Don Corleone who kept his friends close, but his enemies closer? How could Don Trefusis do less?'

Adrian opened his mouth to speak, but decided against it.

'The technical data on Mendax were securely locked in the safe here at the hotel. But Szabó had also built a working Mendax machine, which he had split into two and entrusted to his grandsons, Stefan and poor Martin. Stefan smuggled out his half in a radio set belonging to another member of his chess delegation and presented it to me in a Cambridge public lavatory a fortnight ago. Martin was to have given me the other half this afternoon in the Hotel Österreichischer Hof, but his throat was cut before he was able to do so. It seems that by this time the killer had worked out how Walton's Third Law operated. That, my dears, is the brief history of Szabó's attempt to get Mendax to me. Does anyone have any questions?'

'If you had left the entire business to us, Tre-blasted-fusis, this whole sordid shambles would have been avoided,' said Sir David.

'I wonder. A problem that has been exercising me mightily is the killing of Moltaj. He was an innocent musician delivering a message for a friend. We have no reason to imagine that he knew about Mendax, no grounds for supposing that he presented a threat to anyone. The Hungarians are not nowadays noted for their savagery in these matters – unlike the East Germans or the British. What conceivable ends could the death of Moltaj serve? It seems to me that this is far from being a trivial issue.'

Trefusis lit a cigarette and allowed the import of his question to sink in. Adrian had done with his inspection of the floor and had now started on the ceiling. He tried to believe that he was a thousand miles and years away.

'Well, we will return to the "Why" later,' said Trefusis. 'The "Who" is interesting also. I saw the killer, as it happens. A very fat man with lank hair and a small head.'

'Who cares?' said Pearce. 'Some bloody Hungo knife artist. Probably halfway across Czecho by now.'

'I think not-o, David-o.'

Sir David put his hands behind his head. 'Donald, give me listen. If you press that wonderful mind of yours into service you will find, after due stock-taking, adding up, taking away, knitting, purling and tacking, that the score is one and a half to half in your favour. You are in possession of the technical bumf and the one half of the machine that your chess-playing friend Castor here gave you in your bog in Cambridge. That's the major haul, old darling. The other half, which the Hungoes got ahold of this afternoon, is n.f.g. without the book of words that you have so cunningly kept clasped to your sagging bosom. You're ahead of the game. Give your winnings to us like a good boy and expect a knighthood by return of post. Failing that, shove it on the open market and make yourself a millionaire. But don't fucking horse around with us. We're busy men. You follow me?'

'Now why should you think that I have only the *one* half of Mendax?'

'Donny dear, you just said, did you not, that the knife artist got to Pollux before you? I take it he didn't kill him just for the fun of it – saving your grief, young Stefan.'

'No, as it happens you are right.' Trefusis picked up the medicine bottle from the table and unscrewed the lid. 'The lining of Martin's coat had been ripped open. I am forced to assume that something was taken.'

'There you are then, so why don't you . . . what the Nigel Christ?'

Trefusis was pouring the purple contents of the bottle into the waste-paper bin on the table in front of him.

'A little prestidigitation to entertain you,' said Trefusis. He struck a match and dropped it into the bin. A great ball of blue and green flame blossomed upwards up for an instant and then shrank away into thick smoke.

'And so we say farewell to Bela's Mendax papers,' said Trefusis.

'You great flapping clitoris,' said Sir David. 'You pointless, fatuous, drivelling old man. What the hell do you think you're playing at?'

'I know what's worrying you, David, but you may rest easy. The smoke alarm has been disconnected. I saw to it earlier this evening.'

'Of course you realise now that you can kiss good-bye to any chance you ever had of getting onto the BBC Board of Governors, don't you?'

'I had no idea I was in the running.'

'All you're in the running for now, matey, is ten years of tax inspectors waking you up at dawn twice a week and policemen stopping your car four times for every two miles you drive.'

'Don't be dismal, David,' said Trefusis. 'I have merely eliminated the vigorish. The game is now even. I have one half of Mendax, while the killer would appear to have the other.'

'Damn you to Hull and all points north.'

'Well, possibly. For the meantime, however, perhaps young Simon can help us out with the identity of this knife artist, if that really is the current jargon. Who is the Hungarians' best assassin, Simon? Not your desk I know, but you've worked there.'

'The artist they like to use is actually a German, sir. Sets up his stall under the name of Alberich Golka.'

'I see. And is this man, I wonder, fat at all?'

'Very fat, sir. That's about the only thing we know about him. He's fat, he's German and he's very expensive.'

'So this costly, full-figured Teuton was employed by the Hungarians to intercept Mendax and, it seems, to kill anyone remotely connected with it. I return to my original question. Why? Why kill Moltaj?'

'Well, sir, it's what killers do. They kill.'

'Only to order. Why *order* this Golka to kill an innocent violinist?'

Simon shrugged politely; Humphrey and Lady

Helen shifted themselves into a more upright position, like churchgoers demonstrating their attentiveness to a sermon; Sir David Pearce yawned; Stefan gazed forlornly out of the window and Dickon Lister continued to bar the door. Adrian wondered when attention was going to be paid to him.

'I ask myself,' said Trefusis, 'why people are ever murdered. They are murdered for reasons of revenge, retribution and rage. They are murdered as a means of winning secrecy and silence, they are murdered to satiate a psychotic lust and/or to achieve a material gain. None of these grounds satisfactorily explains the immense expenditure of monies and risk that was involved in putting a period to the existence of a harmless Hungarian fiddler. Consider too the *manner* of the murder. So grisly, so public, so violent, so uncomely.'

'Perhaps the killer didn't like his face,' suggested Pearce.

'Oh, but it was a lovely face. No, there is only one motive that strikes me as necessary and sufficient. Moltaj's murder was directed at *me*.'

'Golka mistook him for you, sir? That's hardly . . .'

'No, no, Simon. I meant precisely what I said. Moltaj was murdered *at* me, to frighten me.'

Sir David rose, stretched and made his way to the sideboard.

'More of this wine anyone?' he called out to no one in particular.

'Yes please,' said Adrian.

Sir David ignored him, poured himself a glass and resumed his seat. Adrian flushed and scrutinised his shoe-laces.

'I believe,' continued Trefusis, 'that the killing of Moltaj was designed to impress upon me the savage and remorseless lengths to which the Hungarians were prepared to go in order to acquire Mendax. If they mean to kill for it, I was supposed to say to myself, then I had better let them have it at once. But what a footling stratagem! I am not, I hope, so old and feeble an old quiz as all that. If I was truly scared – and I must pause here to assure you that indeed I was as pitifully afraid as ever I have been – then surely the natural course of action for me to have taken would have been to deliver the Mendax papers to Sir David and to rely on his department for protection. The Hungarians are not the kind to set murderers on one's tail simply to exact revenge. They are not MI5, for heaven's sake. Then again, nor are they such idiots as to imagine that they could ever panic me into giving Mendax to *them*, they could only panic me into giving it to my own people. That is when I realised, of course, that this is precisely what was intended. I was meant to be cowed into presenting Mendax not to the Hungarians, but to Sir David Pearce. Sir David Pearce had been running Golka. Sir David Pearce had ordered the death of Moltaj as a means of frightening me out of the game and Sir David Pearce had ordered the identical death of Martin Szabó that he might maintain his fiction of bloodthirsty Hungarians running riot throughout Salzburg.'

'I'll call for a nurse,' said Sir David. 'You lot keep him talking. And for God's sake humour the poor bastard before he turns violent.'

Trefusis dipped his head sorrowfully. 'No, David,

I don't think anyone will be calling for nurses. Not just now.'

Sir David met the stares of the others in silence and then burst into laughter.

'Oh for God's sake, look at you all! You can't possibly be serious! The man's babbling and you know it.'

'Perhaps we should ask Golka,' said Trefusis.

'Ooh, yes, *what* a good idea. Let's ask Golka. Or Florence Nightingale perhaps, or the Nabob of Bhandipur.'

'Well, Golka?' said Trefusis. 'You are the one who did the killing. Perhaps you could tell us on whose orders?'

Lister did not alter his expression at all. He shifted his weight from his right to his left leg and remained silent.

Adrian felt his gut churning. Ten minutes ago he had not imagined getting out of this session with his integrity unscathed, now he was beginning to doubt that he would get out of it alive.

Simon Hesketh-Harvey coughed and raised a tentative hand.

'Um, excuse me, sir. I hate to seem dim, but are you suggesting that *Lister* is Golka?'

'Oh, there can be no doubt of that. I recognise him, you see.'

'Mm. He's . . . not very *fat* though, is he, sir?'

'Well of course not. Such a *noticeable* thing to be, isn't it, fat? Far from ideal, one might therefore think, for the successful pursuit of the dreadful trade Golka has chosen. But you see, while a fat man can never make himself thin, a thin man may easily make himself fat.'

'*Padding*, do you mean, sir?'

'Quite. His face might not properly match the corpulence of his body, but it is not uncommon, after all, to see men who are fatter in frame than in feature. Is that not right, Mr Lister?'

Lister said nothing.

Adrian stared at him, trying to picture where on his person a gun might be concealed. Or his knives.

'Are you absolutely certain, sir? I mean . . .'

'Oh for God's sake!' exploded Sir David, his voice setting the bells of the gilt and porcelain clock on the wall to chime. 'You work to *me* Hesketh-Pisshead-Harvey! You sir *me*, do you understand? You do not sir this sack of rotting tweed. You sir me!'

Simon did not turn to look at Pearce during this outburst. 'As you say, sir,' he said stolidly. 'You are suggesting then, Professor, that in order to acquire Mendax, Sir David hired Golka?'

'Yes, because he has been operating privately, I think. He wants Mendax for himself. A supplement to the nugatory pension he might expect from his masters. If he had succeeded in frightening me into offering Mendax to Her Majesty's Government, he would have made sure, I have no doubt, that Golka crashed the handover and took Mendax away, apparently from the both of us. It had to look like the Hungarians had won, you understand.'

'This is so stupid of you, Donald,' said Sir David. 'So very stupid. You see, if your analysis is correct, I already have one half of Mendax, the half that Lister took from Martin this afternoon. It seems natural that I should trouble you for the other half.'

'Oh but you don't have one half of Mendax, David. That is the whole point. I have both halves.' Trefusis looked down at the two radio sets on the table in front of him.

Adrian watched as Uncle David's eyes froze into a momentary stare of panic before slowly relaxing into a smile.

'Bad bluff, Donald. V. bad bluff.'

'I am afraid not. You see, there is something else of which you and Lister or Golka – whichever he prefers – are in ignorance. Walton's *First* Law.'

'Oh hell!' said Humphrey Biffen suddenly.

Everyone turned to stare at him.

'Ever since you mentioned the Third Law I've been sitting here racking my brains trying to remember the others,' said Biffen with an apologetic shake of the head. 'I remember Two and Four of course, but what on *earth* was One?'

'Oh come on, Humpty!' his wife nudged him playfully. '"Whatever is on the person is not true." How could you forget?'

'Oh *yes*!' cried Biffen with satisfaction. 'I *am* an old fool. So sorry, Donald.'

'My dear fellow, not at all. Lady Helen is of course quite right. "Whatever is on the person is not true." I wonder, Sir David, if you ever listen to the little wireless essays with which from time to time I infest the air waves? They may be heard domestically every Saturday morning on Radio 4. They are also broadcast around the globe by the BBC World Service.'

'I know that. Anyone who's ever tried to listen to the cricket knows that. To their bored cost.'

'Ah, then it is possible that you heard this week's essay? It was transmitted in Europe this morning at oh three hundred hours and again at fifteen hundred this afternoon.'

'Yes, I heard it,' said Sir David. 'By God, this had better be leading somewhere.'

'Indeed it is. You might recall a reference to a chaffinch in my piece. Chaffinch is my name for Martin Szabó. Stefan here is Coaltit, I am Bald Eagle, Adrian is Lyre Bird.'

Adrian blushed again. Why 'Liar Bird'? It didn't seem fair.

'And you, Sir David,' continued Trefusis, 'are Duvet, I don't know why, but you are. I hope that doesn't upset you.'

'I've been called worse things.'

'Oh, surely not?'

'Just get on with it, will you?'

'Very well. In this same broadcast I also uttered these words . . . let me see . . . the sentence went like this . . . "reminded me at first of a copy of Izaac Walton's *Compleat Angler* that I have in my possession". Yes, I think that was it. This was an instruction to Martin to obey Walton's First Law: Whatever is on the person is not true. "Reminded me at *first* of a copy of Izaac *Walton's* . . ." I knew, you see, that if you or Golka did intercept Martin you would expect to find your treasure in the lining of his coat. In his last interview with his grandson in Hungary, Szabó had deliberately told Martin that this was where Mendax should be secreted. Your department's man in Budapest has a contact inside the Hungarian secret police. Simon tells me he is called "Locksmith". "What you want will be in the lining of Martin Szabó's jacket," Locksmith no doubt signalled to London, as Bela intended him to. You briefed Golka accordingly: "Expect to find Mendax in the lining of Pollux's coat," you will have said. Martin did indeed create an inner pocket to his jacket in which he hid a piece of microcircuitry. This Lister gratefully took after he had cut the poor boy's throat. I believe you will discover that what you killed that boy to obtain controls the spin cycle of a tumble drier. The wireless set on Martin's dressing table would have yielded a much richer secret. I have it here.'

Trefusis held up the second of the two radios.

'There we have it, you see. Mendax. I know how badly you want it, David, and I am so terribly sorry that I am not in a position to oblige you. Humphrey and Lady Helen, like myself, are old friends of Bela Szabó and we feel that we have the prior claim. Simon's loyalty, naturally, is to his parents-in-law and to me, the devoted godfather of his wife Nancy. Stefan here, as Bela's heir and the brother of Martin, whom you so pitilessly slew, must decide on what punishment should be meted out to you. Lister, I'm afraid, cannot be allowed to live.'

Sir David rose to his feet. 'This has all been most instructive,' he said. 'A tidy operation on your part, Donald. I congratulate you. I must now ask you to present Mendax to me. Mr Lister, *if* you please.'

Adrian watched as Lister's right hand went slowly to his left side and brought out, from under the lapel of his powder-blue safari jacket, an automatic revolver. At least Adrian supposed it was an automatic revolver. It was certainly some form of hand gun, and it was pointed very directly at the head of Professor Trefusis. Adrian had imagined that he had a lifetime before him in which to acquire all kinds of facts, including a basic knowledge of firearms, enough for instance to be able to tell the difference between a pistol, a revolver, an automatic or a semi-automatic. But now he was to be killed by one such instrument before he had the chance to find out what it might be.

'Mendax,' said Trefusis with no indication of concern, 'is of course yours to keep or dispose of as you will, Sir David. I have no argument against bullets. But I must ask you to allow me to finish my address. Then you may kill us all, as kill us all you surely must, for I am sure I speak for everyone in this room when I say that I have every intention of informing your political masters of the entirely reprehensible part you have played in this affair.'

'Oh certainly I shall kill you all,' said Sir David. 'With the greatest pleasure in the world I shall kill you all.'

'Naturally. But I cannot allow you to purchase Mendax, even at the bargain price of six bullets, without offering you a demonstration of its prodigious abilities. You cannot be expected to buy a pig in a poke, Sir David . . . sight unseen. That, after all, is why Adrian is with us here.'

Sir David folded his arms and reflected.

'Very well,' he said. 'If it amuses you.'

'Thank you,' Trefusis bent down over the table. 'Now correct me if I am wrong, Stefan, but I believe that all we need do is connect these two radio sets like so . . .'

Adrian forced his eyes away from the gun in Lister's hand and round towards Trefusis behind him. He had prised open the battery compartments of each radio. From one a ribbon of parallel connecting cable now protruded, ending in a plug. As Trefusis pushed this plug into the battery compartment of the other it snapped home with a soft plastic click. He plugged the headphone jack into one of the radios and looked enquiringly towards Stefan, who was shaking his head.

'Not this, it must be the other. Certainly the other.'

'Thank you, my boy.' Trefusis unplugged the headphones from the first radio and attached them to the minijack socket of the second. 'Two hundred and fifty metres, I think?'

'Sure,' said Stefan. 'You will hear noise.'

Trefusis held the headphones up to one ear and turned the tuning wheel on the first radio set. 'Aha!' he said at length. 'Adrian, if you would be so kind . . .'

Adrian took the headset with trembling hands. He looked up at Trefusis, who returned the gaze affectionately.

'Must be done, my dear,' he said. 'I don't believe you will be harmed in any way.'

As soon as the headphones were over his ears, Adrian felt reassured. A gentle hiss filled his head, foregrounded by brighter, sharper little sounds that were like an aural equivalent of spots in front of the eyes. It was very pleasant, very relaxing; a bath for the brain. He heard too, quite clearly, the real external sound of Trefusis pressing a button on the device behind him. The effect of this was to cause the hiss, and the dancing little sounds in front of it, to be replaced by a wider, deeper hum. Slowly Adrian lost all sensation of physical contact with the world. He knew quite clearly that he was sitting in a chair, but he could not feel which parts of his body were touching it. Somewhere in the centre of this warm, weightless pool of sound hung the voice of Donald Trefusis.

'Tell me how you feel, Adrian.'

Adrian knew how he felt. He knew everything. Suddenly nothing in his mind was mystery; all was open and clear. It was as if he was swimming through the lobes, folds, neurones, synapses, chambers and connectors of his own brain.

'I feel fucking great,' he declared. 'Sort of swimming feeling like the time I had that grass round at Mark's place in Winnet Street – that must have been years ago – I can see the outline of Lister's cock the way he's standing there – very badly cut safari suit I suppose – small circumcised as well – and after we had the grass I was really sick all over Mark's duvet – when Uncle David came to stay and I was twelve I found magazines under his bed I remember – that fluff smell under the spare-room bed – I smelt it again when we stayed in the hotel on Wednesday on our way to Salzburg – I had to pretend I knew the difference between grass and resin which I didn't which is pathetic because it's so fucking obvious isn't it – I wish I hadn't taken Uncle David's fucking money – why on earth Donald calls him Duvet – the word for the unit of thermal insulation in duvets is tog – Donald will know where it comes from – come to think of it I haven't had a wank in two days – Lister can't kill us all can he – I mean this is mad completely mad – they might sell KY jelly in a chemist's somewhere in the Getreidegasse – all that blood – if I *do* die it won't matter anyway because I'm such a cunt I won't notice – Uncle David is listening to me and looking at me as if I was a fish in a tank and I can hear Donald talking to me so I suppose if none of you minds I had better shut up and listen to what he's saying – big helmet but tiny cock – you've hardly said anything Biffo and your wife hasn't said much either – showing through his togs – what are you doing here anyway – I suppose Donald asked you to follow him as well when we were driving here – I'm asking you a question Mr Biffen and you aren't answering – or rather I suppose you *are* answering because your mouth is opening and closing but I can't hear you – awful white spittle you have in the corners of your mouth – I've just had this gross image of you and Lady Helen snogging can you imagine – someone is telling me to be quiet I can hear them – I think I had better stand up now – no I can't because the headphones would slip off – I mean grass looks like grass and resin doesn't but I thought it was a trap I suppose – Lister wearing padding and looking fat – I wonder if Simon is armed and is going to try and shoot Lister before he can fire at Donald – Lister has heard me say that now and he will probably shoot Simon first just in case – me and my big mouth – can't be an automatic revolver come to think of it doesn't sound right – somebody is still telling me to be quiet – thirty-eight that must be it a thirty-eight automatic though whether that's thirty-eight millimetres or inches I have no idea – wasn't there someone called Lister at school – Hugo is turning into an alcoholic because of me – it really is a *very* small cock that Lister has got perhaps that is why he is a killer – if Donald knew all along that I was being paid by Uncle David then he has never liked me and if he has never liked me then perhaps it's just as well Lister is going to shoot us all – do you remember that time when you made me write to Mother Uncle David and I saw Tony Greig – I hope Lister shoots the others first so I can watch – that's disgusting but then I am disgusting I suppose everyone is – I'm so happy – I really like all of you you know that – I simply must have a fuck before I die there was a girl on the footbridge with simply astonishing tits – Stefan's got quite a cute bum it has to be said oh for God's sake Adrian he's just lost a brother – I don't know why but I like you all but I am glad that we are all going to die and be together – I like you too Uncle David I always – the magazine under your bed was called *Lolita* wasn't it completely hairless vaginas – I can't imagine how you spell Golka but it is rather an impressive name – I suppose it gets bigger when he's excited – when he's cutting some-one's throat probably – as big as a thirty-eight slug I suppose – looks like a slug at the moment – this is an amazing experience – I probably love Donald – not like Hugo or Jenny – not like wanting to go to bed with him – ha can you imagine that Donald – me going to bed with you – no I don't mean that but I think I love you in every other way and of course you hate me don't you as you should because I am such a cunt – everyone watching me and listening to me and me making a total arse of myself because I can't help it though it's good to get it off my chest – of course it's never going to end because – '

'Thank you, Adrian, I think that will do.'

Trefusis pulled off the headphones and the air seemed to scream into Adrian's head with a huge kicking electric shock. He gasped like a skin diver breaking the surface. He felt Donald's hand on his shoulder and the stares of everyone else in the room piercing him through to the brain. Rocking backwards and forwards in his chair, he buried his head in his hands and began to cry.

Through the close snivel of his weeping he heard re-establish themselves the sounds of the room: the music in the courtyard below, the ticking of the clock and Uncle David's crude heckling.

'What bloody use is this? The boy's done no more than drool and blub like a maniac. I don't need a machine to make him do that. One swift kick in the balls would be enough.'

'I imagine,' said Trefusis, 'that had we left the machine attached for longer, every truth in Adrian's brain would have been disgorged.'

'What a revolting thought.'

Adrian leant back in his chair and opened his eyes.

'May I stand up please?' he asked in a small voice. 'I think my leg may have gone to sleep.'

'Yes, yes, of course. Walk around the room a little, my boy.'

Avoiding the eyes of Stefan, Simon and the Biffens, Adrian stepped down from the dais.

Sir David gave the wide shrug of a man who believes himself to be surrounded by fools. 'Well I dare say it might work,' he said. 'Just leave it where it is and walk away from the table, will you?'

'In a moment, David,' said Trefusis. 'First I have to do this . . .'

Trefusis raised the gavel like a benevolent judge and brought it down onto the coupled radios. Splinters of broken plastic flew across the room. Sir David stiffened.

'You're dead, Donald,' he hissed. 'Do it, Dickon!'

'No! No, no, no, no, no!'

With a screech that tore his throat Adrian threw himself at Lister, knocking him to the floor. He fell on him with a roar, banging his head down onto his chest, barking and bellowing into his face.

'I'll kill you! Kill you! I'll kill you!'

He felt the sharp profile of the gun against his stomach, and pressure upwards as Lister's gun hand tried to free itself from the weight of Adrian's body.

Through the background clamour of upraised voices, Adrian thought he heard Simon Hesketh-Harvey shout, 'Pull him off!'

Hands pulled roughly at his shoulders, trying to tug him away. Why the hell didn't they run? Why couldn't they leave him be? What was the point of sacrificing yourself like this if your allies stayed around to watch? This was their chance to flee. Did they *want* to be killed?

Adrian kicked his knee into Lister's stomach and the gun exploded with a dull boom.

For a second Lister and Adrian stared at each other. Someone, it could have been Uncle David, said, rather impatiently, 'Oh for heaven's *sake*!'

Adrian felt hot blood surge against his stomach like

a discharge of semen and wondered whether it was his or Lister's.

'Oh shit,' he said as Lister rolled away. 'It's mine.'

'It's not my fault!' someone close to him cried. 'He just . . .'

Adrian's eyeballs slid upwards and he fell forward. 'I'm so sorry,' he said.

As he fell into unconsciousness he thought he heard the voice of Bob, the landlord of the Shoulder of Lamb.

'You silly arse, sir. I had him covered all the time.'

But as Adrian slipped away, Bob's voice, if it had ever been there, tapered and dissolved into the only sound that accompanied Adrian into the darkness, the sound of Trefusis wailing.

Thirteen

Professor Donald Lister's face hung above Adrian like a great white balloon. Adrian forced his eyes wider open and tried to remember who Professor Donald Lister could be. He had not realised that such a person was.

The balloon moved away and split itself into two, like the dividing of a gigantic cell.

'You should sleep, my boy,' said Trefusis.

'Sleep,' echoed Dickon Lister.

The two new balloons separated and disappeared from Adrian's line of vision.

A little while later he opened his eyes again to find Istvan Moltaj and Martin Szabó gazing down upon him. Their throats were pure and unscarred, their brown eyes round with compassion.

'Very pale, Helen. Is it right he should be so pale?'

'Only to be expected,' said the voice of Lady Helen Biffen.

Adrian smiled. 'Thank you for welcoming me here,' he said. 'I had always known that death would never be the finish. I hope we can stay friends throughout eternity.'

He realised with a flick of annoyance that although he had uttered the words quite plainly they had sounded only inside his head. His lips had not moved nor had his larynx stirred. Perhaps there was a special technique up here that he would have to master in order to be able to communicate. He dwelt on the possibility for a while and contemplated with drowsy satisfaction the prospect of the infinite time now available to him.

Adrian awoke from his dreams in some discomfort. The bedroom was very familiar. The dressing table at the end of the bed he had seen before only recently. He hauled himself up onto his elbows to get a better view, then yelped in agony as a sharp pain shot through his stomach. Footsteps hurried towards him from a connecting room. As he sank back, spent, the thought came to him that he was in the same suite of the Hotel Österreichischer Hof that Martin Szabó had stayed in, that he was lying on the very bed that Martin Szabó had sat on when his throat had been cut.

'Adrian, you shouldn't try to move,' said Trefusis.

'No,' said Adrian. 'Sorry.' He closed his eyes in order to concentrate on framing a question but the question eluded him and he fell asleep.

He came round a little later to find Trefusis sitting by his bed.

'Morning, Donald. If it is morning.'

'Yes,' said Trefusis. 'It is morning.'

'I'm alive then?'

'I think we can go that far.'

'What day is it?'

'Wednesday.'

'Wednesday. How long have I been here?'

'No more than a few hours.'

'That's all?' Adrian was surprised. 'They got the bullet out, did they?'

'Bullet? There was no bullet.'

'But I was shot.'

'Yes, you were shot, but there was no bullet.'

Adrian pondered this.

'What's hurting me then?'

'You lost some blood. I should imagine your stomach will be a little sore for a while. The plaster from your dressing will be pulling at your skin.'

'I'm quite hungry.'

'Rudi will bring you something.'

'Good-o,' said Adrian and fell asleep again.

Two days later Adrian sat at the piano in the Franz-Josef Suite and picked his way through Beethoven's Minuet in G. There was a plate of sandwiches and a glass of beer in front of him. His suitcases were assembled in the middle of the room ready to be taken down to reception. He had felt fully fit enough to bear Donald company for the long drive home in the Wolseley but Trefusis had insisted he go by air.

Adrian's stomach was healing very well, the raw little eruptions where the embedded wadding had been picked out with tweezers were capped with fresh scar tissue and he could now touch the long soft tongue of burn-tissue on his left side without wincing.

He closed the piano lid and straightened himself. It was a companionable kind of pain, clean and sharp as Pilsner; a better pain than the crushing leaden ache of guilt he had carried around with him for as long as he could remember.

There was a hearty knock at the door and Simon

Hesketh-Harvey came in, followed by a beaming Dickon.

'*Grüß Gott*,' said Adrian.

'And how's the lad?'

'The lad's fine thank you, Dickon,' said Adrian. 'And looking forward to going home.'

'That's the ticket,' said Simon.

'No,' said Adrian, pulling a travel wallet from his jacket pocket, 'this is.'

A long table had been prepared in the upstairs room of the Shoulder of Lamb. Nigel the barman was serving soup under the vigilant eye of Bob, the landlord. Trefusis sat at one end, with Adrian at his left hand side and Lady Helen Biffen on his right. Martin and Stefan Szabó, Humphrey Biffen, Dickon Lister, Istvan Moltaj and Simon and Nancy Hesketh-Harvey were all present, chattering and laughing with the hysterical bonhomie of businessmen at a Christmas party. There was one empty chair halfway down the table on Lady Helen's side.

'But why did you have to go to such lengths?' Adrian was asking Trefusis. 'I mean why couldn't you just *tell* me what was going on?'

'It was very necessary, I am afraid, that you acted in complete ignorance of the whole affair. David Pearce was paying you to spy on me after all. You believed you were acting in the interests of his department. That was how it had to remain. We knew he wanted Mendax for himself, not for his country but for his own enrichment. It was expedient that you should be unaware of this.'

'What about Lister? Is he really Golka?'

'Lister used to work as a junior official at the British Council in Bonn. Simon found out that Pearce had inexplicably seconded him to the Consulate in Salzburg. This puzzled Simon. He picked Lister up and questioned him with some force. Lister is indeed Golka – between ourselves,' said Trefusis, lowering his voice, 'not a very pleasant man, I'm afraid. It became apparent that Sir David was quite prepared to kill for Mendax. This was wholly unacceptable to us. We made Lister an offer. He was to keep us informed of Pearce's plans, much as you were keeping Pearce informed of ours, and we would arrange that he need only *pretend* to kill Moltaj and Martin.'

'As long as I witnessed these killings?'

'Oh yes, that was very necessary. Your description of them to your Uncle David would be of the utmost importance. It had to seem to him that, although he had just failed to get hold of the Mendax papers, he had at least succeeded in getting hold of one half of the device itself. When he knew that I had the rest he would come out into the open and reveal his true motives.'

'There's one thing,' said Adrian. 'When you attached Mendax to me I heard nothing through those headphones but white sound. I felt no compulsion to do anything but fall asleep. All that guff I came out with, it was just a put on. I made it up.'

'Of course!' said Trefusis. 'Haven't you understood it yet? Mendax doesn't exist.'

'What do you mean?'

'It's a nonsensical notion, absolutely nonsensical. But we had to make Pearce believe it could really work.'

354

'But you hooked me up to it!'

'That's right.'

'I might have blown the whistle. Simply announced that it wasn't doing anything for me, just hissing in my ear. How could you know that I wouldn't?'

'I relied on the fact that you are a chronic liar. Once you were attached to a device that was supposed to make you tell the truth but didn't work, you would naturally do the dishonest thing and pretend that it did. It was mixture of suggestion on my part and appalling dishonesty on yours. Not that it mattered whether you went through that charming and absurd act or not. Pearce had shown his hand by this time. I am only sorry that you decided to behave in such a peculiar fashion as to throw yourself at Lister's gun.'

'It was very brave of the poor darling,' said Lady Helen. 'And it was criminally foolish of Lister to have loaded blank charges. They can be very dangerous.'

'It might have been necessary for him to appear to shoot one of us,' said Trefusis.

'A toast!' cried Simon Hesketh-Harvey. 'To Adrian Healey, saint and hero.'

'Adrian Healey, saint and hero.'

'Thank you,' said Adrian, touched. 'It was nothing, really.' He beamed around the room. 'So the invention of Mendax was merely a ruse.'

'Some of us,' said Simon Hesketh-Harvey, 'had been entertaining doubts as to Sir David's trustworthiness over a number of years. Donald came up with the idea of Mendax. Over a two- year period he corresponded with Bela on the subject, knowing that Sir David would eventually get to hear of it. An old hand like Donald must expect his mail to be interfered

355

with. He never expected that one of his own students would be set to spy on him, however. That was a tremendous bonus.'

'Steady on,' said Adrian. 'David is my uncle you know. Blood is thicker than water after all.'

'Not thicker than friendship I might have hoped,' said Trefusis. 'But there! No recriminations. You acted splendidly.'

Bob, the landlord, leant forward and winked. 'I had a great big gun pointed at Sir David from behind the curtain all the time, Master Adrian, sir.'

'Well, you might have told me,' said Adrian. A wave of tiredness came over him and he gave a huge yawn, the effort pulling at his stomach muscles and reawakening the wound.

Humphrey Biffen must have read the momentary twinge of pain in Adrian's face, for he was instantly on his feet. 'You are still weak, Adrian. One of us should take you back to St Matthew's.'

Adrian rose as steadily as he could. 'That's all right,' he said. 'The walk will clear my head.'

Cambridge in the long vacation had a forlorn, slightly embarrassed appearance, like an empty theatre. It was a warm night. Adrian looked up at St John's College chapel and at the stars beyond. The soft summer air refreshed him. Perhaps he would not go straight home to bed after all. There was a great deal to think about. In his pocket he had a letter from Jenny. It had awaited him in his pigeon-hole at St Matthew's on his return from Gatwick that afternoon. It seemed that she had got herself a job as an assistant director at Stratford. Adrian crossed the road, sat on the low stone wall opposite the pub and lit a cigarette.

He found that the letter could be read both as a farewell and as a plea for his return.

'I cannot decide whether or not you have grown up yet. What *is* this fantasy world that men inhabit? I don't think there is anything so wonderful about hard-nosed realism or remorseless cynicism, but why must you always revert to type? Have you already become an irretrievable "Enemy of Promise"? I was rereading it the other day. What is that final phrase about all Englishmen . . . that they become "Cowardly, sentimental and in the last analysis homosexual"? It was written fifty years ago for God's sake! It can't still be true can it – after a world war, a social revolution, rock and roll and all the rest?

'I was so in love with you last year. I believed we were the most remarkable couple anywhere. All my friends thought I had it made, that's a terrible phrase I know, but you know what I mean. I don't think you quite believe that women exist. To you they're a kind of difficult boy with surplus flesh in some places and missing flesh in others. I'm not even sure if you ever enjoyed my company, but then I don't know if you ever enjoyed anyone else's either, including your own. I know you hate amateur psychology but there it is.

'"Little girls grow up to be women, little boys grow up to be little boys." I can't believe that our generation is growing up to fulfil all the ridiculous stereotypes. So I'll become an earth mother and you will loll in front of the television watching cricket and Clint, is that it? Then why the years of education? Why a youth at all? Why read books and try to puzzle things out if it all ends in the same way?

'To you and your kind your youth and upbringing

357

take on this great mystique, the quality of myth. The first twenty years of my life are an open book, school and home, home and school, some friends here, some friends there. To you they are the backdrop to a gigantic world of fantasy to which you have endlessly to return. "Dearest creature, you do not understand . . ." I hear you say, as generations of men have always whined to their women. But that is the point! I do not understand. Nor, even if you had more persuasive powers of exposition than you already do, could you ever make me understand. Because there is nothing *to* understand. That is what *you* have to understand. You grew up, you went to this school and that one, you made these friends and those. It was nothing. The future is a much bigger deal than the past, Adrian, a much bigger deal. Not just because it has babies in it, but because there are better people in it, who are better behaved and more fun to be with; the scenery is better, the weather is better, the rewards and thrills are better. But I really am not sure that you will ever . . .'

A commotion coming from the Mitre, the pub next door to the Shoulder of Lamb, caused Adrian to look across the road. Both establishments had reached closing time. The landlord of the Mitre was escorting a boisterous group of drinkers into the street. Nigel, next door in the Shoulder, was locking up for the night. Something higher up caught Adrian's attention. One window of the room upstairs, the private dining room which he had just left, was directly above the street entrance of the pub. Adrian could see the clear silhouette of a man standing with his back to the window. Trefusis proposing a toast, perhaps. He looked harder. No, assuredly not Trefusis.

Adrian waited for the pack of drunken rejects from the Mitre to disperse. They stood jeering boozily outside the pub for what seemed an age before at last shouting and kicking their way towards Magdalene Bridge and out of sight. The street was empty. Adrian crossed over and edged his way round to the alleyway that connected the two pubs. The ground floor of the Shoulder of Lamb was empty. Adrian looked around for a box or beer crate that he could stand on. There was a plastic dustbin in the corner of the alley marked 'Mitre Only!' in white paint, the exclamation mark betraying a whole history of bitter inter-pub rivalry that Adrian had time to find both comic and pitiful. He edged the bin under the Shoulder's ground floor window and, setting his left leg onto the lid, tried to haul himself up, but the dustbin buckled and he found himself thigh deep in refuse. Pain ripped across his stomach and he gagged at the stench of garbage that rose to his nostrils. It was an abiding mystery to Adrian that all man-made rubbish smelt the same once it had been in a dustbin for any length of time. Trying hard not to breathe, he turned the bin upside down and tested if the base would be more likely to take his weight. It held and Adrian got his foot to the window ledge and straightened himself. His head was now no more than two feet below the level of the first floor window. He heard the voice of Humphrey Biffen.

'I'm still not quite sure how we score this,' he was saying.

'Excuse me?' said a Szabó.

'Well, it's Donald's victory again. No doubt about that,' said Nancy. 'Even if we take Lyre Bird out of the picture altogether. He was, after all, a shared resource. The same result would have been achieved without him. He merely added zest. You have to admit it, you failed to take Walton's Rules into account and you genuinely believed that you held one half of Mendax: you loused up, didn't you, David?'

'Bollocks to the lot of you,' growled the voice of Uncle David. 'Donald changed the game halfway through! Turned it into some half-baked fiction just so that he could put that dandiprat of a nephew of mine over his knee and give him a spanking. A spanking that he richly deserved, I will grant you.'

'Well, that's what gave you half a chance,' said Nancy. 'You were beaten all ends up and you know it.'

'Ha! You wait. Just you watch my smoke. If you're not all excessively nice to me I'll set the next round in Lebanon and then you'll know what's what.'

'What are you going to tell the department?' asked Humphrey.

'Nothing *to* tell. Wasted a tiny amount of cash on the surveillance of Stefan. A few flights to Salzburg. Activated our man Locksmith in Budapest. An idle bugger who needed a sharp toe up his totsie anyway. No harm done. The world knows you're my Moriarty, Donald. They let me have a fly at you once in a while, to humour the mad dog in me. They're relieved to see that I have a human flaw, is my view of it.'

'And when do you play your next game?' asked the other Szabó.

'We try to make each game run for at least two or

three years,' said Trefusis. 'Like any decent real life engagement. We will take the next year off before starting again. David and I are the antagonists and it is up to us to recruit as we please. I nearly always have Humphrey and Helen on my side, and David likes to use Dickon. I am the spy and David the spycatcher.'

'Donald devises the scenario and I have to stop him. Which I did in seventy-four.'

'David is at liberty to use all the facilities of his Service, but at his own risk.'

'And at yours, old love,' said David. 'The fact that you are now branded a dirty lavatory loiterer is some kind of victory for me, I venture to think.'

'That's a point,' said Simon. 'You did nearly get yourself sent to prison, Donald.'

'An unlooked-for occurrence, I admit, but these things lend lustre to the reputation of a fading don, don't you feel?'

'Can't you do something about that, David?' asked Helen. 'A word in the right ear, a review of evidence, a retraction from the arresting officer . . . *something*?'

'Of course, of course,' Uncle David's voice murmured affably.

'Really David, there's no need . . .'

'When did you start all this please?'

'When the game proper ended,' said David. 'About twenty years ago life in the Service became dull, pompous, sordid and absurd. Bloody good bouillabaisse, Bob.'

'Thank you, sir. Got the trick of it in Marseille.'

'Yum, yum.'

'Tell me a thing,' said Trefusis. 'In the car driving

over to Salzburg, Adrian told me what we might call his life story.'

'Oh ah?'

'He told me about you and Helen at school, Humphrey.'

'Yes, he came to a couple of our Friday afternoon teas, didn't he, dear?'

'He told me too, about bumping into you, David, at Lord's in . . . seventy-five or six it must have been.'

'Oh yes, that'll be the Aussie test. I remember. Don't know what he means by "bumping into me" though.'

'No?'

'His parents were going on holiday. Naturally they didn't want the little rat getting under their feet then. Shoved him onto me.'

'He hadn't . . . then . . . *run away* from home in any way?'

'Good Lord no! That what he told you? No, no. Pretty normal schooling he had as far as I can remember. Got slung out for nobbing half his house and circulating filthy drivel in a school magazine. Couple of years at the local college in Gloucester where he got his "A" levels. Taught at some prepper in Norfolk. Then St Matthew's. Why, tell you something different did he?'

'No, no. That was broadly the story as he told it me. One or two, er . . . embellishments perhaps. A lot of highly entertaining nonsense about Piccadilly and prison and so forth. I'm sure he never intended to be so insulting as to expect me to believe them.'

Adrian's foot slipped on the ledge. Scrabbling wildly to regain his balance, he kicked a toe through the window, knocked the dustbin from under him and fell backwards onto the ground. Without stopping to see what damage he had caused either to himself or to the window, he picked himself up and ran out into the street.

Fourteen

Adrian brought the tips of his fingers together and smiled gently. The girl's voice continued to read.

'*Othello* is a tragedy of privacy, a phrase that itself expresses incongruity, for, as with most Shakespearean tragedy, success is achieved by a treatment unsuited to the form. And it is the lack of suiting which makes the theme perennial; the tearing- down of a privacy is a subject which fits our age, as it might fit any age. It lets in chaos, and lets out love.'

'Oh bravo!' cried Adrian. 'Memorably phrased, Shelagh.'

The girl flushed slightly with pleasure. 'You like it Dr Healey?'

'Indeed! I liked it when I first read it . . . phew, let me see . . . must be getting on for ten years ago now . . . nineteen eighty-one, I'm pretty sure it was . . . and I like it just as much now. If anything age seems to have improved it. John Bayley, *Shakespeare and Tragedy*, published, unless I'm very much mistaken, by Routledge and Kegan Paul.'

'Oh dear,' the girl flushed again, but not this time with pleasure.

'Too memorably phrased I am afraid, my dear.'

'Thing is . . .'

'I *know* you are . . . frantically busy. But believe me, I had far rather listen to that good essay than the bad one you would have contrived without Bayley's help. All's well. I think you will manage to get yourself an adequate degree without my pestering you every fortnight for an essay, don't you?'

'Well . . .'

'Of course you will!' Adrian stood and refilled Shelagh's glass. 'A little more malvoisie for you?'

'Thank you.'

'A smoky volcanic bite that cannot disgust. You act, I believe?'

'Yes . . . that's why I get so behind with work.'

'I don't know why I say "believe" you act, I've seen you in a number of productions. My wife is down from London this weekend, you may have heard of her?'

'Jenny de Woolf, the director? Of course!'

'Then why don't you come round to our house in Trumpington this evening and say hello?'

'Really? I'd love to.'

'All right, my dear. Seven o'clock, shall we say?'

'That would be fine. Thanks!'

Adrian watched with approval as the girl gathered her bag and her scarf and made for the door. 'By the way, Shelagh . . .'

She paused enquiringly in the doorway.

'I note,' said Adrian, 'that you are a member of the University Humanist Society.'

She looked back at him with a hint of defiance and suspicion.

'Yes?'

'You take it seriously?'

'Very.'

'You dislike religion perhaps?'

'I loathe religion.'

'Ah, now that is interesting. I think that tonight I shall invite old Trefusis along as well, you'd like him I'm sure, and I know he'll like you. We are currently working on a . . . on a problem that may interest you.'

'Oh?'

'As you may know, the nineties have been nominated the "Decade of Evangelism" by various functionaries culled from the madder wings of the Christian church.'

The girl's mouth wrinkled in comic disgust. 'Don't remind me.'

'We have discovered that behind this weird and pitiable phrase there lies . . .' Adrian broke off. 'Never mind. I'll tell you the rest tonight. Dryden House, Trumpington. Can't miss it.'

The girl looked intrigued. 'Right. I'll see you then, Dr Healey. Er . . . bye then.'

'Goodbye, Shelagh. Oh and Shelagh?'

'Yes?'

'I'd appreciate it if you didn't mention this to anyone for the moment. You'll find out why.'

Adrian looked out of the window and watched the girl hop across the grass of Hawthorn Tree Court. He smiled to himself as he sat at his desk and wrote a short note on a sheet of writing- paper.

'To Bald Eagle. Gingerbread. Informal. I think the game may well be afoot. Love Liar Bird.'

Adrian leant back in his chair, fed the paper into his fax machine and pressed an autodial key. He watched the sheet chug through the machine before crossing to his window again.

On the other side of the court he could make out the figure of an old man through an open window on the first floor. The figure stooped down for a moment and fiddled with something on his desk and then came up bearing a ripped sheet of paper. He turned in Adrian's direction, flourishing the paper like a Morris dancer waving a handkerchief, and executed a quick little jig.

Adrian laughed and turned back into the room.

Acknowledgements

Donald Trefusis and his Wireless Essays first appeared
on the BBC Radio 4 programme *Loose Ends*. I should
like to thank the producer Ian Gardhouse, and
the presenter Ned Sherrin, for allowing the Professor
a platform for his ideas and observations.

There is no possibility that this book could ever
have been written without the violent threats and
pitiless blackmail of Sue Freestone of William
Heinemann and Anthony Goff of David Higham
Associates.

I'm grateful to my parents for their researches
into Salzburg, to Tim Rice for allowing the quotation
from 'I Don't Know How to Love Him',
to Hugh and Jo Laurie for reading the manuscript
when they had hundreds of better things to do,
and to Jo Foster for everything.

The Hippopotamus

For Kim, *alter ipse amicus*

The author would like to thank Matthew Rice for his invaluable help with the shooting scenes. Any inaccuracies in that quarter are entirely his fault.

The broad-backed hippopotamus
Rests on his belly in the mud;
Although he seems so firm to us
He is merely flesh and blood.

'The Hippopotamus', T. S. Eliot

Foreword

You can't expect an arse like me to tell a story competently. It's all I can bloody do to work this foul machine. I've counted up the words processed, a thing I do every hour, and, if technology can be trusted, it looks as if you're in for 94,536 of them. Good luck to you. You asked for it, you paid me for it, you've got to sit through it. As the man said, I've suffered for my art, now it's your turn.

I don't claim that it has been a wholly grotesque experience. The Project, as you insist on calling it, has kept me from drinking at lunch-time, from drooling after unattainable women and from quarrelling with the unspeakables next door. At your suggestion, I have been leading a more or less regular life these seven months and I am told the benefits can be read clearly in complexion, waistline and eye-whites.

The routine has been fixed and perversely pleasurable. Every morning I have risen at round about the hour most decent people are thinking of one more shot before bed, I have showered, descended the stairs with a light tread, champed through a bowl of Bran Buds and guided my unwilling slippers studywards. I switch on the computer – a procedure my son Roman calls 'jacking into the matrix' – goggle with disgusted eyes at whatever guff I've set down the night before, listen to some more of those bloody interview tapes with Logan, light up a Rothman and just bloody well get down to it. If the day has gone well I'll disappear upstairs for a round of light celebratory masturbation – what Roman would no doubt call 'jacking into the mattress' – and I won't so much as think of a bottle till seven-ish. All in all a proud and pure life.

The problem with renting a house in the country is that suddenly everyone wants to know you. I am endlessly having to fend off Oliver, Patricia and Rebecca and others who seem to think my time is limitless and my cellar bottomless. Every once in a while the Bitch will unload a son or daughter for the weekend, but they are both big enough and ugly enough to look after themselves and don't need me to help them roll their joints or fit their coils. Next week Leonora will be moving into the house I've given her and be permanently off my hands. She's far too old to be clinging to me.

No, on balance I would say the thing's been a huge success. As a process, that is, as a process. Whether the *product* has anything to recommend it is, naturally, for you to say.

I am fully aware that there's a deal of tarting up to be done. I assume you'll make some decision about whether or not to create a unified point of view . . . a consistent third-person narrative, an omniscient author, an innocent eye or an innocent I, all that Eng. Lit. balls. Since half of it's in letter form you could always titivate here, dandify there and call it an Epistolary Novel, couldn't you?

My favourite candidate for a title is *Other People's Poetry*, I have a feeling however that your filthy marketing people will regard this as a notch too poncey. It seems to me to be the best title, the only title. So whatever cheap alternative you dream up instead, to me this book will always be

Other People's Poetry and nothing else. Your suggestion, *What Next?* or *Now What?* or whatever it was, strikes me as a touch too Joseph Heller and a whole smashing upper-cut too market-led, as I believe the phrase is. Otherwise I'm rather fond of *The Thaumaturge*; that would go down as my nap for place. No doubt you'll come up with your own clever-arse idea. Roman thinks *Whisky and Soda* would be rather neat.

The details here below are more or less accurate. If you develop a publisher's yellow streak, you can always change the names and dates – buggered if I care. Meanwhile, on delivery of this, the second quarter of my advance is due: I'm off back to the smoke to find myself a tart and a bar, so sling the cheque over to the Harpo, in which place too a message can be left, delivering itself of your professional opinion, for what little it's worth.

E.L.W.

One

The fact is I had just been sacked from my paper, some frantic piffle about shouting insults from the stalls at a first night.

'Theatre criticism should be judgement recollected in tranquillity,' my wet turd of an editor had shrilled, still trembling from the waves of squeal and whinge that actors, directors, producers and (wouldn't you just believe it) pompous, cowardly prigs of fellow-reviewers had unleashed upon him by fax and phone throughout the morning. 'You know I support my staff, Ted. You know I venerate your work.'

'I know no such bloody thing. I know that you have been told by people cleverer than you that I am a feather in your greasy cap.'

I also knew that he was the kind of anile little runt who, in foyers and theatre bars the West End over, can be heard bleating into their gin and tonics, 'I go to the theatre to be entertained.' I told him so and a full gill more.

A month's salary, deep regret, the telephone number of some foul rehab clinic and my lance was free.

If you're a half-way decent human being you've probably been sacked from something in your time . . . school, seat on the board, sports team, honorary committee membership, club, satanic abuse group, political party . . . something. You'll know that feeling of elation that surges up

381

inside you as you flounce from the headmaster's study, clear your locker or sweep the pen-tidies from your desk. No use denying the fact, we all feel undervalued: to be told officially that we are off the case confirms our sense of not being fully appreciated by an insensitive world. This, in a curious fashion, increases what psychotherapists and assorted tripe-hounds of the media call our self-esteem, because it proves that we were right all along. It's a rare experience in this world to be proved right on anything and it does wonders for the *amour propre*, even when, paradoxically, what we are proved right about is our suspicion that everyone considers us a waste of skin in the first place.

I boarded the boat that plies its fatuous course between newspaperland and real London and watched the *Sunday Shite* building grow upwards in space as slow knots were put between self and dismal docklands and, far from feeling mopey or put upon, I was aware of a great swelling relief and a pumping end-of-term larkiness.

At such times, and such times only, a daughter can be a blessing. Leonora would by now have high-heeled her way, it being half past twelve, to the Harpo Club. You probably know the place I mean – can't use the real name, lawyers being lawyers – revolving doors, big bar, comfy chairs, restaurants, more or less acceptable art on the walls. By day, smart publishers and what used to be called the Mediahedin; by night, the last gasp of yesterday's Soho bohemians and washed-up drunks taking comfort from the privilege of being sucked up to by the first gasp of tomorrow's ration.

In the back brasserie Leonora (hardly my idea, a name

that tells you all you need to know about the child's footling mother) hugged, snogged and squealed.

'Daddee! What brings you here in the daytime?'

'If you take that slithery tongue out of my ear, I'll tell you.'

She probably imagined that a slightly famous daughter and her even more slightly famous father displaying easy affection for one another in such a manner would provoke envy and admiration in those of her tight-arsedly bourgeois generation who only ever saw their parents for tea in hotels and wouldn't think of swearing, smoking and drinking with them in public. Typical bloody Leonora; there are pubs all over the country where three generations of ordinary families drink and swear and smoke at each other every bloody night, without it ever crossing their minds that they are simply sensationally lucky to have such a just brilliantly fabulous relationship with their wonderful daddies.

I dropped the Rothmans and lighter on the table and let the banquette blow off like a Roman emperor as it took my weight. The usual dirt averted their eyes while I took in the room. Couple of actors, nameless knot of advertisers, that queen who presents architecture programmes on Channel Four, two raddled old messes I took to be rock stars, and four women at a table, one of whom was a publisher and all of whom I wanted to take upstairs and spear more or less fiercely with my cock.

Leonora, whom I had never wanted to spear, the gods be thanked in these unforgiving times, was looking thinner and more lustrous-eyed than ever. If I didn't know it was unfashionable I would have supposed her to be on drugs of some kind.

'What's all this?' I asked, picking up a portable tape-recorder on the table in front of her.

'I'm profiling Michael Lake at one,' she said. 'For *Town & Around*.'

'That fraud? His dribble of three-act loose-stooled effluent is the reason I'm here.'

'What can you mean?'

I explained.

'Oh Daddy,' she moaned, 'you are the limit! I saw a preview on Monday. I think it's a perfectly brilliant play.'

'Of course you do. And that's why you are a worthless key-basher who fills in time sicking out drivel for snob glossies until a rich, semi-aristocratic queer comes to claim you for a brood-mare, while I, for all my faults, remain a writer.'

'Well, you're not a writer now, are you?'

'A jessed eagle is still an eagle,' I declared, with massive dignity.

'So what are you going to do? Wait for offers?'

'I don't know, my old love, but I do know this. I need your mother off my back until I'm sorted out. I'm two months behind as it is.'

Leonora promised to do what she could and I skedaddled from the brasserie in case the Lake fake was early. Playwrights more than most are not above throwing good wine or bad fists when the valueless offal they have vomited up before a credulous public has been exposed for what it is.

I sat at the bar and kept an eye on the mirror dead ahead, which gave a full view of the influx from the entrance door behind me.

The lunch crowd twittered around the bar area awaiting

their meal-tickets or their spongers; the daytime scent of
the women and the sunlight pouring through the window
created an interior atmosphere so distinct from the dark,
flitting nimbus that hangs over the place at night that we
might have been lapping in a different room in a different
decade. In America, where boozers are often under the
street, like the cutesy bar in that ghastly television series
they repeat every day on Channel Four, a daytime atmosphere is positively banished. The punter, I suppose, is not
to be reminded that there is a working world going on
outside, lest he start to feel guilty about pissing it away.
Like an increasing number of niminy-piminy Europeans,
Americans bracket drinking with gambling and whoring,
as deeds to be done in the dark. For myself, I have no
shame and don't have to steal off to Tuscany or the Carib-
bean to be able to drink guiltlessly in the sunlight. This
casts me as a freak in a lunch-time world where the fires
of anything vinous are extinguished by spritzing sprays of
mineral water and the blaze of anything hearty is drizzled
in balsamic vinegar or damped down with blanketing
weeds of radiccio, *lollo rosso* and rocket. Christ, we live in
arse-paralysingly drear times.

Once, since we're on the subject of designer lettuce, at
a luncheon for literary hacks, the novelist Weston Payne
prepared a salad of dock, sycamore and other assorted
foliage collected from the residents' garden in Gordon
Square. He dressed these leaves in a vinaigrette and to
universal applause served them up as *cimabue, putana vera*
and *lampedusa*. One grotty little pill from the *Sunday Times*
went so far as to claim that *putana vera* could be bought
in his local Chelsea Waitrose. A bottle of London tap-water
chilled and passed through a soda-stream was slurped with

every evidence of delight under the name of *Aqua Robinetto*. Very fitting really. After all, for twenty years Weston's novels had been palmed off as literature to these same worthless husks without their ever noticing a thing. I sometimes think that London is the world's largest catwalk for emperors. Perhaps it always was, but in the old days we weren't afraid to shout out, 'You're naked, you silly arse. You're stark bollock-naked.' Today you only have to fart in the presence of a dark-haired girl from the *Sunday Times*, whose father is either a sacked politician or a minor poet like myself, and you'll be puffed and profiled as the new Thackeray.

You can't imagine, if you're younger than me, which statistically speaking you are bound to be, what it is like to have been born into the booze-and-smokes generation. It's one thing for a man to find, as he ages, that the generations below him are trashier, more promiscuous, less disciplined and a whole continent more pig-ignorant and shit-stupid than his own – every generation makes that discovery – but to sense all around you a creeping puritanism, to see noses wrinkle as you stumble by, to absorb the sympathetic disgust of the pink-lunged, clean-livered, clear-eyed young, to be made to feel as if you have missed a bus no one ever told you about that's going to a place you've never heard of, that can come a bit hard. All those pi, priggish Malvolios going about the place with 'do you mind, some of us have got exams tomorrow, actually' expressions on their pale prefectorial little faces. Vomworthy.

It seems the popsy up on a stool next to mine read some of the off-pissedness in my face, for she gave me a long sideways stare, unaware that I was inspecting her inspection by way of the mirror. She slipped her bony but appetising buns off the stool and made for a chair in the corner, leaving me the sole occupant of the bar pasture, to graze the gherkins and crop the cashews alone. Knew her from somewhere. Five got you two that she was a diarist for the *Standard*. Leonora would know.

The great dramatist was ten minutes late, naturally, and strode through to the dining area without seeing me. The smirk on his face indicated that he had either fooled the generality of my erstwhile colleagues, no difficult thing, and been praised for his abominations, or he had heard the delightful news of my dismissal. Probably both. He wouldn't remember of course, because they never do, but it was I who discovered the little prick in the first place. That was back in the days when I used to shuttle around the fringe nightly and sit through performances by companies with names like Open Stock and Shared Space; a time when my nod could guarantee transfer from an upstairs pub in Battersea to a plush drama-brothel in the West End. Michael Lake had written what in a better world would have been a perfectly ordinary play, but which was rendered extraordinary by the banality, illiteracy and po-faced sulkiness of just about every other new work that had been written that year and for the last five years before it. In a dung heap, even a plastic bead can gleam like a sapphire. Nineteen seventy-three that must have been or, at a pinch, four. Now, of course, it wasn't possible for the man to write a note to his milkman without it being lavishly mounted to universal praise at the National Theatre . . . the *Royal* National Theatre, I beg its creepy, arse-licking pardon. The few fires of good anger and proper passion that had flickered in his early work had been pissed out by an insufferably pompous state-of-the-nation gravity and a complete indifference to the audience or awareness of the theatre. He, of course, as one of the generation that disdains the definite article, would have said 'a complete indifference to audience or awareness of theatre', as if Audience was a formless notion, instead of a live tangle of coughing, shuffling humanity, and Theatre an intellectual concept entirely divorced from actors, scenery, lighting-rigs and wooden boards. Never mind that Theatre transformed his humourless texts as best it could into just about bearable evenings and Audience funded his Suffolk watermill and lurid collection of Bratbys . . . they shouldn't expect his thanks for it. On the contrary, the general scheme was that we should be grateful to him. Cocky little arse-wipe.

'More of the same,' I said to the barman.

'Let me get this . . .' a voice, female, at my elbow.

'One of the finest phrases in our language,' said I, without turning round. I could see in the mirror that it was the bony-bunned creature, levering herself back up on to her stool. Absolutely *love* small women, they make my dick look so much bigger.

'And a Maker's Mark for me,' she added, pointing to a bottle high on the bar shelf.

A proper drinker, I noted with approval. Your experienced lapper knows that barmen always initially mishear the name of whatever brand you specify. 'Not Glenlivet, Glen*fiddich*! No, you oaf, not a lager shandy, a *large brandy* . . .' Always find the bottle with your eye first and point at it when ordering. Saves time.

A hint of something Floris-ish, or at a pinch Penhaligony, wafted up as she settled herself. Adequate breastage and a slim white throat. Something neurotic in her bearing, you get to spot that quickly in female bar-flies, most of whom are usually on the brink of the kind of hysteria that smashes glassware or slaps innocently by-standing faces.

Roddy poured a large measure into a highball glass and she watched him closely. Another good sign. I was a close chum for a time of Gordon Fell the painter, before he got knighted and began to think himself too high for low company; we went out on the nasty together fairly regularly throughout the Sixties. Gordon always drank Old Fashioneds, had done for thirty years. Never took his eyes off the barman for a second while they were being prepared, like a blackjack player eyeing the deal. One afternoon Mim Gunter, the old witch who wielded the optics at the Dominion Club in Frith Street, a favourite pissery, was off sick and her son Col had to take her stand at the bar. Well, Col was only sixteen, poor lad didn't have the first clue what an Old Fashioned was, and bugger me if Gordon hadn't the foggiest either. I tried later to calculate how many hours of his life Gordon had spent watching while they had been assembled before his unblinking eyes, but ran out of napkins to do the sums on. I knew that Angostura bitters came into the formula somewhere, but that was all I knew. In the end we had to ring Mim in hospital where she was all gowned up and ready to be wheeled into the theatre to have the cancer cut from her throat. Our SOS tickled her pink, of course. Ten feet from the phone, the other side of the bar we were, but we could still hear her screeching the foulest insults at the hapless Col down the line and telling the doctors to bugger off, 'this was business'. She died under the knife two hours

later, Gordon Fell's Proxy Old Fashioned taking its place
in history as the last drink she ever mixed.

The point is, we watch the barman, but we don't take it
in. It's the reassuring movement of the hands, the pleasing
fitness of bar stock and cocktail apparatus, the colours, the
noises, the rich, speaking scents. I've known non-drivers
unable, in the same way, to recall routes they have taken
daily in taxis for years.

The placing of the glass on its paper coaster, the discreet
pushing-forward of the ashtray and Roddy's quiet with-
drawal having been accomplished, we were free to talk.

'Good health, madam.'

'And yours.'

'Have I a feeling,' I wondered, 'that we've met?'

'That's what I was asking myself when I was here before.
I decided you were too forbidding to ask, so I disappeared
to the corner seat.'

'Forbidding?' I've heard this tosh before. Something to
do with jowls, eyebrows and a pugnacious, Bernard
Ingham-like set to the lower lip. 'As it happens,' I said,
'I'm a lamb.'

'And then, sitting there, I realised you were Ted Wallace.'

'The same.'

'You may not remember, but . . .'

'Oh hell, we haven't done the deed, have we?'

She smiled. 'Certainly not. I'm Jane Swann.'

Said as if the name was a reason for my never having
sauced her.

'Jane Swann. And I know you, do I?'

'Cast your mind back to a small font in Suffolk twenty-
six years ago. A baby and a rising poet. The baby cried a
great deal and the rising poet made a promise to turn his

back on the world, the flesh and the devil. A promise that even the baby didn't believe.'

'Well, fuck my best boots! Jane . . . Jane Burrell!'

'That's me. Though in fact it's Swann now.'

'I must owe you any number of silver napkin rings. And a library's worth of moral guidance.'

She shrugged as if to say that she didn't believe me to be the kind of person whose taste in silver napkin rings or moral guidance coincided with her own. Now that I looked there was that in her cast of features which recalled her ghastly parents.

'Never got much of a chance to get to know you,' I said. 'Your mother threw me out of the house not half an hour following the baptism. Barely laid eyes on her or Patrick since.'

'I was always very proud of you, though. From a distance.'

'Proud of me?'

'Two of your poems were set texts at school. No one believed you were my godfather.'

'Bloody hell, you should have written to me. I'd've come and gabbled to the Sixth Form.'

Too true. Nothing like the parted admiring lips of a seminar of schoolgirls to make a man feel wanted. Why else would anyone try to become a poet?

She shrugged and took a sip of her bourbon. I noticed she was trembling. Not trembling perhaps, but shivering. She had about her an air that reminded me of long ago. Leaning forward as if she wanted to pee, leg jogging up and down on the bar-stool stretcher. There was something . . . images of wooden draining boards, Dividend tea stamps and pointy bras . . . something forlorn.

I looked at her again, the little signals came together and I remembered. Jane looked now exactly as girls in the early Sixties did when they returned from visiting an abortionist. An unmistakable confluence of gestures and mannerisms, but one which I hadn't seen in a girl for years. That blend of shame and defiance, of disgust and triumph; the urgent appeal in the eyes that encouraged you either to mourn the desolation of a life utterly ruined or to celebrate the victory of a life made magnificently free, a dangerous look. I remembered only too well that if you guessed the girl's mood wrong in those days and congratulated her when she wanted to be comforted, you got a fountain of tears and a fortnight of screaming recrimination; if you consoled and sympathised when what she fancied she needed was applause and praise for a proud and heroic stand, you got a zircon-edged swipe across the chops and scornful laughter. Why the expression on my new-found god-daughter's face should have put me in mind of the atmosphere of those sordid and unmissed times, I had no idea. Women haven't needed to look as vulnerable and guilty as that for thirty years; that is a man's office now.

I coughed. 'Which poems?'

'Mm?'

'Set texts. Which ones?'

'Oh, let me see. "The Historian" and "Lines on the Face of W. H. Auden".'

'Of course. Of bloody course. The only two that ever make the anthologies. Tricksy rubbish.'

'Do you think so?'

'Certainly not, but you'd expect me to say so.'

She favoured me with a sad-eyed smile.

'Same again, Roddy.' I rapped the bar.

'I often read your theatre reviews,' she ventured, sensing that the smile had been a touch too obviously sympathetic.

'Not any more you won't.'

I told her of my sacking.

'Oh,' she said, and then, 'oh!'

'Not that I give a stuff,' I assured her, in a manner that admitted no condolences. I unloosed my thoughts on the current state of British theatre, but she wasn't listening.

'You've time on your hands then?' she said once I had run down.

'Well . . . I don't know so much about that. There's a more or less open invitation to fill the restaurant column in *Metro* . . .'

'I'm not a writer, you see, and I don't know enough . . .'

'. . . and there's always room for just one more definitive book on the Angry Young Men . . .'

'. . . you are virtually family, after all . . .'

I stopped. There were tears forming in her lower eyelids.

'What is it, my dear?'

'Look, do you mind coming home with me?'

In the cab she stayed off whatever it was that was distressing her. She sketched a short autobiography, enough to show me that she wasn't as bright or pretty or stylish or interesting as she had seemed sitting at the bar. But then, no one ever is, which is why it's always worth having shares in whisky and cosmetics.

Five years earlier, barely twenty-one, she had married a man, Swann, who traded in paintings. No children. Swann was currently in Zurich sharing his duvet with a Swiss girl, degraded enough and powerfully enough built (if Jane's bitchy glossing was to be believed) to appreciate his bruising bedroom habits. Jane's father Patrick had been gathered to God some six summers, which come to think, I knew, and Rebecca, the mother, still gadded about between Kensington and the Brompton Road pretending to be smart. Rebecca's other child, Jane's brother Conrad, whom I remembered as something of a turd, died in a carcrash. Pissed off his head, apparently. Good thing too. There's no excuse for crashing a car sober.

Rebecca was one of the few women I ever met who ... well, it is a fact that women do not enjoy sex. It has become almost a matter of religion for them to deny this, but it remains a fact. Women put up with sex as the price they pay for having a man, for being part of what they like to call a 'relationship', but they can do without. They do not feel the hunger, the constant stabbing, stomach-dropping hunger that tortures us. The bugger of it is that whenever I say this I am accused of being a misogynist. For a man who has spent his entire life thinking and dreaming of women, skipping after them like a puppy trying to please his master, ordering his entire existence so that he might be brought into more contact with them and judging his life and worth solely according to his ability to attract them and make them desire him, it comes a little hard to be accused of a dislike of the sex. All I feel is profound worship, love and inferiority mixed in with a good deal of old-style self-loathing.

I know the arguments ... Lord, who doesn't? Desire, they tell me, is a form of possession. To lust after a woman is to reduce her to the level of creature or quarry. Even worship, according to a reasoning too damned tricksy for me to follow, is interpreted as a kind of scorn. All this is, I need hardly tell you, the supremest bollocks.

Some of my best friends, as you would expect of a
quondam poet, are chutney-ferrets. So too, as you would
also expect of a quondam theatre critic, are some of my
bitterest enemies. You couldn't ask for a better controlled
experiment to help us settle this business of the genders
than the world of the nance, now could you? Gaysexuals,
bottomites, benderists, settle on a name you like, taking
such problems as the queer-bashers, the newspapers, the
virus, the police and society as read, lead a pretty fabulous
life. Lavatories, parks, heathland, beaches, supermarkets,
cemeteries, pubs, clubs and bars vibrate to their music of
simple erotic exchange. A man, bent, sees another man,
bent. Their eyes lock and . . . bang, sex is done. They don't
have to know their partner's name, they don't have to
talk to him, they don't even, in the back rooms of dark
metropolitan nightclubs, have to see his bloody face. It's a
male world, ordered in a precisely male way, according to
the devices and desires of a strictly male sexuality. Do
those big hairy faggots who pose in magazines with leather
collars round their dicks and rubber tubing up their cack-
alleys think of themselves as oppressed? Do gay men tarting themselves up for a night in a club whine about the
vile sexism which insists they must be made attractive in
order to be inspected like cattle? Do they hell.

Sometimes, in my dreams, I imagine a world in which
women enjoy sex: a world of heterosexual cruising areas
in parks and promenades, heterosexual bars, heterosexual
back rooms, heterosexual cinemas, heterosexual quarters
of the town where women roam, searching for chance
erotic encounters with men. Such an image is only conceivable in one's fantasising bedroom, jerked into life by an
angry fist and a few spastic grunts. If women needed sex

as much as men did then – duck, Ted, duck, run for cover – then there wouldn't be so many rapists around the place.

We live in the world as given, and no doubt anthropologists and zoologists can tell us that it is biologically necessary for one of the sexes always to be hungry and the other to be mostly bored. Men have compensations, after all, for the agony of their endlessly unfulfilled desires. By and large, we run the world, control the economies and swank about with laughable displays of self-importance. This isn't a whinge. I merely want the simple truth understood and out in the open: men like sex and women don't. It has to be recognised and faced.

Women's constant rejection of such a self-evident fact doesn't help at all. Whenever I point it out to my women friends they instantly deny it; they will claim to be regular masturbators; they will claim that the idea of a good anonymous fuck is a real turn-on; they will claim that only the other day they saw a man whose bottom reminded them a little of Mel Gibson and that they got really quite juicy thinking about it. *Only the other day?* What about only the other *minute*? What about every damned sodding bloody minute of every bloody damned sodding day? Don't they see that women should pop open the champagne and celebrate the fact that they are not slavering dogs like men, they should revel in the biological luck which allows them to be rational creatures who can think about the benefits a partnership with a man can provide, who can think about motherhood and work and friends . . . who can just plain *think* unlike us poor bastards who spend days that should be spent in work and higher thoughts having to realign the sore and swollen cock under the waistband of our underpants every time a set of tits walks by? Of course women get the itch now and again, we wouldn't be here as a race otherwise; of course they have genital equipment sensitive enough to ensure that sex can, when embarked upon, cause shiverings of pleasure, barks of delight and all the dirty rest of it. But they are not, lucky, lucky, lucky things, for ever *hungry*, for ever *desperate*, for ever *longing* for the base physical fact of getting their bloody rocks off. I mean, the fact is, it's five in the afternoon as I write this, and I've already tossed myself off twice today. Once first thing, in the shower, and again just after lunch, before sitting down to this. Any honest tart will tell you, sympathetically, like a nurse, that men, poor dears, just have to spit their seed. Why women should wish to claim parity in the matter of this gross imperative beats me.

As it happens, because of my trade, I've met a great many famous men, men of good report. Do you know, without exception, those I've known well enough to be able to sit with round a whisky bottle in the small hours have all confided to me that the real motivation behind their drive to become famous actors, or politicians or writers or whatever, has been the hope, somewhere deep inside them, that money, celebrity and power would enable them to get laid more easily? Whisky can rot through the layers that mask this simple truth: ambition to do well, a desire to improve the world, a need to express oneself, a vocation to serve . . . all those worthy and nearly believable motives overlay the bare-arsed fact that when you get right down to it all you want to do is get right down to it.

I owe whisky that. Not a drink many women of my acquaintance are much given to, but it has saved me. Without it I should be even more of a lost and bewildered old cunt than I am. If it weren't for those late scotch-soaked nights I should have gone through life convinced that I was uniquely dirty and uniquely dangerous. The ruination of a promising career, the occasional run-in with the police and the destruction of a couple of marriages is the price whisky exacted for allowing me to see that I was not alone: solid bloody bargain.

But . . . that's enough of that. I can get carried away. If you want catchpenny theories about the Sexes and all that, you can find shelves in bookshops devoted to nothing else. *Men Biting Back, Women Biting Back From Men's Biting Back*, responses to responses to counter-responses: it's like the days of the Cold War, every publication by the other side is read, every posture analysed, every twitch on the web detected and every cultural shift pored over. God knows there are columnists, cultural commentators and semi- academics enough to keep the Gender Wars industry arming and rearming for ever. Anyway, who gives a fuck what a parcel of undereducated journalists have to say about anything?

No, I fart this noxious guff in your faces not because it's important or new, nor because I want to engage in a sterile debate about it, but because you have to understand something of my mood and disposition that day Jane found me and dragged me off to Kensington. Her mother Rebecca, I was about to note before I leapt astride my hobby-horse and galloped off for a few paragraphs, was probably the only woman I've met who really seemed to enjoy sex for sex's sake with a relish and a need that could compare to a man's desire. She was also the only woman I've ever met whose favourite drink was whisky. A connection possibly.

Jane's house found itself somewhere near Onslow

Gardens. There was money in her purse, no question, courtesy of her Uncle Michael no doubt, and, like every rich, ignorant girl these days, she passed herself off as an interior decorator.

'People saw what I'd done with the flat,' she said, as the taxi drew up outside a standard South Kensington white-pillared portico, 'and asked if I could help them out too.'

The interior lived up to my ripest expectations. Hideous flouncing swags for curtains, raw silk instead of wallpaper, you can picture the whole sham shambles for yourself, I'm sure. Barbarically hideous and as loudly wailing a testament to a wholly futile and empty life as can be imagined. Just how fucking idle, just how rottingly *bored*, do you have to be, I wondered, to sit down and dream up this kind of opulent garbage? She was standing in the middle of the room, eyebrows raised, ready for my gargles of admiration. I took a deep breath.

'This is one of the most revolting rooms I've ever stood in in all my life. It is exactly as hideous as I expected, and exactly as hideous as ten thousand rooms within pissing distance of here. It's an insult to the eye and fully as degrading a cocktail of overpriced cliché as can be found outside Beverly Hills. I would no more park my arse on that sofa with its artfully clashing and vibrantly assorted cushions than I would eat a dog-turd. Congratulations on wasting an expensive education, a bankload of money and your whole sad life. Goodbye.'

That's what I would have said with just two more fingers of whisky inside me. Instead, I managed a broken, 'My God, Jane . . .'

'You like?'

'Like isn't the word . . . it's, it's . . .'

'They tell me I have an eye,' she conceded. '*Homes and Interiors* were here last week, photographing.'

'I'm sure they were,' I said.

'You should have seen the place when I moved in!'

'Such a sense of light and space,' I sighed. Always utterly safe.

'Men don't usually appreciate such things,' she said with approval, moving to the drinks table.

'Fuck off, you mad, sad bitch,' I said inside, while 'Even a man couldn't fail to be knocked out by this skilful, tasteful blend of the ethnic and the domestic,' said my cowardly outspread arms.

'It was Macallan, I noticed,' she was saying. 'There is Laphroaig if you'd rather.'

'N-no, the Macallan does.'

She brought them over, folded a leg under herself and sank down on an ottoman, which was moronically tricked out in a design which would turn out, I supposed, to be taken from some Mayan funeral shroud or mystic Balinese menstrual cloth. The grand idea behind such a squalid episode of cultural rape and the other equally feeble, equally impertinent conceits that littered this appalling room, I supposed, was that Jane would dispose herself there, surrounded by friends, the diversity of whose drinking habits would justify the ludicrous range of unopened liqueur, aperitif and spirit bottles on display, while gentle yet probing conversational topics were flicked like shuttlecocks about the room. Instead she sat, still trembling like an adolescent, with nothing more for company than a raddled has-been who once knew her parents. And he, despite the gallons of free whisky on offer, was wishing himself violently elsewhere.

She swirled the drink in its tumbler.

'The first thing you have to know,' she said at last, 'is that I am dying.'

Oh, marvellous. Ideal. Simply perfect.

'Jane . . .'

'I'm sorry.' She lit a cigarette with jerky movements. 'That was crass, actually.'

Damned right. Nobody seems to understand that in such matters the tact and sympathy should come from the one who is about to die, not the poor bugger who has to take the news. She'd come to the right shop, though. I've known enough death not to be nice about the forms of it.

'Are you quite sure?'

'The doctors are unanimous. Leukaemia. I've run out of remissions.'

'That's a smeller, Jane. I'm very sorry.'

'Thank you.'

'Scared?'

'Not any more.'

'I suppose it's hard to tell when the axe might fall?'

'Soon, they tell me . . . within three months.'

'Well, my darling. If you've made peace with your enemies and said goodbye to your friends, you shouldn't be too sorry to leave the party early. It's a grotty world and a grotty age and we'll all be joining you soon enough.'

She smiled a thin smile. 'That's one way of looking at it.'

'The only way.'

Now that I knew, of course, I could see it in her. It was there in the brightness of the eye and the tightness and pallor of the skin. The boniness of body that I had read as neurotic rich girl's pseudo-anorexia, that too might in justice be attributed to sickness.

401

She leaned back, and breathed out. Just showing off now, I thought. The exhalation seemed to me to be designed to demonstrate how mature and wise her death sentence had made her, how it had 'put things in perspective' and set her curiously free.

'I told you that I wasn't scared,' she said, 'and I'm not. But at first I was. Simply hysterical. Tell me . . .'

'I'm listening.'

'I don't really know where to begin. What do you think . . . what do you think of priests?'

I sat down. Here we go, I thought. Here we ruddy go. The laying-on of hands. If not priests, essential oils; if not essential oils, needles; if not needles, herbs; if not herbs, lumps of translucent rock and etheric sheaths.

'Priests . . .' I said. 'Are we speaking of the Romish or the Anglican kind?'

'I don't know. I take it you're an atheist?'

'I sometimes slip, but broadly speaking, yes. I try not to think about it. The cassocked buzzards have been wheeling in the air above you, have they? Fighting for scavenging rights to your soul?'

'No, no . . . it's not that. Oh dear . . .'

She got up and paced about, while I sat, gripped my whisky and waited. I thought about life as a restaurant critic, wondered if there were the seeds of any late-flowering poetry in me and reflected, with the intolerance of the healthy, that leukaemia was an affliction that I would be perfectly capable of snapping out of. Brace up and walk it off, woman, I said to myself. If you can't tell a few white corpuscles to piss off out of it, what are you?

At last she turned, a decision arrived at.

'The point is,' she said, 'that a strange thing has happened. In my family. I don't understand it, but I think it might interest you. As a writer.'

'Oh ah?' Whenever people say, 'as a writer, you'll find this very fascinating,' I prepare myself for thunderous bore-dom and numbing banality. Besides, what kind of writer was I anyway? She was trying to flatter me into attention.

'I thought, as you aren't . . . ah . . . *occupied* at the moment, that you might be able to help me. Something needs investigating.'

'Well, my dear, I don't know exactly what you had in mind. I'm not what you might call an investigative journal-ist. I'm not actually any kind of journalist at all. I can't really imagine what a failed poet, failed novelist, failed theatre critic and only marginally successful failure could possibly offer.'

'Well, you know the people concerned, you see, and . . .'

'Woah!' I held up a hand. 'Jane. My darling. Angel. Poppet. In sappier happier days, your mother and I used to stick it away. That's all. I haven't seen her in a coon's age. She said goodbye to me twenty-odd years ago in a blizzard of flung christening cake and savage abuse.'

'I'm not talking about Mummy, I'm talking about her brother.'

'*Logan?* You're talking about Logan? Jesus suffering fuck, woman . . .' I tried to say more, but the Cough had come upon me, as it does these days. It starts as the smallest tickle in the throat and can build, though I say so myself as shouldn't, into a not unimpressive display. Something between a vomiting donkey and an explosion at a custard factory. Jane watched without sympathy as I choked and wheezed myself to relative calm.

'You knew him,' she repeated, 'you knew him better than most. And you are, don't forget, David's godfather.'

'Well,' I panted, wiping away the tears from my cheeks, 'as it happens I haven't forgotten. Sent him a confirmation present only the other week. Got a cutely pi response.'

'Cutie pie?'

'Pi, as in . . . oh, never mind.'

Nobody can speak English any more.

'So you knew about *David's* confirmation, but not about mine.'

Lord, what a whining old sow.

'I told you,' I explained patiently, 'your mother won't have anything to do with me. I saw her three or four years ago at Swafford and I could see then that she still hadn't forgiven me. Your Uncle Michael, on the other hand, has a large nature.'

'And an even larger bank balance.'

This was not worthy of a reply. It was true that I valued Michael's friendship highly and his sister Rebecca's not a whit, but I liked to think that there was more to it than money. But then, I liked to think that the world venerated poets and that one day wars would end and television personalities be wiped out by a fatal virus. Between what I liked to think and the cold veridical state of things fell one hell of a shadow.

'I would want you to think of this as a commission. I'm not an especially rich woman . . .'

No, of course you aren't, are you? You've pissed it all away on Lalique flacons, Peruvian birthing-blankets and Namibian labia-jewellery, you senseless cow.

'. . . but I could offer you a hundred thousand now and the rest . . . either later or left to you in my will.'

'A hundred thousand?' I caught sight of myself in the artfully, fartfully tarnished mirror above the mantelpiece. I saw a red mullet, gaping, pop-eyed, purple and very, very greedy.

'A quarter of a million all told.'

'A quarter of a million?'

'Yes.'

'This isn't *lire*, is it? I mean, you are talking about pounds sterling?'

She nodded gravely.

'I don't . . . Jane . . . a quarter of a million is a lot of money and is, I won't attempt to deny it, quite monstrously appealing to me. But I don't know if I have it in me to do anything for anyone which, in any kind of honesty, is worth a tenth of that sum.'

'You will have to work hard,' Jane said.

I could see from the set of her mouth that nothing I could say was going to make much difference to her. Her mind, like her face, was fully made up.

'And you will have to work fast. Whatever you uncover I need to know before I die. That is if I do.'

'Er . . . if you do what?'

'If I do die.'

'If you do die?'

'If I do die.'

We were beginning to sound like a couple of pissed Nigerians.

'But you said . . .'

'No, the *doctors* said, the doctors said that I was going to die. I don't believe I am. That is the point.'

Well, there it was. If she did get around to giving me a

cheque, it would in all likelihood be signed 'Jessica Rabbit' or 'L. Ron Hubbard'.

'I believe that I have been saved, you see.'

'Ah. Right. Saved. Yes. Lovely.'

She rose and went over to a lacquered bureau, smiling the seraphic smile of the irretrievably crazed.

'I know what you're thinking, but it isn't like that. You'll see.' She took a cheque-book from the bureau and began to write. 'There!' She tore off a cheque and waved it in the air, a pennant of good faith drying in the breeze.

'Look . . .' I managed. 'Jane. In all honour, or such tatters of it as I have remaining, I shouldn't take your money. I don't understand what it is that you want me to do, I doubt that I have the capacity to do it and it is, to put it nicely, a racing certainty that you are not in your right mind. You should see a . . . a chap.'

What I meant by 'a chap' I wasn't sure. Doctor, psychiatrist or priest, I suppose. Frothing hypocrisy on the part of a man who doesn't believe in such ordure, but what the hell else is one supposed to say?

'I want you to go to Swafford. I want you to tell the family that you are writing Uncle Michael's biography,' she said, handing me the cheque. 'You are probably the only person alive he would allow to do such a thing.'

A properly signed and dated cheque for one hundred thousand pounds lay on my lap in front of me. My bank had a branch near South Ken tube station. I could be out of the house and filling in a deposit slip in ten minutes.

'There are,' I said, 'professional writers who will compile family histories for you at a fraction of that price. Vanity publishing, they call it.'

'You don't understand,' she said. 'You won't be writing a family history, you will be reporting a phenomena.'

'Phenomenon,' I muttered irritably.

'You will be witnessing a *miracle*.'

'A miracle. I see. And what kind of miracle precisely?'

She paused. 'I want you to go to Swafford and make your reports,' she said. 'Write to me constantly. I want to see if you notice anything. You think my mind has gone, but I know that if you go there, you will see for yourself what there is to be seen.'

I left the house and rolled up the Brompton Road, reflecting as busily as a wet mirror on a sunny day. Jane was mad, certainly, but her cheque was crossed and endearingly sane. It was a question now of how to wangle an invitation to Swafford. It was a question of how much work I had to do for the money. It was a question of what kind of work I had to do for that money. I damned the woman for not telling me what to look out for. If she had given me the slightest indication I could then have at least contrived to bolster her delusions by seeming to confirm them. But what were those delusions? My last visit to Swafford had been amusing enough but hardly revealing of miracles.

Two

Lord Logan knelt down between his sons and pointed to the tower. David looked up. Through the night mist he saw the clock face, newly painted gold on blue.

'Very smart, Dad,' Simon was saying. 'Is that real gold?'

Lord Logan laughed.

'Gilt.'

'It is gold in the drawing room though. You said.'

'In the drawing room, yes.'

'And in the Chinese Room, Dad, and the chapel.'

'Gold leaf.'

'Gold leaf,' Simon repeated with satisfaction. 'The decorators showed me the book. Every single page was pure gold.'

David was screwing up his eyes. The electric light spun the mist all around the clock into a yellow ball that suspended itself above the stable yard.

'Now then,' said Lord Logan. 'What's the time?'

'Uh oh,' said Simon, putting his hands over his ears.

David looked too and saw that it was about half a minute to ten o'clock. He counted down the seconds in his head.

Lord Logan hugged the boys to him and made a ticktock noise with his tongue. He felt the warmth of David's hand in his and the chill of Simon's.

David listened for the grinding whir that came before the chime. One of the big hunters was stamping in his stall and, farther away in the kennel block, David heard the whining of the beagle pups.

No sound came from the clock. They were not standing directly in front of it so David supposed their angle made the hour hand look more advanced than it really was. He began a fresh count-down from ten. Simon had told him once that you could accurately count seconds if you put the word 'alligator' between each number.

'Ten alligator, nine alligator, eight alligator, seven alligator, six alligator . . .' David said to himself.

Simon removed his hands from his ears.

'Dad!' he said reproachfully. Only these holidays had he switched from Daddy to Dad and he liked to use the new word as much as possible.

'You see?' Lord Logan jigged with pleasure.

There was no doubt that, whatever their angle to the clock, it was now a clear minute past ten.

'But I *liked* the bong,' said Simon.

'Ah, but you don't understand. There's a control fitted. It still chimes during the day, but when it's dark, it doesn't.'

'Brilliant! That's brilliant, Dad!'

'Something had to be done. The twins were being woken up every hour, on the hour.'

'I know, Dad,' said Simon. 'My room's just down the corridor, don't forget.'

'Ah well,' said Lord Logan, standing up and dusting his knees with the back of his hand. 'That's another thing. Come on, David, you're not too big . . . hup!' David jumped on to his father's shoulders and they made their way back to the house. 'Now that you're thirteen, Simon, we ought to take you out of the nursery and give you a proper bedroom, don't you think?'

'Oh boy,' said Simon.

'I mean, if you're going to be joining the guns on Boxing Day.'

'Daddy!' Simon kicked the gravel in excitement. 'Oh boy, oh boy, oh boy!'

Lord Logan hitched David up further on to his shoulders.

'Woof! I'm getting too old for this, Davey.'

David knew, however, that although he would soon be twelve, he was small and light for his age and that his father could have carried him five miles without a murmur.

A fortnight later David lay on his bed and stared at the ceiling, just as he had the night before. The night before had been Christmas Eve when all children lie awake to surprise their fathers. Not that it would have been Lord Logan himself, Simon claimed.

'He gets Podmore to dress up and dump them in our rooms.'

'No, I bet it is Daddy. He'd enjoy it.'

David had not managed to stay awake long enough to find out. Tonight he would certainly stay awake. He absolutely had to.

The brand-new alarm clock, a Christmas present from Aunt Rebecca, ticked on his bedside table.

Half past one.

The most important thing was not to wake up the twins. They were more than a year old and, since the muffling of the stable clock, they had started, in Nanny's words, to sleep through. But you never knew with the twins. They were always capable of creating an uproar. So that they would be especially tired, David had spent an hour enter-

410

taining them in their cots earlier in the evening. He had drawn pictures for them with crayons and pulled faces, hummed tunes and danced stupidly around the room until it was time for the goodnight visit.

'They seem rather hot, Sheila.'

'Yes, Lady Anne. David has been exciting them.'

'Davey?'

'I was just reading to them, Mummy.'

'Oh. Funny boy. Never mind, at least they'll sleep. Won't you, my darlings? Night night, Edward. Night night, James.'

A quarter to two.

David stood up and pulled a pair of dark brown corduroy trousers over his pyjamas. He put on his games pullover from school, which was navy blue with a roll-over collar, and chose a woolly hat and black plimsolls, also from school.

Looking at himself in the mirror, he wondered if perhaps he shouldn't smear boot polish on his face. He decided not to. It would be simply disastrous if he couldn't wash it off and everybody saw traces next morning.

Two o'clock.

He looked out of the window. Still dry. A clear night in fact, with just a hint of mist. That would mean a good hard frost and that would mean no footprints. God was on his side. God and Nature.

David returned to his bed, shook a pillow out of its slip, folded the slip neatly and pushed it up inside his jumper, securing it behind the waistband of his pyjamas and trousers.

He went to the door and tip-toed out into the corridor. The door of the twins' room opposite was open; a

411

twenty-watt night-light threw a weak yellow glow into the passageway. David could hear the twins breathing in time with each other.

As he passed the door of Simon's old room David edged himself closer to the wall, to avoid a loose board in the middle of the floor. Nanny was the only grown-up who slept near by, but she could wake up at the slightest sound, so he had to be most terribly careful.

David inched along the wall towards the pass door that led into the main part of the house. During the day you could bounce balls, slam cupboards and scream and shout in the nursery wing without ever being heard, but at night the smallest sound was magnified. His breathing alone seemed to make a dreadful amount of noise. The walls, the carpet, the roof, the radiator pipes, everything shifted, clicked and hummed like parts of a machine.

He opened the door. There came to him a faint scent of cigar smoke and the important ticking of a long-case clock. The north passage lay ahead and beyond it the stairs. David let the door swing silently behind him and stole forwards with the great Seven League Boots stride of the stealthy. He couldn't remember exactly how many guests were staying; he thought at least twelve, with another ten or eleven coming the next day for the shooting. To be sure of things, he would have to go by the bedrooms as though each one were occupied by a very light sleeper.

He took the centre of the corridor now because he knew that there were cabinets and tables set along the walls with china and silver and glass on them which would make a lot of noise if he brushed against them.

He was about half-way down, with the marble gleam of the staircase now in view ahead of him, when a sudden sound brought him to a stop. A yellow line of light had appeared under the door of the room he was passing, the Hobhouse Room. Frozen mid-stride, David strained to listen, mouth open, blood hammering in his ears. He heard the silken rustle of a dressing-gown being drawn on.

With a bolt of fright he remembered that there was no bathroom in the Hobhouse Room. He leapt along the corridor in a panic, stopping by the long-case clock at the end where he flattened himself against the wall. He leaned back and panted as quietly as he could, trying to synchronise his breathing with the great gulping beats of the pendulum that swung inside the clock beside him.

He heard the door of the Hobhouse Room open and footsteps approach.

David couldn't understand what was happening. He wanted to scream out 'But the bathroom's the *other* way!'

The footsteps came closer and closer. David held his breath and closed his eyes tight. The vibrations of the clock went through his body, each tick like an electric shock.

The footsteps stopped. 'He's looking at me,' thought David. 'I can hear him breathe.'

Then came the sound of fingernails gently tapping on wood. There was a bedroom door the other side of the clock from David. The Leighton Room, where Aunt Rebecca always stayed. David heard her whispered voice.

'Max? Is that you?'

A man's voice close by David answered, hoarse and cross.

'Let me in, it's bloody freezing out here.'

The door opened and closed.

David waited. Laughter and other sounds came from inside the Leighton Room. He knew that Aunt Rebecca loved games of all kinds. He decided to gamble on the likelihood of her and the man, Max, staying in the room for some time. David took a deep breath, stepped forwards and headed for the staircase.

His route was meticulously planned and rather complicated. He had to go first to the library, then to the kitchen, then outside through the scullery into the stable yard, and finally back through the kitchen to the library again.

It was dark at the top of the stairs. David took off his plimsolls so that their rubber soles wouldn't squeak on the marble. He went down slowly, feeling the corners of the picture-frames on the wall as he descended. His hand found the corner of the last painting, a huge Tiepolo every inch of which he knew, so now he could be sure he was on the last step. At the bottom, he turned left and went quickly across the open hall, the shortest route to the library.

Half-way across the hall he ran into something huge, something sharp and bristly that hugged him and stung his face. The shock was so great, the sense of being so completely in the grip of what he could only suppose to be a ghost or wild animal, that without meaning to he shouted out; a short howl of pain and fright.

At the very moment he cried out, David realised that what he had run into was only the Christmas tree. Disgusted with himself at such cowardice, he spat a needle from his mouth, stepped back from the tree and listened. There were no sounds of any movement upstairs: no shouts, no sleepy grumbles, no wails from the twins, only a gentle tinkle from the decorations as the tree recovered from the collision. David's panicky yell had probably not been so very loud after all. In his head he replayed the sound and realised that really it had been no more than a husky gasp.

Circling the tree warily, David made for the library.

In the library the smell of cigar smoke was so strong it made the hairs at the back of his legs prickle. It was warm too; a faint orange glow in the fireplace showed that the fire had not yet died. David closed the door behind him and felt for the light switch.

Blinking at the sudden brightness, he looked about the room. He was glad to see that the shutters were closed. There would be no oblongs of light thrown on to the South Lawn, which would have been visible to anyone looking out of a window from one of the upstairs bedrooms.

On the fifth shelf, behind Lord Logan's enormous desk, there was a neat line of twelve old books entitled *Crabshawe's History of the Countie of Norfolk*. They were bound in sand-coloured leather and stamped with gold lettering.

David moved his finger along the line, like a browser in a bookshop, until he came to Volume VI, which he pulled out and laid on the desk. He inserted his hand in the gap on the shelf and felt for the lever. He pulled hard and was shocked by the great twang of the spring as it released the catch. By day the mechanism seemed as quiet as a whisper.

The whole section of shelving swung open and David went through the secret doorway and into the room beyond.

He couldn't find a light switch in this room, so he had to work by the light spilling in from the library. He could see enough, however, and sense even more: the heads of fox and stag bearing down on him, the light aroma of gun-oil and the thudding of yet another big clock.

He made for a small bureau against the wall, between

two gun cabinets. On the bureau was a large padded
leather book from Smythson's of Bond Street. 'Game
Book' it said. Simon had given it to Daddy two Christ-
mases ago. David remembered excitedly asking to see it,
expecting it to be a book perhaps like Hoyle's, some sort
of encyclopedia or dictionary of games and pastimes. He
had not been pleased to find out that it was just blank
pages, with ruled ledgers headed 'Date', 'Breed', 'Guns',
'Number killed' and so on.

Behind the game book there was a small drawer. David
pulled it open and stirred the contents with a finger until
he found – amongst the rubber bands, fishing flies and
squares of lint – a key, around which his fist closed with a
relieved and determined clutch. Now it was time to go
down to the kitchen.

He took the greatest care to avoid the Christmas tree as
he crossed the hall. Once he knew it was there he could
see it quite clearly, of course, standing guard over the
staircase like a huge and shaggy bear.

David shivered at the sudden breath of warm air that
met him when he opened the red baize door and went
down the steps into the kitchen.

Moonlight came in through the high semi-circular windows; it gleamed on wickerwork hampers that had been
laid out ready for the great breakfast. David edged round
the central table, sat down on a chair at the end nearest the
stove and put his plimsolls back on. His elbow touched a
piece of grease-proof paper on the table. He lifted a corner
of the paper up and could smell smoked ham. Immediately
his throat began to contract and spasm. He turned away
and breathed deeply, but had to bury his face in his fore-

arm to muffle the sound of his dry retching. After a while he stood and wiped the tears from his eyes.

At the far end of the kitchen was a door which led to the sculleries and pantries. David went through and turned on the light.

The machinery in the cold-room hummed and down the end of the passage a large black cat came up to him, stretching its legs as it walked.

'Sh!' said David.

The cat twined itself around his legs and began to purr.

'Come on, then,' David said and the cat accompanied him to the larder door.

The second shelf of the larder, neatly ordered, contained sugar, flour, tins of baking powder, packets of yeast, sachets of gelatine, spices, cake decorations and cartons of candied peel, all in huge catering-size packs. There were children's party napkins there too, boxes of meringue nests, bags of confetti, waxed paper jelly-bowls and tins of Playbox biscuits.

David took out the pillow-case from under his pullover and began to fill it. He dropped a piece of angelica on the floor for the cat, who sniffed, shook a paw and stalked out, disgusted.

When the pillow-case had been filled with the right things, David left the larder, switched off the light in the passageway and returned to the kitchen.

With his pillow-case over his shoulder like Father Christmas, he let himself out of the back door.

He walked through the night, clouds of vapour coming from his mouth and nostrils. He felt happy and charged with energy and vigour.

The outhouse he was heading for used once to be part

of the laundry buildings and lay between the stable block and the gamekeeper's cottage. Simon called it the 'B and L' room now, for beaters and loaders.

The moon, high in the starlit sky, shone on the door and lit the iron padlock with a lick of silver. David took the key from his pocket and unfastened the lock.

Far away, in the spinneys and copses, the pheasants shifted in their roosts. Rabbits fled from barking vixens, owls swooped on scampering voles and, back in the yard, the black cat that unseen by David had slipped with him out of the kitchen, batted a dying mouse from paw to paw.

Sitting on a large box marked 'Eley', David straddled the machine. He pulled back the brass lever and hummed a little tune to himself as he engaged the treadle.

II

Simon jumped out of the Range Rover with Soda, his spaniel bitch, and looked amongst the crowd of beaters for a sign of his brother. Eventually he saw David standing apart from the others, stroking the head of one of the labradors. At a whistle from Henry the gamekeeper's lad, the dog turned and sprinted towards the group of pickers-up who were making ready to leave. David, deprived of company, looked up in Simon's direction. Simon immediately pretended to be scanning the sky and smelling the wind.

Ahead of him lay the drive, a long avenue of beech, oak and elm. Simon closed up his gun, brought it to his shoulder and sighted into the air above the trees.

'Blam!' he whispered. 'Blam!'

A giant hand landed on his shoulder. 'If a sportsman true you'd be, Listen carefully to me, Never, never let your gun . . .'

Simon joined in, '. . . Pointed be at anyone. When a hedge or fence you cross, Though of time it cause a loss, From your gun the cartridge take, For the greatest safety sake.'

Lord Logan nodded.

'Sorry, Dad,' said Simon, breaking the gun. 'I was just . . . you know.'

His father shrugged with a smile. He looked over his shoulders like a conspirator and drew a silver hip-flask from his coat pocket. 'Chivas Regal,' he said. 'One nip only. Don't tell your mother.'

The whisky stung Simon's throat and tears started in his eyes.

'Whooh!' he said. 'Thanks, Dad.'

Lord Logan screwed the lid back on and looked down at Simon's dog. 'Whisky and Soda,' he said and winked.

Simon laughed. Today he was the only gun with his own dog. Everybody else would have to rely on pickers-up to retrieve their dead game. Soda was Simon's dog and she would bring his kills back to him personally.

'We're numbering eight, we're moving two!' called Henry.

Lord Logan looked in the direction of the drive, where the drawing of numbers was under way. 'Have you drawn?' he asked.

Simon shook his head.

'Good,' said his father. 'Best not. Let the older guns fight it out, eh? We'll double-bank you behind Conrad.'

Simon's face fell. 'But I want to be at the front!'

'Conrad's a dreadful shot. You'll do well.' Lord Logan's mouth wrinkled in the special distaste it reserved for whines and whinges.

Simon blushed. 'Thanks, Dad.'

'Well, then. Let battle commence.'

Simon kept a few paces behind to watch the effect his father had on the others as he joined the main group of guns. Men and women stepped back, eyes sliding covertly in his direction. Everybody smiled. Simon knew that some were smiling because of the preposterously perfect condition of his father's clothes, the shining Purdey guns, the gleaming new leather, the perfectly made hat from Lock's, the hand-warmers, the cartridge belt, the tailored tweed coat and the tight narrow leggings that tapered down from his broad bulk – dark stockings over moleskins. Dad knew too and he didn't care. He liked the best of everything and said so often enough. Mummy's friends and family were in the tattiest old tweeds and muddiest boots and thought highly of themselves because of it. Dad let them smile. He knew they smiled for other reasons too.

David and the other beaters had gone off round to the wood behind the avenue. The guns and loaders, all men, were beginning to arrange themselves, two to a peg. Simon went up to one of the loaders.

'Just chuck us some boxes,' he said.

The grown-ups had a loader each and a pair of guns, so that they could keep shooting with one gun while the other was being loaded. Simon did have two twelve-bore guns, but one was an over-and-under, a present from Aunt Rebecca who, being a woman, had no idea that over-and-unders were not on; they were fit only for foreigners, armed robbers and weekend nobodies. The barrels on a proper shotgun, everybody knew, had to be side by side. To make matters worse, Aunt Rebecca's gun had a box lock instead of a side lock, which put it completely beyond the pale. Therefore, beautiful as it may have been and ideal for a private and solitary rough shoot, Simon had left it behind. He prayed that Aunt Rebecca, who was milling about around the back with Uncle Ted and a group of women and spectators from the village, wouldn't notice. Simon did have another shotgun, a four-ten which he had grown up on, potting at crows and rabbits, but after a long debate with himself he had decided that he should take just his one dependable old twelve-bore and do his own loading.

He filled the pockets of his Barbour with cartridge boxes.

Soda danced around him displaying all the excitement and pleasure that Simon was trying hard to conceal.

He saw his seventeen-year-old cousin Conrad, drawn at number three, and took up a position behind him.

'Oh bloody hell,' said Conrad. 'Don't stand behind me. I don't want to die.'

Simon blushed.

'I'm a good shot,' he muttered.

'Got a bloody dog with you, too, have you? Well, I'm not having any running-in.'

'She won't run in,' said Simon indignantly.

'Well, she'd better not.'

'Sh!' Lord Draycott, an elderly man further along the line, scowled at Conrad from under a rather wide cloth cap.

Conrad snorted contemptuously. 'It's pheasant, for God's sake! They're virtually deaf.'

'These are wild birds, Conrad,' whispered the man next to Conrad, whom Simon recognised as Max Clifford, a friend of his father's. 'Sporting birds. They startle easily. They're not hand-reared as they are in Hampshire.'

Somehow, in Max's soft tones, the word 'Hampshire' came out as a terrible insult. Conrad reddened and turned away. Simon settled himself. Soda sat neatly beside him, tongue out, panting gently. Quiet descended.

Simon continued to recite 'A Father's Advice' to himself, under his breath.

'Keep your place and silent be, Game can hear and game can see. Don't be greedy, better spared, Is a pheasant than one shared.'

A cock pheasant strolled out of the wood and into the

main drive towards them, clucking loudly. Someone laughed.

Simon felt inside his pocket and drew out two cartridges.

'If 'twixt you and neighbouring gun, Bird may fly and beast may run, Let this maxim e'er be thine, Follow not across the line.'

The pheasant continued its strut down the avenue, neck thrusting arrogantly backwards and forwards.

Simon pushed the cartridges into the barrels and closed the gun.

'Stops and beaters oft unseen, Lurk behind some leafy screen. Calm and steady always be, Never shoot where you can't see.'

The pheasant's cheerful walk slowed. He peered doubt-fully ahead and seemed slowly to become aware of a line of pink faces, of brown, green and russet tweed and of shining gun-metal ranged against him. He checked his swagger and set his neck forward in goggling disbelief, which reminded Simon of the cross-eyed barman in Laurel and Hardy films.

Simon breathed hard through his nose and swallowed.

'You may kill or you may miss,' he whispered to himself, 'But at all times think of this, All the pheasants ever bred, Won't repay for one man dead.'

The pheasant threw a glance back into the spinney he had just left. Simon thought the bird had made some connection. With a rising note of outrage in his throat, as if trying to send some desperate warning signal to his family and friends back there in the wood, the pheasant rose.

At the same time, Lord Logan brought to his lips a silver

horn and blew. Deep within the woods a mighty roar went up and the beaters began to stamp and strike the ground.

Simon licked his lips and banged his feet into a solid two o'clock position, weight forward on his left leg. His right thumb flicked the safety catch. The other guns rose from their shooting-sticks. Soda squared herself.

All at once the air was filled with squadrons of rocketing pheasants. Gunshots sounded everywhere like harsh coughs, and little puffs of smoke blossomed in the air.

Simon had practised this in his head so many times. The birds had to come high to clear the trees, which is why the guns were positioned where they were. But they came so fast: three or four hundred flushed in one go. By the time Simon could sight they were already over his head. He followed one bird up from the cover and fired off the first barrel just before his gun reached the vertical. He brought the gun down fifty degrees, followed another bird and managed to loose off again, aiming for the beak.

He had broken his gun and was scrambling to reload when a shout came from the woods.

'Steady boys: whoa, whoa! Hold hard!'

The last few pheasants fluttered past and Simon heard echoes of the closing volleys of gunshot rattle off the windows and brick-work of the house half a mile behind them. The first flush had taken perhaps forty seconds and he had only just managed to get off both barrels. Conrad had fired off fourteen rounds. There rose a barking and yelping through the trees.

'Go on, Soda!' shouted Simon. 'Go on, girl!'

Soda sprang forward and dashed into the woods: Simon thought he might have downed a bird with his second barrel. Soda would have seen.

A shout went up.

'Look! Look!'

Simon saw, now that the gun smoke had cleared, that the air ahead of them was full of what appeared to be falling petals. The pickers-up were standing in bewilderment, their dogs circling them and whimpering as a coloured blizzard swirled about.

Simon heard Aunt Rebecca's voice behind him. 'It's . . . for God's sake . . . it's *confetti*!'

'Bravo! Charming!' said Uncle Ted.

'Bloody hell!' said Conrad.

Soda trotted out of the spinney with a pheasant in her mouth which she dropped at her master's feet.

Simon looked down in disgust. 'It's a runner,' he said. The bird was still alive, its beak opening and closing, its crooked, wrinkled legs working frantically. Simon picked it up and twisted its neck until he heard a crack.

The others gathered round.

'What the hell's going on?'

'This is the only bloody kill!'

Simon looked up in embarrassment as everyone crowded round him.

'What do you mean?' he said.

'We mean,' said Conrad, 'that no one else has bagged a single sodding bird. That's what we mean.'

Simon didn't understand. The first flush in a well-stocked cover like that should mean a kill of at least a hundred birds.

Lord Logan took the pheasant out of Simon's hands. Henry, the gamekeeper's assistant, was hurrying forward towards them, an expression both of wild fury and of complete puzzlement on his face.

Lord Logan examined the pheasant. There were little silver balls caught up in its gorge.

'Silver shot?' someone exclaimed. 'That's going it, even for you, Michael.'

Simon saw his father's eyes flash for a second under his heavy brows.

'This is not shot,' he said, rolling a single ball between his thumb and forefinger. 'Nor is it silver.'

He put the ball in his mouth and crunched it between his teeth.

'Sugar!' he said mournfully. 'Just sugar.'

Simon took a fresh cartridge out of his pocket and began to unpick the end. Into his father's outstretched palm he poured out a heap of coloured hundreds and thousands, silvered sugar balls, rice and a wad of confetti.

'Christ!' said Conrad. 'Sabs. It's the bloody sabs.'

'Sabs?' said Simon. 'They wouldn't . . .'

'Sabs! Sabs! We've been bloody sabbed!'

The cry went up and gathered into a roar that mingled with the chuckling of the pheasants as they settled back in their roosts and mingled too with the weeping, squealing laughter of one of the beaters who had lagged behind the others and now lay on the ground, deep in the wood, wriggling with happiness and, true to his trade, beating and beating and beating the ground with small fists.

Three

Dear Uncle Ted,

This is just a note to thank you so much for your present. I'm very sorry you couldn't make the service itself, but I do understand that your life is immensely busy.

Mr Bridges, my English master, tells me that what you sent is a first edition, which is extremely valuable. I am very touched by your generosity. I have never read the *Four Quartets* before, although we did *The Waste Land* for GCSE which I enjoyed enormously, so I am looking forward very much to reading and understanding these new poems. Are they connected at all to Beethoven's quartets, I wonder? My favourite poet is Wordsworth at the moment.

The confirmation was magnificent. The Bishop of St Alban's spoke to us all beforehand and reminded us of the solemnity of the occasion. When the moment came for him to lay his hand upon my head I found myself crying. I hope you don't think that was wrong of me. I think I was moved more by the idea of the apostolic succession than by anything else. Christ laid a hand on Peter's head, Peter became Bishop of Rome and he laid a hand on the head of everyone else who became a bishop. Even though we broke with Rome in the sixteenth century, the bishops of the Church of England can trace themselves by a hand laid on the head, all the way back to Christ.

When I bit the wafer I was surprised by how tasty it was. I had been told by everyone that it would be disgusting – like cardboard. Actually it reminded me of the rice-paper that you find on the underside of a macaroon. The wine was very sweet, but that's how I prefer it anyway.

You said that you hoped confirmation would live up to its name and that, as well as confirming my faith publicly, the service would confirm something in me privately. Well, I suppose it has, really. Everyone is agreed that the world is getting to be a worse place year by year. There is more crime, more poverty, more corruption, more distress. I think that Grace, which we talked about a lot in confirmation classes, is probably the only thing that can save the world. That's very idealistic I know, but I think it makes more logical sense than anything else. Grace is about looking *inwards* not outwards. If everyone looked inwards to their own souls, or psyches or whatever word you want to use, then all the sins in the world would disappear. If only we could all put up our hands and say 'the problems are all my fault' there would be no problems.

Simon has been made house captain this term and is in the first XV, so we are all very proud of him. He wants to go into the army after school, but Daddy wants him to try for Oxford. I'm not sure what I want to do, not the army anyway. I would truly love, more than anything else, to be a poet like you.

After all, what else is *worth* doing?

The Hippopotamus

The world is too much with us; late and soon,
Getting and spending, we lay waste our powers:
Little we see in Nature that is ours;
We have given our hearts away . . .

It's now after prep and I've just found a very marvellous line in the *Four Quartets* that talks about how the stones of a building don't reflect light, but actually *absorb* it. I think that is saying something about the love of God.

I hope you will absorb my love and thanks for a wonderful present.

Lots of love

David
XXX

I tried my damnedest to recall whether myself at that age, I had been quite such a pi, punchable little shit as this. I remembered listening to illicit jazz and climbing ladders to catch the housemaster's daughter undressing; I remembered all the fights, farts and fidgets of a bog-standard, bog-quality British education; I remembered howling with injustice, roaring with passion and grunting with loneliness; I remembered talking about poetry, certainly, and pledging that the poets of the future would grab mankind by the balls and give such a vicious twist that the whole human race would scream for mercy. But wanking on about Grace and sin? Spraying out pissy dribbles of Wordsworth sonnetry? I don't think so. 'The Bishop of St Alban's spoke to us all beforehand and reminded us of the solemnity of the occasion' indeed. Did the sanctimonious squirt think he was writing a letter to a godfather or an article for the school magazine? 'I would truly love, more than anything else, to be a poet like you.' Did he mean he would love to be, like me, a poet? Or was he crawly (and idiotic) enough to mean that he wanted to be the kind of poet I was? Cold Christ and tangled Trinities, what an anus.

4 Butler's Yard
St James's
LONDON SW1

Dear David,

What a remarkable letter. I am delighted that my little present has hit the mark so surely.

I too was disappointed not to be amongst those present at your confirmation. I recall my own with exceptional clarity. Chichester, not the loveliest of our great cathedrals – squat and ugly as a toad if the truth be out – but holy in my memory. The service took place on one of those afternoons that occur only in the past. Sunlight kissed the altar-table, the chalices, patens and candlesticks, the bishop's mitre and our young neophyte heads with a golden rim-light calculated to cause the sternest atheist among us to whinny with unconditional faith.

Utter balls, naturally. The only thing gleaming with light

that afternoon was the dew-drop depending from the bish's nose.

There is no doubt, whatever one's perspective on these matters, that the numen created by a gathering-together of people united in one common spiritual cause is as palpable as the ground they kneel upon. Whether this is truer in an Anglican cathedral than in a Buddhist temple or a front-parlour séance of crackpot spiritualists is not within my province to say. I *am* pleased, however, that you are getting something out of old Tom Eliot, whom I did indeed know. He published me at Faber and Faber when I was starting out. Said some rather nice things about me – then again, towards the end, he said nice things about a whole fleet of talentless ninnies, none of whom you would have heard of, nor ever will hear of again. There was a man called Botterill he was absolutely sold on. Who reads Botterill today? Why, even fewer people than read me, and that is saying something.

However, that is neither here nor there. I wanted to say, principally, how impressed I was by the sentiments expressed with such courage and conviction in your letter. My only other godchild is your cousin Jane, and as you know, I am not on speakers with that side of your family, so I count myself very lucky in having an intelligent and interesting godchild with whom it is a pleasure to correspond. It'll be your holidays soon, I suppose. It would be a great treat if we could get together and see if between us we can't get to the bottom of this business of art and life. I wonder if it would be possible for me to come over some time in the summer and stay at the Hall? We would be able to read, think, talk, sip cordials and pick daisies together, or as Burns prefers, we can 'pluck the gowans fine'. My own son (you remember Roman?) will be with his respective and disrespectful mother over most of the summer holiday so I shall be alone and in sore need of some intellectual and spiritual stimulus.

Outrageous. Ted, you fucker, is this what you've come to? Cadging country-house visits off your godchildren? Admit it, you sad old bugger, the only 'intellectual and spiritual stimulus' you were ever in need of was a quick shag in the shrubbery with a domestic. I did need a way in to Swafford, however, if I was to earn my lovely lovely money. It was also possible that the company of a mooning romantic might disgust me enough to egg on some new and crunchy verse of my own.

So why not mention the idea to your parents, old lad, and see what they think? It's been an age since I've seen you and, dissipated and disgraceful as I may be, my promises at the font do mean something to me. Perhaps your youth will inspire me to write poetry again. I find that time and age have corrupted my powers and that, as your favourite poet observes, 'the vision splendid' does indeed 'fade into the common light of day'.

> *Whither is fled the visionary gleam?*
> *Where is it now, the glory and the dream?*

P-U! I had to leap up and pace the room whistling and humming and kicking the wainscoting to take the taste of that one away.

So, here's looking forward to a summer of discovery and amusement,

Your affectionate godfather

Ted

Oh, you howling old hypocrite, what a beast you are, what a dread cruel beast. What a great, slavering, wicked and contemptible monster. How can you hold up your head? How can you look yourself in the face? How can you sleep? You horrible, horrible man.

Dear Uncle Ted,

Your letter made me dance. Mummy or Daddy will be in touch soon. I hope you can stay at least a whole month!

> ... *neither evil tongues,*
> *Rash judgments, nor the sneers of selfish men,*
> *Nor greetings where no kindness is, nor all*
> *The dreary intercourse of daily life,*
> *Shall e'er prevail against us, or disturb*
> *Our cheerful faith that all which we behold*
> *Is full of blessings.*

Counting the days,

Love

David
XXX

II

Swafford Hall
Swafford
Norfolk

Sunday, 19th July 1992

Dear Jane,

Your first report, as promised, from within the walls
of Troy. My letter to your cousin and god-brother, if
there is such a thing, worked like a charm. Little Davey
all but sent me his pocket-money to cover my train fare,
so keen was he for me to come. Unless I poo things up
horribly, I'm here for as long as I behave myself.

Liverpool Street Station has been turned into a sinister and unacceptable mixture of an Edwardian amusement pier and a daytime television studio since last I
looked. Absolutely disgusting. Since your cheque seems
inexplicably to have been honoured, I travelled First
Class. There's only one smoking car on the whole train
as far as I can see. In Britrail's futile attempts to ape
airlines (in itself a deranged project – about as sensible
as going into a barber-shop and asking for a Lindsay
Anderson cut) they litter the compartment with a laughable in-carriage glossy called 'Executive' or 'Top Traveller' or some such pukey garbage. Thank Jesus I'll soon
be dead. Sorry, that sounds a little callous in the light
of your illness. You know what I mean.

Anyway, after an hour and a half's worth of scenery
had streaked past my window, the train banged to a

testicle-strangling halt at Diss Station and collapsed the little pyramid of Johnny Walker miniatures I had been constructing on the table in front of me. I saw a youth on the platform, tossing and catching a bunch of car-keys like a gangster with a silver dollar. A glossy black spaniel sat by his side exposing its tongue to the air as is the custom of such creatures. The bungling manner with which I attempted to pull my suitcase widthways through a narrow compartment doorway must have told him who I was. It is unlikely he would have remembered me from four years ago, the last time I infested Swafford.

'Hello, sir,' he said, taking the case and deftly twisting it free. 'I'm Simon Logan. Welcome to Norfolk.'

'Good man. Ted Wallace.'

'This is Soda. My spaniel.'

'It's an enormous pleasure, Soda,' I said, dropping a forefinger on to the animal's muzzle by way of greeting.

Simon led me to the exit.

'David wanted to come too, but I thought you'd enjoy the two-seater.'

A two-tone Austin-Healey stood in the car-park, ice-blue over ivory. A Rank Starlet car, I thought to myself, sort of thing Diana Dors would be photographed in, tossing back her scarfed head with a gleam of teeth and a glitter of winged sun-glasses. You're probably too young to remember Diana Dors, but I put this in at no extra charge. I had been hoping for Michael's well-stocked Rolls-Royce, of course, but the boy was clearly pleased with this machine, so I clucked appropriately.

'I left the roof and window pieces at home to leave room in the boot for your luggage. So long as it doesn't rain, eh?'

I looked up at a huge East Anglian sky, innocent of clouds and blue as . . . my poetic powers have been sucked clean of simile. I can't think what it was as blue as. As blue as blue. As blue as the Virgin's panties. As blue as it was.

Once the town of Diss was behind us, the Austin's engine note and the unmarked lanes created the pleasing illusion of a mild and dusty Dornford Yates England. One half-expected to see horses rearing in shock at the unaccustomed sight of an automobile and slack-jawed villagers nudging one another in wonder. In fact we saw no one. A sheet of stillness lay over everything and we ripped through it like a speedboat across a lake. You probably haven't heard of Dornford Yates either, but there you go.

In the rush of air my forelock flapped in my face as I looked right and left, stinging my eyes. Simon, whose hair is unfashionably short, looked straight ahead, every concentrated second at the wheel sustaining him in something close to orgasm. I judged him seventeen and only newly licensed. He is the kind of boy who would take his driving test the morning of his birthday and find excuses to drive twenty miles to buy a box of matches. Soda was wedged happily behind us, the tip of her tongue whipped back by the wind till it met the base of her ears.

A silver gleam caught my attention in the distance, across a haze of fields whose crops were just on the turn from green to gold.

'What's that?' I bellowed.

Simon cocked his head.

I stabbed a finger and yelled. 'There! Shiny thing, like a church.'

'Oh, that. Silo.'

'What?'

'For grain. Cheaper to build that than reroof an old barn. Better storage.'

'Ugly bugger.'

I noticed too that the country seemed, Noël Coward jokes about Norfolk aside, *flatter* than I remembered it. This wasn't possible, but there was no doubting the increase in width and depth of view. It was the hedgerows of course, or rather the absence of them. It must have been twenty years ago that they had started to pull them down, but my old man's memory still expected them. In the same way, if Westminster council decided overnight to allow traffic in Piccadilly to flow in both directions I would probably never notice, because I always think of Piccadilly as a two-way street, for all that it must be decades since they buggered it up. Now, here in East Anglia, what with the denuded fields and those great giant's bolsters encased in bin-liner that serve the office of straw-bales and these new and nasty aluminium silos, the landscape resembles something frankly American – you know those great wheat fields in Iowa where, line abreast, massed combine-harvesters roll over the horizon like Panzer divisions? I am a city pigeon of course, needing hard paving-stones beneath my feet and air I can bite, but rural England, for all that, has its place in my heart and I don't like the idea of hooligans arsing around with it.

Simon was amused.

'Got to think of the yield,' he shouted and then – the

aggressive cry of despoiling landowners everywhere – 'you want to eat, don't you?'

But hedges are still thickly planted, I noticed, around the approaches to Swafford Hall. There's nothing quite so enlivening to an unregenerate snob such as myself as the sight from a car of flashing parkland trees half-obscuring and half-revealing the chimneys, windows and columns of a great house, like a stripper teasing with a veil. We ate up the lime avenue and the full vulgar glory of the place swung, as L. P. Hartley would say, into view, and then I saw with a stab of regret and self-reproach that there was a boy sitting half-way up the baroque steps that poured from the front portico like a thick stream of molten lava. He stood and shaded his eyes in our direction.

I had deferred any thoughts of how I was going to shake off this wretched child. He had served his purpose by getting me invited here; the last thing I wanted was to trail about the place coping with pretentious adolescent drippery or, worse, being forced to listen to myself dole out my own dime-store apothegms. The answer, perhaps, would be to set him a task of some kind, to devise a devilish assignment that would keep him out of my hair. 'Write me something extensive in *terza rima*,' I pictured myself saying. 'If you're going to be a poet, you must learn to master the forms.'

Simon blew up a cloud of grit and gravel in a sharp and senseless sweeping handbrake turn in front of the house. David came down the steps blinking dust from his eyes.

'Hello, Uncle Edward,' he said, smiling and blushing. He is a comely boy indeed. Never having had any relish for my own gender, such coltish charms increased my blood pressure by not a bar – indeed I consider his looks a little ridiculous in a male – but I can think of any number of writers and artists of my acquaintance who at the very sight of him would swoon and moan and clutch at a passing vodka for support. Simon is handsome in a colourless way, like an old photographic portrait. He is respectably growing out of his spots and into a conventional English – or in his case of course, half-English – manhood. David's complexion, however, is quite astonishingly clear; in all my life I have not seen skin so wholly without blemish. There is something a little freakish there, I think. I assume you know him better than I do? At all events, his downcast eyes and crimson cheeks speak of a virginal modesty rare in the young today. He bids fair to be fully the kind of prig his letters have threatened.

'Davey, you young hound, well met,' said I, heaving my corse from the car.

What is nowadays almost universally called, with mock inverted snobbery, a 'real live butler' was standing at the threshold.

'Ah, Podmore, is it not?' I flapped a hand in his direction after a moment's concentrated hesitation, a hesitation designed to show me sifting my memory, recalling and discarding the names of at least twenty other butlers with whom I was on familiar terms. Comes easily to you, my dear, but we Bohemians have got to strive for the effect of insouciance.

'Good afternoon, Mr Wallace. Nice to see you again, sir.' Not that he was fooled for a minute, I dare say.

David had taken my suitcase from the boot of the

Austin with a proprietorial air that told the world that I was, certainly as far as he was concerned, *his* guest. Simon waved over his shoulder and launched the car, with a crunching spin of the back wheels, away on some other errand.

Well, well. Here I was. How long I would stay depended, I supposed, on the kind of reception Michael gave me. Your idea of telling him that I would like to write a biography is all very well, but.

The fact is, and I didn't tell you this earlier, Jane, but I know for certain that at least two fairly prestigious hacks have tried before now to biograph Michael Logan with little success. Swafford Hall is known in journalistic circles as the Writs Hotel.

I'm not saying it won't work – after all Michael trusts me, trusts me rather as Guy Burgess was trusted, in the belief that anyone of such naked indiscretion and unreliability must be loyal and true – but I feel you should know that some other approach may prove necessary in the end. *Nous verrons ce que nous verrons.*

David had reached the top of the steps, the weight of the case listing his slight frame.

'It's all right, Mr Podmore,' he said. 'I'll show Uncle Edward his room.' *Mister* Podmore? Disquietingly bourgeois.

'Had I better punch in with the parentals before we go any further?' I wondered, sensing the prospect of the long terrace tea that melts seamlessly into veranda cocktails, on which I had set my heart, recede into the distance.

'Mummy's shopping in Norwich this afternoon,' came the happy reply. 'And Daddy's in London. This way.'

I forbore to ask when Michael was expected back. The trick of being a good guest is never to ask any questions about the composition of the household. Hosts, even the grandest, are nervous creatures and interpret curiosity as evidence of dissatisfaction.

'Perfect,' I said, lumbering up the steps.

David had at least, in bagging the Landseer Room for me, swung me first-class accommodation. Have you ever stayed there? The room is huge, comfortably bedded, well supplied with Chippendale and Hepplewhite and generous of view. Of particular interest to me, for I am a man who loves his tub, there is a connecting bathroom stuffed to a level of Babylonian profligacy with costly oils and unguents and whose shower and bath are equipped with taps which can be operated from a console beside the bed. Only Michael Logan could be potty enough to employ servants who have nothing better to do than fill baths and then go to the expense of fitting machinery which can do their job for them. The curtains at least are operated manually, which is a great blessing, there being few pleasures in life higher than that of waking to the sound of a housemaid swishing in the daylight.

There is a price to pay for everything however, and in the case of the Landseer Room the reckoning comes in the form of the preposterous painting that hangs over the fireplace. This disgraceful quarter-acre waste of canvas depicts a spaniel of some kind straining alert and proud on a high castle rampart which gives over a vast Speyside strath or glen or whatever they call valleys in Scotland these days. The work is entitled, if you have a bucket handy, *Lord of All He Surveys*. There are other

441

bedrooms, I know, which offer more acceptable art, including a passable *Deathwish of the Cumaean Sybil* and a more or less juicy *Zeus Ravishing Europa with Dryad and Nymph Standing By in Antic Pose*, but none has the style and comfort of this room, so I am prepared to let the spaniel pass for the sake of the fragrant bathing and amiable views. One of the things I shall have to ask Michael is whether he buys his art by the hundredweight or whether he uses his eye. I am at least denied the unspeakable horrors of the Hobhouse Room, whose dread *For Found Is the Lamb that Once Was Lost* can provoke nightmares and bucking hysteria in all but the most iron-willed. You ever met Oliver Mills? An old crony of your father and me. Screechingest of screeching queens, a depriested director of films and television – you must know Oliver. Anyway, he was once found skittering up and down the corridor outside the Hobhouse Room wrapped in an eiderdown and wailing, 'Lead me to a garret, a servant's hovel, a kennel, a Forte hotel, *anything*!' Naturally, Muggins had to swap rooms with him.

But the lordly spaniel surveying his domain (or should that be demesne?) I can take, especially since the other lordly spaniel, David, had sweetly taken a lot of trouble to cater for my every whim.

'Ah!' I said, sighting the drinks table. 'Everything is as it should be.'

David followed my eye to the tall, green, glittering forest set in its twinkling crystal sea. 'It is whisky you like, isn't it, Uncle Edward?'

'Before we go any further, old darling,' I said, 'shall we dispense with the Uncle? Ted will do, just plain Ted.'

'Right,' said David. 'Ted. As in Heath.'

'A boy of your age has heard of Ted Heath?'

David was startled. 'He was the Prime Minister, wasn't he?'

'Oh, *that* Ted Heath. Thought you meant the band leader.'

'Band leader?'

Christ, I abominate children. And Christ, I abominate my receding memory.

'Well, Davey,' I said, 'think I'll . . . ah . . . take a bath and conceivably a short nap.'

'Oh . . . right.' He hid his disappointment well. 'Absolutely. You know where everything is?'

'Rather.'

He backed to the door. 'I'll . . . when you come down . . . there's the South Lawn which is . . .' he pointed to the wall behind the bed, '. . . that way. I'll probably be hanging about round there if you want to . . . you know. Chat.'

I felt a bit of a swine.

'Davey,' I said, looking at him straight. 'It's simply wonderful to be here. We're going to have a splendid time. Thank you for asking me.'

His face lit up. 'Thank you for coming. There is so much . . .' He paused, shook his head and left the room, closing the door behind him.

Sleek and soft from patchouli oil and glowing with good malt, I sat an hour later, a sheet of Swafford Hall writing-paper in front of me and the view across the lawns and parkland beyond. I would concentrate on the drudgery of writing this letter to you later, but for the moment there was no reason not to tickle the Muse's tits

443

and see if she mightn't start to express. It was unlikely a poem would come in such peaceful circumstances, but you certainly won't get if you don't ask. I listed, as is my custom, such few words as my mood and the scene suggested.

> *Held*
> *Surface*
> *Gaumy*
> *Suspension*
> *Ataractic*
> *Gross*
> *Weight*
> *Mollity*
> *Burst*
> *This*
> *Spread*
> *Suzerainty*
> *Piss-gold*
> *Widened*
> *Hotter*

I examined this list for some quarter of an hour. The rare words often annoy the punter, but they never think, they never stop to *think* about a poet's life. A painter has oils, acrylics and pastels, turpentine, linseed, canvas, sable and hog's hair. When did you last employ such things routinely? To oil a cricket bat or mascara an eyelid, perhaps. Come to think of it, you've probably never oiled a cricket bat in your life, but you know what I mean. And musicians: a musician has entire machines of wood, brass, gut and carbon fibre; he has augmented sevenths, accidentals, Dorian modes and twelve-note rows. When did you ever use an augmented seventh as a way of getting back at your boyfriend or a bassoon obbligato to order pizza? Never. Never, never, never. The poet, though. Oh, yes, the poor poet: pity the poor bloody poet. The poet has no reserved materials, no unique modes. He has nothing but words, the same tools that the whole cursed world uses to ask the way to the nearest lavatory, or with which they patter out excuses for the clumsy betrayals and shiftless evasions of their ordinary lives; the poet has nothing but the same, self-same, words that daily in a million shapes and phrases curse, pray, abuse, flatter and mislead. The poor bloody poet can no longer say 'ope' for 'open', or 'swain' for 'youth', he is expected to construct new poems out of the plastic and Styrofoam garbage that litters the twentieth-century linguistic floor, to make fresh art from the used verbal condoms of social intercourse. Is it any wonder that, from time to time, we take refuge in 'gellies' and 'ataractic' and 'watchet'? Innocent words, virgin words, words uncontaminated and unviolated, the very mastery of which announces us to possess a relationship with language akin to that of the sculptor with his marble or the composer with his staves. Not that anyone is ever *impressed*, of course. They only moan about the 'impenetrability' or congratulate themselves for being hep to the ellipsis, opacity and allusion that they believe deepens and enriches the work. It's a bastard profession, believe me.

Well, well . . . I can make any number of excuses, but I suppose the real truth is that the energy has gone out of me, has been weeping from me for ten years. Too many appearances on 'The Late Show' and Melvyn Bragg, too many easy offers to anthologise and edit, too much regard and petting, and lately, far too much of the old electric soup. I crossed out the list of words, scrawled 'FUSTIAN!' in angry letters across the page and stored the sheet of paper in the desk. I would have screwed it up and tossed it away were it not that a deranged university in Texas has paid me for the rights to all my papers.

'Papers?' I had asked when approached by their Professor of Modern Poetry. 'What do you mean papers?'

'Hell, you know . . . notebooks, drafts, correspondence . . . papers.'

What kind of self-conscious and insufferably twee belle-lettriste ponce keeps *notebooks*? I asked myself. Utterly absurd, but the money was good, so I sat down one weekend and forged dozens of likely-looking rough drafts of my better-known poems. It was the greatest lark alive, scrawling indecipherable Greek in the margin, writing 'but Skelton?????', '*mild und leise wie er lächelt*', 'see Reitlinger's *Economics of Taste* Vol. II, page 136' and 'No, no, no, no, no, no! Close the field, close the field!!!' in different-coloured inks across the pages. At one point I wrote 'posterity can suck my cock' in pencil and then erased it. It took less than four years for an American graduate to uncover this and write to me asking what I had meant by it. She came over to England three months later on a research fellowship and found out.

Forgive me for rambling, my dear, but you've no idea what a relief it is to get all this off my chest. Besides, since you haven't told me what to look for, I've nothing else to write about yet.

Anyway, despairing of poetry, I was pouring myself another glass of scotch when the telephone next to my bed rang.

'Ted, it's Anne.'

'My love!'

'Quite. Settled comfortably in?'

'Snugger than a bugger in a rugger scrum.'

'Then come downstairs, I want to talk to you.'

She was in one of the south-facing drawing rooms, looking out of the window. She turned at the sound of creaking floorboard and favoured me with a welcoming smile.

'Ted, it's actually tremendous to see you.'

I joined her at the window, kissing each cheek and then stepping back to examine her. A taking little creature she has always been; fair hair, good cheekbones, eyes as blue as et cetera. I don't know how much you know about her, she's only your aunt by marriage, so I'll fill in a little for you.

She had met Logan while he and I were still clumping around in uniform. He hadn't a button in those days and she was the daughter of a bust and useless earl. While engaged on some footling divisional exercise in the Thetford Chase area, Michael and I, as the only subalterns in our distinctly shabby regiment who didn't say 'pardon' or hold our knives like pencils, had been taken by the CO for dinner at Swafford Hall, then a mouldering heap so cold that your breath stood out in the drawing room and the women's nipples peaked like bakelite studs. Anne was eleven years old at that time and had been pressed into the traditional child's service of handing out olives and smiling sweetly at the guests before being packed off to bed. I hadn't noticed her much, except to see that she had dog hairs on the back of a rather plain velvet dress.

In the car on the way back, with the CO nuzzled against his shoulder in a rumbling stupor, Michael had turned to me.

'Tedward,' he whispered, 'some day I'm going to marry that girl and buy that house.'

'Not before I've been made Poet Laureate,' I had said. 'It's a deal.'

The driver turned round and winked. 'And I'll be leader of the Labour Party,' he said.

'Shut up, Corporal,' we snapped in chorus, 'and watch the road.'

The CO had woken up and puked fiercely all over Michael's mess-jacket.

What happened to that driver I have no idea. For all I know he did become leader of the Labour Party. I never took much of an interest in these things. It is a certain truth that they didn't make me Poet Laureate and that they wouldn't if I were the only British poet left alive, which, as a matter of fact, I happen to believe I am. Michael left the army, with me, the moment our two years were up. Ten years later he had married Lady Anne and within another two the noble father-in-law's embolism burst and Michael bought Swafford off Alec, the new Lord Bressingham, a sneaky young tyke who looked a cross between Bryan Forbes and Laurence Harvey and was only too pleased to fold the cash in his lizard-skin wallet and skip to a flat in Berkeley Square. It was a kinky little caprice of fate, all of a piece with Logan's guiding star, that Alec Bressingham then spent the next five years giving that money right back in the form of gambling chips at the string of casinos that Michael then ran in Mayfair. Alec even contrived to shoot himself in a Logan-owned hotel. Anne hadn't worried too much, the lad was only the remotest kind of cousin and she had always suspected him of anti-Semitism, a taint she could smell anywhere, like so many who marry into the tribe. She acquitted me of the vice, however, probably because I was so brazen in hailing Michael as 'you old Jew'. She is usually pleased to see me, so long as I behave myself.

I finished my inspection of her.

'And it's just as tremendous to see you, Annie,' I replied. 'You're looking younger. Lost some of that fat.'

'Michael's in town. Hopes to make it down for next week. Sends you a punch in the belly.'

I noticed she had half an eye still on the window. I followed the direction of her gaze. The South Lawn, as I assume you know, slopes down to a lake, in front of which, on rising ground, stands a miniature version of the Villa Rotunda, built as a kind of summerhouse. Anne saw me watching her, shrugged and smiled.

'David's in there,' she said. 'Ted, I think it's simply the best thing that you've come.'

'Ah,' I said, non-committally.

'I'm so worried about him. I ought to tell you . . . it's a little strange . . .'

She broke off. Simon was standing in the doorway.

'Mother, I'm going off to Wymondham to see Robbie. That okay?'

'Yes, darling.'

'I might stay the night.'

449

'Fine, fine. Make sure you tell Podmore you won't be in to dinner . . .'

He nodded and left. Anne sat down.

'Army, I understand?' I said, joining her on the sofa.

She seemed confused. 'Army? What army?'

I pointed to the door. 'Simon.'

'Oh. Yes. Yes, that's right.'

'Seems mad,' I said, waffling on to give her a chance to unburden herself of whatever it was she wished to unburden herself. 'I only went in because they would have hurled me in the slammer if I'd refused. The idea of someone actually wanting to sign up when it isn't compulsory . . . done his Wosbie, has he?'

'No . . . it's not Wosbie any more. It's the . . . the RCB, or some such.'

'Yes,' I growled affably, quite content to play the part of the trumpeting old war-horse. 'Quite. "The Professionals", they call themselves these days. An ability to keep the port decanter from touching the table as it goes around is not enough. You have to be able to speak Cantonese, strip a tank-engine, lead a discussion group on Post-Traumatic Stress Disorder and know your men's Christian names.'

'Ted,' she said at last, a pleading note in her voice, 'you're a poet. An artist. I know you like to . . . to make fun of yourself, but that's what you are.'

'That's what I am.'

'I've never understood much of your work, but then of course one isn't supposed to, is one?'

'Well . . .'

'But I do know that you must think a great deal about . . . about, oh I don't know . . . *ideas.*'

450

'A young poet once said to Mallarmé, "I had the most marvellous idea for a poem this afternoon." "Oh dear," said Mallarmé, "what a pity." "What do you mean?" said the young poet, stung. "Well," said Mallarmé, "poems aren't made of ideas, are they? They're made of words." '

'Oh, do be serious, Ted, just for once. Please.'

I had thought I was being serious, but I duly switched on a pensive expression and leaned forward.

'We're all rather concerned that David is turning out oddly.'

'Oh yes?'

'It's nothing,' Anne put her hands to her cheeks like a flushed maiden, 'it's nothing you can put your finger on. He's an absolute dear. Terribly kind, terribly thoughtful. Everyone thinks him perfectly sweet. He's never in trouble at school. He just doesn't seem to be quite . . . of this world.'

'Daydreamer.'

'Well, that's not quite it. I think he's not . . . *connected* to us. Does that make sense?'

'It's an age when privacy counts, you know.'

'At a dinner party last weekend he said in a very clear voice to the wife of our local MP, "Which animal do you think has the longest penis?" She gave a hysterical laugh and snapped the stem of her wine glass. But he persisted. "No, which do you think? Which animal?" At last, out of desperation, she suggested the blue whale. "No," he said. "The male rabbit-flea. The erect penis of the male rabbit-flea is two-thirds the length of its body. Don't you think that's the most marvellous thing?" Then he saw we were all staring at him and he flushed scarlet and said: "You'll have to forgive me. I'm not very good at conversation." I mean. Ted. Wouldn't you call that extraordinary?'

'Certainly,' I said. 'I mean, poor *female* rabbit-flea. I trust she has been blessed with accommodation elastic enough for such a frantic attachment. But in truth,' I added hastily, for I saw this was not the answer she required, 'David is fifteen. Fifteen-year-olds are always odd. They like to rattle the cage, to tug on the leash, to find their . . . their *space*, I believe the expression is.'

'You'll know what I mean when you've spent any time with him. So distant, so detached. As if he's a visitor here.'

'Well I'm a visitor here,' I said, rising, 'and it's a lovely feeling. But certainly I'll observe him if that's what you want. I expect it'll turn out that he's in love with the gamekeeper's daughter or some such.'

'Hardly. She has a hare-lip.'

'That needn't be a bar to love. There was a whore in Rupert Street had a hare-lip. Gave the most delicious . . .'

I decided to leave the story for another time, bowed a crisp farewell and set my compass for the South Lawn.

David had emerged from the Villa Rotunda and was now on the lawn in front of it, lying on his stomach and chewing a plantain stalk.

'Good bath, good nap?' he asked.

'Didn't manage the latter,' I said, lowering myself on to the bottom step of the stone stairs that ran up to the summerhouse.

He looked at me through squinting eyes. 'The

summerhouse suits you,' he said. 'Same noble proportions.'

Cheeky sod.

'You speak truer than you know,' I replied, looking
over my shoulder at the structure behind. 'John Betje-
man's nick-name for me was the Villain Rotunda.'

He smiled dutifully and removed the stalk from his
mouth. 'Have you been crying?' he asked.

'Touch of hay-fever. The air is thick with pollen and
other unnatural pollutants. My soft-tissues are geared
for London you see, with its wholesome sulphur and
nutritious nitrogen.'

He nodded. 'I saw you through the window with
Mummy.'

'Oh ah.'

'Were you talking about me?'

'What on earth makes you think that?'

'Oh,' he stared down at a money-spider chasing
around his finger tips, 'she worries about me.'

'If you were advertising for a mother in the Situations
Vacant column of a newspaper and wanted to frame the
job description you couldn't come up with a phrase
better than "Must be prepared to worry twenty-four
hours a day." It's what mothers *do*, Davey. And if for ten
minutes they stop worrying, that worries them, so they
redouble their worry.'

'Well I know that . . . but she worries more about me
than about Simon or the twins. I see it in the way she
looks at me.'

'Yes, but the twins have got a nanny, haven't they?
And Simon, with the best will in the world, Simon is . . .'

'Simon is what?'

I hesitated to use the words 'ordinary' or 'dull' or even 'unintelligent' which were probably unfair.

'Simon is more conventional, isn't he? You know, head boy, rugger, army, all that. He's . . . safe.'

'Meaning I'm *unsafe*?'

'I bloody well hope so. I'm not having any godchild of mine going about the place being anything other than wild and dangerous.'

David smiled. 'I suppose Mummy told you about the dinner party the other night?'

'Something about a rabbit-flea?'

'Why are people embarrassed about sexual things?'

'I'm not.'

'No?'

'Certainly not,' I said, taking out a cigarette.

'You have sex a great deal, don't you? So everyone says.'

'A great deal? Depends what you mean. I take it when I can get it, that's for sure.'

'Simon says he saw you with Mrs Brooke-Cameron once.'

'Did he? Did he indeed? I trust we put on an entertaining show.'

He stood up and brushed the grass from him. 'Shall we go for a walk?'

'Why not? You can cut me a stout ash-plant and tell me the names of the wild flowers.'

We headed towards the lake and copses beyond.

'In my opinion,' he said, 'people are more embarrassed about love than about sex.'

'Ah. What makes you think that?'

'Well, nobody talks about it, do they?'

454

'I thought they talked about little else. Every film, every pop song, every television programme. Love, love, love. Make love, not tea. All you need is love. Love is a many-splendoured thing. Love makes the world go to pieces.'

'Well, that's like saying they talk about religion because they say "Christ!" and "Oh my God" a lot. They *mention* love, but they don't actually talk about it.'

'And I wonder,' I said, 'if you have ever been in love?'

'Oh yes,' said David. 'Since I can remember.'

'Mm.'

We walked on in silence for a while, skirting the lake. The skin of the water was twitching with waterboatmen, dragon-flies and a tangle of skating insects I could not identify. A heavy, meaty smell of water, mud and rot rose from the margins. David was looking all around as he walked, eyes darting in every direction. It wasn't quite as if he was looking for anything, I thought. I was reminded instead of a game called Hector's Room I'd played up in Scotland once at the Crawfords' place. You ever played it? You are shown a room for a minute and then you bugger off while everyone else goes in and makes one small adjustment each, they move a lamp, take away a wastepaper-bin, swap a couple of pictures around, introduce a new object, that order of thing. Then you have to go back in and identify as many of the alterations as you can. The Crawfords had first played it in their son Hector's room, hence the name, and the real design, I have always thought, was to show the men and women exactly where each other's bedrooms lay, to facilitate late-night handkerchief-pandkerchief. That's certainly the only benefit I ever got out of it. Anyway, there's a very particular expression on the face of a player when he returns to an altered room, a slow smile, and a sweeping, darting gaze, with sudden suspicious but amused whippings-around of the head, as if the furniture and fitments might still be caught in the act of moving. David's manner reminded me quite precisely of that moment in the game.

'I suppose what I meant,' I said, 'was more "Have you ever been *in* love?" foul phrase though it may be.'

David had stopped and was scrutinising fungus at the base of an alder.

'Of course,' he said. 'Ever since I can remember.'

'Hum. Let me be coarser still, Davey. Have you ever been in lust?'

He looked up at me and said slowly, 'Ever since I can remember.'

'Is that right? And have you ever done anything about it?'

He coloured a little, but said fiercely, 'No. Absolutely not.'

'Is there a particular favoured one?'

'Do you remember,' he said, 'that Boxing Day Shoot four years ago, when those cartridges were tampered with and all that confetti flew out?'

'Vividly.'

'Everyone thought it must have been the New Age types that lived in the East Lodge. The ones that made lutes and kept a goat.'

'It was mentioned, I remember.'

'Anyway, it wasn't them.'

'No?'

As we wound our way back to the house he told me

what he had done. He hasn't sworn me to silence or any such nonsense, but never having been wildly entertained by the pompous ritual of shooting, I have absolutely no intention of telling anyone else anyway. Besides yourself of course. I will, over the weekend, work it up into an amusing anecdote for you and send it separately.

It was only later that evening, while I was changing for dinner, that it occurred to me that he had never answered my last question to him.

III

20th July 1992
too damned early

It's Monday now, getting on for seven in the morning and I've spent a great deal of the night writing this letter.

I was in a foul mood after dinner. Nobody stayed up to drink with me and nobody wanted to play cards or do anything fun. I went upstairs and moped in my room.

It's hard to explain such a fit of the sullens. You can try and rationalise it. It may be that I am blue-devilled because I feel guilty about abusing the Logans' hospitality: I am, let us be frank, acting as your paid spy. This seems an unlikely explanation for my current state of mind, which I think owes more to Anno Domini.

I lay in the room, under the great baldachin of a tester, chasing the summer-night itches around my body. One little prickle awoke another and another, until I was bucking on my bed like that little girl in the exorcism film. The same thing went on in my mind, mental itches popping like bubbles. Not enough whisky before bed, this was the problem.

At sixty-six I am entering, I thought, the last phase of my active physical life. My body, on the move, resembles in sight and sound nothing so much as a bin-liner full of yoghurt; my ability to concentrate, the only skill aside from egotism that a poet needs, has faded. Marriages have gone phut and professionally I am regarded as a joke. The Right-Wing Poet they call me. Typical arsing impertinence. Just because I don't subscribe to all the mealy-mouthed orthodoxies of the academic cosa nostra, just because I am a sucker for a title and a well-bred air, just because I know the difference between politics and poetics, just because I have some sense of national belonging, just because I think Kipling is a better poet than Pound (a view, incidentally, that even boat-shoe-wearing academics have been coming round to of late), just because, in short, I have my own brain on my own shoulders, they choose to ignore and belittle me. Fuck 'em. Fuck 'em all. No need to: they're already fucked. But none the less I have this feeling, this feeling I cannot quite be rid of, a feeling that I have, at this period in my life, been turfed off the newspaper for a good reason – no, that's not it, clearly I have been sacked for a good reason – what I mean is that I got myself sacked quite deliberately.

And the daftness of things – that was keeping me awake too. You must have experienced one of those moments when life seems limitlessly absurd? Especially with your current sentence of death hanging over you. I find they come most often with me when I am looking from the window of a moving car or train. You catch sight of something perfectly ordinary, such as it might be bluebells nodding on an embankment, or a family picnicking in a lay-by, and suddenly your mind can no longer support the notion of a whole world full of life and objects and fellow-humans. The very idea of a universe appears monstrous and you become unable to partici-pate. What on earth does that tree think it is up to? Why is that heap of gravel sitting there so patiently? What am I doing, staring out of a window? Why are all these molecules of glass hanging together so as to allow me to look through them? The moment passes, of course, and we return to the proper realm of our dull thoughts and our duller newspapers: in less than a second we are part of the world again, ready to be irritated into apoplexy by the stupidity of a government minister or lured into caring about some asinine new movement in conceptual art; once again we become a part of the great compost heap. Our absence is so fleeting and our control over it so negligible that an act of will cannot reproduce the experience.

Peter Cambric, whom I knew pretty well in the Seventies, a bit before your time probably, was harried until his death by the story of a hunt he went on in 1964 in South Africa. He bagged a couple of elephants, alone enough to damn him in today's eyes, but managed to pick off a couple of bushmen too, which even back then was considered pushing it somewhat. A hundred years ago one would have been able to round off such an anecdote with the words, 'The whole thing was hushed up, of course.' In 1964, though, things got out and Peter's life was made miserable everywhere he went: his name, rather like that of poor Profumo or one of the Watergate band, was for ever linked with this one scandal. The thing of it was that Peter was always a magnificent shot and rumour would have it that he had taken good aim at these natives. This was a little hard to credit, for Cambric came from a progressive family, spoke from his seat in the Lords in the Liberal interest and consistently voted against hanging. The construction put on the affair was that he had mistaken the Kalahari clicking of the bushmen for the call of an ostrich of some sort. This was enough to allow Cambric entrée into the drawing rooms of the mighty but not quite enough to free him of his whiff of impropriety. Anyway – I draw breath – all this has a point, because one Cheltenham Gold Cup day in the mid-Seventies I shared a car back to London with Peter and we sat in the back getting thoroughly nasty on a clutch of freebie bottles of Hine or Martell or whichever cognac house it was that sponsored the race in those days. Cambric confessed to me that he *had* taken careful and deliberate aim but that he had an excuse. It seems that one of these strange moments I have described stole over him of a sudden. The whole scene, the *veld*, the trees, the game, the bearers, the very sky above, all became quite unreal to him. Existence stopped meaning anything. Life itself was no longer of even passing significance; neither his own nor anybody else's. The moment he had loosed off the second bullet, however, he had come to his senses and dropped the rifle, breathing 'Oh my God, oh my God,' as the truth sank in.

'What I experienced, Ted,' he told me, 'was nothing short of ecstasy.'

'Ecstasy?'

'I've read a lot of Mother Julian and *The Cloud of Unknowing* since that day. The mystics. Ecstasy means "standing outside of yourself". From the Greek.'

'Mm,' I said. 'Yes. You are aware, my old darling, that all this would sound pretty wobbly in court?'

'There is a higher law,' said Peter, with the sententious gush of the well brandied, and we left it at that.

As I lay there itching, I cursed my own disposition which, when confronted with the hopeless nonsense of things, has always succumbed more to accidie than

461

ecstasy. When push-off comes to shove-off, a man must have a reason to get out of bed in the mornings, something more than the threat of bedsores at any rate.

I threw off the covers and waddled with bare cracking feet to the drinks tray. I stared at the bottles.

'God's cock,' I said to myself. 'It's nearly four in the morning. Surely I haven't come to this?'

I stood there staring at those whisky bottles for upwards of an hour. Behind the tall green necks a sliver of light between the curtains whitened and the sound of birds filled the air. Couldn't stop the tears from falling. Petulant tears, frustrated tears, grieving tears, angry tears, maudlin tears, guilty tears . . . I didn't know what kind of tears they were. Just tears, idle tears.

Walkies, I thought to myself, grabbing a full bottle and pushing my feet into a pair of shoes. Best go walkies.

Choosing not to risk the complexities of the great front door, I let myself out through a french window in the drawing room and lingered on the terrace for a while, sniffing the dawn air and trying to convince myself that it was of a superior quality to our own London vapour.

In spite of the evidence of life all around me, the birds as mentioned and the spewing vegetable life of borders, shrubs and trees, I was conscious of an absolute deadness all around. London though, London at half past four in the morning, absolutely zings with life. The blasts of the newspaper vans thundering through empty streets, the hissing micturations of the derelicts, the quick staccato of cheap stiletto clicking down alleys, the rattle of lonely cabs and, in squares and streets, a louder singing of blackbirds and sparrows than the countryside can ever know, all these sounds are animated and given meaning by the quality that all great cities share: an acoustic. Everything rings in town. The rural world is absolutely without resonance, reverberation or echo, absolutely without the ring of civilisation. Which makes it fine for an occasional repairing lease or weekend excursion, but debars it wholly from suitability as a habitat for man. Country people, of course, think otherwise: if they had their way they would carpet Piccadilly and the Strand with moss and set wisteria creeping up the walls of Buckingham Palace, just to stop any sound from being allowed to ricochet. As with sounds, so with ideas. Shout out a thought in the capital one morning and it's printed in the Londoner's Diary in the *Standard* in time for the West End final edition, screeched over in the Harpo Club that same evening and derided as old hat in the pages of *Time Out* the following week. Valueless, beyond question, revolting, certainly, but surely indicative of a livelier atmosphere than obtains in arcadia, where ideas bounce like a punctured tennis ball on a peat-bog.

There is one thing, I concede, that the countryside does very well and that is dew. And the dew it was, as I leant on the terrace balustrade clutching, but not drinking from my whisky bottle, that caught my eye. The wide tract of grass that glides down to a ha-ha, and the rougher grass beyond where the horses sometimes grazed, was, as one might expect and demand, soaked in quantities of pretty and appealing dew. It was a track of darker grass running down the centre of the lawn that drew my attention however, a trail that marked where someone had recently walked. A gardener, gardener's assistant, gamekeeper or indoor servant, even in these unmannerly times, would surely keep to pathways, I reasoned, so who – a quick check of the watch – who from the household would be abroad at three minutes shy of five o'clock?

I followed, drenching a perfectly excellent pair of buckskin brogues as I went. A fig for that, thought I, like a Salvation Army maiden discovering Life in a Sixties screenplay, this is Adventure. I pursued the scuffing spoor of whoever had gone before until I reached the end corner of the lawn where it sloped down to the deep ha-ha. The browner, barer ground here, banked against the sun and starved of irrigation, did not take dew, or if it did, soaked it up instantly, and I could see no more tracks to follow.

Unless my mysterious quarry had springs in his heels powerful enough to enable him or her to carry the ha-ha, they must have struck right, towards a dark, dense area of laurels and rhododendrons. I made my way towards it, feeling, by now, rather an arse.

The place, one of those margins that gardeners cannot do anything with, was so thickly planted with sinister shrubbery that I could see no way to enter. I stood at the edge, brandishing the bottle like a mace, and listened. Not a sound came back. The grass at my feet was lusher again here, but bore no traces of human presence. I turned and made my way back to the corner of the lawn, greatly puzzled. Much against my will, I started to think of your word 'miracle'. Don't think me mad, but tell me, my dear, have you witnessed someone . . . my mind rebels violently against any such thought . . . someone *flying*? Ludicrous, obviously, yet . . . let me know if this squares with what you want me to discover.

I was conscious of a sensation not unlike that which overtakes you when investigating a mysterious night-time noise that denies you sleep. You stand on the stairs, heart pounding and mouth open. You proceed to elimin-ate the obvious: creeper tendrils tapping against the window pane; your dog, wife or child raiding the larder; floorboards creaking as the night-storage heater activates itself. None of those fits the noise, so, fighting a rising panic, you begin to consider less likely causes: a mouse in its death-throes; a bat loose in the kitchen; a child's toy left running; the cat accidentally (or deliberately) treading on the remote-control unit and rewinding a video cassette, but none of those quite explains the par-ticular sound either and so . . . if you are anything like me, you trot hastily upstairs, dive back into bed and cover your face with a pillow, preferring not to know.

I walked back to the edge of the ha-ha and looked over it to the parkland beyond. I could see no sign of footprints there, but perhaps I was at the wrong angle. Feeling like twelve types of dick, I slid down the bank and hauled myself up the steep side of the ha-ha, the full bottle of the ten-year-old my only weapon. Once on the level of the park I walked forward through the thick grass examining it for signs of human passage. Nothing. Not a trace. I looked backwards and saw the clear marks of my own progress. No one could possibly have come this way. I moved forward again and suddenly, with no warning, my toe stubbed into something hard and metallic. Leaping like a Scottish dancer, I let out a muf-fled yell. A hideous pain flew to my cold wet toe and a hideous stream of abuse from my cold wet mouth. It was a bucket, half submerged in a large tuft of longer grass, a heavy galvanised bucket.

I hopped there, wincing; my big-toe nail, which has a tendency to grow in, had jammed viciously into the end of the shoe. I uncorked the bottle and raised it to my lips. As the bouquet of the whisky arrived at my nose, I paused.

There was something inexplicably foolish and bathetic about this incident, yet also something intensely disturbing. A line of footprints leading nowhere: a man following them with a bottle of whisky in his hand: the trail ending with the kicking of a bucket. I am not, as you know, a fanciful man, Jane. I set no store by providential symbols, only symbols devised by man, yet I would be an arse-hole pig-headed bigot of a rationalist indeed if I failed to ponder this dream-like sequence.

I cursed and pushed the cork back in without tasting a drop, raised my arm high and let the bottle fall into the bucket with a clang and a crack. Just for the moment, I decided, I would allow myself a little superstition. Why not, while staying here, ease off the sauce a little?

Having renegotiated the ha-ha, I hobbled back to the house, slapping my thigh with irritation. With every step away from the ha-ha I grew in self-recrimination. What kind of man throws away a full bottle of ten-year-old malt? Perhaps it was not that I had drunk too much, more that I hadn't drunk enough; certainly I hadn't slept enough: above all I had failed to finish this first letter to you. The further drinking I decided to leave until later in the day, the sleep could be postponed too. But now I've said just about everything there is to be said, most

of it inconsequential to a degree, I'm mongrel-bitch tired
and my fist cannot form letters any more, so fuck off,
my darling, and leave me alone.

Your devoted godfather

Ted

IV

David stared at the ceiling with something like reproach. The dreadful thing was upon him once more. No matter down what reeking gutters or up what transcendent steeples he forced his thoughts, still the blood thickened into that aching fibre and still his cheeks burned with that pounding heat.

'Down!' he panted. 'Down, down, down.'

He knew what was about. He knew full well how his balls were packed and straining with seed, how his tubes and coils forced and swelled with a pressure to unload. For a year at least he had experienced the soggy defeat of waking to the knowledge that the dam had burst unbidden during the night. What his body did in his dreams he could not control or be blamed for, but he would not, could not allow his conscious self to fall victim to this vile poking, pressing ugliness.

Four by the stable clock, fooled into action by the summer light of dawn.

David stood. He shivered as the shameful head of the monster rubbed with frictive drag against his pyjamas, for a wincing second prising open the slit at its head as it stabbed blindly at the fabric before finding the freedom of the flap and quivering upwards with a stupid prong of victory.

'Stop it, stop it!' David breathed. 'Oh, please . . . please . . .'

But nothing would stop it; not cold water, not prayer, not threats, not promises.

David stood by the bed and clutched the beast in fury, choking it.

'You . . . will . . . behave . . . !' he snarled, shaking it back and forth in anger.

The bastard thing. It won. Great ropes of semen flew from its tip and dropped to the carpet with a flat triumphant patter.

David threw himself on to his bed, sore, savaged and despairing. He sobbed into the pillow and swore that this thing must never happen again.

After a while, feeling better, he got up and began to dress.

He timed the last five words of his prayer to coincide with the five chimes of the stable clock.

'*Good, sweet, true, strong*, and *PURE*!' he breathed.

He hoped that by adding the word 'strong' he would be able to avoid calamities like that of an hour ago. Purity required strength. Where the strength would come from he could not tell. Not from purity, surely? That would be what his father called a catch–22. Strength came from within.

Well, he must be going. He loved it here, but it would never do to be . . .

He tightened up in alarm. Footsteps! He could hear them distinctly. Someone shuffling towards him. He heard a cough and a retching noise. Uncle Ted! There couldn't be the least doubt that it was Uncle Ted. What was he doing up so early? He was the kind of man, surely, who never rose before ten at the very least. David kept very still and, although it was pitch black where he was, closed his eyes tightly. Uncle Ted coughed once more and walked away towards, David judged, the laurel bushes.

Then Uncle Ted came back once more and stood right over him, wheezing and tutting and banging his foot so that dirt fell on to David's face. David didn't dare brush the crumbs of soil away. He simply lay in the warm earth and waited. He heard a scrambling and a thudding noise. Was Uncle Ted trying to find his way in? David held his breath. The sound stopped. There was silence. A wood louse crawled over David's cheek.

Suddenly there was a loud clang, followed by a great roaring and swearing. Uncle Ted was in the park! What on earth was he doing?

'Cunting, godding hell-bitch fuck-arse shite . . .' David heard, and then a small pop and silence. The small pop sounded like a cork being drawn from a bottle. David wondered if he was going mad. The next sound was another clang and then came the sound of scrambling close to him again. David held his breath once more.

At last, grumbling and puffing with annoyance, Uncle Ted turned and stamped away in the direction of the house.

Ten minutes later, the door of hinged turf neatly shut behind him, David crouched in the ha-ha and scanned the house for signs of life. Lowering his gaze, he saw the marks on the lawn and cursed himself.

'Of course!' he whispered. 'The dew! I really must be more careful.'

Four

Dear Uncle Ted,

Your letter arrived this morning. I have read it over many times. Firstly because your handwriting is so difficult and I have had trouble with some ambiguous phrases. Secondly because there is much in it that puzzles me for other reasons. On the handwriting front, I spent much time wondering, for instance, what you meant by David's 'codfish chums'. I know that Davey is very much an animal lover, but I found this idea intensely peculiar until I realised that you meant 'coltish charms'. Then again, there is a reference to yourself as a Rotarian which struck me as unlikely. I have now decided that the word is 'Bohemian'. When I came upon the phrase 'let us be frank, I am aching as your pansy', I could only imagine that the whisky had got the better of you. I have since, by tracing out the letters and coming to an understanding of your pen-strokes, come to the decision that you actually meant to write 'I am acting as your paid spy'.

This leads me on to my main point. Ted, I do not want you to consider yourself a viper in the Logan bosom or

471

a snake in Swafford grass. You made a reference at the very beginning of your letter to the Trojan horse and that is a bad anallegory too. You are an old friend and now a guest of Michael and Anne Logan. You stand godfather to one of their children. There is nothing so strange in your staying with them for a while, surely? Although it is true that it was I who asked you to stay at the Hall and also true that I am paying you to communicate your impressions to me, I have done so in the certain knowledge, *certain knowledge* that once you have been there for a while you will find that your own instincts as a writer and as a friend of the Logans will keep you there willingly. In fact I am sure that wild horses wouldn't drag you away from the place. You can no more call yourself a paid spy than a serious photo-journalist could call himself a snoop.

You may think that by going along in this business you are simply humouring the whim of a dying neurotic who is mad enough to pay you handsomely for it. That may be true. For a month now I have gone over and over it in my mind and asked myself whether or not I am imagining things. I went to see a priest some time ago and he told me that it was common for 'visions to attend the dying'. I saw a psychotherapist who said the same thing in a different way: 'The hurt mind plays itself realistic images to mediate between its desires and dreaded reality. On a larger scale, society does the same thing with its cinema and television industries.' Some such stuff. But I know that what I know is what I know and that nothing can ever be the same again. I won't embarrass you by telling you that I now know that God exists, and that God is perfect and as real as this pen I am holding. Have you ever been in a hot country, a scorchingly uncomfortably hot place, and then walked into a cool cathedral or temple? Or come in from a bitter, cheek-aching winter day to the warmth of a fire? Imagine such a feeling of relief and welcome and pleasure to the power of ten, the power of twenty, any power you like, and still you haven't come near the sensation of coming into the presence of God.

I said I wouldn't embarrass you, but I probably have. You will say I've only embarrassed myself I expect, but that isn't true. I'll say no more about this for the moment.

I am so grateful that your first letter was so full. I didn't find it 'inconsequential to a degree' at all: absolutely everything you tell me is of interest. I don't even object to your making fun of me in the way that you have been. I suppose you are being rude because you hate me for making you feel like a prostitute or spy. I don't mind in the least, but I am sorry you have been feeling unhappy and 'blue-devilled'. What a charming expression.

Your story about Peter Cambric interested me greatly. I can't really beleive that, if he felt so 'at one' and in a state of 'ecstasy' he would have been able to do something so self-conscious as aim a rifle and then pull a trigger. One of my stranger therapists tried to induce a similar state of mind in me, as part of a process that was supposed to heal or cleanse my blood. Her technique had something to do with alpha and theta waves in the brain. These are necessary for Biofeedback which is the popular name for her technique. A group of us would be in a room together, lying on couches, all leukaemics and AIDS patients, and we had to relax totally until our theta and alpha waves were buzzing or radiating or emitting or whatever it is that they do, and then she made us communicate with our bodies.

'See your blood as a crystal stream, absolutely pure and absolutely clear,' she would say. 'See it gently flow and ripple and glide. But look, look deeper into the blood, there is a tangle of weed just below the surface. You think it's out of reach, but it isn't. You can reach, you can reach into the stream. Lean forward and reach into the stream and take the knot of weed, take it in your hands. It is like jelly. The consistency of jelly. Rub it between your fingers. You can press it and rub it between your fingers and feel it dissolve. As it dissolves you can dip your hands into the water and allow the dissolved residue to be carried down the stream. All the weed is untangled and dissolved and all its tiny particles now float freely and easily down the stream to be lost in the sea. Now the river is pure and free and clear again.'

All this would go on for hours and cost thousands as you can imagine. It works in your head up to a point. But, no matter how relaxed I was, whenever she told me to rub the jelly between my fingers I would look down at my hands (in my mind, this is) and something in my brain would force the weeds to become hard and fibrous and knotted and insoluble. I would force them to return to jelly, to something like the consistency of overcooked spaghetti, and then I would rub and rub, thinking I had won, but at the heart of the soft spaghetti this demon in my head would force me again to see another tangle of coarse, black fibre. And so it would go on, one part of me willing myself to dissolve the weed, another part of me forcing myself to recognise that the heart of the weed was malignant and unbreakable-down. When the session was over, as all the others did, I would smile sweetly at the healer, so as not to hurt her feelings (ridiculous when you think how much money she was making out of us) and say that I felt most amazingly at peace, but I knew that the little knot was still there.

I am the only one of that group alive now.

I must rush to catch the post. I want you to get this before Uncle Michael arrives.

Ted, I know I have done the right thing in sending you to Swafford. The length of your letter and your current state of mind show me that God, in his extraordinary way, has found a means to save both of us together in one action, as it were. You are my 'godfather', the word is not accidental.

Forgive me if all this is, as they say in America, 'too on the nose', but I'm not interested in shirking embarrassment any more. If my younger self could read this letter she could never in a million years beleive that I had written it.

Write as soon as you can and as much as you can. If there is any possibility of your borrowing a type-writer or word-processor it would save me eye-strain and headache . . .

Sending love and awaiting news

Jane

II

Swafford
Friday/Saturday, 24th/25th July

Jane,

Well, as you can see i have reluctantly consented to your request and tracked down a machine. This belongs to simon and appears to be quite unused. it does to words what the KRAFT company does to cheese.

apparently i bang the keys too hard, being used to mechanical type-writers. NOR DO I UNDERStand how the bloody shift key works. it either locks the capitals or denies me any at all. STill at least youll be able to read this if I can get simon or davey to show me how the printer is operated.

i enclose with this letter the story of david and the sabotage of the boxing day shoot for your edification. even if its irrelevant to your needs i thought you might enjoy it.

Your letter, contrary to your expectation, did not embarrass me at all. I dont know who or what you think i am, some sort of Henry wilcox or C. Aubrey Smith figure who goes all pink and stiff at the mention of emotion or faith. I'm a poet for fucks sake, not a treasury official. THE ONLY EMOTION that annoys a poet is cheap emotion, unearned emotion, borrowed emotion, the emotion of wish-fulfilment, emotion that comes from fantasy or guess work and not from the gut. at least that's what it says in the poet's manual.

BUT, pausing only to remark that there is no such

word as 'anallegory' much though there should be, i'm
not presuming here to judge your emotions. the weird
thing (talking of weird you seem to have forgotten the
golden rule 'i before e excepting after c'. You wrote
'beleive' in your letter. Perhaps you knew the right spelling but your subconscious mind couldn't commit itself
to producing such a terrifying word as 'believe' in its
entirety) the weird thing . . . what is the weird thing I
was going to say? OH YES, THe weird thing about this
word-processing affair is that you cannot go back and
cross a word out. with a type-writer you can backspace
and cover your errors in x's. It actually seems to be
impossible here. one can absolve oneself of all one's sins
and nobody will be any the wiser. Except oneself.

Talking of going all pink and stiff at the mention of
things there has been a much fuller house this weekend
than I expected. I mentioned in my last letter that I
thought it rude to ask hosts or hostesses about the composition of a house-party, so i was surprised to discover
that a girl claiming to be your best friend has been down
here since Friday night. Goes under the name of Patricia
Hardy, smells of cucumber juice and is the cause of
much pinkness and stiffness in the undersigned. presumably you knew she was coming. I hope she's not
here to spy on the spy.

I'll come to her and the others later. Where did I leave
off last time? Monday morning. Yes. I finished my first
letter to you, rolled wearily downstairs to post it in the
box in the hall and dozed lightly with my head against
a barometer on the wall for five minutes before managing to pull myself up the banisters, one rail at a time,

finally falling on to my bed five minutes short of eight o'clock.

I AWOKE in time for lunch and managed to brazen out Annie's looks of blended astonishment and reproach in the small sitting room beforehand.

'Couldn't sleep. Bed too comfortable, everything too quiet,' I explained, but I could see that she thought I had been sitting up in my room all night quietly boozing myself into a stupor. Since I believe there are few things more transparently undignified in this world than a drinker making an effort to appear sunny and energetic in order to prove to the world that he is innocent of a hangover, I swallowed the insult of her look and declined her offer of a sherry without further protestations of innocence.

I shan't take you through every hour of every day: it's now Saturday and very little occurred on Monday and Tuesday that I judge worthy of notice. Simon was still away and Anne seemed anxious for me to bear David as much company as I could.

'He's very bright, they tell me,' she said. 'I'm afraid that there's not much stimulus for him in the holidays. Simon is that much older and has . . . different interests. As you know I was never exactly bookish either. Michael is wonderful with him, of course, but he's been so busy lately . . . do you remember his niece Jane? Jane Swann?'

Ha! Your name had come up for the first time. You haven't made it plain whether or not your condition is known to the world so I made no mention of it, anxious to see whether news has reached Swafford.

'I should say so,' I replied. 'She's my other godchild.'

'Oh, of course, so she is. Jane was here in June, part

of which covered Simon and Davey's exeat after exams, and she and Davey got on like a house on fire. All the more remarkable really because . . .' She broke off in some confusion.

'Because?'

'I'm not sure if you *know*,' she said, with the kind of upper-class emphasis which would have told me even if I hadn't.

'The leukaemia? Yes, Jane told me.'

'Really? I didn't know you were in touch. The most appalling thing. Jane invited herself here and . . .'

She thought better of saying whatever it was she had in mind to say. She knew about your mother and me, naturally, so perhaps she felt she was being tactful in not going on about your branch of the Logan family.

So you stayed at Swafford in June, did you? Is that when God smote you, or did you go as a result of being smitten? No doubt you'll let me know in your own good time.

(Extraordinary thing about this machine: when you type an apostrophe or inverted comma it can tell whether it should curl to the left or the right. Thus, when typing the dialogue above I would press the same key for quotes and it would automatically 'type it like this'. Damned smart. I'm beginning to see what all the fuss is about.)

The upshot of this conversation is that Davey has had me more or less to himself. He is a quick lad, no question about that, and I think genuinely interested in poetry and art and thought and the life of the mind. As is natural at his age, he believes that poetry's sole function seems to lie in the description of nature. Keats, Clare,

Wordsworth, selected Browning and Tennyson, that sort of jazz. I delicately put him right.

'No, no, no, you chump. You must have heard the expression "the egotistical sublime"? These people aren't writing about dandelions and daisies, they're writing about themselves. Romantic poets are more obsessed with self than the most therapy-addicted Californian you can imagine. "*I* wandered lonely as a cloud", "*My* heart aches", "*My* heart leaps up".'

'But they love nature, surely?' We were walking through the park on the way to the village, where I wanted to stock up on Rothies. Michael only provides cigars for his guests. This would be Monday afternoon, three-ish. There was a beagle pup in need of exercise with us. Its function was to double the length of the walk, wee on my buckskins and attempt the stylish feat of snapping its jaws shut on darting butterflies.

'Listen, old darling. Nature is the shit we were born in. It's pretty, but it isn't art.'

' "Beauty is truth, truth beauty, – that is all ye know on earth, and all ye need to know." '

'Ye-e-s, but if you imagine that beauty is only available *out there*, you're going to have a grotty young life, you know. Don't imagine that celandine and meadowsweet, ranunculus and clover offer us our only path to truth, beauty and Vedic happiness. John Clare could wander the leas and dells in a loony trance because there were leas and dells to wander in. We have cities and edge-of-town big-shed architecture now. We have television and algae-wrap lymphatic treatments.'

'So we're supposed to write about those, are we?'

Get the 'we', Jane. I was thirty-eight before I dared

put 'poet' in my passport and confess membership of the *genus irritabile vatum*.

'We're not *supposed* to write about anything.'

'Shelley said that poets are the unacknowledged legislators of the world.'

'Yes, and he would have looked ten kinds of idiot if everyone had agreed with him.'

'What do you mean?'

'Well, poets would then have to have been described as the *acknowledged* legislators of the world, wouldn't they? And get off their velvet-clad arses and start enacting. That wouldn't have suited him at all.'

'I don't see that that's a very helpful observation.'

'Well, *ex*cuse me.'

We walked on in silence for a while, the beagle pup leaping like a dolphin in the sea of long grass.

'Look,' I said, 'I love the fact that you want to be a poet. I adore it. But I cannot, in all conscience, imagine an occupation more . . . In fact, let's make a wager. I bet you, David Logan, I bet you that during my stay here you will not be able to name a single profession that has less use, less chance, less future, less point, less status and fewer prospects than the calling of Poet.'

'Sewage engineer,' he replied at once.

'Two scenarios,' I said. 'Scenario A: all the poets in England, Scotland, Wales and Northern Ireland go on strike. Result? It would be fourteen years before anyone outside Gordon Square or the offices of the *TLS* so much as noticed. Hardship, discomfort and nuisance quotient? Nil. Impact? Nil. Newsworthiness? Nil. Scenario B: all the sewage engineers in London alone go on strike. Result? Turds and tampons flopping out your kitchen tap, your feet squelching in scum and ooze where'er you walk. Typhus, cholera, thirst and catastrophe. Hardship, discomfort, nuisance, impact and newsworthiness quotients? High.'

'All right, all right, that was a bad one. Um . . . composer then. Classical music composer.'

'Well, closer. Modern composers do have a small audience, I grant you. But most of them, those who don't make the big money – and there is big money to be made even in what they insist on calling "serious" music – fill in time and earn their rent by writing filmscores, advertising jingles and public domain soundtracks, conducting, teaching harmony and counterpoint at conservatoires, that kind of thing. If they want to they can play bar piano in the evenings in a nightclub. A poet, though, what cabaret skills has he got? He has an even smaller audience, his work is almost exclusively confined, after all, to those who speak the same language: if he wants another job his only choices involve *other people's poetry*. He reviews. My God, how he reviews. In every newspaper, periodical, quarterly and magazine you can think of, he earns his daily Hovis reviewing other people's poetry. Or he teaches. Unlike the composer he doesn't teach the skills of his craft, he doesn't teach prosody and metre and form, he teaches other people's poetry. If he's a big cheese, he can edit the poetry list of one of the few remaining publishing houses that runs such a thing. He'll be publishing other people's poetry and anthologising other people's poetry. No doubt he can make appearances on "The Late Show", "Kaleidoscope" and "Critics' Forum" too, talking about other people's poetry. Jesus God, if I had the

choice between coming back in this century as a poet
or a composer I'd take composer and give half my annual
income to charity in gratitude.'

Davey looked rather rattled by this outburst and I
instantly felt the worst kind of pig. He thought for a
moment, biting his lower lip. 'I know you don't mean
all that,' he said. 'I know you're just testing my vocation.
I know that there is nothing better to be than a poet and
that you know it too.'

By this time we had reached the alleyway that leads
into the main street of the village and I realised that a
strange and wonderful thing had happened, or rather,
a foul and horrid thing had failed to happen. I had
spoken for half an hour with a youth who claimed to be
a poet and he hadn't so much as hinted that he wanted
me to read a single one of his poems. Perhaps this is the
miracle, Jane, to which you have alluded . . .

That was Monday afternoon. Tuesday was a quiet
day. We took a boat out on the lake and I drank Chablis
and, at David's request, read aloud from my *Collected
Verse*. Still no move from him to inflict any of his on me.

He thought 'Lines on the Face of W. H. Auden' was
contrived, which I told him was like complaining that
The Hundred and One Dalmations had a lot of dogs in it.
He liked 'Martha, As Seen in a Slit of Light' and 'Ballad
of the Workshy Man', but his particular favourite, naturally, was 'Where the River Ends', which I hadn't the
heart to tell him was in fact inspired by the news that
Gregory Corso and Lawrence Ferlinghetti's poetry was
being set for school exams. He thought it was an ecologi-
cal poem, a 'green' poem *avant la lettre*, about sewage
outflow into the sea. Youth's a stuff I'll not endure.

Insanely, as if by the power of hypnosis, I found myself asking whether, since I'd shown him mine, he'd show me his.

He blushed like an overripe peach. 'You don't want to see it really,' he said.

'Well, can you recite any? Truly, I'd love to hear some.'

This from Ted Wallace, mind you, who'd been known to hurl himself into moving traffic at the prospect of verse recitation.

The poem was short, which was good. The poem was sweet, which was good. The poem had form, which was good. The poem was bad, which was bad. The poem was called 'The Green Man', which was unpardonable.

The Green Man

I sucked the earth and sucked it dry
Dry earth is dust, powder for the hair
I stretched myself and plucked the sky
Plucked sky is blue, a blue coat to wear

I licked the grass: licked it clean
Clean grass is hay; gold hay for the flesh
I hugged the leaves; squeezed their green
Squeezed sap is blood, and blood must be fresh

I sowed the seed, seed of my own
Sown seed is white, white as the breeze
Soon will be born, blood of my bone
Son of the earth and child of the trees

The Hippopotamus

This man of straw, this god of mud
Blue is his coat, proudly unfurled
The precious green, the green of his blood
Shall bathe us all clean and ransom the world

I did warn you. It's like smelling someone else's farts, isn't it? He seems to be recording, in his own graceful way, a wank in the woods. In case you're wondering whether I lovingly committed this thing to memory, let me assure you I have copied it out from a painstakingly calligraphed manuscript which Davey presented me as a result of my having been (how could I be otherwise?) complimentary.

So much for Tuesday. Wednesday, however, was of the highest significance for Swafford, since it saw Michael's return from town. We understand he now hopes to stay for some time. He has a kind of telecommunications centre installed in his study where he can toil away stripping assets, defrauding pension funds and acquiring whatever it is that big cheeses like your uncle do acquire . . . acquisitions I suppose.

On Wednesday afternoon David and I stood on the leads above the front portico and watched the helicopter land on the South Lawn. Michael clambered out, charged forward towards the house clutching his head (clutching his wig if grubby rumour is to be given house-room. I'll find out about that one day, don't you worry) and as soon as he had safely cleared the beating rotor-blades, looked up to where we stood. David waved, Logan waved back. I waved, Logan peered then waved and pranced. A welcome. A big bouncing welcome from a big bouncing man.

485

Down the wooden rungs we streamed, me gasping in David's wake; we clattered along the old nursery passage, tumbling down the back stairs and hurrahing into the hallway to greet him, like Jo and Amy March in the gooiest Sunday afternoon serialisation you can imagine. Your Aunt Anne, coming from the front drawing room, had won by a length and was first to be kissed. Michael, in his wife's arms, looked up as we braked our heels into the marble and skidded to an embarrassed halt.

'Davey! And Tedward! Ha-ha-ha!'

My God, you can only envy this man. Not his power and his wealth and his position, though frankly one can envy that too, but his authority and his – well yes, his power in that sense – his power within his family and his power over his family and the great radio beams of pure sodding charisma that he gives out so unsparingly and so unceasingly, much as weightlifters and literary editors give off BO.

Compare and contrast:

Last Christmas, Ted is invited to Helen's house, Helen being my second wife and the mother of Leonora and Roman.

Ted, not being a driver, makes landfall on schedule, as advised in writing and by fax to the household, at Didcot Station. Anyone there to meet him? In a pig's arse.

So Ted gets a cab to drive him the twelve miles. He arrives, and presses the doorbell with the tip of his plum-pudding nose, for his arms are all laden with presents.

Nobody comes, so Ted pushes and finds that the door swings open. He heads for the drawing room, staggering under the weight of his parcels. He reaches the threshold, cheeks ruddy with festive cheer, eyes twinkling like fairy-lights. Old Ted is the Spirit of Christmas Present, Henry the Eighth in one of his good moods, Friar Tuck and Clarence the Angel all rolled into one beaming bundle. He is Mirth, Jollity, Paternal Love and Yuletide Joy. He is chestnuts roasting on an open fire, he is a curranty wassail of mulling wine and plump mistletoe. His florid beam of bonhomie promises games, cheek-pinching, larks, piggy-back rides, jokes and mincemeat merriment.

His ex-wife, his only son, his only daughter, his only daughter's boyfriend and his only ex-wife's new husband look up from the television, where Cilla Black is presenting the Christmas edition of 'Blind Date', and say:

'Sh!'

'Oh, it's you.'

'Have you been drinking, Daddy?'

'Hi.'

'God you look awful.'

'Sh!'

Home- is - the -sailor - home - from - sea - and - the - hunter - home - from - the - hill, I don't fucking think.

This was no more than the kind of loutish, graceless, lumpen reception ninety-nine fathers out of a hundred are accorded every day of their lives. Nothing new or surprising in that. The only response to such brute behaviour, naturally, is to get so drunk and unpleasant that you do the bastards the favour of justifying their icy welcome and guarantee another just like it next time.

Moment of whining self-pity over, let me proceed. We had left your Uncle Michael (a man who had never in his life entered a room without everyone in it leaping to their feet and either clustering around him like tame gazelles or jumping out of the window in fright) standing in the hall.

'So, Davey . . . what do you hear, what do you say?'

'The strawberry patch is absolutely bursting. I had a look with Uncle Ted last night.'

'We shall have strawberries for pudding. Yes. A mountain of strawberries. Tedward!' Michael's bruisingest bear-hug. 'I heard.' Outstretched arms, shoulders raised, like Christ crucified.

Suddenly you could see that Christ's stance on the cross was in fact no more than a great middle-European Jewish shrug: 'I'm being crucified, my mother's at the foot of the cross and she's moaning that I'm not wearing a fresh loincloth. Oi!', that kind of shrug. The kind gentiles can't do. I took it to refer to my dismissal from the rag.

'Ah, well,' I said (my shrug, I could see in the hall mirror, gave me a sour and petulant dowager's hump), 'it's only a bloody newspaper.'

'Right! Only a newspaper. That's what I said when I sold it in '82. It's only a newspaper. Mind you . . .' He broke off and looked around him.

'So where's Simon?'

Annie had taken his arm. 'Simon has been staying with Robbie. Tractor racing, as you very well know from the fax I sent you. He'll be back tomorrow morning.'

So Annie sends faxes to Michael telling him of the comings and goings of his brood, does she? I must say, Jane, that surprised me mightily, for I had been there in the drawing room on Monday, if you remember, when Simon languidly announced that he was staying away for the night, and Anne had hardly seemed to take it in at all. They say the only skill needed to be a financial genius is grasp of detail. Perhaps it applies to parenthood too, in which case I'm a dead loss, as it's all I can do to remember the genders, ages and names of my two.

Everyone satisfactorily greeted and hugged, Michael hurried upstairs to bath and change out of his financial suit and into the familial polo-shirt and shorts. The knowledge that he was upstairs made Swafford a different house. Hard to explain how altered the atmosphere was. It was as if we had been doing nothing over the last few days but filling in. I'm a few years older than him but he is still capable of making me feel like a four-year-old. All the more stupid of me, therefore, to break the news to him so suddenly on his first evening back.

'You want to do *what?*' His brows came together to form an expression which could have been either a scowl of thunderous rage or a frown of amused perplexity. In my rather watery fear, I interpreted it as the former.

'Michael, Michael . . . it's not . . .'

'So now you're some kind of hack? Some kind of . . . what is her name? Some kind of dirt-mongering Kitty Kelley? *The Private Life of Michael Logan*. No, no, worse than that, too tame. *The Private* Lives *of Michael Logan*. *The* Very *Private Lives of Michael Logan*. Tedward, Tedward. This is terrible.'

Oh shit. Oh shitey-shitey-shit-shit. I spread my hands.

'Michael, old walrus, I knew this would happen. I've gone and explained myself all wrong. It's not *you*, I'm not interested in *you*. Not you *per se*. It's the whole . . . the whole *thing*.'

'For a poet you have a less than wonderful way with words.'

I leaned back, flustered. The man had been so pleased to see me, so hugely and powerfully delighted. Now I had rushed in and hustled him. We were sitting alone around the dinner table, the covers having been cleared away, Annie having gone into the drawing room and Davey having bedded himself down for the night. There were strawberries and cream in us – Michael's words are never lightly spoken – the proper old-fashioned kind of strawberries at that, late fruiting, the kind you can twist the pith out of as easily as pulling a baby carrot from compost, not the modern travesty whose leaves snap off and which taste of stale cider; there was good wine in us too and a mellow cloud of Michael's Havana and my Rothies hanging in the air. I had thought the moment propitious.

'Bloody hell, Michael, you know me,' I said with a winning smile.

'That's what I'm afraid of,' he replied.

'Unworthy of you. I'm not interested in gossip or scandal . . . not that there is any, I'm sure, and if there is I don't care. I *say* biography, but I'm thinking as much of a kind of history, a kind of *outline*. You see, Michael,' I leaned forward again, 'I think the two great threads of twentieth-century history are the Anglo-Saxon and the Jewish. It may be that next century it will be the Hispanic and the Arab, or the black and the Asian, or the Venusian and the Martian for all I bloody know, but for the last hundred years' (I was improvising madly here, of course) 'the Jew and the Anglo have more or less defined the entire shape of the globe, of intellectual thought, of art, of popular culture, of history, of . . . oh, I don't know . . . of mankind's destiny, if you will. Now, it's not uncommon for Jews to marry out of their race, nor uncommon for an Anglo-Saxon to do so. But you and Anne, you see, you make a particularly intriguing, a particularly *vivid* case-study, the outlines stand out. You're not just *any* Jew, you're maybe the most powerful in Europe. Anne isn't just *any* Anglo, she's from one of the oldest families in Britain, whose ancestors have ruled, rouéd and ruinated for over a thousand years. Her mother's connections mean there's a spot of Russell, as in the Prime Minister and as in Bertrand, in the mix, and there's a helping of Marlborough and Churchill too, with a side-salad of Cecils and Pagets. So your family is a union, an interweaving of the two great threads. Perhaps the tradition of Anglo-Saxon and Jewish dominance in the world is over, from Christ to Marx, Einstein, Kafka and Freud, by way of Shakespeare, Lincoln, Franklin, Jefferson and Colonel Sanders. Your offspring, your marriage, your family, it all becomes almost a symbol, doesn't it? I'm not interested in whether you've been faithful to your wife, Michael, or what dirty deals you may have done in your time. I really think there is a most marvellous book here.'

Fer-rankly . . .

Michael stared at me for what seemed a week. 'I'll think about it, Tedward.'

I smiled. 'That's all I ask.'

'You're staying a good long while. There'll be time to discuss later. Let's go join Anne.'

So we left it at that.

Have I done right, Jane? I think he's swallowed my

491

story – why shouldn't he? It's bloody convincing – and I don't think I've queered the pitch for any other developments. But I wish, I wish, Jane, my dearest of dear, dear things, that you would tell me exactly what it is I'm supposed to be looking out for.

Give me time to stretch and pour myself another whisky and then we'll look at Thursday.

III

Thursday saw what we might call the opening of the house for the summer. When I heard that others were coming, it occurred to me that for Davey I was something in the nature of an advance guard and that the reason he was so especially pleased to have me early was that he could form a prepared alliance against any nasty grown-ups that were coming later and not be relegated to the status of Left-Out Child or Hanger-On. This was a hasty and ill-formed diagnosis, as we shall see.

We had a conversation about people in which we found ourselves pretty much in agreement. I said that I was nervous of meeting anyone new and Davey said he was in much the same case. He remarked that it was hardly surprising we thought the same about things: we were after all, he explained, to all intents and purposes the same age.

'You've gone all funny on me now, young walnut. What do you mean?'

'Well, I'm fifteen years from the cradle and you must be about fifteen from the tomb.'

Not *precisely* the kind of words you expect to hear from neatly brushed and polished youth, but he has a point of course, *bis pueri senes* and all that.

The first house-guest to turn up was your chum, Patricia. My lord, Jane, there's a pair of breasts if you like.

She had come on her own, recuperating from a 'devastating' affair with Michael's underling, Martin Rebak. You probably know this. Rebak, CEO of Logan's (it stands for Chief Executive Officer and is a sort of cross

493

between a managing director and a chairman I believe), was her man for a year: there was talk of marriage and eternal love, but then he cruelly upped and tupped a PR girl leaving Patricia simply squelching in misery. Michael rather sportingly told this CEO that he was a cunt and a beast and he and Annie have, as it were, officially taken Patricia's side. The CEO's still 'in place' in Simon's words (Simon came back from his tractor racing this morning) and slightly miffed to be the recipient of Logan's old-fashioned Mafia boss disapproval. Whether Michael's sympathy for the beazel springs from a desire in him to sauce her himself, only the Lord and yourself (probably) knows. There are *rumours* to the effect that Michael is a consistent and conscientious putter-about, but there are rumours about everybody. That the rumours are nearly always correct is neither here nor there for the moment.

Still, what a piece. She doesn't appear to be wearing the willow for her lost love, in fact she's brighter than a bag of buttons and merrier than a gallery of grigs.

'I remember *you*,' she says to me after bestowing a kiss on Podmore, I mean . . . *Podmore* . . . 'you're Ted Wallace! There was an article about you in the *Evening Standard* yesterday. You've just been sacked from something, haven't you? A. N. Wilson wrote defending you and Milton Shulman said you were a disgrace to the good name of critics.'

'As Myra Hindley is a disgrace to the good name of child-murderers.'

'And we met twice,' she went on. 'Once at a launch for something, was it a Ned Sherrin theatrical-anecdote book at The Ivy?'

'You won't believe this,' I said, 'but I have missed every one of Ned Sherrin's theatrical-anecdote book launches. It goes against the laws of probability, but I've done it. I put it down to rigorous training and self-discipline. The trouble is, you see, if you go to one, you can't stop yourself from going to another, and another, and so on. And before you know it, you're going to one every week. I suppose the only other solution would be for Ned Sherrin to stop writing them, but that would be cheating somehow, wouldn't it?'

'I know! It was at the National Portrait Gallery. Portraits by children, for some charity.'

'Ah, a dim memory is surfacing.'

'There were all these portraits,' Patricia explained to Michael and Anne. 'You know, of Princess Diana and Margaret Thatcher and so on, done by five-year-olds. And Ted said in a loud voice, "Call those paintings? Why, a modern artist could have done them." And then you made a fuss because you couldn't smoke.'

'Yes, well, not above making an arse of myself, I'd be the first to concede . . .'

'But the *first* time we met was at a dinner party in 1987 in Pembridge Square.'

She was beginning to sound like one of those 'Embarrassed by Lapses of Memory?' people who advertise on the front page, bottom right-hand corner, of the *Telegraph*.

'Pembridge Square? Pembridge Square? I don't believe I know anyone who lives in Pembridge Square . . .'

'The Gossett-Paynes.'

'. . . except, of course, for Mark and Candida Gossett-Payne. Well, well, well. Nice to meet you again, Patricia.'

I could see out of the corner of my eye that this is where things were going to get eggy. Davey had slid into the hallway during the latter part of the conversation and was beginning to darkle and glower dangerously. It looked as though he had decided to take against this spirited and charmingly high-breasted creature. He rightly guessed, I suppose, that I would rate her above him as a companion for a walk or boating trip. This is not how things were to be, however.

'Er . . . and of course you must know David,' I said, bringing him forward.

Her reaction was rather extraordinary, looking back. She moved forward and dropped to her knees . . . hardly necessary since she is only six inches taller than him at most.

'David!' she said, gazing into his eyes. 'I'm Patricia. We met, do you remember . . . ?'

She went into her Mrs Memory routine, while Davey fixed her with a liquid stare.

'My *God*, but look at you now!' she cooed. 'Will you . . . David . . . will you give me a kiss?'

Well, I mean for heaven's sake . . . as if he were a toddler or dribbling grandsire. He played up to it very well, I'll give him that: a flirty look from under the lashes and a modestly presented cheek. But stuff my arse with figs if she didn't try and work the head round to a proper lip-to-lip snog . . .

She's your friend, Jane, and I'd give even unto half my collection of bow-ties to prong her where it counts, but I have to say that I'm not quite sure she's balanced.

We all moved into the morning room for coffee, Davey overcoming a marked inclination to simper, while we discussed thoughts for the weekend. Simon trundled in politely: all *he* got from Patricia was a casual wave of the hand. Twigging to the drift of our conversation he remarked that today was the last day of the East of England Show.

'Really?' said Patricia in a slow drawl that betrayed such contemptuous indifference that Simon went red. She turned to Davey and asked him what he thought of David Mamet.

'East of England Show, eh?' I said to Simon, who was standing there, polishing his toe-cap against his calf. 'Sort of agricultural thing, is it?'

'Well . . . oh well, you know . . . I'm sure it's not very interesting to people who aren't . . . very interested in that sort of thing.'

'No?'

'It's very popular here, though. Round here, I mean. In Norfolk and so on.'

'Oh ah. Sheep-dog trials and the like, I suppose?'

'Um, not exactly . . . this is East Anglia, really. Not many sheep.'

'Well, Norwich terrier trials perhaps. Cromer crab racing. Norfolk turkey knobbly-throat competitions.'

'There's rare breeds and there's displays and stalls and some show-jumping and . . . but it's . . . as I say, it's not very interesting, I expect.'

'You love it, Simon, you know you do,' his mother said. She and Michael had been in private conference in the corner. Bedroom and mealtime arrangements, I assume. She turned to me. 'He's absolutely potty about it, you know. Hasn't missed a Show Thursday in years. I'm surprised you aren't on your way there now, darling.'

'No, well I thought I ought to . . . you know, greet our guest and see if anyone else wanted to . . . but it's probably not . . .'

'Simon, old thing,' I said, 'if you've room, I'd love to come along. That is, if it isn't a bore for you?'

David turned round, startled. Patricia gave me what writers used, inexplicably, to call a 'level' look. Of . . . what? Scorn? Relief, possibly? Heaven knows. Anne looked pleased and Michael, rather distracted that morning, nodded benignly. Simon, either out of courtesy or genuine feeling, expressed delight.

'No! Not at all. Be a pleasure. We can go in the Austin-Healey if you like. Unless anyone else . . .'

What on earth had possessed me I really cannot say. An agricultural fair . . . in blazing July . . . in East Anglia. Rare breeds . . . Show-jumping . . . Fat pigs . . . Clay, in all probability, pigeon shooting.

We left straight away, just Simon, Soda and myself. My horror at the prospect of massed farmers aside, I found myself unable to calculate whether I was pleased or piqued to see Patricia and Davey form such an instant bond of apparently mutual devotion. Naturally, I've known girlies form attachments to the younger male before now – there's that icky media notion of the toyboy after all – but in the tennis score of the bedroom most girls in my experience would rather Love Thirty or Love Forty than Love Fifteen. Men, of course, are a whole other issue: they start at Love All and stay there until they're dragged from the court.

The East of England Show, I was disturbed to learn,

takes place outside Peterborough, on the way to being a two-hour drive from Swafford. My face must have betrayed my misgivings.

'You should have come last month instead,' said Simon. 'Last month was the Royal Norfolk Show. That's only in Costessey, half an hour away.' Costessey, it became clear despite its spelling, is pronounced 'Cossy'.

Simon then embarked on a story that will be deeply familiar to you, Jane.

'I took my cousin Jane to the Royal Norfolk,' he said. 'Do you know Jane?'

'My god-daughter,' I yelled above the wind-rush.

'Ah. You probably know then that she's not very well.'

I nodded.

'I had thought that perhaps a day out might be good for her. Unfortunately she collapsed during a baling demonstration. Terrible.'

'Terrible,' I agreed.

'I thought she was a goner, I'm afraid. You've never seen anyone so pale. The St John's Ambulance people wanted to take her to the Norfolk and Norwich. That's a hospital.'

'Sounds a reasonable idea. Probably more appropriate than a restaurant, say, or a football stadium.'

'She came round a bit in the tent, though, and I took her back to Swafford. She didn't want to see a doctor. Just went straight to bed. She was there for a couple of days. Davey read to her every afternoon and Dad hired a proper professional nurse. Dad's her uncle.'

'She seems quite well now,' I ventured. 'I saw her in London.'

'Yup, bit of a recovery. I'm not too surprised. You see that with pigs sometimes.'

Cousinly affection takes strange forms.

As we drove to Peterborough, I mused on the peculiar pronunciation of Costessey and entertained Simon and Soda by improvising a limerick.

> *There was a young girl from Costessey*
> *Whose pubes were curly and glostessey*
> *Her thighs and her arse*
> *Were smooth as mown grass*
> *And her cunt was dark, dank and mostessey.*

'Brilliant!' Simon almost swerved off the road in joy. 'That's absolutely brilliant.'

When we arrived at the show ground, he repeated and repeated the limerick to his chums, of which there were many present. The poetic spirit, as you can see, is capable of flourishing in even the most barren and unpromising soil. Simon, for whom poetry is a closed book in a locked cupboard in a high attic in a lonely house in a remote hamlet in a distant land, kept saying to his friends, 'This is Uncle Ted. He's a famous poet. He actually made up a poem in my car as we were driving over!' And then he would recite it. The circumstance of being a 'proper poet' seemed to transform the limerick and confirm upon it something approaching the status of Art.

Reminded me of a trick we used to pull when hard up in the Dominion days. The Dominion was and still is a drinking club just round the corner from the Harpo, probably not your scene, dear. I used to wastrel there in the late Fifties and early Sixties with Gordon Fell, later 'Sir' Gordon, the painter and cultural icon (or so he was described the other week in an article by my daughter Leonora). The ruse was to get Gordon absolutely tanked up on the syrupy Old Fashioneds that he favoured and then start him talking. As soon as he mentioned in the course of conversation someone who wasn't actually a bosom-buddy of anybody in the room – let's use the name Tiny Winters, for instance – we would ask:

'Tiny Winters ... Tiny Winters ... Remind me, Gordie, who's he?'

And Gordon would splutter out some description of who this chap was. We would look puzzled and then firmly shake our heads.

'Nope. Simply can't place him.'

This would enrage Gordon, as well it might, Tiny Winters or whoever being in fact perfectly well known to us. 'You know Tiny! *Tiny!* Everyone knows Tiny!' Gordon would hoot indignantly.

We would appear to struggle with our memories.

'What does he look like?' someone would wonder at last.

'Well he's ... oh, give us a piece of paper for the Lord's sake ...'

Tra-la! Victory. Out would come the charcoal and within five minutes we would be possessors of a genuine Fell. Even in those days you could get £50 for the crudest of sketches. The cruder the better, in fact.

'Oh *that* Tiny! Gotcha. Yes, of course, how *is* old Tiny then?'

One of us would slip the paper into a pocket and hurl

off in a cab round to Cork Street and come back to share the spoils, old Gordon none the wiser.

Of course that shite-arsed little weasel Crompton Day had to go and tell him all about it one afternoon. Next time we tried the scam, Gordon took extra care over his portrait, tongue out, eyes swimming in concentration. We were simply panting with pleasure, this looked like seventy-five quid in the bag at least. When he finished we went into our usual 'Ah, *now* I know who you mean' routine, but before we could slip the portrait off the bar he had picked it up and was starting to tear it into narrow strips before our horrified eyes.

'There you are, dears,' he said, handing out a thin ribbon to every one of us. 'One each.'

Sod. After that you could never get him to draw so much as a map to show you the way to a restaurant.

Anyway, my limerick did the rounds of the show, much aggrandised, as I say, by its status of being the work of a known poet. Not that it could be sold like a Fell sketch, of course. Poetry doesn't work like that, oh no. It just shoots straight into the public domain. Still, mustn't mount that weary old hobby-horse again.

You don't really want to hear about 'The Day I Went to the East of England Show', so I will skip details of the gripping display of synchronised John Deere tractors, spare you the full story of the Suffolk Punch competition and save my descriptions of the titanic struggle between the Dereham and District Beet Growers and the Neane Valley Mangel-Wurzel Breeders (Incorporating the North Cambridgeshire Tap Root Association) for another time.

Simon, paucity of imagination and dullness of wit

aside, is at least a civil figure and he never yielded to any temptation to abandon me to the depredations of the numerous hat-wearing ladies who skimmed and dipped from tea-tent to tea-tent like dragon-flies in August. In as much as agricultural fairs were a new experience for me, and every man in his sixties should take especial pleasure in any new experience however apparently grotesque, I cannot claim that it was the grisliest afternoon of my life. Simon allowed Soda and me numerous pitstops in the beer-tents and sandwicheries and even suggested that we track down a Rothman's bus which he knew would be in attendance. I stocked up on armfuls of free Rothies, filled in a questionnaire and charmed the sashes off a couple of the heavily fucused popsies who were staffing the bus, a converted double-decker gaily trimmed in the Rothman's livery of blue, white and gold. Reminded me of my youth when cigarette girls were as common a sight at theatres, cinema premières and nightclubs as charity-beggars are today. Thing is, the chances were you could shag a ciggie girl in the lavvies for a fiver in those days: I've a strong feeling that the sticker-vendors of the Save the Children Fund and the bucket-shakers of the Cystic Fibrosis Society would scream for the police and sue you for optical rape if you so much as flicked an eye below the level of their necks in today's caring Britain. There has been a relentless and disturbing rise in moral standards over the years. It worries me.

We left the jamboree at six, trailing many shiny floating balloons that bore the glamorous logos and exotic colourings of cattle-feed suppliers and manufacturers of slow-release fungicides – it would appear that Michael

503

likes to sit round after dinner and giggle at helium-enhanced voices.

As we drove back, Simon pestered me for more limericks. 'Do one for Swafford,' he insisted.

> *There was an old woman of Swafford*
> *Whose hair was gigantically coiffured*
> *When asked for the reason*
> *She said 'In this season*
> *I need all the shade that is offered.'*

'Not bad. It wasn't very rude, though, was it?'

'Soda liked it,' I replied, wounded.

'Now do a limerick on me.'

'Hum . . .'

> *There was a young man named Simon*
> *Who hated the art of rhyming*
> *He thought it a shame*
> *That his very own name*
> *Could only be mated with hymen.*

'You're absolutely bloody right, there. Hymen was my nick-name at school. Did you know?'

'Let's call it an inspired guess,' I said.

'Okay, what about one for yourself?'

> *There was an old lecher named Ted*
> *Who was known to be useless in bed*
> *When parting a bush*
> *He'd fumble and push*
> *And screw the poor mattress instead.*

504

Simon was fascinated by this concept. 'Does that really happen?'

'What, missing the opening, you mean? Certainly. All the time.'

Not to have known that, it seemed to me, meant that the boy must either be a virgin or else have been seduced by a woman experienced enough to guide him in without so much as a moment of outslip. Lucky beggar.

The homebound trek from Peterborough, as so often happens, seemed appreciably shorter than the outward haul.

Davey, in a replay of the moment of my arrival on Sunday, was drooping on the front steps.

'Hello, young beast. And where's your girlfriend?'

He turned his head away to disclaim the appellation.

'We bear gifts,' I said. 'Look, for you a fat pig fashioned of rarest homespun and with finest kapok stuffed.'

He took it. 'It's rather funny,' he said. 'Thank you.'

'The lady who sold it to me wondered if I had sat for the artist. This was a little rich as she herself favoured nothing so much as a common cormorant or shag struggling in an oil-slick. None the less, I think you will agree there is a more than passing resemblance between this excellent pig and my wise and wicked self. If you were to stick a pin in it I should leap and yowl.'

'I would have liked to have come, you know.'

Ha! Where is an outreach counsellor with a diploma from the University of Dunstable and a government grant, when you need one? I waited until Simon and Soda were out of earshot, smoothed Davey's ego with descriptions of how turgid and unamusing the afternoon had been and toddled into the house to dress for dinner. For tonight was to see the Logans playing host to the county, a black-tie event.

No one else was about, so it wasn't until we foregathered in the foregathery that I discovered Mother Mills was to be of our party.

Oliver Mills. I don't know if you've met him. He was padre of our regiment back in National Service days. He's seen the dark since and defrocked himself. That at least is his story: it is my belief, founded in idle gossip, that he became frankly too hot for the army or the church to handle. His taste for butch subalterns and zesty young rankers knew no bounds. There was an episode I heard about in '59 that may well have been the straw that broke the camel's back. A general, inspecting a platoon of glowing cadets, soon to be passed out, stopped in front of one especially doll-like ephebe.

'You, sir! Name?'

'Cyprian Manlove, sir.' (Or whatever)

'You a gentleman of sound moral fibre?'

No reply.

'Well, sir?'

Whereat the unfortunate boy burst into tears and scampered from the parade ground. Hanged himself by his Sam Browne, leaving a note that begged his mother's forgiveness. Nothing proved, naturally, but he was known to serve at the altar in chapel and it wasn't long before Oliver folded up his stole and plunged head first into the secular. The boy hadn't been exactly Mother Mills's type, but in those days buggers couldn't be choosers.

Oliver's first lay billet was with the BBC, a haven for

the bent and faithless if ever there was one, where he directed most of those dreary kitchen-sinkers that everyone pretends were the golden produce of the golden age of television, though frankly I'd rather watch John Major dry than sit through any of that self-righteous ullage ever again. Most of the playwrights responsible have died from alcohol poisoning and socialist disillusionment by now, thank God, and Oliver, as you know, specialises these days in rich and loving period adaptations of the classics and fuck the workers, though he wouldn't thank you for saying so. You never knew such a one for writing priggish round robins to the press: 'Sir, We the undersigned are horrified at the government's attempts to cut the Arts Council grant/impose VAT on corduroy trousers/privatise Dickie Attenborough', you know the sort of mealy-mouthed sludge I'm talking about: he'll round up all the usual suspects at the Harpo Club and get them to agree to be set down as co-signatories. Once tried to get me to append my name to a screed wailing about the Net Book Agreement, whatever the badgery fuck that might be. Thoroughly amiable and amusing companion (if you like your wit tied in frilly bows) but, when the socialist bit's clamped between his expensively capped pegs, as humourless a lump of dough as ever held a torchlight vigil outside the South African Embassy or stuck an AIDS Awareness ribbon on an unwilling first-nighter.

'Quid pro quo,' I had said. 'First, you sign a letter I'm writing that urges the government to bring back town-square flogging for graffiti and littering . . .' I had notably crabby views on that head just then, the wall opposite me in Butler's Yard having recently been sprayed in lettering that looked like upside-down Arabic.

Naturally, Mother Mills had stalked away baffled. For all that, he and I were on good terms and he greeted me heartily on Thursday night at Swafford when I pottered in, freshly tubbed and scrubbed, for my pre-dinner glass of the nasty.

'Well, if it isn't the Happy Hippo,' he said – Christ, I hate that old nick-name – 'and beaten to the watering trough by a better man.'

'Hello, Oliver,' I wheezed, 'and what plucks you from Kensington?'

'Same as you, angel. R&R. Mother's been as busy as a big brown bee these last few months. She's come to replenish her tissues.'

'But still sucking up the vodka, we note.'

'Not since Barbara Cartland described Fergie as vulgar have we heard such a grubby pot have the Nigella Nerve to call such a Katie Kettle black.'

I ignored him and poured myself a few fat fingers of the Macallan as he twittered on about his new love.

'Dennis. A name as romantic as fly-spray, but so sweet and trusting and heavily cocked. I'll take another voddie while you're there.'

'What does he do, this Dennis?'

'Anything I ask.'

'For a living.'

'He's a social-security clerk if you must know. I met him on a Pride march.'

There are times when you envy faggotry, and times when you don't. At least we plain old hetters never have to set up house with clerks and welders and shop assistants. Call me a snob and call me unkind, but how Oliver can bear the idea of ignorant dull-witted oafs from Clapham or Camberwell farting in his bed and scratching their balls in front of his cheval-glass, I cannot imagine.

'And what about you, Ted? We understand you've been squiring love's young dream about the lawns and meadows.'

'Barely spoken to her.'

'No, no. Not the breeder. I'm talking about the caramel-thighed Hylas of the fens. The Rupert Graves of the Iceni, as you very well know.'

I did, but had affected to misunderstand.

'Are you by any chance referring to my godson?'

'Please, Ted. You're a poppet when you're yourself, but not fit for firewood when you're all stiff and grumpy. Throw your mother some line or she'll have a miserable time.'

Well, put like that, a man can hardly in all charity keep up a chilly front.

'You'll find him a pretty little piece, I'll not deny,' I conceded, easing myself into a chair. 'Intense as all get out, mind you.'

'Don't I know it. While you and Simple Simon were dwile-flonking with the rough bumpkinry, he took me out on his little dinghy, *much* to the chagrin of the Patricia element, who was too scared or too high-heeled or too tightly stockinged or too lah-di-Mayfair-dah to climb aboard, but wanted sinful Davey all for herself none the less. And *we* know why, don't we?'

'We do?'

'Well, of course we do!' Oliver looked at me in amaze-

509

ment, saw that I was genuinely adrift and then became puzzled himself. 'Don't we? I mean, darling. I assumed you were here for the same . . .'

At this point the door opened and Max and Mary Clifford strutted in.

'Ah, Ted . . . returned from your adventures.' Max extended a languid hand. Born in Liverpool, yet with an accent and manner that makes the Duke of Devonshire sound like Ben Elton. A self-made man who worships his creator, as someone said about somebody else, or somebody else said about someone. His wife Mary is of Welsh stock – Wrexham, if memory doesn't deal me a dog-turd, and is also possessed of vowels like a line of Lalique icicles.

She proffered a powdery cheek and wagged a waggish finger. 'Now Ted, I hope you're going to be *very* well behaved and *very* sober tonight. The Bishop and his wife are coming over this evening and the Draycotts will be here too, so best party manners.'

Un-yippee and un-hurrah.

'That goes for you too, Oliver. No atheistical talk, we beg.'

Said as if *she* were throwing the party and this was *her* house.

'Is he Heidi or Lorraine?' Oliver wanted to know.

Mary looked blank. 'He's Ronald, Oliver. Ronald and Fabia, I think their names are. They used to be at Ripon.'

'I think what Oliver wants to know,' I said, 'is whether the Bishop is High Church or Low Church.'

'Thank you, precious,' said Oliver.

'Oh, nothing like that,' Max pronounced with authority, taking two sherry glasses deftly in one hand. 'Solid public-school hymnbook. No nonsense.'

'Looks like Molly Moderate,' I said to Oliver.

'Hm . . .' Oliver looked at his nails dreamily. 'Pity. I'm best at twitting the low rent, as it happens. Bishop-baiting,' he explained to Mary, 'is one of Mother's specialities.'

'Now Oliver,' Mary screeched. 'I absolutely *forbid* . . .'

'Forbid what?' Michael had arrived, hair sleekly brushed back, sapphires winking in his shirt front.

'Oliver's threatening to tease the Bishop this evening.'

'Really?' Michael looked towards Oliver, who jiggled the ice in his glass in lazy salute. 'I think he's more likely teasing you, Mary.'

'Oh.'

'But, you're welcome to try your luck, Oliver. I believe Ronald used to box for the army. Isn't that right, Max?'

'So they tell me, Michael. So they tell me.'

Max has mastered a particular tone of voice with which he addresses Michael. It tells the world of a special relationship, a close and secret bond that shares its own private joke about the world. It drives me absolutely potty, as you can imagine. I knew Michael long before Max and his kind. There is a simultaneous envy (I know that Max, as a fellow boxwallah, can talk turkey with Michael in a way denied to me) and a protectiveness. I feel like Piggy in *Lord of the Flies*, left behind when Ralph is borne off with the others to explore the island. 'But I was with him before anyone! I was with him when he found the conch,' I want to cry.

In the event the Bishop went largely unbaited. Twenty

of us sat down to dinner. I suppose I had better give the guest list and you can tell me in your letter back whether you need further details.

Michael and Anne
Ted
Patricia
Max and Mary Clifford
Rose (Michael's ancient Austrian aunt, never said a
    word)
Oliver
Simon
David
Ronald and Fabia ✛ Norvic (the Bish and Bishess)
John and Margot Draycott
Clara (the Cliffords' daughter – skinny, wears a brace)
Tom and Margaret Purdom (local squirearchy)
Malcolm and Antonia Whiting (local literati, to please
    me. Ha!)
YOUR MOTHER

Yes, I thought that was worth leaving to the end. You could have felled me with a cocktail-stick. Your mother. Rebecca Burrell, née Logan. In the flesh.

Five minutes before we went in to dine, the full complement, as I thought, having been mustered, a peal was heard from the doorbell and there she stood. With luggage, with presents for the boys, with all the useful clever gifts from Fortnum's that city-dwellers bestow on their deprived country cousins – rustic pies, stoneground loaves, Norfolk honey, grain mustard and wind-dried lavender – with, in short, all the paraphernalia that betokens a long and cosy stay.

'Bex!' cries Michael, falling on her neck. Then he beams at me. 'So, kiss my sister, Ted.'

She was sporting a beady, I-know-you're-wearing-dirty-underpants sort of face but with the trace of a smile lurking in its margins. I'd seen her four years ago, at Christmas. Michael had been hoping to forge a rapprochement then I suspect, but it hadn't really worked. I was too rebarbative, Rebecca was at her spiky worst and Pamela Pride, as Oliver might say, had woven her wicked web all too easily. With so many people there it had been possible for us to ignore each other. It's going to be harder these next weeks.

So Jane, give it to me straight: did you or did you not know that the She-Beast of Phillimore Gardens would be coming? If so, I hate you and hate you and hate you for not warning me.

We were seated apart at dinner which was some kind of a relief. I had been given the treat of walking Patricia in and sat between her and the squire's wife, Margaret. Simon sat at his mother's end of the table next to Clara Clifford and engaged her in conversation without vomiting at the sight of the particles of food that were getting caught in her brace, which is more than I could have managed. David sat at Michael's end, unostentatiously avoiding meat. He had to parry the ludicrous remarks of Antonia Whiting, some of which drifted over to my end.

'Malcolm and I are trying to set up a South Norfolk Festival of Poetry and Prose. We think Jeyes of Thetford might sponsor it. Malcolm's worried that the "J-Cloth Festival" might not sound right. What do you think?'

Oliver, largely thanks to Mary Clifford's witless proscriptions earlier on, was at his most disgraceful. Talk of festivals reminded him of an anecdote and he discoursed at length about the erotic adventures that had attended his visit to the Venice Film Festival last year.

'You won't *believe* the trade that you can find trolling up and down the Dorsoduro,' he said. 'After a week my back-pussy was like a wind-sock.'

'What's a back-pussy?' Davey wanted to know.

'We were rather disappointed in Venice, weren't we, Tom?' Margaret Purdom put in hastily.

'The prices in Harry's Bar were ridiculous. Absolute scandal. For two Bellinis you had to pay . . .'

'There was one boy,' Oliver continued, 'who worked behind the guichet at the Academia. I got him to come back to the Gritti with me only to have him deliver the sweetest warning. You see, he was possessed of the most enormous . . .'

The door opened and Podmore came in to clear away the soup plates. Oliver was equal to the occasion. He knows better than to talk loosely *devant les domestiques*. Barely pausing for breath, he put up a hand to one side of his mouth, as if to shield Podmore from corruption, and continued, '. . . the most enormous C-O-C-K . . .' spelling the word out in a loud and frantic whisper. Podmore's chin wobbled a fraction and Margaret Purdom let out a small scream, but Oliver looked pleased with his social adroitness.

'It was so sweet,' he went on, once Podmore had departed, 'Gianni, for such was his name, anxiously explained, in one of those divinely dusty Italian voices, that he was afraid he might hurt me. "Carissimo," I said, "I'll grant you it's a monster, but after what I've been through this last week you'll be lucky if it touches the sides. It'll be like a paper boat up the Grand Canal." Still, that's enough of me. You much of a traveller, Bishop?'

Patricia nudged me. 'Oliver makes it all up of course, doesn't he?' she whispered.

'Naturally,' I said. 'Nobody has sex any more, straight or bent.'

'What on earth do you mean?'

'It's the great paradox of the age. Before permissiveness came in, everyone everywhere was at it like randy goats. But the moment the young started to insist on talking about it all the time, you couldn't get laid if you were a table at the Savoy. As soon as something becomes a Right you can't bloody do it any more. Self-consciousness, you see.'

'In *Gerald's Fortnight*, my third novel . . .' Malcolm Whiting said.

'I just think it's all so unnecessary,' the Purdom offered from my right.

'Unnecessary?' Oliver's ears had pricked up at the other end of the table.

'Hear, hear,' said Max.

'The protagonist of *Gerald's Fortnight* . . .'

'The day sex becomes unnecessary,' said Michael, 'will be a dark one indeed.'

I was glad he had decided to join in. There is nothing worse than a Jew sitting and listening to a conversation. They nod their heads with a fraudulent air of rabbinical

515

wisdom that makes you want to set about them with staves.

'Do you mean sex is now unnecessary because of artificial insemination?' asked Simon, having a pitiful stab at sounding sophisticated.

'I'm not saying hex itself is unnecessary . . .' Margaret Purdom is one of those ghastly upper-middle-class people who can't quite bring themselves to pronounce the 's' in sex. 'I just mean the endless *talking* about it and showing it on television and rubbing our noses in it.'

'Does it shock you, Mrs Purdom?' asked Oliver.

'Of course not . . . it's just so uncalled for. There was a thing on the other day . . .'

'What about tea-drinking?'

'I beg your pardon?'

'Tea-drinking,' said Oliver. 'Do you object to that on television?'

'Well, of course not. I don't see . . .'

'Nobody *calls* for tea-drinking though, do they? I mean, in television dramas, the camera could easily show the kettle boiling on the hob and then cut discreetly away. But no, they have to show the whole thing. The warming of the tea-pot, the pouring-out, the plopping of the sugar-cube and the slow sipping from the cup. Isn't that "unnecessary" too? Isn't that completely uncalled for?'

'Hardly the same thing, Oliver,' said Max.

'No, of course not! Because no one is shocked by tea-drinking, are they? They are shocked by sex but they daren't admit it. I could respect that Mary Whitehouse creature and her moral minority if they had the Betty Balls to admit that they were in fact frankly and deeply shocked by the spectacle of naked coupling on a public screen. Shocked to their winceyette knicky-knicks. But, instead, they think it's more impressive to give off a tiresome worldly air. "I'm not *shocked*," they say, "oh good heavens no. I just find it all rather boring," as if Tessa Tedium were the Chrissie Crime.'

While Ma Purdom struggled for a reply (to an argument that I suspect Oliver had trotted out many times before . . . probably on one of those 'The People Grill the Producers' shows that the BBC now inflict endlessly on us in a futile attempt to crawl to the audience), bold husband Tom leapt to her defence.

'Yes that's all very clever-clever,' he said, 'but you can't argue that the world isn't in an unhealthy moral state.'

'Wouldn't think of it, dearest. People lie, cheat, rape, swindle, kill, maim, torture and destroy. Bad thing. People also pop into bed together and cosy up. Good thing. If we imagine fucking is a sign of moral decay we're being just a little bit stupid-stupid, aren't we?'

'I still don't see why we have to go *on* about it all the time,' said Margaret.

'*Gerald's Fortnight* was accused by critics of . . .'

'If you really want to crack down on promiscuity among the young,' said the Bishop, 'then you should surely fight for sex scenes on television to be more realistic. Show the whole thing with actors that look like real people instead of like models. Once children know about the squelch and the stench and the whole slippery mess of it they may become less anxious to try it out until they have to.'

Bit hard on the Lady Bishop I felt, but a point well

made. Patricia at this point, heated by such saucy talk, started consciously or unconsciously to rub her leg against mine. It was good to have a woman's thigh pressing against me and, victim of the primal curse on man, which is a need to show off to women, I embarked on holding the company spellbound for a while with my sparkling theories on art and life.

Oliver, being the bitch he is, tried consistently to undermine me with bitter little interjections. I held my own, naturally, but refused to allow the conversation to sink into sterile mud-slinging.

'Returning to the subject of sex for a moment,' said Michael, during a pause which followed a more than usually platitudinous observation from Simon. 'When I bought Newsline Papers Ltd, I called a conference of interested parties to see whether we should stop showing naked women in the pages of our tabloids.'

'Interested parties being bricklayers and spotty teenagers, no doubt?' said Oliver.

'Being psychologists, sociologists, feminists, moralists and representatives of religions,' said Michael. 'The bricklayer and the teenager I can cope with. I said to these experts, "Pretend you own this newspaper. If you can't turn it into profit in six months you're out of a job. What do you do?" Well, you never heard such nonsense in your life. "Let's have more *good* news", "Make it a *family* paper", "Show women in a positive light", "affirmation", "family values" . . . I slapped on the table in front of them a copy of the rival paper. "This is the competition," I said. "It sells millions every day. It is the opposite of everything you have mentioned, but it sells. Why? Tell me please, why? Because people are stupid? Because people are cruel? Because people are ignorant? Because people are savage? Why?" And they answered, "Because it's there. It sells because it's there." "The *Independent* is there too," I said, "and the *Christian Science Monitor* and *Spare Rib* and the *Morning Star*. They are there too, but they don't sell. Give me a better answer." But no better answer came.'

'Of course not. Because what they wanted to say,' said Max, 'is that newspapers should be under *their* control. *They* know better.'

'Well, who's to say they don't know better, Max?' Michael said. 'Perhaps they do know better about many things. About selling newspapers they don't know better, that I will say. I tried running for a few weeks without naked ladies and the circulation dropped. We put the naked ladies back in and the sales rose. What else could I have done?'

'You could have gone into another fucking business,' said David with sudden and extraordinary ferocity.

The whole table froze in a fraught and deathly silence. There was something terrible about such savagery from such a source. Few things are more sphincter-winkingly embarrassing than a family row at the best of times. I could hear Patricia beside me holding her breath.

'Well, Davey,' said Michael, 'I did go into another business, if you remember. I sold the newspapers.'

'And someone else bought them and is profitably printing pictures of naked ladies to this very day,' said Max.

'Well, thank God it isn't my father!' David was trembling at his own courage but otherwise he managed to maintain a steadfast front.

519

'Davey is very concerned with the whiteness of my soul,' said Michael ruefully, much as a husband might joke about his wife's solicitude for his waistline.

There was a sudden outbreak of little local conversations and no single topic dominated the party again for the rest of the dinner.

Davey left the table with the ladies but Simon stayed for the port, his demeanour failing hopelessly to project an air of being simultaneously grown-up, respectful, blasé, grateful and impassive.

Max slid down to my end of the table and put an arm to my shoulder.

'Well, that was a sticky one, I think,' he said in a low voice. 'Of course, little Davey can do no wrong, can he? The sun shines out of little Davey's rear end, doesn't it? If Simon had said such an unctuous and insolent thing, not that he would, there would have been hell to pay.'

I remembered that Max was Simon's godfather and found myself amused that he should show such loyalty. I felt bound to reciprocate and soon we were at it like a couple of old generals taking sides over a rematch of Waterloo.

'Well, he may have been a tad unctuous, but it was brave, it was spirited and it was felt.'

'Sodding cheek and you know it, Ted.'

'So, it's better to be drained of imagination and ideals at birth than to risk losing them later on, is that it?'

'Simon isn't devoid of imagination *or* ideals. It's just that he has manners and decency enough to respect others.'

'The kind of manners and decency that question nothing, challenge nothing and achieve nothing.'

'Oh pish, Ted. As if you believe a word of that. You're the most cynical man in Britain and you know it.'

'Never, Max,' I said, 'never, ever tell a man he is cynical. Cynical is the name we give those we fear may be laughing at us.'

'Don't get all gnomic with me, you old fraud.'

The trouble with Max, repellent as he may be, is that he is not quite as stupid as one would like him to be. Not that he's brilliant, it's just that he's always just a tiny bit brighter than would be convenient.

'This is a silly conversation, Max.'

'You're right. If the truth be told, I just came over to steal a cigarette off you. Can't cope with Michael's enormous cigars.' I obliged him and he puffed on it like a schoolboy. 'Heard about your dishonourable discharge from the rag. Sorry about that. Quite agree with you over the Lake man. His plays get worse and worse. Pleased that Rebecca's arrived, are you? You and she . . . weren't you . . . once upon a long ago?'

'I believe I'm not the only one,' I said, then wished I hadn't.

Max flashed his eyes at me and then down to the stem of his glass. 'Well, well. Now who on earth can have told you that, I wonder?'

'These things get about.'

'No they don't. Oh no they don't. Only happened once. A Christmas some years back. In this very house. And I thought we'd been so very discreet. Well, well, well. *There's* a mystery. Can't be the lady in the case, can it? Fancy that, just fancy that.'

I wriggled a bit on this hook. It was hardly my intention to land David in the poo; in his relation of the Great

Shooting Sabotage (you'll have read that by now, Jane) he had only told me the story of Rebecca and Max in the night-time as an incidental detail. He hadn't even understood it himself at the time.

In casting about for a convincing way to change the subject, I recalled something that Donald Pulsifer the wild-life photographer had once told me. The way to confuse and pacify an angry gorilla, he said, is to start hitting yourself. If you make a blistering assault upon your own person, slapping your cheeks, punching yourself in the stomach, tearing at your hair and clawing at your face, the animal will stop in its tracks, tilt its head and – likely as not – come forward to cuddle and caress you in sympathy, licking your wounds and cradling you like a baby.

'Can't deny it was a shock to see Rebecca coming through the door this evening,' I said, deciding to test Pulsifer's theory. 'We had a furious row at Jane's christening. Well, that's what I tell the world. The fact of the matter is I was drunk and I was dreadful. A couple of years earlier Rebecca had nourished something of a *tendre* for me, you see. To her I was rather more than a casual bedmate. My first wife Fee had run off with that American Open Field poet and I had become a sodden and available mess. Then Patrick Burrell started lapping and sniffing around her loins and she gave me an ultimatum. "If you don't marry me, I'll up and marry Patrick," she said. "Then marry the daft turd," says I. "What the fuck do I care?" That was bad. Very bad. She kept to her word, duly wed the oily rat and out popped Jane, for whom I was chosen as godfather, as much, I believed, to prove to me that she was "Happy! Ha, ha! Blissfully, blissfully happy," as anything else, and I accepted to show that there were no hard feelings on my side either. And then at the . . . what do you call them . . . wakes? That can't be right, at the christening party . . . there must be a proper name for them . . . I did a very stupid thing.'

'Oh yes?' Max was sucked in now and seemed to have lost interest in my knowledge of his own little secret.

'I found Rebecca alone in the conservatory. I said to her that I missed her. I said to her that I wished I hadn't let her marry Patrick.'

'Oh, you idiot.'

'It was true. Damnation, it was true.'

'What use was that to her?'

'Well I know that now, don't I? I had imagined, in my champagne blur, that she would be touched. Instead of which she smashed fifteen panes of conservatory window and roof in her fury. I let it be put about that she had been repelling my unwanted advances.'

'Well, that certainly explains a great deal,' said Max. 'Do you know, I have always wondered why Rebecca freezes at the sound of your name?'

'Well, now you know.'

'Lord, Ted, I'd've thought you knew women better than to have made a blunder like that.'

This egregious man-of-the-world matiness hardly qualified in my book as cradling my head and licking my wounds, but it was an improvement on the icy stare of a minute ago.

'Let's have you down this end, you two,' called Michael. 'We're going to have some fun with the ladies and those balloons.'

So we filled our lungs with helium, crept into the drawing room and made the women scream.

An evening of games followed, the details of which you won't be anxious to hear. I rather shone in charades, fooling everyone with my vivid portrayal of an army of rabbits calling a truce.

'It *must* be *Watership Down!*' everyone cried.

Ha, ha. It was *War and Peace*. Warren Peace, do you see?

Simon made an arse of himself as guesser in a round of 'In the Manner of the Word', on account of never having heard of the word 'archly'. I'm afraid he is rather an oaf, that boy.

I tried to get Oliver alone to quiz him about our earlier, interrupted, conversation, you remember the one I mean?

'*Patricia . . . wanted sinful Davey all for herself . . . And we know why, don't we?*'

'*We do?*'

'*Well, of course we do! Don't we? I mean, darling. I assumed you were here for the same . . .*'

But Oliver proved elusive, and after bidding goodnight to the non-resident guests, we all wound our ways to our several beds.

And now it is Saturday morning, an equestrian party has departed for trottings, canterings and gallopings about the park, my neck is stiff, Podmore has promised to provide a late breakfast and this letter is done.

Yours aye

Ted

Five

Dear Ted,

What a long letter. How beautifully printed. How absorbing. How alarming. I shall answer your numerous questions one at a time.

Patricia: Yes, I did know that she would be joining you at the weekend. I saw no special reason to tell you. She is not spying on the spy if that has been worrying you. She is there simply because she wants to be. As you discovered, she is recovering from an unhappy love affair. I am *very* interested in her comings and goings, however, and would beg you to watch closely there. Patricia is very vulnerable and I want her to come to no harm.

Mummy: I had no idea that she would be coming down, although I am not surprised to hear it. I am very grateful for the elliptical (is that the word?) way in which you have filled me in about your relationship with her. She often moves from place to place without telling me,

there is nothing unusual in that. She knows nothing of
the reason for your visit (nor does Patricia) although
both of them are aware of my leukaemia, as are the
Logans.

Michael: I am sure he will consent to your request. If
he doesn't it hardly matters, you will just have to be an
unofficially inquisitive guest instead of a licensed writer-
in-residence.

There are now a number of specific things that you
can do for me.

Firstly: Please stop using Latin tags in your letters.
You should by now be beyond the stage of having to
demonstrate your superiority over me. The same goes
for pointing out spelling mistakes and incorrect usages.

Secondly: Enquire about the twins, Edward and
James. You have hardly mentioned them. You say they
are 'staying with family'. What family? Where? Why?
When are they returning? This may be important.

Thirdly: Find out how Oliver is and what brings him
here.

Fourthly: I need more information about Aunt Anne.
You told me nothing for instance of her reaction to
David's outburst about Michael's newspaper holdings at
the dinner-table on Thursday.

Fifthly: On no account mess around with Patricia.
She is very special and not to be trifled with.

Sixthly: You have talked only about the guests. The
house is full of other men and women. There are indoor
and outdoor servants, there is Podmore. I have heard
nothing of them.

Seventhly: Constant vigilance; constant awareness;

constant observation; constant openness.

I shall write no more because I want you to get this as soon as possible.

Much love

Jane

II

Swafford Hall
Swafford
DISS
Norfolk

25th July 1993

Jane –

As you can see, I'm at Swafford! You'll never *imagine* who's here too! Your mother for one, looking fantastically elegant, and ... wait for it ... Ted Wallace, your long-lost godfather. I *wish* you could make it over too. You've always said you wanted to get to know him. As far as I can tell he's here for simply ever, so why don't you come on down? He and your mother seem to be getting on rather well, which is a bit of a surprise – David tells me they used to hate each other.

And what *about* David?! Everything you said seems to be absolutely true, though there is the veritablest *queue* for his attentions. I'm having to fight off that dreadful Oliver Mills as well as Ted and even, I think, your mother, just to get five minutes alone with him.

Who else is here? Oh, Max and Mary Clifford, natch, and their daughter Clara who's rather squinty and peculiar and unfortunate. Michael's been a bit quiet but we had an incident-packed dinner party on Thursday, lots of local worthies present, including Ronald Leggatt, the Bishop of Norwich, and his fat wife, Fabia. The Draycotts were there naturally, those dreary literary people the Whitings, and some other couple I couldn't place.

As soon as we sat down, Oliver started behaving dreadfully, telling all kinds of shatteringly inappropriate stories and talking about sex in a loud voice, so I gave Ted who was sitting beside me a swift kick to get him to try and change the subject. Big mistake! I think you have been well off not knowing that man. There are football hooligans in gaol who could fairly claim to be more sensitive and less piggish.

'I blame this ghastly obsession with therapy,' he said, on the subject of everybody's obsession with sex. 'It's a short space between "therapist" and "the rapist", after all.'

'What's wrong with therapy, Ted?' I asked – I hope not too snappishly. I didn't want to give the impression that I'd been under one myself.

'Well, it comes down to which damned language you choose, doesn't it?' he said, in an extravagantly patient voice, as if I were a two-year-old. I think he is one of those kind of men who would talk to Marie Curie as if she were a drooling illiterate.

'Are you talking about sexual discourse here?' Malcolm Whiting asked.

'No, he's discoursing about sexual talk,' said Oliver.

'I wrote a book called *The Love Tree* which you may have . . .' the Whiting idiot started to say.

'I'm saying this,' Uncle T. interrupted. 'In the old days, when we thought that our souls were at stake, Latin had all the authority and it was the curate or the curé who did the curing. Now, in the technical age, we say psyche for soul, and therapist for curate, Greek being the language of science. Mind you, with all this New Age wank around, we've turned to Anglo-Saxon too and the world has started to blather on about "healing". Same process – holy, sane or healthy: cure, therapy or healing.'

'You really don't see a difference, Mr Wallace?' asked the Bishop. 'You don't perceive different kinds of ill-health?'

'Different kinds of "unholiness", you mean? Well. If I break my leg I go to see my old friend Doctor Posner. If I break my heart I go to see my old friend Doctor Macallan.'

'Doctor Macallan?'

'He means whisky,' your mother explained, while directing an acid "Why-can't-you-shut-up-and-leave-well-alone?" look at Ted.

'Ah,' said the Bishop, 'and suppose one of your children were sick in some way?'

'Loopy?'

'If you like. I assume you wouldn't fill *them* up with whisky?'

'It's always struck me,' said Max, 'that if someone believed they were Napoleon I'd send them to someone else who believed that they were the Duke of Wellington. That'd sort them out.'

'Few people are spiritually unhealthy in quite such a clear-cut way, however,' the Bishop said.

'Ah well, "spiritually" is your word, you see,' replied Ted. 'One man's "spiritual ill-health" is another man's "lack of self-esteem" is another man's "oversupply of blood-sugar" is another man's "holistic imbalance". You pays your exorbitant fee and you takes your worthless choice. The fact is nothing can ever be truly cured *or* therapied *or* made whole.'

'Whatever do you mean?' Michael asked. This was getting dangerous.

'Everything rots. At the risk of special pleading, only art can halt the process.'

'What a load of pompous balls, darling,' said Oliver. 'Gone are the days when art bestowed immortality. "So long lives this, and this gives life to thee" and all that wank. The invention of the camera gave us all eternal life. The Dark Lady and the Golden Boy of the sonnets are no more immortal now than Oprah Winfrey or the contestants on the "Wheel of Fortune".'

Ted wasn't having any of that. 'You don't believe that for a moment and besides, it isn't what I meant. You must surely confess that artists, certainly dead ones, are more intelligent, sensitive and intuitive than any therapist with a degree in psychogibber from Keele university or any scurfy outreach parson with a diploma from King's or for that matter any mad Druid channelling energy with hot hands and a lump of amethyst.'

'But honey, we all know that art is what drives people mad.'

'Oh, artists are mad, Oliver, I'll give you that. Every man Jack and every woman Jill of them. All practitioners of the spirit are mad. Show me a sane psychotherapist and I'll show you a charlatan, show me a holy priest, saving the Bishop's reverence, and I'll show you an apostate, show me a healthy New Age healer and I'll show you a mountebank. But who's to say that sending a patient to a recital or an art gallery isn't a better balm for hurt minds than forcing them to talk about their relationship with their mothers or stuffing them full of Holy Bread?'

'But you do distinguish between the mind and the body I suppose?' Rebecca said. 'I mean, you wouldn't send a man with a physical disease to an art gallery, surely?'

'Of course he would. That's why the Tate is already so full of lepers,' said Max, earning rather a cheap and obvious laugh, I thought.

'The anti-hero of *The Love Tree* is brought down by . . .'

'No, no.' Ted was getting het up now. 'A mechanical fault can be corrected and medicine is perfectly competent at that. But it isn't healing, it isn't *making whole*.'

'And healing can only come from art?'

I felt we were drowning in precisely the sort of conversation we shouldn't be having, but I honestly couldn't see any way out of it. All the Logans, David, Simon, Michael and Anne, were staring at Ted, practically open-mouthed.

'Put it this way,' replied Ted, 'we're all grown-ups. Even the religious amongst us are no longer superstitious. Nobody happy and confident believes in ghosts or telepathy or miracles. But art abides. It is the only thing that not only cannot be disproved, but can actually be tangibly and incontrovertibly proved.'

He looked round with an indecently smug expression on his face, as if challenging us to disagree. Most of us just gawped down at our dinner-plates in embarrassment. It couldn't have been more killingly awful if he had taken out his whanger and stuffed it in Lady Draycott's ear. David stared at me in consternation and

Rebecca shook her head sorrowfully. Then Simon, stupid clod-hopping Simon, above whose head the whole undercurrent had flowed (if that makes sense), started to speak.

'Well, I think that there are *some* things that can't be explained . . .' he began, but mercifully Michael galloped to the rescue by talking about his newspapers.

Even that wasn't safe ground, mind you. It provoked a very strange scene with David blurting out how he'd always hated Michael owning tabloids. The young can be so puritanical, can't they? I can remember being a bit like that at his age, but not quite as daring. Michael took it like a lamb, but all in all it had turned into a very odd dinner party.

But what was Ted up to? I mean he does *know*, I assume? Perhaps I should take him aside and tell him not to meddle? Unless his slobbery grins mean nothing, he's desperate to sleep with me, so I should be able to get him to behave. He spent all of yesterday banged up in his room 'writing', which probably means drinking his shame away.

It's such a pity you aren't here, Jane. Surely those doctors will have finished their tests by now? I don't know how you can bear to miss all the fun. I reluctantly confess that Oliver ought to be first in the queue as his need is greater than mine, but my Lord I'm looking forward to it all . . .

All my love

Pat

PS: Blast, I've missed the Saturday post, so you won't get this till Tuesday at the earliest.

III

Swafford
28.vii.92

Jane,

Disaster. Absolute fucking disaster. I don't know how it happened and I don't know how I'm going to tell you. I am tempted to run from Swafford squealing the words 'Fly, fly! All is lost!' It may be that flight will be pre-empted in any case, by a swift and savage ejection. The threat hangs over me like the sword of Damocles. That's Greek by the way, so it's allowed . . . which brings me to this point: where the *hell* do you get off telling me to avoid Latin tags? Amongst the dwindling number of perks that come with old age are included:

A) a literal and metaphorical presbyopia which allows distant schoolgirls and distant schoolboy Latin to come sharply into focus

B) a contempt for self-image and the opinion of others

C) the respect and deference of one's juniors (or – if that is too Latinate for you – 'the high thought and fealty of one's youngers').

Or so I had fondly imagined.

We'll make a deal: I will lay off the Latin if you promise never EVER to use words like 'special' again. Thank you.

Now, to explain the disaster.

How much do you know about computers? A great deal more than me, I should imagine. The machine I'm using at the moment is the first I have ever touched. I think of it really as no more than a socially ambitious type-writer. It belongs to Simon and has been transported to my room together with its printer and a simply baroque quantity of cabling. It lives on the writing-desk and hums irritably like the engine-room of a submarine. When I haven't used it for a while the monitor succumbs to a fit and gaudily coloured fish swim quietly to and fro across the screen, which eccentric mannerism I find strangely endearing. The computer has a device attached to it called a MOUSE, on account of the squeaking noise it makes when it is grabbed and rubbed along a hard surface.

All I know about the use of the thing is that I have to SAVE all the time. This soterial requirement has no evangelical basis, but is said to keep me from accidentally erasing the things that I am typing. You give the work you are saving a FILENAME. My letters to you are stored by the computer in a little envelope on the screen. The envelope is called TED'S FOLDER and the letters are called JANE.1 and JANE.2. I may call them letters, but the computer calls them FILES. This is something of a misnomer as they are nothing like a file, but that is neither here, there nor anywhere. Be patient. This is getting somewhere.

When I sat down at the computer this morning to write this I decided first to reread my last letter to you so as to remind myself of its contents. The procedure for this is relatively simple. I point my mouse at the FILE I need to look at, then twice in rapid succession I depress a button on the mouse's head and, as if by technology, the text of the letter appears on the screen.

As I was preparing for this operation, I noticed for

the first time that on the screen, inside TED'S FOLDER, next to the FILENAME of every document, there is printed a lot of incidental information of a wearisome technical nature: SIZE, KIND, LABEL, things of this kind, followed by numbers and abstruse acronyms. There are another two columns which say 'CREATED' and 'LAST MODIFIED'. I realised that these descriptions refer to DATES. In other words, just by looking at a file you can see when it was first written and when you last made alterations to it.

Well, blow me down if I didn't discover that JANE.2, my last letter to you, claimed that it was 'Modified on 27/07/92 at 20.04' – or five past eight yesterday evening. Now, I know for a fact that I was sucking down pre-dinner cocktails in the library with Rebecca, Oliver and Max at five past eight yesterday evening. I also know for a fact that I haven't so much as looked at the computer since my marathon session on Friday and Saturday, the 24th and 25th.

I looked through the text to see if it had indeed been 'modified'. I couldn't *find* any alterations, but then you see, anybody could have accidentally pressed the space-bar while reading the letter through and this would have counted as modification enough to change the ascription under the FILENAME heading.

Well, next I thought I was being absurdly paranoid. How could I be sure that the computer knows the date anyway? For all I know it believes that this is a cold December night in Heidelberg at the height of the Holy Roman Empire. To test this (as I could find no way of instructing the computer to divulge to me its idea of the day of the week) I wrote a brand-new letter and then looked to see what date it was stamped with. There is no doubt about it, the computer is accurate to the minute.

This can only mean that SOMEBODY has read my last letter to you. This would never have happened if you'd allowed me to communicate in MANUSCRIPT (that's English for handwriting).

I don't know who the culprit can be. This machine belongs to Simon and he certainly knows how to work it . . . he has some ridiculous program stored here which lists the Swafford estate's game-chick population and records the progress of the shooting season. His familiarity with computers might be said to count in his favour perhaps, since he is unlikely to have been so dumb as to have made an alteration to the text of my letter and then saved it in such a way that I, a complete novice, can tell that it has been tampered with. On the other hand, we do know that Simon is not one of nature's brightest specimens.

David perhaps? Perfectly possible, except that he is so obsessively honest and 'good' and strait-laced that I imagine he would pluck out his eyes rather than catch himself reading another man's letters. The bottom-bitingly horrible thought that occurs to me, if it turns out that it was Davey, however, is that he has therefore read my less than complimentary remarks about his fucking poem. Ooya.

It cannot have been Oliver, Max or Rebecca, that we can say with certainty. They were with me from seven fifty-five until the end of dinner. The rest of the house-party, Simon, David, Clara, Michael, Anne, Mary and Patricia, were all downstairs by twenty past I reckon, so unless I can prove that the Butler Did It we may have to send for Poirot.

But that's not the point really, is it? The worry is not *who*, but *what next*? It was a damnably long letter and besides being stuffed with the indiscreetest of gossip, it would reveal to anyone that I am being paid by you to sniff around: hence my fear that I may be about to be shown the door. For the moment I am brazening the thing out. Damn technology. Damn you. Damn me and damn whoever is responsible.

Next we come to the Seven Proclamations of Onslow Terrace which you nailed up in your last communication.

1. *Stop using Latin*

We've dealt with that one.

2. *Enquire about the twins*

Hum. The twins have been staying, in answer to your question, with Anne's sister Diana, who lives, as I'm sure you recall, near Inverness. Edward suffers from asthma and the air in Scotland is believed, at this time of year, to be less harmful than the air in Norfolk. James and Edward are inconsolable if parted: therefore they have gone together. But you'll hear more on that subject under Proclamation Four.

3. *Find out how Oliver is and what brings him here*

I really didn't know at first what you meant by 'find out how he is'. He is . . . Oliver, I thought. As to what brought him here: his exact explanation last Saturday was 'R&R', which perhaps you didn't understand. It is

Eighties-speak and means Rest and Recreation or possibly Rest and Recuperation, at a pinch Rest and Relaxation. *Not* Rock and Roll, nor Rhyme and Reason, nor Rough and Ready, nor Radicals and Revolutionaries, nor Rum 'n' Raisin: not any other damned thing, just plain Rest and Recreation.

There is a pleasing American saying: 'If it looks like a duck and walks like a duck then it probably is a duck.' Oliver looks like a man in need of R&R and walks like a man in need of R&R, I reasoned. Therefore he probably is in need of R&R. I couldn't imagine why you wanted me to find out more.

Ever your obedient, however, I bearded him yesterday morning after breakfast. He sat in the library, filling a shaft of light with cigarette smoke and emptying the newspapers of gossip.

'Morning, heartsworth. Guess which little play at the Nash is sold out to the end of its run?'

He was referring of course to Michael Lake's *Demi-paradise*, the cause of my fall, currently wowing them at the National Theatre.

'It would hardly have been worth my making a fuss about it,' I said, defending my attack on the piece, 'if I thought it was going to fold in a fortnight. It was because I *knew*, absolutely knew, that the public would eat it whole. That's the point.'

'If there's one thing Teddy can't bear, it's a successful left-winger who's stayed left-wing. Every time you think of Michael Lake and his kind, Gertie Guilt scampers up and swings her handbag right into your solar plexus, doesn't she?'

'Oh, Oliver, not this conversation.' I sank into a chair opposite him, the slant of sunlight falling between us.

Oliver and I had been on an Aldermaston march together, had joined the same Labour club (West Chelsea, naturally . . . nothing too hairy or tattooed) and contributed to the same periodicals, which in those days were so left-leaning they needed the support of Moscow to keep them from falling over. I couldn't have been happier than to seize upon the Prague Spring in 1967 as a perfect excuse to leave, in every sense, the party. Oliver always pretends that I betrayed him, betrayed my principles and betrayed that non-existent heap of prejudice and ignorance, the 'people'. Of course we all know that the real traitor, Oliver's necessary Judas, was none other than his beloved History. He has got to the age now when he considers it worth foisting on the world lamentably evasive and heavily edited editions of his journal, or 'Daisy Diary' as he refers to the work privately. The years 1955 to 1970 have just been published, lots of sanctimonious ordure heaped on *my* head, but very little about his disgusting basement-nightclub activities, naturally. Just a few mealy-mouthed phrases about the 'awakening of the gay identity' and arse-wash of that nature. Most of 'Daisy' consists of media gossip and his usual monocular interpretation of politics. 'Them' are callous and shiftless, 'Us' are heroes of the people.

'Not this conversation?' he said. 'What would you rather speak about? The smelliness of the working man and his ingratitude in refusing to have heard of you?'

'My breakfast is just digesting,' I said. 'I refuse to have it brought to the surface by a man lecturing me on political morals from the comfort of a rich leather chair in a millionaire's country-house library.'

'A political truth is a political truth whether spoken from a working man's pub or a gentleman's club, dearest, and well you know it. But,' he added sweetly, sensing that I was ready to confound him with a reply, 'you're right. Let's talk of cabbages, not kings. Simon tells me that without rain, the winter barley is going to be looking pretty jolly silly soon. What's more, Hetty the Hose-Pipe Ban will shortly be paying a visit unless Clara Cloud can be pinched and made to cry.'

'Talking of Clara,' I said, wondering whether there was some accidental significance in Oliver's choice of that Christian name. 'What's going on with the Clifford product? Is she . . . I mean . . .'

'If you mean, is she two faggots short of a *corps de ballet*, then no, darling. She's fourteen, she's got a little bit of a squint, her teeth stick out, she has no friends and no bust and nothing can make her happy. You could hardly expect her to be the life and soul of the party, now, could you?'

'What about you? Everything up to snuff?'

'Oh lor, we're about to be quizzed on Safety, I can tell. Mother's very safe, thank you, baby, and very sound. Socialism is still her only communicable disease.'

'You've lost a bit of weight, though.'

'In the days when I grew up, when Fitzrovia was the heartland of the civilised world and Quentin was still Crisp, losing weight was held to be rather desirable. Nowadays it would appear to be a flag of shame. Just because we like to take it up the Gary Glitter, darling, it doesn't mean we have to grow fat to satisfy the fears of our friends.'

'Oh, for goodness' sake will you stop expecting me to tread everywhere with precious little tippy-toes of political correctness.'

'Darling, the real political correctness in this country, as you very well know, is to stuff the minorities and howl "Sanctimony, sanctimony" at anyone who dares suggest different.'

We just can't help it, Oliver and I. We wouldn't be able to discuss prospects in the Danish football league without bickering.

'Well, it's wonderful to see you looking so fit, then,' I offered.

'Ha, well, that's where you're wrong, you fat Ted. The real reason I'm losing weight is because my Dennis won't let me eat anything worth eating. I may have a cute figure, but I've also got acute angina.'

'Oh, my dear Oliver, I'm very sorry.'

'It's only chest pains, not the real thing. But my sweet Dennis chooses to interpret it as a Warning.'

'So you've come here to escape his eagle eye and stuff yourself as full of good food as you can?'

'Something like that, Ted, yes.'

So. There you have it, Jane. That answers Proclamation 3, I hope.

4. More information about Aunt Anne

Later that same morning Davey dragged me off round to the stables to say hello to the horses and hounds. Annie came clattering into the yard on her return from the morning gallop.

'This is a first,' she said, dismounting. 'Are we about to see you ride, Ted?'

'Given our respective weights, it would probably be fairer if the horse got on my back and rode me,' I said.

A groom came to take Annie's mount.

'Could I have a word, Lady Anne?' he asked.

'What is it, Mr Tubby?'

'That's Lilac. Simon reckon she's sick.'

We clustered round the stable door of the horse in question. Lilac is a large bay mare belonging to Michael. She stood at an angle, her head pressed against the side wall, a forlorn attitude that may or may not have betokened illness, and certainly seemed to indicate a rather depressed outlook on life. Horses strike me as being so perpetually dull of eye and stupid of demeanour that it is never easy to determine, as it might be with dogs, what state of health they are in.

'Simon was here for the morning rounds and noticed she want taking her feed and she was circling round and round and there was blood in her spittle,' said Tubby.

'But she was all right yesterday, was she?'

'She was ever so well yisty, Lady Anne.' (Forgive the attempts at rendering the dialogue, Jane dear. It's rather a challenge.) 'She come in from pasture full of spirit.'

'Oh dear, have you any idea what it might be?'

'Simon want certain, he's afraid that might be ragwort poisoning or maybe grass fever.'

'Oh, dear, I do hope he's wrong. Surely we would have noticed if it was ragwort? It takes time, doesn't it?'

'That can come sudden, Lady Anne, so Simon say.'

Who was supposed to be the expert, I wondered, Simon or this paid professional? A case of passing the buck, I supposed. If the horse suddenly went mad and bit everybody, it would be Master Simon's fault not the groom's.

Davey stroked the horse's muzzle and blew gently up its nose. 'I wonder,' he said, starting to open the stable door, 'if . . .'

'*NO*, Davey! No!' Annie screamed. 'Come away from there *at once*!'

David leapt back from the gate as if it had been surging with high-voltage electricity. Tubby looked discreetly away, but I felt free to goggle.

'I'm sorry, darling, I didn't mean to shout.' Anne's breath, like the mare's, was snorting from her nostrils as she wound down from her peculiar outburst. 'Ill horses can be very dangerous. Very temperamental.'

David was scarlet with bafflement or embarrassment or fear or rage or frustration. 'Lilac knows me as well as anyone . . .' he managed to say.

Anne gained full command of herself, anxious to preserve a front before Tubby and myself. 'I know, darling, I know. But until we know what's wrong with her, there's always the danger of infection. There are a number of things horses can get which humans can catch, you see.'

'When did I last catch *anything*?' asked David.

Annie turned to me brightly. 'I'm popping into Norwich to see my dentist in half an hour,' she said. 'Why don't you both come along? David can show you the sights.'

I sat in the front of the Range Rover next to Anne, with a subdued, if not sulky, David in the back.

'The twins will be coming home tomorrow,' she said. 'Angus and Diana are off on their hols.'

'And Edward?'

'He's been taking a new treatment out of his asthma season, all through the winter and spring. So far there's been no trouble, so we do feel we can risk him coming home. If it starts up again we may have to rethink. There's a place in Switzerland Margot was telling me about. I miss them dreadfully.'

She had surprised the world and herself when, at the age of forty-eight, she had waxed pregnant with twins. I remembered them as eighteen-month-old blobs at Christmas '88 when last I had visited Swafford.

'They'll be on their way to being five soon, I suppose?'

'That's another reason to have them back. Their birthday comes in another fortnight.'

David perked up after Anne had dropped us off somewhere near the centre of town and driven off to keep her appointment.

'Do you know an interesting thing about Norwich?' he asked as we stood about on the pavement.

I doubted there was one, unless he was referring to its distance from London, but expressed the required ignorance.

'There are exactly fifty-two churches in Norwich and three hundred and sixty-five pubs.'

'Is that right?'

'So they say. That means you can get drunk in a different bar every night of the year, and repent at a different altar every week of the year.'

The odds, then, were a pleasant six-to-one on that we would stumble across a pub before we encountered a church. Probability took a powder that day however, and I found myself being marched by Davey into the close and asked to admire the flying buttresses and exquisitely proportioned apsidal east end of the great cathedral. The flying buttresses and exquisitely proportioned apse of a great barmaid would have exerted infinitely more powerful a pull, but I allowed myself to be led. I mused that it had in all probability been twenty years since I had last stood inside a cathedral. The smell of the stone and the particular perfection of temperature and atmosphere, neither warm nor cool, neither dry nor humid, is common to all Norman and Gothic ecclesiastical interiors and contributes much to the mystery and grandeur of such creations. He says.

David took me outside to the cloisters where he showed me the armorial bearings of his mother's family.

'And where do you think your father's ancestors might be recorded?' I asked.

'In the Bible, I suppose.'

'Do you like being the seed of Abraham?'

'You don't count as Jewish if it's only your father, you know.'

'So I believe.'

'The trouble with Jews,' said David, settling himself on a small ledge within an open archway that looked on to the central lawn of the cloister, 'is that they don't have any sense of nature. It's all towns and businesses.'

'Are you talking about Jews in general, or one Jew in particular?'

'Well I think Daddy is actually more rurally minded than most, wouldn't you say?'

He can afford to be, I thought.

Interpreting my silence as disagreement, David folded his arms and thought for a while.

'Why don't you sit down?' he asked at length.

'Do you really want to know?'

'Yes,' he said, surprised.

'The reason I don't sit down,' I said, 'is that lately I have been growing the most luscious and luxuriant crop of piles.'

'Piles?'

'You must have heard of piles. Haemorrhoids.'

'Oh, haemorrhoids. Yes. Daddy gets those. He has a cream and an applicator. I've seen them in his bathroom cupboard. He says I'll get them one day because piles are a Jewish man's affliction. Piles and mothers. What causes them?'

'They come with age and sedentary habits. The only cure is to have them lanced with a knife. A cure that is crueller than the disease.'

'I thought you said on Thursday night that nothing could be cured.'

'Touché, you young sod.'

'*You* aren't Jewish are you?' asked David after a pause.

'Sadly not. Despite the piles.'

'You are a pretty urban sort of person though, wouldn't you say?'

'Only nor'-nor'-east,' I said. 'I know a fox from a fax machine.'

'Simon thinks *I'm* the urban one in the family because I don't approve of killing. He says city people have lost all idea of the importance of life, so they concentrate on the importance of death.'

'That sounds to me a little too sophisticated to have come from Simon.'

David laughed. 'Well, he probably read it in the *Shooting Times*.'

I felt in a pocket for a Rothie. David looked scandalised.

'What's the matter?' I said. 'The Victorians used to fit ash-trays in their pews, you know. Sermons were judged by cigar length. A four-inch sermon, a five-inch sermon, a full Corona and so on.'

'Never!'

'Swear to God.'

'Try telling that to a tour-guide.'

I conceded the point and went without.

David gazed up at me. 'Do you know why Mummy wouldn't let me go into the stable to tend to Lilac this morning?'

I shook my head.

David sighed and chewed his lower lip. 'She doesn't like me to use . . . she's *afraid*, you see.'

'Afraid?'

'I can . . . sometimes . . . almost . . . I know you'll laugh . . .'

'I won't laugh,' I promised. Not audibly, at any rate.

'I can sometimes *talk* to animals.'

Well, I thought, I sometimes talk to the wall. But I knew that was not what he meant. He meant, of course, that the animals talked back.

My son Roman, who is not far off Davey's age, once claimed that he could understand a mouse he kept in a cage in his bedroom.

'And what does this mouse talk about?' I had asked.

'He tells me how much he would like a friend.'

A feebly transparent plea for another pet mouse, I

had thought, and duly shogged off to Horrids to buy one, on the strict understanding that they guaranteed its masculinity. It occurred to me later that perhaps it had really been a plea from Roman himself. He often grew lonely in London, once the initial excitement had worn off, on those occasions when his mother packed him off to stay with me in school holidays: too young for his sister Leonora – he had been conceived, after all, as a last-ditch attempt to create something that might hold Helen and me together – too young to accompany me to the theatre, too old to be entertained by a nanny.

It struck me now that, idyllic as Davey's childhood might seem from the outside, he too had cause to be lonely. He does not share the agricultural or sporting interests of his brother and (presumably) his local age-mates; his manner, while not precisely forbidding, does give off an air of remoteness, of separation from the herd, of – to use Annie's word – disconnectedness. It is natural for a child of sensitivity and intelligence to withdraw. Better to flaunt your independence than risk rejection. Animals are welcome friends because they never judge. Adolescent girls, as is well known, become so infatuated with their ponies that they have been known to wedge the morning sugar lump in their labia and lie back to have it nibbled from their drooling quims. The unconditional love an animal can offer, love without guilt, rejection, violence or demands, has great appeal for the young. They are of course too stupid to see that even the most intelligent creature does things only for food. Love, for an animal, begins and ends with din-dins.

'So you talk to animals?' I said.

'They trust me. They know I don't want their eggs, or their milk, or their coats, or their strength, or their flesh, or their obedience.'

'A large number of them want each other's flesh though, don't they? Or do you only talk to vegetarian animals?'

I could have kicked myself when I saw how sarcastic that question had sounded in David's ears. I had meant it quite seriously.

He stood up. 'We are meeting Mummy at the Assembly House,' he said. 'It's a bit of a walk. We should be on our way.'

Anne and I sat munching flap-jacks in the tea-rooms of the Assembly House. David had begged to be allowed to trot across the road to the City library.

'I never thought I'd be doing this,' said Annie.

'Doing what?'

'Biting. I had quite made up my mind that I was in for all sorts of terrible injections and fillings.'

'Clean bill of health, then?'

' "If I have teeth like that at your age, Lady Anne, I shall count myself a lucky man." '

'Double-edged compliment.'

'Any compliment will do at our time of life, don't you find?'

'It's been such a while since I received one,' I said, 'that I can't really answer the question.'

'Oh, poor little Tedward. I'll offer you one then. You've been in Norfolk only a week and you already look a thousand times better than you did when you arrived.'

'That's a compliment to yourself and your hospitality, my love, not to me.'

'Oh poo, you're quite right. Well, I'll tell you how wonderful it is to have you around, then.'

'Angel.'

'No really, Ted. It is. I do hope you're enjoying yourself. You must say if there's anything you need.'

I opened my hands to indicate that not princes nor popes could provide me with more.

'What about you?' I said. 'A happy bunny?'

'Blissful.'

'No storms on the horizon?'

'Why should you say that?' She frowned a little and became busy with the tea-pot.

'No reason, no reason. I just sometimes think it's a strange life for you. Living in the house you grew up in, but . . .'

'But with a husband from another world? Oh Ted, really! I get the best of everything. My own lot and all the financiers and politicians and artists and writers and odd-balls that Michael attracts.'

'That's a list that would make many in this world vomit.'

'Well, put like that, it does sound rather dreadful, but I'm so lucky really. Let's face it, I'm not awfully bright and Michael is such a good husband. I mean, it would be obscene if someone in my position complained. Simply obscene.'

I let her pour out another cup for me.

'I'm not saying,' she went on, 'that I don't get upset when the newspapers write awful things about him. Comparing him to that ghastly Bob Maxwell, for instance. Calling him a corporate raider or a financial pirate and an asset-stripper. If they *knew*, Ted! They haven't seen him in tears when he has to sack people.'

Haig used to weep over the casualty lists, I thought to myself. Never stopped him from sending them over the top though, did it?

'He cares, Ted. He's decent. I'm so proud of him. The boys are so proud of him.'

'That much is very clear, my love. *I'm* proud of him too if it comes to that.'

'I mean, Ted, it is enough for me just to be a mother and wife, isn't it? If you can say, at the end of things, that your life's achievement was a family, that doesn't mean you failed. Not everybody has to create things, like Michael and you.'

So Anne was at that stage, I thought. 'I may not have composed the Ring Cycle or founded ICI, but I brought up four children.' Brought up four children with the help of a quantity of maids, nannies, nurses and hirelings that would have been better employed running a medium-sized boarding school.

'My dearest of dear, dear old things,' I said, and I may even have patted her hand. 'Firstly you have to confess that, in fact, you do a great deal. I don't suppose there is a committee, a trust or a charity that doesn't have you on its board. People may laugh at Lady Bountiful, but what you do needs to be done, is done, and couldn't have been done without you.'

'Thank you for saying that, Ted. I must confess one does feel underappreciated sometimes. They have such awful types around on the charity committees and school boards and councils these days. So snide and picky and sneery. They just expect me to smile and nod like the Queen. So often, when I suggest things, I simply get laughed at, as if my job is only to appear on the letter-head and wear a big hat.'

I could picture those meetings all too readily. The ginger-tached, tinted-lensed, cheap-suited, signet-ringed, loafer-shod nobodies suffering from razor-burn and irritable-vowel syndrome who import Korean strimmers or run golf driving-ranges and now populate all the boards and committees and magistrates' benches of the country, what would they see in this Lady Anne Ponsonby-Smythe-Twistleton-Lah-di? Conservative, Labour or Liberal, they would consider her a useless joke.

'Wouldn't it be lovely,' I could imagine Annie saying brightly, 'to ask the Duchess of Kent to open the borstal's new lavatory-complex?'

Sniggering glances are exchanged and dandruff rains down on the agenda-papers as heads shake slowly in disbelief.

'With respect to the lady chairman, that would be highly inappropriate,' says some builder of executive homes, by which he means, 'We'll do the thinking, thank you, pet. You just shut your posh mouth and sign the frigging cheques.'

Poor old darling, committing the crime of doing no more than trying to be nice.

'What you do,' I said, 'is valued. Good God, your family alone! Wouldn't I rather have four fine sons ready to do something in the world, than four flabby poems mouldering in the *Oxford Book of Modern Poetry*.'

'But you've got children as well!'

'Helen's got them. I'm a Bad Influence. I think I know my godchildren better than I know Roman or Leonora.'

'Ted, that's a terrible thing to say. I know you must be a wonderful father, if the way you treat Davey is anything to go by. You treat him as an equal.'

'That's conceited of me. I should be treating him as a superior.'

'Oh dear, I do know what you mean. He isn't being a nuisance, is he?'

'Good Lord, as if! I should imagine that child's school reports would compare favourably with those of St Agnes.'

'Do you understand what I was talking about when I said I was worried about him? Am I just being hysterical? You see, it's so difficult for him. Growing up under the shadow of someone like Simon. I sometimes.... here he is!'

David hove into view, swinging a carrier-bag full of books.

'And what have you two been talking about?'

'The characteristics that distinguish the ten-year-old Macallan from the eighteen. I was telling your mother that the ten-year-old, cheaper as it may be, is the better glass.'

'I quite agree,' said David. Saucy thing.

As we walked to the car-park I asked him what he had taken out from the library.

'Oh, just books.'

As it happens, I managed to catch a glimpse of one of the titles when he slung the carrier-bag into the back of the Range Rover.

Staunton's Equine Anatomy was the title. Hah-lah.

That completes my report, for the time being, on Lady Anne, although I would like the chance to quiz her on what she had meant by 'the shadow of someone like Simon'.

5. *On no account mess around with Patricia. She is very special and not to be trifled with.*

This is unworthy of you in every particular. I ought, I suppose, to be flattered that you imagine Patricia would *allow* me to 'mess around' with her. Or do you imagine that I would stoop to rape? Or in her case, stretch up on tip-toe to rape?

I have no doubt she is 'special'. Who the bloody hell isn't? It's a short step from using the word 'special' to ending conversations on the telephone with 'I love you' instead of the more usual and desirable 'Good-bye' or 'Fuck off, then'.

Your warnings were redundant in any case, for it is she who has been messing with me.

She found me on the hammock after lunch, relaxing with the *Telegraph* and a glass of the particular.

'Game of croquet, Ted?'

'Well,' I replied, laying down the paper, 'I can see the hoops, but where are the mallets and balls? Or are we to use flamingos and hedgehogs?'

'They're kept in a trunk in that hut,' she said pointing to the simulacrum of the Villa Rotunda. Hut, for good-ness' sake.

I happen to be rather good at croquet. I don't know why this should be, there is no other game at which I am anything less than an embarrassment. I played tennis with Simon yesterday: the boy had only to stand solemnly in the centre of the court and pat the ball gently over the net to have me wheeling, slapping, panting and thrashing like a Newcomen engine. Oliver, who was watching, said the spectacle put him in mind of a windmill tilting at Don Quixote.

The gentle, spiteful art of croquet, however, is more suited to my low centre of gravity and high sense of malice. We played, as is best, with two balls each, I with my fascistic favourites black and red, Patricia taking yellow and blue. My skills took her a little by surprise, I think; she is adept at the game herself, and the first circuit of the lawn was completed in a concentrated silence, broken only by the thlunk-shimm of roqueted balls fizzing out of bounds.

As we approached the final hoops however, Patricia gave up all attempts at winning and became inclined to coze. It seemed she had what I believe is known as an agenda.

'Ted, why did you behave like that on Thursday night?'

'Behave like what?'

'You know perfectly well.'

Thursday was the night of the big dinner party. As you will see from my chronicle of the event, I behaved in exemplary fashion throughout. As far as I can see, it was Oliver, and to some extent Davey, who crapped in the salad on that occasion, not me. I said as much to Patricia.

'Whatever it is that is going on here,' she said, 'can only be ruined by your scepticism and contempt. You

557

may think it's all very funny, but I should have thought you had more respect for a godchild than that.'

Respect for you, Jane, or respect for Davey? I really was completely lost by now.

'Thoughts, Patricia,' I said, 'as you may imagine, are beginning to burgeon and bubble in the primal soup of my mind, inchoate and confused, like protozoic life-forms. Some of the more likely-looking specimens might one day evolve into sentient beings, but for the moment my planet seems to be eons behind everyone else's in the race for civilisation. When you say "whatever it is that is going on here", you mean precisely . . . ?'

'If you want to sit and snipe from the sidelines, then fine, Ted. But I'm warning you, if you blow it for the rest of us, I'll . . . I'll kill you.'

'Blow *what*?'

'Oh, for goodness' sake . . .' Patricia threw down her mallet and glared at me. 'You're just a wart-hog, aren't you? A great fat vicious wart-hog!'

Turning on her heel she stamped off to the house, muttering and choking with emotion. As I watched her go, I became aware of a figure looming towards me from the corner of the lawn. Rebecca approached, a trugful of strawberries on her arm, a broad grin on her face.

'Still the same magical touch with women, Ted?'

'Some people,' I said, bending to gather the croquet-balls, 'cannot take defeat.'

'Oh, come now, Ted, it was more than that surely? You tried to goose her while she bent to play the ball.'

'Certainly not,' I replied. 'Nothing can have been further from my mind.'

'Then you are not Ted Wallace but an imposter and I shall go and ring the police.'

'Well, naturally any bending woman in a short skirt causes some kind of reflex on a summer's day, but I assure you it is a reflex buried deep by years of frustration and remains fully under my control.'

'Then what was it all about? Come and sit on the steps and tell me everything.'

We sat with the roundhouse behind us.

'What is going on here, Rebecca? Just what the hell is going on?'

'Darling, you've been here longer than I have. You tell me.'

I'm afraid at this point, Jane, I half gave away our little conspiracy.

'Well, it starts for me like this,' I said. 'Bumped into Jane a couple of weeks ago. She knew me, but I felt the completest fool not recognising her.'

'I think we know whose fault that is, darling.'

'Yes, well, whatever. Went back to her place and she told me about the leukaemia and such like.'

'Did you get an earful of God?'

'There was talk of miracles certainly. Something emanating from here, from Swafford. She claims to be . . . well . . . cured.'

'Don't I know it? Ecstatic letters have arrived at Phillimore Gardens praising the Lord and rejoicing in many wonders.'

'Do you believe her?'

'Like you, that's why I'm here, darling. To find out. As it happens, we share the same doctor, Jane and I.'

'And what does he say?'

'Well, you know doctors. He is surprised by the remission but cautious as cautious can be.'

'There definitely has been a remission then?'

'No doubt about that.'

'Hum.' I sat and thought for a space while Rebecca started in on the strawberries.

'But what has any of that,' she asked, 'got to do with Patricia's splendid description of you as a wart-hog, a great fat vicious wart-hog?'

'Does she know about Jane's miraculous recovery?'

'Sure to. Best buddies.'

'Who else knows?'

'Search me, darling. It was last June I understand. Simon brought her back prostrate to this house from the Norfolk Show, white corpuscles practically oozing from her pores. Michael and Anne were here of course, Simon and Davey had an exeat from school to celebrate the finishing of their exams, can't be sure who else. Oh, Max and Mary, they were staying at the time, I'm almost sure.'

'So do any of them believe in this miracle?'

'Don't ask me.'

I grabbed a fistful of strawberries and thought for a while.

'Well, I don't think Simon believes. He told me the other day about Jane's collapse. Compared her overnight recovery to that of pigs he had known.'

'Romantic bugger.'

'Oliver on the other hand . . . He seems to know something. I'm almost certain he does.'

'If there's truffle, Oliver will snuffle it out, you can be sure of that.'

560

'And Patricia clearly thinks that I am in on it, but scoffing sceptically up my sleeve.'

'Well, that's certainly how you sounded the other night at dinner, isn't it?'

Rebecca was alluding to a conversation I had with the Bishop and others about 'healing' and 'therapy'.

'You do see, don't you, my dear, that this talk of miracles is preposterous?'

'Well, I know one thing, darling, and that is that Jane should have been dead by the end of June.'

'Why did you never let me know? Why did I only find out by chance that my only god-daughter had leukaemia?'

'Fat lot you'd've cared. It would have taken more than a dying god-daughter to get you to raise your red eyes from the whisky glass. I know what you've been like. Oliver tells me of your exploits. Not that he needs to – I read the newspapers. A glitterati drunkard rampaging around Soho and the West End insulting everyone you meet and sweating your fat arse over a bar-stool with your fellow has-beens, puking bile at everyone under fifty and tearing great chunks off hands that dare to feed you.'

'Rebecca . . .'

'But of course you've been sacked now, haven't you? Suddenly you need your rich and powerful friends to help you out of the tank of bitter piss you've been drowning in for the last twenty years. You'll slobber with doe-eyed sympathy and moon with paternal concern – why, darling, you'll even cut down on your drinking and go boaty-woaty with your godson like a white-haired old saint – so long as underneath you can remain the same cynical, evil-minded old turd that the world knows and loves.'

There, in a nutshell, you have your mother. I suspect I am the only man in this world who has dared to spurn her. It may have been all of two decades ago but to a mind like hers this is no time at all. Revenge for Rebecca is a dish best served ice-cold, nestling in a *coulis* of vitriol, garnished with sprigs of belladonna and thrown hard into the poor bastard victim's face.

I arose, brushed the strawberry stalks from my lap and walked away, saying not a word.

On my way to the house I collided with Clara the cross-eyed Clifford.

'Good afternoon, Mr Wallace,' she said, 'I was just coming to fetch you.' At least, that is what I think she said. I won't try and emulate her lisp, poor dear.

'Oh yes? And why is this?'

She looked steadfastly at me (and at some other unidentified object a hundred and twenty degrees to the west). 'Uncle Michael would like to see you in his study.'

The visitor to Lord Logan of Swafford's study is put in mind of Ernst Stavro Blofeld's headquarters. Control consoles, electrically operated curtains and projection screens, telecommunication devices, globes containing whisky decanters and large-screen videophones represent only the visible and identifiable elements of gadgetry.

'Choose a city for destruction, Mr Bond. Which is it to be? New York? Leningrad? Paris? No, wait! London! Of course! Goodbye Piccadilly, farewell Leicester Square, as you British are so fond of saying.'

'Ted!' Michael half-rose from his chair, a cigar in his mouth. 'Forgive me for summoning you like a disorderly corporal. I'm awaiting a call from South Africa.'

'Business or politics?' Michael is well known for dabbling his hands in the affairs of nation states. Around the walls there are hung photographs of him beaming at the camera in varying postures of intimacy with World Leaders: an arm around Walesa, stiffly side by side by Mandela, toasting Yeltsin with a shot-glass of vodka, sharing a preposterous gilded Louis XVI sofa with Arafat, on the golf course with James Baker and George Bush.

'So what's the difference? There's a tobacco company I'm looking at in Johannesburg. South Africa's the coming state, you know.'

'I admire your optimism.'

Michael backhanded away a waft of cigar smoke and with it the reservations of any so small-minded as to doubt him. 'So. Tedward. What do you want to know?'

I didn't understand what he meant at first. Then I saw and a big smile spread across my face. 'You'll do it? You'll co-operate?'

'My lawyers and I receive an absolute right to veto?'

'Certainly.' I nodded vigorously. As if it would ever come to that.

Instantly, Michael pushed across the desk a sheaf of papers, densely type-written in narrow margins, secured with green thread fasteners.

'Read and sign,' he said. 'Initial where I have initialled, full signature where I have signed in full.'

Ah, the ways of the mighty. 'Do I *have* to read it?' I asked.

'Tedward, so plaintive, like a child with homework. Your "Ballad of the Workshy Man", that must have come from the heart. Me, I read documents twenty times this size on the crapper before breakfast.'

'No wonder you've got piles,' I said.

'You knew I have piles?' Michael frowned.

'Fellow-sufferer,' I said hastily. 'One sees it in the way you sit down.'

'You writers! Not workshy at all. All your work is done observing people.'

Sweet of him to choose to believe that. 'So tell me,' I said, mimicking one of his favourite opening phrases, 'what exactly is in all this?'

'Standard contract for an authorised biography. Rights of injunction. Don't worry, there's nothing that stops you from making full royalties. Talking of which, you owe me one penny.' He opened the palm of his hand and stretched it across the desk.

'I do?' I looked up in surprise.

'In law,' said Michael, 'a contract is meaningless without consideration. Someone must pay someone. You will see in the document you are signing that in consideration for the sum of one penny, I agree to co-operate in your biography, known hereafter as The Material. So. One penny please.'

Fazed by the combination of legalese and earnestness, I fumbled in my trouser pocket for a coin.

'Do you have change for a five-pence piece?'

'Certainly.' Michael caught my shilling, opened a drawer, took out a small strong-box, shook inside it with his fingers and drew out two tuppenny bits. 'And four is five,' he said. 'Shake, business-partner. We have a deal.'

I stood to shake his hand and was disconsolate to see him burst out laughing.

'Tedward! Smile! Deals are causes for celebration.'

'I'm sorry,' I said. 'I think I am overawed by your solemnity.'

'It was your first lesson in how we work. Up to the moment of signature and handshake is grim determination. The moment the ink is on the paper and the hands are clasped together, we are locked in an ecstasy greater than love.'

Michael placed two tape-recording machines on the desk and pressed their record buttons.

'One for each of us,' he said. 'Just so we know where we stand.'

Thus, interrupted only by two calls from Johannesburg, fourteen faxes from there and elsewhere and a call to tea, we sat while Michael embarked on the story of his life.

I will save the details of the conversation for a long weekend, Jane. Let it just be said that Much Has Become Clear.

This morning however, an oddity.

I slouched in to brekker, hoping to catch the bacon before it had turned to leather in the tureen, and sat myself down, as usual, alone with the *Telegraph* at the end of the dining-room table.

Patricia came in, flushed and excited.

'Ted!' she cried. 'I'm so glad to have caught you.'

'Have a coffee,' I said, a little frigidly. I find it difficult to treat a girl who has recently called me a wart-hog with any real warmth of manner, however much I may want to jam my cock up her funnel.

She was not much interested in coffee, however. She had something on her chest. Lucky something.

'Ted, I want you to forget everything I said to you yesterday afternoon.'

'Ah.'

'I'm just so terribly sorry. I really don't know what came over me. I was quite unbearably rude.'

'Not at all, not at all.'

'And I talked such a great deal of nonsense.'

At this point, Simon loomed in looking for Logan, a worried look on his customarily vacant face.

'I think he's working in his study,' said Patricia. 'Anything wrong?'

'Oh, not really. Well, it's Lilac, actually. Dad's hunter. She seems no better. Just wanted to let him know, that's all.'

And off he lumbered, leaving Patricia and me alone once more. She continued with her rather strained apology.

'I can't think why I was so horrid to you. I've been under a lot of pressure lately. I think that must be it. You've probably heard that my . . . that Martin, the man I've been living with, he left me. I get very . . .'

'My dear old girl,' I said. 'Please. Think no more about it.'

'I suppose I imagined at that dinner that you were getting at me. All your talk about therapists. I've been seeing one, you see, and I thought you must have known and were mocking me.'

'Patricia, I would never for a moment . . .'

'Well, of course I realise that, now. I lay awake last night thinking what a brute I'd been to you. You were just talking in general. How could you possibly have known?'

'It was entirely my fault for jabbering on in such a thoughtless fashion. I should be apologising to you.'

She smiled. I smiled back. Somewhere deep in the trouser region the neglected old worm twitched and wriggled in his sleep.

She kissed me on the cheek. 'No hard feelings?'

'Of course not, my dear,' I lied.

I watched that magnificently constructed arse swing out of the room and allowed those hard feelings to subside in my lap. A high arse, ledging out from the coccyx; the kind of arse you can stand a tea-pot on.

But Jane, what the deuce had she been talking about? Didn't fool me for a second. The smile was too bright, the kiss on the cheek too theatrical. I recognise pride thwarted when I see it. She was apologising because she had been told to. Hm. Thinks.

I return now to my schedule and address Proclamation the Sixth:

You have talked only about the guests. The house is full of other men and women. There are indoor and outdoor servants, there is Podmore. I have heard nothing of them.

What do you want, blood? I am not one of those easy aristocratic types who can walk with kings nor lose the common touch. I'm a tight-arsed bourgeois masquerading as *déclassé*. Give us a break, baby-doll.

Of the servants I know by name I can tell you this. There is Podmore, first name Dick, who looks and behaves more like a disbarred time-share salesman than a butler, but then that is how all butlers have looked for years now, even in ducal households (as if I really know). Upper servants have lost the knack of seeming to have no provenance, no private life, no family and no sexuality. One look at Podmore and you can surmise all too readily that he was born in Carshalton Beeches, that he flirted with the Teddy Boy movement in the 1950s before moving with his wife Julie to Norfolk (just great to get away from all that traffic and what was then called the rat-race . . .), that he has his eye on a retirement condo hard by a golf course in Florida and that he can't understand why Logan hasn't replaced the french windows in the main drawing room with sliding patio doors.

Not much else to say about him really except that I suspect him of being a closet nance, Mrs Podmore or no Mrs Podmore. He has a way of eyeing Davey up that argues something of the gaysexualist.

Julie Podmore acts as housekeeper, her duties largely comprise bossing the maids shrewishly and lowering her head whenever she passes a house-guest. She is in her fifties, of medium height, weight and fuckability: she dyes her hair. Beyond that I know nothing to her credit or detriment.

The only maid whose name I can remember is called Joanne. I remember her name because she has a combination of ample thighs and noisy tights. As a result she makes a frishing noise whenever she climbs the stairs or walks the corridor. To match the thighs she sports a cantilevered bust: I should imagine she has to make an effort to lean backwards at all times in order not to fall over. The other maid is woundingly plain and will never rise in her profession until she learns that guests are unlikely to be interested in her brother's exploits on the speedway track.

There are kitchen staff into whose eyrie I have not penetrated, but I can tell you that the cook's name is Cheryl and that she bakes a sinful egg custard. Liberality with the nutmeg is the key here, I fancy.

Venturing outside we encounter Alec Tubby, the chief groom. He is stoutly Norfolk and entirely without discernible character. His son Kenny assists him in the muckings-out and rubbings-down around which stable life revolves. He will be a bit depressed at the moment on account of the vet expressing dark forebodings this afternoon as to the chances of Lilac pulling out of her decline.

A splendour called Kate supervises the kennels and, as is traditional with such specimens, presents to the world a handsome beard and moustache. It must take at least a square yard of stout blue corduroy to trouser her arse alone. She is rather fun as a matter of fact, and a pleasure to talk to. She has persuaded me to puppy-walk some of the young hounds, which is a thing that needs doing at this season and which I find highly enjoyable. There is something tirelessly entertaining about the way puppies widdle.

Further afield we find Tom Jarrold, the gamekeeper. He is aggressively jealous of his cocks, hens and chicks and can spot a no-good townie like me a mile off. We have little to say to each other. Henry, his assistant, aspires to be no more than a carbon-copy of Tom. Simon seems to be the only person alive who can communicate with either of them. Jarrold has a hare-lipped daughter, Katrina. Not just hare-lipped, actually, but hairy-lipped too. Nature can be unbearably cruel.

The only other member of staff to mention is Valerie, Michael's secretary or PA. She keeps herself very much to herself and is only here on certain days. I have not determined if there is a pattern. When she is here she dines alone, in Michael's study, guarding the telephones. This is her choice apparently, since she has been offered a place at table amongst persons of rank and tone.

I really am afraid, my angel, that there is nothing more I can tell you. But, as required by the last of your dictats, Proclamation Seven, the Four Constants will ever be my guide.

Constant vigilance; constant awareness; constant observation; constant openness.

So rest assured that I shall not cease from mental strife, nor shall Simon's computer sleep by my hand, till we have built Jerusalem in Norfolk's green and peasant land.

Assuring you, madam, of my good faith in this and all matters.

Yours (for Logan-Wallace Biogs Plc)

Ted Wallace (CEO)

*O*nslow *I*nteriors

12a Onslow Terrace • South Kensington • LONDON SW7

URGENT FACSIMILE TRANSMISSION

To: Patricia Hardy, c/o Logan, Swafford Hall, Norfolk
From: Onslow Interiors Ltd
My fax: 071-555 4929
Your fax: 0653-378552

For the private and personal attention of Miss Hardy

Dear Miss Hardy,

You suggest in your letter that you might consider
making an approach to E.L.W. to raise the question of
his recent remarks on the subject we discussed.

We would recommend with _extreme_ force that you do not
make such a move. T. is not an expert in this field and
has no knowledge of the details.

I trust this warning has come in time to save you
making an unfortunate mistake.

Unable for the moment to join you for meeting as
suggested.

Letter follows

Yours

J.S.

LOGANGROUP plc

To..Jane Swann
Company...Onslow Interiors
Fax No. 071 555 4929
From ....Patricia
Fax No. 0653 378552
Page..1 of 1

Jane,

Bother! If your fax means what I think it does, then I've screwed up. Gave Ted an earful yesterday. Called him a foul and ugly old wart-hog. Hard to take those kind of words back but I had a go just now in the breakfast room.

I told him that I've been behaving irrationally on account of Martin leaving me and that I had had a go at him because I thought <u>he</u> had been having a go at me. <u>Think</u> he swallowed it. He leered what he imagines is a debonair smile and started dripping egg-yolk down his shirt, which I think is a sign of forgiveness.

You really should have warned me though. Does he really not know what's going on? And why are you concerned with what he thinks or believes anyway? He's not here on a commission from a <u>newspaper</u> is he? The mind boggles. Come to think of it, Michael announced last night that Ted is writing his biography. They've been closeted together for hours and hours. What's <u>that</u> all about?

Wildest apologies, do come down soonest

Pat

IV

David closed the book and let his eyes lose focus as he gazed up at the ceiling-rose. By eleven o'clock the light had faded enough to silence the chimes of the stable clock. Two hours had passed by since then. In an hour he would be ready. For the moment it was safest, so excited was he, to relax his whole body and concentrate on nothing.

He thought of a circle and within that circle, another circle, within that another and another and another, allowing his inner eye to zoom at speed through the endless ring of rings, finding a central glowing spot that in its turn changed into another circle which itself contained yet more and more circles. It was like a dive into the centre of things and diverted the mind from any base or worldly thoughts. The technique came from a book on yogic meditation he had bought last holidays and worked extremely well so long as one was capable of concentrating with the utmost force while at the same time remaining entirely relaxed.

The time went surprisingly quickly in this state and David already knew, without looking at his bedside clock, when it was two o'clock precisely.

He stood naked before a tall mirror, breathing deeply. The night was warm but he would need some protection. He chose a T-shirt, baggy track-suit bottoms and a pair of trainers. No socks or pants. Taking from the bedside table a torch, an apple and a small jar wrapped in sheets of Kleenex, he left the room.

A gibbous moon, he had heard it called. Half and half. Enough light to see, enough dark to conceal. Light was not important, really. In his present state he felt he could accomplish the mission blindfold.

His trainers loomed white beneath him in the shadow of the house and against the greasy black of the grass, white flashes pumping back and forth. Looking up, he saw Orion's belt twinkling on its waist and the dog star spinning blue to the east. The sound of his trainers scuffing the grass died in the velvet deep of the night.

'All the air,' he whispered to himself in the rhythm of the running and panting, 'a solemn stillness holds. All the air . . . a solemn . . . stillness . . . holds. All the air . . . a solemn . . . stillness . . . holds!'

He was there. The long shadow of the clock fell on the stable yard and a warm savour of horse manure rolled towards him.

Soft as a moth he flitted to the door of the corner tack room. Inside, another smell awaited him, the perfume of saddle-soap and dubbin, so rich that it made him cough. Holding his breath, he felt for the wooden stool, picking it up by the carved hole in the centre of its seat. A loose item of tack, a bridle or unfastened martingale, fell to the ground with a brittle ring as he lifted the stool clear, but he knew that the sound penetrated no ears but his own and those of the horses, who knew what he was up to and approved.

He reached Lilac's stall and unlatched the top section of the gate. Lilac, as though she had been waiting, moved her head forward to welcome him.

'Hello,' said David, mind to mind, with no movement of lips and no stirring of breath or vocal cords. 'I've brought you an apple.'

Lilac took the present, like a patient with no appetite

who knows they must eat to keep up their strength. While she was slowly masticating the apple, slewing it from cheek to cheek, David pulled off his T-shirt and slipped out of his track-suit bottoms. Feeling that it was ridiculous to be naked but for a pair of trainers, he took those off too and stood bare in the moonlight.

He shivered a little and felt a colony of goose-pimples start up around his legs.

'Are you ready, old girl?' he asked, again without use of his voice. 'I am.' He stooped to take the jar and its tissue wrapping from the pocket of his track-suit. The torch he could do without.

He exerted the gentlest pressure on Lilac's shoulders as he opened the lower gate and stepped in clutching the stool, but she made no move to make for the open yard. Slowly, he closed both gates together and they were alone in the absolute dark.

She was very peaceful, only a light sweat testifying to her terrible illness. She stood in silence, one rear hoof from time to time clopping the flagstones. David moved down her side, his body touching hers as he felt his way to the end of the stall. The heat from her flanks awoke the great heat in him and as he raised himself up on the stool he felt his glans push through the foreskin and his whole cock stand higher and straighter and harder than it had ever stood before. He straightened up on the stool, a hand steadying himself on Lilac's hindquarters, and slowed his lungs to the rhythm of Lilac's own breathing. She was oestrous and would not kick back with her legs as she might when off heat. Even had she been, David knew that she would welcome him.

When he was ready and he knew they were as one, he

pushed two fingers into the jar and gathered up a thick lump of Vaseline. With his other hand he brushed Lilac's tail to one side. Obediently she gave a twitch and the tail hung high above, leaving him free to work with both hands. Below the dock and anus the outer lips were easy to find and within them he could feel the clitoral hood and below it the soft tissue of the inner labia. Delicately pushing with his finger he found what he thought must be the urethra and gently he traced his finger down to the easy tender squash below. As if to confirm his discovery, Lilac blew gently from her nose and stamped a foot.

David worked the bolus of jelly into the vaginal opening, finding that his fingers slipped easily in and out. What Vaseline was left over he used to anoint himself, although he was already supplying himself with his own thin stream of juice.

The cock went in with splendid ease, its straight slicked hardness pulled further through by a quick spasm from Lilac. The wall closed all around to suck him deeper in and David gasped with the blinding joy of what he felt. A hand either side of the root of her tail, he experimented tentatively by pulling himself marginally back and pushing himself marginally forward. The sensation blinded his head with stars. A millimetre this way, a millimetre that, hooves thundered in his brain and the hot crystals in his stomach were smashed into billions of burning grains. The absolute rightness and holiness and perfection and beauty of life charged through him. In this position he could stay for ever, he and the whole kingdom of life – animal, plant or human, locked in a whirlwind of love. The other time it had all been too quick for him to feel this ecstasy: that had been with a woman and there had been tension and the need to talk in words.

'You are whole, Lilac,' his voice inside him called to her. 'With this gift of pure spirit I pronounce you whole and healed.'

The lights in his head spilled and toppled and spun in desperate agony as he pushed and pushed, unable to believe the unsurpassable depth and intensity of the tumult of pleasure that was overwhelming him, and then there flashed one great white sheet of light in his head and he felt the surge of his spirit course and course and course and course and course as though it would never stop.

As he finished, forcing the last drop, the Vaseline jar tumbled to the ground with a clatter and Lilac whinnied in alarm, pulling in her great ring of muscle with a bruising clench.

David winced but stayed calm, knowing that Lilac would subside too if he was still. The tension in her flanks eased away and she relaxed the muscle, letting David pull out.

He stood there for a moment, hot hands on her side, exultant and exhausted. At last he stepped down to pick up the wad of tissues that had wrapped the jar and began with care to wipe Lilac down, talking to her all the while.

Out in the stable yard he shivered sharply as he put on his T-shirt. He looked down at the spongy dangle of his cock.

'You must be sparing of this great gift,' he said to himself, 'very, very sparing.'

Six

Albert and Michael Bienenstock grew sugar beet in a part of Hungary that in 1919 was redesignated Czechoslovakia. This act of cartographical tyranny had transformed Michael into an overnight Zionist and, inspired by a childish sense of adventure and the inflammatory writings of Chaim Herzog, he took a boat to Haifa in 1923, under a proud new name, Amos Golan. Golan, Michael had satisfied himself after extensive, and in Albert's view preposterous, researches into family history, was the Bienenstocks' true Israelite patronymic. Golan was a fit name for a man travelling to claim his homeland for his people.

'Sailing into trouble,' said Albert, words with which he was later to mock himself.

Albert's own son was named Michael in honour of his foolish uncle, to the great consternation and scandal of Albert's cousins in Vienna. Tradition held it to be bad luck for members of the same family to share a given name. Albert was not a traditionalist. He had no religion, he had no real sense of Jewishness. He was a farmer and a horseman, closer to the anti-Semitic Magyars of the old Habsburg Empire than to the scholarly gabardine beetles of shtetl and city, who scuttled about the streets with their heads down, cravenly hugging the walls when the gentiles walked by, as if fearful of catching or perhaps transmitting some terrible disease.

As a young man in 1914, Albert had fought for his Emperor. Rigged up like a chocolate soldier in gleaming cuirass and nodding plume, Albert the Blue Hussar was among the first to charge the Serbian guns in the early weeks when the Great War was a small Balkan affair that nobody believed could matter. Later, the proud troops of horse humbled by the titanic ordnance of the twentieth century, Albert was appointed to their reassignment as no more than drays and dispatch ponies, pulling with lowered heads the carriages and ambulances that shuffled behind the lines in the frozen Carpathian mountains or relaying fatuous messages between staff and field. With ironic resignation he told himself that loyalty to a great moustache in Vienna was no more stupid than loyalty to a great beard in Jerusalem. By the end however, he had seen too many white worms crawling in the eye-sockets of too many dead comrades, and too many living comrades frying up the livers and lights of too many slaughtered Cossacks with baby faces. He exaggerated the symptoms of some light shell-shock he sustained during a bombardment and was happy to be transferred to a remount division in that district of Romania known as Transylvania, where he was to sit out the war processing the remnants of the cavalry.

Albert possessed a very special gift with horses. He understood them far better than did the equestrian instructors and veterinary surgeons of the Imperial Army, a fact which generated ill-feeling in some of his brother officers. Others preferred to trumpet Albert's skills as a healer, making extraordinary claims which he was always quick to repudiate.

'There is nothing so mysterious about what I do,' he

said. 'I am patient with the animals. I show them that they are loved. I keep them calm. The rest is up to nature.'

Such protestations were so much spitting in the wind. Albert's reputation grew and was even extended to humans, the result of a stupid incident over his batman, Benko. This foolish soldier had allowed his foot to be stamped on by a frightened stallion one afternoon. Instead of reporting the injury immediately to an orderly, Benko had kept quiet and allowed the wound to fester overnight. The next morning, when he hobbled in with the morning coffee, Albert had questioned him.

'Why are you limping so badly, Benko?'

Benko had burst into tears.

'Oh, sir!' he cried. 'Would you take a look at it? I daren't go to the surgeon, for I know he will amputate from the knee. He never does anything else.'

It was certainly true that there existed many standing jokes about soldiers who had made the mistake of visiting the regimental sawbones. There was one private, they said, who rather lost his head and went to see this doctor with nothing more than a migraine – after which he lost his head completely. This joke worked better in Romanian than in Hungarian. Another story concerned Jana, the local whore. One day a soldier called Janos had gone to see the doctor with a genital wart. He was never seen again, but Jana set up her stall only a week later.

Understanding Benko's reluctance to make an official appointment, Albert agreed to examine the foot, but could not help wincing with disgust when Benko gingerly pulled off his boot and sock. He was not a hygienic soldier, indeed had not in all likelihood separated that boot from that foot in many weeks. Benko saw Albert's gagging reaction and immediately began to gibber with fear.

'It's gangrene, isn't it, sir? It's gangrene and I shall lose my leg! I know it, I know it.'

'There, there, you stupid boy. Let me see.'

'No, no! I'm done for, I'm done for!'

Albert took him by the shoulders and spoke into his eyes. 'Listen to me. You must be very calm now. You must breathe slowly and deeply. Breathe very slowly and very deeply for me.'

Trembling, Benko tried to obey. Albert kept on talking to him, firmly but with kindness, until he was satisfied that the boy had wound down from his hysteria. Horses were easier, you could communicate such confidence without words.

'Now I'm going to look at your foot. Be sure there is no real problem with your foot. It is sore and it smarts, but that is not the end of the world.'

Benko turned his head away in squeamish terror as Albert took a deep breath, stooped and pressed his hand to the swelling, which was purple with poison. Immediately, a small splinter flew from the centre of the wound, followed by a jet of pus.

'There,' said Albert, 'that's better.'

Benko turned round to stare at Albert. 'Better?'

'Yes, I'm sure you will find that your foot will mend now.'

'You place your hand on my foot and you say it will mend?'

'No, no, I merely . . .'

But it was too late. Around the barracks the rumour flew.

'Benko's foot was black with gangrene . . .'

'Bienenstock himself nearly fainted at the stench . . .'

'Just put a hand . . .'

'A hand that seared with heat, Benko says . . .'

'Nearly burned him . . .'

'Just rested it for a second . . .'

'Would have had to amputate from the knee . . .'

'Look at the boy now . . .'

'Skipping like a terrier . . .'

'Bienenstock is a strange man, I've always said so . . .'

'Not Christian, you know . . .'

'Not even a proper Jew . . .'

'Never seen in synagogue, according to Corporal Heilbronn . . .'

After a while even Albert himself began to wonder what he had done. He was sure that he had seen that splinter fly, he was sure that the smell he recoiled from was nothing more than the Limburger reek of filthy socks, he was sure that his 'skill' lay in no more than the ability to comfort, to comfort in the proper sense, to make strong, to fortify. But the damage had been done, and from that day Albert never knew a moment's ease amongst his men. A horse that he had 'miraculously' nursed to health had later gone mad, throwing a recruit, who broke his back and never walked again. Everywhere that Albert went he saw the sign of the cross or of the evil eye. Then Benko, silly superstitious Benko, made an appointment with his commanding officer and asked to be reassigned to other duties. Serving Captain Bienenstock made him nervous. A week later Benko died after stepping on a landmine.

'He trod with *that* foot,' the men said. 'Bienenstock's curse.'

*

Albert's loyalty would never be given again: so he swore when he returned in 1919 to his neglected Hungarian fields, soon to become his neglected Czechoslovakian fields. Michael his brother, who had stayed behind with Imperial blessing to tend those fields that the people of the Empire might have something to sweeten their war, had not been a good farmer. The Zionist bug had bitten him early in the Gentile's Quarrel, as he called it, and he had higher things to think of than the husbandry of, as it were, alien corn.

After Michael's departure, Albert spent the next ten years working to become the largest grower of beet in all of Czechoslovakia. In 1929 he set the seal on the triumphant achievement of this ambition by building a small refinery on his land and marrying the daughter of his foreman, a small girl with brown eyes and lustrous hair. Within a year she bore him a son, Michael, and in the spring of 1932 perished in the delivery of a daughter, Rebecca. Albert tried, but he could not save her. Grieve as he might, he could still reflect that it was perhaps as well that he had not succeeded in nursing her back to health after the doctors had pronounced her all but dead. His reputation as an unholy sorcerer had followed him back home and even rabbis, who were supposed to be above the credulous herd, shunned his society.

Albert needed no one. He had proved his point. He was a superb agriculturist. Now, alone with his two tiny children, his wide fields of beet and his sugar refinery, he yearned to leave the country that was no longer his own. Besides Yiddish and Hungarian, his mother tongues, he had had to learn German and Romanian for service in the

Hussars and since then the languages of his new government, Czech and Slovak.

'I am leaving before Prague is taken over by the French,' he told his factotum, Tomasz. Albert held, all his life, a peculiar horror of the French tongue, unaccountably believing it to be far more difficult to master than any other in Europe.

But how could Albert leave? Who would buy his beet fields? Who would give him a good price for a private refinery? Where would he go? Many in his village spoke of America, but America meant only New York; Jews were not welcome in the farmlands. Albert's brother Michael, or rather Amos, urged him by letter to come and join him in Palestine, where he and his new wife Nora had given the world a pair of brand new sabra children, Aron and Ephraim, who were growing up to be the new Jews of the new Jerusalem.

'After all, you're something of a sabra, yourself, Albert,' he wrote.

Albert was puzzled by this remark. A Jew could only call himself a sabra, he had understood, if he was born in the land of Israel. A learned friend explained Amos's meaning.

'Your brother is making a friendly joke, Albert. "Sabra" is also a word for a kind of fruit. A prickly pear, spiky on the outside but sweet and soft on the inside.' As good a description of Albert as anyone ever found. He had been forced to be prickly however, for his estate was large and took a great deal of energy and skill to run, with markets so deeply corrupt, inflation so crazily high and the people so grindingly poor. He had been forced to be prickly because his real, calm, loving and rational self was mistaken for the black soul of a hypnotic wizard.

A week after this letter from Amos had arrived, Adolf Hitler was elected by the German people to be their new Chancellor. Albert was disappointed. Hitler did not seem to him to be a suitable leader for the Germans; the anti-Semitism, he supposed, like everybody's anti-Semitism, was an unpleasant noise that meant very little. Albert was rarely bothered by anti-Semitism. He had often felt a little that way himself when he heard Hasidim sounding off on the subject of the law or Amos and his friends sounding off on the subject of Zion. It was not that Albert was ashamed of being Jewish, it was rather that he was damned if he was going to make a big fuss about it. He was a father and a farmer, that was all.

Another week later a very surprising thing happened. An English gentleman arrived at Albert's house, accompanied by an interpreter from Prague. Albert was beside himself with excitement to have a real Englishman within his walls. Of all the peoples of the world the English were quite his favourite. It had been a matter of great relief to him that he had not come into any hostile contact with them during the course of the war, for he was sure that he would have been greatly tempted to cross the lines and join them. He liked their formality, their tweed suits, their respect for horsemanship, their ironic humour and their lack of show.

Albert seated the Englishman and the interpreter in leather chairs in his study. He rang for Tomasz, his servant.

'The gentleman will take tea?' he asked the interpreter. He hoped that the Englishman would not think that his ringing for a servant amounted to ostentation. It really was perfectly usual for Albert to drink tea at this hour and for

Tomasz to be summoned by a bell and commanded to prepare it.

'Tea would be delightful, my dear sir,' the translator replied in grand Hungarian. He seemed to Albert to be attempting to out-anglify the Englishman with his pre-war pomposity and pre-war whiskers.

Once tea was poured, Albert sat politely upright and waited for the purpose of this visit to be revealed. Sipping from his cup as though he were attending the smartest party on the smoothest lawn in Berkshire, the English gentleman delivered himself of a short sentence and then cocked his head good-naturedly towards the interpreter. The voice was light and pleasant, with soft 'r's and a gentle falling inflection. The interpreter smiled broadly and declared:

'Mr Bienenstock, I represent His Majesty's Government in London.'

What splendid words! Albert's head became dizzy with excitement, then dizzier still as, over the next hour, the Englishman explained his mission.

The British Empire – another splendid phrase! – was deeply sensible, the Englishman said, of her complete dependence upon the cane sugars that originated in her far dominions of Australia and the West Indies. Were there ever to be another war in Europe – and the Englishman protested that this eventuality was held by his masters to be quite discountably remote – naval tacticians were of one mind in their agreement that the seas that bounded the British shores might be all but cut off from vital supplies of hot-weather commodities, of which sugar was the most vital . . . well, after tea perhaps. The British had never in all their long history – really a most unpardonable oversight

– grown sugar beet on any domestic basis. They had no expertise on the subject whatsoever. That it could be grown was not a matter that admitted of the least doubt. Sugar from cane, they were fully aware, was not a realistic possibility, owing to their weather, which Mr Bienenstock doubtless knew was capricious to a nationally celebrated fault. Sugar beet however, the staple of Mr Bienenstock's fertile native plains, seemed perfectly suited to the British climate. It was after all, was it not, akin to the carrot, the turnip and – one must assume – the beetroot? The British farmer was known for the splendour of his carrots, his turnips and his beetroots; surely the cultivation of their close cousins *Beta Rapa* and *Beta Vulgaris* could not be beyond him? The Ministry did feel, however, that someone was needed to guide them, a man who knew all aspects of the vegetable, as it were from field to sugar-bowl. Mr Bienenstock's name had been put forward to Ministry representatives in Prague as being one of the most authoritative in the sugar world. Would Mr Bienenstock consider making the journey to England, in two years' time, to counsel and instruct the ignorant farmers there, to manage test beds, to supervise refinery construction and to oversee Britain's first tentative production of the crop? To use a meteorological metaphor, the British Isles were in drought and needed a man like Mr Bienenstock to shower them with his knowledge and expertise. Her Majesty's Government would pay a generous salary for this work and take pleasure in defraying any such expenses in the matters of travel and resettlement as might arise. The English gentleman himself was in no doubt that should Mr Bienenstock be desirous of such status, he could during this time apply to become a full subject of King George and be assured of a favourable outcome.

The government of this same majesty would also be pleased, subject to Mr Bienenstock's agreement, over the next two years to buy, at a fair market price, all his fields and his refinery in Czechoslovakia and to send out a number of British agriculturists to experience with him two full cycles of the beet, in growth, harvest and refinement. The government of Czechoslovakia was most anxious to help in this matter, Britain's friendship with the vigorous young democracy being an established fact in a fickle world, a relationship to be relied upon in these trying times for Europe.

The Englishman and Czech translator would leave Mr Bienenstock now to digest this proposal. His decision could be given over the next few weeks. Really most excellent tea. The best the Englishman had tasted on the Continent. Good afternoon to you, Mr Bienenstock. Such charming children.

If Albert had got down on his knees and covered his head to beseech God to grant him all that he desired he could not have framed a prayer that so exactly delineated his requirements. Albert managed to maintain his dignity enough not to reply there and then, sending word to Prague three days later that he would be pleased to assent to the English gentleman's scheme and that he was looking forward to offering his hospitality to the agricultural experts London chose to send out to him.

The English farmers, Mr Northwood, Mr Aves and Mr Williams, arrived later that year. They impressed Albert as being both intelligent and respectful, proving themselves attentive and exceptionally apt pupils in the art of sugar.

Harry, Paul and Vic, as they insisted they be called, were kind to Michael and Rebecca, who responded by taking to English as though the language had been planted inside them at birth and had been only waiting for this one chance to flourish. Albert picked up the spirit and substance of the language very quickly too, but suffered great teasing from young Michael, who could not understand his father's inability to master its textures.

'No, Father. It's not "Wick Villiams" or a "vunderful willage". It's "Vic Williams" and a "wonderful village".'

'I can't say those letters.'

'That's mad!' Michael would hoot, outraged by such absurdity. 'If you can say "Villiams" and "willage", of course you can say Williams and village.'

'Old weterans stick to old vays,' Albert would say with deliberate cussedness.

During those two exciting years for the Bienenstock household, all the talk was in English and of England. The visitors spoke of pubs and clubs, of cricket and soccer, of Oxford and Cambridge, of Leslie Howard and Noël Coward, of crossword puzzles and fox-hunting, of Huntley and Palmer biscuits and Mazawattee tea, of the BBC and the GPO, of Guy Fawkes Night and Derby Day, of the Prime Minister of Mirth and the Prince of Wales. Albert unearthed in a bookshop a copy of *Der Forsyte Saga von John Galsworthy* and found himself growing ever impatient to become part of this kindly, ordered world with its town-squares and sea-side hotels, its cosy fogs and rattling taxis, its politicians in top-hats and duchesses in white gloves.

On the boat over from Bremerhaven (one last look at poor Germany and poor, poor Europe), while Rebecca was being sick over the rails, little Michael raised the subject of their names.

'Harry says . . .' every statement of Michael's for the last year had begun with those words, 'Harry says that English people might laugh at the name Bienenstock. Harry says it sounds like a kind of bean soup.'

'Oh dear,' said Albert. 'We don't want people to laugh at our names. We must think of something else.'

It was a year later, when they were already well settled i just outside the town of Huntingdon, that Michael himself came up with the splendid idea. His best friend at kindergarten was called Tommy Logan and Michael, writing Tommy's name many times all over his exercise book, as best friends do, noticed that 'Logan' was really 'Golan' rearranged.

Albert was delighted. 'Logan,' he kept repeating to himself, 'Logan . . . Logan . . . Logan.'

'You see, Father!' said Michael. 'We have made an *Anglo* version of *Golan*!'

Six months later the two children walked with their father from the Naturalisation Department of the Home Office towards the Lyon's Corner House in Trafalgar Square.

'Uncle Amos will be so pleased,' said Albert Logan, subject of the King.

Tommy Logan's reaction however, back at the Huntingdon kindergarten, had been one far removed from pleasure.

'You've stolen my name!' he howled. 'You horrid *Jew*, you've stolen my name. How dare you! I'll never talk to you again, you stinking *Jew*.'

'However did they know that you are Jewish?' Albert

had wondered when Michael related this falling-out to his father.

'Miss Hartley told them on my first day,' Michael said. 'She said that everyone was to be nice to me, because decent people have forgiven us for killing Christ.'

'Is that so?' said Albert and a small furrow appeared on his brow.

But furrows were not for Albert's forehead, they were for his fields. The government test beds in Huntingdonshire were the sensation of the day and for a short season the talk of England.

'BRITAIN TO BEET THE WORLD!' a page-five headline in the *Daily Express* had declared above a photograph of Albert and a government agriculturist standing proudly in front of their 'experimental' acres.

'This unprepossessing vegetable, no more in reality than a turnip with a sweet tooth, could be the key to Britain's future prosperity,' a leader writer declared.

The members of the British public were less sure.

'Will sugar from beet be purple?'

'Can it be turned into proper English cubes?'

'Is it more fattening?'

'Will it taste of soil?'

'Can beet be baked in a pie?'

'Can I grow it in the garden and make my own sugar?'

'Is it fair on the colonies?'

'You can bet they won't be serving it in the Tate Gallery tea-rooms.'

Over the next four or five years, the smiling Hungarian in tweed plus-fours toured the south coast and East Anglia in his holly-green Austin, bestowing government grants and agricultural advice on puzzled but welcoming farmers. Michael and Rebecca continued with their studies at Miss Hartley's kindergarten in Huntingdon, a town to which Albert was by now greatly attached, despite initial misgivings.

'Oliver Cromwell?' he had cried, when first he had heard. 'Oliver Cromwell came from here? The king-killer?'

He simply could not believe that the otherwise loyal and respectable townspeople of Huntingdon could be so sincerely proud of their wicked son, that disgrace to English history, the British Lenin. In time however, he learned to forgive the Lord Protector who was, after all, a gentleman farmer like himself and had been pushed by dread circumstance, not by Bolshevism or bloodlust, into the events that led to that awful January morning in Whitehall. The people of Huntingdon, in their turn, learned to love the strange Czechoslovakian with the charming manners, perfect English children and inexplicably Scottish surname. They were less sure about the refinery whose construction he had supervised and which he now ran. It gave off a sickly smell of burnt peanut-butter which would hang over the whole town on windless days. The creation of a second refinery in Bury St Edmunds gave young Michael his first lesson in management technique, however, and can be thanked for that.

One rainy afternoon, when Rebecca and Michael were playing on the floor of their father's study, an engineer came to call on Albert. He left a 600-page report, full of technical drawings and scientific data, which he was anxious for Mr Logan to approve.

Michael watched that evening as Albert sat with the report on his lap.

'Have you got to read all that?'

'Read it? What do I know from pressure-gauges and amps? This is what I do.'

Albert riffled his thumb through the pages of the report and opened a page at random. With a red-inked pen he underlined a few words and flipped through to another page where he circled some numbers, writing a large question mark in the margin. He did this four or five times before scrawling at the bottom of the last page the words, 'Can the sub-station take the extra load?'

Michael happened to be outside the study a week later when the engineer called again.

'I've checked and checked and checked the figures you queried, Mr Logan, and so have my colleagues, but we're blowed if we can find any error.'

'Ah. I'm so sorry, my dear fellow. I must have made a mistake. I should not have been doubting you.'

'Well, we do like to be thorough, sir. We were pretty sure about the sub-station too. Then, you'll never guess, but the contractors telephoned to say they had made a miscalculation with their tolerances. They should have been greater by ten per cent.'

After Albert had shown the grateful and admiring engineer from the house, he addressed Michael, whom he had seen lurking in the corridor.

'You see? Now they have checked so many times that everything is sure to be fine.'

'But the sub-station? How did you know?'

'Sometimes you make a lucky guess. Believe me, you can always rely that sub-stations cannot take the load and you can always rely that another man's pride will do much of your work for you.'

II

One day, it was during the holidays, the very week before Michael was due to start his first term at boarding school in Sussex, Albert summoned the children to his study. He was looking very serious and spoke in Hungarian, a sure sign of distress.

'I have just had a letter from your Uncle Amos,' he said. 'It means that I shall have to go away for a little while. This is a good time for me to take a holiday. You, Michael, will have to go early to your new school. I have telephoned the headmaster and he will be happy to look after you. You will stay at home, Rebecca, and be looked after by Mrs Price.'

'What is it, Father?' asked Michael. 'What has happened?'

'Our cousins living in Vienna, your Uncle Rudi, your Uncle Louis and your Aunts Hannah and Roselle and all the children, they would like to leave Austria and come to England. I can help because I have my British passport. But I must go there myself. A tiresome necessity, but a necessity all the same.'

The next day Albert had gone to London to see his old friend in the Foreign Office, the English gentleman who had visited him in 1933. Albert forbore from making any reference to Britain's 'firm friendship with your vigorous young democracy', the 'established fact in a fickle world' of which the gentleman had spoken on that afternoon in Czechoslovakia. It was not for Albert to question Mr Chamberlain's tea-party with Hitler.

The gentleman from the Foreign Office listened to

Albert's story and confessed the matter to be a little out of his sphere. He recommended a man he knew in another department and was kind enough to write Albert a letter of introduction.

The man from the other department, perhaps because his name was Murray, had not taken to this Logan with a middle-European epiglottis.

'Really, sir, I am not sure what you mean by "taking a stance". We have a large number of British Jews like yourself coming here every week, all making representations of this nature. I say to all of them what I am going to say to you. There are wheels within wheels. You must understand the precarious state of diplomacy currently obtaining on the continent of Europe. After recent hard-won successes in Munich, His Majesty's Government is hardly in a position to make demands on Germany as that long-suffering country struggles to express a coherent sense of her national identity and establish a proper place at the world's table. It is precisely the sort of hysterical rumour-mongering that you and your fellow . . . that you and your fellows are engaged in that can upset the delicate balance of negotiations and threaten peaceful relations.'

'But my peaceful relations are already being threatened,' said Albert with the unselfconscious wordplay that only a non-native speaker of English can achieve.

'Really! If you insist on founding your understanding of a power such as the new Germany on the hearsay of a brother in Jerusalem . . .'

Albert knew enough to hold his tongue in the presence of a triumphalist Munichois.

'You are of course free to travel where you will, Mr "Logan", but I must warn you that if you transgress any law of the German Reich you cannot expect protection or immunity from us. I would recommend that you wait a little while. If your family is sincere about coming to England they must satisfy firstly the requirements for emigration laid down by their home government.'

'But they have no home government, sir!' Albert cried, sounding, he was painfully aware, exactly like the kind of whining Jew that he and much of the world most despised.

He never told Michael or Rebecca how completely his faith had been shattered by the indifference and disapproval that he met at the hands of His Majesty's Government that day and on the four days following, as he wore out the waiting-room chairs of Whitehall and the patience of the few functionaries who consented to see him. Had he lived to see the Battle of Britain and the Blitz, Michael persisted in believing, Albert's belief in the British might have been at the very least partially restored. Michael was to find out later from Uncle Louis the full extent of his father's disillusion and despair during that painful week, as he was to find out the details of all that followed.

Arriving in Vienna, Mr Albert Logan, famed grower and refiner of beet, summoned his cousins by messenger to the hotel he had chosen to favour with his custom. Here he met his first reversal, here the sharp point of the Truth began to press against his new-grown English hide.

The messenger returned half an hour later with a letter. Albert took some notes from his pocket with which to pay the youth and was astonished to see the money being snatched roughly from him without a word of thanks.

'Steady there, young fellow,' said Albert in his most patrician officer's Viennese.

The messenger spat on the carpet, a fleck of yellow

spittle landing on Albert's shining brown brogues. 'Jew-lover,' he said with contempt and stalked from the room.

Albert shook his head with disbelief and opened the letter. Now the sharp point of the Truth pierced the skin and started to push through. His cousins could not attend such a meeting, they explained with profuse apology. In order to comply with the laws of Austria under the recent Anschluss, they were obliged to wear yellow stars on their coats. Persons with yellow stars on their coats, they assured Albert, were not allowed inside hotels like the Franz Josef.

Mohammed took a cab to the mountain. Cousins Louis and Rudi and their families were all crowded together in one small room in a part of the town that Albert, who knew Vienna well from his old days in the Hussars, had never thought to visit. He was shocked to see them, shocked beyond bearing, more shocked than he had ever been before. The white worms in the eye-sockets of his comrades and the frying livers of the young Cossacks had not shocked him more: in this small room the sharp point of the Truth finally forced itself deep inside him until it tore at the walls of his heart. Albert leant on his Swaine, Adeney and Brigg's umbrella and cried like a baby for a full quarter of an hour while his cousins clustered about him in concern.

Albert had known and then forsworn loyalty to the Emperor Franz Josef, whose cavalry he had loved; he had known and now forswore loyalty to two King Georges and a King Edward, whose country and people and history he had revered. In that awful little room with its imponderably hateful smell, a smell that took all the dignity and colour and strength away from his family and all the dignity and colour and strength away from him, his tweeds, his expensive luggage and his small blue passport, in that dreadful stinking room he swore a new loyalty, to his people – his stupid, moaning, helpless and cosmically irritating people, whose religion he scorned, whose culture he despised, whose mannerisms and prejudices he abominated.

With lies, with cunning, with the use of old army contacts and above all, of course, with the use of money, Albert procured the papers necessary to allow his cousins to leave Vienna. Besides Louis, Rudi, Hannah and Roselle, there were four children, Danny, Ruth, Dita and Miriam. He took them by train to Holland and thence by boat to Harwich in England. He stayed in Huntingdon long enough to introduce them to Rebecca and her nanny Mrs Price, and then he drove down to Sussex to call on Michael's headmaster, Dr Valentine.

'Here is money enough to pay for his schooling for the rest of time,' he said. 'You shall see it please that he acquires an excellent scholarship to his public school.'

'Well, I think that rather depends, Mr Logan, on how intelligent the boy is and with what diligence he applies himself to his work. Scholarships are hardly something you can . . .'

'Michael is most intelligent and most hard-working. I will see him now please.'

A boy was dispatched to fetch young Logan.

While they awaited him, Albert addressed the headmaster once more. 'Another thing to say, Dr Walentine. It is possible that you may imagine my son and myself are Jewish people.'

'Really, Mr Logan, I had given it no . . .'

'It is to understand that we are *not* Jewish people.

Michael is not a Jewish boy. He is a Church of England boy. I am going away into Europe now, but I have friends here in England. If it arrives in my ears that any one single person of the school suggests or makes it said that Michael is a Jewish boy it is possible that I shall come back to take him away and that I strike you with my fists, Dr Walentine, with strength enough to kill you.'

'Mr Logan!'

'Here he comes now. We shall go to a walk, he and me . . . him and I.'

The flabbergasted Dr Valentine was left to ponder this alarming threat while Michael showed his father the lake, the pony paddocks, the cricket field and the woods where he and his friends played cowboys and Indians.

Albert spoke in a mixture of Yiddish and Hungarian. Michael replied in English.

'You are seven years old now, Michael. Plenty old enough to know the facts of the world.'

'It's all right, Father. I've already been told.'

'You've been told?'

'The man wees inside the woman and she has a baby. Wallace told me. He's the senior boy in my dorm.'

'What a child. I'm not talking about *those* facts, which you can tell your friend Vollis, have nothing to do with urination. I am talking about the real facts.'

'The real facts?'

'Tell me, Michael Logan. What is your country of birth?'

'Hungary,' said Michael, puffing up his chest.

'NO!' Albert turned and gave his son a violent shake. 'Not correct. Tell me again. What is your country of birth?'

Michael stared at his father in amazement.

'Czechoslovakia?' he suggested, frightened.

'NO!'

'No?'

'No! You come from England. You are English.'

'Yes, of course, but I was born . . .'

'You were born in Huntingdon. You grew up in Huntingdon. What is your religion?'

Michael had never seen his father like this before. So strong and so angry. 'Church of England?'

'YES!' Albert kissed him. 'Good boy. You have the idea. You must never, ever, upon pain of your life and my eternal curses, tell a living soul that you are Jewish. Do you understand?'

'But why not?'

'Why not? Because the Germans are coming, that is why not. They will tell they are not coming, but believe me they are coming all the same. The Nazi Germans are coming and they will take anyone away who is Jewish. So you are not Jewish and your sister is not Jewish. You know no Jews, you see no Jews, you have conversation with no Jews. You are Michael Logan of Wyton Chase, Huntingdon. Your uncles and aunts from abroad live'with you. They are Lutheran Christians.'

'And you live with me too, of course.'

'Of course,' said Albert. 'I live with you too. Of course.'

Six months later Michael had received a letter with an exotic postmark.

'Jerusalem!' one of his friends shouted. 'Logan's got a letter from Jew-rusalem.'

'My uncle's with the army in Palestine,' Michael said nonchalantly. 'The Mandate, it's called.'

'Logan's a Jew!'

'Bloody am not!'

'Miserly jewy Jew!'

'What's going on here?'

Michael turned in fear as Edward Wallace shouldered his way to the front of the press. Wallace was a senior boy and known to be capable of merciless mental bullying.

'Loganstein's got a letter from Jew-land.'

'He's a Jew. You can tell. Look at his nose.'

'He's a Roundhead, that's for sure.'

Roundheads, in school slang, meant those who were circumcised, as distinct from Cavaliers, who were not.

Wallace looked down on Michael, his eyes darting wickedly back and forth across the boy's face as if coming to a decision. Michael braced himself. His mouth was dry and he felt faint with apprehension.

Wallace spoke at last. 'Don't be stupid,' he said. 'Logan's not a miserly Jew, he's a miserly Scot like me. And I happen to know, Hutchinson, that you are a Roundhead too and what's more your nose is bigger than anyone in the civilised world's. It's so big in fact, that there's talk in the papers of East End children being evacuated into your left nostril until the end of the war.'

A tidal wave of mocking laughter swept over Hutchinson at this and Michael had to clamp his muscles tight to avoid wetting himself with relief. Wallace turned to him with a sly smile.

'Bags I have those stamps, McLogie, I collect 'em.'

Michael tore the corner from the envelope and handed them over with a beam of gratitude. Wallace clipped him round the ear and told him not to grin at him like a monkey or he'd kick him in the slats.

'Sorry, Wallace.'

Michael had then run to the school rears to read the letter in private. It was from his Uncle Amos. To this day he regrets never having read it more closely. The quickest glance was all he would allow himself before tearing it into tiny shreds and flushing it down the lavatory.

All he would ever be able to recall of the letter were a few phrases. Uncle Amos wrote that Michael's father had been shot by the Nazis two days after Chamberlain had declared war on Germany. Something about Berlin. Something about living in the ghettos and spreading warmth. Albert Golan was a hero of the Jews and a great man. Moisha Golan, his son, should be very proud and should always remember.

The next day Uncles Richard and Herbert, as Louis and Rudi now called themselves, came to pick Michael up from school.

III

All the money had gone, naturally. All the money from the sale of the farm in Czechoslovakia, all the money earned from his work over the last few years for the Ministry, all the money raised against his interests in the two refineries. Michael's next three years at Dr Valentine's prep school were assured. After that . . .

'I shall certainly get a scholarship,' said Michael. 'And I shall get a job in the holidays and pay for Rebecca's schooling too.'

'You aren't yet ten years old, Michael,' said Aunt Roselle, now Aunt Rose. 'We will pay for your school. We all have work, we will look after you both. We will be proud to have you as a son and daughter.'

Michael had found jobs however. Every day of his school holidays was engaged in earning money. Firstly he had worked for a bakery in Huntingdon as delivery boy and then, after his scholarship took him to public school, he called the family together and made a suggestion.

'Mrs Anderson is getting very old,' he said. 'She wants to sell her shop. Why don't we buy it?'

'How could we afford to do such a thing?'

'We can sell this house and be able to live over the shop. I've made enquiries. There is room enough for all of us. It's a tight squeeze – Rebecca, Ruth, Dita and Miriam will have to share a room, Danny and I will sleep behind the counter – but we can manage.'

Logan's Sweets and Smokes was known in the family as Michael's Shop. Michael did the books, having the most mathematical turn of mind in the family. He understood coupons and the rationing system, he understood how to barter and he understood how to keep customers loyal.

One evening Aunt Rose knocked on his bedroom door.

'Michael, it's Happidrome on the wireless. What are you doing there? Come downstairs.'

She opened the door and saw Michael holding a large book.

'This is my customer book,' he explained. 'Every time a customer comes into the shop I talk to them and find out what they like. I list their favourite tobacco, or cigarette, or brand of sweets, and each night I make sure I have learnt it. Take the book. Ask me.'

A bewildered Rose had opened a page and offered the name 'Mr G. Blake'.

'Godfrey Blake,' said Michael, 'lives in the Godmanchester Road and smokes forty Player's Weights a day. He buys one packet of Craven A a week for his wife, who only smokes at weekends. He has a son in the army in North Africa and a daughter in the WAAF. He's an assistant ARP warden, injured his hip at Passchendaele and is secretly in love with Janet Gaynor. He has a weakness for humbugs and I always give him one or two if he's out of coupons. He gives me half a crown for cleaning his car on Sundays.'

'Woosh!' said Aunt Rose. 'Mr Tony Adams?'

'*Wing-Commander* Anthony Adams,' said Michael, 'flies a desk at RAF Wyton. He has a sweetheart named Wendy, a land-army girl working near Wisbech, and he rides there to see her twice a week on his motor-cycle. He smokes Parson's Pleasure ready-rubbed, which they don't sell in the Officers' Mess, and he likes aniseed balls for himself and Fry's Five Boys chocolate for Wendy.'

'Michael. Why have you learnt all this?'

'Because these people smoke and eat sweets. The first time Mr Blake came into the shop he was just passing. Now he walks the extra half-mile to us twice a week. When the business grows after the war, people like that will be important.'

'When the business . . . ? Listen to him. Michael, it's just a shop.'

'It's a seed, Aunt Rose. Now, I have to go back to school next week. You and Aunt Hannah will be looking after things weekdays. I will leave this book for you. See if you can try to learn everything in it too. Everyone should know it off by heart – Danny, Dita, Miriam, everyone – so when they help out at weekends and after school they can make the customers feel important.'

In the family's eyes, Michael's destiny was as inevitable as if he had been born Prince of Wales. He was a force and that was that.

During subsequent school holidays, as the war came to a close, so the proper expansion of the business, the full germination and growth of the seed, began. A paper round was added, early-morning work for Danny and his sister and cousins; bread, potatoes, flowers and an increasing range of tinned foods began to crowd the shelves of the small retail area until Michael and Richard decided that it would be worth their while to buy the house next door, knock through the party-wall and create a small version of a Home and Colonial Store.

In 1947 Michael won a scholarship to Cambridge which he turned down.

'We can really concentrate on things now,' he said.

A call-up the following year to National Service could not be turned down however. His old protector from prep

605

school, Edward Wallace, who had deferred service until after Oxford where he was now finishing, persuaded him to join him in applying to the Royal Norfolk regiment.

'Not a very smart outfit, which is perfect as we'll be cocks of the roost. Plenty of time for race-meetings and women.'

One afternoon, during his officer training in Wiltshire, Michael read a short story by Somerset Maugham which gave him the idea he had been looking for. It concerned a young man who found himself in need of a packet of cigarettes in a Midlands town one afternoon. He walked along the streets searching for a tobacconist: the better part of a mile he walked before he found one. Instead of going on his way and thinking no more about it, as an ordinary person might, this young man retraced his steps to the place where he had first stood. 'I shall open a tobacconist's here,' he said to himself, 'there is clearly a need.' His shop was a magnificent success. 'How childishly simple,' thought the young man. For the next twenty years he travelled Britain walking the streets looking for cigarettes. Whenever he had to walk far, there he would open another shop. He was a millionaire by the age of thirty-five.

'Well, Tedward,' said Michael to his friend Wallace, 'God bless Mr Maugham.'

'Don't you think,' said Wallace, 'that others might have tried it first?'

'What you have to understand, Tedward, is that "others" don't try anything. They leave it to people like us.'

'You can count me out, darling one,' said Wallace. 'Sounds like work.'

A year and a half later Michael met Lady Anne Bressingham, which gave him something to work towards. She was eleven when they met and Michael not quite twenty, but he knew as surely as any man ever knew a thing that she would grow into the woman for him.

Wallace accused him of being a pervert.

'No, no, Tedward, you don't understand. It is in the smile. She has the right smile. At the moment she is a bony girl, but I know what she will become. It is never the eyes alone, or the beauty, or the figure, it is always the smile. When she smiled I knew at once. It is that clear.'

By 1955, Wallace had cause to remark that Logan newsagent-tobacconists were as familiar a sight in every English high street as dog-turds and Belisha beacons.

'Clothes rationing will end soon,' said Michael. 'People will want good, well-made clothes, brightly coloured and cheap. These new teenagers will want jeans from America. It is time we looked into the matter.'

At a party in 1959 to celebrate the publication of Edward Lennox Wallace's *Odes of Fury*, Logan took the rising poet aside.

'I'm going into publishing, Tedward. We've bought APC Magazines Ltd. What do you think of that?'

'Women's magazines and children's comics.'

'Chiefly. But we have other titles too. *New Insights*, for instance.'

'*New Insights* is older than God and just as dead.'

'So tell me, who should I employ to nurse it back to life? They say Mark Onions is a coming talent.'

'Stanley Matthews knows more about poetry and literature than Mark Onions. Mark Onions couldn't nurse a sick vole.'

'Perhaps I should ask my best man.'

'Your *what*?'

'Anne and I are to be married. I was hoping your waist-coat would be the one to hold the ring.'

Over the next sixteen years Logan's collection of companies was transformed into a kingdom and then into what the world could only call an empire. The genius, everyone agreed, lay in the grasp of detail, in the flexibility of strategy and in the remorseless gathering of comprehensive and grindingly technical intelligence. In the Fifties Michael had picked up a telephone to sell his highly profitable valve-manufacturing plant the moment he had heard from a friend in America about the development in the labs of an object called the transistor.

'But it will be a long time before they come on to the market,' the friend had warned. 'Vacuum tubes have years in them yet.'

'So I'll get a good price for the factory now. Do you think I will get such a good price next year when everybody knows about this transistor of yours?'

Logan bought into vinyls and man-made fibres in the early Sixties and sold out five years later, just before wool and cotton and leather came triumphantly back into fashion. The teenage daughter of a management employee had told him that nylon was definitely out, square and dud.

The high-street outlets were redesigned, at massive cost, to include aisles and trolleys so that the customers could help themselves to their goods and pay at a cash desk. An unpleasant proceeding, but one which Logan was convinced showed the way forward. The name of these new supermarkets was changed from Logan's to Lomark Stores. All companies, in fact, that Michael acquired

traded either under their original names or under new
titles which had nothing to do with their owner. The word
'Logan' was used only by the parent corporation in the
stock-market listings. 'Nobody likes a smart-arse,' Michael
said. 'If my customers thought that the man who sold
them marshmallows and cigarettes was the same man who
published their magazines and manufactured their televisions, they would start to desert me. They have their
pride after all.'

The financial world knew, naturally, and smiled on what
was then a rare treat for the markets, a diverse group of
businesses controlled by one holding company; a company
that was not afraid to borrow and to expand; to divest here
and reinvest there. Every skin Logan shrugged off left
pickings on the Stock Exchange floor, every corporate
marriage or rape was blessed with profitable issue.

Michael's family of second and third cousins proved a
sore trial to him, however. Only the ageing Richard showed
any aptitude for business: he died in 1962, followed soon
by his brother Herbert. Their children were uninterested
in the empire. Michael wanted very much to help them,
as his father had helped them, but they preferred to help
themselves, moving to London, marrying into established
Jewish families and making a quieter way in the world.

'You're not our father,' Danny had said to Michael,
refusing an offer of money. 'You mean well, but you will
keep trying to swallow everything and everyone up.'

Michael was hurt by this. He had a great gift, to make
work for thousands, to make money for thousands. It was
his duty, surely, to use this gift. Certainly to use it with
kindness and consideration. No one treated their workers
better. No magnate of comparable power and standing

could claim to know the first names and family histories of so many of his employees. No magnate of comparable power welcomed so enthusiastically the arrival of a Labour government. He paid his supertaxes like a man, never grumbling in public, however horrified he might have been in private. After the disasters of devaluation and the rising inflation of the 1970s he could never feel again any great respect for party politicians or interest in their short-term squabbles. He reserved his political energy for global matters, preferring crafty Third World statesmen with their fly-whisks and djellabas to the dull-witted borough councillors of Westminster. His style of beneficent paternalism was regarded with contempt by the domestic political parties but his even-handedly distributed money was welcomed by all.

Michael's sister, Rebecca, he never expected to be involved in business. He had high hopes that she might be a perfect second wife for his friend Wallace, whose poetry Michael could not begin to understand or enjoy, but whose successful editorship of *New Insights* had given him real pleasure. She married instead a man called Patrick Burrell, a perfectly ghastly fellow in Michael's estimation who incessantly and gracelessly bothered him for money but at least provided the closest thing Michael ever had to a daughter, his niece Jane.

'Since you always claim that you need money for her sake,' Michael said to Burrell at last, 'I will settle money on her once and for all. A million pounds is hers and hers alone. I will start an account tomorrow. She can have the cheque-book herself when she is twenty-one. If any school fees need to be paid or clothes to be bought for her meanwhile, you will let me know, Patrick, won't you?'

Burrell had taken this badly and some years later sent a telegram to Rebecca from New York informing her that he had found someone else. Michael had been unhappy for his sister, but relieved to be rid of the connection.

A connection he was sorry to sever had come a little more than a year after Rebecca's marriage. It had been drawn to Michael's attention that Edward Wallace had been stealing money from the magazine; not a great deal, it was true, but it was not the scale of the embezzlement that had been at issue so far as Michael was concerned. It took him some time to forgive his old friend. He watched in great despair as the poet declined in creativity and charm while increasing in girth and drunken misanthropy.

In 1966, Michael knelt before the Queen and arose a knight. In 1975, he stood to make his maiden speech in the House of Lords as Baron Logan of Swafford. A year later, at the age of forty-six, he came to the decision that he had earned the right to divert his magisterial powers of concentration into the matter of starting a family. He began with a son, Simon. Two years later Anne obliged him with another boy, David. It was after this birth that she persuaded Michael to pardon and absolve Wallace his peculations.

'I can see that you miss him, darling. Let's ask him to be David's godfather.'

Nine years following this, when a woman might reasonably forgive or even thank her uterus for slipping quietly into desuetude, Anne found herself pregnant again, this time with two boys at once.

IV

In 1991, with the twins approaching their fifth birthday, Edward, the younger by fifteen minutes, showed signs of developing serious problems with his asthma. This inspired Lady Anne to order a regular nightly patrol to monitor his breathing.

One hot night, with the air thick with pollen and spore, the twins' nanny, Sheila, was heard to shriek in horror. She ran down the nursery passage howling for Lady Anne.

Edward, she wailed, was blue and lifeless in his bed. Dead, not breathing at all. Quite dead. Most awfully dead. Anne and Michael ran for the stairs, their hearts jumping with panic and terror.

Meanwhile the two older boys had been awoken by the same screams and commotion. They hurried straight to the twins' bedroom in equal alarm. Simon took one look at Edward's immobile form and started to pump the lifeless child's arms and legs back and forth, perhaps in some dimly remembered re-enactment of first-aid instructors at school or more probably in imitation of the procedure of vets when dealing with suffocating piglets.

'No!' David had shouted. 'Let me!'

He pushed aside his older brother, who was now pummelling the ribs with some violence. Anne and Michael arrived in time to see Simon being elbowed roughly away.

Then they saw, they all saw, David kneel at the bedside and lay a hand gently on Edward's chest. Immediately, absolutely at once, they are all agreed on this, the child twitched and started to choke and whoop. Michael and Anne were too excited at first, too concerned with calling

the doctor and seeing Edward to hospital, to ponder much
on what they had witnessed. Michael remembered,
though, that when he had taken his older sons aside and
told them that they must go to bed, David's hand in his
felt scorchingly hot, where Simon's was cold.

Some weeks later Michael took David aside.

'Davey, we must talk about your talent.'

'My talent, Daddy?'

'You know what I mean when I use that word. Your
healing. I should have spoken before.'

Michael related to David those episodes from the life of
Albert Bienenstock that he had previously kept from him:
the healing and then the death of Benko, the persecution
that followed and the suspicion and ostracism of the com-
munity and its rabbis.

'Your gift, you see, is not something that the world will
welcome.'

'But why does Mummy look at me sometimes as if I'm
ill or as if I've done something wrong?'

'She's confused, Davey. You must try to understand.'

David nodded. Michael went next to speak to his wife.

'Tell me truly, what are your feelings about Davey's gift?'
he asked.

'Gift?' Anne looked at him in surprise.

'The gift he used to bring Edward back to life.'

Anne turned away, but Michael took her by the
shoulders and brought her round to face him.

'You know what we saw, Anne.'

'I know . . .' she said.

'It confuses you and worries you.'

Anne nodded.

'We must make sure,' Michael said, 'that Davey's life

will not be disrupted. We cannot allow the thing to be known.'

Anne considered this in silence.

'You're thinking of your father, aren't you?' she said.

'I'm thinking of Davey. Just of Davey. He is not to be treated as a freak.'

'But darling, you can't really . . .'

'We'll say no more.'

'I agree,' said Anne. 'We should say no more.'

More had to be said, however, the following year. Michael's niece Jane arrived in the midsummer of 1991 for her last stay at Swafford. She had spent many months fighting the exhausting cruelty of her disease and was not expected to survive for many weeks longer. All she wanted now, she said, was the peace of the countryside and the love of her uncle and cousins; these she would take away as a memory to comfort her last few sterile days in hospital.

Her collapse at the Royal Norfolk Show was held to be the onset of a terminal and irreversible decline. Simon had been forced to drive her back to Swafford himself despite being too young for a licence and surer of tractors than of Jane's twitchy BMW. He had carried her white and feeble form easily up the stairs, 'light as a plucked partridge, really,' and laid her on the bed of the Landseer Room. The room, the doctors agreed, in which she would shortly die.

During the first week of her confinement David and Simon were able to visit her. Simon would look in each morning with fruit, flowers and stories of life on the estate, and in the afternoons David would come with a book and sit by the bed, reading and chatting until dinnertime, never minding if Jane drifted in and out of sleep while he talked.

On the boys' last morning at Swafford they went in

together to the sick room, solemn and elegant in their school uniforms, to bid her farewell.

'You look like dreadful pale undertakers,' she said. 'You shouldn't. I feel so much better today.'

The boys departed feeling greatly hopeful. A week later Jane was out of bed, professing herself not just better but truly cured. Cured not only in body, but cured all through. She felt more well now than she ever did before the leukaemia had come. She claimed that her previous life had been that of a caterpillar and that now she was reborn as a free and perfect butterfly.

Anne asked her, very seriously and in private, if she believed that there was any tangible cause or agency involved in this cure. Jane prevaricated, hiding behind a wide and tangled linguistic bush. Her words were of angels and grace and purity and becoming. Anne went away puzzled and alarmed.

Michael's visit was more straightforward.

'My love, we are so happy. So happy that you are better. However this may have happened, it is best, do you not think, to celebrate it in peace as a quiet and wonderful thing that took place in the privacy of what I hope you will always think of as your family home?'

'Whatever you say, Uncle Michael.'

Logan's friend Max Clifford was staying at this time and Michael wanted to speak to him on the subject too.

'It's just this, Max. You know what devils journalists can be.'

'We've sacked plenty in our time between us, eh?'

'Jane is going to London for tests. It may be that she is right and, as does sometimes happen with leukaemia, she has truly managed to overcome the illness. We don't want, we *really* don't want any publicity attached to this. Newspapers are so hysterical when it comes to anything connected to cancer and there are always religious or mystical freaks who have something to sell. Jane herself is not quite in her right mind about things yet . . .'

'There have been rumours, Michael. Mary tells me she heard her praying in the woods yesterday.'

'Max,' said Michael, 'this is precisely what I mean. While she is so disturbed it is essential that everything is played down.'

'Mm,' said Max. 'She was kneeling there on the ground. A lot of Druidical guff apparently and a great deal about David.'

'If you are my friend, Max,' Michael was very sharp now, 'you will say no more on this subject. Not to me, not to anyone.'

The following year however, it was made clear that, despite Logan's injunctions, word *had* spread. Firstly, Ted Wallace arrived with a quaint story about wanting to write Michael's official biography, a claim that Michael frankly found absurd and a typical, Tedwardly piece of transparent deviousness. Anne had the idea in her head that Wallace might prove a 'steadying influence' on David, but it was clear to Michael that he was there, as usual, to upset apple carts and set pumas among pigeons. The Logans found it difficult to talk to each other about David. Michael wondered if his wife might be in some submerged way envious of the genes David had inherited from Albert Bienenstock. Perhaps she found Ted's worldly cynicism a welcome relief. Perhaps she even welcomed the idea of Ted corrupting David with alcohol or initiating him into Norwich's few sad specimens of harlotry, anything to upset the delicate balance of the qualities in her son that she found so disquieting. Michael considered all these possibilities carefully. To appease her and because it was better to have a man like Ted inside his tent pissing out, than outside pissing in, Michael concealed his misgivings and made a show of being pleased to see the old drunkard at Swafford. He never went so far as to *trust* him; that would be insanity. Instead, he required Podmore to maintain a discreet watch and found out from this that Ted appeared to be in constant postal communication with Jane. Podmore had been quite happy to take it upon himself to do some dusting around the computer currently installed in the Landseer Room and as a result of this zealous housework Michael had discovered, much to his surprise, that the contents of Ted's letters revealed an apparent ignorance of what had been going on as far as Davey was concerned.

Meanwhile, Oliver Mills had invited himself for a few weeks, then Max and Mary Clifford had asked if they might come with their daughter Clara, a girl they never usually took anywhere if they could help it, embarrassed as they were by her unfortunate appearance. Jane's close friend Patricia Hardy was the next to arrive. When Rebecca rang her brother to see if she might too 'pop down for a week or so', Michael began to grow seriously worried. He felt the thing was growing too fast. He knew, in business terms, how hard it was to keep things secret. You cannot cap a volcano. True, the house-party now convened at Swafford constituted none but close, if not trusted, friends, but for how long could such a state of affairs be maintained?

Encouraged by his discovery of Ted's ignorance and

innocence in the matter therefore and suddenly acutely aware that a best friend is a best friend, however many times he might lie to you and steal from you, Michael decided to accede to the original request and tell his life story to that old fraud Edward Lennox Wallace. It was, perhaps, the best and clearest way to get Ted up to speed and on-side.

On the second day of their talk, which Michael found he was enjoying immensely, Ted revealing himself to be a surprisingly appreciative listener, the news about Lilac broke and the urgency and importance of their collaboration impressed itself all the more clearly on Michael's mind. There was no *evidence* that David was behind the recovery in Lilac that had the vet scratching his head in astonishment, but there could be absolutely no doubt whatsoever, so far as Michael was concerned, as to the provenance of this miracle, nor, it would seem, was anyone else in the house uncertain. The business of Lilac, coming when it did, destroyed whatever illusion Michael may have had that he was controlling the situation. He broke with all restraint and told Ted everything, not even omitting his differences with Lady Anne in the matter or the details of his sordid involvement in the reading of Ted's letter to Jane. Since the day he had read Uncle Amos's letter from Jerusalem telling him of his father's death, Michael had never placed himself at another's mercy. He did so now.

'There you have it, Tedward. The unvarnished truth. So what do I do? Is Davey's gift meant for the world? Do I roar it from the battlements? Or is it a curse that should be hidden away in shame? Do we call for a priest? A doctor? A shrink? You are the boy's godfather. Advise.'

'Hum,' said Wallace. 'Hah.'

618

'Well?'

'I shall need some time. I have ideas. For the moment I'd recommend you sit tight and do nothing.'

'Do nothing.'

'Often the wisest course. In my case, I must think.'

'Think? Think? What's to think?'

'Well, to be truthful, Michael, a man doesn't like to learn at the age of sixty-six that everything he's always believed in makes no sense.'

'And what have you ever believed in, Edward Wallace?'

'Oh, you know, little things. Little things, like how hard it is to write a poem.'

Seven

Dear Ted,

I think you must be there now. Patricia tells me that you and Uncle Michael have been 'closeted together' for some time.

It's time for me to come down. You can give me the fruits of your conversations with Uncle Michael when I arrive tomorrow, after my final tests. Can you understand now why I have been so excited? I'm so pleased that you have been sharing in this with me.

You can talk to Patricia and Mummy now and let them know what you've been up to. But not a word to anyone outside Swafford, of course.

Look after Davey though. Make sure he keeps up his strength and isn't made to feel isolated or used.

When Davey first told me how he had healed Edward I knew that my decision to come to Swafford had been meant. Was 'miracle' really too strong a word? I don't think so. Surely you can't now either. Tell me this isn't going to change your life, Ted, and I'll call you a liar.

Much, much love

Jane

PS: My most urgent and final 'proclamation' as you like to call them is this: Smile! We are loved. We are loved. Everything is going to be wonderful. Everything shines. Everything is as it could only be and must be.

II

From the diary of Oliver Mills:
29th July 1992, Swafford Hall

Everything has come to a head, dearest Daisy Diary. I write this in tumbling confusion. It's eleven at night and in three hours' time I shall . . . well I don't know what I shall, but it will be the terror of the earth and that's a fact.

I mentioned yesterday that the Hearty Hetties of the household were getting all dismal about some horse, a hunter owned and ridden, as they say on race cards, by Michael himself. The name of the beast, Lilac, besides being camper than a jamboree of Danish scouts in Spandex briefs, betrays the Jenny Gender. Lilac is a big brown mare and the Cox's Orange Pippin of Logan's eye. Yesterday, as I made most meticulous mention, she began to display symptoms of something madly amiss. Vera Vet pronounced that it had all the hallmarks of Ragwort Poisoning. The common ragwort, dread thing, possesses some alkaloid which degenerates the liver: no Auntie Dote is known to man. Horses don't usually eat Rachel Ragwort as she's bitterer than a forgotten poet, but Lilac was grazing in the park at the front of the house last week and might have nibbled away without noticing. Yesterday she was seen to be bleeding from the mouth like Chopin, circling round and round and leaning her head against the wall looking dismal: this means a Dysfunction of the Liver, sure as eggs are oval. Terminal. Incurable. Why horses possess livers I can't for a moment imagine. I've yet to see one with a voddie and tonic. However, I mustn't rattle on, there's lots to write and do before beddies: oh my, is there ever lots to write and do. Dysfunctions of the liver, according to Vera Vet – real name Nigel Ogden, and rather a choice arrangement, as it happens, amber corduroys sheathing the second most provoking bottie in Norfolk – are a guaranteed one-way ticket to Horsy Heaven. Nige would leave Simon and Michael with a day to think what they wanted to do with Lilac and return on the morrow (i.e. today) with a humane killer, should disposal – which Vera Vet frankly recommended, so excitingly harsh, so maddeningly cruel, so thrillingly unsentimental these country people – be the preferred Oprah Option.

Dinner last night, Daisy, was thuswise rather a forlorn affair. Simon, naturally, was all for a bash on the head and a quick sale to the glue factory. Probably would have bought a jar of reconstituted Lilac and used it to mend his wellies too, heartless beast.

I was thinking 'Go on, Davey boy! Lay on with your hands. Don't just sit there . . .' and so I bet were Patricia and Rebecca. Annie was looking daggers at all of us and at Davey especially, so he stayed quiet. If there is such a thing as telepathy then my silent screaming entreaties should have deafened his cute little inner ear. There was a sparkle in that velvet eye and a flush to those nectarine cheeks that bespoke something, I'm sure of that. There could not be a more clearly heaven-sent and angel-scented opportunity to test his powers than the War of Lilac's Liver and he must know it.

Michael was very quiet, as he has been most of the week. He looks worn out, poor lug. He spent the afternoon and early evening closeted with Ted Wallace which, let's face it, would shag out a Jack Russell. I give up with Ted. When I think back to the merry piglet I knew in the Sixties and early Seventies and then look at the mud-encrusted lump that confronts us today I want to weep. He won't let anyone in. The cheap pose of the cantankerous old griffin is bad enough in the talentless journalists and layabouts he associates with, but in Ted, who once had a real helping of that thing called talent, it's heartbreaking. You try and talk to him, try just to bring him out of his private hell and he can't bear it, as if emotional frankness were a distasteful social boo-boo, like saying 'pardon' or fitting a candlewick cover to your loo-lid. All I want to do is see him break down. Whoops, sounds cruel. I mean by it that I just want to hear him say, *once*, 'I know, Oliver. It's awful. I've lost it and I hate it and you must forgive me if I get all choleric and sour. Inside, I'm still the Happy Hippo with a heart. Help me.' Would that be too much? It would transform him, I'm sure it would. But you can't get in. The bolts are drawn.

Aside from anything else his attitude is far from simpatico on the Davey front. I cannot understand why Annie encourages his attentions in that quarter. If anything is guaranteed to break the spell it will be Ted's crapulent can't-impress-*me* scepticism.

All in all, with Ted wearing his worst 'what boring children you are' face, Michael glowering at one end of the table, Annie nervous as a grass-hopper at the other, and the rest of us in varying states of electric tension in between, a pretty glum dinz all round. I shot off to bed early. Cheryl Chest was beating her terrible tattoo and I needed my pills and the soft snog of Sandra Sleep.

A strange waking this morning. I thought at first that Vesta Vision was playing the giddy goat with me. 'This is it,' I moan to myself. 'Next, the tingle down the arms, then the tightness in the throat, finally the big cardiac club that fells me once and for all.'

I stared at the vision helplessly. It was that of a fiendish child, or rather two fiendish children, for it was doubled, like the split-field effects they used to employ to indicate drunkenness in zany Tony Randall comedies. You were supposed, in that tradition, either to clutch your head and groan 'Uh-oh, too many Martinis,' or to gurgle, hiccup and ask the barman for another and another, all on account of how Doris Day doesn't understand you.

I was not drunk, however, and was certain, as I always have been, that Doris Day understands me perfectly. Nothing symptomatic of coronary unpleasantness, just the double demons.

I closed my eyes tight and opened them again. Still the same identical child-beasts. The one on the left spoke.

'He's awake.'

The image on the right giggled and I realised that Mother had been reacting like a hysterical old ninny. It was all simply explained.

'You're the twins,' I manage to croak.

'Yes we certainly are,' says the one on the left.

'Which is which?'

'He's Edward and he's James,' they chirrup simultaneously, which is no help.

'Can't you wear badges with letters on them so we know?' I suggest.

'Ha, ha! We like people not knowing.'

I look at them for a while.

'You're James,' I decide, pointing at the one on the left.

'How do you know?' he says, disappointed.

'Ha, ha! I just knew.'

'No, go on, tell.'

'Well,' I say, 'your breathing isn't as dramatic as Edward's and I happen to know that Edward has asthma.'

They glare at each other with recrimination. James starts to try and imitate Edward's gulping breaths. I know I will always be able to tell them apart though, because now that I look, Edward's chest is notably larger than James's and his shoulders set more upright.

'You had quite a bad turn last year, didn't you?' I ask.

Edward responds with great pride. 'Simon thought I was a sodding goner. Looked very bad he said. Blue as a still-born runt.'

'But somehow you pulled through?'

James and Edward exchange glances. 'Mummy says we're not supposed to talk about it.'

'Never mind,' I say. 'I'm Oliver, by the way.'

'We know that. How do you do?'

'How do you do?' I reply, with matching ceremony.

'Do you want to hear a good joke?' asks James.

'Always want to hear a good joke.'

He clears his throat grandly, as if about to recite 'Gunga Din'.

'Knock knock.'

626

'Who's there?'

'I done up.'

I pray this isn't going to be one of those tiresome non-jokes that children inflict upon us without understanding them themselves.

'I done up who?'

'Eurgh!!' They scream with delight. 'You done a poo! You done a poo!'

So pleasing to have someone on my level at Swafford at last.

'Well, you must leave me now while I dress. Any idea of the time?'

With the practised ease of synchronised swimmers they each inspect a watch.

'Twenty-five past nine,' they chorus.

'Anyone still at breakfast?'

'Everyone else is round the stables. We're not allowed because the horses make Edward wheeze.'

'The stables?'

'Mr Tubby came round to say that Lilac's ever so better.'

Yippy-dido! I fling on my clothes and streak round to the stable yard. Vera Vet is stepping into his Volvo. Lovat green cords this time, not quite such a good colour for him, it seems to me. Simon, Davey, Michael, Anne, Patricia, Rebecca, Ted and the Cliffords are all there.

'Let me know if there's any change. It's really most . . .' He shakes his brown curls. 'I've seen recovery before, but never so fast.'

We watch his car disappear. Michael turns towards Lilac's kennel or whatever they're called, where Simon stands stroking Lilac herself: she certainly looks in my

ignorant estimation as bright of eye and glossy of coat
as one could wish. David lurks modestly in the background, tracing patterns in the dust with the point of
his shoe. The Cliffords, Rebecca and Patricia are staring
at him.

'So what are we all hanging around here for, then?'
Michael wants to know. He claps his hands. 'She's a
mare, not the Mona bloody Lisa. Let's go inside. Ted,
we'll get on, shall we?'

Michael and Ted return to the house. Simon pats
Lilac and goes off to talk to Tubby the groom. I take
my courage in both hands and snaffle David, much to
the boiling rage of the others.

'Well,' I say brightly, 'there's a mercy. I don't have a
thing in black. If there'd been a funeral I should have
looked horribly festive.'

Annie trolls over. 'Any plans today, Oliver?'

'Well . . .' say I.

'Like to come on the lake again?' Davey suggests, eyes
round and lovely.

Annie checks this move.

'Looks like rain,' she says, scanning the cloudless sky.
'There's talk of it anyway. Today or tomorrow. Why not
go into town? See a film or something?'

I get the sitch. She wants her boy-child safe in a city,
not standing on the lawn laying hands on her guests like
Bernadette at a fête.

'Good idea,' I say.

Whatever happens I plan to ask Davey about the
horse. Did he press a hand to her flank, pop a crystal in
her ear . . . what?

'All right then.' Davey doesn't look too excited, but

628

he's game. It may be my turn. Nothing wrong with Rebecca so far as I can tell, Patricia's in a bate because that Rebak piece jilted her and Clara just needs a squint corrected and her teeth pushed in. I could do that myself with enough follow-through. No question in my mind or, I hope, Davey's: Mother's angina comes first.

Bitch it . . . I'm out of voddie now. I shall steal down for a bottle . . .

. . . Betterness. Much of betterness. No one saw me, full flask of Stolly by my side, now I can concentrate. Where had I got to? Davey and Mother's Day Out. *Much* to tell.

We walked round the corner to where my Saab was quartered.

'What's on?' I asked.

'On?'

'At the cinema, bum-brain.'

'Oh . . .' He kicked a stone. 'Who cares?'

I started in on the questioning as soon as the car had cleared the driveway. 'Now, Davey. Darling. I want to know everything.'

He looked across at me with a smile. An overwhelming urge to run my tongue around and into his lips threatened to unseat my reason. Dreadful. Simply dreadful. I'm an Esau girl, these days. Give me an hairy man, not an smooth, that's my glad cry. Davey has a power though, oh Jessie, does he ever have a power. Mother knew that she was going to have to be very, very careful.

'Look,' I said. 'Time for Trudie Truth and her cheerleader chums Connie Candour and Fanny Frankness. I know and you know about Jane. I know and you know

629

about Edward and his asthma. And now we have Lilac and her magic liver.'

David breathed out deeply and drummed his heels in the footwell.

'I have to find out, Davey. I'm sick myself, as you know. I must find out what's been going on.'

There was a pause while he wrestled with his . . . I don't know, conscience or pride I suppose. 'I have very hot hands,' he said at last. 'Feel.'

He offered me his hand. It was a warm day so I wouldn't have expected a cold feel from a fish, but Davey's hand . . . cub's honour, Daisy . . . it scorched. Not a wet heat, nothing sweaty, but Lord, hotter by far than 98.4°F, I would swear to that.

'Bloody hell, darling! That's, that's . . .'

'I've always had very hot hands, you see. When I saw Edward lying there I knew that my hand on his chest would help.'

'So that's it, is it? That's all you have to do?'

Davey shook his head. 'No. You see I tried that with Jane when she was here last month and nothing happened.'

'Nothing?'

'Not a thing. The leukaemia is deep in the bones you see, the platelets of the blood are manufactured in the marrow. I knew I would have to . . . have to get right inside her.'

Oh my God, thinks Mother. He fisted her. The little darling fisted her.

'When you say . . . get right inside her?'

Davey hovered on the brink. He's never told anyone,

630

I think to myself. He's on the verge of pouring it all out. All the secrets of his sorcery.

'You see . . . there's . . .'

He dries up.

I take the next turning in the road, down a little lane and towards a wood. Fuck the cinema, we can find out what was on and pretend we saw it.

The sound of the ratchets of the handbrake bring him out of his trance.

'Where are we?' he whispers.

'Let's go for a ramble and you can tell me everything.'

A sign on the fence surrounding the wood says 'Private', but I figure we're unlikely to run into anyone. David springs over like an antelope as I straddle the wire clumsily, snagging a perfectly good pair of Ralph Lauren chinos.

The copse is no more than three or four acres. Beech, ash, oak, brutes like that. Very quiet in that muffled way that woods have.

'You were saying, Davey,' I say as we penetrate the gloom, 'that Jane's leukaemia wasn't sensitive to touch alone?'

'I've always known you see . . . and you swear you'll keep all this to yourself?'

'Swear, swear and double-swear. Cross my heart and hope to go bald.'

'I've always known,' he says, 'that the gift – I call it *the* gift not *my* gift – I've always known that the gift comes from here.'

He stopped, knelt and pressed a palm against the earth.

631

I nodded. David looked like staying on the ground so I got down and sat beside him.

'It's the power of Everything. The word is "channelled". The power of Everything can be channelled through me. But I have to be strong, you see. I have to be . . . pure.'

'You see' was becoming his trademark phrase. He wants me to see. He desperately wants me to see.

'Pure, Davey? What do you mean by pure?'

'I'm very healthy myself, you see. I'm never ill and I never get spots or infections or anything like that. This is because I only eat pure food. Not the meat of animals or plant matter that has been artificially forced. My family used to think I was a crank when I was younger. Most children go through a phase of vegetarianism, but they aren't as committed as I have always been. Now I think they understand. They never talk about it though.'

'So you believe that this diet in some way makes your body purer for this channelling?'

'That's only part of it. You see, there are other kinds of purity. My spirit must be pure. It cannot afford to be contaminated by anything impure.'

'So you think there are spiritual equivalents to meat and non-organic vegetables?'

'You could put it that way, I suppose.' Davey lay back and looked at the roof of the wood.

'A pure mind in a pure body, then?'

'Yes. But you see I am human, aren't I? I mean, I am a human being.'

I was glad he was sure of that. I couldn't have coped if he'd claimed to be an angel.

'And as a human being,' he went on, 'I feel hunger

and cold and pain like everyone else. All kinds of hunger.'

Ah. I dimly saw what he was trying to say. He needed assistance, here, I felt. Mother came to the rescue with polished ease.

'You mean that you worry about your other hungers? Fleshly hungers, shall we call them?'

'Mm hm.' He nodded. 'When I first had a wet dream . . . it was only a year ago, which is late, but so what?'

He threw out this embarrassing fact like a challenge, giving me the impression that he had been teased at school for lagging behind in development.

'So what indeed? I didn't mature in that way till I was sixteen,' I lied helpfully.

Davey was not interested in Mother's genital development. 'I caught up anyway,' he mumbled. Mother was aware of this. Mother knows how to inspect a trouser bulge, I hope.

'Anyway,' said Davey, 'I had one of those dreams. When I woke up I didn't know what to do. I knew that I couldn't allow such a terrible waste.'

'Er . . .'

'It's not just my hands, you see. I knew that every part of me could heal. My blood and my . . . my . . .' He broke off, unable to find a word.

'Seed?' I suggested.

'Mm. My seed. So I couldn't afford to waste any of it with cheap . . . you know.'

Wow!

'So, are we perhaps saying, Davey,' I said carefully, as if I were Socrates exploring a premise with Alcibiades,

633

'that the "way in" to someone's body you talked about earlier might in fact be through your seed?'

'Of course,' said David. 'But just so long as I am pure and only use its grace to heal. I must never use it to give pleasure to myself.'

'So . . .' again the utmost delicacy seemed to be required, '. . . so in Jane's case the only way to help her was . . .'

David sat up and looked straight into my eyes. Hypnotic little baggage.

'We talked about it very fully,' he said. 'Jane understood what I was suggesting. She decided that even if the gift were not to work, at least it would be something . . .'

'At least it would be a kind and helpful experience for you and a comfort and pleasure for her?'

'Exactly!' Davey smiled. 'I wasn't very . . . anyway it doesn't matter, the whole point was to heal Jane, not to "make love" in that sense.'

'And so your seed entered her body.'

'That was on my last night before I had to go back to school. We'd arranged I should visit her bedroom late.'

So intrigued had I been, Daisy, by the prospect of these two cousins at it like knives in the stilly watches that the other, obvious, thought hadn't entered my head. Lilac . . .

I'd have to tread carefully here.

'And we know,' I said, 'how wonderfully that particular . . . er, treatment . . . worked in Jane's case. So when it came to helping Lilac, you no doubt . . . ?'

'The same thing, that's right.'

All inhibition gone now. Said as matter-of-factly as you could wish. Amanda Amazement and Diana Disgust

634

were denied any access to my features as I reacted to this. It was necessary to react as though he were telling me about nothing more remarkable than a trip to the sea-side.

'So that would have been last night,' I said.

'Yes. Last night.'

A wistful grin now, true love recalled.

'I know some people would find it disgusting,' he went on. 'A human and a horse, I mean. But they don't understand the connection between life and nature and grace. It was truly the most natural thing in the world.'

I hastened to agree with him and he lay back again, content to have his secret shared.

Where did all this leave Mother, you'll be wondering, Daisy mine. Well, Mother was heating up like a milk pan in a kiln. If this fifteen-year-old faun with the curling lashes and take-me-now lips was the future of medicine in Great Britain, then a lot of people were going to be queuing up for a cure if ever word got out.

'And Michael and Anne. Your parents. They don't know about this . . .' I searched for a neutral phrase, 'this aspect of your healing?'

He shook his head.

'It would worry them. Daddy's quite proud of me, I think. He values the gift. But Mummy's frightened, I can tell.'

She'd be frightened a whole size bigger if she knew, thought I.

There he lay and there I sat. All that power swimming in his fuzzy little ball-sack: all that fatty deposit lining my aorta and waiting to be cleansed away.

I've always tried to be honest with you, dear Daisy. I

told you about the felching episode in the Finsbury Park nightclub. I was manly and frank on the subject of the bondage queen who tried to bite off my nipples in his flat in Hyde Park Gate. I confessed openly that I allowed that gorilla of a policeman in New York to slap my legs with a towel and call me his bitch-pig slave. I can be honest here too, and admit that even if I had not been diagnosed as suffering genuinely from angina pectoris I should have laid claim to it there and then without a moment's thought.

God, it has to be faced, can be astonishingly sweet. When I was a priest, and I'd be the first to admit that I only joined up because I liked the bells-and-smells aspect, the cotters, the thuribles and the sung versicles, I thought God was a capricious prig. Here was I, burning and yearning to serve, and there was the horrid, horrid Bible, never a book that I thought much of, telling me how damned and abominable I was. Couldn't have been pleaseder to hand in my notice and flounce from the chancel never to return.

But – and you know this, Daisy, better than anyone, you who know my inmost heart – there was what we can only call a Void in Mother's life. I've tried my bloody best, I've fought with my tiny fists for the oppressed and the hurt in the world, I've put my talent into things that matter and I've made an effort – unlike Wallace – to live a decent life. I know lots of nasties wouldn't think being pissed on in New York or rimmed behind a bush on Hampstead Heath is decent, but you and I know, Daisy, what decent means.

Now, here was Glenda God giving me the chance to be physically whole in a way that exactly suited the very passion that Big Brenda Bible had always claimed to be unclean. God makes things fit, you have to hand it to Her.

I said to David.

'I'm unwell. Do you think . . . do you think you could help *me*?'

I prayed a little prayer that angina wasn't the kind of affliction that a laying-on of hands could cure.

Davey smiled. 'Of course I can help you, Oliver. It's what I'm here to do.'

A great smarting wave of blood rushed up the nape of my neck. When I spoke, my voice was husky.

'Here? Now?'

David shook his head. 'I don't think so. I'll visit you tonight. That would be better.'

'I'm in the Fuseli Room, slap next to Ted Wallace. I can hear his snoring clearly enough so . . .'

'All right then, you come to my room. You know where it is?'

I nodded, not liking the way such practicalities lent the tryst a squalid air.

We got back in the car, tea-ed at the Scole Inn and returned to Swafford singing the praises of *Unforgiven*, which I'd seen and in whose details I gave David a good briefing.

Well, Daisy. Here we are. It's a quarter to two. Thank God I never travel without my breath-spray or a spare tube of Man Glide. I'm off to Davey's Den. Wish me luck, my darling.

III

Astonishingly, Mother Mills came down to breakfast after me on Thursday morning. A man takes pride in always being the last one down and I didn't enjoy being beaten.

'Morning, Ted,' Oliver trilled as he came into the dining room.

'You're revoltingly cheerful,' I said, propping the *Telegraph* against the marmalade jar.

'Am I? Am I? Yes, I suppose I am,' he replied with a giggle, practically skipping to the sideboard. 'I could eat a horse. Which, let's face it darling, we all may well have been forced to do had little Lilac not made such an am-az-ing recovery yesterday.'

Hell and turds, I thought. Here we go. 'With the best will in the world, Oliver,' I said with a firm rasp, 'can we please find something to talk about this morning other than bloody miracles?'

'You still can't bear it, can you, baby? The proof that there truly are more things in heaven and earth than your puny, fusty, narrow philosophy ever dreamed of.'

'I wonder if a man in your condition should be stuffing himself with quite so much fried food,' I said, eyeing with revulsion the heaped kidney and sausage that he plonked down on the table next to me.

'Ho-ho!' he said, returning to the sideboard. 'A man in my condition?' He began to fill another plate, flourishing the serving-spoon like a cocktail waitress. 'I'm sure I don't know what you mean by "a man in my condition". What condition?'

I stared up at him, quite unable to hide my dismay. 'Oh, no . . .'

He beamed with what he no doubt considered an inner radiance and I considered a vile smirk.

'Oh yes. Oh yessy-yes-yes.'

'Don't tell me *you've* had the bloody laying-on-of-hands treatment as well?'

'I'm whole, Ted. As cured as this bacon and twice as hot and sizzling.'

'Well,' I gave him a sour look as he sat down beside me with a wince, 'the little Miracle Worker doesn't seem to have had the kindness to heal *all* your infirmities, does he?'

'Meaning?'

'You've got the piles that afflict us all, I note.'

'Oh *those*,' he said, with a smile, 'they'll pass in time no doubt.'

'Humph. I'd be more inclined to trust good old Preparation H myself.'

He waded in on his gargantuan breakfast. Despite my irritation I found myself impressed by the confidence of his demeanour and the unquestionably genuine sparkle in his eye.

'Be serious, Oliver,' I said. 'Do you honestly believe that you have been cured? Completely cured?'

'I've thrown away my pills, Ted. I feel . . . oh, it's impossible to put into words how I feel. Davey is a gift from God. A gift from Glenda herself.'

'And his touch . . . did you feel this warmth that everyone talks about?'

'Darling,' said Oliver, a forkful of kidney hovering in front of his mouth, 'it is simply the hottest thing I have ever felt in my life. It burns like a soldering iron. My word, how it burns. Right inside the deepest deeps it burns.'

I knew now that I had to do that thing that I hate most to do. I had to think. I had to sit, close my eyes, press my hands to my ears and analyse, like a chess-player or a code-breaker. The most dreaded activity a man can undertake. I hadn't done it since last I wrote a decent poem.

I decided that the Villa Rotunda would make the ideal cogitarium, but that it would be madness to go there without fortification. I left Oliver to swim in the riotous grease of his breakfast and his self-satisfaction and made my way to the library.

Morning drinking times are matters of great debate. The threshold moves inexorably the more alcohol becomes a habit. I can remember a time when I thought it was impossible to take a glug of anything stronger than tomato juice before twelve o'clock. Twelve o'clock became half past eleven, became eleven, became half ten, became ten and so on. This was before the great puritan backlash of course which has made drinking a private vice never to be shown the light at lunch-times. Alcohol is the great secret of our age. If the public knew, if they had the remotest idea of the amount of drinking done by our politicians and leaders, they would be shocked to their boxers. Fortunately, journalists, as is better known, are inebriates too, so they have an interest in keeping a lid on things. The number of Members of Parliament who aren't what doctors would call a functional alcoholic is astoundingly small. Alan Beith is a teetotaller, I seem to remember, and Tony Benn gets by on tea and pipe-tobacco; they are the only dry parliamentarians I can think of for the moment. Any others are doubtless abstemious because they have been told by their doctors that one more smell of brandy would kill them. I've seen Chancellors and Prime Ministers pissed as rats, judges too and news-readers and chairmen of transnational giants. A well-known television political commentator told me at the Harpo once that the war in Bosnia, from which he had just returned, was run exclusively on alcohol. Skirmishes and strategies are entirely ordered according to supplies of slivovitz and vodka.

Alcohol is the prime determining factor of human history: the dethronement of British Prime Ministers, civil strife in Russia and the ruin of whole financial structures can be traced back to the glass. We are led to believe that it is only football hooligans who can't handle it; the fact is that it's too big an issue even to think of confronting. Thank God. For, having said all that, we get by on it far better than we manage without. Total abstainers make rotten leaders of men and incompetent husbands, lovers and fathers. Drunkards hiccup, belch, fart, vomit and stain the front of their trousers with piss. Puritans never reveal any of their functions, and it's a short step from denying the world access to your own base physicality to denying others the right to any base physicality of their own.

Special pleading on my part, no doubt. Perhaps we hear once more the light footfall of Pudoria, Goddess of Guilt. I think, as much as anything, that I had become annoyed with myself for taking such a noticeable drop in drinking since I had arrived at Swafford. Not annoyed with myself, more infuriated by the kindly approval of everyone else.

'Ted, you look so well!'

'This seems to have been something of a rest cure for you, Ted.'

'Wendy Whisky is becoming offended by your inattentions, dear.'

That kind of junk. It took a considerable effort to remember to have an ostentatious drink from time to time, merely in order to stop them from strewing rose-petals in my path and chalking up another cure to Davey.

I headed for the library therefore to see if I couldn't push a couple down my throat before giving myself over to thought.

I believed I had the place to myself, but a snivel from a deep wing-chair in the corner told me that I had female company.

'You all right, Patricia?' I said, coming up behind her. Should have coughed my approach, I suppose, for I gave her one hell of a turn.

'Please, Ted! You shouldn't sneak up like that.'

She had been crying steadily for some time.

'Very sorry,' I said. 'Everything all right?'

'Well, what does it look like, you fat idiot?'

'Contrary to popular belief,' I said, 'it only makes it worse to take it out on someone else. I don't think you'll find insulting me very helpful.'

'Is that your attempt at sympathy?'

'It's practicality, which is kinder than sympathy.'

She wiped her nose. 'Well I certainly don't need a cross between G. K. Chesterton and a fucking calendar motto.'

'You still thinking of that Martin Rebak?' He was the underling of Michael's who had ditched Patricia.

She nodded. 'Got a letter from him this morning. I thought perhaps he might have tired of his new infatuation. He's just married her.'

'Then clearly he has tired of her,' I said.

642

'Oh, give it a rest, Ted.'

'Well, what do you want me to say? That he is not worth your tears? That you'll get over it? That it's always darkest just before the dawn and that time heals all wounds?'

'I need David, that's what I need.'

'And what do you think he can give you?'

'Hope,' she said. 'A sense of worth.'

There you have the modern Briton. It drives me to a frothing frenzy when politicians return from inner cities saying, 'What the people of this town need is Hope,' as if we could all respond with a glad cry of 'No sooner said than done, old sport,' as we gather up a handful of Hope from the sideboard, stuff it into a Jiffy-bag and send it off to Liverpool 8 by the First Class post. What these bleeding hearts mean is Money, but they're too greasy to say so. Hope may spring eternal in the human breast, but you can't suck it off another's tits, it has to lactate in your own. Not the kind of message to give a girl in Patricia's state, I supposed. As for a sense of worth . . .

'The best way to mend your spirits,' I offered instead, 'is to do something for someone else.'

'Meaning?' she asked coldly.

'Meaning, why not do me a favour?'

'Such as?'

'Such as, when this strange little holiday is over and we're back in London, why not oblige me by allowing yourself to be taken out to dinner? Le Caprice is an olive-stone's throw from my flat. We could eat a good dinner and then you could let me lie you on a litter and lick you like a lolly.'

She stared at me. 'I'm young enough to be your daughter.'

'I'm not fussy.'

'This is your idea of grief therapy is it, Ted? Coming on like a randy goat?'

'I'll leave you to think it over. My evenings get pretty booked up, so you'll have to be quick.'

'You're serious, aren't you?' she said, stopping me with a hand, which I took in mine.

'I'm a fat old man, Patricia. It's hard enough to find women of my own age who aren't prostitutes, but a young thing like you . . . well it would be a rare treat. Possibly my last ever. Thighs unpitted by cellulite, breasts that stand up like begging dogs. How often do you think I am granted such pleasures these days?'

'And what makes you think I would consent to being slobbered over by you?' she asked, withdrawing her hand.

'Your innate kindness,' I said, going over to pour myself a large glass of sherry. 'The knowledge that you would be making me quite cretinously happy.'

'It's a hell of a thing to ask.'

'Ha ha!' I said triumphantly. 'And just why is it such a hell of a thing to ask?'

'What do you mean?'

'You said that it was a hell of a thing to ask. Why should you think that?'

'Well, for your information, my body is not something I offer around like a tray of canapés.'

'And why not?'

'Why not? Why not? Because I happen to set some store by it.'

'So,' I trumpeted, 'why do you need Davey to give you a sense of worth if you already have one?'

'Oh, for heaven's sake. Of all the cheap . . .'

'You've made it extremely plain that my offer of love and companionship is a far lower offer than you consider you have the right to expect. You value your body and your favours far above mine.'

'There's a big difference between valuing my body and valuing myself. You didn't offer me love and companionship, you asked me to lie out and be licked.'

'Which is a man's clumsy way of asking for love, as well you must know. If I had said that you were the most beautiful woman I had laid eyes on for years and that I most desperately wanted you near me, you'd think I was taking pity on you. Thursdays are pretty good for me,' I said and buggered off, leaving her to stew.

I headed for the Villa Rotunda, notebook and pencil in one hand, sherry-glass in the other. Clouds were gathering on the sky-line and the long-promised bad weather looked to be approaching at last. Clouds boiled in me too and rumbles of thunder sounded in my head.

It was dark and cool inside the summerhouse. I sat on the wooden box of croquet mallets and fired up a Rothie. The last two days, I make no bones about it, had left me feeling bewildered and isolated. On the first page of the notebook I began to write down a list of the contradictions that were driving such hard nails into my mind.

They say writing lists is anal, the mark of an 'anal retentive'. I am almost certain no one who uses that moronic phrase has the least idea what it means. The critic Edward Wilson once described Charles Dickens as an 'anal dandy'. I don't suppose he knew what the fuck he was talking about either. Listing things, as I do with words when preparing a poem for instance, seems to me to be a far cry from a compulsion to store objects in my bottom. Only the other day Oliver and I had been admiring the new Swafford Hall writing-paper that Michael had ordered from Smythson's in Bond Street and which Podmore had distributed on bureaux and tables in the bedrooms, book rooms and drawing rooms of the house.

'Ooh, I just think stationery is so delightfully anal!' he had squeaked. Oliver that is, not Podmore.

'Why *anal*?' I had asked testily. 'Why not renal or cranial or pulmonary or nasal or testicular? I mean, what on earth has it got to do with arses? It makes no sense.'

'Don't be difficult, dear. Everyone knows that stationery is anal. It's an established fact.'

We go through phases in infancy of wanting to lodge things either in our mouths or in our bottoms, we are told. We develop into orally or anally retentive types. As a smoker, drinker, guzzler and biter of biro ends, I might be considered oral. I can understand that: the above-stated itemries are all taken by mouth. Apparently, however, as a drawer-up of lists and a lover of good-quality paper, I am also anal. Does that make sense? Of course not. What possible use do such categorisations have, beyond providing people like Oliver with an opportunity to make flip dinner-party remarks?

Anal, my arse. I like my lists. This particular list was very important. Compiling a list for me is like laying out a formal garden in the rubbishy wilderness of my mind. Anal. Pah.

I chewed the end of the pencil, orally retaining several cedar-wood splinters, and then I began to write.

1. Edward, Jane, Lilac and now, possibly, Oliver have

apparently been cured by David's placing his hands upon them.

2. A hot hand placed on a human body is, surely, no different to a hot compress, a hot flannel or, come to that, a hot buttered tea-cake placed on a human body. If heat alone could treat cancer and asthma and heart disease, then the medical world would have told us about it.

3. Therefore David's hands are transmitting some power other than heat.

4. My understanding is that electricity, magnetism and gravity are the only physical fields of force in the universe. A molecule or an atom, or whatever they are called, cannot be moved by any other power. Well, there are a couple of others, but they only exist on paper.

5. The only other force worth considering, I have always held, is the creative force in man, such as might write a poem or right a wrong.

6. There is such a thing as the power of suggestion, however. One human mind is capable of being hypnotised or persuaded by another. We have faith, we have Hitler, we have advertising. But faith *healing*? Come off it. Pain may be mental illusion, but tumours and clotted arteries are not. Besides, there's the vet and, it would seem, Jane's doctors.

7. If all this is true: if David is capable of changing molecular structure – for this is what we are discussing – then the world should know about it.

8. I am David's godfather. What do I think of the morality of allowing him to be (a) splashed all over the newspapers, (b) pushed back and forth between scientists and fanatics determined either to prove him a fraud or to overblow his gifts?

9. What do I mean 'gifts'? Gifts are things that are given. That necessitates a giver. Why should God waste his time giving the power to heal? What happened to free will and the duty of man to get on with life without the impertinent interference of his creator? And what about the millions who will die every year never having been given a chance to be healed by David? Children in Africa with eaten-away faces? Paraplegics in Peru? Lepers in Libya? The blind in Bali and the deaf in Delhi? It's senseless, senseless, absolutely senseless. Even the flawed and spiteful God we have wouldn't be cruel enough to give his children just a handful of healers to go around four billion.

10. And if God did give us a healer he'd be damned sure that the one chosen would do more than heal. They'd preach abstinence and salvation and hell-fire or some such damned thing to go along with it. Whereas all David does is witter on about half-arsed namby-pamby Green crap and dribble a load

of maundering pantheistic bollocks about Nature and Purity.

11. There again. Music is a gift. Painting is a gift. Even poetry is a gift. Palpable talents and charisms enough exist which improve man's fate on earth, why not one of healing? It may be that the giver is not God, but genetics and evolution. After all, there is evidence that David's power is congenital, inherited indeed, as are the gifts of many musicians.

12. But. But, but, but. To be a great musician the gift alone is not enough. You must live amongst men and suffer and understand. Above all you must WORK. Nothing of any value that I've ever seen man achieve on this earth has ever been accomplished without work.

13. Oh yeah? Why are you fighting it so hard, Ted? What's your problem? Face the evidence of your own eyes.

14. Evidence of my eyes? What have I actually seen?

15. Oh, come on. Evidence of your own ears, then.

16. Hearsay.

17. It's 'hearsay' to you that Mexico exists. Do you really doubt it?

18. All right. All right. But that still leaves the problem
    of David. I swore an oath at the font. His father,
    my friend, looks to me for guidance. For once in
    his life he doesn't know what to do. I can help.

19. That's right, you can help. You can . . .

I broke off. The sound of voices was approaching. Two
people, deep in conversation. They stopped under the
open window of the Villa, the rear window that gave out
on to the lake.

'This, I think, is a quiet spot.' The voice of Max Clifford.

'Very quiet.' The voice of Davey.

I locked myself into a kind of gaping immobility, like an
uncoordinated child playing musical statues. They were
only yards from where I sat and the smallest sound from
inside the summerhouse would be as audible to them as
their speech was to me.

'Now then. I'll get right down to it, David. I've seen
Oliver this morning.'

No reply.

'He wouldn't say what had happened, but it's clear that
something has. Something of a similar nature to the
extraordinary recovery that Mary and I witnessed in your
cousin Jane earlier this year.'

'It's quite true. Oliver's heart is mended now.'

Clifford gave an admiring laugh.

'Amazing. Quite amazing.'

'It's not really amazing, you know. Not to me.'

'I suppose these activities take something out of you?'

'Yes. As a matter of fact they do take something out of
me.'

'It's merely . . . I feel rather absurd making this request. I appreciate it's not like asking someone to lend you a book or to baby-sit for the evening.'

'You can ask me anything you like, Max.'

'My daughter Clara has . . . certain things wrong with her.'

'I'm sure I can help her, Max.'

'She's not *ill* exactly, but she is, well, odd. She's so awkward and clumsy and . . .'

'And unhappy.'

'Very difficult to take her out anywhere. People stare, you know. The strabismus and the buck-teeth are bad enough. But she makes absolutely no effort to be graceful or . . .'

'Yes, I know. I would be very happy to see her and do what I can.'

'I don't know exactly what your technique is. If Mary and I could help in any way?'

'Well, the thing is, Max. You have to trust me, you see. I would rather that you weren't present when I am with her.'

'Of course, of course. Whatever you say. But you are fully up to strength? I mean, you're not an especially strong boy by the looks of you. We don't want to exhaust you.'

'I am quite strong really. My spirit is very quickly replenished. So long as I don't waste it.'

'Splendid.'

They fell into a silence. I stretched a cramped leg out as noiselessly as I could. Perhaps they had walked away. I contemplated rising and going over to the window to peep down. Then I heard the sound of a pebble splashing into the lake and decided that they were still there. Another couple of pebbles were thrown before David spoke.

'What have you said to Clara about me?'

'Well, we did mention that it was a possibility that you would like to help her.'

'And how does she feel about that?'

'Clara is fourteen years old and will do as she is told,' Max said sharply. He must have realised how callous this sounded, for he quickly added, 'Not that she *needs* to be told, I should say. No, she's very keen. Her squint and her teeth and her bloody uncoordinated gawking. They are a great trial to her. To all of us.'

'Where is she now?'

'With Simon somewhere, according to her mother. Mucking around in the stables. Mucking *out* in the stables, more likely. Would you like me to send her to you?'

'This afternoon if that would be all right. After lunch.'

'Yes. Yes, you should eat first, I expect. Er, where exactly will you do it?'

'I'm not sure, Max. Perhaps we might go for a walk. But it really has to be private. We must be absolutely alone.'

'As you say, as you say . . . I'm very grateful. Mary and I are both very . . .'

Max's voice faded and I was left, once more, to myself.

I turned back to my notebook and completed, for the time being, my list.

20. I may have the evidence of my own eyes soon. Best, I think, to suspend judgement until then.

I looked in on Michael before lunch. He was dictating a

letter. Smoother and more assured he looked than when last we had talked. His business face, I supposed. He appeared to be pleased to see me. There again, he had appeared to be pleased to see me the week before when, as I now knew, he had in fact been excessively vexed by my presence. For all I know, no one in the world has ever been pleased to see me, but some have been better at hiding it than others.

'Ahoy, Tedward! And how goes the morning?'

'Just wanted a word, Michael.'

'Thank you, Valerie. I'll talk to Mr Wallace now.'

'Yes, Lord Logan.'

Valerie slipped out, closing the door behind her.

'So, what do you hear, what do you say?'

I sat down in the chair opposite the desk. 'You've heard about Oliver?'

Michael sighed and drummed his fingers against the side of his head.

'Annie was in here. Very upset. She said she had told Davey yesterday not to see anyone without telling her first. She is furious that he disobeyed. "Of course he disobeyed!" I said to her. "If my Uncles had told me, when I was his age, 'Don't do any more work on the shop, Michael. Sit and listen to the wireless or read a book, but no more thinking about business and customers and money,' do you think I would have taken any notice? Never on your life." But Annie was not satisfied.' Michael sighed again and unzipped a fresh cigar. 'So tell me, Tedward, what do you think now?'

'What do I think? I don't know. However . . .' I smiled a conspiratorial smile, 'I may know later today.'

He frowned. 'Later today? So what happens later today?'

'Michael, do you mind if I don't tell you? I won't let anything occur which shouldn't occur, you have my word.'

'And do I have your word that your word is worth anything?'

'I like to think it's worth at least the air it's spoken with.'

Logan grunted his assent.

'You're going to talk to Davey, then?' he asked.

'Perhaps,' I said. 'I'll let you know this evening.'

'Jane will be here by then. She comes down this afternoon.'

'Yes, I know,' I said. 'We shall have a full house: queens and knaves.'

Logan rose and we repaired for a pre-lunch sip in the library, where Oliver's friskiness and excessive show of good health quite put me off my schooner of fino.

IV

Meals at Swafford gather in formality during the day. This is common in the grander houses of the kingdom. I expect Lévi-Strauss or Margaret Mead, were they living, could explain this phenomenon by stripping away the lacquer of smart country-house tradition to reveal a solid anthropological teak of tribal taboo beneath – as it is we shall no doubt have to look to arse-witted Sunday-paper style-writers for explanation. Breakfast, to the delight of my traditionalist self, is, as it should be, a more or less servant-less affair, Podmore only coming in with fresh coffee and toast when summoned by screams or bells. The sideboard is topped with a row of gleaming tureenery containing, in addition to the bacon, eggs, sausages, mushrooms and wrinkly fried tomatoes we might expect, the three great K's of English breakfast lore – Kedgeree, Kippers and Kidneys (keenly devilled); the length of the dining-table is rhythmically dotted with dishes of marmalade, with pots of coffee and tea, with silver toast-racks and jugs slopping to their crystal brims with the juice of orange, tomato and grapefruit. A Hepplewhite satinwood side table is matutinally spread by Podmore into a fan of national and local newspapers. Periodicals are provided too, *The Spectator*, *Private Eye*, *The Oldie*, *Country Life*, *The Field*, *Norfolk Fair*, *The Illustrated London News*, *The Economist*, *Investors Chronicle* and *Beano* for the twins. It is my custom, as I have said, to contrive to come down last and have the room to myself. I stay there for an hour or so, until the first easings of mid-morning flatulence push me to the lavatory. If St Peter were to ask in what time or place I should like eternally to be suspended for the infinite length of my heavenly career, I could certainly choose half past ten on a summer's morning in the dining room of Swafford Hall.

Dinner, when guests are invited from outside, is a formal full-fig feast. The ladies slip into off-the-shoulder frocks and the staff into over-the-shoulder modes of food dispensal – white gloves, fork-and-spoon service, effulgent napkins wrapped about the bottle necks. Wine and conversation flow, cheeks and candles glow. Even when the house interns alone are present, a certain elegance of protocol is maintained. The women are taken in draped on the arms of their men at eight and shag off *en masse* for coffee in the drawing room at elevenish, leaving the hairy element to crack nuts and jokes over the port. This much-maligned procedure, Simon told me the other day, originated in Victorian days when women were anxious to keep from their husbands, brothers and sons the alarming news that they possessed bladders and urinary tracts. Whatever its basis, I find the custom highly satisfactory. Anne has the delightful habit of calling us into the drawing room, when she believes the sexes have been segregated for long enough, by performing gentle Schumann sonatas on the piano. One loves to play at being civilised, but one does need rich friends to meet the rising costs of such an exercise. Civilisation, after all, is not an attitude of mind, it is an attribute of wealth. Dinners at Swafford, to my mind, are very nearly as fine as breakfasts.

Luncheon lies between these two in ceremony as in chronology. The library serves as the muster station and pre-prandial lapping-pool of choice; thence we are gonged to the dining room for solids. Podmore brings in the dishes and dumps them at Anne's end for her to dole out down the table. It is the quickest meal, puddings are often sent back untouched, the imbibal of anything stronger than iced water is uncommon and conversation tends to the stilted. The British are uneasy about domestic weekday lunches; the work ethic is in us ingrained so deep that even the leisured classes like to behave as though midday eating is a tiresome intrusion on a life of toil and honest diligence.

As we made our way into the dining room on this day, my appetite already ruined by Oliver's rude health and Anne's distraught demeanour, the atmosphere within doors crackled with the same kind of tension as prevailed without. It is a mark, I have often noticed, of God's cheap sense of literary cliché that he so often chooses to provide climatic conditions that reflect our inmost moods. The day of Jane's christening, for instance, which I think of as the Day of Rebecca's Curse, was a streaming, soaking day, to match the sodden weeping that attended it. The weather that accompanied the scene of Helen's departure from my house and life with a screaming Roman and a coldly sniffing Leonora was bone-chillingly frosty, imparting an iced numbness that exactly suited my mood. And the day, if we cast our minds back all those pages ago, that saw my expulsion from the *Sunday Shite* was clear and warm and free and bright. Today's bristling electric menace, while overdone like all God's effects, could not be said to be inappropriate.

Michael was silent, Anne brittly garrulous. I watched Clara, who in turn cast quick covert glances towards a flushed and expectant David. Simon was, rarely for him, moody and unresponsive. Max contented himself with suave responses to Anne's chatter. Patricia, Rebecca and Oliver wittered about London things. The twins, who might have brought some zest to the table, ate in the nursery. Mary Clifford said nothing, until towards the end of dinner when she tried to press pudding on a reluctant Clara.

'You really should, dear.'

'I'm not very hungry, Mummy.'

'No, but I think a slice of treacle-pie would be a good idea. Don't you, Davey?'

This megalithically foolish remark caused Max to bite his lower lip and Oliver to raise his eyebrows. Davey was about to reply when Simon butted in.

'It's pretty good pie actually, Clara. If you don't finish yours I'll have it, don't you worry.'

'Simon is one of those who can gorge himself like a pig and not have an ounce of flesh to show for it,' said Anne, cutting Clara a slice. 'He's already had three helpings.'

'It's two actually, Mum,' said Simon sending his plate along for the third. 'Got to keep my strength up, we're moving the pigs out to the fields to glean this afternoon. Do you want to come along, Clara?'

Clara looked helplessly at Simon, her eyes big and watery under their thick lenses.

'Clara and I thought we might go for a walk, Simon,' Max said. 'When you say "glean",' he went on effortlessly, 'do you mean they actually get by foraging for themselves, or do you supplement their diets? I've always wanted to know.'

While Simon explained I watched Clara turn with lowered head back to her bowl and poke at her pie in misery. I fancied, this forlorn moment aside, that in fact she looked a little better than she had on arrival at Swafford the previous week. Nature, it seemed to me, was sure to right

Clara's defects in time without Davey's mystical interference. Look at American girls. At the age of fourteen they look as if they're recovering from a traffic accident: their mouths are caged with wire, their legs and backs strain in corrective stockings and splints, their skin is lumpy from acne, their upper lips fuzz with down, their sad little bras are stuffed with Kleenex and their eyes slither independently in all directions but forwards. Yet by the time they reach eighteen they have become almost too beautiful to bear, with teeth like indigestion tablets, eyes to dive into, skin you want to lick all over, fresh boobs and postures new. No armpit hair, however, which I believe to be a calamitous error. Have you ever let honey-suckle live up to its name? Ever drained its honey? When you take the flower and pull the stamen through, a delicate shining drop of nectar swells up at its head. A bead of sweat bulging at the tip of a woman's axillary hair is as beautiful. Your true connoisseur of women delights in the great meaty reek of the female essence, not the sterile lemon top-notes of deodorants and creams. The French understand this, about the only thing they do understand – apart from French of course. Think of those giddy Baudelairean *amants* burying their heads in comedy actresses' sweat-soaked how-dare-yous. Haaa . . .

Please excuse me. We return to the luncheon.

Michael stood. 'You'll forgive my leaving,' he said. 'I have work to do this afternoon. But I trust we'll all be here at four to welcome Janie when she arrives?'

Nods all round.

I left as soon as possible to commence my stake-out in secrecy. It was a difficult undertaking to reach the Villa Rotunda without being seen from the house. A number of the guests, I knew, would be in the drawing room that overlooked the South Lawn at the back of which the villa stood. I had, therefore, to skirt the entire lawn in a wide loop and achieve the summerhouse from the rear. This necessitated the negotiation of much thick vegetation. The bushes and shrubs had set themselves the happy afternoon task, it soon came to my notice, of attempting to knock from my hand, by the use of cunningly upthrust roots and protruding twigs, the cup of coffee I had foolishly decided to take with me on the journey. By the time I had grunted myself through the rear window of the Villa there was no more than an inch of coffee remaining, much supplemented by garden detritus. An inch of after-luncheon coffee, I reflected, is better than a centimetre and I drank it gratefully down, leaf-fragments, thunder-flies, twig-bark and all. None the less, the spillage of so much was shortly to cause me a moment of panic, as I was to discover.

Settling cosily on the croquet trunk once more, I watched a spider swing from the ceiling and pondered, like Robert the Bruce before me, on the problem of effort. To stand up takes effort, to move about takes effort: simply to be still, to do no more than endure, even that takes effort. Effort is expended strength. Strength comes from food. We carry on because we eat. But *creative* effort? How is that expense replenished? Where does creative energy *come from*? From food also? Then how can it be that a poet, say, who once could write, can suddenly write no more? Not, surely, because he has stopped eating spinach? David thinks he has a creative energy that comes from . . . from God knows what. From nature, from some intricate connecting web, a sustaining field of force such as they talk about in that absurd science-fiction story with Alec

Guinness, the one that Roman amazed me by calling an
'old' film . . . may the force be with you . . . if that was
an old film to Roman – *Star Trek*, was it called? Something
like that – then what was *Duck Soup*? . . .

'It's burning! It's burning!'

An excited voice outside the window. I leapt to my feet.
The coffee cup fell from my lap and smashed on the floor.

Not David's voice. Nor Clara's.

I went to the window and looked out.

There below me were the twins, squatting on the path-
way that ran between the rear of the Villa Rotunda and
the edge of the lake. One of them had a magnifying-glass
in his hand, the other was holding a snail. A sizzle of steam
rose from a small hole in the snail's shell.

'Hoi!' I shouted.

They turned in guilty alarm and then smiled when they
saw who it was.

'Hello, Uncle Ted.'

'We're experimenting.'

'Well, you shouldn't experiment here,' I said.

The twin holding the magnifying-glass frowned.

'Why not?'

'Because . . .' I sought for a reason. 'Suppose your
brother David were to see you. You know what he thinks
of cruelty to animals.'

'That's all right.'

'Davey's in the woods somewhere.'

'He went with Clara.'

'Ages ago.'

Ages ago? *Ages* ago? I looked at my watch. Ten past
three.

Damn you, Ted, you fat buffalo. Damn you, you great

661

wallowing tit. You've slept for forty minutes. If you'd had a whole, full cup of strong coffee, perhaps . . .

I hurled myself down the front steps of the Villa and round to the twins.

'Where?'

'Where what?'

'Davey and Clara. Where in the woods did they go?'

They shrugged.

'*We* don't know.'

They pointed across the lake.

'Somewhere.'

'Shall we go and hide and seek them, do you think?'

'No, no. You stay here. I just wanted to . . . catch up with them. Have a word.'

'Right ho.'

'We'll stay here.'

'You bet. We'll be here.'

'Right here.'

'Just exactly here.'

I marched off around the lake, cursing my lazy old body. It was entirely my point. Energy. Effort. Where does it go?

I stamped through the damp pong of the lake's edge, my feet tearing up the tangle of glasswort, marshwort, mallows and kingcups beneath. Ahead lay the small woodland copse where Davey and I had walked on our first day. It was more humid now, the air bursting with vapour and, above, the clouds thickening to the colour of cuttlefish ink.

I stood in this spinney and listened. Larks, chaffinches, thrushes and flies squeaked, chirruped, throstled and buzzed. Small pockets of midge eddied and bounced in the gloomier thickets. I walked towards the darkest, densest part of the copse as quietly as a heavy man can when

662

the ground beneath him is carpeted with dried twig and crackling bark.

Somewhere ahead of me I heard David's voice, very low and husky. Bending double, I edged towards the sound, lifting each foot high off the ground and placing it down with all the strained delicacy I could manage. The effort caused me to pant and blow like a steam-roller. Sweat gathered in my eyebrows.

'So you see, the spirit must find a way in,' I heard David's voice explain.

'Spirit like air?' Clara asked.

I came to a stop behind a briar bush and peeped through. In a small clearing, less than the length of a long cocktail bar away from my cover, I could see Clara and David, seated on the ground. Clara was sideways on to me but I could see David's face clearly. He was wearing charcoal-coloured jeans and a white T-shirt. His knees were drawn up a little and he had laid a hand on Clara's shoulder. I breathed as quietly as I could.

'No, not like air, exactly. You must know about men's spirit. The spirit that makes life.'

Clara giggled. 'What, you mean like . . . *sperm*?'

A bead of sweat rolled down and stung my eyes. The light was fading and the air was charged enough to make the skin prickle.

'It isn't a joke, Clara. If this spirit is very pure and very holy, it can make the person receiving it very holy and very pure too.'

Clara stared at him. 'You aren't going to . . .'

I swallowed. This was not what I had been expecting. Not what I had been expecting at all.

'I've been thinking. You see, the problems you would like me to help you with are all up here.'

David traced his fingers around her face.

'Usually, you see, I would implant the spirit deep within you . . .'

I suddenly thought about Oliver's piles at breakfast and wanted to choke. A warm fat drop fell on my head with a slap. Blast, I thought. Some fucking wood-pigeon. Another drop landed on my arm. Rain.

'. . . but I think what would be best in your case,' David continued, 'would be for the spirit to be introduced here.'

He ran a thumb between Clara's lips.

'You mean I'd have to *drink* it?'

David sighed. It was apparent to me that he was not finding the naïveté of Clara's response at all sympathetic.

'Your father explained, didn't he? He told you that I have the power to help people. He told you to trust me and to do what I said, didn't he?'

Clara nodded. She did not appear to be happy.

'The way to take in the spirit is for me to suckle you, as a loving mother might suckle her young.'

Clara did not reply.

'You must think of how the pure living spirit will enter you and make you whole. It will heal your eyes and your teeth. It will fill you with power and beauty.'

'What will it taste like?'

Splendid child. I found myself taking to her very much. Poetry lies in practical detail.

'It will taste of everything you love. Of honey and sweet warm milk.'

'Aniseed?'

'If you like aniseed it will taste of aniseed.'

'I *hate* aniseed.'

'Well then, it won't taste of aniseed. What is your favour-ite flavour?'

'Worcester sauce.'

'Mm . . .' David paused. I could imagine him wondering how much conviction it would carry if he claimed that his pure holy river of spirit would indeed taste of Worcester sauce. 'Your mind will create whatever flavour it desires,' was the best he could come up with.

'Will it *look* like Worcester sauce, then?'

'Never mind how it will look!' David was becoming exasperated.

'It's starting to rain, now.'

'The rain is good. It's clean and pure and quite warm.'

I edged further forward for shelter in the bush; the bramble around me combing my hair with violent scratches.

David had mastered his irritation and spoke now in a calm hypnotic coo.

'Clara. You have been told to trust me and you trust me. You have been told I will help and I will help. I will lie back like this, all right? Now, I'm going to take your hand and put it here, just on my jeans like this.'

'What's that?'

'You know what that is. You must know, surely? Just feel it for a moment. Feel how warm and firm it is. It is where the spirit comes from. That's right.'

Clara's body obscured my view of the details of this woodland scene. I could see David's face looking up to the trees and his toes curling in their shoes. I could see Clara's shoulders and the back of her arm. A rumble of thunder sounded far away and the rain began to spank the leaves.

'Now,' he said. 'Just undo me here and . . . that's it. Gently though.'

'Is this what they all look like?'

'Surely you've seen one before?'

'A girl at school showed me a magazine. It didn't have this loose skin though.'

'OW! CAREFUL!'

'What have I done? What have I done?'

'No, no. It's all right. But you must be more gentle. It's extremely sensitive, you see. So, nice and easy.'

'It's very hot.'

'Yes, that's right. It is. Very hot. The heat comes from the spirit that is going to make you well and whole. Now, I want you to bring your head down.'

'I don't like to . . .'

'Clara . . . it's very simple.'

'But that's where you do . . .'

'What?'

'That's where you do pee-pees.'

'Clara, please! It is completely clean. So clean that it can purify your whole body. You have to trust me. What would your father say if I told him you had failed to trust me?'

'All right, then . . .'

Through the riot of brambles I saw her head dip down and David's right hand press against the nape of her neck.

'Easily,' said David. I imagine he was grateful that the girl's teeth protruded outwards, not in.

'Wimbledon,' she replied, or so it sounded to my ears. It may be that she said something else. I supposed that any word spoken under those circumstances would come out as Wimbledon.

'Birmingham!' she said, proving me wrong.

'Drain the spirit,' said David, the downward-facing palm of his free hand clutching and releasing the litter of the spinney floor. The rain was falling fast now, bouncing from a tree-stump beside his head. 'Yes. Don't stop. Keep going. Yes. At any moment . . . at any moment you will feel the spirit . . .'

Any moment? Christ the young are extraordinary. I would have had to lie there for half an hour just to warm myself up.

'Yes . . . yes . . . yes . . . *yes*!' David's voice rose into song. But suddenly, with a violence more powerful than that of the thunder rolling in the distance, a deep voice bellowed from out of the darkness behind them.

'NO!! NO!! LET HER GO!!'

Four things happened at once.

Ted Wallace fell forward into the bramble bush in surprise and tore his wrist on the brambles.

David howled in agony.

Clara tore her face from David's lap, a stream of crimson and cream bubbling in her mouth.

Simon crashed through the bushes and hurled himself into the clearing, his face white with rage.

I pulled myself free of the thorns and watched as Clara staggered forwards into Simon's arms, gagging and sobbing. David sat up and stared down at the torn and bleeding mess in his lap. His magic pecker seemed, luckily for him, to be in one piece, but Clara's lower teeth had scraped a gash along the underside and peeled back a curl of flesh.

Simon, one hand holding Clara's head against his

shoulder, looked across at his brother. His shoulders heaved and his tongue flicked across his lips as he searched for words. The rain streamed down between them and the wild electric smell of freshly soaked forest rose from the floor.

At last Simon found utterance.

'Physicist . . .' he shouted, '. . . heal thyself.'

Poor old Simon, illiterate as ever.

He turned and spoke in Clara's ear, as the approaching thunder shook the copse.

'We can't have you going into the house looking like this. Come on, I'll take you to Jarrold's cottage. You can clean up there.'

Clara clung to him as they left the clearing. The front of her dress was soaked and stained with rainwater, blood, semen and lumps of freshly vomited treacle-pie.

'You can't leave me like this!' Davey shouted after them. 'Simon! Come back!'

They disappeared into the wood. David rocked himself backwards and forwards, the rain flattening the hair against his scalp.

There sat a child, I supposed, much in need of a god-father. Sighing, I took a handkerchief from my pocket and stood up. He watched my approach silently, quivering like a snared rabbit. His breath caught the upper register of his vocal cords as he inhaled with huge gasps.

'You saw?' he managed to say.

'Don't talk,' I said. 'Not a bloody word. Can you stand?'

He took my arm and struggled upwards, wincing like the very dickens. Poor fucker.

Eight

When Gordon Fell was knighted in 1987 he threw a celebration binge afterwards at the Savoy. Not the Dominion Club of course, as it should have been, but the Savoy. Well, no matter. During the party he described to us the ceremony at Buckingham Palace. Gordie hadn't been the only man there that morning to be knighted, naturally. The Queen contrives to process dozens of candidates in one hit. They are disposed, it would seem, in rows of chairs, as at a lecture, while a band of the Guards plays anus-contractingly inappropriate tunes like 'A Spoonful of Sugar' and 'Chitty Chitty Bang Bang' in the background. Gordon was due to kneel and be dubbed next in line after the self-important fool sitting beside him. This pompous little pip-squeak had wriggled his way into the chairmanship of some large charity or another and was now coming to collect what he regarded as his due reward.

The figure had introduced himself with pride and whispered, after Gordon had told him his name, 'And what do you do, then? The diplomatic, is it?'

'I'm a painter,' Gordie said.

'Really?' said the fellow. 'Not one of those awful moderns, I hope.'

'Oh no,' said Gordon. 'Of course I'm not a modern painter. I was born in the sixteenth fucking century, wasn't I? I'm an Old Master, me.'

Not quite Buck House language perhaps, but justifiable under the circumstances. The chap turned his shoulder on Gordie, disgusted that he could be sharing an honour with such an animal. Gordon pointedly scratched his groin and yawned.

Anyway, the turn came for the charity weasel to kneel and be serviced. It so fell out that his investiture into the Knights Commander of the Crawling Toads, or whatever order it was that he was in line for, took place unaccompanied by melody, the band being engaged in taking the sheet music of 'Consider Yourself' off their stands and replacing it with 'Born Free'. Her Maj's sword tapped the man's shoulders in hushed silence and he rose to an upright position with becoming dignity, bowing his head with a crisp snap that would have shamed an equerry. As he did so his nervous, uptight and excitable system delivered itself of an astoundingly sustained and quite startlingly loud fart. The monarch stepped backwards, which was all part of the programme as it happened, but which seemed to everyone present to be an involuntary reaction to the man's violent rip. The expression on his face as he trailed miserably down the aisle was one of deepest woe. Every person in the room stared at him or, worse, waited until he was level with them and then averted their eyes. Gordon, passing him in the aisle as he made his own way to the steps of the throne, murmured in a growl audible to all, 'Don't worry, old boy. She'll be used to it. Keeps plenty of dogs and horses, don't forget.'

The lips of the Queen, according to Gordie, were seen to curve into a smile at this and she detained him in conversation for longer than anyone else. When he returned to his seat next to the still-scarlet farter, Sir

Gordon rasped out, in time with the band which was now operative again, 'Bo-orn free, a-free as the WIND BLOWS.'

Being the vindictive sod he is, Gordie didn't stop there, naturally. In the mêlée of press that gathered outside the palace and especially around him, he was asked how the occasion had gone.

'That man over there,' Gordon said, pointing at the chap, who was standing with his wife and only a photographer from a local Hampshire newspaper to bolster his self-esteem, 'let out the most extraordinary fart, virtually in the sovereign's face. Quite astonishing. Some kind of anarchist, I suppose.'

The pack flew to the spot like flies to a cow-pat and the pathetic creature was last seen streaking down the Mall, his silk topper bouncing on the pavement behind him. He lost his hat, his reputation and in all probability his wife in one Gordon Fell swoop. Never insult a painter. Not worth it.

I had always reckoned that this man's experiences counted as the most embarrassing a human being could undergo. I had not known, however, what God had in store for me that stormy Norfolk afternoon.

I walked a wincing David to the edge of the west drive as the rain streamed down upon us. Slow progress: he was bent forward, the handkerchief pressed to his groin, and capable only of shuffling geriatric steps. We got there in the end and I told him to shelter under a tree until I returned. Back at the house the first person I bumped into was Rebecca.

'Ted, for heaven's sake!' she hooted. 'You look as if you've just emerged from a swamp.'

'Don't have time to talk, Rebecca,' I said. 'Can you save a life and lend me your car?'

'Why?'

'I'll explain later. Bloody urgent. Please.'

She shrugged. 'Help yourself, darling. It's round the back.'

'Bless you. And, Rebecca? Another boon. Simon will be returning to the house in the next half-hour or so. I wonder if you could give him this note?'

I grabbed a sheet of house writing-paper, scribbled a message for Simon and sealed it in an envelope.

'Dark, dark mysteries,' said Rebecca.

'Terribly important, old carrot. You won't forget? Promise?'

She promised.

'And the car-keys?'

'Under the visor.'

I hadn't driven since the army, and even then sparingly. In those days you passed your test by going to the adjutant and signing a piece of paper which entitled you to command any vehicle from a motor-bicycle to a three-ton lorry. I didn't doubt I would manage, however. When I considered the number of dickwits who seemed capable of perfectly competent driving, Simon for example, I couldn't believe that it would be beyond me.

Rebecca's Mercedes was under cover in the garage behind the stable yard, a convertible with the blasted roof down. Electric roof at that. After fiddling hopelessly with the ignition key for five minutes – fucking thing wouldn't even *turn* – I hared off to find Tubby. He got the car started and roof up, quick as pigshit.

I contrived, with great discomfort, to fit my belly under the steering-wheel only to encounter my first problem.

'The fucking thing's only got two pedals!' I yelled.

'That's automatic,' said Tubby.

He wasted ten valuable minutes in painstakingly explaining the workings and I edged out of the garage and headed for the west drive as fast as I could. I reached it without actual collision on the way, but it was a near thing, the edge of the park being liberally furnished with stone Portland vases and quaint rustic benches. I could barely see: the rain was still coursing down and I hadn't the faintest idea where the windscreen-wiper switch could possibly be hidden.

I slewed to a halt at the end of the drive, churning up mud as the car skidded on to the grass of the park itself.

Davey was lying under a cedar, motionless.

Fuck, I thought. He's been struck by lightning. Should never have told him to shelter under a tree.

It was not as bad as that. He had fainted, but not, I decided, from loss of blood. The handkerchief was stained, but not swamped. I bent down and tried to lift him. Not a heavy boy, but too much for me. Matters would not be helped by discs slipping and joints locking up.

'Davey!' I called in his ear. 'Wake up. Wake up, Davey, wake up.'

His eyes flickered open and he stared at me.

'Come on, boy. You've got to try and stand. I've got us a car and we're going to a hospital. Get you put right.'

He tried to get to his feet too quickly, as though there had been nothing wrong with him. The pain caught up with him sharply and he fell against me with a whimper. From that half-standing position I was able at least to drag him to the car and push, lever and pack him into the passenger seat.

'Oh, Uncle Ted,' he kept saying. 'Uncle Ted, Uncle Ted.'

'Sh! I've got to concentrate on this fucking car.'

'On the string common,' he woozed like a drunkard.

'What?'

'On the ... steering ... column. The windscreen-wipers. There.'

The wipers helped, but it was still a nightmare drive. The road threw up the most tremendous mist of water and some deep memory inside me kept prompting my left foot to attempt a clutch manoeuvre when I wanted to slow down. The only pedal for it to meet was the brake, on which it would stamp with great force, causing us to aqua-plane on the spray to the hooting terror of the traffic.

David seemed to be amused by my oaths and grunts and remained alert enough to direct me to the Norfolk and Norwich Hospital.

It was only as we slid to a stop outside the doors of the casualty entrance that a true realisation of the fraught nature of this call impressed itself upon me. Michael would expect me to manage this without involving him or his family in any publicity. I turned to David.

'Whatever I say by way of explanation, Davey, you must remember and repeat. Do you understand?'

He looked at me dumbly.

'What?'

'I will explain who you are and how you came by this accident. You will not diverge from my explanation by one syllable. Do you understand? We don't want Clara dragged into this. Nor your parents if we can help it.'

'What are you going to say?'

'I don't fucking know yet, love, do I? Oh, now what?'

A knuckle was being rapped against the glass on my side of the car by a man in a bright-yellow plastic waistcoat. Unable to find a way to wind down the window, I opened the door, pushing the man off balance and into a puddle. I heaved myself out of the car and went to his aid.

'I'm terribly sorry . . . terribly sorry. Oh dear, oh God. You're all wet.'

'You can't park here,' he said, ignoring this frippery incidental. 'Ambulances only.'

'This is an emergency,' I said. 'Besides, I don't know how to park. If I left the car here, you wouldn't be kind enough to put it somewhere for me, would you?'

'I *beg* your pardon?'

I went around the bonnet and helped Davey out of the car.

' 'Ere!' the fellow shouted. 'I'm not going to . . .' He caught sight of the crimson hankie pressed to the fork of David's jeans and the words of recrimination died on his lips. 'You'd best hurry in,' he said. 'The car'll be round the back. You can pick the keys up from my booth.'

One is always hearing a great deal of liberal waffle about the terrible state of the National Health Service. Waiting lists, cuts, low morale: you can't help but soak up the thrust of the moronic yapping we have to put up with every day from the professionally disenchanted and humour-lessly self-righteous wankers of the left. Even a sceptical old reactionary like me is, willy-nilly, influenced by this kind of talk into imagining that all NHS institutions are crowded with desperately sick patients lying about in the corridors on straw palliasses waiting for the health authority's one overworked, under-rested teenage doctor to come and tell them to pull themselves together.

Not a bit of it. Not a bloody bit of it. It may be that the Norfolk and Norwich Hospital is an exception – East Anglia, it must be admitted, cannot be described as an area of massive inner-city tension; one supposes the average medical emergency involves bumpkins bitten by coypus or tourists overdosed on flapjacks and churches. I expected, none the less, to find at least a measure of squalor and overworked hysteria. But when Davey and I walked in through the automatic electrically operated doors and reported to the reception desk I felt less like a soldier dragging his wounded comrade into the filthy Crimean field-hospital of popular left-wing imagination and more like Richard Burton checking in to a five-star hotel in Gstaad with a tipsy Elizabeth Taylor on his arm.

'Oh dear oh dear,' clucked the little granny behind the desk. 'Someone's been in the wars, haven't they?'

'This young fellow has met with an accident,' I said with a hearty wink. 'Usual thing, you know. Caught the old man in his zipper, poor sod.'

'Whoops!' she said. 'I'd better have your names then.'

'Ah, Edward Lennox.'

Davey's eyebrows rose.

'And your son's name?'

'David,' I said. 'His name is David.'

'Do you have David's National Insurance card with you, by any chance?'

'Oh lor, came straight out without thinking of it, I'm afraid.'

'That's all right, dear. You can fill in a form later. Meanwhile, if you wouldn't mind taking a seat, a doctor will be out to see you as soon as possible.'

'Got that?' I hissed to David as we sat down. 'David Lennox. Accident while peeing.'

He nodded. He was very pale, his hair was still damp and his lower lip oozed blood from where he had been gnawing at it in pain.

He sat there not speaking, just staring blankly at the clock on the wall.

'You'll be fine,' I said, interpreting his silence as fear. 'They'll know what to do. Probably happens every day.'

'The thing is . . .' said David.

'Yes?'

'These jeans. They are 501's.'

'501's? I don't understand.'

A nurse was walking towards us, radiating welcome, confidence and disinfectant.

'David Lennox?'

'The thing about 501's,' whispered David urgently into my ear as he stood, 'is that they have a button-fly, not a zip.'

He was led away and I sat there punching my thigh with an angry fist.

Bloody American fashion. Fuck it. Fuck them all. *Button-fly?* Who ever heard of such a thing? Button-flies were for demob suits and old wedding trousers. *Button-fly?* Buggering fuckety-cunt, this was going to be just wonderful. Button-fly. Absurd.

After twenty minutes of this lonely fury, a tall white-coated woman with steel-grey hair gathered in a vicious bun strode towards me, a dangerous light in her cold blue eyes.

'Mr Lennox?'

'Yup, that's me.'

'Dr Fraser. I wonder if I might have a word with you?'

'Yes, yes. Absolutely. Absolutely. How's Davey doing?'

'This way, please. I have a small office.'

I followed obediently, beguiling the time on our short walk by making amusing observations on the weather and the state of the traffic, just like a real grown-up daddy.

Dr Fraser – Margaret Fraser if the identity tag attached to her coat was to be believed – closed the door of the office behind her and pointed to a seat.

'Mr Lennox,' she said as I sat down, 'I wonder if you would be good enough to tell me the nature of your relationship with David?'

'Well,' I said breezily, 'some days good, some days bad. You know what adolescents are like.'

'That's not quite what I mean, Mr Lennox,' she said, going round to sit behind the desk. 'You are the boy's father, is that correct?'

'For my sins.'

'Perhaps you can explain, then,' she unclipped a biro from her breast pocket, 'why David should say to me: "The pain got worse in the car, partly because Uncle Ted is such a terrible driver." Those were his words, Mr Lennox. "Uncle Ted".'

'Really?'

'Really. Now why should a son call his father "Uncle", I wonder?'

'Well, I *say* "father", but I mean *god*father, obviously.'

'Godfather?'

'Godfather,' my voice sounded dry and reedily inadequate, 'you know, which is *like* a father, isn't it?'

678

'You are not related to David?'

'Not really.'

'Not really. I see.'

As if making out a prescription, she took a small white notepad from a drawer in the desk and started to write on it.

'Why,' she asked as she wrote, 'obviously?'

'I'm sorry?'

'You just told me that when you said father you meant godfather, "obviously". Why obviously?'

'Well . . .' I began to feel a great need for a Rothie, 'I suppose it isn't that obvious, now you come to mention it. You being outside the family, nothing would seem obvious to you, would it? I mean, other people's lives . . . mystery. Blank mystery. Wouldn't you say?'

'But *you're* outside the family too, it would seem.'

'Ah well . . . yes. In that sense. Mm.'

'David's injury, according to the papers from the front desk, was sustained when he caught his penis in a zipper.'

Penis, what a ghastly word. Not right from a tall woman with chilly eyes and solid breasts.

'Yes, zipper, that's right.'

'Although the jeans he is wearing . . .'

'Have a button-fly. Yes, well, obviously he changed out of the original trousers.'

'Obviously again?'

'Well, there he is, you know. Having a pee, catches the pecker. *I* didn't know what to do. So I rushed and got another pair of trousers for him and then . . .'

'You were present when he was urinating?'

'No, well, obvi . . . *naturally*, he called out, didn't he? I rushed up . . .'

'*Up?*'

'To the bathroom . . .'

'All this took place in a bathroom?'

'Yes! In a bathroom. What did you expect, a bakery? A hair-dressing salon?'

She wrote down a few words.

Her silence and patience were excessively irritating. I moved a hand to the pocket of my jacket.

'I hope you aren't thinking of smoking, Mr Lennox?' she said without looking up. 'This is a hospital.'

I sighed. She spoke again, still writing.

'Why are David's clothes so soaked, I wonder?'

'It's been raining, Dr Fraser. It's been raining for most of the afternoon. Or hadn't you noticed?'

'Yes, Mr Lennox. I had noticed. Such weather causes us to be very busy with serious accidents, Mr Lennox.' I was beginning to hate the way she kept repeating the name. 'But to return to your story. As I understand it, David's little misadventure took place in a bathroom? I can understand, at a stretch, why he might change trousers after his accident, but why he should then stand outside in the rain . . .'

'I had to get the car out, didn't I? Look, why all these questions? Surely this kind of thing must happen often enough . . .'

'I am happy to be able to tell you, Mr Lennox, that it is in fact pleasantly rare for a child to be admitted to this hospital with human bite-marks to the penis.'

'Ah.'

'Yes. It is even more rare for a busy casualty surgeon to be obliged to listen to stories of bathrooms, urination, zippers and changed trousers when it is plain to the meanest intelligence that the mud-, semen- and blood-stained jeans and hysterical state of the boy in question tell quite another story.'

'Ah,' I said, 'well . . .'

'What makes this case rarer still is the fact that the child has been brought into casualty by a man I immediately recognised as the poet E. L. Wallace, but who gives his name as plain Edward Lennox.'

'Well, for goodness' sake, if you knew who I was in the first place . . .'

'This E. L. Wallace claims to be the boy's father,' she went on, 'and when this is exposed as a complete fabrication, he asks me to believe that it was "obvious" that he meant he was really only the godfather.'

'Which I am.'

'I think, Mr Wallace,' she said, resting her chin on her hands, 'that you should tell me the name of the child's real parents now, don't you?'

I ignored this question. 'I'd like to speak to Davey, please.'

'I am sure that the police, when I ring them, would disapprove of my allowing you to do any such thing.'

'The police? Have you run mad? What on earth have the police got to do with anything?'

'Please don't shout, Mr Wallace.'

'I'm sorry, but look . . .' I leaned forward and lowered my voice. 'All right. Let's talk as grown-ups and mature people of the world now, shall we? I confess that the story about the zip was a little bit of a white lie. But surely, just because a pair of lovers suffer an unfortunate mishap . . .'

'David is fifteen years old, Mr Wallace. I have no doubt that in the Bohemian world that you inhabit . . .'

'Yes, yes, yes. Never mind about your rancid second-hand ideas of Bohemia. The young must be allowed to experiment surely? I mean . . .'

'I have a boy of David's age myself, Mr Wallace!'

'Well, if it comes to that, Dr Fraser, so do I.'

She looked at me aghast. 'You do?'

'Certainly. And if the same thing happened to him, do you think I would kick up a great stink about it? Of course not. Make a fuss and the whole thing gets blown up out of proportion. You know what the young are like. Guilt, resentment, anger, aggression. No, no. The last thing in the world you should do is make some big deal out of it. That's not Bohemianism, that's plain common sense. I absolutely forbid the involvement of the police. And leave the parents out of it too, that's my advice. I'll see him now, if I may.'

She stared at me with round eyes, the notepad forgotten.

'Well!' she said finally. 'I must say for sheer bloody nerve you take first prize, Mr Wallace. This is what is meant by "poetic licence", is it?'

'Oh, for hell's sake!' I had frankly had it with this stiff-bosomed prude. 'You're a doctor, not a damned social worker. Don't you have some oath that forbids you from gossiping about the private lives of your patients? I mean, Jesus, woman, what is it with this country? Why do bossy creatures like you insist on sticking your inquisitive noses into other people's affairs all the time? Just stitch the boy's prick up, give him some pills and send him on his way. What the hell business is it of yours how he got his injuries and with whom? Just leave us alone, will you?'

'It may interest you to know, Mr Wallace, that I am a magistrate. A Justice of the Peace.'

'And a member of Calvinists Against Cocksucking and Housewives Against Fellatio, no doubt. What you do in your private life is a matter of complete indifference to me. And what a young boy does in his should be of equal unimportance to you. You're a doctor, your job is to heal, not to preach.'

She gave me another hostile glare and reached out her hand for the telephone. 'If I don't have the name and address of David's parents this minute, Mr Wallace, I shall call the police.'

I sighed. 'Oh, very well. Very well. And I suppose you want the name of the parents of the girl too, so you can fuck up two families at once, is that it?'

'Girl? What girl?' She stared at me in astonishment.

'What girl, what girl? What do you mean "what girl"? Did you think he was being sucked off by a giraffe, for God's sake?'

'No, Mr Wallace. I assumed that *you* were the other party.'

It was my turn to give the look of pop-eyed amazement.

'WHAT? You thought *what*?'

'Please, Mr Wallace, lower your voice.'

'You thought *I* . . .'

I've spent a lifetime having people of Dr Fraser's stamp throw words like 'Bohemian' at me, but I truly believe that if I have a fault it's that I'm not as dirty-minded as most. They call me a cynic and sceptic too, but that's because when I see a thing I call it what it is, not what I want it to be. If you spend your life on a moral hill-top, you see nothing but the mud below. If, like me, you live in the mud itself, you get a damned good view of clear blue sky and clean green hills above. There's none so evil-minded as those with a moral mission, and none so pure in heart as the depraved. All the same, it was probably stupid of me not to have seen what she had been driving at.

'If there has been a mistake, Mr Wallace,' she was saying, 'I assure you I am very sorry, but you must see that it is my duty to establish the facts in cases like these. The parents are . . . ?'

'When I tell you,' I said, 'you will understand why I am worried about any police involvement and subsequent publicity. The boy's parents . . .' I paused dramatically, '. . . are Michael and Anne Logan.'

Her mouth dropped open.

I nodded heavily. 'Precisely.'

'Do you know, Mr Wallace,' she said, 'I thought David looked familiar from the first. I've met him. Lady Anne and I serve on the same bench.'

'Is that right?' Big bloody surprise. I could picture her sentencing poachers and flashers to death with relish. 'Well, it so happens that there is a young girl staying at Swafford at the moment, Clara Clifford. She is the daughter of Max Clifford, whom perhaps you also know?'

'I know *of* him of course . . . I didn't know he had a daughter.'

'She's fourteen. Now, to cut a long story short, I was walking in the woods at Swafford this afternoon and I heard a scream. When I got there I discovered that youthful eagerness and inexperience had brought Davey to the pass you have witnessed. Unfortunate and embarrassing, but hardly a matter for the police.'

She gave me another long look.

'And you really are David's godfather?'

I raised my right hand. 'Poet's honour.'

She smiled and for the first time I saw the ghost of something attractive and even erotic lying behind her skeweringly blue eyes.

'If you like,' I offered, 'you can take an impression of my bite-mark. Isn't that usual forensic practice?'

'I think what I'll do,' she said, rising to her feet, 'is go and have another word with David. Would you mind staying here for a moment?'

'No, no. I can read your letters.'

'Nothing very interesting there,' she said with a laugh. 'You will find an ashtray in the middle drawer however.'

I composed a little present for her in the notepad.

> *There's a beautiful doctor called Fraser*
> *With a glance like a surgical laser;*
> *If you're guilty of sin*
> *She'll stare at your chin*
> *And save you the price of a razor*

Underneath I wrote, 'Limericks are the best I can come up with these days. I'm only sorry there are no good rhymes for "Margaret" . . . with love, Ted Wallace.'

Under that thick ice, I thought, lay the perfectly preserved remains of a passionate heart. I believed I knew exactly the kind of sounds she would make at the moment of orgasm. Something between a creaking gate and a pouncing jaguar. Humby-ho. I would never get a chance to prove myself right.

Davey stood a little sheepishly by the reception desk while she took charge of his paperwork. A thoughtful nurse, or perhaps Dr Margaret herself, had given him a handful of glossy magazines to hold in front of his groin. Behind them protruded a thick white bandage.

'I've used sutures,' she told me. 'They will dissolve in one or two days.'

'No permanent damage?'

'He'll find it a little painful to pass water for a while and even more painful to . . .'

'Quite.'

'Otherwise he'll be fine. I'm sure he's a good healer.'

'You speak truer than you know,' I said, to a thunderous look from David.

'I've also given him a tetanus booster and some anti-biotics.'

'And he can redress the bandage himself after each piddle, can he?'

'Oh, he'll have no trouble, will you, Davey?' she said, laying a hand on his shoulder.

'I'll be okay,' he mumbled, writhing like a pint of live bait at the embarrassment of being talked about over his head as though he were a five-year-old.

The journey out of Norwich passed in silence. I was too pre-occupied with avoiding bollards and lorries to talk and David had his own thoughts to contend with. Once we had cleared the city boundary and settled ourselves behind a pleasantly slow-moving van, I felt relaxed enough to speak.

'Fortunately,' I said, 'that doctor is a friend of your mother's.'

'She said. Will she tell Mummy anything?'

'No,' I said. 'I don't think so.'

'I might,' said Davey, greatly to my surprise.

'Well, if you think that would be a good idea.'

He shifted uncomfortably in his seat. 'She has to know what Simon did. It was wicked. It was evil.'

'Now, hang on.' I took my eyes off the road for a second to look at him. 'What would you expect Simon to do? I mean he comes upon a scene like that . . .'

'He knew. He knew perfectly well what was happening. He knew and he was jealous. He wanted to humiliate me and destroy me. He's always been jealous, you see. He's like the brother in the parable of the Prodigal Son. He can't bear being ordinary and he can't bear Mummy and Daddy thinking I'm different and special.'

'And that's what you are, is it? Different and special?' It still stuck in my craw to repeat that ghastly word.

'You know I am, Ted.'

'At the risk of sounding obvious, isn't everyone?'

'Well, that's true as well. I don't actually believe that what I do is anything so extraordinary. I think anyone could have my power if they really wanted it.'

'Even me?'

'Especially you! You've already had that power, when you were a poet. You wrote "Where the River Ends", didn't you?'

'I've always thought my power as a poet came from studying form and metre and, of course, the poems of others, not from tapping some mystical source. And,' I thought it was about time to give it to him straight, 'I hate to disappoint you, but "Where the River Ends" is not about the purity of nature and its contamination by man.'

'Yes, it is. It's about pollution.'

'It's about the fact that the poetry of Lawrence Ferlinghetti and Gregory Corso was included on the school syllabus.'

'What?' He stared at me as if I had gone mad.

'Poems are inspired by real things, real shitty, concrete things. I was making a bitter joke about how the pure well-springs of poesy were being fouled by people I thought of as inadequate and talentless nobodies. I deliberately used the tired old metaphor of rivers running to the sea just to satisfy my desire to describe those poor harmless American poets as floating turds.'

'Well,' said Davey, shifting again, 'I don't see what difference that makes. Your poem still has my meaning, doesn't it? The river starts as pure and then, as it goes through each town and through the city and to the sea, it becomes darker and dirtier and more disgusting. Your poem still says that. I don't suppose anyone who reads it knows about those poets. It *is* about purity.'

'Yes, but the point is you can't start a poem by wanting to write about some capital-letter idea like Purity or Love or Beauty. A poem is made of real words and real things. You start with the base physical world and your own base physical self. If some meaning or beauty comes out of it, then that is, I suppose, the wonder and relief of art. You want gold, you have to go down a mine to hack it out of the ground, you have to sweat your guts out in a filthy forge to smelt it: it doesn't fall in gleaming sheets from the bar of heaven. You want poetry, first you have to muck in with humanity, you have to fight with paper and pencil for weeks and weeks until your head bleeds: verses aren't channelled into your head by angels or muses or sprites of nature. No, I don't see that my "gift", such as it ever was, has anything in common with yours at all, Davey.'

David chewed on this for a while. 'So what exactly are you saying?'

'I don't know, my old darling. That's the bugger of it. I don't know.'

A car behind me honked its horn and I noticed that I had slowed down to under thirty miles an hour. It occurred to me that with clever gadgetry you could easily chart the emotional state of a driver from his variations in speed and aggression at the wheel. I considered the idea of cars having sensors installed which would pick up driving inconsistencies and calculate their cause by reference to some electronic table compiled by a competent psychologist. The data selected from this table would then send signals to a display on the roof. 'Attention! The driver of this car has just had a terrible row with his wife.' 'This driver is besotted with his new mistress.' 'This driver is in a foul bate after being unable to find his spectacles this morning.' 'This driver is in an even, equable temper.' I was convinced, as that retired police commissioner used to say, that it would constitute a major contribution to road safety. The only flaw, I supposed, lay in the possibility that experienced drivers were more adept than me at driving consistently whatever their mood.

We caught up with the van ahead and I shook myself from this pointless reverie. This is the worst of driving, your thoughts get sucked into long tunnels, as into a sleep. You don't, as it were, breast the waves of thought, you are borne along by them and you end up drifting.

I glanced across at Davey. He was slumped in his seat in that slack-jawed, eye-glazed lolling stupor at which adolescents excel.

'Perhaps it would help,' I said, 'if you told me more about the exact nature of your powers. I think I have a goodish idea, but you can fill in the gaps.'

'All right.'

By the time the hedgerows had leapt up by the roadside and the gables of the hall were flashing behind the parkland trees, I believed myself to be more or less, as Max Clifford would say, 'up to speed', Lilac and all.

I dropped Davey off at the back of the house before re-stabling the car. He was to slip upstairs, unseen if he could help it, while I explained to the household that the poor angelic mite was all fagged out after a hard day's mending bumblebee wings, healing bruised buttercups, smiling sweetly at the raindrops and generally being David. Once he was safely between the sheets he could be visited without anyone being the wiser as to the local details of his injuries.

Simon was waiting for me in the garage yard. I stopped the car and pulled myself out, leaving the engine running.

'It's nearly seven,' he remarked, a hint of complaint in his voice. I had arranged in my note to him that we should RV here at half past five.

'Never mind about that,' I said. 'You manoeuvre this bastard thing into its hangar. My driving days are over.'

His enthusiasm for cars got the better of his grumpiness. He climbed in, nosed the Mercedes into the garage and switched off the motor. I stood in the yard waiting for him to come out. The rain had stopped and everything shone and dripped, fresh as a washed salad.

Simon remained in the gloom of the garage for an inexcusably long time.

'What are you doing in there?' I shouted into the darkness. 'Singing the bloody thing to sleep?'

He emerged two or three minutes later, edged round the car and closed the double doors of the garage.

'There was blood on the front passenger seat,' he said. 'I wiped it off.'

'Ah. Good man. Now, if it's seven, I had better go to my room and change.'

We walked back towards the house.

'I got your note, Uncle Ted. I haven't told a soul. I wouldn't of anyway.'

'Wouldn't *have*,' I muttered.

'Oh, sorry. I never get that right.'

'Well don't *apologise* for it, for God's sake.'

Simon had a quality that seemed to bring out the mental bully in me. All bullies become more and more irritated by their victim's acquiescence in being bullied, which inclines one to bully all the more.

'Are you cross with me?' Simon asked.

'I am excessively annoyed with myself, as it happens,' I said. 'Annoyed with myself for being irritable with you, annoyed with you for allowing me to be irritable with you, annoyed with myself for allowing myself to be annoyed, and most of all annoyed with myself for being stupid.'

There were too many 'annoyeds' and 'irritables' in that sentence for Simon to be able to decipher its meaning, so he changed the subject.

'Is Davey all right?'

'He'll live. I banished him to his bedroom. And what of Clara?'

'She'll be okay. I sent her to bed too.' He bent down to pull up a weed from under the cotoneaster that grew along the wall around the side of the house. 'I suppose Davey is furious with me?'

'He thinks you're jealous of his powers. He thinks you

deliberately chose your moment to crash through the woods and humiliate him. He thinks you are evil.'

Simon gaped. 'That's pathetic.'

'Well, perhaps. And what's your point of view? What do you think of Davey?'

He thought about this.

'He's my brother.'

'Yes, yes. But what do you think of him? What's it *like* to have him for a brother?'

'I can't really remember *not* having him as a brother. He can be a pain. I mean, let's face it, he is a bit weird. And he really pisses me off with all that bloody anti-blood-sports stuff. I mean, he claims to love nature so much, but surely he can see that we wouldn't have all these copses and spinneys if it weren't for the pheasants. Everything would be flat fields for thousands of square miles. The woodland doesn't just support game-birds, you know. There's wild flowers and wild mammals and insects that completely depend on shooting.'

'Of course, of course, of course.' I wasn't in the mood for a lecture on killing. 'I'm talking about the other side of Davey.'

'Look, here's Max,' said Simon and I received the impression that he was relieved to be spared the necessity of answering.

Max was standing outside the front door in a dark suit, looking up at the sky with benevolent approval, as if it were a junior management executive who had successfully cut back on their workforce without provoking a strike.

'Ted. Simon. Splendid,' he said as we approached. 'Rain's stopped. Glorious evening.'

'More on the way, actually,' said Simon.

'You seem very cheerful, Max,' I remarked.

'And you look like shit, old boy.' Which, I suppose, I did. My skin and scalp were scratched by brambles and my clothes were devastated by rain, sweat and mud.

'I'll go in now,' Simon said. 'See you at dinner.'

Max took my arm and walked me to the lawn. 'As a matter of fact, Tedward, I *am* cheerful.'

'Really?' I said, frigidly. I hated it when Max used Michael's name for me.

'I might as well tell you, if you hadn't already guessed, that I asked Davey to see what he could do about Clara.'

'Has she been ill?'

'Oh, come off it, Tedward, you know perfectly well what I'm talking about. Anyway, David did see her. Always found the boy an intolerable little prick, if you must know. Hated having to ask him a favour. So goody-goody. Nothing in this world less bearable than an anti-business snob. He'll spend his father's nasty money when the time comes, right enough, don't you worry. But, well . . . I can't deny his ability. I don't know what he did. It must have been very intense. Clara's absolutely knocked out by it.'

'And it's worked?' I stared at him. It had never crossed my mind that, after Simon's intervention, David's cure might actually have been effective. Aside from anything else, in crude physical terms, she had not appeared from my angle so much to have swallowed her medicine as to have spewed it down her front.

'I've just spent half an hour with her in her room.'

'You mean her teeth are straight and her eyes look in the same direction?'

'Well, no. Obviously he can't alter her appearance just like that. But *inside*, Tedward! I've never seen her so cheerful and so . . . confident. It's absolutely miraculous. We've sent that girl to psychiatrists and nuns and summer camps and God knows what. It's unbelievable.'

I agreed and nodded enthusiastically while he gibbered on.

'She wouldn't tell me how he did it, but I wouldn't care if he fed her eye of newt and ear of bat. The squint will correct itself soon, apparently, and the teeth too. And she's just so much . . . oh, you'll see. You'll see.'

'Fabulous,' I said. 'Bloody marvellous. But look, I must bath and change if I'm not going to be late for dinner. See you at the bin.'

Oliver was gliding up the stairs as I made the hallway.

'Well!' he said, turning at the sound of the front door. 'Another happy meeting of the Somme Re-enactment Society, I see.'

'Yes, most amusing. I got caught in the storm, if you must know.'

'I think the storm got caught in you, dear.'

I headed up the stairs towards him. 'By the way,' I said, 'has Jane been asking after me?'

'No, heart. There was a message to say she can't come till tomorrow.'

'Why not?'

'More tests. Doris Doctor just refuses to believe. They probably want to exhibit her at the Royal College of Surgeons. Shall we bustle? We mustn't be late for din-dins.'

I wallowed in my bath, gazing at the sky and clouds painted on the ceiling, a tumbler of the ten-year-old clutched in my fist. I wished I could wash myself clean of everything. I wished Jane were here. I wished I was back in London. I wished I wasn't so old, so confused and so cross. At least there was whisky. A bottle, that's all I asked for, a full bottle of . . .

As I peered through the mist of steam at the angels looking down on me from their *trompe-l'œil* heaven, a small thought arose somewhere in my mind like a bubble of marsh gas. I dropped my whisky glass in surprise. Other thoughts began to pop to the surface, each lighting the other in a lightning path like will o' the wisp. Could it be possible, I wondered? Did these sudden zig-zags of light lead anywhere, or was the parallel of ignis fatuus appropriate and the whole burst of thoughts nothing more than a false trail into the swamp? Hum . . .

I reached out an arm for the telephone handily placed in an alcove by the bath.

Nine

Podmore's felt hammer gonged the conversation to an end. I replaced the receiver and hauled myself from the tub. Years ago I discovered, and you may find this useful, a trick which enables one to dress quickly after a bath. The problem with clothing oneself when not fully dry is that one's shirt and especially one's socks will frot and rub frictively against the skin. They won't slide easily on: a man can pull a shoulder muscle or crick a neck trying to wrestle with clothes in a damp post-balneal state. My discovery is that the use of a good old-fashioned bath-oil will solve this problem. It leaves the skin smooth and sleek as a seal's and sir's shirtings and half-hosements will practically leap from the floor and wrap themselves around him in a gladsome twinkling.

I was therefore able to glide serenely into my underlinen and stand before the mirror, patting my well-rounded tummy while I considered the little errands that had to be completed before dinner. Just two essential visits would . . .

I was distracted by the sound of moans and gasps floating through the wall from the Fuseli Room next door, where Oliver was billeted. I finished dressing, brushed my hair and came out into the corridor. Oliver emerged at the same time. He looked guiltily towards the door of his room.

'Ted, you double beast. Were you listening just now?'

'Listening? To what?'

'I'm afraid Mother was enjoying a quick one off the wrist. I'm a noisy lover when it comes to myself.'

'My dear old Oliver,' I said. 'When my life is so impoverished that I find I have nothing better to do than listen to an old man wanking, I will put a bullet in my head.'

I had been listening, however. A man does. I parted from Oliver at the top of the stairs.

'Just have to pop back and check something,' I said. 'Think I left a packet of Rothies in my room.'

I hurried back along the corridor and towards the passageway where the children slept. Having paid my respects to Clara, a fruitful conversation, I slipped down the stairs and out of the front door. I skimmed across the drive, panting like a dog on a hot day, crossed the front lawn, skirted the west drive and achieved the park from the side. After all, I didn't want to scramble up and down that bloody ha-ha again. The sky was thickening to charcoal as new storm clouds gathered, but the light, although mucky for a July evening, was perfectly good enough to see by. I picked my way carefully through isolated heaps of horse dung, confident that Tubby would have stabled the horses against the bad weather and that I would escape rape or trampling from a loose stallion. I found what I was looking for and bent down to get a closer look. Satisfied, I straightened myself with a grunt and returned to the house.

Only Max, Mary, Michael and Oliver were in the small drawing room when I arrived. Michael and Mary were sitting on a sofa in the corner, talking quietly while Oliver presided over the drinks tray.

Max was peering out of the window. It gave out in the

direction of the Villa Rotunda and the lake beyond, so I
knew he couldn't have seen me crossing the front lawn.

'Simon was right,' he told the room. 'More storms on
the way.'

'Ar, these country folk, they ben know,' Oliver croaked.

'That is the worst Norfolk accent I have ever heard,' I
said.

'Then you haven't heard real Norfolk people talking,
dear. Their accents are *much* less convincing than mine, I
can assure you. Pour you a whisky?'

'Larger the better,' I said.

I approached the sofa where Michael and Mary sat.

'But Michael, *everyone* should know,' she was saying.

'Mary, believe me, I'm delighted. Delighted. Let's leave
it at that.'

'But Michael, don't you feel that you have a duty? I
mean this gift is something remarkable, something that
must be *used*.'

I hovered behind the sofa, not wanting to interrupt.

'I don't know, Mary. I just don't know. You see Annie
doesn't like . . .'

'What doesn't Annie like?' said the woman herself from
the doorway. Acutest bloody hearing you could think of.

There was a fractional pause – too short for a court
of law to read anything into, but long enough to embarrass
Michael – before Oliver came to the rescue.

'Voddie dear, that's what you don't like. You're a gin
girl. Voddie makes you grumpy. So I'm pouring you a full
Jilly Gill of lovely Jenny Gin.'

'Thank you, Oliver.'

I caught Anne's eye, which was filled with a pleading
expression that I found hard to interpret. She gestured to

the far corner of the room, away from the others. I joined her there and we pretended to inspect an Oakshett acrylic portrait of the Logan family.

'I've just seen Davey,' she said in a low voice. 'What's wrong with him?'

'Ah,' I said. 'Bit knocked up, that's all. You might as well know that he . . . he had a session with Clara this afternoon.'

'Oh, no . . .'

'They got caught in the rain. Both fine. Just a bit tired. As a matter of fact, Max believes Clara is wonderfully improved.'

'She is?' Annie shook her head sorrowfully. 'Davey said something about a row with Simon, but he wouldn't tell me any more. What happened?'

'You might as well face it, Anne. No point fighting. That boy is a miracle worker. There can be no question about it. Don't you agree?'

She started to speak.

'Don't you agree?' I repeated slowly.

She looked at me and caught her breath.

'Oh, Ted!' she whispered. 'Oh, Ted, you wonderful man!' She tugged at my sleeve like a child. 'I *knew* I could rely on you. I *knew* it!'

'Rely on Ted?' Oliver's voice burst in on us. 'I find that hard to believe,' he said and presented Annie with her gin.

'Ted has been an angel and promised to take the twins ballooning at Brockdish tomorrow,' said Annie brightly. 'So sweet of him.'

'Balloonists at Brockdish? They sew up the end of a pair of Ted's drawers and then fill them with hot air, do they?'

'No, Oliver,' I said. 'They take a life-sized nylon replica

of your ego and ask you to talk into it on any subject.
That's how it's done.'

'Wit isn't quite your thing, my love,' said Oliver. 'Just a
little too cumbersome, you see.'

Rebecca, Patricia and Simon were the last to arrive,
Patricia giving me a secret little grin as she came in. She's
been considering my offer, I thought. How delightful.

II

'There should have been twelve of us to dinner tonight,' Annie announced as we filed into the dining room. 'But Jane hasn't come yet and Davey and Clara are having early nights. So we'll have to have Max, Oliver, Mary and Simon on that side and Rebecca, Ted and Patricia on this.'

'It's dark enough to be winter,' said Michael, closing the shutters.

'Cosy,' said Oliver.

'Gloomy,' said I.

The first course was a smoked goose-breast, and things were going well conversationally until Patricia asked whether Lilac was still healthy.

'She's fine,' said Simon. 'Perfectly all right.'

'The most wonderful thing,' Patricia said. 'I mean, that vet was so absolutely sure, wasn't he? Ragwort poisoning. I looked it up in the library. It's a chronic condition that causes irreversible liver damage. How *can* Lilac be all right?'

Simon mumbled something about vets being as capable of making mistakes as anyone else.

'We must face facts, Anne,' said Mary. 'I know you don't like talking about it, but something has got to be said, hasn't it? Apart from anything else, Max and I are just so *grateful* to Davey.'

Simon cut into a slice of goose-breast with a violent scrape of his plate.

'I'm very glad that you are happy,' Anne said. 'And I'm very glad Clara is happy.'

'And Oliver,' said Max. 'Oliver's happy, too.'

'Oh, yes,' said Oliver. 'I'm happy. I can eat disgusting food again and voddie up without fear.'

'And I'm happy,' said Rebecca. 'Happy about my daughter.'

'And you must be happy too, Anne, Michael? You must be happy about Edward,' said Patricia.

'And Simon must be happy about Lilac,' said Mary.

Simon nodded uncomfortably.

'It's so *silly* not to talk about it!' Mary went on, her eyes shining. 'As if it's a guilty secret, instead of a wonderful, wonderful miracle that has made everyone happy.'

I laid down my knife and fork with a clatter. Now. It might as well be now.

'Well, I'm sorry to piss on this parade,' I said. 'But I'm not fucking happy. I'm not fucking happy at all. In fact I'm as miserable as bloody sin.'

'Of course you are, you miserable old shit,' snapped Oliver. 'And you deserve to be, too. Christ almighty, what a piece of work you are.'

'Hold it, hold it!' Michael thumped his hand down on the table. 'What is going on here? This is a dinner table. Please!'

'I'm sorry, Michael. You're the host and whatever you say goes, but I think Edward Pissing Wallace has it coming to him.'

'Hear, hear,' said Rebecca on my left.

Oliver pointed a spoon at me. 'You still don't believe in Davey's power, do you, Ted?'

I looked across at Anne and shrugged my shoulders. 'If you must have it, then I'll tell you. No, I don't believe in Davey's powers.'

'You see! He just can't take it.' Oliver's voice was rising

in pitch. 'He is granted this one chance, as we all have been here, a chance which most people would never be permitted in a thousand lifetimes, he's granted this *one* chance to pull himself up by his boot-straps, this one chance to lever himself out of the swamp he's been stuck in for all these years, this one chance to raise his eyes upwards and see the beauty of things, and what's his reaction? "I'm not fucking happy. I'm miserable as bloody sin." Of course he's not happy. What we've experienced this last week is nothing less than a divine revelation. A divine fucking revelation and we can all see it, all of us can see it and celebrate it. We've got at least that little inch of humility that allows us to shout and weep with unreserved joy. All of us but bloody-minded, pig-headed, stone-blind, stone-deaf, Doubting Ted.'

There were tears in his eyes. I looked down at my plate in embarrassment.

'I'm sorry,' Oliver said. 'I'm sorry, Ted. But the fact is, I love you, you stupid turd. You're a friend that I love. We all love you. But you're such a . . . such a . . .'

'It's all right, Oliver,' said Rebecca, 'we all know what he is. It's just this, darling,' she said, turning to me, 'why won't you accept what you can see? Why would it hurt you so much just to face the truth?'

'What truth?' I asked.

'The truth,' said Oliver, 'that there is such a thing as the Operation of Grace.'

'The truth,' said Rebecca, 'that there really is something out there.'

'I'm not interested in what's out there,' I said. 'I'm interested in what's in here.' I thumped my chest.

'*Christ!*' Oliver banged down his fork. 'Why do you have

to say things like that? Why do you have to say things like that? This isn't a fucking sixth-form debate. There are no prizes for smart-arsed remarks here.'

'I must say,' said Max, 'it's a bit odd that a poet of all people should be the only one unconvinced by all this. What's happened to your sense of mystery, your imagination?'

'No,' I said, 'it's not odd at all. If I was interested in mysteries and the imagination, I would have become a physicist. I'm a poet because I'm very mundane. I'm only good with what I can taste and see and hear and smell and touch.'

'Oh here we fucking go again, Pamela Fucking Paradox . . .'

'It's not a paradox at all, Oliver.'

'So is that why you came here, then? Just to pour cold water all over us? Just to sneer up your snotty sleeve? If you can't take it seriously, why try and ruin our happiness?'

'Of course I take it seriously. I take it very seriously indeed. Jane is my god-daughter and Davey is my godson. Whether you believe it or not I am very serious about that. Very serious indeed.'

'Well then, why . . .' Rebecca began, but was interrupted by Anne.

'I'm pressing the bell for Podmore,' she said. 'I would rather we didn't say anything while he is in the room.'

We sat in stiff and strained silence while Podmore cleared away the plates and served up the main course. I drank down two big glasses of wine. I was hot and uncomfortable. Oliver, opposite me, alternately glared and shook his head in sympathy. I had been touched when he had said he loved me.

Michael was revolving the stem of his wineglass and frowning. He threw little puzzled glances at me from time to time. Simon was scarlet and deeply uncomfortable. Max, Mary, Rebecca and Patricia had formed a strong bond and twittered loudly about the weather and politics. Every silly assertion seemed deliberately aimed in my direction, as if daring me to challenge their united front. It was like being sent to Coventry at school.

At last Podmore departed.

'Seconds away,' said Oliver. 'Round Two.'

'Tedward,' Michael said, sawing at a roast potato. 'I don't understand. You are denying everything? Everything that I told you?'

'It's not a question of denying, Michael. I don't deny anything you said about your father, I don't deny anything you . . .'

'Woah, woah!' said Oliver. 'Just a Molly Moment. Michael's *father*?'

I looked towards Michael, who shrugged and nodded his assent. I told the story of Albert Bienenstock and his horses and Benko, his batman. Not news to Rebecca or Anne, obviously, but everyone else, even Simon, was amazed.

'Well, you see!' said Patricia, nudging me. 'It's inherited. Skipping a generation. The whole thing's inherited.'

'Oh, I don't doubt that,' I said. 'I'm sure of it, in fact.'

'Well what *do* you doubt, for God's sake?' demanded Oliver, thoroughly exasperated.

'Look,' I said, 'you might as well all know the reason I came here. I was asked.'

'Asked?'

'By Jane. I bumped into her in London a couple of

705

weeks ago. She told me . . . well, she didn't tell me very much in fact. She told me that her leukaemia had gone and that there had been some kind of miracle at Swafford last month while she had been staying here. That's all she told me. She wanted me to find out the rest for myself.'

'Which you have.'

'Which I have.'

'So what's the problem?' asked Michael.

'There's no problem,' I said. 'No problem at all.'

'But Davey?' said Oliver. 'What do you think about Davey?'

'Do you really want to know?'

'*Yes!*' Oliver screeched.

'Steady on, Oliver,' said Michael.

I could well appreciate the note of hysteria in Oliver's voice. I tried to sound as neutral and dispassionate as possible. I really had no idea how anyone would react to what I had to say.

'I think that Davey . . .'

The door opened.

'What is it, Podmore?' Annie asked in a tone of voice that, for her, was distinctly sharp.

'I beg your pardon, Lady Anne. There is a telephone call for Lord Logan in his study.'

The annoyance around the table was colossal. I was relieved. The diversion gave me a few minutes to collect my thoughts and arrange what I had to say in some kind of coherent order. If I'd had a piece of paper and a pencil I would probably have jotted down headings. Anal old Ted.

Michael stood up. 'Damn,' he said. 'I'm sorry. If it has come through on my study line it must be America and it must be urgent. I shall be as quick as I can. Please hang on for me, Ted. I want to hear everything that you've got to say.'

We passed a fraught three minutes in silence. I drank another glass of wine, to looks of recrimination from everyone.

Michael returned and closed the door behind him.

'I'm sorry about that,' he said, resuming his seat. 'Ted, go on, please.'

'What was I saying?'

'Oh, Lord save us, he's drunk now,' said Oliver. 'You were going, Teddy bear, to give us the benefit of your expert opinion of Davey.'

'That's right,' I said. 'Well, I think the key is this. David is a sensitive boy and a proud boy.'

Max laughed and the others joined in. Oliver snorted his contempt.

'That's it, is it? "David is a sensitive boy and a proud boy." End of analysis. I think you've said enough, dear. If anybody is proud and sensitive, it's Edward Wallace. Too proud and sensitive to believe what conflicts with his lumpish theories or to admit it when even he can see that he's wrong.'

'Leave it, Oliver!' said Michael in a tone fierce enough to make everyone jump. 'I want to hear what Ted has to say. Now more than ever I have to hear it. You'll find out why. For the time being, just be quiet.'

I stared at him in some puzzlement. He looked back at me with an expression of great intensity and – I believe I recognised it even then – of great fear. With the benefit of hindsight, it must certainly have been fear. At the time I couldn't understand the look at all.

'Well,' I said, slowly, 'as I say, David is proud and sensitive. He loves poetry and he loves what he thinks of as Nature with a capital "N". He is not quite as intelligent as he would like to be, but then which of us is? He is not unintelligent, you understand, he is intelligent enough to glimpse valuable and serious ideas and to be maddened that they are beyond his reach. Because so much that he prizes is out of his intellectual grasp he imagines he can leap at the truth of things by intuition or with the help of some deeper agency, some spirit of nature. He cannot believe that God could have granted him the sensitivity to respond to beauty and ideas without also giving him the mental equipment or artistic talent to participate actively in them. I don't think any of this is uncommon with a fifteen-year-old. It would be bizarre and horribly inappropriate if David was in fact as intelligent and precocious as he wanted to be. The intellect grows, like any other part of the mind or body. Davey is different from most children, however, because he is so extraordinarily sensitive. Some sensitive children just suffer in silence. But David is extraordinarily proud as well as extraordinarily sensitive. He hates his inadequacy. He cannot bear it. It has driven him to a miserable and dangerous hysteria. Some proud and sensitive children in similar situations fantasise that their parents are millionaires. Davey's father already is, so that would hardly be feasible. Some fantasise that they are foundlings, or aliens, or special agents, or capable of unsupported flight, or invisible, or possessed of supernatural powers. And that is what David has chosen. Supernatural powers. It wouldn't usually matter, because under normal circumstances everyone around such a child would tease or straight-talk its delusions away. But you have all fed them, which is absurd and irresponsible and, I believe, immensely dangerous. Davey's hysteria has grown and grown and overtaken the entire household.'

I took a giant swig from my glass of claret.

It was Oliver, naturally, who broke the silence. He stared at me with disbelief. 'How can you sit there and say all that? We know what we have seen.'

'No you don't,' I said. 'You haven't the faintest idea what you've seen. Believe me when I say this. David is possessed of no extraordinary powers whatsoever. There is nothing miraculous he has done or can do. He is a very, very, very ordinary child with a more than ordinary helping of, as I said, pride and sensitivity . . .'

There was a noise outside the door and we all straightened into silence again.

The door did not move.

'Come in!' shouted Michael.

Still no response. With a click of irritation, Michael strode to the door and opened it. The corridor was empty. Michael looked down it to right and left.

'Oh dear,' said Anne, 'do you think Podmore has been listening?'

'Probably just the wind,' said Michael, closing the door and returning to the table. 'There's another storm on the way.'

It was true that wind had begun to howl around the windows and down the flues.

'Carry on, Ted,' said Oliver, with a savage growl. 'I think you were saying that we are all very irresponsible and absurd and that Davey is a very, very, very ordinary child.'

'A very ordinary child who needs a great deal of kindness

709

and understanding if he is not to slide into hysterical chaos,' I said.

'But you're a mass of contradictions,' said Max. 'You've just admitted that Michael's father's powers could have been inherited and now you say that there aren't any powers.'

'I have said no such thing.'

'He is drunk,' said Patricia. 'If anyone needs kindness and understanding, it's *you*, Ted.'

'I need my share, certainly,' I said.

'We can all play armchair psychiatrists, can't we, Ted?' said Rebecca. 'We could, for instance, examine the mind of the ageing poet.'

'Quite,' said Oliver, 'the man who believes that spirituality is his province and his alone. The man who thinks that a glimpse of art and the infinite is only granted to hairy-arsed curmudgeons who drink hard liquor and understand Ezra Pound. The man who struggles so hard for his own poetry that he has developed a theory that denies the possibility of inspiration in others. "If I have to flounder in the mud sweating and straining, then it must be true that everyone else on earth has to as well." That's your grand "philosophy", isn't it? The sight of an innocent child given grace as a divine free gift just chokes you to death, doesn't it?'

'You may think I appear very graceless,' I said. 'But you must . . .'

'Graceless, darling? Why ever should we think that? Your own inspiration dried up years ago and you've lived on rotten credit ever since. As an ugly old fraud yourself, anything of any beauty or authenticity has to be mocked and rejected. Graceless? Lordy Lord, no.'

'Let's leave character out of it for the moment,' said Max, with boardroom crispness, 'and concentrate on facts. Do you deny, Ted, that Edward's life was saved?'

'No,' I said. 'I have to confess that I cannot deny that.'

'And Lilac?' said Oliver. 'And Jane? And me? And Clara? Can you deny us? Look at what's in front of your great fat nose, man!'

'All right, Oliver, calm down,' said Michael. 'Let's get this straight, Ted. Are you saying that my son has absolutely no powers whatsoever?'

'*No!*' I cried. 'No, I am *not* saying that! I think he is a remarkable and wonderful boy. I think he is, in his own way, a miracle. Not magical, but uncommon enough to be a miracle in this world. I think he has powers that are as rare as they are beautiful.'

'I'm going mad!' said Patricia clutching her hair. 'You said a moment ago, "David is possessed of no extraordinary powers whatsoever. He is a very, very, very ordinary child." Your exact words. And half a minute later . . .'

'I stand by every word I have spoken,' I said.

There was an almost unanimous shout of rage at this perversity. It was brought to a shocked silence by Anne.

'Oh be quiet, all of you!' she stormed. 'You just don't see, do you? You just don't see! You told Ted that he couldn't see the truth when it was right under his nose, but it's not Ted, it's you. It's all of you. Ted is absolutely right. Everything he has said is absolutely right and consistent and you just can't see it.'

'Annie! My love, I don't understand!' Michael stared across at his wife in bewilderment.

'I'm sorry, Michael,' I said. 'I've been playing games with you.'

'Games? You've been playing games?'

'Well, not games precisely. Just getting a bit of my own back perhaps. *Allowing* you to misunderstand. You asked me whether or not I thought your son had any powers whatsoever and I said that he did. I said that he was a remarkable and wonderful boy. What you don't understand, what only Annie understands, is that *I wasn't talking about Davey.*'

Still he couldn't see. None of them could see.

'Not talking about Davey?'

'No,' I said. 'I was talking about *Simon.*'

'What?' Oliver whipped round on Simon, who sat there, fork hovering in front of his face, and mouth open in consternation and alarm.

'Oh look . . .' he said. 'Come on, Uncle Ted . . . I mean . . .'

'I'm sorry, Simon,' I said, 'but the truth must be told.'

Anne leant forward and placed a hand on Simon's arm.

'Ted! Annie! Explain . . . please, tell me what's going on,' said Michael.

'You saw yourself how it all began two years ago, Michael,' I said. 'For the time being we'll call it the first miracle. You came into the room when Edward was lying suffocated and almost unconscious from asthma. Simon did what any sane human being would do. He pumped the boy's arms back and forth and tried to get the breathing started. He pummelled the ribs. A few seconds later, sentimental hysterical David elbows him out of the way, frightened by such violence and completely ignorant of the need for it. He has just laid a hand on his chest when you and

Annie walk in, at the very moment that the results of Simon's commendable first-aid became apparent and Edward is starting to cough and splutter. You see the hand laid on the chest and you instantly think of your father, who despite his own obvious good sense was very nearly bamboozled himself into thinking that he had done something extraordinary with his batman's sore foot. Some time later you tell Davey this story and the stupid boy, who had probably only laid his hand on the chest to feel for the boy's heart-beat or something equally useless, believes he has inherited a mystical power from his grandfather.'

'But . . . you can rationalise *anything* like that,' said Patricia. There was a hint of doubt in her voice, however.

'Rationalising a sunset doesn't make it any less beautiful,' I said. 'Nor is it designed to. Simon is thoughtful, practical, unsentimental and kind. He is also entirely without ego. It never occurred to him to take credit or demand thanks for what he did. Davey on the other hand . . . well, just think about it. Just consider the sequel. Michael and Annie decided that Davey's miraculous healing of Edward should remain a secret. Michael because he didn't want his son to be hounded or feared in the way Albert had been, Annie because she could see what Michael believed and how much it delighted his sense of separate family pride. She was also afraid that Michael might think she was in some way jealous of Davey's apparent gifts. Which, of course, is precisely what you *did* think, isn't it, Michael?'

Michael nodded.

'And the point is this. In spite of the pact of secrecy and silence, word of Davey's powers did get out. How? I'll tell you. Davey made damn sure word got out, that's how. I had it in a letter from Jane recently. "When Davey first told me how he had healed Edward," she wrote. It wasn't part of Davey's plan that his magical gifts should go unrecognised. Jane told Patricia and Rebecca, they told Max and Mary and Oliver. Davey announced his status as healer and miracle worker to the whole bloody world.'

'I think I'll go now, if I may, please,' Simon said, half-rising from the table. He had been listening to all this with acute dismay and unease.

'No, Simon . . . I beg of you,' Michael said. 'I beg you, stay.'

Simon dropped reluctantly back into his seat. Everyone was looking at him and he hated it.

'So you are saying that it is really *Simon* who has done all this healing?' said Patricia. 'He is the one who inherited his grandfather's gifts?'

'Certainly Simon has inherited Albert Bienenstock's powers,' I said.

'Simon. A healer . . .' said Michael shaking his head.

Simon himself sat there, simply squirming with embarrassment, poor lad.

'Michael, can't you see what I've been saying?' I said. 'Your grandfather wasn't a healer. His powers were the powers of calm good nature, amiability, decency, selflessness, courage, modesty and sense. Prosaic you may think, but what is poetry if not the compression of the prosaic? Such qualities as Albert Bienenstock possessed may have seemed as dull as coal, but taken all together, concentrated in one man, they refined themselves into a diamond. That is what Simon has inherited. Isn't that enough for you?'

It was *not* enough for them.

'I'm sorry to go on about this,' said Patricia, 'but you're

avoiding the obvious point, Ted. What about Jane and Lilac and Oliver and Clara?'

'Exactly,' said Oliver. 'If modesty and calm good nature can cure leukaemia and liver failure then I think the world should know about it, don't you?'

I poured myself another glass of wine. The stuff was going down me by the gallon and swishing in my belly. The wine, together with the unaccountable nervousness I was feeling and the adrenaline that was pumping around me, was starting to cause my guts to bubble and squelch with wind.

'Davey really believed that he could cure sickness,' I said, suppressing a wet fart. 'I think we can be sure of that. He concocted some weird fantasy about having to be pure in order to channel his mysterious power.'

'Pure?' asked Michael.

This was going to be extremely difficult.

'I suspect he had discovered somehow, perhaps with wounded animals, that he could not always effect a cure with a laying-on of hands. He developed a bizarre theory. Pure and natural were the keywords. What he meant by them, God knows. Nothing more coherent or convincing than what an advertising copy-writer means by them, I suppose. Davey decided that he had to be as pure and natural as an animal. Pure and natural as a ladybird, of course, not pure and natural as the ladybird's cousin, the dung-beetle. Pure and natural as a gazelle, not pure and natural as the hyenas that bite into the gazelle's eyeballs and feast on its intestines. His ideas of purity and natural-ness seem to have more in common with a Victorian hymn-book for children than any real understanding of the physical world. All things bright and beautiful and no things dark and foul. But at the same time Davey was undergoing puberty, don't forget, an event not covered by Victorian hymnbooks, an event as dark and foul as you could imagine. Davey happens to be a voraciously sensual child. Those of us around the table who are male can remember what our gonads and gametes were up to when we were fifteen, I'm sure. In my case they're still up to it, but without the up-springing violence of old. Davey was mortified to discover one morning that he had succumbed to a wet-dream. This presented him with a problem. Why had God and Nature packed his body with this nasty fluid? How could he remain a pure, pretty little buttercup while such a squirting horror dwelt within him? He reconciled it this way. Semen was a life-giving spirit, he knew that much. So long as he avoided the lustful outflow of this spirit, it would remain pure, would in fact be the purest, most potent essence imaginable. He decided that his semen . . . I hope you're ready for this, Annie . . . was the ideal channel for his healing. When his cousin Jane arrived for her stay at Swafford he was presented with the ideal test-case for this belief. He persuaded Jane that the laying-on of hands would not be enough and that he needed to impregnate her with his spirit. It's a technique many a leader of religious cults has found invaluable. In Davey's case, desire and appetite were submerged and I am sure he sincerely believed that his only motivation was to heal and to help.'

'Oh, Davey . . .' Annie whispered. She had been completely unaware of this feature of her son's mission and mission and I felt a bit of a pig letting her know so publicly.

'I'm sorry to have to tell you that it is highly probable he tried the same trick with Lilac,' I added.

Jaws hit plates and Oliver started to throw mental daggers at me.

'Only Oliver can tell you,' I said, feeling he deserved it, 'what technique was employed in his case.'

Heads swung towards him. Poor Oliver, not a good dissembler.

'Look,' he said, licking his lips. 'We all believed, didn't we? Some of us still do. Everything Ted has said has been bigoted and circumstantial. He hasn't disproved a thing.'

'You seduced my son?' said Michael.

'No, bugger it, he seduced me! He told me . . . Jesus, it sounds absurd if put like that . . . Look, if you have to have it described in language that Wallace would understand, then yes, Davey fucked me up the arse. And I'm better, aren't I? It was Davey, though. *Simon* hasn't done a thing for me. I've barely spoken to the oaf all week. It's Davey! Of course it's Davey. Why the hell are you listening to this fat sod? What about Jane and Lilac?'

Mary and Max exchanged horrified glances. They were thinking about Clara, poor dears.

'I can explain about Lilac,' I said. 'I'm afraid the whole episode was entirely my fault.'

'*Your* fault?' Michael frowned.

'Yes, it's the stupidest thing on earth. I telephoned the vet, Nigel Ogden, this evening. I asked him to confirm that Lilac really had been suffering from ragwort poisoning. He said it was the only condition that could explain the depression, the bleeding from the mouth, the aimless circling, the leaning against the wall, the abdominal pain, the loss of appetite, the diarrhoea, the raging thirst, everything.

But I had had an inspiration in my bath this evening, you see. Like Archimedes. I may not be a vet, but no one could deny that I am a drunkard. What if, I asked the vet, what if Lilac had been *drunk*? Really, really soused. Off her saddle and pissed out of her mane. Nigel thought about it for a bit and had to confess that he had never seen a horse drunk, but that he supposed the symptoms might be similar to those he witnessed. It would affect a horse badly, he imagined, since it is very difficult for them to vomit. It wouldn't explain the bleeding from the mouth, however. But I had an answer to that, too. I won't go into the reasons, but early in the morning on the second day of my stay here I dropped a full bottle of ten-year-old malt whisky into a bucket in the west park, where Lilac and her fellow four-footers have since been grazing.'

'You did *what*?' gasped Patricia.

'Yes, I know it sounds mad, but it seemed the right thing to do at the time. We can go into it later. The point is, this evening in the bath, the moment I remembered that incident, things clicked into place. I crept out before dinner to inspect this bucket. The bottle had cracked open and whisky had oozed out. There were blood marks on the cracked glass. Lilac, with irreproachable taste, must have discovered this unexpected treasure while out in the park the day before yesterday and licked and sucked and lapped at it happily for most of the afternoon. Barley can never have been presented to her in so pleasurable a form. She didn't get all of it, you'll be pleased to know, just enough to give her a good time and a really vicious hangover. It truly is as simple as that.'

They all stared at me in silence. Then Simon began to laugh.

'Drunk!' he said. 'So Lilac was drunk. Do you know I *thought* it couldn't be ragwort! Alec and I spent a whole day checking the field, because it does grow round here. You have to check, you know. It's no good using a weed-killer, because funnily enough they just make the plant more palatable to horses. Drunk!'

Oliver banged the table. 'All right!' he said, face whitened in anger. 'That might be true. *Might* be. But . . .'

'Clara,' interrupted Max heavily. 'What about Clara? Are you saying that boy dared to . . .'

I thought I would have to tread carefully here.

'You will be pleased to know that Davey did not attempt to do to Clara what he had done to Jane and Oliver and Lilac. He tried this afternoon to feed her some stuff to do with his spirit . . .' I thought that was near enough the truth to be acceptable, they could take the phrase as literally or metaphorically as they chose. 'But Simon prevented him. What you thought you were doing sending that poor girl to Davey I have no idea.'

'We wanted to do what was best,' said Mary helplessly. 'It seemed the right thing.'

'Look, far be it from me to lecture you both,' I said, 'but Clara is the most downtrodden young thing I have ever seen in my life. You make it abundantly plain to everyone that you are ashamed of her, you tick her off in public for her awkwardness, which naturally makes it ten times as bad, and you give her, it seems to me, absolutely no indication whatsoever that you love her or enjoy her company.'

'How dare you?' Max shouted across the table. 'How bloody dare you?'

'Oh be quiet, Max, he's right and you know it,' said

719

Mary. 'Of course he's right. Clara doesn't match up to your idea of the perfect accessory and it maddens you.'

Max thought about answering back, but the idea of a public row clearly didn't square with his self-image, so he shrugged his shoulders and relapsed into silence.

'Simon has worked a miracle on Clara this last week,' I said. 'He's had her helping in the stables, feeding the chicks, walking the puppies, swimming in the lake. He's given her confidence and he's shown her that he likes her for herself.'

'No, really, I haven't done anything . . .' Simon started to say.

'She was very shaken by her experience with David this afternoon,' I went on. 'She told me about it when I visited her in her bedroom just before dinner.'

'My, we have been busy this evening, haven't we?' said Oliver. 'Quite the . . .'

'What do you mean "her experience" exactly?' Mary interrupted.

'Well, as I say, Davey can be very intense in his manner. She was a little frightened by it all. As well as demeaned, I should imagine. You've sent her to doctors and shrinks and specialist summer-camps and religious retreats as though she were sicker and madder than a rabid dog. Now you instruct her to go into the woods with Davey to be healed like a leper. Simon happened to see them together and took Clara away. He told her that there was absolutely nothing wrong with her. He told her that he adored her exactly the way she was and that if she dared change a thing about herself he would never forgive her. She worships Simon of course and for the first time in her life she felt loved, simply and properly loved. I think, as far as she is concerned, that is a miracle.'

Mary looked across at Simon.

'Look . . .' he said. Big tears had started to roll down his face. 'Don't be . . . don't be angry with Davey. He never meant any harm. He was just trying to help. He's not bad or anything. He's just a bit confused, really.'

Annie stroked his arm.

Oliver was trembling now. 'What is the *matter* with everyone?' he cried. 'You haven't explained the most important fact of all. Jane. You can't, can you?'

I raised my shoulders apologetically. 'Remissions occur, Oliver,' I said.

'Remissions occur! Loaves of bread will sometimes turn into fishes. Dead men will sometimes walk. Pigs have been known to fly. Balls to "remissions occur".'

'I can tell you all about Jane,' said Michael in a voice so heavy that we all turned to him. 'Bex, I'm very sorry. That telephone call just now. Jane has died. At the hospital. In her sleep. I had to wait until I had heard what Ted was going to say.'

I stared into my wineglass. I suppose somewhere in the back of my mind I had guessed that there was something wrong. When I thought of the over-bright phrases that ended her last letter to me. 'Smile! We are loved. We are loved. Everything is going to be wonderful. Everything shines. Everything is as it could only be and must be.' Silly child.

'Let's go through,' said Anne. 'I don't think we want anything more to eat.'

We rose from the table in silence and processed to the

drawing room. Michael comforted Rebecca who sobbed into his shoulder and I put an arm around Patricia.

I felt curiously to blame, as though my breaking of Davey's spell had been the cause of Jane's death and the sudden misery in the household. We sat in a ring of sofas surrounding the large central ottoman, which we all gazed at glumly to spare us the hardship of meeting one another's eyes. With the wind whipping around the house and the rain batting the window panes, our huddled group resembled frightened cavemen staring into a fire.

'She had a relapse this morning,' Michael said at last. 'She thought it must be a mistake. Kept telling the doctors that she was fine and that she had to travel to Norfolk. She died at ten minutes to eight this evening.'

Ten to eight. Exactly the moment the memory of the whisky bottle in the bucket popped into my head. Oh, be quiet, Ted, I said to myself. Get a grip, man.

'And all the time,' said Michael. 'All the time, she thought she was well. Never said goodbye because she thought she was cured.'

'But *me*!' said Oliver, unable to suppress it for any longer. 'What about me? I'm cured, aren't I?'

'Oh, Oliver,' I said. 'Did you really throw those pills away?'

'I don't need them. I don't *need* any fucking pills. Can't you understand that?'

'Then why were you shouting in agony in your bedroom this evening?'

'I wasn't shouting in agony, I was . . .'

Poor old bugger.

'I was *groaning* in agony,' he said at last, with an attempt at dignity. 'There's a big difference.'

722

'I'll send someone out to Norwich to get some more pills,' said Michael.

'It's only angina,' Oliver said. 'If I stick enough vodka down me to deaden the pain, it can wait till morning.'

Annie slipped out of the room and Oliver looked up at me with reddened eyes.

'Why, Ted? Why did you have to spoil it all? It *could* have been true. Why couldn't you let it be true?'

'Oh, Oliver, I don't know. You're the priest, not me. Isn't it something to do with letting man get on with things on his own?'

'But it was such a beautiful idea. It gave us hope.'

'Don't imagine,' I said, 'that just because you can't be cured by the laying-on of hands or the injection of holy semen that life and the world are therefore hopeless. If you want to talk about the Operation of Grace, why not talk about Simon?'

'Oh, please . . .' Simon stood up. 'Uncle Ted, I'd much rather you stopped talking about me like that. Please.'

I waved a hand at him.

'I'm sorry, old darling. It's been very fraught for you. The more one ages, you will find, the less afraid of sentimental language one becomes. Didn't mean to embarrass you.'

'I have to walk Soda now,' he said backing out of the room.

'Good idea.'

He stopped in the doorway.

'Um, Aunt Rebecca. I'm very sorry about Jane. You have my . . . you know. Deepest . . .'

He turned to go but his path was blocked by Annie.

'Simon!' she said with alarm. 'Davey isn't in his room.'

723

III

Mary Clifford's first thought was for her daughter.

'What about Clara?' she wailed.

Fatuous woman. As though Davey might have kidnapped her or eloped to Gretna Green with the helpless creature lashed to his saddlebow and struggling to be free. I doubted he wanted to see her or her big buck teeth ever again in his life.

'Clara is in bed, fast asleep,' said Annie.

'Tedward,' said Michael. 'That noise we heard outside the dining-room door . . .'

The same unwelcome thought had crossed my mind. If David had been listening to my pompous and pitiless analysis of his disordered psyche, then the Lord alone knew how he would react. Such a clumsy arse I am, such a hopelessly clumsy arse.

'Oh hell,' I said. 'He can't have gone out on a night like this. He can't have done. Not in his condition.'

'Condition?' Annie grabbed my arm. 'What do you mean condition?'

'Look, there's no time to explain,' I said. 'Davey injured himself this afternoon. He's perfectly all right, but he should be in bed.'

'Dad, why don't you and Mum and Mary and Rebecca and Patricia search the house?' said Simon. 'I'll get Soda and the rest of us can take a look outside.'

Simon took Max and me through to the boot room where he issued us with wellington boots, waxed jackets and torches.

Armed with these, we trooped down into the kitchens

and out of the back door, past the astonished kitchen staff. I, as back marker, was the member of the party detained by Podmore.

'Is anything wrong, Mr Wallace?'

'Everything's fine, my old. We're going on a treasure hunt. Such fun.'

Out in the kitchen yard Simon shouted to us above the roar of the wind and the hissing of the rain.

'We'll go first to the kennels. Get Soda.'

Max and I nodded and followed him round the back of the house. Rainwater streamed down the back of my neck.

'Do you really think he might have run away?' Max asked me.

'No idea,' I answered. 'Christ, I hope not. But if he was listening at the door while I was talking about him, he might well feel unable to face us all.'

'And how exactly is he injured?'

'Well,' I said. 'Your daughter bit him.'

Max nodded. 'I see,' he said. 'Yes, I see. The stupid thing is, I never liked the little shit anyway. Always relieved that Simon was my godson, not him. Should have gone on instinct.'

'Not a little shit,' I said, fumbling for the hood of my Barbour. 'Hardly his fault everyone encouraged him to believe he was Jesus Christ, is it?'

We had arrived at the kennels. Soda lived apart from the beagles, who were baying and whimpering in the sheltered part of their accommodation. Max and I talked to them and told them that thunderstorms were a harmless lark, while Simon let Soda out and attached a long lead to her collar.

'She's got a super nose,' he said. 'Davey and I used to

play hide and seek with her. Manhunts and that kind of
thing. You know.'

He bent down and spoke to Soda in the rushed, excited
tones humans reserve for dogs. 'Seek Davey, Soda! Go on,
girl. Seek Davey! Seek Davey! Where's he gone, Soda?
Where's he gone?'

Soda jumped and barked with pleasure. Never occurred
to her to wonder what the fuck we were doing playing
games like this late at night in the middle of a thunder-
storm. Still, I suppose if you're a dog and are used to
watching humans zooming around at high speed in metal
boxes, staring at large sheets of paper at breakfast-time
and breathing in smoke from short white tubes, then
nothing the species does has the power to surprise you.

We followed Simon and Soda out of the kennel yard and
round the side of the house. Soda's nose bounced along
the ground, snorting and sniffing. Every now and again
she would dance off in a wide loop, following some false
scent, before returning to the main path.

'Nothing yet,' said Simon.

I looked up at the windows of the house and watched
the lights being switched on in rooms on every floor. The
indoor search party seemed to be having no luck either. I
wondered whether they would have the courage to ask the
servants for help.

We arrived at the front door and immediately Soda
began to snuffle around the steps, barking excitedly and
spinning about in frenzied circles.

'I think she's got something,' said Simon. 'Go on, girl!
Find Davey! Find Davey!'

Soda yapped twice and tore off towards the front lawn,
Simon holding on to the lead. Max sprinted after them,

anxious to show he could keep pace with a spaniel and a seventeen-year-old. I rolled along at a more leisurely jog and caught up with the trio at the end of the lawn. Max and Simon's torches were flashing back and forth, but it was light enough to see that of David there was absolutely no sign. Perhaps he had climbed over the ha-ha and into the park. That is where I had been earlier in the evening, peering at the bucket of whisky. The association gave me an idea.

'False alarm,' said Simon.

Soda was barking and circling furiously in the ditch of the ha-ha.

'Wait a moment,' I panted. 'I was here the other week. It was morning.'

'So?' said Max.

'Well, I followed a trail of foot-prints in the dew across the lawn and this is exactly where they ended. I couldn't understand it. That's the morning I went on into the park and dropped that whisky bottle. Thought I'd been going mad. Just a trail of foot-prints up to here and then nothing.'

Simon looked at the lawn and then down into the ditch where Soda still leapt frantically back and forth barking fit to bust. He slid down the ha-ha and shouted at Soda.

'Seek Davey! Go on, girl! Find him, find Davey!'

Soda kept up a stream of excitable yapping and began to scrabble with her paws against the bank. Simon watched for a moment and then took hold of Soda's collar and pulled her back.

'Look!' he shouted, pointing. 'Here!'

We were still on the lawn level, so Max lay on his stomach and looked down, tracing with the light of his torch a line in the turf that Simon was indicating, a line which formed three sides of a large square.

Simon grasped a handful of the grass and heaved. A heavy turf rectangle, about three feet by three, started to come away from the bank. It was uncut at the top edge, which formed a kind of hinge, but Simon wrenched until the whole piece worked free. Max and I, reaching down, helped take the weight of it and drop it into the ditch beside Simon.

As soon as the entrance was revealed, Soda tried to jump in, but Simon kept hold of her.

'Leave, Soda. Leave. Good girl, you're a good girl. Stay there.'

He shone his torch into the hole.

Max and I, lying on the grass above and peering down, could make out the doorway of a tunnel cut into the bank beneath us and see in the light of Simon's torch two bare feet in the mud.

'Is he all right?' I shouted down. 'How is he?'

Simon put his hands around the ankles and began to pull. 'I can't tell,' he said. 'I'll need a hand.'

Max and I dropped into the ditch to help. Max pointed with the torch as Simon and I heaved and more and more of Davey emerged. He had been lying lengthways and unclothed in a tunnel scarcely big enough to contain him. Air-holes, if he had bothered to construct any, would have been penetrated by the rainwater and blocked by wet earth. He cannot have lain there for more than an hour, I thought. None the less, the air would have become appallingly fetid and the soil would have dampened into mud.

I heard footsteps and shouts from the direction of the

house. Michael and Annie were running up the lawn, with Rebecca, Patricia and Mary not far beyond.

'You've found him,' cried Annie. 'Where was he?'

They looked down into the ha-ha, where Simon and I were laying David's body in the ditch. Soda licked the mud from his arm and moaned like a rusty gate.

'What's that bandage,' asked Michael. 'There's blood on it! What in God's name has he tried to do to himself?'

'Don't worry about that,' I said.

'He's not breathing!' wailed Annie. 'Michael, his eyes are closed and he's not breathing.'

Simon took one of David's arms, which were lying by his side, and I took the other. We raised them, pulling them back behind Davey's head. We did this several times, slowly at first and then with a quicker and quicker rhythm. Then Simon laid the palms of his hands on David's chest and bore down with all his weight, pushing and pushing. Annie began to cry.

Finally Simon, shaking his head, pinched his brother's nose with one hand and with the other opened his mouth. He leant down and blew into the lungs.

IV

'Look, for fuck's sake, keep up, the pair of you,' I growled. 'I'm ten minutes late as it is.'

'We'll run then,' said Roman. 'Yes sir, we'll bloody run.'

'Abso-sodding-lutely. We'll only bloody run.'

They barged past me and ran up the pavement, turning left and out of sight into Great Marlborough Street.

By the time I caught up three minutes later they were swinging around a lamp-post outside the back of Marks and Spencer's and tutting at imaginary wrist-watches as I approached.

'I'll be over there,' I said. 'In that building. I shan't be more than half an hour.'

'There's a McDonald's in Oxford Street,' said Davey.

'Yeah, can we go over and get a Big Mac?'

'Ten Big Macs.'

'Come on, Dad! It's the last week before school.'

'Yes, yes, yes. Don't badger me. Here . . .' I handed them each a fiver. 'And don't throw up in the street.'

'We'll see you in there. It's just in Oxford Street.'

'See you . . .'

I crossed the street and pressed the buzzer.

'Ted Wallace to see Lionel Greene.'

'Second floor.'

Greene didn't have a great deal to say. Nothing that Michael, as executor, hadn't already told me.

'The estate consists in its entirety of the South Kensington property, four hundred thousand pounds in shares and one hundred and thirty thousand pounds on deposit with the Chelsea branch of Coutts Bank.'

'Seems rather a lot.'

'Would you prefer the shares to be sold?'

'Not sure.' If I donated it all to some leukaemia society I would end up regretting it. Gestures are all very well but they don't fill bellies. Besides, it would look so smug and greasy.

'It's entirely up to you as the sole beneficiary.'

'Yes. I know.'

'And the house, Mr Wallace? Will you be selling that?'

'I'm certainly not going to live there,' I said. 'You should see the wallpaper.'

'I am also instructed to give you this letter,' Greene added, handing me an envelope. The handwriting was appalling and it took me some time to make out a single one of the words. Greene turned discreetly away to allow me to read it unobserved.

Dear Ted,

I'm so sorry. I can't understand what has gone wrong. I need you to send Davey to me at the hospital. I'm suddenly very weak. It doesn't make sense. It doesn't make any sense at all.

The doctors say it is the leukaemia, but we know that can't be the case, don't we? We know that they must have made a mistake.

Thank you for all your letters and for throwing your-self into the work so whole-heartedly. I wasn't wrong in sending you and I haven't forgotten that we have a bar-gain. I have made a new will which the nurses have witnessed. Spend the money on bringing Davey's gifts to the notice of the world.

731

As soon as you get this, come with Davey. He will make it all right again.

Love

Jane

'I understand,' Greene said, 'that she died no more than half an hour after writing it. Very sad. I had a brother who died of leukaemia. Terrible thing.'

'Very terrible,' I said, standing.

'Just two things before you go, Mr Wallace. I have the keys to Onslow Terrace here. Would you like them?'

'I suppose so. There are some papers there that I ought to go through.'

I pondered the strange custom by which people's letters, bills and scraps of useless rubbish instantly become dignified with the word 'papers' the moment they are dead. Objects like house-keys, of course, become 'effects'.

Greene handed them over with a ceremonial dip of the head.

'And the second thing?' I asked.

'The second thing is this,' he said, picking up a book from his desk with a shy smile. 'I wonder if you would do me the inestimable favour of signing my copy of your *Collected Works*?'

The boys were sitting in an upstairs section of the 'restaurant', as it liked to call itself.

'Everything hunky-dory, Dad?'

'Yes, thank you,' I said. 'My God, do you really enjoy those things?'

'No, Dad,' said Roman, 'we eat them because we hate them. Of course we bloody enjoy them. Have one yourself.'

'I think not.'

'Go on, Ted,' Davey urged. 'You've got to at least try them, you know. Otherwise you've no right to criticise them.'

'Oh, now hang on . . .'

'I'll nip down and buy you one,' he said.

'Why couldn't he have asked a waitress?' I asked, watching him shoot downstairs.

'Come off it, Dad,' said Roman. 'Don't pretend to be more ignorant than you are.'

'Hum.'

'Do you know, Davey had never had a Big Mac in his entire life until two weeks ago?'

'Yes, I did know,' I said.

'Bloody addicted to them now.'

'Roman,' I said.

'Yup?'

'I know we never really get much of a chance to talk about anything, but I just wanted to say . . .'

'Say what?' he burped.

'Well, I just wanted to say that it's bloody good having you around. I hadn't realised what a . . . what a splendid chap you are.'

He smiled. 'Dad, you've been watching too many bloody American TV movies,' he said.

'I have watched as many American TV movies as I've eaten Large Macs,' I replied. 'At least let me *try* and be fatherly, however badly I may do it. The thing is this, though. I know Helen only carts you off to London when

733

she and Brian go on their August holiday, but if ever you want to hang around the flat at any other time, well . . .'

'Yeah, I don't mind,' he said.

'Good man.'

'So, what's the plan for the rest of the afternoon?'

'Well, it's a rather busy day for me, as it happens. I've got to cut over to the Harpo Club in half an hour. Your sister Leonora wants to see me. I think her boyfriend's run out on her.'

'Again?'

'Again. She hasn't got anywhere to live. I might be able to put a house her way. After that, I've got a meeting with a publisher.'

'You writing poems again?'

'This is for a novel, based on . . . based on an idea that came to me last month when I was staying at Swafford.'

'And how long will that take?'

'I've no idea. I've never written one before.'

'No, the meeting. With the publisher person. How long will that take?'

'Oh, no more than half an hour I don't suppose. But then I really ought to zip over to visit Oliver in hospital.'

'Blimey, and what are we supposed to do all this time?'

'Ah, well. I'm coming to that. Let me see . . . hold out your hand.' I took out my wallet. 'I reckon thirty pounds each ought to do it.'

'Yes please!' said Roman. 'Ought to do what?'

'This afternoon's task,' I said, counting out six ten-pound notes into his hand, 'is for the two of you to go along Brewer Street and see if you can get admitted into a dirty movie or bed show. You have to bring me the ticket stubs as proof.'

'And what's the prize if we manage it?'

'The prize, Roman, you ungrateful bastard, is the pleasure of having seen a dirty movie or a bed show. Isn't that enough?'

'All right. You're on.'

'Fine.'

'What exactly is the point, though?' Roman asked, pocketing the cash. 'Is it just to annoy Mum if she ever finds out?'

'It has absolutely nothing to do with your mother. Nothing whatsoever. It's for the good of your immortal souls, if you must know.'

'Fair enough. Just wondered.'

'And the pair of you had better find something to do this evening as well. I'm taking Patricia out to Le Caprice and she may want to come back afterwards.'

'We're going to need more than thirty quid, then.'

'You are one of the few people,' I said, handing him another four tenners, 'who can accurately be called a son of a bitch.'

'Your Big Mac, sir,' said Davey, depositing a plastic tray on the table in front of me. 'With Regular Fries and a Diet Coke.'

'There's no cutlery,' I protested.

'Fingers and thumbs are nature's cutlery,' he replied with a self-conscious smile.

I opened the brown polystyrene box and stared gloomily at the contents.

'Do I really have to do this thing?'

'Yes, sir, you do!' they said.

'A good trick,' Davey offered, 'is to empty the fries into the open lid of the box. There, like that. Neat, isn't it?'

I raised the bun to my face and sniffed. 'What's that pink sauce?'

'Ah, nobody knows. It's the best-kept secret in the world.'

I bit into the warm squashy mess.

They watched me anxiously, like laboratory technicians monitoring a guinea-pig.

'Well, Dad? What do you reckon?'

'Absolutely dis*gusting*.'

'So, another one?' Davey suggested.

'Why not?' I said.